D1738878

THE
JACK
VANCE
READER

THE
JACK
VANCE
READER

EMPHYRIO

THE LANGUAGES OF PAO

THE DOMAINS OF KORYPHON

Edited by
Terry Dowling
and
Jonathan Strahan

First Edition

ISBN
978-1-59606-156-9

Subterranean Press
PO Box 190106
Burton, MI 48519

www.subterraneanpress.com

CONTENTS

DEDICATION

To John Vance

ACKNOWLEDGEMENTS

The editors extend sincere thanks to Ursula K. Le Guin, Mike Resnick and Robert Silverberg for their heartfelt and enthusiastic tributes, as well as to Tom Kidd, John Schwab and the other members of the Vance Integral Edition team. Special thanks, once again, to Jack Vance, Norma Vance and John Vance for their enthusiastic support and assistance.

WORLDS OF WONDER

INTRODUCTION

by Terry Dowling & Jonathan Strahan

'Give 'em the old human angle—glamor, mystery, thrills!'
—Howard Frayberg, 'Sjambak'

I told of force and time and space,
I told of hence and yonder;
I asked if she would come with me,
To know my worlds of wonder.
—Navarth, *The Palace of Love*

There was a time soon after World War II, back when science fiction was still finding its space legs and learning what it could be, when the term science fantasy came into fashion. It encompassed that burgeoning grab-bag of works that dealt less and less with the hardline science and gimmick stories prized by veteran editor John W. Campbell Jr. and magazines like *Analog Science Fiction: Science Fact* and shifted the focus to adventures in all manner of exotic settings, but with enough of a foot in reality that suspending disbelief was easily possible. Edgar Rice Burroughs could have John Carter travel safely and effortlessly to Barsoom, Philip José Farmer could send Alan Green across space to the rolling grasslands of the Xurdimur, and the term science fantasy was there to cover it.

It was a label suited to its time. Like the SF pulp adventure readership of the 30s and 40s, post-War readers wanted to go places and experience new things. By the time *Science Fantasy*, a magazine of that name, was first published in the UK in 1950, those often wild and unfettered space adventures were coming into full maturity, being smartened up and made much more sophisticated. As in the pulps, distant worlds were still settings for exotic adventures, but increasingly—in publications like *Amazing, Fantastic, Galaxy* and *The Magazine of Fantasy & Science Fiction*—the focus was on the settings as *real* places, living, breathing venues for solving colorful and often fascinating mysteries, for glossing the human condition in surprising ways and, in turn, making our lives larger in the process.

As these exotic adventures took on a more rigorous, rational feel at the expense of the conveniently simplistic and the magical, the dedicated planetary adventure came into its own—what is often called the planetary romance. With the steady shift towards exploring *alien* sociology, *alien* behavior, *alien* ways of thinking, now there were stories that *Analog* magazine *could* publish—and did, famously, with Frank Herbert's "Dune World" and "The Prophet of Dune" serialisations and Anne McCaffrey's "Weyr Search" and "Dragonrider" tales— stories that had more than just some ingenious scientific idea as their reason for being.

It was a liberating, forgiving time. What matter if faster-than-light travel was automatically treated as a given or that uniformity of language was often an improbable constant in those heady, pre-universal translator days? The point, as ever, was to get the protagonist on the ground and into the adventure as soon as possible, just as savvy storytellers have always done. But now there was something extra: the sense of truly being in another place in an allowable universe. Now, at the heart of the very best of these planetary adventures, there was usually a xenological mystery of some kind, the sort found in shorter pieces like James Blish's "And Some Were Savages" or novels like Niven and Pournelle's *The Mote in God's Eye*. The scales were being tipped away from mere magic to 'reasonable' scientific possibility, and with it came sense of wonder in spades.

A quick sampling of authors using the form says it all: Poul Anderson, Ursula K. Le Guin, Robert Silverberg, Leigh Brackett, Frank Herbert, Anne McCaffrey, Philip José Farmer, Marion Zimmer Bradley, Dan Simmons, Larry Niven, Brian W. Aldiss, James Blish, Andre Norton, George R.R. Martin, C.J. Cherryh, Gene Wolfe, the list goes on.

Pre-eminent among these world-builders, of course, was Jack Vance. In dozens of novels, many of them in series, and in stories like "The Moon Moth" and "Assault on a City," he has been a master of the planetary romance for the greater part of his 59-year writing career, returning to the form again and again and becoming SF's world-builder par excellence. It is hardly surprising that, as an inveterate world traveller who so keenly savored the experience of new places, new sensibilities, new ways of seeing, he should go on to build fanciful destinations for his and our enjoyment.

This volume celebrates this special achievement by offering three novels that show why this particular creator of worlds is so admired, respected and imitated. The fact that they are accompanied by new introductions from fellow luminaries in the field, Robert Silverberg, Ursula Le Guin and Mike Resnick, only serves to highlight the level of achievement on display here.

Why these three works with so many titles to choose from? The answer is simple. Chronologically and conceptually, *The Languages of Pao, Emphyrio* and *The Domains of Koryphon* (aka *The Grey Prince*) show the range, preoccupations and strengths, the signature melding of wonder, terror, humor and possibility in the author's preferred story form. Plainly and simply, they show Vance doing what he does best.

Emphyrio is considered by many to be Jack's finest novel. First published by Doubleday in April 1969 and serialised in *Fantastic Science Fiction–Fantasy* for June and August that year, it takes us to the city of Ambroy on the planet Halma and shows us, typically, small events becoming increasingly larger in an elegant and effective story filled with humor and sorrow, courage and wonder, triumph and sacrifice. On the one hand *Emphyrio* is merely a vigorous space opera with alien worlds and strange customs, exotic planetary treks and a satisfying central mystery; on the other it is a rich and touching coming of age tale that anticipates works like *Araminta Station* and *Night Lamp*. As such it stands as an easy contender for the title of classic planetary romance.

The Languages of Pao first appeared in *Satellite Science Fiction* for December 1957 and was reworked for its Avalon Books appearance in November 1958. Though an earlier title in the Vance world-building canon, appearing soon after *Big Planet* (1957), it shows the blending of outright adventure, cultural design and motivating central premise splendidly. The result is an intriguing enactment of the author's fascination with the notions of language theory.

The Domains of Koryphon is another fine example of the mature Vancean planetary adventure and comes from the same fertile decade that gave us the Durdane Trilogy (1971, 1972 and 1973), *Trullion: Alastor 2262* (1973), *Showboat World* (1975), *Marune: Alastor 933* (1975), *The Dogtown Tourist Agency* (1975), *Maske: Thaery* (1976) and *Wyst: Alastor 1716* (1978). First serialized in *Amazing Science Fiction Stories* for August and October 1974 under its preferred title (and subsequently published in book form that same year as *The Grey Prince*, a title not of Vance's choosing), it has an ingenious twofold xenological mystery at its heart and not one but two planetary treks. It brings center-stage two human-derived 'alien' cultures (the Uldras and the Wind-runners), two non-human races (the erjins and the morphotes), plus an assortment of paranormal skills and the Vance signature touch of having a viable 'enlightened medievalism' in all planetary societies save that of the Outkers of Szintarre. Like *Emphyrio* before it, it is a blueprint for so much that the author has returned to again and again: having a taciturn, resourceful hero, a cultural crisis (often intensely personal as well) that requires an understanding of alien ways, the hint of mental powers at work. As such, it too is a ready contender for the title of classic xenographical adventure.

And adventure remains the keynote here, let us not forget. The three fine works that follow are entertainments, not xeno-anthropological treatises, simply three diversions from a writer so drawn to the planetary romance that he kept envisaging new journeys to go on, new worlds to visit. Thank our luckiest stars that he found a way to take us with him.

Terry Dowling & Jonathan Strahan
Sydney and Perth, October 2007

EMPHYRIO

INTRODUCTION

by Robert Silverberg

Jack Vance's slender, elegant fable *Emphyrio* was first published in
1969, capping one of the most productive decades of Vance's long
and distinguished career. Earlier in the 1960s had come the award-
winning novellas "The Dragon Masters" and "The Last Castle," the
superb novel *The Blue World*, the first three novels in his *Demon Princes*
series, the first volume of the *Planets of Adventure* series, and *Eyes of the
Overworld*, a successful continuation of his classic *The Dying Earth*,
along with an assortment of short stories and several mystery novels. In
that flurry of remarkable work, *Emphyrio*, which Doubleday & Co.
launched in hardcover as part of a science-fiction line famous for the
virtual invisibility of its publications, received rather less attention than
it deserved, and over the years has been reissued less frequently than
many of Vance's other titles. But it is quintessential Vance, displaying
his considerable virtues in splendid fashion.

I called it a "fable," and that is, I think, what it is: a story intended
not as a realistic representation of a speculative situation, as is the science fiction of, say, Robert A. Heinlein, Frederik Pohl, or Arthur C.
Clarke, but as an airy excursion into the non-real, depending for its
peculiar strength on the solid substructure of human insight that lies
beneath its airy conceptualizing. As is the case in much of his work,

Vance does not ask us to believe in any very serious way in the literal reality of the world he creates here, though he does supply it, in his ever-punctilious way, with a history, a sociology, a religion, and all the other necessary details. The story itself is built on a fable, one that is ancient in the era its characters are living in, and it is a fable in its own right as well, a self-contained work of imaginative fabulism that does not even try to make the pretense of offering literal extrapolation from our own reality.

Vance's style is, as ever, a key element in this fabulation. He writes as though he had never so much as encountered the crisp, fast-paced pulp-magazine sort of prose that has been typical of most science fiction since the early 1940s. In an unhurried manner that owes more to Rider Haggard or Rudyard Kipling than it does to Hemingway or Heinlein, he sets forth his narrative in rich, baroque cadences, laden with descriptive color, from his very first paragraph onward:

"In the chamber at the top of the tower were six individuals: three who chose to call themselves 'lords' or sometimes 'remedials'; a wretched underling who was their prisoner; and two Garrion. The chamber was dramatic and queer: of irregular dimension, hung with panels of heavy maroon velvet. At one end an embrasure admitted a bar of light: this of a smoky amber quality, as if the pane were clogged with dust—which it was not; in fact, the glass was a subtle sort, producing remarkable effects. At the opposite end of the room was a low trapezoidal door of black skeel."

His handling of dialog similarly eschews the naturalistic moderne. Vance characters speak calmly even when under stress, and always with a certain archaic formality of tone. "My motives are sufficient," one of them says, "and concern you more directly than you know. Proceed." And another declares, "My ambitions are not ignoble. I intended to learn the truth of the Emphyrio legend. Emphyrio is a great hero; the truth would inspire the people of Ambroy, who are sorely in need of truth." Such a measured manner of speaking would seem weirdly stilted if it cropped up in the middle of a Heinlein novel; but Vance writes that way throughout, and such is the perfection of his ear that he achieves great consistency of tone and this quaintly formal sort of dialog, sustained as it is through the whole book, takes on a kind of fantastical grandeur against which the quick, clipped interchanges of standard pulp fiction would sound brusque and inarticulate.

His narrative method, too, ignores most of the pulp canon of tricks. The accelerated line-by-line pace of the hard-boiled story, that quick interplay of dialog and description, is not for him; nor is he afraid to halt a story wherever he pleases to present us with a leisurely dollop of exposition. It was the great achievement of Robert A. Heinlein, beginning in 1940, to demonstrate how the unfamiliar background details of a futuristic world could be demonstrated to readers by showing them in use as the story moves along, rather than by pausing the story for detailed explanation. Vance knows how to do that well enough: in the opening paragraph I quoted above, we meet "remedials" and "Garrion" and "skeel," no details provided, and on many another occasion throughout the book he is just as deliberately inexplicative. (A grand feast, for example, is described as being made up of "roast biloa-bird with wickenberry sauce, rag-fish, candied sea-calch, bowls of whelk, corpentine, hemmer garnished with that purple-black seaweed known as livret, a profusion of cakes, tarts and jellies, and jugs of edel wine.") Of all of that, only the cakes, tarts, jellies, and whelks resonate with anything we know, though the reader readily gets the general idea of a gorgeous adventure in gourmandiserie. Heinlein would have managed the effect in much the same way, if he had been given to setting up alien feasts of that degree of plenty.

But there is nothing Heinleinesque about what we meet on the second page of *Emphryio*'s second chapter, and again on several pages of Chapter Three and in the seventh chapter: footnotes! Bland explanatory footnotes! Having introduced the unfamiliar term "noncup," for example, Vance tells us bluntly by means of a footnote that it means "noncuperatives," and those are "nonrecipients of welfare benefits, reputedly all Chaoticists, anarchists, thieves, swindlers, whoremongers." In science fiction's primitive past, when the pioneering magazines of Hugo Gernsback dominated the field, page after page of the stories would be festooned with lengthy footnotes of this sort, spelling out anything that might puzzle the uninitiated reader. The Heinlein revolution swept all that away; but here is Vance serenely telling us in small type what "noncups" are, or how many kinds of written script have been in use in his land of Fortinone, or what the honorific abbreviation "Rt." stands for. Is it because the limitations of his skills are such that he is unable to explain such matters in the context of the story? Hardly. Like the manneristic descriptive prose and the stylized rhythms of the dialog, Vance's use of footnotes is part of the distancing technique that is at the core of his art—holding the reader at bay, reminding him at every turn that what he is experiencing is not a realistic representation of mundane life but a tale of fabulous imaginings, a verbal object, an artificial construct of its maker's mind.

He no more wants us to take it as literal reality than H.P. Lovecraft wants us to believe in the actuality of Cthulhu or Lord Dunsany the marvelous city of Babbalkund.

On the most superficial level, the story-as-told is familiar stuff. Vance presents us with a world of oppressed plebeians coolly and cruelly dominated by heartless aristocrats, with social restrictions that verge on the totalitarian, with foolish, meaningless religious observances, and an earnest young rebel eager to bring about reform. There is a bit of space-piracy; there is a brief adventure on an alien world. None of this is startling in its originality, nor is Vance's swift resolution of his casually presented plot particularly convincing: the young rebel pushes, and the villains fall down.

Beneath the overt story, though, all sorts of interesting Vancean things are going on. There is a quiet advocacy of individual craftsmanship, for instance, something we meet in many Vance works, Vance himself being a remarkable craftsman not only in words, but the theme has stronger than usual force here, where young Ghyl and his father Amiante are portrayed as inspired artists in wood, and we believe their artistry. We believe, too, in the hostile forces of their society that constantly press against them, and see them as the sort of necessary checks on individuality that such a jerry-built society would have to impose. The book's characters are touching and plausible ones: idealistic Ghyl, his enigmatic father Amiante, his flamboyant friend Floriel, his bête noire Nion, and the two contrasting love objects, sluttish Sonjaly and aristocratic Shanne, all swim upward toward us out of the mannered prose and stylized dialog with remarkable vividness. When Amiante suffers at the hands of the government investigators, we feel for him; when he dies, swept away by Vance in a two-line paragraph, we mourn his disappearance. (Despite Vance's rigorous employment of distancing techniques, he strikes a quiet note of powerful emotion, when, near the end, Ghyl rediscovers an elaborate screen that

Amiante had carved when Ghyl was a child. Hundreds of small, individualized, disturbing faces peer from it, including that of Ghyl himself; and above them, near Amiante's own, his guarded, mysterious father had inscribed the phrase, REMEMBER ME. Ghyl's eyes blur at the sight; and, at that moment, so do the reader's.)

Ghyl, whom we meet at the age of seven and follow through the unfolding of his adolescence to his maturity, is an appealing and sympathetic figure, whose puzzled view of his father and whose tentative adventures in early love ring completely true. Ghyl's untrustworthy friends, who push him this way and that toward his ultimate sense of himself, are a lively, roguish bunch. The universe in which they all live is no more realistically depicted than that of a fairy-tale, but takes on an odd sort of fairy-tale reality that is as memorable in its way as any of the carefully thought out imaginary worlds of a Poul Anderson or a Hal Clement, complete as they are down to the last technical detail of atmospheric composition and gravitational pull. The neighborhoods of Ghyl's native city, known to us only by their evocative names—Brueben, Gisely, Vashmont, Foelgher—become as real to us as any planet invented for us by the writers of the hard-science school.

Such science-fiction writers as Anderson, Clement, and Heinlein gave us scores of memorable novels that are ornaments to our field. Jack Vance, working with similar material in his own very different mode, has done the same, as we see here in *Emphyrio* and a host of other books written over a span of some six decades. His unique artistry produces rare and beautiful things.

EMPHYRIO

CHAPTER I

In the chamber at the top of the tower were six individuals: three who chose to call themselves 'Lords' or sometimes 'Remedials'; a wretched underling who was their prisoner; and two Garrion. The chamber was dramatic and queer: of irregular dimension, hung with panels of heavy maroon velvet. At one end an embrasure admitted a bar of light: this of a smoky amber quality, as if the pane were clogged with dust—which it was not; in fact, the glass was a subtle sort, producing remarkable effects. At the opposite end of the room was a low trapezoidal door of black skeel.

The unconscious prisoner was clamped into an intricately articulated frame. The top of his skull had been removed; upon the naked brain rested a striated yellow gel. Above hung a black capsule, a curiously ugly object, if only a contrivance of glass and metal. Its surface was marked by a dozen wart-like protuberances: each projected a quivering thread of radiation into the gel.

The prisoner was a fair-skinned young man, with features of no great distinction. Such hair as could be seen was tawny. The forehead and cheekbones were broad, the nose blunt, the mouth easy and generous, the jaws slanting down to a small firm chin; a face of innocent impracticality. The lords, or 'Remedials'—the latter term was somewhat obsolete and seldom heard—were of another sort. Two were tall and thin, with arsenical skins, thin long noses, saturnine mouths, black hair varnished close to their heads. The third was older, heavier, with

21

vulpine features, a glaring heated gaze, a skin darkly florid, with an unwholesome magenta undertone. Lord Fray and Lord Fanton were fastidious, supercilious; Grand Lord Dugald the Boimarc seemed oppressed by worry and chronic anger. All three, members of a race notorious for its elegant revels, appeared humorless and dour, with no capability for ease or merriment.

The two Garrion at the back of the room were andromorphs: blackish purple-brown, solid and massive. Their eyes, black lusterless bulbs, showed internal star-refractions; from the sides of their faces extended tufts of black hair.

The lords wore black garments of refined cut, caps of jeweled metal mesh. The Garrion wore black leathern harness, russet aprons.

Fray, standing by a console, explained the function of the mechanism. "First: a period of joinings, as each strand seeks a synapse. When the flashes cease, as now they are doing, and the indicators coincide—" Fray indicated a pair of opposed black arrows "—he becomes nothing: a crude animal, a polyp with a few muscular reflexes.

"In the computer, the neural circuits are classified by range and by complexity of cross-connection into seven stages." Lord Fray examined the yellow gel, where the scanning beams aroused no further motes of light. "The brain is now organized into seven realms. We bring him to a desired condition by relaxing control of specific realms, and, if necessary, damping, or squelching, others. Since Lord Dugald does not intend rehabilitation—"

Fanton spoke in a husky voice: "He is a pirate. He must be expelled."

"—we will relax the stages one at a time until he is able to provide the accurate statement Lord Dugald requires. Though, I confess, his motives are beyond my comprehension." And Lord Fray brushed Grand Lord Dugald with a flickering glance.

"My motives are sufficient," said Dugald, "and concern you more directly than you know. Proceed."

Fray, with a subtle gesture, touched the first of seven keys. On a yellow screen an amorphous black shape twisted and writhed. Fray made adjustments; the shape steadied, diminished to a coin-sized disk quivering to the prisoner's pulse. The young man wheezed, moaned, strained feebly against the bonds. Working with great facility, Fray superimposed a pattern of concentric circles over the dot and made a final adjustment.

The young man's eyes lost their glaze. He saw Lord Fanton and Lord Dugald: the black disk on the screen jerked. He saw the Garrion: the black disk distorted. He turned his head, looked out through the embrasure. The sun hung low in the west. By a curious optical property of the glass it appeared a pale gray disk surrounded by a pink and green aureole. The black spot on the screen hesitated, slowly contracted.

"Phase One," said Fray. "His genetic responses are restored. Notice how the Garrion disturb him?"

"No mystery," snorted old Lord Dugald. "They are alien to his genetic background."

"Why then," demanded Fanton coolly, "did the spot react similarly to the sight of us?"

"Bah," muttered Lord Dugald. "We are not his folk."

"True," said Fray, "even after so many generations. The sun however works as a reference point, the origin of mental coordinates. It is a powerful symbol."

He turned the second key. The black disk exploded into fragments. The young man whimpered, jerked, became rigid. Fray worked at the adjustments and reduced the shape once more to a small disk. He tapped the stimulator button. The young man lay quietly. His eyes roved the room, from Lord Fray to Lord Dugald, to the Garrion, to his own body. The black disk held its shape and position.

"Phase Two," said Fray. "He recognizes, but he cannot relate. He is aware but not yet conscious; he cannot distinguish between himself and the surroundings. All is the same: things and their emotional content are identical. Valueless for our purposes. To Phase Three."

He turned the third key; the tight black circle expanded. Fray again made adjustments, constricted the blot to a small dense disk. The young man heaved himself up, stared down at the metal boots and wristlets, looked at Fanton and Dugald. Fray spoke to him in a cold clear voice, "Who are you?"

The young man frowned; he moistened his lips. He spoke and the sound seemed to come from far away: "Emphyrio."

Fray gave a short curt nod; Dugald looked at him in surprise. "What is all this?"

"A rogue linkage, a deep-lying identification: no more. One must expect surprises."

"But is he not enforced to accuracy?"

"Accuracy from his experience and from his point of view." Fray's voice became dry. "We cannot expect cosmic universals—if such exist." He turned back to the young man. "What, then, is your birth-name?"

"Ghyl Tarvoke."

Fray gave a brusque nod. "Who am I?"

"You are a lord."

"Do you know where you are?"

"In an eyrie, above Ambroy."

Fray spoke to Dugald: "He now can compare his perceptions to his memory; he can make qualitative identifications. He is not yet conscious. If he were to be rehabilitated, now would be the starting point, with each of his associations readily accessible. To Phase Four."

Fray turned the fourth key, made his adjustments. Ghyl Tarvoke winced and strained at his boots and wristlets. "He is now capable of quantitative appraisals. He can perceive relationships, make comparisons. He is, in a sense, lucid. But he is not yet conscious. If he were to be rehabilitated, there would be further adjustment at this level. To Phase Five."

Phase Five was concluded. In consternation Ghyl Tarvoke stared from Fray to Dugald, to Fanton, to the Garrion. "His time-scale has been restored," said Fray. "He has, in effect, his memory. With considerable effort we could extract a statement, objective and devoid of emotional color: skeletal truth, so to speak. In certain situations this is desirable, but now we would learn nothing. He can make no decisions, and this is a barrier to lucid language, which is a continuous decision-making process: a choice between synonyms, degrees of emphasis, systems of syntax. To Phase Six."

He turned the sixth key. The black disk spattered violently apart, into a set of droplets. Fray stood back in surprise. Ghyl Tarvoke made savage animal sounds, gnashed his teeth, strained at his bonds. Fray hurriedly made adjustments, constrained the squirming elements, compressed them to a jerking disk. Ghyl Tarvoke sat panting, gazing at the lords with detestation.

"Well then, Ghyl Tarvoke," spoke Fray, "and what do you think of yourself now?"

The young man, glaring from lord to lord, made no reply.

Dugald took a fastidious half-step to the side. "Will he speak?"

"He will speak," said Fray. "Notice: he is conscious; he is in full control of himself."

"I wonder what he knows," mused Dugald. He looked sharply from Fanton to Fray. "Remember, I ask all questions!"

Fanton gave him an acrid glance. "One might almost think that you and he share a secret."

"Think as you like," snapped Dugald. "Remember only who holds authority!"

"How can there be forgetting?" asked Fanton, and turned away.

Dugald spoke to his back. "If you wish my position, take it! But take responsibility as well!"

Fanton swung back. "I want nothing of yours. Remember only who was injured by this sullen creature."

"You, me, Fray, any of us: it is all the same. Did you not hear him use the name 'Emphyrio'?"

Fanton shrugged. Fray said lightly, "Well then, back to Ghyl Tarvoke! He is not yet a total person. He lacks the use of his free connections, the flexible web. He is incapable of spontaneity. He cannot dissemble, because he cannot create. He cannot hope, he cannot plan, therefore he has no will. So then: we will hear the truth." He settled himself on a cushioned bench, started a recording machine. Dugald came forward, planted himself flat-footed in front of the prisoner. "Ghyl Tarvoke: we wish to learn the background to your crimes."

Fray interceded with gentle malice: "I suggest that you ask questions of a more categorical nature."

"No, no!" retorted Dugald. "You fail to understand my requirements."

"You have not set them forth," said Fray, still waspishly polite.

Ghyl Tarvoke had been straining uneasily at his harness. He said fretfully, "Take loose these clasps; I will be more at ease."

"Your comfort is of small consequence," barked Dugald. "You are to be expelled into Bauredel. So speak!"

Ghyl Tarvoke pulled at his bonds again, then relaxed and stared at the wall beyond the lords. "I don't know what you want to hear."

"Exactly," murmured Fray. "Precisely."

"The circumstances contributing to your abominable crimes!"

"I remember a lifetime of events. I will tell you everything."

Dugald said, "I prefer that you speak somewhat more to the point."

Ghyl's forehead creased. "Complete the processing, so that I can think."

Dugald looked indignantly at Fray, while Fanton laughed. "Is this not a manifestation of will?"

Fray pulled at his long chin. "I suspect that the remark derives from ratiocination rather than emotion." He spoke to Ghyl. "Is this not true?"

"True."

Fray smiled faintly. "After Phase Seven you will be capable of in-accuracy."

"I have no wish to dissemble: quite otherwise. You shall hear the truth."

Fray went to the control board, turned the seventh key. The black disk disintegrated into a fog of droplets. Ghyl Tarvoke gave a moan of agony. Fray worked the controls; the drops coalesced; the disk at last was as before.

Ghyl sat quietly. He said at last, "So now you will kill me."

"Certainly. Do you deserve better?"

"Yes."

Fanton burst out, "But why have you performed such evil, on folk who have done you no harm? Why? Why? Why?"

"'Why?'" Ghyl cried out. "To achieve! To make capital of my life, to stamp my imprint upon the cosmos! Is it right that I should be born, live and die with no more effect than a blade of grass on Dunkum's Heights?"

Fanton gave a bitter laugh. "Are you better than I? I live and die with equal inconsequence. Who will remember either of us?"

"You are you and I am I," said Ghyl Tarvoke. "I am dissatisfied."

"With good reason," said Lord Dugald with a dour grin. "In three hours you are to be expelled. So speak now, or never be heard again!"

CHAPTER II

Ghyl Tarvoke's first insight into the nature of destiny came upon his seventh birthday, during a visit to a traveling pageant. His father, usually vague and remote, somehow had remembered the occasion; together they set off on foot across the city. Ghyl would have preferred to ride Overtrend, but Amiante, for reasons obscure to Ghyl, demurred, and they ambled north across the old Vashmont Development, past the skeletons of a dozen ruined towers, each supporting the eyrie of a lord. In due course they arrived at the North Common in East Town where the gay tents of Framtree's Peripatezic Entercationers had been erected. A rotunda advertised: *Wonders of the Universe: a magnificent tour without danger, inconvenience or expense, depicting the spectacles of sixteen enthralling worlds, arranged in tasteful and edifying sequence.*

There was a puppet show with a troupe of live Damar puppets; a diorama illustrating notable events in the history of Halma; exhibits of off-world creatures, living, dead, or in simulacrum; a comic ballet entitled

Niaiserie; a mind-reading parlor featuring Pagoul the mysterious Earthman; gaming stalls, refreshment counters, hucksters of gewgaws and trifles. Ghyl could hardly walk for looking this way and that, while Amiante with patient indifference pushed through the crowds. Most were recipients of Ambroy, but many had come in from the back regions of Fortinone; and there were a certain number of foreigners as well, from Bauredel, Sauge, Closte, distinguished by the cockades which allowed them complimentary welfare vouchers. Rarely they saw Garrion, odd animals tricked out in human clothes and always a sign that lords walked among the underfolk.

Amiante and Ghyl visited first the rotunda, to travel vicariously among the star-worlds. They saw the Battle of the Birds at Sloe on Madura; the ammoniacal storms of Fajane; tantalizing glimpses of the Five Worlds. Ghyl watched the strange scenes without understanding; they were too foreign, too gigantic, at times too savage, for his assimilation. Amiante looked with a subtle bittersweet half-smile. Never would Amiante travel, never would he accumulate the vouchers for so much as a three-day excursion to Damar, and knowing as much, he seemed to have put all such ambitions to the side.

Leaving the rotunda they visited a hall displaying in diorama famous lovers of myth: Lord Guthmore and the Mountain Wilding; Medié and Estase; Jeruun and Jeran; Hurs Gorgonja and Ladati the Metamorph; a dozen other couples in picturesque costumes of antiquity. Ghyl asked many questions which Amiante for the most part evaded or answered glancingly: "The history of Halma is over-long, over-confused; it is enough to say that all these handsome folk are creatures of fable."

Upon leaving the hall they passed into the puppet* theater, and watched as the small masked creatures jigged, scampered, chattered, sang their way through *Virtuous Fidelity to an Ideal is the Certain Highroad to Financial Independence*. In fascination Ghyl observed Marelvie, the daughter of a common wire-drawer, at a Foelgher Precinct street dance, where she attracted the attention of Lord Bodbozzle the

---

*The regulations of Fortinone and indeed of all the North Continent prohibited both the synthesis and the importation of sentient creatures, as tending to augment the recipient rolls. The Damarans, native to the moon Damar, fabricated small creatures of a docile eager intelligence, with furry black heads, black beaks and laterally-placed eyes; so long as the creatures performed only as puppets, or served as pets to lord-children, the welfare agents tended to ignore their presence.

Chaluz, a lecherous old power tycoon of twenty-six fiefs. Lord Bodbozzle wooed her with agile capering, a comic discharge of fireworks and declamation, but Marelvie refused to join his entourage except as legal spouse, with full acknowledgment and the settlement of four choice fiefs. Lord Bodbozzle agreed, but Marelvie first must visit his castle to learn ladyship and financial independence. So the trusting Marelvie was conveyed by air-weft to his castle, high on a tower above Ambroy, where Lord Bodbozzle immediately attempted seduction. Marelvie underwent various vicissitudes, but at the critical instant her sweetheart Rudel leapt in through a window, having scaled the naked girders of the ancient tower. He thrashed a dozen Garrion guards, pinned whimpering Lord Bodbozzle to the wall, while Marelvie performed a skipping dance of glee. To buy his life, Lord Bodbozzle forfeited six fiefs in the heart of Ambroy and a space-yacht. The happy couple, financially independent and off the rolls, bounded happily away on their travels, while Lord Bodbozzle massaged his bruises…

Lamps flared on, signaling intermission; Ghyl turned to his father, hoping for but not expecting an opinion. It was Amiante's tendency to turn his feelings inward. Even at the age of seven Ghyl sensed an unorthodox, almost illicit, quality to his father's judgments. Amiante was a big man, slow of motion in a fashion which suggested economy and control rather than ponderousness. His head was big and brooding, his face wide at the cheekbones and pale, with a small chin, a sensitive mouth characteristically twisted in a musing half-smile. Amiante spoke very little and in a soft voice, although, stimulated by some apparently trivial incident, Ghyl had seen him erupt words, spewing them forth as if they were under physical pressure, to halt as suddenly, perhaps in mid-sentence. But now Amiante had nothing to say; Ghyl could only guess his feelings in regard to the misfortunes of Lord Bodbozzle.

Looking around the audience, Ghyl noted a pair of Garrion in a splendid livery of lavender, scarlet and black leather. They stood to the rear of the hall, manlike but non-human, hybrids of insect, gargoyle and ape, immobile but alert, eye-bulges focused nowhere but observing all. Ghyl nudged his father. "Garrion are here! Lords watch the puppets!"

Amiante turned a brief glance over his shoulder. "Lords or lordlings."

Ghyl searched the audience. No one resembled Lord Bodbozzle; no one radiated that near-visible effulgence of authority and financial independence which Ghyl imagined must surround all lords. He started to ask his father whom he presumed to be the lord, then stopped, knowing that Amiante's only response would be a disinterested shrug. Ghyl looked along the rows, face by face. How could lord or lordling not resent the crude caricature of Lord Bodbozzle? But no one seemed perturbed...Ghyl lost interest in the matter; perhaps the Garrion visited the pageant by their own inclination.

The intermission was to be ten minutes; Ghyl slipped from his seat, went to examine the stage at closer vantage. To the side hung a canvas flap; Ghyl pulled it open, looked into a side-room, where a small man in brown velvet sat sipping a cup of tea. Ghyl glanced over his shoulder; Amiante, preoccupied with his own inner visions, paid no heed. Ghyl ducked under the canvas, stood hesitantly, prepared to leap back should the man in brown velvet come to seize him, for somehow Ghyl had come to suspect that the puppets were stolen children, whipped until they acted and danced with exact precision: an idea investing the performance with a horrid fascination. But the man in brown velvet, apart from a civil nod, seemed uninterested in capturing Ghyl. Emboldened, Ghyl came a few steps forward. "Are you the puppet-master?"

"That I am, lad: Holkerwoyd the puppet-master, enjoying a brief respite from my labors."

The man was rather old and gnarled. He did not appear the sort who would torment and whip children. With added confidence Ghyl—not knowing precisely what he meant—asked: "You're...*real?*"

Holkerwoyd did not seem to find the question unreasonable. "I'm as real as necessary, lad, at least to myself. There have been some who have found me, shall we say, evanescent, even evaporative."

Ghyl understood the general essence of the response. "You must travel to many places."

"There's truth indeed. Up and down the great North Continent, over the Bight to Salula, down the peninsula to Wantanua. All this on Halma alone."

"I've never been from Ambroy."

"You're young yet."

"Yes; someday I want to be financially independent, and travel space. Have you visited other worlds?"

"Dozens. I was born beside a star so far that you'll never see its light, not in the sky of Halma."

"Then why are you here?"

"I often ask myself the same. The answer always comes: because I'm not somewhere else. Which is a statement more sensible than it sounds.

And isn't it a marvel? Here am I and here are you; think of it! When you ponder the breadth of the galaxy, you must recognize a coincidence of great singularity!"

"I don't understand."

"Simple enough! Suppose you were here and I elsewhere, or I were here and you elsewhere, or both of us were elsewhere: three cases vastly more probable than the fourth, which is the fact of our mutual presence within ten feet of each other. I repeat, a miraculous concatenation! And to think that some hold the Age of Wonders to be past and gone!"

Ghyl nodded dubiously. "That story about Lord Bodbozzle—I'm not so sure I liked it."

"Eh?" Holkerwoyd blew his cheeks. "And why not?"

"It wasn't true."

"Aha then. In what particular?"

Ghyl searched his vocabulary to express what was hardly so much as an intuition. He said, rather lamely, "A man can't fight ten Garrion. Everyone knows that."

"Well, well, well," said Holkerwoyd, talking aside. "The lad has a literal mind." Back to Ghyl: "But don't you wish it were so? Is it not our duty to provide gay tales? When you grow up and learn how much you owe the city, you'll find ample dullness."

Ghyl nodded wisely. "I expected the puppets to be smaller. And much more beautiful."

"Ah, the captious one. The dissatisfaction. Well then! When you are larger, they will seem smaller."

"They are not stolen children?"

Holkerwoyd's eyebrows puffed like the tail of a startled cat. "So this is your idea? How could I train children to gambols and artless antics, when they are such skeptics, such fastidious critics, such absolutists?"

Ghyl thought it polite to change the subject. "There is a lord in the audience."

"Not so, my friend. A little lady. She sits to the left in the second row."

Ghyl blinked. "How do you know?"

Holkerwoyd made a grand gesture. "You wish to plunder me of all my secrets? Well, lad, know this: masks and masking—and unmasking—these are the skills of my trade. Now hasten back to your father. He wears the mask of leaden patience, to sheathe his soul. Within he shakes with grief. You shall know grief too; I see that you are fey." Holkerwoyd advanced, making ferocious gestures. "Hence! Hup! Hah!"

Ghyl fled back into the hall, resumed his seat. Amiante turned him a brief quizzical glance, which Ghyl avoided. Many aspects of the world were beyond his understanding. Recalling the words of Holkerwoyd he looked across the room. Indeed, there in the second row: a small girl with a placid woman of middle-age. So this was a lady! Ghyl examined her carefully. Pretty and graceful she was beyond question, and Ghyl, in the clarity of his vision, saw also a Difference. Her breath would be tart and perfumed, like verbena or lemon. Her mind moved to unfathomable thoughts, wonderful secrets...Ghyl noticed a hauteur, an ease of manner, which somehow was fascinating...A challenge...

The lights dimmed, the curtains parted, and now began a sad little tale which Ghyl thought might be a message to himself from Holkerwoyd, even though such a possibility seemed remote.

The setting of the story was the puppet theater itself. One of the puppets, conceiving the outside world to be a place of eternal merriment, escaped the theater and went forth to mingle with a group of children. For a period there was antic and song; then the children, tiring of play, went their various ways. The puppet sidled through the streets, observing the city: what a dull place compared to the theater, unreal and factitious though it was! But he was reluctant to return, knowing what awaited him. Hesitating, delaying, he hopped and limped back to the theater, singing a plaintive little commentary. His fellow puppets greeted him with restraint and awe; they too knew what to expect. And indeed at the next performance the traditional drama *Emphyrio* was presented, with the runaway puppet cast as Emphyrio. Now ensued a play within a play, and the tale of Emphyrio ran its course. At the end, Emphyrio, captured by the tyrants, was dragged to Golgotha. Before his execution he attempted to deliver a speech justifying his life, but the tyrants refused to let him speak, and inflicted upon him the final humiliation of futility. A grotesquely large rag was stuffed in Emphyrio's mouth; a shining axe struck off his head and such was the fate of the runaway puppet.

Ghyl noticed that the lord-girl, her companion and the Garrion guards did not stay for the finish. When the lights came on, showing white staring faces throughout the audience, they were gone.

Ghyl and Amiante walked homeward through the dusk, each occupied with his own thoughts. Ghyl spoke. "Father."

"Yes."

"In the story, the runaway puppet who played Emphyrio was executed."

"Yes."

"But the puppet who played the runaway puppet also was executed!"

"I noticed as much."

"Did he run away too?"

Amiante heaved a sigh, shook his head. "I don't know. Perhaps puppets are cheap…Incidentally, that is not the true tale of Emphyrio."

"What is the true tale?"

"No one knows."

"Was Emphyrio a real man?"

Amiante considered a moment before replying. Then he said: "Human history has been long. If a man named Emphyrio never existed, there was another man, with a different name, who did."

Ghyl found the remark beyond his intellectual depth. "Where do you think Emphyrio lived? Here in Ambroy?"

"This is a problem," said Amiante with a thoughtful frown, "which some men have tried to solve, without success. There are clues, of course. If I were a different man, if I were once again young, if I had no…" His voice dwindled.

They walked in silence. Then Ghyl asked, "What is it to be 'fey'?"

Amiante scrutinized him curiously. "Where did you hear the word?"

"Holkerwoyd the puppet-master said I was fey."

"Ah. I see. Well then. It means that you have about you the air of, let us say, important enterprise. That you shall be remarkable and do remarkable deeds."

Ghyl was fascinated. "And I shall be financially independent and I shall travel? With you, of course?"

Amiante laid his hand on Ghyl's shoulder. "That remains to be seen."

CHAPTER III

Amiante's shop and residence was a tall narrow four-story structure of old black timbers and brown tile facing on Undle Square to the north of the Brueben Precinct. On the ground floor was Amiante's workshop, where he carved wooden screens; on the next floor was the kitchen where Amiante and Ghyl cooked and ate, as well as a side room in which Amiante kept a desultory collection of old manuscripts. On the third floor Amiante and Ghyl slept; and above was a loft full of unusable objects, too old or too remarkable to throw away.

Amiante was the most noncommittal of men: pensive, almost brooding, working in fits of energy, then for hours or days occupying himself with the detail of a sketch, or perhaps doing nothing whatever. He was an expert craftsman: his screens were always Firsts and often Acmes, but his output was not particularly large. Vouchers, therefore, were not plentiful in the Tarvoke household. Clothes, like all the merchandise of Fortinone, were hand-made and dear; Ghyl wore smocks and trousers stitched together by Amiante himself, even though the guilds discouraged such 'fringe encroachment'. Seldom were there coins to be spared for sweets, and none for organized entertainment. Every day the barge *Jaoundi* pushed majestically up the Insse to the holiday village Bazen, returning after dark. For the children of Ambroy this was the most delightful and hoped-for excursion imaginable. Once or twice Amiante mentioned the *Jaoundi* excursion, but nothing ever came of it.

Ghyl nonetheless considered himself fortunate. Amiante imposed few restraints. Other children no older than himself were already learning a trade: at guild-school, in a home workshop or that of a relative. The children of scriveners, clerks, pedants, or any others who might need advanced reading and writing skills were drilled to second or even third schedule.* Devout parents sent their children to Infant Skips and Juvenile Hops at the Finukan Temple, or taught them simple patterns at home.

Amiante, whether through calculation or perhaps absentmindedness, made no such demands upon Ghyl, who came and went as he pleased. He explored all Brueben Precinct, then, growing bolder, wandered far

---

*In Fortinone and across the North Continent five schedules or systems of writing were in use:
1. A set of twelve hundred and thirty-one pictograms derived from ancient interplanetary conventions, taught to all children.
2. A cursive version of the pictograms, used by tradesmen and artisans, with perhaps four hundred additional special forms.
3. A syllabary, sometimes used to augment the pictograms, sometimes as a graphic system in its own right.
4. A cursive form of the syllabary, with a large number of logographs: the system used by the lords; by priests, ordained saltants, lay leapers, expostulants; by scriveners and pedants.
5. An archaic alphabet, with its many variants, used with archaic dialects or for special effects, such as tavern signs, boat names and the like.

afield. He explored the docks and boat-building shops of Nobile Precinct; clambered over hulks of old barges on the Dodrechten mud-flats, eating raw sea-fruit for his lunch; crossed to Despar Island in the estuary, where there were glass factories and ironworks, and on several occasions continued across the bridge to Breakman's Point.

South of Brueben, toward the heart of old Ambroy, were the precincts most thoroughly demolished in the Empire Wars: Hoge, Cato, Hyalis Park, Vashmont. Snaking over the forlorn landscape were rows and double-rows of houses built of salvaged brick; in Hoge was the Public Market, in Cato, the Temple; elsewhere were vast areas of broken black brick and mouldering concrete, ill-smelling ponds surrounded by slime of peculiar colors, occasionally the shack of a vagabond or noncup.* In Cato and Vashmont stood the gaunt skeletons of the old central towers, preempted by the lords for their eyries. One day Ghyl, recalling Rudel the puppet, decided to test the practicality of the exploit. Selecting a tower, the property of Lord Waldo the Flowan**, Ghyl started to climb the structure: up the diagonal bracing to the first horizontal girder, across to another diagonal, up to the second horizontal, and the third, and the fourth: up a hundred feet, two hundred feet, three hundred feet, and here he stopped, hugging the girder, for the distance to the ground had become frightening.

For a space Ghyl sat looking out across the old city. The view was splendid, in a still, melancholy fashion; the ruins, lit at an angle by the gray-gold sunlight, showed a fascinating wealth of detail. Ghyl gazed off across Hoge, trying to locate Undle Square...From below came a hoarse harsh voice; looking down, Ghyl saw a man in brown trousers and flared black coat: one of the Vashmont welfare agents.

Ghyl descended to the ground where he was sternly reprimanded and required to state his name and address.

Early the following morning a Brueben Precinct welfare agent, Helfred Cobol, stopped by to have a word with Amiante, and Ghyl became very apprehensive. Would he be rehabilitated? But Helfred Cobol said nothing about the Vashmont tower and only made gruff recommendations

---

*Noncuperatives: non-recipients of welfare benefits, reputedly all Chaoticists, anarchists, thieves, swindlers, whore-mongers.

**The lords derived their cognomens from the public utility fiefs which constituted their primary holdings. These, in the language of the time, were Spay, Chaluz, Flowan, Overtrend, Underline and Boimarc: communications, energy, water, transit, sewerage, trade.

that Amiante impose stricter discipline upon Ghyl, which Amiante heard with polite disinterest.

Helfred Cobol was stocky and barrel-shaped with a pudgy pouchy head, a bump of a nose, small gray eyes. He was brisk and business-like, and reputedly conceded special treatment to no one. Still he was a man of wide experience and tended not to interpret the Code too narrowly. With most recipients Helfred Cobol used a breezy manner, but in the presence of Amiante he was cautious and watchful, as if he found Amiante unpredictable.

Helfred Cobol had hardly departed before Eng Seche, the cantankerous old precinct delegate of the Wood-carvers' Guild came by to inspect the premises, to satisfy himself that Amiante was conforming to the by-laws, using only the prescribed tools and operations, making use of no jigs, patterns, automatic processes or multiple production devices. He remained over an hour, examining Amiante's tools one by one, until finally Amiante, in a somewhat quizzical voice, inquired precisely what he sought.

"Nothing specific, Rt. Tarvoke*, nothing especial; perhaps the impression of a clamp, or something similar. I may say that your work of late has been peculiarly even of finish."

"If you wish, I can work less skillfully," suggested Amiante.

His irony, if he intended such, was lost on the delegate. "This is counter to the by-laws. Very well then; you are aware of the strictures."

Amiante turned back to his work; the delegate departed. From the slope of Amiante's shoulders, the energy with which he plied mallet and chisel, Ghyl realized that his father was exasperated. Amiante finally threw down the tools, went to the door, looked across Undle Square. He turned back into the shop. "Do you understand what the delegate was saying?"

"He thought you were duping."

"Yes. Something of the sort. Do you know why he was concerned?"

"No." And Ghyl added loyally, "It seemed silly to me."

"Well—not altogether. In Fortinone we live or die by trade, and we guarantee hand-crafted wares. Duplicating, molding, casing—all are prohibited. We make no two objects alike, and the Guild Delegates enforce the rule."

"What of the lords?" asked Ghyl. "What guild do they belong to? What do they produce?"

---

*Rt: abbreviation for *Recipient*, the usual formal or honorific title of address.

Amiante gave a painful grimace: half-smile, half-wince. "They are folk apart. They belong to no guilds."

"How do they earn their vouchers?" demanded Ghyl.

"Very simply," said Amiante. "Long ago there was a great war. Ambroy was left in ruins. The lords came here and spent many vouchers in reconstruction: a process called investment. They restored the facilities for the water supply, laid down the Overtrend tubes, and so forth. So now we pay for use of these facilities."

"Hmmf," said Ghyl. "I thought we received water and power and things like that as part of our free welfare benefits."

"Nothing is free," remarked Amiante. "Unless a person steals, whereupon, sooner or later, in one way or another, he pays for his stealing. So there you have it. The lords take a part of all our money: 1.18 percent to be exact."

Ghyl reflected a moment. "Is that a great deal?"

"It seems adequate," said Amiante drily. "There are three million recipients in Fortinone and about two hundred lords—six hundred counting ladies and lordlings." Amiante pulled at his lower lip. "It makes an interesting calculation...Three million recipients, six hundred noble-folk. One noble for each five thousand recipients. On a basis of 1.18 percent—call it one percent—it would appear that each lord receives the income of fifty recipients." Amiante seemed perplexed by the results of his computation. "Even lords must find it hard to spend so lavishly...Well, then, it is not our affair. I give them their percentage and gladly. Although it is indeed somewhat puzzling...Do they throw money away? Give to far charities? When I was correspondent I should have thought to ask."

"What is a 'correspondent'?"

"Nothing of importance. A position which I held a long time ago, when I was young. A time long past, I fear."

"It does not mean being a lord?"

Amiante chuckled. "Certainly not. Do I resemble a lord?"

Ghyl examined him critically. "I suppose not. How does one become a lord?"

"By birth."

"But—what of Rudel and Marelvie at the puppet play? Did they not receive utility fiefs and become lords?"

"Not really. Desperate noncups, and sometimes recipients, have kidnaped lords and forced them to yield fiefs and great sums of money. The kidnapers would be financially independent, they might call themselves lords, but they never dared mingle with the true lords. Finally the lords bought Garrion guards from the Damar puppet-makers; and now there are few kidnapings. Additionally the lords have agreed to pay no more ransom if kidnaped. So a recipient or a noncup can never be a lord, even should he wish to be."

"When Lord Bodbozzle wanted to marry Marelvie, would she have become a lady? Would their children have been lords?"

Amiante put down his tools and carefully considered his answer. "Very often the lords take mistresses—lady-friends—from among the recipients," he said, "but are careful never to breed children. They are a race apart and apparently intend to keep themselves so."

The amber panes of the outside door darkened; it burst open and Helfred Cobol entered the shop. He stood frowning portentously toward Ghyl, whose heart sank into his shoes. Helfred Cobol turned to Amiante. "I have just read my noon briefing sheet. There is a red notation in reference to your son Ghyl: an offense of trespass and careless risk. The apprehension was made by the Ward 12B, Vashmont Precinct, welfare agent. He reports that Ghyl had climbed the girders of Lord Waldo the Flowan's tower to a dangerous and illegal height, committing an offense against Lord Waldo, and against the precincts of Vashmont and Brueben by incurring risk of hospitalization."

Amiante, brushing chips from his apron, blew out his cheeks. "Yes, yes. The lad is quite active."

"Far too active! In fact, irresponsible! He prowls at will, night and day. I have seen him slinking home after dark drenched to the skin with rain! He roams the city like a thief; he learns nothing but shiftlessness! I cannot believe that this is a benign situation. Do you have no concern for the child's future?"

"No hurry there," replied Amiante in an airy tone. "The future is long."

"A man's life is short. High time he was introduced to his calling! I assume you intend him for a wood-carver?"

Amiante shrugged. "As good a trade as any."

"He should be under instruction. Why do you not send him to the guild-school?"

Amiante tested the edge of the chisel against his thumbnail. "Let him enjoy his innocence," he said in a gruff voice. "He will know drudgery enough in his lifetime."

Helfred Cobol started to speak, then stopped. He gave a grunt which might have meant anything. "Another matter: why does he not attend Voluntary Temple Exercises?"

Amiante put down his chisel, frowned rather foolishly, as if he were puzzled. "As to that, I don't know. I have never asked him."

"You teach him leaps at home?"

"Well, no. I do small leaping myself."

"Hmmf. You should enjoin him to such matters regardless of your own habits."

Amiante turned his eyes toward the ceiling, then picked up his chisel and attacked a panel of aromatic arzack which he had just clamped to his bench. The design was already laid out: a grove of trees with long-haired maidens fleeing a satyr. The apertures and rough differences of relief were indicated by chalk-marks. Using a metal straight-bar as a guide for his thumb, Amiante began to gouge into the wood.

Helfred Cobol came across the room to watch. "Very handsome... What is that wood? Kodilla? Boligam? One of those South Continent hardwoods?"

"Arzack, from the woods back of Perdue."

"Arzack! I had no idea it gave so large a panel! The trees are never more than three feet through."

"I pick my trees," Amiante explained patiently. "The foresters cut the trunks into seven-foot lengths. I rent a vat at the dye-works. The logs soak in chemical for two years. I remove the bark, make a single two-inch cut up the trunk: about thirty laminae. I peel off the outer two inches entirely around the trunk, to secure a slab seven feet high by six to nine feet long. This goes into a press, and when it dries I scrape it flat."

"Hm. You peel the layer off yourself?"

"Yes."

"With no complaints from the Carpenters' Guild?"

Amiante shrugged. "They can't or won't do the work. I have no choice. Even if I wanted any." The last was a muttered afterthought.

Helfred Cobol said tersely, "If everyone acted to his own taste we'd live like Wirwans."

"Perhaps." Amiante continued to shave wood from the arzack slab. Helfred Cobol picked up one of the curls, smelled it. "What is the odor: wood or chemical?"

"A little of both. New arzack is rather more peppery."

Helfred Cobol heaved a sigh. "I'd like a screen like that, but my stipend barely keeps me alive. I don't suppose you have any rejects you'd part with."

Amiante glanced expressionlessly sidewise. "Talk to the Boimarc lords. They take all my screens. The Rejects they burn, the Seconds they lock in a warehouse, the Acmes and Firsts they export. Or so I suppose, since I am not consulted. I would earn more vouchers if I did my own marketing."

"We must maintain our reputation," declared Helfred Cobol in a heavy voice. "In the far worlds, to say 'a piece from Ambroy' is to say 'a jewel of perfection'!"

"Admiration is gratifying," said Amiante, "but it gains remarkably few vouchers."

"What would you have? The markets flooded with brummagem?"

"Why not?" asked Amiante, continuing with his work. "Acmes and Firsts would shine by comparison."

Helfred Cobol shook his head in dissent. "Merchandising is not all that simple." He watched a moment or two longer, then laid his finger on the straight-bar. "Better not let the Guild Delegate see you working with a guide device. He'd bring you before the committee for duping."

Amiante looked up in mild astonishment. "No duplicating here."

"The action of the bar against your thumb allows you to carry along or duplicate a given depth of cut."

"Bah," muttered Amiante. "Pettifoggery. Utter nonsense."

"A friendly warning, no more," said Helfred Cobol. He glanced aside to Ghyl. "Your father's a good craftsman, lad, but perhaps a trifle vague and unworldly. Now my advice to you is to give over this wandering and prowling, by day and by night. Apply yourself to a trade. Wood-carving, or if you want something different, the Guild Council can offer a choice where shortages exist. Myself, I believe you'd do best with wood-carving. Amiante has much to teach you." Helfred Cobol turned the briefest of glances at the straight-bar. "Another matter: you're not too young for the Temple. They'll put you at easy leaps, and teach you proper doctrine. But keep on like you're going, you'll end up a vagrant or a noncup."

Helfred Cobol gave Amiante a curt nod and departed the shop.

Ghyl went to the door, watched Helfred Cobol cross Undle Square. Then he slowly closed the door—another slab of dark arzack into which Amiante had set bulbs of crude amber glass—and came slowly across the room. "Do I have to go to the Temple?"

Amiante grunted. "Helfred Cobol is not to be taken altogether seriously. He says certain things because this is his job. I daresay he sends his own children to Saltation, but I doubt if he leaps any more zealously than I do."

"Why are all welfare agents named Cobol?"

Amiante drew up a stool, poured himself a cup of bitter black tea. He sipped thoughtfully. "Long ago, when the capital of Fortinone was at Thadeus, up the coast, the Welfare Supervisor was a man named Cobol. He appointed all his brothers and nephews to good jobs, so that shortly there were only Cobols in the Welfare Department. So it is today; and welfare agents who are not born Cobols—most of them are, of course—change their names. It is simply a matter of tradition. Ambroy is a city of many traditions. Some are useful, some not. A Mayor of Ambroy is elected every five years, but he has no function; he does nothing but draw his stipend. A tradition, but useless."

Ghyl looked at his father respectfully. "You know almost everything, don't you? No one else knows such things."

Amiante nodded rather glumly. "Such knowledge earns no vouchers, however...Ah well, enough of this." He drained his cup of tea. "It seems that I must train you to carve wood, to read and write...Come here then. Look at these gouges and chisels. First you must learn their names. This is a plow. This is a No. 2 elliptical gouge. This is a lazy-tang..."

CHAPTER IV

Amiante was not a demanding taskmaster. Ghyl's life proceeded much as before, though he climbed no more towers.

Summer came to Ambroy. There were rains and great thunderstorms, then a period of beautiful clear weather during which the half-ruined city seemed almost beautiful. Amiante aroused himself from his musing and in a great burst of energy took Ghyl on a walking-trip up the Insse River, into the foothills of the Meagher Mounts. Ghyl had never before been so far from home. In contrast to the dilapidations of Ambroy, the countryside seemed remarkably fresh and open. Tramping along the riverbank under the purple banion trees, they would often pause to gaze wistfully at some especially pleasant situation—an island, shaded under banion and water-willow, with a little house, a dock, a skiff; or perhaps a houseboat moored to the bank, with children swimming in the river, their parents lounging on the deck with mugs of beer. At night they slept on beds of leaves and straw, their fire flickering and glowing to coals. Overhead burned the stars of the galaxy and Amiante pointed out those few he knew: the Mirabilis Cluster, Glysson, Heriartes, Cornus, Alode. To Ghyl these were names of sheer magic.

"Someday," he told Amiante, "when I am bigger, we'll carve lots of screens and save all our vouchers; then we'll travel: to all those stars, and the Five Jeng Worlds as well!"

"That would be very nice," said Amiante with a grin. "I'd better put more arzack down into chemical so that we'll have sufficient panels."

"Do you think we could buy a space-yacht and travel as we wished?"

Amiante shook his head. "They cost far too much. A hundred thousand vouchers, often more."

"Couldn't we save that much, if we worked very hard?"

"We'd be working and saving all our lives, and still never have enough. Space-yachts are for lords."

They passed Brazen and Grigglesby Corners and Blonnet, then turned aside into the hills. At last, weary and footsore, they returned home, and indeed Amiante spent precious vouchers to ride Overtrend the last twenty miles through Riverside Park, Vashmont, Hoge.

For a period Amiante, as if himself convinced of the soundness of Ghyl's proposals, worked with great diligence. Ghyl helped as best he could and practised the use of chisels and augers, but vouchers came in with discouraging slowness. Amiante's diligence waned; he resumed his old habits of working and musing, staring into space for minutes at a time; and presently Ghyl lost interest as well. There must be some other, faster, system by which to earn vouchers: gambling, for instance. Kidnaping of lords was irregulationary; Ghyl knew that his father would never hear of such a proposal.

The summer proceeded: a halcyon time, perhaps the happiest of Ghyl's life. In all the city, his favorite resort was Dunkum's Heights in Veige Precinct, north of Brueben, a grassy-topped shoulder of ground beside the estuary. Dozens of fresh mornings and as many hazy afternoons Ghyl climbed Dunkum's Heights, sometimes alone, sometimes with his friend Floriel, a big-eyed waif with pale skin, fragile features, a mop of thick black hair. Floriel lived with his mother, who worked in the brewery, sectioning and cleaning big purple hollips, from which the brew derived its characteristic musty flavor. She was a large ribald woman, not without vanity, who claimed to be second cousin to the Mayor. Hollip odor permeated Floriel's mother, her person and all her belongings, and even attached itself to Floriel, and ever afterward, whenever Ghyl drank beer, or caught the tart musk of hollips at the market, he would recall Floriel and his wan ragamuffin face.

Floriel was a companion exactly suited to Ghyl's tastes: a lad mild and acquiescent, but by no means lacking in energy or imagination, and ripe for any adventure. The two boys spent many happy hours on Dunkum's Heights, basking in the tawny sunlight, chewing the soft grass, watching the flight of shrinken-birds over the mud-flats.

Dunkum's Heights was a place to laze and dream; in contrast, the space-port, in Godero Precinct, east of Dunkum's Heights, was the very node of adventure and romance. The space-port was divided into three sections, with the depot at the center. To the north was the commercial field, where two or three freight ships were usually loading or discharging. To the south, lined up along an access avenue, were space-yachts belonging to the lords: objects of the most entrancing verve and glitter. To the west was the passenger terminus. Here hulked the black excursion ships, serving those recipients who, by dint of toil and frugality, had been able to buy off-world passage. The tours were various. Cheapest and most popular was a five-day visit to the moon Damar, a strange little world half the diameter of Halma where lived the Damaran puppet-makers. At Garwan, on Damar's equator, was a tourist node, with hotels, promenades, restaurants. Puppet plays of every description were presented: legends of Faerie, fables of gothic horror, historical reenactments, farces, displays macabre and erotic. The performing puppets were small human simulacra, far more carefully bred, far more expensive than the wry little creatures exported to such enterprises as Framtree's Peripatezic Entercationers. The Damarans themselves lived underground, in circumstances of great luxury. Their pelts were black; their bony little heads were tufted with coarse black bristles; their eyes shone with curious glints, like the lights of a star sapphire; in short, they were not unlike their own export puppets.

Another tourist destination, somewhat more prestigious, was the planet next out in orbit: Morgan, a world of wind-swept oceans, table-flat steppes, pinnacles of naked rock. On Morgan were a number of rather shabby resorts, offering little recreation other than sailing high-wheeled cars across the steppes. Nonetheless, thousands paid hard-won vouchers to spend two weeks at Tundra Inn or Mountain House or Cape Rage Haven.

Far more desirable were the Wonder Worlds of the Mirabilis Cluster. When folk returned from the Wonder Worlds they had fulfilled their dreams; they had traveled to the stars; they would talk of the marvels they had seen to the end of their time. The excursion however was beyond the financial reach of all but the highly compensated: guild-masters and delegates, welfare supervisors, Boimarc auditors and bursars, those noncups who had gained wealth through mercantilism, gambling or crime.

Worlds more remote than the Wonder Worlds were known to exist: Rodion, Alcantara, Earth, Maastricht, Montiserra with its floating cities, Himat, many others, but no one fared so far save the lords in their space-yachts.

To Ghyl and Floriel nothing was impossible. Noses pressed to the fence which surrounded the spaceport, they vowed that financial independence and space-travel was the only life for them. But first to gain the vouchers, and here was the stumbling block. Vouchers were hard to come by, Ghyl well knew. Other worlds were reputedly rich, with vouchers distributed without stint. How to take himself and his father and Floriel to a more lavish environment? If only by some marvelous exploit, by some miracle he could come into possession of a space-yacht! What freedom, what romance and adventure!

Ghyl recalled the exactions imposed upon evil Lord Bodbozzle. Rudel and Marelvie had gained financial independence—but it had only been a puppet-play. Was there no other way?

One amazing day toward the end of summer Ghyl and Floriel lay on Dunkum's Heights sucking grass stems and talking largely of the future. "What, really, do you think you'll do?" asked Ghyl.

"First of all," said Floriel, cradling his girlishly delicate face in his hands, "I'll hoard vouchers: dozens. Then I'll learn to gamble, like the noncups do. I'll learn all the best ways to win and then one day I'll gamble and earn hundreds and hundreds of vouchers. Thousands even. Then I'll turn them in for a space-yacht and fly away! away! away! Out past Mirabilis!"

Ghyl nodded reflectively. "That would be one way."

"Or," Floriel went on, "I might save a lord's daughter from danger. Then I'd marry her and be a lord myself."

Ghyl shook his head. "That's never done. They're much too proud. They just have friends among the underfolk. Mistresses, they're called."

Floriel turned to look south, across the brown and gray crumble of Brueben to the towers of Vashmont. "Why should they be proud? They are only ordinary people who happen to be lords."

"A different kind of people," said Ghyl. "Although I've heard that when they walk the streets without Garrion no one notices them as lords."

"They're proud because they are rich," declared Floriel. "I'll earn wealth too, and I'll be proud and they'll be eager to marry me, just to count my vouchers. Think of it! Blue vouchers, orange vouchers, green vouchers! Bundles and boxes of all colors!"

"You'll need them all," observed Ghyl. "Space-yachts cost a great deal: a half-million vouchers, I suppose. A million for the really good ones: the Lixons or the Hexanders with the promenade deck. Just pretend! Fancy that we're out in space, with Mirabilis behind, heading for some wonderful strange planet. We dine in the main saloon, on turbot and roast bloorcock and the best Gade wine—and then we go along the promenade to the after-dome and eat our ices in the dark, with the Mirabilis stars behind and the Giant's Scimitar above and the galaxy to the side."

Floriel heaved a deep sigh. "If I can't buy a space-yacht—I'll steal one. I don't think it's wrong," he told Ghyl earnestly, for Ghyl wore a dubious expression. "I'd steal only from the lords, who can well afford to lose. Think of the bales of vouchers they receive and never spend!"

Ghyl was not sure that this was the case, but did not care to argue.

Floriel rose to his knees. "Let's go over to the space-port! We can look at yachts and pick one out!"

"Now?"

"Of course! Why not?"

"But it's so far."

"We'll use Overtrend."

"My father doesn't like to give vouchers to the lords."

"Overtrend doesn't cost much. To Godero, no more than fifteen checks."

Ghyl shrugged. "Very well."

They went down from the bluff by the familiar train, but instead of turning south, skirted the municipal tanneries to the Veige No. 2 West Overtrend kiosk. They descended by escalator to the on ramp, boarded a capsule. Each in turn punched the 'Space-port' symbol and held his under-age card to a sensor plate. The capsule accelerated, rushed east, decelerated, opened; the boys stepped forth upon the up-escalator, which presently discharged them into the space-port depot: a cavernous place, echoing to every footfall. The boys slunk over to the side and took stock of the situation, conversing in low voices. For all the comings and goings, the atmosphere of suppressed excitement, the depot was a cheerless place, with walls of dust-brown tile, a great dim vault of a roof.

Ghyl and Floriel decided to watch the passengers boarding the excursion ships. They approached the embarkation wicket, tried to pass through the field gate but a guard waved them back. "Observation deck through the arch; passengers only on the field!" But he turned away to answer a question and Floriel, suddenly bold, seized Ghyl's arm, and they slipped quickly past.

Amazed and delighted at their own audacity, they hurried to the shadow of an overhanging buttress where they crouched to take stock of the situation. A sound from the sky startled them: a sudden high-pitched roar from a Leamas Line excursion ship, settling like a great portly duck on its suppressors. The roar became a whine as the force-field reacted with the ground, then passed beyond audibility. The ship touched ground; the hyper-audible sound returned into sensible range, then sighed away to silence, and the ship was at rest firm against the soil of Halma. The ports opened; the passengers slowly filed forth, vouchers spent, heads bowed, ambitions sated.

Floriel gave a sudden gasp of excitement. He pointed. "The ports are open! Do you know, if we went through the crowd right now we could go aboard and hide? Then when the ship was in space we'd come out! They'd never send us back! We'd see Damar at least and maybe Morgan as well."

Ghyl shook his head. "We wouldn't see anything. They'd lock us in a little room and give us bread and water. They'd charge our fathers for the passage—thousands of vouchers! My father couldn't pay. I don't know what he'd do."

"My mother wouldn't pay," said Floriel. "She'd beat me as well. But I don't care. We'd have traveled *space*!"

"They'd list us for inclination," said Ghyl.

Floriel made a gesture of scornful defiance. "What's the difference? We could toe the line in the future—until another opportunity like this came along."

"It's no opportunity," said Ghyl. "Not really. In the first place they'd catch us in the act and pitch us out. We'd do ourselves no good whatever. Anyway, who wants to travel in an old excursion ship? I want a space-yacht. Let's see if we can get out on the south field."

The space-yachts were ranked in a line along the far end of the field, with an access avenue running in front of them. To reach this avenue meant crossing an open area where they would be in plain view of anyone who cared to look down either from the observation deck or the control tower. Ghyl and Floriel, huddling beside the wall, discussed the situation, weighing pros and cons. "Come," said Floriel. "Let's just make a run for it."

"We'd do better just walking," said Ghyl. "We wouldn't look so much like thieves. Which we're not, of course. Then, if we were caught, we could say truthfully that we meant no harm. If they saw us running, they'd be sure that we were up to mischief."

"Very well," grumbled Floriel. "Let's go then."

Feeling naked and exposed they crossed the open area, and gained the comparative shelter of the access avenue without challenge. And now, near at hand, were the fascinating space-yachts; the first, a hundred-foot Dameron CoCo 14, jutting its prow almost over their heads.

They peered cautiously down the avenue, which was the way the lords came when they wished to embark upon their yachts. All seemed placid, the marvellous yachts crouched on rolling gear and nose-blocks as if dozing.

No Garrion were in sight, nor any lords, nor any mechanics—these latter generally men from Luschein on South Continent. Floriel's daring, drawn more from an active mind and a high-strung temperament than any real courage, began to peter out. He became timid and fretful, while Ghyl, who would never have come so far on his own, was obliged to supply staying-power for both.

"Do you think we should go any farther?" Floriel asked in a husky whisper.

"We've come this far," said Ghyl. "We're doing no harm. I don't think anyone would mind. Not even a lord."

"What would they do if they caught us? Send us to rehabilitation?"

Ghyl laughed nervously. "Of course not. If anyone asks, we'll say we're just looking at the yachts, which is the truth."

"Yes," said Floriel, dubiously. "I suppose so."

"Come along then," said Ghyl.

They started south along the avenue. After the Dameron was a Wodze Blue, and next beside it a slightly smaller, more lavish, Wodze Scarlet; then a huge Gallypool Irwanforth; then a Hatz Marauder, then a Sparling Starchaser in a splendid hull of gold and silver: yacht after yacht, each more wonderful than the last. Once or twice the boys walked up under the hulls, to touch the glossy skins which had known so much distance, to examine the port-of-call blazons.

Halfway along the avenue they came upon a yacht which had been lowered off its nose-block, apparently to facilitate repair, and the boys walked furtively close. "Look!" whispered Ghyl. "You can see just a bit of the main saloon. Isn't she absolutely wonderful?"

Floriel acknowledged as much. "It's a Lixon Triplange. They all have those heavy cowls around the forward ports." He walked up under the hull to examine the port-of-call blazons. "This one's been everywhere. Triptolemus…Jeng…Sanreale…Someday, when I read I'll know them all."

"Yes, I want to read too," said Ghyl. "My father knows a great deal about reading; he can teach me." He stared at Floriel, who was making urgent gestures. "What's the matter?"

"Garrion!" hissed Floriel. "Hide, back of the stanchion!"

With alacrity Ghyl joined Floriel behind the prow support. They stood scarcely breathing. Floriel whispered desperately, "They can't do anything to us, even if they catch us. They're just servants; they don't have a right to give us orders, or chase us, or anything. Not unless we're doing damage."

"I suppose not," said Ghyl. "Let's hide anyway."

"Certainly."

The Garrion came past, moving with the rolling purposeful step characteristic of the race. He wore livery of light green and gray, with gold rosettes, a cap of green-gray leather.

Floriel, who took pride in his knowledgeability, hazarded a guess regarding the Garrion's patron: "Green and gray…might be Verth the Chaluz. Or Herman the Chaluz. Chaluz lords use the gold rosette, you know: it means power."

Ghyl did not know, but he nodded acquiescence. They waited until the Garrion entered the terminal and was gone from sight. Cautiously the boys came out from behind the stanchion. They looked left and right, then proceeded along the line of yachts. "Look!" breathed Floriel. "The Deme—the gold and black one! The port is open!"

The two boys halted, stared at the fascinating gap. "That's where the Garrion came from," said Ghyl. "He'll be back."

"Not right away. We could climb the ramp and look inside. No one would ever know."

Ghyl gave a grimace. "I've already been reprimanded for trespass."

"This isn't trespass! Anyway, what's the harm? If anyone asked what we were doing, we'd say we were just looking."

"There's sure to be someone aboard," said Ghyl dubiously.

Floriel thought not. "The Garrion is probably fixing something, or cleaning. He's gone to get supplies and he'll be away ever so long! Let's take a quick look inside!"

Ghyl gauged the distance to the terminal: a good five minutes walk. Floriel tugged at his arm. "Come along; as if we were lordlets! One peek inside, to see how the lords live!"

Ghyl thought of Helfred Cobol; he thought of his father. His throat felt dry. Already he and Floriel had dared more than was proper...Still, the Garrion was in the terminal, and what could be the harm in looking through the entrance? Ghyl said, "If we just go to the door..."

Floriel now became reluctant; evidently he had been counting on Ghyl to veto so mad a proposal. "Do you really think we should?"

Ghyl made a signal for caution and went quietly toward the space-yacht. Floriel followed.

At the foot of the ramp they stopped to listen. There was no sound from within. Visible only was the inside of the air-lock and, beyond, a tantalizing glimpse of carved wood, scarlet cloth, a rack of glass and metal implements: luxury almost too splendid to be real. Drawn by fascinated curiosity, almost against their wills, certainly against their better judgment, the boys gingerly ascended the ramp, furtive as cats in a strange house. They peered in through the port, to hear a murmur of machinery, nothing else.

Now they backed away to look toward the terminal. The Garrion had not come forth. Hearts thumping in their throats the boys stepped into the air-lock, peered into the main saloon.

They let out their breath slowly in delight and wonder. The saloon was perhaps thirty feet long and sixteen feet wide. The walls were paneled in gray-green sako-wood and tapestry cloth; the floor was covered with a thick purple rug. At the forward end of the saloon four steps rose to a control platform. Aft, an arch opened upon an observation deck under a transparent dome.

"Isn't it marvelous?" breathed Floriel. "Do you think we'll ever have a space-yacht? One as fine as this?"

"I don't know," said Ghyl somberly. "I hope so…Yes. Some day I will have one…Now we had best go."

Floriel whispered, "Think! If we knew astrogation, we could take the space-yacht right now—up and away from Ambroy! We'd own it, all to ourselves!"

The idea was tantalizing but preposterous. Ghyl was now more than ready to leave, but to his dismay Floriel skipped recklessly across the saloon, up the steps to the control platform. Ghyl called to him in an anxious voice, "Don't touch anything! Don't move a single lever!"

"Come now. Do you take me for a fool?"

Ghyl looked longingly back at the entrance port. "We'd best be going!"

"Oh but you must come up here, you can't imagine how grand it is!"

"Don't touch anything!" Ghyl warned him. "You'll cause trouble!" He came a couple steps forward. "Let's go!"

"As soon as—" Floriel's voice became a startled stammer.

Following the direction of his gaze, Ghyl saw a girl standing by the aft companionway. She wore a rich suit of rose velvet, a square soft flat cap of the same material with a pair of scarlet ribbons hanging past her shoulders. She was dark-haired; her face was piquant, mobile, bright with vitality, but at this moment she looked from one ragamuffin to the other in outrage. Ghyl stared back in fascination. Surely this was the same small lady the puppet-master had pointed out at the puppet show? She was very pretty, he thought, with the same fascinating hint of Difference: that peculiar quality which distinguished lords from men.

Floriel, arousing from his petrifaction, began to slink down from the control deck. The girl came a few steps forward. A Garrion followed her into the saloon. Floriel froze back against a bulkhead. He stuttered, "We meant no harm, we only wanted to look—"

The girl studied him gravely, then turned to inspect Ghyl. Her mouth drooped in disgust. She looked back at the Garrion. "Give them a beating; throw them away."

The Garrion seized Floriel, who chattered and howled. Ghyl might have retreated and escaped, but he chose to remain, for a reason not at all clear to him: certainly his presence was no help to Floriel.

The Garrion dealt Floriel a series of disinterested blows. Floriel yelped and writhed in dramatic fashion. The girl gave a curt nod. "Enough; the other."

Sobbing and panting Floriel fled past Ghyl, and down the ramp. Ghyl stood his ground against the Garrion, trying to control his shrinking flesh as the creature loomed over him. The Garrion's hands were cool and rough; the touch sent an odd chill along Ghyl's nerves. He hardly felt the blows, which were carefully measured. His attention was fixed on the girl who watched the beating critically. Ghyl wondered how someone so delicate and pretty could be so unfeeling. Were all the lords so cruel?

The girl saw Ghyl's gaze and perhaps sensed the import. She frowned. "Beat this one more severely; he is insolent!"

Ghyl received a few additional blows and then was shoved roughly from the ship.

Floriel stood a fearful fifty yards down the avenue. Ghyl picked himself up from the ground where he had fallen. He looked back up the ramp. There was nothing to see. He turned away and joined Floriel; wordlessly they trudged back along the avenue.

They gained the interior of the depot without attracting attention. Mindful of his father's antipathy toward the Overtrend, Ghyl insisted on walking home: a matter of four miles.

Along the way Floriel burst out in a spasm of fury. "What abominable people the lords! Did you sense the girl's glee? She treated us as if we were muck! As if we stank! And my mother is second cousin to the Mayor! I will have my own back some day! Hear me, for I am resolved!"

Ghyl heaved a mournful sigh. "She certainly could have used us more kindly. Still—she also might have used us worse. Far worse."

Floriel gazed at him in amazement, hair tousled, face distorted. "Eh? What's all this? She ordered us beaten! While she watched, smirking!"

"She could have had our names. What if she had given us to the welfare agents?"

Floriel lowered his head. The two boys trudged on into Brueben. The setting sun, entering a band of ale-colored haze, cast amber light in their faces.

CHAPTER V

Autumn came to Ambroy, then winter: a season of chilling rains and mists, which started a black and lavender lichen growing over the ruins, to lend the old city a dismal grandeur it lacked in the dry season.

Amiante completed a fine screen which was judged 'Acme' and which also received a Guild Citation of Excellence, with which he was quietly pleased.

He also received a visit from a Guide Leaper of the Temple, a sharp-featured young man wearing a scarlet jacket, a tall black hat, brown breeches tight around heavy legs, knotted with muscle after a lifetime of leaping. He came to remonstrate in regard to Ghyl's carefree life. "Why does he not participate in Soul Endowment? What of his Basic Saltations? He knows neither Rite nor Rote nor Doxology; nor Leaps nor Bounds! Finuka requires more than this!"

Amiante listened politely, but continued to work with his chisel. He spoke in a mild voice, "The lad is hardly old enough to think. If he has a mind to devotion, he'll know fast enough; then he'll more than make up for any lack."

The Leaper became excited. "A fallacy! Children are best trained young. Witness myself! When I was an infant, I crawled upon a patterned rug! The first words I spoke were the Apotheosis and the Simulations. This is best! Train the child young! As he stands now he is a spiritual vacuum, susceptible to any strange cult! Best to fill his soul with the way of Finuka!"

"I'll explain all this to him," said Amiante. "Perhaps he may be encouraged to worship; who can say?"

"The parent bears the responsibility," intoned the Guide Leaper. "When have you done your last leaping? I suspect months have passed!"

Amiante calculated a pensive moment. He nodded. "Months at the very least."

"Well then!" exclaimed the Leaper in triumph. "Is this not an explanation in itself?"

"Very likely. Well then, I'll have a discussion with the boy later in the day."

The Guide Leaper started to expostulate further, but, observing Amiante's absorption in his work, he shook his head in defeat, performed a holy sign and departed.

Amiante glanced up expressionlessly as the Leaper passed through the door.

Time and welfare regulations pressed in upon Ghyl. On his tenth birthday he joined the Wood-carvers' Guild, his first choice, the Mariners' Guild, being closed to all save sons of existing members.

Amiante dressed for the occasion in formal guild-meeting wear: a brown coat flared wide at the hips, peaked up at the shoulders, with black piping and carved buttons; tight trousers, with rows of white buttons down the sides, a complicated billed hat of tan felt with black tassels and guild medals. Ghyl wore his first trousers (having heretofore gone only in a gray child's smock) with a maroon jacket and a smart polished leather cap. Together they walked north to the Guild Hall.

The initiation was a lengthy affair, consisting of a dozen rituals, questions and responses, charges and assurances. Ghyl paid his first year's dues, received his first medal, which the Guild-master ceremoniously affixed to his cap.

From the Guild Hall Ghyl and Amiante walked east across the old Mercantilikum to the Welfare Agency in East Town. Here there was further formality. Ghyl was somatyped; his Beneficial Number was tattooed upon his right shoulder. Henceforth, by Agency reckoning, he was an adult, and would be counseled by Helfred Cobol in his own right. Ghyl was asked his status at the Temple, and was forced to admit to none. The Qualification Officer and the Department Scrivener looked with raised eyebrows from Ghyl to Amiante, then they shrugged. The scrivener wrote upon the questionnaire: "No present capability; status of parent in doubt."

The Qualification Officer spoke in a measured voice: "To achieve your most complete fulfillment as a participating member of society, you must be active at the Temple. I will therefore assign you to Full Operative Function. You must contribute four hours voluntary cooperation per week to the Temple, together with various assessments and beneficial gifts. Since you are somewhat—in fact, considerably—retarded, you will be enrolled in special Indoctrination Class...Did you speak?"

"I was asking if the Temple was necessary," stammered Ghyl. "I just wanted to know—"

"Temple instruction is not 'fully compulsory'," said the officer. "It is of the 'Strongly Recommended' category, inasmuch as any other course suggests noncuperativity. You will therefore report to the Temple Juvenile Authority at ten o'clock tomorrow."

So, willy-nilly, and with Amiante keeping his own counsel, Ghyl presented himself at the Central Temple in Cato Precinct. The clerk issued him a dull red cloak with high hitches for leaping, a book which displayed and explained the Great Design, charts of uncomplicated patterns; then assigned him to a study group.

Ghyl made but fair progress at the Temple, and was far outshone by others younger than himself, who skipped easily through the most complicated patterns: bounding, dancing, whirling, flicking a toe to touch a sign here, an emblem there, swinging contemptuously wide over the black and green 'Delinquencies', coursing swiftly down the peripheries, veering past the red demon spots.

At home Amiante in a sudden fit of energy taught Ghyl to read and write the third-level syllabary, and sent him to the Guild instruction chambers to learn mathematics.

It was a busy year for Ghyl. The old days of idleness and wandering seemed remote indeed. On his eleventh birthday Amiante gave him a choice panel of arzack, to be carved into a screen of his own design.

Ghyl looked among his sketches and chose a pleasant composition of boys climbing fruit trees, and he adapted the composition to the natural grain of the panel.

Amiante approved the design. "Quite suitable: whimsical and gay. It is best to produce gay designs. Happiness is fugitive; dissatisfaction and boredom are real. The folk who gaze upon your screens are entitled to all the joy you can give them, even though the joy be but an abstraction."

Ghyl felt impelled to protest at the cynicism of his father. "I don't consider happiness an illusion! Why should folk content themselves with illusions when reality is so pungent? Are not acts better than dreams?"

Amiante gave his characteristic shrug. "There are many more excellent dreams than meaningful acts. Or so it might be argued."

"But acts are *real*! Each real act is worth a thousand dreams!"

Amiante smiled ruefully. "Dream? Act? Which is illusion? Fortinone is old. Billions of folk have come and gone, pale fish in an ocean of time. They rise into the sunlit shallows; they glitter a moment or two; they drift away through the murk."

Ghyl scowled off through the amber panes, which allowed a distorted view of the comings and goings in Undle Square. "I can't feel like a fish. You're not a fish. We don't live in an ocean. You are you and I am I and this is our home." He threw down his tools and marched outside to draw a breath of air. He walked north into Veige Precinct and by force of habit mounted Dunkum's Heights. Here to his annoyance he found two small boys and a little girl, perhaps seven or eight years old. They were sitting in the grass tossing pebbles down the slope. Their chatter seemed much too boisterous for the spot where Ghyl had spent so much time musing. He gave them a glare of outrage, to which they returned puzzled stares. Ghyl strode off to the north, down the long descending ridge which died upon the Dodrechten mud flats. As he walked, he wondered about Floriel, whom he had not seen for some time. Floriel had joined the Metal-benders' Guild. When Ghyl had seen him last, Floriel had sported a little black leather skull-cap from under which his hair curled out in a manner almost too charming for a boy. Floriel had been somewhat remote. He had finally, so Ghyl decided, been caught up in a sensible career, for all the wild talk of his childhood.

Ghyl returned home during the late afternoon, to find Amiante sorting through a portfolio of his private treasures, which he generally kept in a cabinet on the third floor.

Ghyl had never seen at close hand the contents of the portfolio. He approached and watched over Amiante's elbow as Amiante pored over the objects, which were old writings: manuscript, calligraph, ornaments and illustrations. Ghyl noted several extremely ancient fragments of parchment on which were characters indited with great regularity and uniformity. Ghyl was puzzled. He squinted down at the archaic documents. "Who could write so careful and minute a hand? Did they employ mites? No scrivener today could do so well!"

"What you see is a process called 'printing'," Amiante told him. "It is duplication a hundred times, a thousand times over. Nowadays, of course, printing is not allowed."

"How is it accomplished?"

"There are many systems, or so I understand. Sometimes carved bits of metal are inked and pressed against paper; sometimes a jet of black light instantaneously sprays a page with writing; sometimes the characters are burnt upon paper through a pattern. I know very little about these processes, which I believe are still used on other worlds."

Ghyl studied the archaic symbols for a period, then went on to admire the rich colors of the decorations. Amiante, reading from a little pamphlet, chuckled quietly. Ghyl looked around curiously. "What does it say?"

"Nothing of consequence. It is an old bulletin describing an electric boat which was offered for sale by the Bidderbasse Factory in Luschein. The price: twelve hundred sequins."

"What is a sequin?"

"It is money. Something like welfare vouchers. I don't believe the factory is in operation any more. Perhaps the boats were of poor quality. Perhaps the Overtrend lords laid an embargo. It is difficult to know; there are no dependable chronicles, at least not in Ambroy." Amiante heaved a sad sigh. "One can never learn anything when he so desires…Still, I suppose that we should count our blessings. Other eras have been far worse. There is no want in Fortinone, as there is in Bauredel. No wealth, of course, except for that of the lords. But no want."

Ghyl examined the printed characters. "Are these hard to read?"

"Not particularly. Would you like to learn?"

Ghyl hesitated, considering the many demands upon his time. If he were ever to travel to Damar, to Morgan, to the Wonder Worlds (already the dream of owning a space-yacht was becoming remote) he must work with great industry, and earn vouchers. But he nodded. "Yes, I would like to learn."

Amiante seemed pleased. "I am not overly well-versed, and there are many idioms which I fail to recognize—but perhaps we can puzzle them out together."

Amiante pushed all his tools to the side, spread a cloth over the screen upon which he had been working, arranged the fragments, brought stylus and paper and copied the crabbed old characters.

During the days which followed Ghyl struggled to master the archaic system of writing—not so simple a matter as he had originally supposed. Amiante could not transliterate the symbols into either primary pictographs, secondary cursive, nor even the third level syllabary. And even after Ghyl could identify and combine the characters, he was forced to learn archaic idioms and constructions, and sometimes allusions regarding which Amiante could provide no enlightenment.

One day Helfred Cobol came to the shop to find Ghyl copying from an old parchment, while Amiante mused and dreamed over his portfolio. Helfred Cobol stood in the doorway, arms akimbo, a sour look on his face. "Now what occurs here in the wood-carving shop of old Rt. Tarvoke and young Rt. Tarvoke? Are you turning to scrivening? Don't tell me you evoke new patterns for your screens; I know better." He came forward, inspected Ghyl's exercises. "Archaic, eh? Now what will a wood-carver need with Archaic? I can't read it, and I'm a welfare agent."

Amiante spoke with a trifle more animation than he was accustomed to show. "You must remember that one does not carve wood every hour of the day and night."

"Understood," responded Helfred Cobol. "In fact, judging from the work performed since my previous call, you have carved wood very few hours of either day or night. Much more of this and you will be existing on Base Stipend."

Amiante glanced at his nearly finished screen, as if to appraise how much work remained. "In due course, in due course."

Helfred Cobol, coming around the heavy old table, looked down at the portfolio. Amiante made a small motion as if to fold up the covers, but restrained himself. Such an act would only stimulate a man trained to curiosity and suspicion.

Helfred Cobol did not touch the portfolio, but leaned over it with hands behind his back. "Interesting old stuff." He pointed. "Printed material, I believe. How old do you reckon it?"

"I can't be sure," said Amiante. "It makes reference to Clarence Tovanesko, so it won't be more than thirteen hundred years old."

Helfred Cobol nodded. "It might even be of local fabrication. When did anti-duping regulations go into effect?"

"About fifty years after this." Amiante nodded at the bit of paper. "Just a guess of course."

"One doesn't see much printing," ruminated Helfred Cobol. "There's not even any contraband off the space-ships, as there used to be in my grandfather's day. Folk seem to me more law-abiding, which of course, makes life easier for the welfare agents. Noncups are more active this year, worse luck: vandals, thieves, anarchists that they are."

"A worthless group, by and large," agreed Amiante.

"'By and large'?" snorted Helfred Cobol. "Altogether, I would say! They are non-productive, a tumor in the society! The criminals suck our blood, the small-dealers disrupt the Agency's book-work."

Amiante had no more to say. Helfred Cobol turned to Ghyl. "Put aside the erudite uselessness, boy; that's my best advice. You'll never gain vouchers as a scrivener. Also, I've been told that your Temple attendance is spotty, that you're only leaping a simple Honor-to-Finuka Half-about. More practise there, young Rt. Tarvoke! And more time with chisel and gouge!"

"Yes sir," said Ghyl meekly. "I'll do my best."

Helfred Cobol gave him a friendly slap on the shoulder and left the shop. Amiante returned to the portfolio. But his mood was broken, and he twitched the papers with quick petulant jerks.

Ghyl heard him mutter a peevish curse, and, looking up, saw that in his annoyance Amiante had torn one of his treasures: a long fragile sheet of low-grade paper printed with wonderful caricatures of three now-forgotten public figures.

Amiante, after his outburst, sat like a rock, brooding over some matter which he obviously did not plan to communicate to Ghyl. Presently, without a word, Amiante rose to his feet, slung his second-best brown and blue cape around his shoulders and set forth upon an errand. Ghyl went to the door, watched his father amble across the square and disappear into an alley which led away into Nobile Precinct and the rough dock area.

Ghyl, also restless, could concentrate no longer on the old writing. He made a half-hearted attempt to master a rather difficult Temple exercise, then set to work on his screen, and so occupied himself the remainder of the day.

The sun had fallen behind the buildings across the square before Amiante returned. He carried several parcels which he put without comment into a cabinet, then sent Ghyl out to buy seaweed curd and a leek salad for their supper. Ghyl went slowly and reluctantly; there was a pot of left-over porridge which Amiante, who was somewhat frugal with food expenditures, had been planning to use. Why the unnecessary expenditure? Ghyl knew better than to ask. At best Amiante might give him a vague and irrelevant response. At worst Amiante would pretend not to have heard the question.

Something peculiar was in the wind, thought Ghyl. In a heavy mood he visited the greengrocer's, then the marine paste dealer's. Over the evening meal Amiante, to anyone other than Ghyl, might have seemed his ordinary self. Ghyl knew differently. Amiante, not a talkative man, alternated periods of staring glumly down at his plate with attempts at contriving an easy conversation. He inquired as to Ghyl's progress at the Temple, a subject regarding which he had heretofore shown little interest. Ghyl reported that he was doing fairly well with the exercises but found difficulty with the catechism. Amiante nodded but Ghyl could see that his thoughts were elsewhere. Presently Amiante asked if Ghyl had recently seen Floriel, and it so happened that Ghyl had come upon Floriel at the Temple, where he took instruction on much the same basis as Ghyl.

"A peculiar lad, that one," Amiante remarked. "Easily persuaded, or so I would say; and with a streak of perversity to make him uncertain."

"That is what I feel too," said Ghyl. "Although now he seems to be buckling down to guild work."

"Yes, why not?" mused Amiante, as if the reverse—indolence, non-cuperativity—were standard conduct.

There was another silence, with Amiante frowning down at his plate as if for the first time he had become aware of what he was eating. He made an offhand reference to Helfred Cobol. "He means well enough, the agent; but he tries to reconcile too many conflicts. It makes him unhappy. He'll never do well."

Ghyl was interested in his father's opinion. "I've always thought him impatient and rude."

Amiante smiled, and looked off into his private thoughts. But he made another comment. "We are lucky with Helfred Cobol. The polite agents are harder to deal with. They offer smooth surface; they are impervious...How would you like to be a welfare agent?"

Ghyl had never considered the possibility. "I'm not a Cobol. I suppose it's very cuperative, and they gain bonus vouchers, or so I hear. I'd rather be a lord."

"Naturally; who wouldn't?"

"But it's not possible in any way?"

"Not here in Fortinone. They keep themselves to themselves."

"On their home world were they lords? Or ordinary recipients like ourselves?"

Amiante shook his head. "Once, long ago, I worked for an off-world information agency and I might have asked, but during these times my thoughts were elsewhere. I don't know the lords' home world. Perhaps Alode, perhaps Earth, which I've been told is the first home of all men."

"I wonder," said Ghyl, "why the lords live here in Fortinone. Why did they not choose Salula or Luschein or the Mang Islands?"

Amiante shrugged. "The same reason, no doubt, that we live where we do. Here we were born, here we live, here we will die."

"Suppose I went to Luschein and studied to be a space-man; would the lords hire me aboard their yachts?"

Amiante pursed his mouth dubiously. "The first difficulty is learning to be a spaceman. It is a popular occupation."

"Did you ever want to be a spaceman?"

"Oh indeed. I had my dreams. Still—it may be best to carve wood. Who knows? We shall never starve."

"But we will never be financially independent," said Ghyl with a sniff.

"True." Amiante, rising, took his plate to the wash-table where he scraped it very carefully and cleaned it with a minimum of water and sand.

Ghyl watched the meticulous process with detached interest. Amiante, so he knew, begrudged every check he was forced to pay over to the lords. It was a process which puzzled him. He asked: "The lords take 1.18 percent of everything we produce, don't they?"

"They do," said Amiante. "1.18 percent of the value of imports and exports alike."

"Then why do we use so little water and power, and why do we walk so much? Is not the money paid regardless?"

Amiante's face took on a mulish cast, always the case when he spoke of vouchers paid to the lords. "Meters are everywhere. Meters measure everything except the air you breathe. Even the sewage is metered. The Welfare Agency then withholds from each recipient, on a pro-rated basis of use, enough to pay the lords, together with enough to pay themselves and all other functionaries. Little enough is left for the recipients."

Ghyl nodded dubiously. "How did the lords first come into possession of the utilities?"

"It happened perhaps fifteen hundred years ago. There were wars—with Bauredel, with the Mang Islands, with Lankenburg. Before were the Star Wars and before this the Dreadful War, and before this: wars without number. The last war, with Emperor Riskanie and the White-Eyed Men, resulted in the destruction of the city. Ambroy was devastated; the towers were destroyed; the folk lived like savages. The lords arrived in space-ships and set all in order. They generated power, started the water, built transit tubes, reopened the sewers, organized imports and exports. For this they asked and were conceded one percent. When they rebuilt the space-port they were conceded an additional eighteen hundredths percent, and so it has remained."

"And when did we learn that duping was illegal and wrong?"

Amiante pursed his delicate mouth. "The strictures were first applied about a thousand years ago, when our crafts began earning a reputation."

"And all during past history men have duped?" asked Ghyl in a voice of awe.

"As much as they saw fit." Amiante rose to his feet and went down to the workroom to carve on his screen. Ghyl took his dishes to the sink and as he washed he contemplated the bizarre old times when men worked without reference to welfare regulation. When all was tidy, he also went down to his bench and for a period worked on his own screen. Then he went to watch Amiante, who burnished surfaces already glistening, cleared burrs from grooves smooth beyond cavil. Ghyl tried to resume the conversation, but Amiante had no more to say. Ghyl presently bade him goodnight and climbed up to the third floor. He went to the window, looked out across Undle Square, thinking of the men who had passed along these ancient streets, marching to triumphs and defeats now forgotten. Above hung Damar, mottled blue, pink and yellow, casting a nacreous sheen on all the old buildings.

Into the street directly below shone light from the workroom. Amiante worked late—an unusual occurrence, Amiante preferring to use the light of day in order to deprive the lords. Other houses around the square, following a similar philosophy, were dark.

As Ghyl was about to turn away, the light from the workroom flickered and became obscured. Ghyl looked down in puzzlement. He did not consider his father a secretive man: merely a person vague and given to fits of brooding. Why, therefore, would Amiante pull the blinds? Would there be a connection between the uncharacteristic secrecy and the parcels Amiante had brought home that afternoon?

Ghyl went to sit on his couch. Welfare regulations put no explicit ban upon private or secret activity, so long as there was no violation of social policy, which meant, in effect, prior clearance with a welfare official.

Ghyl sat stiffly, hands by his side clutching the coverlets. He did not want to intrude or discover something to embarrass both himself and his father. But still...Ghyl reluctantly rose to his feet. He walked quietly downstairs, trying simultaneously to avoid furtiveness and noise; to go down unnoticed but without the uncomfortable feeling of being a sneak.

The cooking and living quarters smelled warm of porridge, with also a sharp tang of seaweed. Ghyl went across to the square of yellow light barred by balusters which marked the staircase...The light went off. Ghyl froze in his tracks. Was Amiante preparing to come upstairs?...But there were no footsteps. Amiante remained in the dark workroom.

But not quite dark. There came a sudden flash of blue-white light, which persisted a second or so. Then, a moment later, came a dim flickering glow. Frightened now, Ghyl stole to the staircase, looked down through the balusters and into the workroom.

For several moments he stared in puzzlement, pulse thudding so loudly he wondered that Amiante did not hear. But Amiante was absorbed in his work. He adjusted a mechanism which apparently had been contrived for the occasion: a box of rough fibre two feet long, a foot high and a foot wide, with a tube protruding from one end. Now Amiante went to a basin, peered down at something in the liquid: an object which glimmered pale. He shook his head, clicked his tongue in patent dissatisfaction. He extinguished the lights, all save a candle, and uncovering a second basin dipped a sheet of stiff white paper into what appeared to be a viscous syrup. He tilted the paper this way and that, drained it carefully, then set it on a rack in front of the box. He pressed a switch; from the tube came an intense beam of blue-white light. On the sheet of wet paper appeared a bright image.

The light vanished; Amiante swiftly took the sheet, laid it flat on the bench, covered it with a soft black powder, rubbed it carefully with a roller. Then lifting the paper he shook off the excess powder, dropped it into the basin. Then he turned on the lights, bent anxiously to examine the sheet. After a moment he nodded in satisfaction. He removed the first sheet, crumpled it, threw it aside. Then he returned to the table, repeated the entire process.

Ghyl watched fascinated. Clear, all too clear. His father was violating the most basic of all welfare regulations.

He was duplicating.

Ghyl examined Amiante with terrified eyes, as if here were a stranger of unknown qualities. His conscientious father, the expert wood-carver, duping! The fact, while undeniable, was incredible! Ghyl wondered if he were awake or dreaming; the scene indeed had something of the grotesque quality of a dream.

Amiante meanwhile had inserted a new item into his projection box and focused the image carefully on a blank sheet of paper. Ghyl recognized one of the fragments from Amiante's collection of ancient writings.

Amiante worked now with more assurance. He made two copies; and so he continued, duplicating the old papers in his portfolio.

Presently Ghyl stole upstairs to his room, carefully restraining himself from speculation. The hour was too late. He did not want to think. But one dreadful apprehension remained: the light leaking through the shutters into the square. Suppose someone had observed the flickering, the peculiar fluctuations, and wondered as to the cause. Ghyl looked down from his window, and the light, going on, going off, then the blue flash, seemed inordinately suspicious. How could Amiante be so careless, so sublimely absent-minded, as not to wonder or worry about such matters?

To Ghyl's relief Amiante tired of his illicit occupation. Ghyl could hear him moving here and there around the workroom, stowing away his equipment.

Amiante came slowly up the stairs. Ghyl feigned slumber. Amiante went to bed. Ghyl lay awake, and it seemed to him that Amiante likewise lay awake, thinking his strange thoughts...Ghyl finally drowsed off.

In the morning Amiante was his usual self. As Ghyl ate his breakfast of porridge and fish-flakes, he pondered: Amiante had duped eight, or even ten, items of his collection on the previous evening. It seemed not unlikely that he would dupe the rest. He must be made aware that the lights were visible. In as artless a voice as he could manage Ghyl asked, "Were you fixing our lights last night?"

Amiante looked at Ghyl with eyebrows first raised in puzzlement, then drooping almost comically in embarrassment. Amiante was perhaps the least expert dissembler alive. "Er—why do you ask that?"

"I happened to look out the window and I saw the lights going on and off. You had pulled the blinds but the light leaked past into the street. I suppose you were repairing the lamp?"

Amiante rubbed his face. "Something of the sort...Something of the sort indeed. Now then—do you go to the Temple today?"

Ghyl had forgotten. "Yes. Although I don't know the exercises."

"Well—do your best. Some folk have the knack, others don't."

Ghyl spent a miserable morning at the Temple, hopping awkwardly through simple patterns, while children years younger than himself, but far more devout, sprang about the Elemental Pattern with agility and finesse, winning commendation from the Guide Leaper. To make matters worse, the Third Assistant Saltator visited the hall and saw Ghyl's hops and sprawling jumps with astonishment; to such an extent that presently he threw his hands into the air and strode from the hall in disgust.

When Ghyl returned home he found that Amiante had started a new screen. Instead of the usual arzack, he had brought forth a panel of costly ing as high as his eyes, wider than his outstretched arms. All afternoon he worked transferring his cartoon to the panel. It was a striking design, but Ghyl could not help but feel a glum amusement at Amiante's inconsistency: that he could counsel Ghyl to gayety, and then himself embark upon a work pervaded with melancholy. The cartoon indicated a lattice festooned with foliage, from which peered a hundred small grave faces, each different, yet somehow alike in the disturbing intensity of their gazes. Across the top were two words: REMEMBER ME, in a loose and graceful calligraphy.

Amiante left off work on his new panel late in the afternoon. He yawned, stretched, rose to his feet, went to the door, looked out across the square, now busy with folk returning to their homes from work about the city: stevedores, boat-builders, mechanics; workers in wood, metal and stone; merchants and servicers; scriveners and clerks; food processors, slaughterers, fishermen; statisticians and welfare workers; house-girls, nurses, doctors and dentists—these latter all female.

As if struck by a sudden thought, Amiante examined the blinds. He stood rubbing his chin, then turned a brief glance back to Ghyl, who pretended not to notice.

Amiante went to the closet, brought forth a flask, poured two glasses of mild reed-blossom wine, put one by Ghyl's elbow, sipped the other. Ghyl, glancing up, found it hard to reconcile this man, a trifle portly, calm of face, somewhat pale, somewhat inward-turned but wholly gentle, with the intent figure which had worked at irregulation the preceding night. If only it were a dream, a nightmare! The welfare agents, helpful and long-suffering, could become relentless when regulations were flouted. One day Ghyl had seen a wife-murderer being dragged away for rehabilitation, and the idea of Amiante being treated so caused him such terror that his stomach churned over.

Amiante was discussing Ghyl's screen: "—trifle more relief, here in this bark detail. The general idea is vitality, young folk romping in the country; why diminish the theme by over-delicacy?"

"Yes," muttered Ghyl. "I'll carve somewhat deeper."

"I think I'd like less detail in the grass; it seems to rob the leaves… But this is your interpretation, and you must do as you think best."

Ghyl nodded numbly. He put down his chisel and drank the wine; he could carve no more today. Usually he was the one to initiate conversation, to talk while Amiante listened; but now the roles were reversed. Amiante was now considering their evening meal. "Last night we used seaweed; I thought it somewhat stale. What do you say to a salad of plinchets with perhaps a few nuts and a bit of cheese? Or would you prefer bread and cold meat? It shouldn't be too dear."

Ghyl said he'd as soon eat bread and meat, and Amiante sent him off to the shopkeeper. Looking over his shoulder Ghyl saw with dismay that Amiante was inspecting the blinds, swinging them to and fro, open and shut.

❂

That night Amiante once more worked his duplicating machine, but he carefully muffled the blinds. Light no longer flickered out upon the square, to excite the wonder of some passing night agent.

Ghyl went miserably to bed, thankful only that Amiante—since he seemed determined upon irregulation—at least was taking precautions against being caught in the act.

CHAPTER VI

In spite of Amiante's precautions, his misconduct was discovered— not by Helfred Cobol who, knowing something of Amiante's disposition, might have contented himself with unofficial outrage and a close watch upon Amiante thereafter, but unluckily by Ells Wolleg, the Guild Delegate, a fussy little man with a dyspeptic yellow owl's-face. In making a routine check of Amiante's tools and work conditions, he lifted a scrap of wood and there, where Amiante had carelessly laid them, were three faulty copies of an old chart. Wolleg bent forward frowning, his first emotion simple irritation that Amiante should untidily mingle charts with guild-sponsored work; then, as the fact of duplication became manifest, he emitted a comical fluting yell. Amiante, straightening tools and cleaning away scrap at the opposite end of the table, looked around with eye-brows twisted in sad dismay. Ghyl sat rigid.

Wolleg turned upon Amiante, eyes glittering from behind spectacles. "Be so good as to Spay-line the Welfare Agency, at once."

Amiante shook his head. "I have no Spay connection."

Wolleg snapped his fingers toward Ghyl. "Run, boy, as fast as you can. Summon here the welfare agents."

Ghyl half-rose from his bench, then settled back. "No."

Ells Wolleg wasted no time arguing. He went to the door, looked around the square, marched to a public Spay terminal.

As soon as Wolleg had departed the shop, Ghyl jumped to his feet. "Quick, let's hide the other things!"

Amiante stood torpidly, unable to act.

"Quick!" hissed Ghyl. "He'll be back at once!"

"Where can I put them?" mumbled Amiante. "They'll search every-where."

Ghyl ran to the cabinet, pulled down Amiante's equipment. Into the box he piled rubbish and scrap. The lens tube he filled with brads and clips and stood it among other such containers. The bulb which fur-nished the blue flash and the power block were more of a problem, which Ghyl solved by running with them to the back door and throw-ing them over the fence into a waste area.

Amiante watched for a moment with a dull brooding gaze, then, struck by a thought, he ran upstairs. He returned seconds before Wolleg re-entered the shop.

Wolleg spoke in stiff measured tones: "My concerns, strictly speak-ing, are only with guild by-laws and work standards. Nevertheless I am a public official and I have done my duty. I may add that I am shamed to find duplicated stuffs, undoubtedly of irregulationary origin, in the custody of a wood-carver."

"Yes," mumbled Amiante. "It must come as a great blow."

Wolleg turned his attention to the duplicated papers, and gave a grunt of disgust. "How did these articles reach your hands?"

Amiante smiled wanly. "As you guessed, from an irregulationary source."

Ghyl exhaled a small sigh. At least Amiante did not intend to blurt forth everything in a spasm of contemptuous candor.

Three welfare agents arrived: Helfred Cobol and a pair of supervi-sors with keen and darting eyes. Wolleg explained the circumstances, displayed the duplicated papers. Helfred Cobol looked at Amiante with a sardonic shake of the head and a curl of the lips. The two other wel-fare agents made a brief search of the shop but found nothing more; it was clear that their suspicions did not range so far as the theory that Amiante himself had been duplicating.

Presently the two supervisors departed with Amiante, in spite of Ghyl's protests.

Helfred Cobol drew him aside. "Mind your manners, boy. Your father must go to the office and respond to a questionnaire. If his charge is light—and I believe this to be the case—he will escape rehabilitation."

Ghyl had heard previous references to one's charge being high or low, but had assumed the phrase to be a colloquialism or a figure of speech. Now he was not so sure. There were menacing overtones to the words. He felt too depressed to put any questions to Helfred Cobol, and went to sit at his bench.

Helfred Cobol walked here and there around the room, picking up a tool, fingering a bit of wood, looking occasionally toward Ghyl, as if there were something he wished to say but found himself unable to verbalize. Finally he muttered something unintelligible and went to stand in the doorway, looking out upon the square.

Ghyl wondered what he was waiting for. Amiante's return? This hope was dashed by the arrival of a tall gray-haired female agent, whose function apparently was to assume authority over the premises. Helfred Cobol gave her a curt nod and departed without further words.

The woman spoke to Ghyl in a terse clear voice: "I am Matron Hantillebeck. Since you are a minor, I have been assigned to maintain the household until such time as a responsible adult returns. In short, you are in my charge. You need not necessarily vary from your normal routine; you may work, or practise devotionals, whichever is customary for you at this time."

Ghyl silently bent over his screen. Matron Hantillebeck locked the door, made an inspection of the house, turning on lights everywhere, sniffing at Amiante's less-than-meticulous housekeeping. She came back to the workshop, leaving lights ablaze everywhere in the house, even though afternoon light still entered the windows.

Ghyl essayed a timid protest. "If you don't mind, I'll turn out the lights. My father does not care to nourish the lords any more than necessary."

The remark irritated Matron Hantillebeck. "I do mind. The house is dark and disgustingly dirty. I wish to see where I am putting my feet. I do not care to step in something nasty."

Ghyl considered a moment, then offered tentatively: "There's nothing nasty about, really. I know my father would be furious—and if I may turn off the lights, I'll run ahead of you and turn them back on whenever you care to walk."

Matron Hantillebeck jerked about and fixed Ghyl with so fero-cious a glare that Ghyl moved back a step. "Let the lights stay on! What care I for the penury of your father? The next thing to a Chaoticist, or so I reckon! Does he want to throttle Fortinone? Must we eat mud on his account?"

"I don't understand," Ghyl faltered. "My father is a good man. He would hurt no one."

"Bah." The matron swung away, made herself comfortable on a couch and began to crochet silk web. Ghyl slowly went to his screen. The matron took a rope of candied seaweed from her reticule, then a flask of soursnap beer and a slab of curdcake. Ghyl went up to the liv-ing quarters and thought no more of Matron Hantillebeck. He ate a plate of broad-beans, then in defiance of the matron, extinguished the lights throughout the upper stories and went to his couch. He had no knowledge of how the matron passed the night, for in the morning when he went below-stairs, she was gone.

Not long after Amiante shuffled into the shop. His scant gray-gold hair was tousled, his eyes were like puddles of mercury. He looked at Ghyl; Ghyl looked at him. Ghyl asked, "Did—did they harm you?"

Amiante shook his head. He came a few steps further into the room, looked tentatively here and there. He went to a bench, seated himself, ran his hand across his head, further rumpling his hair.

Ghyl watched in apprehension, trying to decide whether or not his father was ill. Amiante raised a hand in reassurance. "No need for con-cern. I slept poorly...Did they search?"

"Not well."

Amiante nodded vaguely. He rose, went to the door, stood looking out across the square, as if the scene—the heelcorn trees, the dusty annel bushes, the structures opposite—were strange to him. He turned, went to his bench, considered the half-carved faces of his new screen.

Ghyl asked: "Can I bring you something to eat? Or tea?"

"Not just now." Amiante went upstairs. He returned a minute later with his old portfolio, which he put down upon the workbench.

Ghyl asked in terror: "Are the duplicates there?"

"No. They are under the tiles." Amiante seemed not to wonder at Ghyl's knowledge of his activities.

"But—why?" asked Ghyl. "Why did you duplicate these things?"

Amiante slowly raised his head, looked eye to eye with Ghyl. "If I did not," he asked, "who would?"

"But—the regulations..." Ghyl's voice trailed off. Amiante made no remark. The silence was more meaningful than anything he could have said.

Amiante opened the portfolio. "I had hoped for you to discover these for yourself, when you had learned to read."

"What are they?"

"Various documents from the past—when regulations were less irksome, and perhaps less necessary." He lifted one of the papers, glanced at it, set it aside. "Some are very precious." He sorted through the documents. "Here: the charter of old Ambroy. Barely intelligible, and now all but unknown. Nonetheless, it is still in force." He put it aside, touched another. "Here: the legend of Emphyrio."

Ghyl looked down at the characters, and recognized them for old Archaic, still beyond his comprehension. Amiante read it aloud. He came to the end of the page, halted, put down the paper.

"Is that all?" asked Ghyl.

"I don't know."

"But how does it end?"

"I don't know that either."

Ghyl grimaced in dissatisfaction. "Is it true?"

Amiante shrugged. "Who knows? The Historian, perhaps."

"Who is he?"

"Someone far from here." Amiante went to the cabinet, brought down vellum, ink, a pen. He began to copy the fragment. "I must copy these all; I must disseminate them, where they will not be lost." He bent over the vellum.

Ghyl watched a few minutes, then turned as the doorway darkened. A man came slowly into the shop. Amiante looked up, Ghyl stood back. The visitor was a tall man with a big handsome head, a brush of fine gray hair. He wore a jacket of black broadcloth with a dozen vertical ruffles under each arm, a white vest, trousers of black and brown stripe: a rich dignified costume, that of a man of position. Ghyl, who had seen him before at guild-meetings recognized Rt. Blaise Fodo, the Guild-master himself.

Amiante rose slowly to his feet.

Fodo spoke in a rich earnest voice, "I heard of your difficulties, Rt. Tarvoke, and I came to extend you the good wishes of the Guild, and wise counsel, should you require it."

"Thank you, Rt. Fodo," said Amiante. "I wish you had been here to counsel Ells Wolleg from turning me in. That would have been 'counsel' when I needed it."

The Guild-master frowned. "Unluckily I can't foresee every indiscretion of every member. And Delegate Wolleg of course performed his duty as he saw it. But I am surprised to see you scrivening. What do you do?"

Amiante spoke in a voice of the most precise clarity. "I copy an ancient manuscript, that it may be preserved for the times to come."

"What is the document?"

"The legend of Emphyrio."

"Well, then, admirable—but surely this is the domain of the scriveners! They do not carve wood, we neither indite nor inscribe. What would we gain?" He waved his hand at Amiante's inexact writing with a small smile of indulgent distaste, as if at the antics of a dirty child. "The copy is by no means flawless."

Amiante scratched his chin. "It is legible, I hope…Do you read Archaic?"

"Certainly. What old affair are you so concerned with?" He picked up the fragment and tilting back his head puzzled out the sense of the text:

> On the world of Aume, or some say, Home, which men had taken by toil and pain, and where they had established farmsteads along the shore of the sea, came down a monstrous horde from the dark moon Sigil.
>
> The men had long put by their weapons and now spoke gently: "Monsters: the look of deprivation invests you like an odor. If you hunger, eat of our food; share our plenty until you are appeased."
>
> The monsters could not speak but their great horns yelled: "We do not come for food."
>
> "There is about you the madness of the moon Sigil. Come you for peace? Rest then; listen to our music, lave your feet in the waves of the sea; soon you will be allayed."
>
> "We do not come for respite," bayed the great horns.
>
> "There is about you the forlorn despair of the outcast, which is irremedial, for love we cannot provide; so you must return to the dark moon Sigil, and come to terms with those who sent you forth."
>
> "We do not come for love," raved the very horns.

"What then is your purpose?"

"We are here to enslave the men of Aume, or as some say, Home, to ease ourselves upon their labor. Know us for your masters, and he who looks askance shall be stamped beneath our terrible feet."

The men were enslaved, and set to such onerous tasks as the monsters devised and found needful. In due course, Emphyrio, the son of fisher-folk, was moved to rebellion, and led his band into the mountains. He employed a magic tablet, and all who heard his words knew them for truth, so that many men set themselves against the monsters.

With fire and flame, with torment and char, the monsters from Sigil wrought their vengeance. Still the voice of Emphyrio rang down from the mountain, and all who heard were moved to defiance.

The monsters marched to the mountains, battering rock from rock, and Emphyrio retired to the far places: the islands of reed, the forests and murks.

After came the monsters, affording no respite. In the Col of Deal, behind the Maul Mountains, Emphyrio confronted the horde. He spoke, with his voice of truth, and his magic tablet, and sent forth flashing words: "Observe! I hold the magic tablet of truth! You are Monster; I am Man. Each is alone; each sees dawn and dusk; each feels pain and pain's ease. Why should one be victor and the other victim? We will never agree; never shall you know gain by the toil of man! Submit to the what-must-be! If you fail to heed, then you must taste a bitter brew and never again walk the sands of dark Sigil."

The monsters could not disbelieve the voice of Emphyrio and halted in wonder. One sent forth his flashing words: "Emphyrio! Come with us to Sigil and speak in the Catademnon; for there is the force which controls us to evil deeds."

(end of fragment)

Blaise Fodo slowly laid the paper on the desk. For a moment his eyes were unfocused, his mouth pushed forward into a thoughtful pink oval. "Yes...Yes, indeed." He gave his shoulders a twitch, settled his black jacket. "Amazing, certain of these old legends. Still we must maintain a sense of proportion. You are an expert wood-carver; your screens are excellent. Your fine son, too, has a productive future before him. So why waste valuable work-time inditing old tales? It becomes an obsession! Especially," he added meaningfully, "when it leads to irregulationary acts. You must be realistic, Rt. Tarvoke!"

Amiante shrugged, put the vellum and ink to the side. "Perhaps you are right." He took up a chisel and began to carve at his screen.

But Rt. Blaise Fodo was not to be put aside so easily. For another half hour he paced back and forth across the workroom, looking down first across Ghyl's shoulders, then Amiante's. He spoke further of Amiante's trespass and chided Amiante for allowing a collector's avidity to overcome him, so that he bought illicit reproductions. He also addressed Ghyl, urging industry, devoutness and humility. "The path of life is well-trod; the wisest and best have erected guide-posts, bridges and warning signals; it is either mulishness or arrogance to seek from side to side for new or better routes. So then: look to your welfare agent, to your Guild Delegate, to your Guide Leaper; follow their instructions. And you will lead a life of placid content."

Guild-master Fodo at last departed. As soon as the door closed behind him, Amiante put down his chisel and returned to his copying. Ghyl had nothing to say, though his heart was full and his throat hurt with premonition. Presently he went out upon the square to buy food, and as luck would have it met Helfred Cobol on his rounds.

The welfare agent looked down at him with a quizzical stare. "What has come over Amiante, that he behaves like a Chaoticist?"

"I don't know," said Ghyl. "But he is no Chaoticist. He is a good man."

"I realize as much, which is why I am concerned. Surely he cannot profit by irregulationary acts; and you must realize this as well."

Ghyl privately thought Amiante's conduct somewhat queer but by no means hurtful or wrong. He did not, however, argue this with Helfred Cobol.

"He is too bold, alas, for his own good," the welfare agent went on. "You must help him. You are a responsible boy. Keep your father safe. Dallying with impossible legends and inflammatory tracts can only richen his rod!"

Ghyl frowned. "Is that the same as 'increasing his charge'?"

"Yes. Do you know what is meant?"

Ghyl shook his head.

"Well then, at the Welfare Agency are trays of small rods, each numbered, each representing a man. I am represented by such a rod, as well as Amiante and yourself. Most of the rods are pure inactive iron; others are magnetized. At every offense or delinquency a carefully calculated magnetic charge is applied to the rod. If there are no new offenses the magnetism presently wanes and disappears. But if offenses continue, the magnetism augments and at last pulls down a signal, and the offender must be rehabilitated."

Ghyl, awed and depressed, looked away across the square. Then he asked, "When a person is rehabilitated, what happens?"

"Ha ha!" exclaimed Helfred Cobol dourly, "you ask after our guild secrets. We do not talk of these things. It is enough to know that the offender is cured of irregulationary tendencies."

"Do noncups have rods at the Agency?"

"No. They are not recipients; they are outside the system. When they commit crimes, as often they do, they find no understanding or rehabilitation—they are expelled from Ambroy."

Ghyl clutched his parcels to his chest, shivered, perhaps to a gust of cold wind which dipped down out of the sky. "I had best be home," he told Helfred Cobol in a small voice.

"Home with you then. I'll look in on your father in ten or fifteen minutes."

Ghyl nodded and returned home. Amiante had fallen asleep at his workbench, head down upon his arms. Ghyl stood back in horror. To right and left, spread out on the bench, was duplicated material: every item that Amiante had processed. It seemed as if he had been attempting to organize his papers when drowsiness had overtaken him.

Ghyl dropped the parcels of food, closed and bolted the door, ran forward. It was useless to awaken Amiante and expect alertness. Frantically he gathered all the material together, stacked it into a box, covered it over with shavings and scrap and thrust it under his desk. Only now did he try to arouse his father. "Wake up! Helfred Cobol is on his way!"

Amiante groaned, lurched back, looked at Ghyl with eyes only half-aware.

Ghyl saw two more sheets of paper he previously had missed. He seized them, and as he did so there came a knock at the door. Ghyl shoved the papers down into the shavings, made a last survey of the room. It appeared to be bare, innocent of illicit paper.

Ghyl opened the door. Helfred Cobol looked quizzically down at him. "Since when do you bar the door against the arrival of the welfare agent?"

"A mistake," stammered Ghyl. "I meant no harm."

Amiante by this time had come to his wits and was looking back and forth along the bench with a worried expression.

Helfred Cobol came forward. "A few last words with you, Rt. Tarvoke."

"'Last words'?"

"Yes. I have worked this ward many years, and we have known each other just so long. But I am becoming too old for field duty and I am being transferred to an administrative office in Elsen. I came to say goodbye to you and Ghyl."

Amiante slowly rose to his feet. "I am sorry to see you go."

Helfred Cobol gave his sardonic grimace of a smile. "Well then: my last few words: attend to your wood-carving, try to lead your son into the ways of orthodoxy. Why do you not go leap with him at the Temple? He would profit by your example."

Amiante nodded politely.

"Well then," said Helfred Cobol, "I'll say goodby to you both, and commend you to the best attention of Schute Cobol, who will take over in my place."

CHAPTER VII

Schute Cobol was a man with a style distinctly different from that of Helfred Cobol. He was younger, more punctilious in manner and dress, more formal in his interviews. He was a man brisk and precise, with a lean visage, a down-drooping mouth, black hair bristling up behind his head. On his preliminary rounds he explained to all that he intended to work by the strict letter of Welfare Agency regulations. He made clear to Amiante and Ghyl his disapproval of what he considered a lax way of life. "Each of you, with above-average capacity, according to your psychiatric rating, produces well under the norm for this rate. You, young Rt. Tarvoke, are far from diligent at either guild-school or Temple—"

"He takes instruction from me," said Amiante in measured voice.

"Eh? You teach what, additional to wood-carving?"

"I have taught him to read and write, such calculation as I know and hopefully a few other matters as well."

"I strongly suggest that he prepare more earnestly for his Secondary Status at the Temple. According to my records, he attends without regularity and is not proficient in any of the patterns."

Amiante shrugged. "Perhaps later in life…"

"What of yourself?" demanded Schute Cobol. "It appears that during the last fourteen years you have visited the Temple but twice and leapt but once."

"Surely more than that. Are the Agency records accurate?"

"Of course the Agency records are accurate! What a thing to ask! Do you have records in conflict, may I ask?"

"No."

"Well then, why have you leapt only once during these last fourteen years?"

Amiante ran his hands fretfully through his hair. "I am not agile. I do not know the patterns…Time presses…"

Schute Cobol at last departed the shop. Ghyl looked to Amiante for some comment but Amiante merely gave his head a weary shake and bent over his screen.

Amiante's screen of the hundred faces received a 9.503, or 'Acme' rating at the Judgment*, and his total submission averaged at 8.626, well into 'First Class' or export category.

Ghyl's single screen received a 6.855 rating, comfortably within the 6.240 limit of the 'Second-Class' or 'Domestic Use' category and so went to the holding warehouse in East Town. Ghyl was complimented upon the ease of his design but was urged to greater finesse and delicacy.

---

*The Judgment, from the standpoint of the Ambroy craftsman, was the year's most important event, establishing as it did his stipend for the following year. The judgments were conducted in accordance to an elaborate ritual and generated vast drama—to such an extent that the judges were applauded or criticized for the ceremonial richness of their performances.

Three separate teams of judges worked independently, at the great Boimarc warehouse in East Town and rated each item of work produced by the Ambroy craftsmen. The first team included the master of the Craftsman's Guild, an expert on the particular class of item from one of the trans-stellar depots, and a Boimarc lord, presumably selected also for his expertise. On the second team were the chairman of the Inter-Guild Benevolent Association, the Craft Guidance Director of the Welfare Agency, the Arbiter of Comparative Beatitudes from the Main Temple. The third team consisted of two Boimarc lords and an ordinary recipient chosen by random lot from the population, who received the title Independent Dignitary and a doubled stipend.

The first team investigated only a single category of objects, with ratings weighted double. The second and third teams inspected all articles.

Ghyl, who had been hoping for a 'First Class' rating, was dejected. Amiante refused to comment upon the judgment. He said merely: "Start another screen. If we please them with our screens, we produce 'Firsts'. If we do not, our screens are 'Seconds' or 'Rejects'. Therefore, let us please the judges. It is not too difficult."

"Very well," said Ghyl. "My next screen will be 'Girls Kissing Boys'."

"Hmm." Amiante considered. "You are twelve years old? Best wait a year or so. Why not produce a standard design: possibly 'Willows and Birds'?"

So the months passed. Despite Schute Cobol's explicit disapproval, Ghyl spent little time at Temple exercises, and avoided guild-school. From Amiante he learned Archaic One and such human history as Amiante himself knew: "Men originated on a single world, a planet called Earth, or so it is generally believed. Earthmen learned how to send ships through space, and so initiated human history, though I suppose there was previous history on Earth. The first men to come to Halma found colonies of vicious insects—creatures as big as children—living in mounds and tunnels. There were great battles until the insects were destroyed. You will find pictures of the things at the Hall of Curios—perhaps you've seen them?"

Ghyl nodded. "I always felt sorry for them."

"Yes, perhaps…Men have not always been merciful. There have been many wars, all forgotten now. We are not a historical people; we seem to live for the events of the day—or more accurately, from one Judgment to the next."

"I would like to visit other worlds," mused Ghyl. "Wouldn't it be wonderful if we could earn enough vouchers to travel elsewhere, and make our living by carving screens?"

Amiante smiled wistfully. "Other worlds grow no such woods as ing and arzack, or even daban or sark or hacknut…And then the crafts of Ambroy are famous. If we worked elsewhere—"

"We could say we were Ambroy craftsmen!"

Amiante shook his head doubtfully. "I have never heard of it being done. The Welfare Agency would not approve, I am certain."

On Ghyl's fourteenth birthday he was accepted into the Temple as a full member, and enrolled in a class for religious and sociological indoctrination.

The Guide Leaper explained the Elemental Pattern more carefully than had Ghyl's previous instructors: "The pattern, of course, is symbolical; nonetheless it provides an infinite range of real relevancies. By now you know the various tablets: the virtues and vices, the blasphemies and devotions which are represented. The sincere affirm their orthodoxy by leaping the traditional patterns, moving from symbol to symbol, avoiding vices, endorsing virtues. Even the aged and infirm endeavor to leap several patterns a day."

Ghyl leapt and skipped with the others and finally managed a fair degree of precision, so that he was not singled out for derision.

During the summer of his fifteenth year his class made a three-day pilgrimage to Rabia Scarp in the Meagher Mounts to inspect and study the Glyph. They rode Overtrend cars to the farm village Libon, then, accompanied by a wagon which carried bed-rolls and provisions, set out on foot toward the hills.

The first night the group camped at the foot of a rocky knoll, beside a pond fringed with reeds and water-willow. There were fires and singing and talking; Ghyl had never known so merry a time. The adventure was given spice by the not-too-distant presence of Wirwans, a race of semi-intelligent beings about eight feet tall with heavy snouted heads, black opal eyes, rough hard skins mottled purple, black and brown. The Wirwans, according to the Guide Leaper, were indigenous to Halma and had existed in the Meagher Mounts at the time of the human advent. "They are not to be approached should we sight them," warned the guide, an intense man who never smiled. "They are inoffensive and secretive, but have been known to strike out if molested. We may see some among the rocks, although they live in tunnels and holes and do not range very far."

One of the boys, a brash youngster named Nion Bohart, said, "They throw their minds; they read thoughts; isn't that so?"

"Nonsense," said the guide. "That would be a miracle, and they have no knowledge of Finuka, the single source of miracles."

"I have heard that they do not talk," Nion Bohart insisted with a kind of flippant obstinacy. "They throw their thoughts across far distances, by a means no one understands."

The leader turned sharply away from the conversation. "Now then, all to your blankets. Tomorrow is an important day; we climb Rabia Scarp to see the Glyph."

Next morning, after a breakfast of tea, biscuits and dried sea-plum, the boys set forth. The country was barren: rocks and slopes covered with a harsh thorny scrub.

About noon they reached Rabia Scarp. During some ancient storm the scarp had been struck by lightning, with the result that a boss of black rock was traced with a set of complicated marks. Certain of these marks, which priests had enclosed in a gold frame, bore the semblance of Archaic characters, and read:

FINUKA DISPOSES!

Before the sacred Glyph a large platform had been built, with an Elemental Pattern inlaid in blocks of quartz, jasper, red chert, onyx. For an hour the guide and the students performed ritual exercises, then taking their gear, moved on up to the crest of the scarp, and there pitched camp. The outlook was glorious. Ghyl had never known such far vistas. To the east was a deep valley, then the lowering mass of the Meagher Mounts, the haunt of Wirwans. To north and south the ridges thrust and bulked away, at last to become indistinct, in Bauredel to the north, in the Great Alkali Flats to the south. To the west lay the inhabited areas of Fortinone, an expanse of muted brown, gray, black-green, all toned yellow-brown by the sunlight, as if under a transparent film of old varnish. Far away shone a quicksilver glimmer, like a heat vibration: the ocean. A moribund land, with more ruins than inhabited buildings, and Ghyl wondered how it had seemed two thousand years ago when the cities were whole. Sitting on a flat rock, knees clasped in his arms, Ghyl thought of Emphyrio and imposed the locale of the legend upon the landscape. There, in the Meagher Mounts, Emphyrio had confronted the horde from the mad moon Sigil—which might well have been Damar. There: that great gouge to the northeast: surely the Col of Deal! And there: the field of battle where Emphyrio had called through his magic tablet. The monsters? Who but the Wirwans?...A peremptory summons broke into Ghyl's musings; it was the group leader announcing a need for firewood. The spell of the moment was broken, presently to be replaced by another: the spectacle of the sunset, with the land and sky to the west drowned in a sad effulgence, the color of antique amber.

Pots hanging over tripods gave off a savory odor of ham and lentils; bramblewood fires crackled and spat; smoke drifted off against the dusk. The scene twitched a deep-lying node in Ghyl's mind, sent peculiar chills across his skin. In just such a manner, by just such fires, had crouched his primeval ancestors: on Earth, or whatever far planet men had first asserted their identity.

Never had food tasted so good to Ghyl. After the meal, with fires burning low and the heavens awesomely immediate, he felt as if he were on the verge of some wonderful new comprehension. Regarding himself? The world? The nature of man? He could not be sure. The knowledge hung at the brink of his mind, trembling...The Guide Leaper also was inspired by the wonder of the night sky. He pointed and stated: "Before us, and I wish all to observe, is magnificence beyond human conception! Notice the brilliance of the Mirabilis stars, and there, somewhat above, the very rim of the galaxy! Is it not glorious? You, Nion Bohart, what do you think? Does not the open sky enthrall you to your very marrow!"

"Yes indeed," declared Nion Bohart.

"It is grandeur of the most excellent and majestic sort. If no other indication offered, here at least is vindication for all the leaping done in praise of Finuka!"

Recently, among the bits and fragments in Amiante's portfolio, Ghyl had come upon a few lines of philosophical dialogue which had haunted him; and now, innocently, he spoke them:

'In a situation of infinity, every possibility, no matter how remote, must find physical expression.'
'Does that mean yes or no?'
'Both and neither.'

The group leader, irked by the interruption and by the break in the mood he was trying to establish, asked in a cold voice, "What is all this obscurantist ambiguity? I fail to understand!"

"Simple really," drawled Nion Bohart, a year or so older than Ghyl and inclined to impertinence. "It means that anything is possible."

"Not quite," said Ghyl, "it means more than that; I think it's an important idea!"

"Bah, rubbish," snorted the leader. "But perhaps you will deign to elucidate."

Ghyl, suddenly in the focus of everyone's attention, felt awkward and tongue-tied, the more so that he did not fully comprehend the proposition he had been called upon to explain. He looked around the circle of firelight, to find all eyes upon him. He spoke in a diffident stammer: "As I see it, the cosmos is probably infinite, which means— well, infinite. So there are local situations—a tremendous number of them. Indeed, in a situation of infinity, there are an infinite set of local conditions, so that somewhere there is bound to be anything, if this anything is even remotely possible. Perhaps it is; I really don't know what the chances—"

"Come, come!" snapped the leader. "You are blithering! Declare us this dramatic enlightenment in plain words!"

"Well, it might be that in certain local regions, by the very laws of chance, a god like Finuka might exist and exert local control. Maybe even here, on the North Continent, or over the whole world. In other localities, gods might be absent. It depends, of course, upon the probability of the particular kind of god." Ghyl hesitated, then added modestly, "I don't know what this is, of course."

The leader drew a deep breath. "Has it occurred to you that the individual who attempts to reckon the possibility or probability of a god is puffing himself up as the spiritual and intellectual superior of the god?"

"No reason why we can't have a stupid god," muttered Nion Bohart in an undertone which the leader failed to catch. With no more than a glare for Nion Bohart, he continued: "It is a posture, may I say, of boundless arrogance. And also, the local situation is not under discussion. The Glyph reads, 'Finuka disposes!'. This clearly means that Finuka controls *all*! Not just a few acres here and a few acres there. If this were the case the Glyph would read 'Finuka disposes across the township of Elbaum, in Brueben Precinct, likewise along the Dodrechten mudflats' or some such set of qualifications. Is this not obvious? The Glyph reads 'Finuka disposes!', which means Finuka rules and judges—*everywhere*! So then—let us hear no more logic-chopping."

Ghyl held his tongue. The leader once again turned his attention to the skies and pointed out various celestial objects.

One by one the boys dropped off to sleep. Early the next morning they broke camp, leapt a final exercise before the Glyph and marched back downhill to the Overtrend depot at a nearby mining town.

During the entire return trip the leader said nothing to Ghyl or to Nion Bohart, but upon their next visit to the Temple both were transferred to a special section for difficult, obstreperous or recalcitrant boys, in charge of a resolute special indoctrinator.

The class, to Ghyl's surprise, included his old friend Floriel Huzsuis, now a gentle unconventional lad, almost girlishly handsome.

Floriel was reckoned a problem not from obstinacy, or insolence, but rather from day-dreaming vagary, compounded by an involuntary half-smile, as if he found the class irresistibly amusing in all its aspects. This was far from the truth, but poor Floriel, by reason of his expression, was continually upbraided for facetiousness and levity.

The indoctrinator, Saltator Honson Ospude, was a tall grim man with a clenched passionate face. Intensely dedicated to his profession, he was without lightness, flexibility or humor and sought to compel the minds of his charges by the force of his own fervent orthodoxy. Nonetheless he was an erudite man, widely read, and introduced dozens of interesting topics into the classwork routine.

"Every society is constructed upon a foundation of assumptions," stated Honson Ospude on one occasion. "There is a multiplicity of such assumptions, from which each society selects: hence the multitude of galactic civilizations, all different. The society of Fortinone, of course, is one of the most enlightened, based as it is upon the most lofty aspirations of the human spirit. We are a lucky people. The axioms which shape our lives are ineffable but indisputable; equally important, they are efficacious. They guarantee us security from want, and offer each of us, so long as he be diligent, the chance to become financially independent."

At this, Nion Bohart could not restrain a caw of laughter. "Financial independence? If you kidnap a lord, perhaps."

Honson Ospude, neither outraged nor nonplussed by the interruption, met the challenge, for such it was, head on. "If you kidnap a lord, you'll gain not financial independence but rehabilitation."

"If you get caught."

"The chances are strong for rehabilitation," stated Honson Ospude. "Even if you succeeded in kidnaping a lord, you could no longer profit. The lord would not pay. Conditions are no longer barbaric. The lords have bound themselves to pay no further ransoms; hence there is no longer a financial incentive to the crime of kidnaping."

Ghyl remarked, perhaps inadvisedly, "It seems to me that if the lords had to choose either payment or death, they would ignore the compact and pay."

Honson Ospude looked from Nion Bohart to Ghyl, then around the class, all of whom were attending with great interest. "It seems that we have here a fine collection of would-be bandits. Well, my lads, a word of warning: you'll encounter grief and woe by working for chaos.

Regulation is the single frail barrier between savagery and welfare; break down the barrier and you destroy not only yourselves but all else besides. Enough for the day. Think well upon what I have told you. All to the Pattern."

Over the course of time certain members of the class—among them Floriel Huzsuis, Nion Bohart, Mael Villy, Uger Harspitz, Shulk Odlebush, one or two others—drew together to form a clique, with Nion Bohart, a swaggering, restless, reckless youth, the informal leader. Nion Bohart was a year or two older than the others: a tall broad-shouldered youth, handsome as a lord, with beautiful green eyes, a thin mouth twitching first down the right side and up the left, then down the left and up the right. In many ways Nion Bohart was an amusing companion, always ready for deviltry, although he never seemed to be apprehended in mischief. It was always the obstinate Uger Harspitz or dreamy Floriel who were discovered and punished for mischief conceived by Nion Bohart.

Ghyl held himself apart from the group, though he was fond of Floriel. Nion Bohart's mischief seemed to verge on irresponsibility, and Ghyl thought his hold upon Floriel's imagination to be both unfortunate and unhealthy.

Honson Ospude detested Nion Bohart, but tried to deal as fairly as possible with the contumacious youth. Nion Bohart, however, and others of the clique took pains to attack his equanimity: doubting his assumptions, weighing the value of universal orthodoxy, marking as if by mistake incorrect or even blasphemous symbols during the leaping which opened and closed each class. Ghyl, anxious only to attract a minimum of notice, conducted himself with discretion, to the disgust of Floriel and Nion Bohart, who wanted him to take an active part in their mischief. Ghyl merely laughed at them and his association with the group became so tenuous as to be non-existent.

❖

The years passed. At last, according to statute, the class was terminated. Ghyl, now eighteen years old, was sent forth as a full recipient of Fortinone.

To celebrate Ghyl's discharge from the school Amiante consulted the victuallers and ordered in a grand feast: roast biloa-bird with wickenberry sauce, rag-fish, candied sea-calch, bowls of whelks, corpentine, hemmer garnished with that choice purple-black seaweed known as livret, a profusion of cakes, tarts and jellies, and jugs of edel wine.

To the feast Ghyl invited Floriel, who had no father and whose ribald mother had refused to take note of the occasion. The two lads gorged themselves on delicacies while Amiante picked at this and tasted that.

Somewhat to Ghyl's annoyance Floriel, immediately after the meal, began to show signs of restlessness and hinted that best he should be on his way.

"What?" exclaimed Ghyl. "The sun's hardly down on the afternoon! Stay on for supper."

"Supper, bah; I'm so stuffed I can't move...Well, to tell the truth, Nion spoke of a little get-together at a place we know and made sure that I'd be on hand. Why don't you come along as well?"

"I'd fear to go to a house where I wasn't invited."

Floriel smiled mysteriously. "Don't trouble yourself on that score. Nion gave orders to bring you along." This latter was transparently a fabrication, but Ghyl, after half a dozen mugs of wine, felt rather in a mood for further celebration. He looked across the room to where Amiante was assisting the victualler in the repacking of pots, pans and trays. "I'll see what my father has in mind."

Amiante made no objection to the outing, so Ghyl arrayed himself in new plum-colored breeches, a black coat with scarlet sculptury, a jaunty black hat with the rim aslant. In his new clothes Ghyl felt that he cut a passably fine figure, and Floriel made no bones about endorsing his opinion. "That's an absolutely smashing outfit; beside you I look a frump!...Oh well, we can't all be rich and handsome. Come along then; the sun is down in the west and we don't want to miss any fun."

To mark the occasion they rode Overtrend south through Hoge and into Cato. They surfaced and walked east into a district of peculiar old houses of stone and black brick which by some freak had stood against the last devastation.

Ghyl was puzzled. "I thought Nion lived across Hoge, toward Foelgher."

"Who said we were going to his house?"

"Where are we going then?"

Floriel made a cryptic sign. "In a moment you'll see." He led the way along a dank alley smelling of the ages, through a gate on which hung a lantern with green and purple bulbs, into a tavern which occupied the whole ground floor of one of the old houses.

From a table across the room Mael Villy raised a call. "There's Floriel, and Ghyl as well! Over here, this way!"

They crossed to where their friends had been making free with ale and wine, found seats and had mugs pressed into their hands. Nion Bohart proposed a toast: "Here's a pimple on the tongue of Honson Ospude, sore feet for all the Guide Leapers: may they try the Double Sincere Eight-Nine Swing, fall flat and slide to rest with their noses upon Animal Corruption!"

With bravos and catcalls the group drank the toast. Ghyl took occasion to inspect his surroundings. The room was very large, with carved posts supporting an elegant old ceiling of green sapodilla and yellow tile. The walls were stained dull scarlet, the floor was stone. Light came from four candelabra supporting dozens of little lamps. Sitting in an alcove an orchestra of three men, with zither, flute and tympany, played jigs and reels. Below the orchestra twenty young women lolled on a long couch, wearing a variety of costumes, some flamboyant, others severe, but all characterized by an element of fantasy, setting them apart from the ordinary women of Ambroy. At last Ghyl fully realized where he was: in one of the quasi-legal taverns offering wine and food, music and good cheer, and also the services of a staff of hostesses. Ghyl looked curiously along the line of girls. None were particularly comely, he thought, and a few were actually grotesque, with garments of incredible complication and cosmetics all but concealing their faces.

"See any you fancy?" Nion Bohart called over to Ghyl. "They're all here tonight. Business is poor. Pick out the one you favor; she'll tingle your toes for you!"

Ghyl shook his head to indicate disinclination, and looked around the other tables.

"What do you think of the place?" Floriel asked him.

"It's splendid, certainly. But isn't it very expensive?"

"Not so much as you might think, if you drink only ale and stay away from the girls."

"Too bad old Honson Ospude isn't here, eh, Nion?" called Shulk Odlebush. "We'd pour him so full he wouldn't know up from down!"

"I'd like to see him tackle that fat woman!" remarked Uger Harspitz with a lecherous grin. "Her with the green feather neck-piece. What a tussle that would be!"

Into the room came three men and two women, the men somewhat cautious of step and gaze, the women by contrast bold, even insolent. Nion nudged Floriel, muttered into his ear and Floriel in turn spoke to Ghyl: "Noncups: those five just taking a table."

Ghyl stared in surreptitious fascination at the five men and women, who, after quick glances into all corners, were now relaxing into their chairs.

Ghyl asked Floriel, "Are they criminals—or just ordinary non-recipients?"

Floriel put the inquiry to Nion, who replied tersely, with a flicker of a cynical grin. Floriel reported to Ghyl: "He doesn't know for sure. He thinks they deal in 'scrap': old metal, old furniture, old artware—probably anything else they lay their hands on."

"How does Nion know all this?" asked Ghyl.

Floriel shrugged. "He knows all sorts of things. I think his brother is a noncup—or was. I'm not really sure. The folk who own this tavern are noncups too, for that matter."

"What of *them*?" Ghyl nodded to the girls on the long bench.

Floriel put a question to Nion, received a reply. "They're all recipients. They belong to the Matrons, Nurses and Service Workers' Guild."

"Oh."

"On occasion lords come in here," said Floriel. "Last time I was here with Nion there were two lords and two ladies, drinking ale and chewing pickled skauf like longshoremen."

"Not really!"

"Really and absolutely," stated Nion who had hitched around to join the conversation. "There may be lords in tonight, who knows? Here, old fellow, fill your mug—good strong ale!"

Ghyl allowed his mug to be replenished. "Why would lords and ladies come down to a place of this sort?"

"Because here is life! Excitement! Real people! Not flat-nosed voucher-douchers!"

Ghyl gave his head a marveling shake. "I thought that when they dropped to the ground they always flew to Luschein or the Mang Islands, or someplace out of Fortinone for their fun!"

"True. But sometimes it's as easy to drop down to good old Keecher's Inn. Anything to escape the boredom of the eyries, I suppose."

"'Boredom'?" Ghyl tested the word.

"Certainly. You don't think the life of the lords is all Gade wine and star travel, do you? A good many of them find time hanging heavy on their hands."

Ghyl considered this novel perspective regarding the life of the lords. What with air-boats to sweep them here and there, not only to Luschein and the Mangs, but to Minya-judos, or the wild Para Islands, or the Wewar Glaciers, the idea was not wholly convincing. Still—who could say? "Do they come without Garrion?"

"As to that I don't know. You'll never see Garrion here in the tavern. Perhaps they watch from behind that lattice yonder."

"So long as it's not a Special Agent," suggested Mael Villy with a glance over his shoulder.

"Don't worry, they know you're here," said Nion Bohart. "They know everything."

Ghyl grinned. "Maybe the Garrion and welfare agents sit together behind the screen."

Nion Bohart spat upon the floor. "Not much. The agents come to play with the girls, like all the rest."

"The lords too?" asked Ghyl.

"The lords? Ha! You should see them. *And* the ladies! They vie in lechery!"

"Have you heard of Lord Mornune the Spay?" asked Uger Harspitz. "How he inveigled my cousin's fiancée? It was at a place up the Insse— some resort. Brazen? Grigglesby Corners? I forget the name—anyway my cousin was called aside on a false message and when he returned Lord Mornune was with the girl, and next morning she never appeared for breakfast. She wrote that she was well, that Mornune was taking her traveling, to the Five Worlds and beyond. Isn't that the life?"

"All one needs is 1.18 percent," said Nion Bohart grimly. "If I had it I'd inveigle the girls no less."

"You could try with your one voucher and eighteen checks," suggested Shulk Odlebush. "Inquire of that fat one with the green neck-piece."

"Bah. Not even one check...but hello! Here's my friend Aunger Wermarch. Hi Aunger! This way! Meet my friends!"

Aunger Wermarch was a young man dressed in the most extreme style, with pointed white shoes and a black-tasseled yellow hat. Nion Bohart introduced him to the group: "A noncup is Aunger and proud of the fact!"

"Right and correct!" declared Aunger Wermarch. "They can call me Chaoticist, thief, pariah—anything they want—so long as they don't put me on their damned welfare rolls!"

"Sit, Aunger—drink a mug of ale! There's a good fellow!"

Aunger pulled a stool up under his splendid shanks and accepted a mug of ale. "A merry life to all!"

"And sand in the eyes of all the water-watchers!" proposed Nion. Ghyl drank with the rest. When Aunger Wermarch turned away, he asked Floriel for an explanation. Floriel gave back a significant wink, and Ghyl suddenly understood the reference to 'water-watchers', those welfare agents who patrolled the shoreline to apprehend smugglers of duplicated items, cheap elsewhere but hand-made and expensive in Fortinone. So here was a smuggler: an anti-social leech and blood-sucker—so Ghyl had learned at guild-meetings.

Ghyl gave a silent shrug. Perhaps. Smuggling violated welfare regulations, just as Amiante's duplicating had done. On the other hand Amiante had not been motivated by profit. Amiante was hardly an anti-social leech, certainly no blood-sucker. Ghyl sighed, shrugged once more. Tonight he would withhold all judgments.

Perceiving the jug to be empty, Ghyl provided replenishment, and filled mugs all around the table. Then he sat back to watch the events of the evening.

Two other young men came to speak to Aunger Wermarch, and presently drew up chairs. Ghyl was not introduced. Sitting at the far end of the table, he was somewhat removed from the node of conversation, which suited him well enough. His head was becoming light, and he decided to drink no more ale. It might be a good idea to think about leaving for home. He spoke to Floriel, who looked at him with a vacant face, mouth looped in a loose grin. Floriel was drunk, in a facile ready fashion that suggested long habit. Floriel said something about hiring girls, but Ghyl had no enthusiasm for the project. Particularly so used and forlorn a set of drabs as these. He said as much to Floriel, who recommended that Ghyl drink a mug or two more ale. Ghyl pulled a wry face.

He was preparing to leave, when at the other end of the table he noted tension. Aunger Wermarch was speaking from the corner of his mouth to his two friends; surreptitiously they studied a group of four somberly dressed men who had just entered: Welfare Specials. This was clear even to Ghyl. Nion Bohart sat looking interestedly into his mug of ale, but Ghyl saw his hand flicker under the table.

Events moved with great swiftness. The Welfare Specials approached the table. Aunger Wermarch and his two friends sprang away, tumbled over two of the agents, ran for the door and were gone, almost before the mind could appreciate the fact. Nion Bohart and Shulk Odlebush rose to their feet in outrage. "What does this mean?"

"What does it mean, indeed?" said one of the Special Agents drily. "It means that three men have departed the premises without our permission."

"Why shouldn't they?" demanded Nion hotly. "Who are you?"

"Welfare agents, Special Department—who do you suppose?"

"Well then," said Nion virtuously, "why didn't you say so? You came in so furtively my friends considered you criminals and decided to leave."

"Come along," said the agent. "All of you. Certain questions must be answered. And if you please," he told Nion Bohart, "be so good as to pick up the parcel you threw to the floor and hand it to me."

The group was marched to a wagon and conveyed to the Hoge Detention Center.

Ghyl was released two hours later. He was questioned only cursorily; he told the precise truth and was instructed to go home. Floriel, Mael Villy and Uger Harspitz were released with warnings. Nion Bohart and Shulk Odlebush, with parcels of contraband material in their possession, were required to expiate their anti-social behaviour. Their Base Stipends were diminished by ten vouchers a month; they were obliged to work two months on the Cheer and Cleanliness Walkabout Squad, removing rubbish from the streets, and they were enjoined to one day a week of intensive Temple exercises.

CHAPTER VIII

Undle Square was cool and absolutely quiet when Ghyl arrived home. Damar, a thin sickle, hung low, backlighting the featureless black hulks to the east. No light showed; the air was cool and fresh; the only sound to be heard was the scrape of Ghyl's footsteps.

He let himself into the workroom. The odor of wood and finishing oil came to his nostrils: so familiar and secure and redolent of everything that he loved that tears came to his eyes.

He stopped to listen, then climbed the stairs.

Amiante was not asleep. Ghyl undressed, then went over to his father's bed and described the events of the evening. Amiante made no comment. Ghyl, peering vainly through the dark, was unable to sense his opinion of the scrape. Amiante finally said, "Well then, go to bed; you've done no harm and suffered none; you've learned a great deal: so we must count the night a success."

Somewhat cheered, Ghyl laid himself down on his couch, and fell asleep from sheer weariness.

He awoke to Amiante's hand on his shoulder. "The welfare agent is here to discuss the events of last night."

Ghyl dressed, washed his face in cold water, combed back his hair. Descending to the second floor, he found Schute Cobol and Amiante sitting at the table, drinking tea, apparently on a basis of courtesy and good-fellowship, though Schute Cobol's mouth was even tighter and paler than usual and his eyes had a far-off glint. He greeted Ghyl with a curt nod and a glance of careful appraisal, as if he found himself face to face with a stranger.

The discussion began on a note of polite restraint, with Schute Cobol asking only for Ghyl's version of last night's events. Presently his questions became keener and his comments cutting; Ghyl became angry rather than abject. "I have told you the truth! To the best of my knowledge I did nothing irregulationary; why do you imply that I am chaotic?"

"I imply nothing. You are the one who draws inferences. Certainly you have been irresponsible in your friendships. This fact, coupled with your previous lack of orthodoxy, compels me to an open mind, rather than the trust I automatically extend to the typical recipient."

"In this case, not enjoying your trust, it is pointless for me to say more. Why waste my breath?"

Schute Cobol's mouth tightened; he looked toward Amiante. "And you, Rt. Tarvoke—you must realize that you have been remiss as a father. Why have you not inculcated in your son a more abiding respect for our institutions? I believe that you have been reproached on this score before."

"Yes, I recall something of the sort," said Amiante with the ghost of a smile.

Schute Cobol became even more brittle than before. "Will you answer my question then? Remember, on you rests the ultimate responsibility for these sad events. Truth is what a father owes to his son, not evasion and ambiguity."

"Ah, truth indeed!" mused Amiante. "If only we could identify truth when we perceived it! Here would be reassurance!"

Schute Cobol snorted in disgust. "This is the source of all our difficulties. Truth is orthodoxy, what else? You need no reassurance beyond the regulations."

Amiante rose to his feet, stood with his hands behind his back, looking from the window. "Once there lived the hero Emphyrio," said Amiante. "He spoke such truth that monsters halted to hear him. Did he, I wonder, expound Welfare Agency regulations through his magic tablet?"

Schute Cobol also rose to his feet. He spoke in a voice passionless and rigidly formal. "I have carefully explained what the Welfare Agency expects in return for the benefits you derive. If you wish to continue to derive these benefits, you must obey regulations. Do you have any questions?"

"No."

"No."

Schute Cobol gave a curt bow. He went to the door and, turning, said, "Even Emphyrio, were he alive today, would be obliged to obey regulations. There can be no exceptions." He departed.

Amiante and Ghyl followed him down to the workroom. Ghyl slumped upon his bench, put his chin on his hands. "I wonder if this is true? Would Emphyrio obey welfare regulations?"

Amiante seated himself at his own bench. "Who knows? He would find no enemy, no tyranny—only inefficiency and perhaps peculation. No question but that we work hard for very little return."

"He would hardly be a noncup," mused Ghyl. "Or would he? One who worked hard and honestly, but off the welfare rolls?"

"Possibly. He might choose to be elected Mayor of the City, and try to increase everyone's stipend."

"How could he do that?" asked Ghyl with interest.

Amiante shrugged. "The Mayor has no real power—although the Charter names him the city's chief executive. He could at least demand higher prices for our goods. He could urge that we build factories to produce things we need but now import."

"That would mean duplication."

"Duplication is not inherently wrong, so long as it does not diminish our reputation for craftsmanship."

Ghyl shook his head. "The Welfare Agency would never permit it."

"Perhaps not. Unless Emphyrio were, in fact, Mayor."

"Someday," said Ghyl, "I will learn the rest of the tale. We will know what happened."

Amiante gave his head a skeptical shake, as if his thoughts had many times coursed the same road. "Perhaps. But more likely Emphyrio is legend after all."

Ghyl sat brooding. Presently he asked, "Is there no way we could learn the truth?"

"Probably not in Fortinone. The Historian would know."

"Who is the Historian?"

Amiante, becoming uninterested in the conversation, began to strop one of his chisels. "On a far planet, so I am told, the Historian chronicles all the events of human history."

"The history of Halma and Fortinone, as well?"

"Presumably."

"How would such information reach the Historian?"

Amiante, bending over the screen, plied his chisel. "No difficulty there. He would employ correspondents."

"What a curious idea!" remarked Ghyl.

"Curious indeed."

Across Undle Square, a few steps up Gosgar Alley to a door with a blue hourglass painted on the panel, up four flights of steps to a pleasant little penthouse: here was the home of Sonjaly Rathe and her mother. Sonjaly was a small slight girl, extremely pretty, with blonde hair and innocent gray eyes. Ghyl thought her enchanting. Unfortunately Sonjaly was something of a flirt, well aware of her charms, always ready with a provocative pout or a clever tilt of the head.

One afternoon Ghyl sat with Sonjaly at the Campari Café trying to make earnest conversation, to which Sonjaly would only give back pert irrelevancies, when who should appear but Floriel. Ghyl frowned and slumped back in his seat.

"Your father told me you'd probably be here," said Floriel, dropping into a chair. "What's that you're drinking? Pomardo? None for me. Waitress, a flask of edel wine, please: the Amanour White."

Ghyl performed introductions. Floriel said, "I suppose you've heard the news."

"News? A Mayor's election in a month or so. I've finished a new screen. Sonjaly thinks she'll change from the Marble-Polishers to the Cakes, Tarts and Pastry-Makers."

"No, no," complained Floriel. "I mean *news!* Nion Bohart is free of the Cheer Squad. He wishes to celebrate, and has called for a party tonight!"

"Oh indeed?" Ghyl frowned down into his goblet.

"Indeed. At the Twisted Willow Palace, if you know of it."

"Naturally," said Ghyl, not wishing to appear stupid in front of Sonjaly.

"It's in Foelgher Precinct, on the estuary—but then I'd better take you; you'd never find your way."

"I'm not certain of going," said Ghyl. "Sonjaly and I—"

"She can come too; why not?" Floriel turned to Sonjaly, who was practising her most outrageous beguilements. "You'd enjoy the Twisted Willow; it's a delightful old place, with a marvelous view. The most interesting and clever folk go there, and many noncups. Even lords and ladies: on the sly, of course."

"It sounds delightful! I'd so like to go!"

"Your mother would object," Ghyl stated more gruffly than he intended. "She'd never allow you to such a tavern."

"She doesn't need to know," declared Sonjaly with a sauciness Ghyl found astonishing. "Also, as it happens, she works tonight, catering a guild banquet."

"Good! Fine! Excellent! No problems whatever," declared Floriel heartily. "We'll all go together."

"Oh very well," said Ghyl crossly. "I suppose we must."

Sonjaly drew up her shoulders. "Indeed! If you find my company so disturbing, I need not go."

"No, no, of course not!" protested Ghyl. "Do not misunderstand!"

"I misunderstand nothing," declared the outrageous Sonjaly. "And I'm sure Rt. Huzsuis would tell me the location of the Twisted Willow Palace, so that I might find my own way through the dark."

"Don't be ridiculous!" snapped Ghyl. "We'll all go together."

"That's better."

Ghyl brushed his plum-colored breeches, steamed and pressed the jacket, inserted new stiffeners into his boots, polishing to a glitter the articulated bronze greave. With a side-glance toward Amiante—who maintained a studious disinterest—he fixed to his knees a pair of black ribbon rosettes, with streaming ends, then pomaded his golden-brown hair almost dark. With another quick glance toward Amiante, he teased the ends, where they hung over his ears into gallant upturned curls.

Floriel was unflatteringly surprised at Ghyl's elegance. He himself wore an easy graceful suit of dark green, with a soft black velvet cap. Together they went to the house with the blue hourglass on Gosgar Alley. Sonjaly anticipated their knock and cautioned them to silence. "My mother is still home. I've told her I'm out to visit Gedée Anstrut. Go to the corner and wait."

Five minutes later she was with them, somewhat breathlessly, her face more charming than ever for its mischief. "Perhaps we can take Gedée with us; she's very jolly and she'd love a party. I don't think she's ever been to a tavern. No more than I, of course."

Ghyl grudgingly assented to Gedée's presence, although it would void all hope of a private hour or two with Sonjaly. She also would impose a strain on his wallet, unless Floriel could be persuaded to act as her escort—a dubious hope, since Gedée was tall and spare, with a keen beak of a nose and an unfortunately sparse head of coarse black hair, which she wore in symmetrical fore and aft shingles.

Still Sonjaly had proposed and if Ghyl disposed, she would pout. Gedée Anstrut eagerly assented to the party and Floriel, as Ghyl had assumed, quickly made it clear that he did not intend to participate in Gedée's entertainment.

The four rode Overtrend to South Foelgher, only a few yards from Hyalis Park. They climbed a little hill: an outcropping of the same ridge which further north in Veige became Dunkum's Heights. But here the river was close below, reflecting the tawny violet, gold and orange dust of the sunset. The Twisted Willow Palace was close at hand—a rickety structure open to the air in warm weather, screened and shuttered when the wind blew. The specialty of the house was grilled mud-eel, esperges in spice-sauce, and a pale light wine from the coastal region south of Ambroy.

Nion Bohart had not yet arrived; the four found a table. A waiter approached, and it developed that Gedée was tremendously hungry, having not yet dined. Ghyl watched glumly while she devoured vast quantities of eel and esperges. Floriel mentioned that he hoped to build or buy a small sailing craft, and Sonjaly declared herself keenly interested in sailboats and travel in general, and the two became involved in a spirited conversation, while Ghyl sat to the side dispiritedly watching Gedée attack the platter of eel which he had ordered for Sonjaly, but which she now decided she didn't care for.

Nion Bohart arrived, in company with a somewhat overdressed young woman a year or two his senior. Ghyl thought to recognize her as one of the girls who had sat on the bench at Keecher's Inn. Nion introduced her as 'Marta', without reference to her guild. A moment later Shulk and Uger arrived, and presently Mael Villy, escorting a girl of rather coarse appearance, far from inconspicuous by reason of flaming red hair. As if to emphasize her disdain for orthodoxy, she wore a tight sheath of black fish-skin which concealed few, if any, of her bodily contours. Sonjaly raised her eyebrows in disparagement; Gedée, wiping her mouth with the back of her hand, stared blankly, but seemed to care nothing one way or the other.

Pitchers of wine were brought; goblets were filled and emptied. Evening became night. Colored lanterns were lit; a lutist purportedly from the Mang Islands played lilting Mang Island love songs.

Nion Bohart was strangely taciturn. Ghyl suspected that his experience had chastened him, or at least had made him less flamboyant. But after a goblet or two of wine, a glance toward the door, a quick look at Sonjaly, Nion hitched his chair forward and became something like his old self: grim and cynical, yet easy and expansive and gay, all at once. To Ghyl's relief Shulk Odlebush engaged Gedée in conversation and went so far as to pour her goblet full of wine. Ghyl moved his chair closer to Sonjaly, who was laughing at something Floriel had said, and turned Ghyl an unseeing glance, as if he were not there. Ghyl took a deep breath, opened his mouth to speak, shut it again, and sat back sulking.

Now Nion was speaking, telling of his experience at the Welfare Agency. Everyone quieted to listen. He told of how he had been conveyed to the office, of his questioning, of the stern injunctions against further trafficking with smugglers. He had been warned that the charge of his rod was high, that he risked rehabilitation. Gedée, chewing on the last of the esperges, asked, "Something I've never understood: the noncups aren't recipients, so they aren't on the welfare rolls and they don't have deportment rods. Well then—can a noncup be rehabilitated?"

"No," said Nion Bohart. "If he is determined a criminal he is expelled, over one of the four frontiers. A simple vagrant is expelled east into Bayron. A smuggler fares worse and is expelled into the Alkali Flats. The worst criminals are expelled into the first two inches of Bauredel. The Special Investigator explained all this to me. I told him I wasn't a criminal, that I had committed no great wrong; he said I had disobeyed the regulations. I told him that maybe the regulations should be changed, but he refused to laugh."

"Isn't there a way to change regulations?" asked Sonjaly.

"I've no idea," said Nion Bohart. "I suppose the Chief Supervisor does what he thinks best."

"Strange, in a way," said Floriel. "I wonder how it ever started."

Ghyl leaned forward. "In the old days Thadeus was the capital of Fortinone. The Welfare Department was a branch of the state government. When Thadeus was destroyed there wasn't any more government, and there wasn't anyone to change Welfare Department regulations. So there never was change."

Everyone turned now to look at Ghyl. "Eh, then," said Nion Bohart. "Where did you learn all this?"

"From my father."

"Well, if you're so knowing, how *are* regulations changed?"

"There's no state government. The Mayor headed the city government until the Welfare Department made a city government unnecessary."

"The Mayor can't do anything," grumbled Nion Bohart. "He's just the custodian of city documents: a nonentity."

"Come now!" cried Floriel in mock outrage. "I'll have you know the Mayor is my mother's second cousin. He is bound to be a gentleman!"

"At the least he can't be expelled or rehabilitated," said Ghyl. "If a man like Emphyrio were elected—the elections, incidentally, are next month—he might insist on the provisions of the Ambroy City Charter, and the Welfare Department would have to obey."

"Ha ha!" chuckled Mael Villy. "Think of it! All the stipends raised! Agents cleaning the streets and delivering parcels!"

"Who can be elected Mayor?" asked Floriel. "Anyone?"

"Naturally," jeered Nion. "Your mother's cousin managed to land the job."

"He is a very distinguished man!" protested Floriel.

Ghyl said, "Generally the Council of Guild-masters nominate one of their elders. He is always elected and then re-elected and usually holds the job till he dies."

"Who was Emphyrio?" asked Gedée. "I've heard the name."

"A mythical hero," said Nion Bohart. "Part of the interstellar folklore."

"Perhaps I'm stupid," said Gedée with a determined grin, "but where is the advantage in electing a mythical hero Mayor? What is gained?"

"I didn't say we should elect Emphyrio," explained Ghyl. "I said a man *like* Emphyrio would perhaps insist upon changes."

Floriel was becoming drunk. He laughed rather foolishly. "I say, elect Emphyrio, mythical hero or not!"

"Right!" called Mael. "Elect Emphyrio. I'm all for it!"

Gedée wrinkled her nose in disapproval. "I still can't see what would be gained."

"Nothing real is gained," Nion Bohart explained. "It just becomes a bit of nonsense: tomfoolery, if you like. A thumb to the nose toward the Welfare Agency."

"It seems silly to me," sniffed Gedée. "A childish prank."

It only needed Gedée's disapproval to stimulate Ghyl's endorsement. "If nothing else, the recipients might become aware that existence is more than waiting for welfare vouchers!"

"Right!" exclaimed Nion Bohart. "Well spoken, Ghyl! I had no idea you were such a firebrand!"

"I'm not, really…Still, the ordinary recipient could stand a bit of stimulation."

"I still think it's silly," snorted Gedée, and seizing her goblet, turned a great gulp of wine down her throat.

Floriel said, "It's something to do, at least. How does one go about becoming Mayor?"

"Peculiarly," said Nion Bohart, "I can answer that, even though my mother has no cousins. It is very simple. The Mayor himself is in charge of the election, since, in theory, the office is outside the province of the Welfare Agency. A candidate must pay a bond of a hundred vouchers to the Mayor, who then is required to post his name on the bulletin board in the Municipal Parade. On election day, all who wish to vote go to the Parade, inspect the names on the bulletin board and announce their choice to a scrivener who keeps a tally."

"So then, all that is needed is a hundred vouchers," said Floriel. "I'm good for ten."

"What?" giggled Sonjaly. "You'd put your mother's cousin from his job?"

"He's a dim-witted old mountebank. Not a month ago he walked past my mother and me as if he failed to see us. In fact, I'll pledge fifteen vouchers!"

"I wouldn't give a tainted check," sniffed Gedée. "It's ridiculous, and childish to boot. It might even be irregulationary."

"Put me down for ten," Ghyl immediately declared. "Or fifteen, for that matter."

"I'll give five," said Sonjaly, with a mischievous glance toward Nion Bohart.

Shulk, Mael and Uger all volunteered ten vouchers and the two girls who had come with Nion and Shulk laughingly promised five vouchers each.

Nion sat looking from face to face with hooded eyes and a half-smile. "As I count it, the pledges come to seventy-five vouchers. Very well, I'll go twenty-five, to make up the hundred, and what's more I'll take the money to the Mayor."

Gedée sat up straight in her chair and muttered something into Sonjaly's ear, who frowned and made an impatient sign.

Floriel filled goblets all around and proposed a toast. "To the election of 'Emphyrio' as Mayor!"

Everyone drank. Then Ghyl said, "Another matter! Suppose, by some fantastic chance, that 'Emphyrio' is elected? What then?"

"Bah! No such thing will happen," retorted Nion Bohart. "And what if it did? It might set people to thinking."

"People had best be thinking of how to behave themselves," declared Gedée stiffly. "I think the whole idea is beastly."

"Oh come now, Gedée," said Floriel. "Don't be so hoity-toity! What's a little jollity, after all?"

Gedée spoke to Sonjaly, "Don't you think it about time we were going home?"

"Why the rush?" demanded Floriel. "The party is just beginning!"

"Of course!" echoed Sonjaly. "Come now, Gedée, don't fret. We can't go home so early! Our friends would think we were ridiculous."

"Well, I want to go home."

"And I don't!" snapped Sonjaly. "So there!"

"I can't go by myself," said Gedée. "This is a very boisterous part of town." She rose to her feet and stood waiting.

Ghyl muttered, "Oh very well. Sonjaly, we'd better leave."

"But I don't want to leave. I'm having a good time. Why don't you take Gedée home, then come back?"

"What? By the time I got back here everyone else will be ready to leave!"

"Hardly, my boy," said Nion Bohart. "This is a celebration! We're good for the whole night! In fact, from here we'll presently move on to a place I know, where we'll meet some other friends."

Ghyl turned to Sonjaly. "Wouldn't you like to come along? We could talk along the way…"

"Really, Ghyl! It's such a little matter, and I'm having fun!"

"Oh very well," Ghyl said to Gedée. "Come along."

"What a coarse crowd!" declared Gedée as soon as they had left the tavern. "I thought things were to be nicer; otherwise I never would have come. I believe your friends are all noncups! They should be reported."

"They're nothing of the sort," said Ghyl. "No more than I myself."

Gedée gave a meaningful snort and said nothing more.

Back to Brueben Precinct they rode, then walked to Undle Square, across to Gosgar Alley and Gedée's home. She opened the door and looked back at Ghyl with a coy gap-toothed grin. "Well then, we're here, and well away from that disreputable crowd. Not Sonjaly, of course, who is simply spoiled and perverse…Would you care to come in? I'll brew a nice pot of tea. After all, it isn't too late."

"Thank you, no," said Ghyl. "I had better be returning to the party."

Gedée closed the door smartly in his face. Ghyl turned and marched back across Undle Square. In the workshop a dim light burned; Amiante would be carving at a screen or poring over an old document. Ghyl slowed his steps, and wondered if his father would like to come to the party. Probably not…but, as he crossed the square, he looked several times back over his shoulder at the lonely light behind the amber glass panes.

Back to the Overtrend, back to South Foelgher, up the ridge to the Twisted Willow Palace. To Ghyl's dismay the lights were turned down; the tavern was empty save for the janitor and the waiter.

Ghyl went to the waiter. "The party I was with, at that table yonder—did they say where they were going?'

"No, sir; not to me. They were all jolly and laughing; much wine they'd been drinking. I'm sure I don't know."

Ghyl walked slowly back down the hill. Would they have gone to Keecher's Inn in Cato? Unlikely. Ghyl gave a hollow laugh, and set out afoot across the dark echoing streets of Foelgher: past stone warehouses and huts of ancient black brick. Fog blew in off the estuary, creating moist auras around the infrequent street lamps. Finally, gloomy and sagging of shoulder, he tramped into Undle Square. He halted, then slowly crossed to Gosgar Alley and proceeded to the door with the blue hourglass. Sonjaly lived on the fourth floor. The windows were dark. Ghyl sat on the step and waited. Half an hour passed. Ghyl heaved a sigh, rose to his feet. She probably had come in long ago. He went home and put himself to bed.

CHAPTER IX

The next morning Ghyl roused himself to find Amiante already up and busy. He washed and dressed in his work smock and went below to his breakfast.

"Well then," asked Amiante, "how did the party go?"

"Nicely. Have you ever heard of the Twisted Willow Palace?"

Amiante nodded. "A pleasant place to visit. Do they still serve mud-eel and esperges?"

"Yes." Ghyl sipped his tea. "Nion Bohart was at the party, and Floriel, and several others from the special class at the Temple."

"Ah, yes."

"You know that there is a mayoralty election next month?"

"I hadn't thought of it. I suppose it's about time."

"We spoke of raising a hundred vouchers and putting up the name 'Emphyrio' to be voted upon."

Amiante raised his eyebrows. He sipped his tea. "The welfare agents will not be amused."

"Is it any of their affair?"

"Anything which concerns the recipients is the Welfare Agency's affair."

"But what can they do? It is certainly not irregulationary to propose a name for Mayor!"

"The name of a dead man, a legend."

"Is this irregulationary?"

"Technically and formally, I would think not, since there would seem to be no intent to deceive. If the public wished to elect a legend to the Mayor's office...Of course, there may be age or residence or other qualifications. If so, then of course the name cannot even be placed on the boards."

Ghyl gave a terse nod. After all, it meant little one way or another...
He went down to the workroom, honed his chisels and began carving
upon his screen—with all the time an eye cocked on the door. Surely
there would come a knock, Sonjaly would look in, tearful, meek, to make
amends for the previous evening.

No knock. No wan face.

Halfway through the afternoon, with the door open to the amber
sunlight, Shulk Odlebush appeared. "Hello, Ghyl Tarvoke. Hard at
work then?"

"As you see." Ghyl put down his chisels, swung around on the
bench. "What brings you here? Is anything wrong?"

"Nothing whatever. Last night you mentioned fifteen vouchers for
a certain project. Nion asked me to drop by to collect."

"Yes, of course." But Ghyl hesitated. In the full light of day the
prank seemed somehow pointless. Even malicious. Or more properly:
mocking and jeering. Still, as Amiante had pointed out, if the population wished to vote for a legend, why should the opportunity not be
extended to them?

Ghyl temporized. "Where did everyone go from the Twisted Willow?"

"Up-river to a private home. You should have come. Everyone
had a wonderful time."

"I see."

"Floriel certainly has good taste in girls." Here Shulk cocked his
head to look at Ghyl sidewise. "I can't say the same for you. Who was
that fearful goat you brought?"

"I didn't bring her. I just had to take her home."

Shulk gave an uninterested shrug. "Give me the fifteen vouchers,
I'm in a bit of a hurry."

Ghyl frowned and winced, but could see no help for it. He looked
toward his father, half-hoping for some sort of admonition against
foolishness, but Amiante seemed oblivious to all.

Ghyl went to a cabinet, counted fifteen vouchers, handed them to
Shulk. "Here."

Shulk nodded. "Excellent. Tomorrow to the Municipal Parade and
post up our candidate for Mayor."

"Who is going?"

"Anyone who wants. Won't it be great? Imagine the fuss!"

"I suppose so."

Shulk gave a casual wave and departed.

Ghyl went to the work bench, seated himself across from Amiante. "Do you think I am acting correctly?"

Amiante carefully put down his chisel. "You certainly are doing no wrong."

"I know—but am I being foolish? Reckless? I can't decide. After all, the mayoralty isn't an important office."

"To the contrary!" declared Amiante with a vehemence which Ghyl found surprising. "The office is specified by the Civic Charter, and is very old indeed." Amiante paused, then gave a soft grunt of disparagement—toward whom or what Ghyl could not divine.

"What can the Mayor do?" Ghyl asked.

"He can, or at least he can try to enforce the provisions of the Charter." Amiante frowned up at the ceiling. "I suppose it could be argued that Welfare Regulation effectually supersedes the Charter—though the Charter has never been abrogated. The mayoralty itself testifies to the fact!"

"The Charter is older than Welfare Regulation?"

"Indeed yes. Older and rather more general in scope." Amiante's voice was again dispassionate and reflective. "The mayoralty is the last functional manifestation of the Charter, which is a pity." He hesitated, pursed his lips. "In my opinion the Mayor might usefully take it upon himself to assert the principles of the Charter...Difficult, I suppose. Yes, difficult indeed."

"Why difficult?" asked Ghyl. "The Charter is still valid?"

Amiante tapped his chin thoughtfully and stared through the open door out into Undle Square. Ghyl began to wonder if Amiante had heard his question.

Amiante at last spoke—obliquely, hyperbolically, so it seemed to Ghyl. "Freedom, privileges, options, must constantly be exercised, even at the risk of inconvenience. Otherwise they fall into desuetude and become unfashionable, unorthodox—finally irregulationary. Sometimes the person who insists upon his prerogatives seems shrill and contentious—but actually he performs a service for all. Freedom naturally should never become license; but regulation should never become restriction." Amiante's voice dwindled; he picked up his chisel and examined it as if it were a strange object.

Ghyl frowned. "You think then that I should try to become Mayor and enforce the Charter?"

Amiante smiled, shrugged. "As to this, I can't give advice. You must decide for yourself…Long ago I had the opportunity to do something similar. I was dissuaded, and I have never felt completely comfortable since. Perhaps I am not a brave man."

"Of course you're brave!" declared Ghyl. "You're the bravest man I know!"

But Amiante only smiled and shook his head and would say no more.

At noon the following day Nion, Floriel and Shulk came to visit Ghyl. They were excited, keyed-up, alive. Nion, wearing a suit of black and brown, looked older than his years. Floriel was casually friendly. "What in the world happened to you the other night?" he asked ingenuously. "We waited and waited and waited. Finally we decided that you had gone home, or maybe—" he winked "—had stopped to cuddle a bit with Gedée."

Ghyl turned away in disgust.

Floriel shrugged. "If you want to be that way about it."

Nion said, "There was a minor difficulty. We couldn't register the name 'Emphyrio' for election unless it was attached or affixed to a recipient in residence, of good moral standing. Naturally, just off Cheer and Health Squad, I was out. Floriel and Shulk are in trouble with their guild. Mael was expelled from Temple. Uger—well, you know Uger. He just wouldn't do. So we nominated you, under the cognomen 'Emphyrio'." Nion came forward, slapped Ghyl jovially on the back. "My lad, you may be the next Mayor!"

"But—I don't want to be Mayor!"

"Realistically, the chances are small."

"Are there no age qualifications? After all…"

Nion shook his head. "You're a full recipient, you're in good standing with your guild, you're not listed by the Temple. In short, you're an acceptable candidate."

From the bench Amiante chuckled; all turned to look at him, but Amiante said no more. Ghyl frowned. He had not wished to become so intimately involved with the program. Especially since, with Nion involved, he had no real control over events. Unless, again, he exerted himself to exercise leadership, which meant contention with Nion, or, at the very least, a test of wills.

On the other hand—as Amiante had pointed out—the candidacy was neither irregulationary nor disreputable. There was no reason whatever why, if he so chose, he should not become a candidate, using the name 'Emphyrio' as a cognomen, after clearly identifying himself as 'Ghyl Tarvoke'.

Ghyl said, "I have no objection—if one condition is met."

"Which is?"

"That I am in control of the entire affair. You will have to take orders from me."

"'Orders'?" Nion's mouth twisted wryly. "Really, now!"

"If you want it otherwise—use your own name."

"As you know, I can't do that."

"Well then, you will have to agree to my conditions."

Nion rolled his eyes up toward the ceiling. "Oh well, if you want to be pompous about the situation…"

"Call it what you like." From the corner of his eye Ghyl could see that Amiante had been listening intently. Now Amiante's mouth curved in the smallest of smiles and he bent over his screen.

"Do you agree to my conditions?"

Nion grimaced, then smiled, and at once was as before. "Yes, of course. The main thing, of course, is not authority or prestige, but the whole great farcical situation."

"Very well then. I want no noncups or criminals involved, directly or indirectly. The affair must be totally regulationary."

"Noncups are not necessarily immoral," argued Nion Bohart.

"True," intoned Amiante from his bench.

"But the noncups you know are," Ghyl told Nion, after a look toward his father. "I don't care to be at the mercy of your acquaintances."

Nion drew his lips back, to show, for an instant, sharp white teeth. "You certainly want things your own way."

Ghyl threw up his hands in a gesture of heartfelt relief. "Do without me! In fact—"

"No, no," Nion Bohart cut in. "Do without you—the originator of the whole wonderful scheme? Nonsense! A travesty!"

"Then—no noncups. No statements or expositions or activity of any kind without my prior endorsement."

"But you can't be everywhere at once."

Ghyl sat for ten seconds looking at Nion Bohart. Just as he opened his mouth to disassociate himself irrevocably from the project, Nion shrugged. "Whatever you say."

Schute Cobol made a heated protest to Amiante. "The idea is absolutely ridiculous! A stripling, a mere lad, among the candidates for

Mayor! And calling himself 'Emphyrio' to boot! Do you consider this social conduct?"

Amiante asked mildly, "Is it irregulationary?"

"It is certainly bumptious and improper! You mock an august office! Many people will be disturbed and distracted!"

"If an activity is not irregulationary, then it is right and proper," said Amiante. "If an activity is right and proper, then any recipient may indulge in it to his heart's content."

Schute Cobol's face flushed brick-red with anger. "Do you not realize that you are bringing difficulty, if not censure, down upon me? My superior will ask why I do not control such antics! Very well. Obduracy works both ways. It so happens that the orders for your yearly stipend increases are in my office for discretionary recommendation. I must make a 'Not approved' indication on the basis of social irresponsibility. You gain nothing by affronting me!"

Amiante was unmoved. "Do as you think best."

Schute Cobol swung around to Ghyl. "What is your final word?"

Ghyl, previously the most lukewarm of candidates, could hardly control his voice from outrage. "It is not irregulationary. Why should I not become a candidate?"

Schute Cobol flung himself from the shop.

"Bah!" muttered Ghyl. "Maybe Nion and the noncups are right after all!"

Amiante made no direct response. He sat pulling at his little chin, an unimpressive foundation to his massive face. "It is time," said Amiante in a heavy voice.

Ghyl looked at him questioningly, but Amiante was talking to himself. "It is time," he intoned once more.

Ghyl went to his bench, seated himself. As he worked he turned puzzled glances toward Amiante, who sat staring out the open doorway, his mouth occasionally moving as he made soundless but emphatic utterances to himself. Presently he went to the cabinet and brought forth his portfolio. With Ghyl watching in disquietude, Amiante turned through his papers.

That night Amiante worked late in his shop. Ghyl tossed and turned on his couch, but did not go down to learn what his father was doing.

The following morning a curious sour odor permeated the shop. Ghyl asked no questions; Amiante volunteered no explanation.

During the day Ghyl attended a Guild outing to Pyrite Isle, twenty miles to sea: a little knob of rock with a few wind-beaten trees, a pavilion, a few cottages, a restaurant. Ghyl had hoped that his involvement with the mayoralty campaign—a relatively obscure and unpublicized affair—might escape attention, but such was not the case. All day he was patronized, taunted, inspected covertly, avoided. A few young men and a few girls inquired regarding his eccentric cognomen, his motives, his plans if elected. Ghyl was unable to supply intelligent answers. He did not care to identify his candidacy either as a prank, or a Chaoticist ploy, or an act of drunken bravado from which he was unable to disengage himself. At the day's end he felt humiliated and angry. When he arrived home, Amiante was out. In the shop was yet a trace of the sour odor he had noticed that morning.

Amiante did not return home until late, an unusual occurrence.

On the following day it was discovered that throughout the precincts Brueben, Nobile, Foelgher, Dodrechten, Cato, Hoge, Veige and out into Godero and East Town placards had been posted. In dark brown characters on a gray background a message read:

Let us promote change for the better
EMPHYRIO SHOULD BE OUR NEXT MAYOR

Ghyl saw the placards with amazement. They clearly had been printed by some manner of duplication; how else to explain the large number of placards?

One of the placards hung on a wall across Undle Square. Ghyl went close to the printing, sniffed the ink, and recognized the sour smell which had permeated the workroom.

Ghyl went to sit on a bench. He looked blankly across the square. A harrowing situation! How could his father be so irresponsible? What perverse motivation could so obsess him?

Ghyl started to rise to his feet, then sank back. He did not want to go home; he did not want to talk to his father…And yet, he could not sit on the bench all day.

He pulled himself upright, walked slowly across the square.

Amiante stood at his bench blocking out the pattern for a new screen: a Winged Being plucking fruit from the Tree of Life. The panel was a dark and glossy slab of perdura which Amiante had been saving for this specific design.

Seeing his father so placid Ghyl stopped short in the doorway to stand staring. Amiante looked up, nodded. "So then—the young political aspirant arrives home. How goes the contest?"

"There is no contest," muttered Ghyl. "I'm sorry I ever agreed to the foolishness."

"Oh? Think of the prestige—assuming of course that you are elected."

"Small chance of that. And prestige? I have more prestige as a wood-carver."

"If you were elected as 'Emphyrio', the situation would be different. The prestige would derive from the extraordinary circumstances."

"'Prestige' or ridicule? More likely the latter. I know nothing about being Mayor. It is absurd."

Amiante shrugged, returned to his design. A shadow fell across Ghyl's bench. He turned. As he had feared: Schute Cobol with two men in dark blue and brown uniforms—Special Agents.

Schute Cobol looked from Ghyl to Amiante. "I regret the necessity for this visit. However I can prove that an irregulationary process has occurred in this shop, resulting in the duplicated production of several hundred placards."

Ghyl leaned back on his bench. Schute Cobol and the two agents stepped forward. "Either one or both of you are guilty," declared Schute Cobol. "Prepare…"

Amiante stood looking from one to the other in a puzzled fashion. "'Guilt'? In printing political placards? No guilt whatever."

"You printed these placards?"

"I did, certainly. It is my right to do so. There is no guilt involved."

"I choose to think differently, especially after you have been warned. This is a serious offense!"

Amiante held out his hands. "How can it be an offense, when I exercise a right guaranteed by the Great Charter of Ambroy?"

"Eh then? And what is this?"

"The Great Charter: are you not familiar with it? It provides the basis for all regulation."

"I know nothing of any charter. I know the Welfare Code of Regulations, which is sufficient."

Amiante was more than courteous. "Permit me to show you the passage to which I refer." He went to his cabinet, brought forth one of his ancient pamphlets. "Notice: the Great Charter of Ambroy; surely you are acquainted with it?"

"I have heard of such a thing," Schute Cobol grudgingly admitted.

"Well then, here is the passage. 'Any citizen of virtuous quality and good reputation may aspire to public office; furthermore he and his sponsors may present to public attention notice of such candidacy, by means of advertisement, public posting of printed bulletins or placards, verbal messages and exhortation, on or off of public property...' There is more, but I believe this is sufficient."

Schute Cobol peered at the pamphlet. "What gibberish is this?"

"It is written in Formal Archaic," said Amiante.

"Whatever it is, I can't read it. If I can't read it, it can't bind me. This trash might be anything! You are trying to swindle me!"

"No indeed," said Amiante. "Here is the basic law of Ambroy, to which the Welfare Code and Guild Regulations both must yield."

"Indeed?" Schute Cobol gave a grim chuckle. "And who enforces the law?"

"The Mayor and the people of Ambroy."

Schute Cobol made a brusque motion to the agents. "To the office with him. He has performed irregulationary duplicating."

"No, no! I have not done so! Do you not see this passage? It avows my rights!"

"And have I not told you I cannot read it? There are hundreds, thousands, of such obsolete documents. Get along with you! I have no sympathy for Chaoticists!"

Ghyl leapt forward, striking at Schute Cobol. "Let my father alone! He has never done a wrong act!"

One of the agents thrust Ghyl aside, the second tripped him and sent him sprawling. Schute Cobol stood above him with flared nostrils. "Luckily for you, the blow did not strike home; otherwise..." He did not finish his sentence. He turned to the agents. "Come along then; to the office with him." And Amiante was hustled away.

Ghyl picked himself up, ran to the door, followed the welfare agents to their five-wheeled car.

Amiante looked from the window, his expression strained and wild, but in some curious manner, calm. "Make a representation to the Mayor! Demand that he enforce the Charter!"

"Yes, yes! But will he heed?"

"I don't know. Do what you can."

The agents thrust Ghyl aside; the car departed; Ghyl stood looking after it. Then, ignoring aghast stares of friends and neighbors, he returned to the shop.

He thrust the charter into a folder, took money from the cabinet, ran forth once more to the Undle Overtrend kiosk.

Eventually Ghyl located the Mayor, cousin to Floriel's mother, at the Brown Star Inn. As Ghyl had expected he had never heard of the ancient Charter and squinted at it with less than no interest at all. Ghyl explained the circumstances and implored the Mayor to intervene, but the Mayor shook his head decisively. "The case is clear-cut, or so it seems to me. Duping is prohibited, for good and sufficient reason. Your father seems a capricious sort to violate such an important regulation."

Ghyl glared into the bland face, then turned furiously away and strode through the dusk back to Undle Square.

Once more in the shop he sat brooding for hours as the sepia gloom of twilight became darkness.

At last he stumbled up to bed, to lay staring into nothing, his stomach churning at the thought of what was being done to his father.

Poor innocent Amiante! thought Ghyl. He had trusted the magic of words: a sentence on one of his ancient bits of paper.

But presently, as the night wore on, Ghyl became doubtful. Recalling Amiante's actions of the last few days, Ghyl began to wonder if, after all, Amiante had not done what he felt he had to do, in full cognizance of his risks.

Poor foolish brave Amiante, thought Ghyl.

Amiante was brought home a week and a half later. He had lost weight. He seemed dazed and listless. He came into the shop, and at once went to a bench and sat down as if his legs were too weak to support him. "Father!" said Ghyl huskily. "Are you well?"

Amiante gave a slow heavy nod. "Yes. As well as can be expected."

"What—did they do?"

Amiante drew a deep breath. "I don't know." He turned to look at his screen, tentatively picked up a chisel in fingers which seemed suddenly blunt and clumsy. "I don't even know why they took me away."

"For printing placards!"

"Ah yes. Now I recall. I read something to them; what was it?"

"This!" cried Ghyl, trying to keep the heartbreak from his voice. "The Great Charter! Do you not remember?"

Amiante picked it up without great interest; turned it this way and that, returned it to Ghyl. "I seem to be tired. I cannot read."

Ghyl took his arm. "Come along upstairs, and lie down. I'll fix supper and we'll talk together."

"I am not very hungry."

Jaunty footsteps sounded along the sidewalk. There was a rap at the door and Nion Bohart, wearing a tall green cap with a pointed bill, a green suit, black and yellow boots, stepped into the shop. At the sight of Amiante he stopped short, then came slowly forward, shaking his head dolefully. "Rehabilitation, eh? I was afraid of that." And he looked down at Amiante as if he were an object of wax. "They showed little restraint I must say."

Ghyl slowly straightened himself, turned to face Nion. "You are the cause of all this."

Nion Bohart stiffened in indignation. "Come now! Let's have no abuse! I wrote neither the regulations nor the Great Charter! I've done nothing wrong!"

"Nothing wrong," echoed Amiante in a small clear voice.

Ghyl gave a small skeptical snort. "Well then, what is it you want?"

"I came to discuss the election."

"There is nothing to discuss. I am not interested."

Amiante's mouth moved as if once again he were repeating what he had heard.

Nion Bohart threw his cap to a bench. "Now look here, Ghyl, you're distressed, justifiably. But put the blame where it belongs."

"And where is that?"

Nion Bohart shrugged. "Hard to say." He glanced through the window, made a quick movement as if to depart the room. "More visitors," he muttered.

Into his shop came four men. Only Schute Cobol was known to Ghyl.

Schute Cobol nodded curtly to Ghyl, turned a quick flash of a glance toward Nion Bohart, gave Amiante a grim inspection. "Well then, as a rehabilitate you are entitled to special counsel. This is Zurik Cobol. He will help provide you a healthy new basis of existence."

Zurik Cobol, a small round man with a round bald head, gave a small nod and stared at Amiante intently.

Nion Bohart, as Schute Cobol spoke, had been unobtrusively edging toward the door; but now a sign from a man standing behind Schute Cobol—a tall man in black, with a keen haughty face, wearing a great black much-beribboned hat, compelled Nion Bohart to remain.

Schute Cobol turned from Amiante toward Ghyl. "Now then, I must inform you that your charge is high. Expert opinion has defined your conduct as verging upon felonious."

"Indeed?" asked Ghyl, a harsh, acid flavor rising in his throat. "Why is this?"

"First: your candidacy is clearly a malicious prank, an attempt to demean the city. Such an attitude is irreverent and intolerable.

"Secondly, you are attempting obfuscation of the welfare rolls by naming yourself with the name of a legendary and non-existent man.

"Thirdly, by associating yourself with this legend of rebellion against established order, you implicitly advocate chaoticism.

"Fourthly, you have consorted with noncuperatives—"

Nion Bohart swaggered forward. "And what, may I ask, is irregulationary about consorting with noncups?"

Schute Cobol spared him a glance. "Noncuperatives are beyond welfare regulations, hence irregulationary, though not actively proscribed. The candidacy of 'Emphyrio' is undoubtedly a noncuperative conception.

"Fifthly, you are the son and associate of a man twice admonished for duplicating. We cannot prove collusion, but surely you were aware of what was transpiring. You made no report of the crime. Purposeful failure to report a crime is a felony.

"In none of these five instances is your delinquency definite enough to be brought home to you; in this regard you are a subtle young man." (At this, Nion Bohart turned Ghyl a look of searching new appraisal.) "Still, be assured that you deceive no one, that you will be subjected to careful observation. This gentleman—" he indicated the man in black "—is Chief Executive Investigator of Brueben Precinct, a very important person. His interest has been attracted, and from your point of view this is not a propitious circumstance."

"Indeed not," said the official in a light pleasant voice. He pointed to Nion. "This would be one of the accomplices?"

"It is Nion Bohart, a notorious ne'er do well," said Schute Cobol. "I have his dossier at hand. It is not appetizing."

The official made a negligent gesture. "He is warned. We need not proceed further."

The welfare agents departed, with the exception of Zurik Cobol, who took Amiante out into the sunlight of the square, seated him on a bench, and spoke earnestly to him.

Nion Bohart looked at Ghyl. "Phew! What a hornet's nest!"

Ghyl went to sit down at his work-bench. "Have I done something terribly wrong? I can't decide…"

Nion, finding nothing more to interest him, went to the door. "Election tomorrow," he called over his shoulder. "Don't forget to vote!"

CHAPTER X

There were five candidates for the office of Mayor. The incumbent received a plurality of the votes and was returned to his sinecure. 'Emphyrio' was a surprisingly strong third with approximately ten percent of all votes cast—enough to disturb the Welfare Agency anew.

Schute Cobol came to the shop and demanded all of Amiante's private papers. Amiante, sitting at his work-bench, working listlessly at his screen, looked up with a peculiar light in his eyes. Schute Cobol came a stride closer; Amiante, to Ghyl's astonishment, sprang erect and struck Schute Cobol with a mallet. Schute Cobol fell to the ground; Amiante would have struck again, had not Ghyl taken away the mallet. Schute Cobol, moaning and holding his head, tottered from the shop and out into the golden afternoon light.

Amiante said to Ghyl in a voice Ghyl would never have recognized, "Take the papers. They are yours. Keep them safe." He went into the square and sat upon a bench.

Ghyl hid the portfolio under the roof-tiles. An hour later welfare agents came to take Amiante away.

When he returned after four days, he was bland, easy, indifferent. A month later he fell into a dull mood and slumped into a chair. Ghyl watched him anxiously.

Amiante dozed. When Ghyl brought him a bowl of gruel for his lunch, Amiante was dead.

Ghyl was alone in the old shop. It was full of Amiante's presence; his tools, his patterns, his mild voice. Ghyl could hardly see for eyes full of grief. What now? Should he continue to work as a wood-carver? Go noncup and live the life of a vagabond? Perhaps he should emigrate to Luschein or Salula? He brought Amiante's portfolio down from the roof, went through the papers which Amiante had handled so lovingly. He puzzled through the ancient charter, shook his head sadly at the idealistic vision of the city's founders. He re-read the Emphyrio fragment, from which he drew courage. "Emphyrio strove and suffered for truth. I shall do likewise! If only I can find the strength within myself! This is what Amiante would want!"

He removed the fragment and the charter from the portfolio and hid them separately; the portfolio he put in the accustomed place.

He went back to stand in the workshop. The building was quiet, except for strange little noises he had never before noticed: creaks of the ancient timbers, a flutter of wind in the tiles. Afternoon came; a flood of mellow light poured in through the amber windows. How often had Ghyl sat in this light, with his father at his own bench across the room!

Ghyl fought the tears back from his eyes. He must use his strength, he must develop, gain knowledge. There was no single focus for the great dissatisfaction he felt. The Welfare Agency worked, by and large, for the benefit of the recipients. The guilds enforced the standards of excellence by which Ambroy survived in relative ease and security. The lords extracted their 1.18 percent from the economy, but the amount hardly seemed excessive.

What then was wrong? Where was truth? What course would Emphyrio have taken? In desperation, to ease his need for activity, Ghyl seized up chisels, and going to Amiante's bench worked on his great perdura panel: the Winged Being plucking fruit from the Tree of Life. He worked with feverish energy; chips and scrapings covered the floor. Schute Cobol passed outside the shop, rapped, opened the door, peered within. He said nothing. Ghyl said nothing. The two looked into each other's eyes. Schute Cobol nodded slowly, departed.

Time passed: a year, two years. Ghyl saw none of his old friends. For recreation he took long hikes in the country, often sleeping the night under a hedge. Living by himself he became a different person: a young man of average height, with hard shoulders, taut muscles. His features were blunt but hard and compressed; there were ridges of muscle around his mouth. He wore his hair cropped short, his garments were plain and devoid of ornamentation.

One day in early summer he finished a screen and by way of relaxation walked south through Brueben and Hoge, into Cato, and by chance passed Keecher's Inn. Obeying a random impulse, he went in, ordered a mug of ale, a plate of steamed whelks. All was precisely as he remembered, though the scale seemed smaller and the decorations not quite so splendid. Girls from the bench looked him over, approached; Ghyl sent them away, and sat watching the folk come and go...A face he knew: Floriel! Ghyl called out; Floriel turned and, seeing Ghyl, evinced astonishment. "What in the world do you do here?"

"Nothing unusual." Ghyl indicated his ale, his plate. "I eat, I drink."

Floriel cautiously pulled up a chair. "I must say I'm surprised...I heard that after your father's death you had—well, become quiet, distant. Even a recluse. A real voucher-grabber for work."

Ghyl laughed—the first time in how long? Years, it seemed. It was good to laugh again. Perhaps the ale was responsible. Perhaps a sudden yearning for companionship. "I've been pretty much alone. What of you? You've changed since I saw you last." And indeed Floriel had become, not a new person, but an augmented version of his previous self. He was as handsome as ever, as debonair, with added control, craft, alertness. He said, with a trace of complacence, "I've changed a bit, I suppose. At heart the same Floriel, of course."

"You're still in Metal-benders?"

Floriel gave Ghyl a glance of injured surprise. "Of course not. Haven't you heard? I've gone noncup. You're sitting with a man outside organized society. Aren't you ashamed?"

"No, I hadn't heard." Ghyl looked Floriel up and down, noting the signs of prosperity. "How do you live? You don't seem to be deprived. Where do you get your vouchers?"

"Oh, I manage, one way or another. I fell into a little cottage up the river, a lovely place. I rent this out over the weekends, and do a fair business. And, to be candid, sometimes I bring up girls for men on a bit of a tear. Nothing absolutely criminal, you understand. One way or another I make out. And you?"

"Still carving screens."

"Ah then, you'll continue in the trade?"

"I don't know...Remember how we used to talk of travel?"

"Yes, of course. I've never forgotten."

"Nor I." Ghyl leaned forward, gazing down into his ale. "Life here is futility. We'll live and die, and realize no glimmer of truth. There's something terribly wrong here in Ambroy. Do you realize this?"

Floriel looked at him askance. "Still the same old Ghyl! You haven't changed a bit!"

"How do you mean?"

"You always were idealistic. Do you think I care a whit for truth or knowledge? No. But I'll travel, and in style too. In fact—" Floriel looked right and left "—you remember Nion Bohart, of course."

"Certainly."

"I see him often. He and I have some grand ideas. The only way to get is to take—from those who have: the lords."

"You mean: kidnaping?"

"Why not? I don't consider it wrong. They take from us; we must redress the balance and take from them."

"One difficulty: if you are caught, you'll be expelled into Bauredel. What good is wealth to a man an inch thick?"

"Ha ha! We won't be caught!"

Ghyl shrugged. "Go ahead, with my blessings. I don't mind. The lords can stand to lose a few vouchers. They extract enough from us."

"That's the way to talk!"

"Has Nion gone noncup?"

"Certainly. He's been quietly noncup for years."

"I always suspected as much."

Floriel ordered more ale. "To Emphyrio! What a marvelous put-on, that election! So many folk in a dither, welfare agents out looking here and there, simply wonderful!"

Ghyl put down his mug with a grimace. Floriel rattled on, unheeding. "I've had good times as a noncup, I tell you! I recommend it! You live by your wits, true, but there's no bowing and scraping to welfare agent and Guild Delegate."

"So long as you don't get caught."

Floriel nodded owlishly. "One must be discreet, of course. But it's not too hard. You'd be astounded by the opportunities! Cut the twig! Go noncup!"

Ghyl smiled. "I've thought of it, many times. But—I don't know how I'd make a living."

"There are hundreds of chances for clever men. Nion chartered a river barge, let it be known that indiscreet behavior was quite all right, and earned three thousand vouchers over one weekend! There's the way to operate!"

"I suppose so. I don't have the golden touch."

"I'll be glad to show you the ropes. Why don't you come up to my cottage for a few days? It's right on the river, not far from County

Pavilion. We'll do nothing—just lounge about, eat, drink, talk. Do you have a girl friend?"

"No."

"Well, I might be able to fix you up. I'm living with a girl myself; in fact, I think you know her: Sonjaly Rathe."

Ghyl nodded with a grim smile. "I remember her."

"Well, then what do you say?"

"It sounds pleasant. I'd like to visit your cottage."

"Good! Let's say—next weekend. An opportune time, just right for the County Ball!"

"Very well. Do I need new clothes?"

"Of course not! We're very casual. The County Ball is costume, of course, so buy some sort of whack-up and a domino. Otherwise—just a swim-suit."

"How do I find the place?"

"Ride Overtrend to Grigglesby Corners. Walk back two hundred steps, go out a plank bridge to the blue cottage with the yellow sun-strike."

"I'll be there."

"Er—should I ask along an extra girl?"

Ghyl considered a moment. "No," he said at last. "I think not."

"Oh come," teased Floriel. "Surely you're not puritanical!"

"No. But I don't want to become involved in anything. I know myself. I can't stop halfway."

"Don't stop halfway! Why be a coward?"

"Oh, very well. Do as you like."

CHAPTER XI

The ride along the Insse was pleasant. The Overtrend cars slid on magnetic cushions without jar or sound; through the windows the Insse reflected back the sunlight. From time to time thickets of willow or horsewhistle intervened, or banks of sponge-tree or black-web. To the other side were pastures where biloa birds grazed.

Ghyl sat back, lost in reverie. It was time, he thought, to broaden his life, to take in more territory. Perhaps here was the reason he had so readily accepted Floriel's invitation. Schute Cobol would certainly disapprove. A fig for Schute Cobol. If only it were easier to travel, to achieve some measure of financial independence…

The car halted at Grigglesby Corners; Ghyl alighted, received his bag from the ejector. What a pleasant spot! he thought. Enormous sad-apple trees towered above the brown buildings of the little depot and store, the yellow-green foliage streaming in the smoky sunlight, filling the air with a pleasant acrid scent.

Ghyl walked back along the riverbank on a cushion of old leaves. Along the other shore a dark-haired girl in a white frock lazily paddled a skiff; she saw him watching; she smiled and waved her hand; then the current eased her around a bend and into a dark little inlet, away from sight. It was as if never, never, had a girl in a white dress floated along the sunlit river...Ghyl shook his head, grinned at his own vagaries.

He continued along the bank, and presently came to a trestle leading through the reeds to a pale blue cottage under a water-cherry tree.

Ghyl walked out along the precarious planks, to a porch overlooking the river. Here sat Floriel in white shorts, and a cool pretty blonde girl whom Ghyl saw to be Sonjaly Rathe. She nodded, smiled with simulated enthusiasm; Floriel jumped to his feet. "So you've arrived! Good to see you. Bring your bag on in; I'll show you where to chuck your gear."

Ghyl was assigned a small chamber overlooking the river with yellow-brown ripples of light coursing across the ceiling. He changed to loose light clothes and went out to the porch. Floriel thrust a goblet of punch into his hand, indicated a sling chair. "Now, simply relax! Laze! Something you recipients never know how to do. Always striving, cringing when the delegate points his dirty fingernail at a flaw! Not for me!"

"Not for me either," sighed Sonjaly, snuggling against Floriel, with an enigmatic glance toward Ghyl.

"Not for me either," confessed Ghyl, "if I knew how to live otherwise."

"Go noncup!"

"What if I did? All I know is carving screens. Where would I sell? Certainly not to the Guild. It looks after its own."

"There are ways, there are ways!"

"No doubt. I don't care to steal."

"It all depends," stated Sonjaly, with the air of one reciting a liturgy, "from whom one steals."

"I regard the lords as fair game," said Floriel. "And perhaps a few other portly institutions as well."

"The lords, yes," said Ghyl, "or almost yes, at any rate. I'd have to consider each case on its merits."

Floriel laughed, waved his goblet. "Ghyl, you are far too serious, far too earnest! Always you want to delve to some impossible fundamental, like an impet diving for a mud-eel."

Ghyl laughed also. "If I'm too serious, you're too irresponsible."

"Bah," retorted Floriel. "Is the world responsible? Of course not! The world is random, vagrant, heedless. To be responsible is to be out of phase, to be insane!"

Ghyl pondered a moment. "This is perhaps the case, in a world left to itself. But society imposes order. Living in a society, it is not insane to be responsible."

"Total bosh!" And Floriel went on to detail the irrationality of certain Guild practices, of Temple ritual, of Agency regulation: none of which Ghyl could refute. "I agree, much of our society is absurd. But should we throw out the baby with the bath? The guilds, the Agency, no matter how insane at times, are necessary instruments. Even the lords serve a purpose."

"We need a change!" declared Floriel. "The lords originally provided valuable capital and expertise. Undeniable. But they have earned back their capital many times over. Do you realize how much 1.18 percent of our gross product is? Have you ever calculated the sum? No? Well, it is enormous. Over the course of years, it becomes stupendous. In fact, it is incredible how so few lords are able to spend so much money. Not even space-yachts cost so much. And I've heard it said that the eyries are by no means paved with gold. Nion Bohart knows a plumber who services eyrie drains, and, according to this plumber, some of the eyries are almost austere."

Ghyl shrugged. "I don't care where or how they spend their money—though I'd prefer they bought my screens rather than, say, Lu-Hang stain-silk. But I don't think I'd care to abolish the lords. They provide us with a spectacle, with drama, with vicarious elegance."

"My dearest goal is to live like a lord," declared Floriel. "Abolish them? Never! Parasites though they may be."

Sonjaly rose to her feet. She wore only a brief skirt and a bit of a loose blouse. Walking past Ghyl she swung her slender body provocatively. Floriel winked at Ghyl. "Pour us all more punch and less strutting back and forth. We know you're beautiful!"

Sonjaly languidly poured punch. "Beautiful, yes. What good does it do me? I want to travel. Floriel won't take me even so far as the

Meagher Mounts." And playfully she put her hand under Ghyl's chin. "Would you?"

"I'm as poor as Floriel," said Ghyl, "and not even a thief. My traveling must be by shank's mare, which you're very welcome to share."

Sonjaly made a wry face and went off into the house. Floriel leaned toward Ghyl and muttered hurriedly, "About that girl I wanted to invite: the one I had in mind was busy elsewhere. Sonjaly tried Gedée—"

"What?" cried Ghyl in consternation.

"—but she is studying to pass a fish-packing examination."

"'Fish-packing'?"

"You know—packing preserved fish in cans and cartons. There is an art to the process—so Gedée tells me. You curl the dear little toe fins and place the specimen just so, and with a sweeping motion pull the feelers down into the oral cavity."

"Spare me the details," said Ghyl. "Spare me, likewise, Gedée."

"It's all for the best," Floriel assured him. "You can go to the ball unencumbered, and your eye can rove as far as it likes. There's bound to be lords and ladies present."

"Really now! How do you know?"

Floriel pointed. "Look yonder, around the bend. See that bit of white? That's the County Pavilion. Off beyond is a vast park, the estate of Lord Aldo the Underline. During the summer many lords and ladies—especially the young ones—come down from the eyries, and they all dote on the County Ball! I wager there'll be fifty on hand."

"With a hundred Garrion," said Ghyl. "Will the Garrion be in costume, with dominoes and all?"

Floriel laughed. "What a sight! We shall see. Naturally you brought a costume?"

"Yes. Nothing very much. I'll be a Zambolian Warrior."

"Good enough. I'm a pierrot. Nion is coming as a Jeng serpent-man."

"Oh? Nion will be here also?"

"Of course. Nion and I are associates, so to speak. We do quite well, as you may imagine."

Ghyl sipped his punch with a faint frown. Floriel was easy and amiable; Ghyl could relax and enjoy Floriel's nonsense. Nion, on the other hand, always aroused in Ghyl a vague and formless challenge. Ghyl drained his goblet. He would ignore Nion completely; he would remain calm in the face of all provocation.

Floriel took the pitcher, went to pour punch, but the pitcher was empty. "Inside there!" he called to Sonjaly. "Mix us punch, there's a good girl."

"Mix it yourself," came a petulant voice. "I'm lying down."

Floriel went inside with the pitcher. There were a few muffled words of altercation, then Floriel came forth with a brimming pitcher. "Now tell me about yourself. How are you making it without your father? Isn't that great old house lonesome?"

Ghyl responded that he lived modestly but adequately; that indeed the shop was sometimes lonely.

The hours passed. They ate cheese and pickles for lunch and later all plunged into the river for a swim. Nion Bohart arrived just as they were emerging from the water. "Halloo, halloo! All you wet creatures! Ghyl too I see! It's been a long time! And Sonjaly! Adorable creature—especially in that wet clinging trifle. Floriel, you really don't deserve her."

Sonjaly turned Floriel a rather spiteful glance. "I keep telling him the same thing. But he doesn't believe me."

"We'll have to do something about that...Well then, Floriel, where shall I stow my bags? The usual little den? Anything's good enough for old Nion, eh? Well, all right, I don't mind."

"Come now," said Floriel. "You always demand and receive the best bed in the house."

"In that case—better beds!"

"Yes, yes, of course...You've brought your costume?"

"Naturally. This shall be the most exalted County Ball of all time. We'll make it that way...What is that you're drinking?"

"Montarada punch."

"I'll have some, if I may."

"Allow me," said Sonjaly. And bowing sinuously she handed Nion a goblet. Floriel turned away in disgust, obviously not amused.

Floriel's disapproval failed to influence either Sonjaly or Nion, and during the remainder of the afternoon they flirted with ever more daring, exchanging glances, casual touches which were barely disguised caresses. Floriel became increasingly disturbed. At last he made a sarcastic comment, to which Sonjaly gave a flippant rejoinder. Floriel lost his temper. "Do what you like!" he sneered. "I can't control you; I wouldn't if I could; I've seen too much control!"

Nion laughed in great good humor. "Floriel, you're an idealist, no less than Ghyl. Control is necessary and even good—so long as I do the controlling."

"How strange," muttered Floriel. "Ghyl tells me the same thing."

"What?" asked Ghyl in surprise. "I said no such thing. My point was that organization is necessary to social living!"

"True!" stated Nion. "Even the Chaoticists agree to that: paradoxical as it may seem. And you, Ghyl, you're still a staunch recipient?"

"Not really...I don't know what I am. I feel I must learn."

"A waste of time. There's your idealism again. Life is too short for pondering! No indecision! If you wish the sweets of life, you must reach forth to take them!"

"And also be prepared to run when the owner comes to punish you."

"That too. I have no false pride; I'll run very fast. I have no desire to set anyone a good example."

Ghyl laughed. "At least you are honest."

"I suppose so. The Welfare Agency suspects me of rascality. However they can't prove it."

Ghyl looked across the brimming river. This sort of life, in spite of Sonjaly's waywardness and Floriel's bickering, seemed much more gay and normal than his usual routine: carving, polishing, a walk to the shop for food, eating, sleeping, more of the same. All for the sake of a monthly stipend! If Floriel could earn enough to live in ease and leisure, in a cottage on the river, why could he not do the same?

Ghyl Tarvoke, a noncup? Why not? He need not steal nor blackmail nor procure. Undoubtedly there were vouchers to be earned legitimately—or almost legitimately. Ghyl turned to Nion: "When a person goes noncup, how in the world does he stay alive?"

Nion looked at him quizzically, obviously well aware of what was going on in Ghyl's mind. "No trouble whatever. There are dozens of ways to stay afloat. If ever you make the decision, come to me. You'd very likely do well, with your air of respectability. No one would suspect you of sharp practice."

"I'll keep you in mind."

The sun declined; the sky burnt with such a sunset as Ghyl had not seen since his childhood, when he had often watched the sun sink into the ocean from Dunkum's Heights. "Time we were dressing for the ball," said Floriel. "The music starts in half an hour, and we want to be on hand for everything. First, I'll bring up the skiff, to ferry us across the river."

He walked ashore by the trestle. Ghyl went to his room, then came out to surprise Nion and Sonjaly locked in an unmistakably ardent embrace. "Excuse me," said Ghyl.

Neither heeded him and he returned to his room.

CHAPTER XII

Floriel Huzsuis, Sonjaly Rathe, Nion Bohart, Ghyl Tarvoke: wearing fantastic costumes, with normal personalities suppressed by their dominoes, the four stepped into the skiff.

Floriel sculled across the river to the pavilion already aglow from flares of chalk-green, pink and yellow, and thousands of tiny sparkling white coruscations.

Floriel held the skiff while his passengers alighted, then tied the painter to a ring and clambered up to the dock. The pavilion lay before them: an expanse of polished wood, with private boxes and observation areas to either side. At the floor-level a double row of exquisitely decorated booths provided wine and other refreshment for the celebrants.

An officer accosted the four, collected admission fees. They wandered out upon the floor in company with perhaps a hundred others. Lords? Ladies? Recipients from the surrounding countryside? From the city? Noncups like Floriel, Sonjaly, Nion? Ghyl could not identify one from the other and he wondered if Nion, usually so knowledgeable, would be able to do so.

At a booth all provided themselves with green crackle-glass flasks of edel-wine and stood watching the spectacle. Now musicians mounted to a dais, all wearing buffoon's garments of checkered black and white. They tuned instruments: a sound thrilling and premonitory of gayety, as sweet as music itself. Then they scraped their fiddles, droned on their concertinas and struck up a gay tune.

The dances of the time were extremely sedate, a far cry from the caracoles of the Last Empire or the orgiastic whirling and twitching to be seen at the seaports of the South Continent. There were several types of pavannes, as many promenades, and for the young, a kind of a swinging hand-in-hand skipping dance, of considerable vivacity. In all cases the couples stood side by side, holding hands or locking elbows.

This first tune was an adagio, the corresponding dance consisting of a slow step, a shuffle, a bow forward, another far back, the knee raised as high as possible, and held stationary, while the music played a fluttering little figure, whereupon the whole series was repeated.

Ghyl, with neither skill nor inclination, watched as Nion moved purposefully toward Sonjaly, only to have Floriel step quickly in front of him and take the half-amused, half-petulant Sonjaly out upon the floor.

Nion went back to stand by Ghyl, his grin benign and indulgent. "Poor Floriel, when will he learn?"

Back and forth along the floor stepped the dancers, graceful-grotesque, grotesque-graceful. There were simulations of a hundred sorts: clowns, demons, heroes; folk from far stars and ancient times; creatures of fantasy, nightmare, faery. The pavilion was rich. There was glitter of metal, the soft sheen of silk; gauze in every color; black leather, black wood, black velvet. Nion touched Ghyl's arm: "There gather the lords and their ladies, by the archway. Look at them peering this way and that; a shame they must be so cautious. Why cannot they mingle more freely with ordinary folk?"

Ghyl refrained from pointing out that fear, as well as pride and haughtiness, was at work. He asked curiously, "How do you know them for lords?"

"Mannerisms. They are distinct in many ways. Look how they stand by the walls. Some say they have learned a fear of space from living so long in the upper air. Their equilibrium is also affected; should you dance with a lady, you'd know at once; she'd be supple but erratic, without feeling for the music."

"Oh? Have you danced with ladies?"

"Danced, and more, if you'll believe me...Look, watch them now: preening, twittering, debating advisabilities—oh, they're a sage fastidious people!"

The lords and ladies had come in several groups, which now fragmented. One by one, they slipped out upon the pavilion, like magical creatures daring a voyage on a perilous sea.

Ghyl scanned the upper tiers. "Where are the Garrion? Do they stand in the dark booths above?"

"Perhaps." Nion shrugged ignorance. "Look at them, those lords! Watch how they stare at the girls! Randy as buck wisnets! Give them ten minutes, they'd impregnate every female in the pavilion!"

Ghyl followed his gesture, but now all looked alike; lords and ladies were lost in the crowd.

The music stopped; Sonjaly brought Floriel across the floor.

"The lords are here," Nion told them. "One contingent at any rate, and there may be more."

Sonjaly wanted the lords pointed out, but now even Nion was hard put to differentiate lord from recipient.

The music started again: a slow pavanne. Floriel instantly took possession of Sonjaly but she gave her head a shake. "Thank you, no; I'd like to rest."

Ghyl, watching the dancers, decided that the step was within his capabilities. Determined to prove himself as rakehelly and gallant as the others, Ghyl presented himself to a shapely girl in a costume of green scales with a green domino, and led her out upon the floor.

He acquitted himself well enough, or so he congratulated himself. The girl had little to say; she lived in the outlying suburb of Godlep, where her father was a public weighmaster.

"Weighmaster?" pondered Ghyl. "Does that go to Scriveners' Guild or Instrument-tenders'? Or Functionaries?"

"Functionaries." She signaled to a young man in overlapping rings of black and red stripes. "My fiancé," she told Ghyl. "He's a Functionary also, with excellent prospects, though we may have to move south to Ditzim."

Sonjaly had recovered from her fatigue; she and Nion were dancing now. Nion moved with a sure precision and far more gusto than Ghyl could summon. Sonjaly clasped his arm and leaned against him without regard for Floriel's sensibilities.

The music ended; Ghyl relinquished the girl in green scales to her fiancé, drank a cup of wine to calm his nerves.

Nion and Sonjaly strolled off to the far side of the pavilion. Floriel scowled and muttered.

At the far end of the pavilion appeared another contingent of lords and ladies, the lords costumed variously: Rhadamese warriors, druids, Kalks, barbaric princes, mermen. One lady wore gray crystals; another blue flashes of light; another white plumes.

The musicians readied their instruments; once more there was music. A person in a cuirass of black enamel and brass, breeches striped ocher and black, a bronze and black morion came to bow before Sonjaly. With an arch glance toward Nion, Sonjaly swept away on the stranger's arm. A lord? wondered Ghyl. So it seemed. A prideful quality of conduct, a poise of head, identified him as such. Ghyl thought Nion appeared vexed.

So went the evening. Ghyl attempted the acquaintance of several girls with indifferent success. Sonjaly, when visible, kept to the company of the young lord in black, brown and brass. Floriel drank more wine than was good for him and glowered here and there. Nion Bohart seemed even more vexed by Sonjaly's frivolity than did Floriel.

The atmosphere at the pavilion loosened. The dancers moved more freely, performing the measures with verve, toes splayed smartly aside, knees crooking sometimes grotesquely high, heads tilting and leaning, this way and that. Ghyl, through perversity or crochet, would not fall in with the general mood. He became disturbed and angry with himself. Was he so dour then, so tightly clenched, that he could not abandon himself to pleasure? He gritted his teeth, determined to out-gallant the gallants, through the exercise of sheer will, if by no other means. He walked around the periphery of the pavilion, to stop short near a delightfully-shaped girl in a white gown, wearing a white domino. She was dark-haired and slender, and very graceful; Ghyl had noticed her previously. She had danced once or twice; she had drunk a certain amount of wine; she had seemed as gay and wild as Ghyl wanted to be. Every movement pressed her gown against her body, which evidently, below the gown, was nude. Observing Ghyl's attention, she tilted her head teasingly sidewise. Ghyl's heart expanded, rose into his throat. Step by step he came forward, suddenly shy, though scenes of this sort had occurred a hundred times in his imagination: the girl seemed dear and familiar, and the instant fraught with déjà-vu. The feeling became so intense that, a step or two away, Ghyl halted.

Shaking his head in perplexity, he considered the girl from the toes of her little white sandals to her white domino.

She made a sound of amused dismay. "You are so critical! Am I grotesque or startling?"

"No, no!" stammered Ghyl. "Of course not! You are absolutely enchanting!"

The corners of her mouth twitched, and she thought to beguile him even more utterly. "Surely others here are beautiful, but you stare only at me! I feel sure that you think me strange or remarkable!"

"Of course not! But I felt that we have met, that we have known each other…Somewhere…But I can't imagine the circumstances. I certainly would have remembered!"

"You are more than polite," said the girl. "And I would have remembered you, as well. Since I don't—" here she turned him her most

bewitching glance "—Or do I? I seem to recognize—as you say—
something familiar, as if somewhere we have known each other."

Ghyl stepped forward, his heart pounding, his throat heavy with a
wonderfully sweet ache. He took her hands, which she yielded readily.
"Do you believe in dreams of the future?"

"Well...yes. Perhaps."

"And predestination and mysterious kinds of love?"

She laughed, a delightful husky sound, and gave his hands a tug. "A
hundred wonderful things I believe in. But won't folk think us strange,
standing here at the ball and declaring our philosophies?"

Ghyl looked this way and that in confusion. "Well, then—will
you dance? Or, if you like, we could sit over yonder and drink a cup of
wine together."

"I would as lief drink wine...I really don't care to dance."

A startling new thought came to Ghyl, or rather, a bubble of cer-
tainty floating up from his subconscious. This girl surely was no recipient; she was a lady! The Difference was manifest! In the quality of her
voice, the poise of her head, the tart perfume which surrounded her!

Exalted, Ghyl procured goblets of Gade wine and led the girl to a
cushioned bench in the shadows. "What is your name?"

"I am Shanne."

"I am Ghyl." He turned her a searching side-glance. "Where do you
live?"

She made an extravagant gesture; she was a vivacious girl, with
hundreds of gay tricks and wry expressions. "Here, there, everywhere.
Wherever I am, this is where I live."

"Of course. And I, as well. But do you live in the city—or up on
an eyrie?"

Shanne held out her hands in mock despair. "Would you rob me of
all my secrets? And if not secrets, my dreams? So I am Shanne, a girl
vagabond, with no reputation or money or hope."

Ghyl was not deceived. The Difference was evident: that indefinable
apartness which distinguished lords and ladies from the underfolk. A
parapsychic umbra? An almost imperceptible odor, clean and fresh, like
ozone, perhaps from long intimate contact with the upper air?
Whatever the case, the effect was delightful. Ghyl squirmed at an
uncomfortable thought. Might not the reverse be true? Might not the
common folk seem louts, dull and lumpish, exhaling a stale reek? The
lords who were so keen to seduce recipient girls could not think so.

They panted after honest and unaffected passion. Perhaps the same situation prevailed *vis-à-vis* ladies and undermen...The idea was unwelcome, in fact vaguely repugnant. Ghyl had never been seriously in love. His infatuation with Sonjaly now seemed stupidity. At this moment Sonjaly herself, again with Nion, danced close by. How coarse was Sonjaly in contrast to Shanne!

Shanne seemed at least favorably disposed toward him, for—wonder of wonders! she tucked her hand under his arm and leaned back with a sigh of relaxation, her shoulder touching his.

"I love the County Ball," said Shanne in a soft voice. "There is always such excitement, such wondering who you will meet."

"You've come before?" asked Ghyl, aching for all the experiences he had not shared with her.

"Yes, I came last year. But I was not happy. The person I met was—gross."

"'Gross'? How so? What did he do?"

But Shanne only smiled cryptically and gave his arm a companionable squeeze.

"The reason I ask," said Ghyl, "is so I won't perform any of the same errors."

Shanne only laughed, with just the slightest sense of restraint, so that Ghyl was left to wonder what indelicacies and crudities the man had performed.

Shanne jumped to her feet. "Come; this is music I like: a Mang serenade. I would like to dance."

Ghyl looked dubiously out at the floor. "It seems very complicated. I know almost nothing of dancing."

"What? Aren't you trained to leap and skip at the Temple?"

The girl was a tease, thought Ghyl. Well, he didn't mind. And his instinct was correct: she was certainly a young lady. "I have done very little leaping," said Ghyl. "As little as possible. In retribution Finuka has cursed me with a heavy foot, and I would not like you to think me clumsy. But there is a skiff at the dock; would you like me to row you out on the river?"

Shanne gave him a quick glance of calculation, ran the tip of her pink tongue over her lips. "No," she said in a thoughtful voice. "That would not be—advantageous."

Ghyl shrugged. "I'll try to dance."

"Wonderful!" She pulled him to his feet, and for a breathless second leaned against him so that he felt all the contours of her body.

Ghyl's skin tingled; his knees felt warm and weak. Looking down into Shanne's face he saw her smile to the side, a slow secret smile, and Ghyl did not know what to think.

Ghyl danced no better than he had promised, but Shanne seemed not to notice and indeed did very little better, apparently not attending the rhythm of the music; once again Ghyl was assured that she was a young lady.

Of course! She would not row with him on the river for fear of kidnap; obviously she could not bring a Garrion into the skiff! Ghyl chuckled. Instantly Shanne's head bobbed up. "Why do you laugh?"

"Exhilaration," said Ghyl gravely. "Shanne the girl vagabond is the loveliest creature I have ever known."

"Tonight at least I am Shanne the girl vagabond," she said, somewhat wistfully.

"Tomorrow?"

"Sh." She put her hand across his lips. "Never say the word!" With a quick look to right and left she led Ghyl through the crowd and back to their bench.

The revelry was approaching abandon. Dancers swayed, kicked, pranced, eyes glittering through their dominoes. Some made extravagant pirouettes; others paused to embrace, feverishly, oblivious to all else.

Intoxicated by color and sound and beauty as much as by the wine, Ghyl put his arm around Shanne's waist; she laid her head on his shoulder, looked up into his face. "Did you know that I can read minds?" she said in a husky whisper. "I like yours. You are strong and good and intelligent—but you are far, far, far too severe. What do you fear?" As she spoke her face was close to his. Ghyl, feeling as if he walked in a dream, bent close, close, closer; their faces met, he kissed her. Ghyl's whole inner being exploded. Never would he be the same, never again! How craven, how dull had been the Ghyl Tarvoke of old! Now nothing exceeded his competence; his previous goals—how abject they seemed!...He kissed Shanne again; she sighed. "I am shameless. I have known you only an hour."

Ghyl reached to her domino, lifted it, gazed into her face. "Much longer." He raised his own domino. "Do you recognize me?"

"Yes. No. I don't know."

"Think back—eight years? Perhaps nine. You were on your space yacht: a black and gold Deme. Two ragamuffins skulked aboard. Now do you remember?"

"Of course. You were the defiant one. You rascal, but you deserved your beating."

"Very likely. I thought you so heartless, so cruel...So remote."

Shanne giggled. "I don't seem so remote now?"

"You seem—I can't find the word. But that wasn't the first time we met."

"No? When before?"

"When I was small my father took me to see Holkerwoyd's puppets. You sat in the front row."

"Yes. I remember. How strange that you should notice me!"

"How could I avoid it? I must have foreseen this moment."

"Ghyl..." She sighed, sipped her wine. "I do so love the ground! Here are the strong things, the passions! Oh you are lucky!"

Ghyl laughed. "You can't really mean that. You wouldn't trade your life—for, say, hers." He pointed to Sonjaly. The music had just stopped; Nion and Sonjaly were walking from the floor. Nion spied Ghyl; his stride slowed, he turned his head, stared, continued.

"No," said Shanne. "I would not. Do you know her?"

"Yes. Also the young man."

"The swaggerer. I watched him. He wasn't what—" Her voice dwindled away. Ghyl wondered what she had started to say.

For a period they sat quietly. The music started again; Sonjaly danced past with the lord in black and brown. In a kind of dreamy curiosity Ghyl looked for Floriel and Nion, but neither was visible.

"There goes your friend," whispered Shanne, "with someone I know. And shortly they will be gone..." She squeezed his arm. "I have no more wine."

"Oh! I'm sorry. Just a moment."

"I'll come with you."

They went to a booth. "Buy a whole flask," whispered Shanne. "The green."

"Yes, of course," said Ghyl. "And then?"

She said nothing—a meaningful silence. Ghyl secured the wine, took her arm. They walked outside, along the riverbank. A hundred yards along Ghyl halted, kissed Shanne. She responded fervently. They wandered on, and presently found a stretch of grassy bank. Damar, at the quarter, laid a quivering trail of tarnished copper on the water.

Shanne removed her domino, Ghyl did the same; they drank wine. Ghyl stared at the river, then up to the moon. Shanne said, "You are quiet; are you sad?"

"In a way. Do you know why?"

She put her hand across his mouth. "Never speak of it. What must be, will be. What can never be—can never be."

Ghyl turned to look at her, trying to divine every last scintilla of her meaning.

"But," she added in a soft voice, "what can be—can be."

Ghyl drank from the wine bottle, set it down, turned to her, held out his arms. She held out hers, the two were one, and what ensued was as far beyond Ghyl's fantasies and musings as a magical reappearance of Emphyrio himself.

There was a pause, while the two sat pressed together. They drank wine. Ghyl's head whirled. He started to speak but once again Shanne halted him and rising on her knees hugged his head to her bosom, and once again for Ghyl the skies reeled and Damar blurred in and out of focus.

At last there was calm. Ghyl held the flask up against the moonlight. "Enough for you and for me."

"My head whirls," said Shanne.

"Mine as well." He took her hand. "After tonight, what?"

"Tomorrow I fly back to my tower."

"But when will I see you?"

"I don't know."

"I must see you! I love you!"

Shanne, sitting forward, clasped her knees with her arms, smiled up toward Damar. "In one week from today I travel. I travel, I travel, I travel! To distant worlds, beyond the stars!"

Ghyl cried out, "If you go, I'll never see you again!"

Shanne shook her head, her smile wistful. "Very likely that is so."

A harsh cold effluvium seethed up through Ghyl's veins and there turned to ice. He felt stiff, vaguely terrified: aghast at the prospect of the future. He recovered control of his voice. "You provoke me to all sorts of outrageous conduct."

"No, no," said Shanne in her sweet whisper. "Don't ever consider it! You might be rehabilitated, or whatever dreadful thing they do to you."

Ghyl gave a slow fateful nod. "There is that chance." He turned to Shanne once more; he took her in his arms, kissed her face, her eyes, her mouth. She sighed, melted against him. Ghyl's mood was now less tender; he felt as old as Damar, wise in the lore of all the worlds.

At last they rose to their feet. Ghyl asked, "Where will you go now?"

"To the pavilion. I must find my father; he will be wondering where I am."

"Won't he be worried?"

"I don't think so."

Ghyl put his hands on the girl's shoulder. "Shanne! Can we go off together, away from Ambroy? To South Continent! Or the Mang Islands! And there live our lives together?"

Shanne once more touched his mouth with her hands. "It would never be feasible."

"And I will never see you more?"

"Never more."

There was a sound behind them, a quiet footstep. Ghyl turned to look, to see a black hulk standing patiently beside the moonlit river.

"Just my Garrion," said Shanne. "Come, let us return to the pavilion."

Ghyl turned away. They walked back along the riverbank. Behind, at a discreet distance, came the Garrion.

CHAPTER XIII

At the pavilion Shanne kissed Ghyl on the cheek, then, donning her domino, slipped off through the colored shadows to a group of lords and ladies.

Ghyl watched a moment, then turned away. How different seemed the universe! How strange seemed his life of a week ago! There was Floriel. Ghyl went to him. "Well then, here I am. Where is Sonjaly? Where is Nion?"

Floriel gave a mirthless laugh. "You missed all the fun."

"Oh?"

"Yes. A lord in armor—perhaps you noticed him—took interest in Sonjaly. Nion resented his attentions. When the two went outside to walk along the riverbank Nion ran after them, though really it was no affair of his. Mine, if anyone's. Well, I went behind to watch. Nion challenged the lord; the Garrion seized him, beat him and threw him in the river. The lord went off with Sonjaly. Nion floated off downstream, splashing and cursing. Splendid! I've seen no more of him."

Ghyl laughed: a caw of such harsh mirth that Floriel looked at him in wonder. "And how did you fare? I saw you earlier with a girl in white."

"Are you ready to leave?"

"Why not? A miserable evening. I'll not come to the County Ball again. It's all froth and frivolity, with not an ounce of true entertainment. Well, let us go."

They walked through the night to the dock, and Floriel sculled the skiff across the river. Damar had set; an ash-colored light welled up into the eastern sky. A lamp flickered in the main room of the cottage. Here sat Nion, huddled under a blanket, drinking tea. He looked up as Floriel and Ghyl entered, and gave a grunt of mingled greeting and disapproval. "So you've finally returned. What kept you so long? Do you know that the Garrion beat me and threw me in the river?"

"It serves you right," said Floriel. He poured tea, handed a cup to Ghyl. The three sat in brooding silence. Ghyl at last made a sound, halfway between a sigh and a groan. "Life at Ambroy is futile. It is life wasted."

"Are you just now becoming aware of that?" asked Nion bitterly.

"Life is probably futile anywhere," remarked Floriel with a sniff.

"That's all that's keeping me at Ambroy," declared Nion. "That, and the fact that I can make a decent living here."

Ghyl clenched his hands around the cup. "If I had any courage—if any of us had courage—we'd go forth to find…something."

"What do you mean—'something'?" asked Nion in a cantankerous voice.

"I'm not sure. Something meaningful, something grand. The chance to work a remarkable good, to right a terrible wrong, to do high deeds, to inspire men for all time! Like Emphyrio!"

Nion laughed. "Emphyrio again? We worked him once for what he was worth, which wasn't much."

Ghyl paid no heed. "Somewhere the truth regarding Emphyrio exists. I want to learn the truth. Don't you?"

Floriel, more perceptive than Nion, surveyed Ghyl curiously. "Why does this mean so much to you?"

"Emphyrio has haunted me all my life. My father died on the same account; he thought of himself as Emphyrio. He wanted to bring truth to Ambroy. Why else did he dare so much?"

Nion shrugged. "You'll never grease your pan with 'truth'." He glanced at Ghyl appraisingly. "The girl you were sitting with—wasn't she a lady?"

"Yes. Shanne." Ghyl uttered the name softly.

"She seemed attractive, judging from her figure. Are you seeing her again?"

"She's going traveling. I'll be left behind."

Nion looked at him with raised eyebrows. He gave a sour little bark of a laugh. "I do believe," he told Floriel, "that the lad's smitten!"

Floriel, still smarting over Sonjaly's faithlessness, was not particularly interested. "I suppose it happens."

Nion addressed Ghyl in an earnest, if condescending, voice. "My dear fellow, you should never take these people seriously! Why do you think they come to the County Ball? No other reason but to have a little fling. They purge themselves of tension and emotion; after all, they live unnatural lives up on those eyries. They detest each other's vanity and arrogance and chill. Hence they come down to the County Ball and warm themselves at the fire of honest passion!"

"Nonsense," muttered Ghyl. "The situation was not at all like this."

"Ha! Did she say she loved you?"

"No."

"Did she show any shyness or reluctance?"

"No."

"Did she agree to see you again?"

"No. But she'll be traveling in a short time. She explained it all to me."

"Oh?" Nion pulled thoughtfully at his chin. "She told you when she was departing?"

"Yes."

"And when will it be?"

Ghyl looked sharply at Nion Bohart whose voice had suddenly become far too casual. "Why do you ask?"

"I have my reasons…Peculiar that she should be so confiding. They're usually the most secretive of folk. You must have plucked at her heart-strings."

Ghyl gave a hollow laugh. "I doubt if she has a heart."

Nion considered a moment, then looked at Floriel. "Would you be ready?"

Floriel grimaced. "As ready as I'll ever be. But we don't know when they debark, or from where."

"Presumably at the Godero space-port."

"Presumably. But we don't know the boat." Floriel looked at Ghyl. "Did she mention what kind of space-yacht she would travel in?"

"I know the space-yacht."

Nion jumped to his feet. "Do you then? Wonderful! Our problems are solved. What about it? Would you care to join us in a venture?"

"You mean, to steal the space-yacht?"

"Yes. It is an unusual opportunity. We know, or rather you know, the departure date: when the yacht will be fueled and victualed and crewed and ready for space. All we need do is step aboard and take charge."

Ghyl nodded. "What then?"

Nion hesitated a barely perceptible instant. "Well—we'll try to ransom our captives; that's only reasonable."

"They won't ransom themselves any more, they've compacted together."

"So I'm told. Well, if they won't pay, they won't pay. We can drop them off on Morgan or some such spot, and then fly off in search of wealth and adventure."

Ghyl sipped his tea, and looked out at the flowing river. What was left for him in Ambroy? A lifetime of wood-carving and Schute Cobol's admonitions? Shanne? Had she, after all, thought him no more than a maudlin brute? If she thought of him at all.

Ghyl winced. He said slowly, "I'd like to take the space-yacht, if only to find the Historian who knows the entire history of the human race."

Floriel gave an indulgent laugh. "He wants to scrutinize the life of Emphyrio."

"Why not?" asked Nion easily. "This is his privilege. Once we've taken the space-yacht and earned a few vouchers, there's nothing in the way."

Floriel shrugged. "I suppose there's no reason why not."

Ghyl looked from one to the other. "Before I listen to another word, an absolutely fundamental matter: we must agree: no killing, no looting, no kidnaping, no piracy."

Nion laughed in exasperation. "We're pirates the minute we take the space-yacht! Why mince matters?"

"True."

"The lords will be carrying a large sum of money for their expenses," Floriel pointed out. "There is no reason why we should leave that to them."

"I agree there also. Lords' property is fair game. If we steal their space-yacht it is foolishness to boggle at dipping into their pouches. But thereafter we prey on no one, perform no harmful acts; agreed?"

"Yes, yes," said Nion impatiently. "Now then, when does the space-yacht depart?"

"Floriel, what of you?"

"I agree, certainly. All we want is the yacht."

"Very well; a solemn compact. No killing—"

"Unless in self-defense," inserted Nion.

"—no kidnaping, or plunder, or harm."

"Done," said Floriel.

"Done," said Nion.

"The space-yacht leaves in less than a week—a week from yesterday. Floriel knows the craft very well. It is a black and gold Deme, from which long ago we were ejected."

"Well, well, well," marveled Floriel.

"One other point," Ghyl went on. "Assuming that we succeed in seizing the yacht, who can navigate? Who can operate the engines?"

"No problem there," said Nion. "The lords don't navigate either; they use a crew of Lusch technicians, who will serve us obediently, so long as their salaries are paid."

"So there," said Floriel, "all is decided. The space-yacht is as good as ours!"

"How can we fail?" demanded Nion. "We'll need two or three others, of course: Mael and Shulk, and Waldo Hidle; Waldo will find us our weapons. Wonderful! To a new life for all of us!" He held up his mug; the conspirators toasted their desperate venture in tea.

CHAPTER XIV

Ghyl returned to Undle Square with the feeling of revisiting a place he had known long ago. A high overcast shrouded the sky, allowing an umber light to seep into the square. An unnatural silence hung in the air, the stillness before a thunderstorm. Few recipients were abroad, and these hurried to their destinations, cloaks drawn up around their heads, like insects fleeing the light. Ghyl let himself into the shop, closed the door. The familiar odor of shavings and polishing oil came to his nostrils; bots buzzed against the windowpane. As always Ghyl turned a glance toward Amiante's bench, as if he half-expected someday to find there the dear familiar hulk. He went to his own bench, and for several minutes stood contemplating the screen which now he would never complete.

He had no regrets. Already his old life seemed remote. How dull and constricted seemed that old life!...What of the future? It was formless, vacant: a great windy space. He could not begin to imagine the direction of his existence—presuming, of course, that the forthcoming act of piracy turned out successfully. He looked around the shop. His tools and belongings, Amiante's accumulation of oddments—all must be abandoned. Except Amiante's old portfolio, which Ghyl could never give up. He took it from the cabinet, stood holding it irresolutely. It was too large to carry in its present condition. He made a parcel of the most valuable contents, those which Amiante had prized most dearly. As for the rest—he would simply walk away and never return. It was heart-wrenching. There were many memories to this room with the amber-paned windows, the shavings on the floor.

The next morning Nion, Floriel, Mael and Waldo Hidle came to the shop and the group formulated plans. Nion proposed a scheme which was simple and bold, with all the virtues of directness. He had noticed that Garrion were never halted at the wicket controlling access to the south area of the space-port, but passed back and forth unchallenged. The group would disguise themselves as Garrion and thereby gain access to the avenue along which the space-yachts were parked. They would conceal themselves near the black and gold Deme. When the Lusch crew came aboard, probably with a Garrion or two, the group, with due discretion and minimum violence—this at Ghyl's insistence—would overpower the Garrion, intimidate the crew, and take control of the yacht. Nion and Floriel wanted to wait for the lords, to let them board the ship, to take them as hostages and hold them for ransom. Ghyl argued against this proposal. "In the first place, the longer we wait the greater our chances of failure and rehabilitation. Secondly, the lords won't pay ransom; this is their compact, to protect themselves from kidnaping."

"Bah," said Nion. "They'll pay, don't worry about that. Do you think they'd be all that self-sacrificing? Not much."

Waldo Hidle, a tall sharp-featured young man, with rust-orange hair and pale yellow eyes, took Ghyl's side. "I'm for taking the ship and leaving fast. Once we make our move we're vulnerable. Suppose a message arrives and we don't make the correct response, or suppose we neglect some trifling formality? The patrol would be on us at once."

"That's all very well," said Nion. "Let's assume we escape with the ship. What are we going to use for money? We must be practical. Kidnaping is a means to earning the money."

Floriel added, "If they refuse to pay ransom, as Ghyl suggests, then we're in no worse ease. We'll simply set them down somewhere."

"Also," said Nion, "they'll undoubtedly have sums of money on their persons, which we can use very nicely."

Ghyl could summon no convincing counter-argument, and after a good deal of further discussion, Nion's plan was adopted.

Every day the conspirators met in the shop, to practise the Garrion stance and mode of walking. Waldo Hidle and Nion secured Garrion masks and costumes; thereafter the rehearsals were done in costume, with each criticizing inaccuracies or falsities in the other's deportment.

On three occasions they paid discreet visits to the spaceport and planned their precise mode of action.

The night before the critical day all gathered at the wood-carving shop and tried to sleep, with little success; all were tense.

Before dawn they were awake, to tone their skins the purple-brown of the Garrion, and strap themselves into the now-familiar Garrion harness. Then, muffling themselves in cloaks, they departed.

Ghyl was last to leave. For a moment he stood in the doorway looking back across the familiar old benches and tool-racks, tears making his eyes heavy. He shut the door, turned, followed his comrades.

Now they were committed. They were abroad in Garrion costume, which was irregulationary. If they were apprehended they would face a very searching inquiry at the very least.

Overtrend took them to the space-port, each touching his Garrion shoulder to the registry plate. At some time in the future each would be billed for the ride, but none would be on hand to pay: or so they hoped. Coming up into the depot they crossed the echoing old chamber, using their much-practised Garrion stride. No one glanced twice at them.

At the control wicket came the first test. The guard glanced across the counter with a blank expression, pressed the unlock button. The door slid ajar; the conspirators stalked out upon the south sector of the field.

They marched down the access avenue, past space-yacht after space-yacht, and took up stations behind the nose-block and rear structure of the ship next to the Deme, that same black and gold space-yacht from which Ghyl and Floriel so long ago had been ejected.

Time passed. The sun rose into the sky; a small red and black freighter sank down upon the north sector, to be met by landing authorities.

Nion spoke in a husky voice: "Here they come." He indicated a group coming along the avenue: six Lusch crew-men, two Garrion.

The plan now devolved upon who entered the ship first: the crew or Garrion. The crew would not be armed, but if they witnessed a struggle they would surely raise an alarm. In the optimum situation the crew would board the ship while the Garrion paused outside an extra few seconds to release the nose chock or some other such small duty.

The optimum situation did not occur. The Garrion mounted the ramp, unlocked the port, turned and stood facing the avenue, as if alert for just such an assault as the conspirators had planned. The crew scrambled up the ramp and entered the ship. The Garrion followed. The port swung closed.

The marauders watched silently, taut with frustration. There had been no opportunity to act. The instant they had showed themselves, the Garrion would have brought weapons to bear.

"Well, then," hissed Nion, "we wait for the lords. Then—we must *act!*"

An hour passed, two hours, the conspirators fidgeting with nervousness. Then along the avenue came a little dray, loaded with gay cases and parcels: personal baggage. The dray halted under the Deme; an after hatch opened, a cargo flat descended, the cases and parcels were transferred and hoisted into the belly of the Deme. The dray returned the way it had come.

The air became heavy with imminence. Ghyl's stomach began to pull and jerk; it seemed that all his life had been spent crouched under a space-yacht's nose-block.

"Here come the lords," muttered Floriel at last. "Everybody back."

Three lords and three ladies came along the avenue. Ghyl recognized Shanne. Behind marched two Garrion. Nion muttered to Floriel on one side of him, to Mael on the other.

The party turned off the avenue, ascended the Deme's boarding ramp. The entry port opened.

"Now!" said Nion. He stepped forth, stalked up the ramp, the others behind him. The Garrion instantly seized their weapons, but Nion and Mael were ready. Energy struck from their guns; the Garrion toppled, rolled to the ground.

"Quick!" snapped Nion to the lords. "Into the ship! Cooperate as you value your lives!"

The lords and ladies retreated aghast into the ship; behind came Nion, Mael and Floriel, then Ghyl and Waldo.

They burst into the saloon. The two Garrion who had come aboard with the crew stood glowering and indecisive; then they rushed forward, clicking their mandibles. Nion, Mael and Floriel fired their weapons and the Garrion became steaming wads of dark flesh. The ladies began to wail in horror; the lords made hoarse sounds.

From the depot came the wail of a siren, hoarse and wild by turns; it appeared that someone in the tower had glimpsed the attack. Nion Bohart ran to the engine room, waved his weapon at the Luschein crew. "Take the ship aloft! We have taken control; if we are threatened you will die first!"

"Fool!" cried one of the lords. "You will kill us all! The tower has orders to shoot down any seized ships, no matter who is aboard; did you not know that?"

"Quick!" bellowed Nion. "Up with the ship! Or we're all dead!"

"The coils are barely warm; the trans-gain system has not been checked!" wailed the Luschein engineer.

"Take us up—or I'll burn off your legs!"

Up went the ship, weaving and tottering on its unbalanced propulsors, and so perhaps was saved from destruction when the energy guns directed from the tower were brought to bear. Before this, the ship gained velocity and vanished into space-drive.

CHAPTER XV

Nion Bohart had assumed command of the ship, a fact tacitly accepted by his fellows and enforced upon the lords. He wore his authority with a swashbuckling swagger; but there was no doubting his earnestness, his dedication, and his pure pleasure in the success of the exploit.

He held his weapons upon the lords while Floriel searched them. He found no weapons, nor the large sums of money which had been expected.

"Well then," said Nion in a dire voice. "Where are your funds? Do you carry vouchers or valuta or whatever?"

The lord who owned the ship, a thin-faced saturnine individual in a suit of silver foil and pink velvet, with a gallant hat of silver mesh, turned a sneer of disgust upon Nion. "The money is in our luggage; where else?"

Nion, not at all disturbed by the lord's contempt, shoved his weapons back in his belt. "Names please?"

"I am Fanton the Overtrend. This is my consort, the Lady Radance; this is my daughter, the Lady Shanne."

"Very well. You, sir?"

"I am Ilseth the Spay; my consort, the Lady Jacinth."

"You, sir?"

"I am Xane the Spay."

"Good. You may all sit, if you are so inclined."

The lords and ladies remained standing a moment; then Fanton muttered something, and the group went to settees along the bulkhead.

Nion looked around the saloon. He gestured to the Garrion corpses. "You, Ghyl, you, Waldo: eject this rubbish."

Ghyl stood stiffly, burning with resentment. Certainly, in any group such as this, there was need for a leader; nonetheless, in Ghyl's opinion, Nion had arrogated this privilege to himself somewhat high-handedly. If now he obeyed the order without complaint, he thereby conceded Nion's authority. If he did not obey, he initiated contention. And he would gain Nion's instant and abiding hatred. So—submit or fight.

He decided to fight.

"The emergency is over, Nion. We began this venture as a group of equals; let's keep it that way."

"What's this?" barked Nion. "Do you object to unpleasant work?"

"No. I object to your giving orders in regard to the unpleasant work."

For a tense moment the two faced each other, Nion smiling but obviously discomfited. He snarled, "We can't bicker over every little detail; somebody has to give orders."

"In that case, let's rotate the leadership. Floriel can start, I'll take it next, or Mael, or you or Waldo—it makes no great difference. But let's keep our group an association of equals, rather than a captain and his followers." Ghyl, sensing that now was the appropriate time to seek support, looked around to the others. "Do you fellows agree?"

Waldo spoke first, hesitantly. "Yes, I agree. There is no need for anyone to give orders, so long as we are not faced with emergency."

"I don't like orders," Mael agreed. "As Ghyl says, we're a group. Let's make the decisions together, then act."

Nion looked at Floriel. "What of you?"

Floriel licked his lips. "Well—I'll go along with whatever everyone else thinks."

Nion gave in gracefully. "Good enough. We're a group, we'll act as a group. Still, we've got to have rules and direction, otherwise we fall to pieces."

"No argument there," said Ghyl. "I suggest then that we confine our guests, passengers, prisoners—whatever they are—in staterooms, and hold a conference."

"Very good," said Nion, and then with heavy sarcasm: "Perhaps, Mael, you and Floriel will so confine our guests. I and Waldo, and Ghyl, if he so decides, will eject the corpses."

"A moment before you hold your conference," spoke Lord Fanton. "What are your designs in regard to us?"

"Ransom," said Nion. "As simple as that."

"In that case, you must revise your plans. We will request none. If we did, none would be paid. This is our law. Your piracy is in vain."

"Not altogether," said Nion, "even if what you say is true, we have possession of the ship, which represents wealth. If you pay no ransom we will take you to the man-markets in Wale. The women will go to brothels, the men will work in the mines or gather silicon flowers on the desert. If of course you prefer this to ransom."

"'Preference' is not involved," said Ilseth the Spay, who seemed less absolute than Fanton. "This is the law, imposed upon us."

Ghyl spoke, to forestall Nion. "We'll discuss the situation at our conference. We intend no harm upon you, if you give us no trouble."

Nion said, "To the staterooms then, if you please."

The ship floated quietly in space, propulsors at rest, while the five young pirates sat at conference.

The question of leadership was first discussed. Nion Bohart was all sweet reason. "In a situation of this sort someone has to act as the coordinator. It is a matter of responsibility, of competence, of confidence and mutual trust. Does anyone want the job of leader? I don't. But I'm willing to tackle it because I feel responsible to the group."

"I don't want to be leader," said Floriel virtuously, with a rather malicious glance toward Ghyl. "I am quite content to let anyone competent take over the job."

Mael grinned uncomfortably. "I don't want the job, but on the other hand I don't want to do the dirty work, to run here and there while somebody plays king."

"Nor I," echoed Waldo. "Perhaps we do not really need a leader. It is easy enough to discuss and reconcile differences and arrive at a consensus."

"It means a constant argument," grumbled Floriel. "Much easier to give the job to a man we know to be competent."

"There won't be arguments if we establish a set of rules and abide by them," said Ghyl. "After all, we are not pirates; we intend no pillage or desperate work."

"Oh?" inquired Nion. "How do you expect to exist? If we don't get ransom money, we have a space-yacht but no means to maintain it."

"Our original compact was explicit," said Ghyl. "We agreed not to kill. Four Garrion are dead, unavoidably I suppose. We agreed to try for ransom; and why not, after all? The lords are parasites and fair game. But most importantly we agreed to use the space-yacht not for pillage or plunder but for travel! To the far worlds all of us have longed to visit!"

"All very well," said Floriel, with a glance at Nion, "but what do we eat when the provisions run out? How do we pay port fees?"

"We can let the ship for charter, we can convey folk here and there, perform explorations or special ventures. Surely there must be honest profit to be gained from a space-yacht!"

Nion shook his head with a quiet smile. "Ghyl, my friend, this is a cruel universe. Honesty is a noble word, but meaningless. We can't afford to be sentimental. We have committed ourselves; we can't back down now."

"This is not our original agreement!" said Ghyl. "We pledged: no killing; no plunder."

Nion shrugged. "What do the others think?"

Floriel said easily, "We have to live. I have no qualms."

Mael shook his head uncomfortably. "I don't object to theft, especially from the rich. But I don't care to kill, or enslave, or kidnap."

"I feel about the same," said Waldo. "Theft in one way or another is a law of nature; every living thing steals from another, in the process of survival."

A slow quiet smile was forming on Nion's face. Ghyl cried passionately, "This is not our compact! We agreed to live as honest men, after taking the yacht. To break the compact would be intolerable! How could we trust each other? Did we not embark upon this venture to search for truth?"

"'Truth'?" barked Nion. "Only a fool would use such a word! What does it mean? I don't know."

"One aspect of truth," said Ghyl, "is the keeping of promises. That is what concerns us most at the moment."

Nion began: "Are you suggesting—" but Mael, jumping to his feet, held up his hands. "Let's not quarrel! It's insanity! We've got to work together."

"Exactly," said Floriel, with a scornful glance toward Ghyl. "We've got to think of the common good, and profit for everyone."

Waldo said, "But let's be honest with each other. No denying that we did make the compact, exactly as Ghyl states."

"Perhaps so," agreed Floriel, "but if four of us wish to make certain changes, must we all be thwarted because of Ghyl's idealism? Remember, the search for 'truth'—"

"Whatever that is," interjected Nion.

"—won't put food in our stomachs!"

"Forget my 'idealism' for a moment," said Ghyl. "I insist only that we keep to the terms of our compact. Who knows? We might do better as honest men than as thieves. And isn't it better not to have to worry about apprehension and punishment?"

"Ghyl's got a sound point there," admitted Waldo. "At least we should give it a try."

"I've never heard of anyone making a good living with only a space-yacht," grumbled Nion. "And be sensible: who's to trouble us if we indulge in a few quiet confiscations?"

"Our compact was clear and definite," Ghyl reminded him. "No theft, no piracy. We've succeeded in our main enterprise: we now own a space-yacht. If five men such as we can't make a good honest living for ourselves, we deserve to starve!"

There was a silence. Nion made a mulish grimace of disgust. Floriel fidgeted and looked up and down, every which way but at Ghyl.

Mael said heavily, "Very well then. Let's give it a trial. If we don't make a go of it, we'll have to try something else—or perhaps split up."

"In that case," demanded Nion, "what of the space-yacht?"

"We could sell it and divide the money. Or cast lots."

"Bah. What a sorry state of affairs."

"How can you say that?" cried Ghyl. "We've succeeded! We've got our space-yacht! What more could we ask?"

Nion turned his back, went to look out the forward port.

Floriel said, "We can still try for ransom. I say, tax the lords one at a time; winkle the truth out of them. I can't believe that they won't pay to save themselves from Wale."

"Let's talk to them, by all means," agreed Waldo, anxious to restore the bonds of cooperation and good-fellowship.

Lord Fanton was the first brought back to the saloon. Eyes snapping with rage, he looked from one face to the other. "I know what you want: ransom! You will have none."

Nion spoke in a suave voice, "Surely you want to save yourself and your family from the man-markets?"

"Naturally. But I can pay no ransom, nor can my friends. So do your worst. You will get no more wealth from us."

"Only the value of your persons," said Nion. "Very well, return to your stateroom."

Xane the Spay was brought forth, Nion swaggered forward, hands on hips, but Ghyl spoke first. "Lord Xane, we wish to cause no one undue hardship, but we were hoping to collect ransom for your safe return."

Lord Xane held out his hands helplessly. "Hopes are cheap. I also have hopes. Will mine be realized? I doubt it."

"Is it literally true that you can command no ransom?"

Xane the Spay gave an embarrassed laugh. "In the first place we control very little ready cash."

"What?" demanded Mael. "With 1.18 percent of all the income to Ambroy?"

"Such is the case. Grand Lord Dugald the Boimarc is a strict accountant. After he deducts for expenses, taxes, overhead, and other costs, there is little residue, believe me or not."

"I for one do not believe you," spat Floriel. "'Expenses', 'taxes'—do you take us for fools?"

Nion asked in a silky voice: "Where does all the money go? It is a sizeable sum."

"You must put your question to Grand Lord Dugald. And remember, our law forbids the payment of as much as a twisted sequin in ransom."

Lord Ilseth the Spay made a similar statement. Like Fanton and Xane he declared that not a sequin of ransom could be paid.

"Then," said Nion grimly, "we will sell you on Wale."

Ilseth made a despairing gesture. "Isn't this carrying vindictiveness too far? After all, you have Lord Fanton's space-yacht and our funds."

"We want an additional two hundred thousand vouchers."

"Impossible. Do your worst." Ilseth departed the saloon. Nion called after him, "Don't worry; we will!"

Mael said gloomily, "They certainly are an obdurate group."

"Curious that they should plead poverty," mused Ghyl. "What in the world becomes of all their money?"

"I consider the statement an insolent lie," sniffed Floriel. "I feel that we should show them no mercy."

"It certainly seems strange," agreed Waldo.

"They'll bring a thousand vouchers apiece on Wale," said Nion briskly. "Five thousand or better for the girl."

"Mmph," said Floriel. "Nine thousand is a far cry from two hundred thousand, but it's better than nothing."

"So then: to Wale," said Nion. "I'll give orders to the Lusch."

Ghyl declared, "No, no, no! We agreed to put the lords off on Morgan! These are the terms of our compact!"

Floriel gave a wordless cry of outrage. Nion turned a smiling face toward Ghyl which was more sinister than a glare. "Ghyl, this is the third time you have obstructed the common will."

"The third time, rather, that I have reminded you of your promises," retorted Ghyl.

Nion stood negligently, with folded arms. "You have brought dissension to the group, which is absolutely intolerable." He unfolded his arms and it could be seen that he held a hand-weapon. "An unpleasant necessity but…" He aimed the weapon at Ghyl.

Waldo cried, "Have you gone mad?" He struggled to his feet, grabbed for Nion's arm. The weapon discharged, directly into Waldo's open mouth, and he fell forward. Mael, clawing at his own weapon, jumped to his feet; he pointed the gun at Nion, but could not bring himself to shoot. Floriel dodged behind Nion, fired, and Mael spun to the deck. Ghyl leapt back into the engine room, drew his own weapon, aimed at Nion, but held his fire for fear of missing and sending a bolt through the hull. Floriel, against a settee, was more vulnerable; but again Ghyl could not bring himself to fire; this was Floriel, his childhood friend!

Nion and Floriel retreated to the forward part of the saloon. Ghyl could hear them muttering. Behind him the Luschein crew watched with terrified eyes.

Ghyl called out, "You two can't win. I can starve you. I control the engines, the food, the water. You must do as I say."

Nion and Floriel muttered at length together. Then Nion called out, "What are your terms?"

"Stand, with your backs toward me, hands in the air."

"Then what?"

"I'll lock you in a stateroom, put you down on a civilized planet."

Nion laughed harshly. "You fool."

"Starve then," said Ghyl. "Go thirsty."

"What of the lords? The ladies? Do they starve and go thirsty as well?"

Ghyl considered. "They can come aft one at a time to eat, when necessary."

Again came Nion's jeering laughter. "Now I'll tell you our terms. Surrender, and I'll put *you* down on a civilized planet."

"Surrender? What for? You don't have any bargaining power."

"But we do." There was the sound of motion, a scuffle, low voices. Into the saloon walked Lord Xane the Spay, stiffly.

"Halt," said Nion. "Right there." And he raised his voice to Ghyl. "We have no great bargaining power, perhaps—but we have enough. You dislike killing, so perhaps you'll try to prevent the death of our guests."

"How do you mean?"

"We will kill them, one at a time, unless you agree to our terms."

"You would do no such heartless deed!"

The gun cracked; Lord Xane the Spay collapsed with his head burned black. "Do you now believe?" called Nion. "Next: the Lady Radance!"

Ghyl wondered: could he run forward and kill the two of them before he himself was killed? No chance whatever.

Nion spoke, "Do you agree? Yes or no?"

"Do I agree to what?"

"Surrender."

"No."

"Very well; we will kill the lords and ladies one by one, then blow a hole in the side of the ship, and all of us will die. You cannot win."

"We will proceed to a civilized planet," said Ghyl. "You may go ashore. These are my terms."

There was more noise, footsteps, a whimper of fear. The Lady Radance staggered into the saloon.

"Wait!" cried Ghyl.

"Will you surrender?"

"I'll agree to this. We will proceed to some civilized planet. The lords, the ladies, and I will go ashore. The ship will be yours."

Nion and Floriel muttered a moment. "Agreed."

✦

The space-yacht descended upon the world Maastricht, fifth planet of the star Capella: a destination chosen after careful and emotion-charged discussion between Lord Fanton, Ghyl and Nion Bohart.

Air composition and pressure had been justified; those who were to disembark had dosed themselves with toners, ameliorators and anti-gens specific against the biochemical complexes of Maastricht.

The saloon port opened, to admit a flood of light. Fanton, Ilseth, Radance, Jacinth and Shanne went into the entry chamber, alighted, to stand blinking and dazzled.

Ghyl did not dare to cross the saloon. Nion Bohart was vindictive and wicked; Floriel, now completely under his control, was no better. Ghyl retired into the engine room, opened the heavy-goods port. He dropped out parcels of food and water, then the lords' luggage, from which he had previously abstracted all the money: a large sum. Tucking his own bundle of belongings into his jacket, he dropped to the ground, and dodged behind the bole of a nearby tree, prepared for anything.

But Nion and Floriel seemed content to leave well enough alone. The ports closed; the propulsors hummed; the yacht raised into the air, gathered speed and disappeared.

CHAPTER XVI

The gold and black Deme was gone. Solitude was complete. The group stood on a vast savannah, confined somewhat to east and west by low sugarloaf humps of bald granite or limestone. The sky was a rich soft blue, completely unlike the dusty mauve sky of Halma. An ankle-deep carpet of coarse yellow stalks tipped with scarlet berries spread as far as the eye could reach, the color muting to mustard-ocher in the dis-tance. Here and there stood clumps of dark shrubs, an occasional heavy black tree, all shags and tatters. It soon became apparent that the time was morning. The sun, Capella, hung halfway up the sky, surrounded by a zone of white glimmer: something like the light over an ocean, and the landscape to the east was shrouded in a bright haze.

Well, then, thought Ghyl: here was the far world he had yearned to visit all of his life. He gave a sardonic chuckle. Never in his wildest

145

imaginings had he anticipated being marooned with two lords and three ladies. He appraised them, where they stood in the shade of a sponge bush, the lords still wearing their splendid garments and proud wide-brimmed hats. Again Ghyl was impelled to a snort of amusement. If he felt discomfited it was clearly nothing compared to the incongruous, almost farcical, spectacle presented by the lords. They spoke quickly among themselves, making nervous gesticulations, looking this way and that, but seeming to bend their most serious attention toward the hills. Now they took note of Ghyl, inspecting him with glares of detestation.

Ghyl went to join them; they moved fastidiously back. Ghyl asked, "Does anyone know where we are?"

"This is Rakanga Steppe, on the planet Maastricht," said Fanton tersely and turned away, as if to exclude Ghyl from the conversation.

Ghyl asked politely, "Are there cities or towns nearby?"

"Somewhere; we do not know where," said Fanton over his shoulder.

Ilseth, a trifle less brusque than Fanton, said, "Your friends did their best to make our lot difficult. This is the wildest section of Maastricht."

"I suggest," said Ghyl, "that we let bygones be bygones. True, I was part of the group which confiscated your ship, but I meant none of you harm. Remember, I saved your lives."

"We are sensible of the fact," said Fanton coldly.

Ghyl pointed off across the far savannah. "I see a watercourse in the distance; at least a line of trees. If we go to this, and if it is a stream, it should eventually lead us to a settlement."

Fanton appeared not to hear and engaged Ilseth in an earnest discussion, both staring toward the hills with an expression almost of longing. The older women muttered together. Shanne looked at Ghyl with an unfathomable expression. Ilseth turned to the ladies. "Best that we verge to the hills, to escape these hellish open plains. With luck we can find a grotto or covered shelter of some kind."

"Aye," said Fanton. "We would not be exposed to the sky during the whole of a strange night."

"Ah no!" whispered Lady Jacinth in a voice of hushed horror.

"Well then, let us be off." Fanton bowed to the ladies, extended his arm in a brave flourish. The ladies, casting apprehensive eyes at the sky, scurried off across the savannah, followed by Lords Fanton and Ilseth.

Ghyl looked after them non-plussed. He called out, "Wait! The food and water!"

Fanton spoke over his shoulder: "Bring it."

Ghyl stared in mingled rage and amusement. "What! You want me to carry all of it?"

Fanton paused, inspected the parcels. "Yes, all. Even so, I doubt if there will be sufficient."

Ghyl laughed incredulously. "Carry your own food and water."

Fanton and Ilseth looked around, eyebrows lofted in irritation.

"Another matter." Ghyl pointed toward the hills, where a large hump-backed black beast stood watching. As they looked, it lifted up on its hind-quarters to gaze more intently. "That is a wild beast," said Ghyl. "It is quite possibly ferocious. You have no weapons. If you value your lives, do not march off by yourselves, without food or water."

Ilseth grumbled. "There is something in what he says. We have not much choice."

Fanton grudgingly returned. "Give me the weapon then, and you may carry the provisions."

"No," said Ghyl. "You must carry your own provisions. I am walking north, toward the river, which undoubtedly will lead to a human settlement. If you go to those hills you will suffer hunger and thirst, and will probably be killed by the wild beasts."

The lords frowned up toward the sky, looked north across the open savannah without enthusiasm.

Ghyl said politely, "I discharged your luggage from the yacht. If you have garments more durable I suggest you change into them."

The lords and ladies paid him no heed. Ghyl divided the provisions into three lots; with vast distaste the lords slung their share of the parcels over their shoulders, and so they set out.

As they trudged across the savannah, Ghyl thought: "Twice now I have saved these lords from death. Beyond all doubt, on the instant that I deliver them to civilization, they will denounce me for a pirate. I will be expelled, or whatever the local penalty. So then, what shall I do?"

Had Ghyl been less concerned for the future he might have enjoyed the journey across the savannah. The lords were a constant source of wonder. By turns they patronized and insulted Ghyl, then refused to acknowledge his existence. He was continually surprised by their superficiality and petulance, by their almost total inability to come to rational terms with their environment. They were in awe of open spaces and ran to reach the shelter of a tree. Their heritage, so Ghyl decided, was responsible for their conduct. For centuries they had lived like pampered children, required to make no decisions, to meet no emergencies. They were concerned, therefore, with little beyond the immediate moment. Their emotions, though dramatic, were never profound. After the first few hours Ghyl accepted their foibles with equanimity. But how to deliver them safely to civilization and at the same time escape with a whole skin? The prospect of becoming a fugitive on a strange planet caused Ghyl foreboding.

The lords immediately made it clear that they preferred night to day as a time for travel. With disarming candor they informed Ghyl that the spaces seemed not so vast, and the glare of brilliant Capella would thereby be avoided. But a number of sinister beasts roamed the savannah. Ghyl feared one in particular: a sinuous creature twenty feet long with a thin flat body and eight long legs. This he thought of as 'the slinker', from its mode of movement. In the dark it could slide up to them unobserved and seize them in its claws. There were other creatures almost as horrid; short bounding beasts like metal barrels studded with spikes; giant serpents gliding on a hundred minuscule legs; packs of hairless red wolves, which twice forced the group to climb into trees. So despite the inclination of the lords, Ghyl refused to travel after dark. Fanton threatened to go forward without him, but after hearing a set of ominous calls and hoots decided to remain near the protection of the weapon. Ghyl built a roaring fire under a big sponge tree and the group ate a portion of the food.

Now Ghyl broached the subject which was at the top of his mind. "I am in a peculiar position," he told Fanton and Ilseth. "As you know, I was a member of the group which thrust these inconveniences upon you."

"The fact is seldom out of my mind," said Fanton curtly.

"This then is my dilemma. I meant no harm for you or the ladies. I wanted only your yacht. Now I feel it my duty to help you to civilization."

Fanton, looking into the fire, responded only with a grim and ominous nod.

"If I left you alone," Ghyl went on, "I doubt if you would survive. But I also must think of my own interests. I want your word of honor that if

I help you to security you will not denounce me to the authorities."

Lady Jacinth sputtered in outrage. "You dare make conditions? Look at us, our indignities, discomfort, and yet—"

"Lady Jacinth, you misunderstand!" exclaimed Ghyl.

Ilseth made an indifferent gesture. "Very well, I agree. After all, the man has done his best for us."

"What?" demanded Fanton in a passionate voice. "This is the spiteful lout who robbed me of my yacht! I promise only that he'll be well punished!"

"In that case," said Ghyl, "we shall separate, and go different ways."

"So long as you leave the weapon with us."

"Hah! I'll do nothing of the sort."

Ilseth said, "Come, Fanton, be reasonable. This is an unusual situation. We must be large-hearted!" He turned to Ghyl. "So far as I am concerned the piracy is forgotten."

"And you, Lord Fanton?"

Fanton gave a sour grunt. "Oh, very well."

"And the ladies?"

"They will remain discreet, or so I suppose."

A soft breeze came out of the dark, wafting a vile scent which caused Ghyl a prickling uneasiness. The lords and ladies seemed not to notice.

Ghyl rose to his feet and peered out into the darkness. He turned back to find the lords and ladies already composing themselves for rest.

"No, no!" he said urgently. "For safety we should climb the tree, as high as possible."

The lords gazed stonily at him, making no movement.

"As you wish," said Ghyl. "Your lives are your own." He stoked the fire with the limbs of a dead tree, evoking a peevish complaint from Fanton. "Must you make such a furious blaze? Fire is detestable."

"There are beasts out yonder," said Ghyl. "The fire will at least allow us to see them. And I urge that everyone climb the tree."

"Ridiculous, perched in the branches," declared Lady Radance. "How could we rest? Is there no consideration for our fatigue?"

"You are very vulnerable on the ground," said Ghyl politely. "In the tree you will not rest as well but you will be more secure." He scrambled up into the branches and wedged himself into a high crotch.

On the ground the lords and ladies muttered uneasily. At last Shanne jumped to her feet and climbed the tree. Fanton assisted Lady Radance; together they scrambled to a branch near Ghyl. Lady Jacinth, complaining bitterly, refused to climb higher than a heavy limb ten feet from the ground. Ilseth shook his head in exasperation and perched himself on another branch somewhat higher.

The fire burnt low. From the darkness came a set of thudding sounds, a far wail. Everyone sat quietly.

Time passed. Ghyl dozed fretfully. Halfway through the night he became aware of a vile stench. The fire was almost dead.

There came a sound of heavy slow footsteps. A huge dark creature came padding across the turf. It paused beneath the tree with one foot in the embers. Then it reached up, plucked Lady Jacinth from the low branch and carried her off screaming horribly. Ghyl could not see to aim the weapon. All climbed higher and slept no more.

The night was long indeed. Fanton and Ilseth crouched in silence near the top of the tree. Lady Radance made an intermittent fluting sound, like the warbling of a petulant bird; from Shanne came an occasional forlorn wail. The air became cold and clammy with settling dew; Lady Radance and Shanne became still and stiff.

Finally a ribbon of green light formed across the eastern sky, expanding upward to become the rim of a pink suffusion: then a spark of intense white light, then a dazzling cusp, then a disk, as Capella cleared the horizon.

Down from the tree came the haggard group. Ghyl made a fire, which he alone seemed to find cheerful.

After a glum breakfast, the five once more set off toward the north. To Ghyl's perplexity Lord Ilseth displayed neither grief nor shock at the loss of Lady Jacinth, nor did any of the others seem overly concerned. "What strange folk!" marveled Ghyl. "Do they have feelings or do they just play at life?" And he listened as the lords and ladies, recovering something of their aplomb, began to converse among themselves, ignoring Ghyl as if he did not exist. Fanton and Ilseth once more gestured toward the hills and began to veer west, until Ghyl called them back to the original course.

About midmorning black clouds boiled up from the south. There were whistling gusts of wind; then a hail storm surpassing any of Ghyl's experience pelted the travelers with pebbles of ice. Ghyl stood with his arms over his head; the lords and ladies ran back and forth beating at the hailstones as if they were insects, while Ghyl watched in amazement.

The storm passed as suddenly as it had come; in an hour the sky was clear again; Capella blazed down upon the glistening savannah.

But the lords and ladies had become dismal, forlorn, black-hearted. Their wonderful broad-brimmed hats drooped, their slippers were torn, their filigreed garments were stained. Only Shanne, perhaps because of her youth, failed to become venomously cantankerous, and she began to trail back with Ghyl. For the first time since the pirates had taken the ship they spoke together. To Ghyl's utter amazement, he found that she had not recognized him as the young man of the County Ball; indeed she seemed to have forgotten the episode. When Ghyl recalled it to her memory she looked at him in perplexity. "But—what a coincidence! You at the Ball—and you here now!"

"A strange coincidence," agreed Ghyl sadly.

"Why are you so evil? A pirate, a kidnaper! You seemed so trusting and innocent, if I remember rightly."

"Yes, you remember rightly. I could explain the change, but you would not understand."

"It makes no difference, one way or another. My father will denounce you as soon as we reach civilization. Do you realize that?"

"Last night he and Ilseth agreed not to do so!" cried Ghyl.

Shanne gave him a blank look, and for a space said no more.

At noon they reached the line of trees, which indeed bordered a dank trickle of water. Late in the afternoon the trickle joined a shallow river, with a faint trail along the bank, and not long after the travelers came upon an abandoned village, consisting of a dozen huts of bleached gray timber leaning every which way. In the soundest of these Ghyl proposed to spend the night, and for once the lords agreed without controversy. The inner walls of the shack were sealed with a pasting of old newspapers, printed in characters illegible to Ghyl. He could not restrain a pang of illogical awe at the sight of so much duplication. Here and there were faded pictures: men and women in peculiar costumes, space-ships, structures of a sort unfamiliar to Ghyl, a map of Maastricht which Ghyl studied half an hour without enlightenment.

Capella sank in a glorious coruscation of gold, yellow, scarlet, vermilion, totally unlike the sad mauves and ale-brown sunsets of Halma. Ghyl built a fire on the old stone hearth, which irritated the lords.

"Need it be so warm, so bright, with all those little whips and welts of flame?" complained Lady Radance.

"I suppose he wants to see to eat," said Ilseth.

"But why must the fool toast himself like a salamander?" demanded Fanton crossly.

"If we had maintained a fire last night," Ghyl returned, "and if the Lady Jacinth had used my advice to climb high in the tree, she might be alive now."

At this the lords and ladies fell silent, and their eyes flickered nervously up and down. Then they retreated into the darkest corners of the shack and pressed themselves to the walls: a form of conduct which Ghyl found startling.

During the night something tried the rickety door of the cabin, which Ghyl had barred shut. Ghyl sat up, groped for his gun. From the embers in the fireplace came a faint glow. The door shook again; then outside Ghyl heard steps, and they seemed like the steps of a man. Ghyl followed the sound around the walls to a window. Silhouetted against the starlit sky he thought to see the shape of a human or near-human head. Ghyl threw a chunk of wood at the head. There was a thud, an exclamation. Then silence. Somewhat later Ghyl heard sounds at the front door: heavy breathing, scratching and scraping, a small squeak. Then once again silence.

In the morning Ghyl went cautiously to the door, opened it with the utmost care. The ground outside seemed undisturbed. There was no booby-trap over the lintel, no trip-string, no barbs or hooks. What then had been the meaning of last night's activity? Ghyl stood in the doorway, searching the ground for signs of a deadfall.

Lord Ilseth came up behind him. "Stand aside, if you will."

"A moment. Best make sure it's safe."

"'Safe'? Why should it not be safe?" Ilseth pushed Ghyl aside and strode forth. The ground gave way under his foot. He snatched up his leg, and fixed to his ankle was a plump purple-cheeked creature like a fat fish or an enormous elongated toad. Ilseth ran wailing through the village, kicking and clawing at the thing on his ankle. Then he gave a sudden great caw of agony and bounded off across the landscape in great wild hops. He disappeared behind a row of feathery black bushes and was seen no more.

Ghyl drew a deep breath. He prodded with a stick and discovered four additional traps. Fanton, watching over his shoulder, said nothing.

Lady Radance and Shanne, moaning in perplexity and terror, at last were prevailed upon to come forth from the hut. The group cautiously departed the dreadful village and set forth along the bank of the little river. For hours they walked in the shade of tremendous trees with fleshy russet trunks and succulent green foliage. Hundreds of small openwork creatures, like monkey-skeletons, hung in the branches, rasping and chittering, occasionally dropping twigs; in and out of the sunlight shimmered air-snakes. Behind, from time to time, Ghyl thought to notice someone or something following. On other occasions a ripple, a turbulence in the water, seemed almost to keep pace with them. At noon these indications disappeared, and an hour later they came to cultivated country. Fields were planted to vines and bushes yielding green pods, bulbs of black pulp, gourds. Soon after they entered a small town: huts and cottages of unpainted timber in a long untidy straggle along the river, which at this point connected with a canal. The townspeople were small and brown-skinned, with round heads, black eyes, harsh heavy features. They wore coarse brown and gray cloaks with conical hoods, long-toed leathern slippers; each displayed cabalic signs tattooed on his cheeks. They were not an affable people, and eyed the travelers with surly incuriosity. Fanton spoke to them sharply, and was answered in a language which Ghyl was surprised to find that he could understand, though the accent was thick.

"What town is this?"

"Attegase."

"How far is the nearest large city?"

"That would be Daillie—a matter of two hundred miles."

"How does one reach Daillie in the swiftest manner?"

"There is no swift manner. We have no reason for haste. Five days from now comes the water bus. You can ride to Reso and take the air-float to Daillie."

"Well then, I must communicate with the authorities. Where is the Spay system?"

"Spay? What is that?"

"The communication device. The telephone, the long-distance radio."

"We don't have any. This is Attegase, not Hyagansis. If you want all those trinkets and gimcracks, you better go there."

"Well then, where is this 'Hyagansis'?" demanded Fanton, at which the man and all the bystanders set up an uproar of laughter. "Isn't any Hyagansis! That's why!"

Fanton sucked in his cheeks, turned away. Ghyl asked, "Where can we stay for five days?"

"Bit of a tavern over by the canal, used by the tipplers and canal-tenders. Maybe old Voma will take care of you. Maybe not, if she's been eating reebers. She gets too bloated to do much more than take care of herself."

The travelers limped to the tavern beside the canal: a strange place built of stained wood, with an enormous high-peaked roof, grotesquely high, from which crooked dormers thrust out in all manner of unexpected angles. One corner was cut away to provide a porch and diagonally in the corner of this porch, under a tremendous beam, was the entrance.

The tavern was more picturesque from without than within. The innkeeper, a slatternly woman in a black apron, agreed to house the group. She held out her hand, rubbing thumb to forefinger. "Let's see your money. I can't spare good food for those who will not pay, and I've never seen a more clownish set of loons, excuse my saying so. What happened to you? You jump from an air-dock?"

"Something of the sort," said Ghyl. With a side-look toward Fanton, he brought forth the money he had taken from Fanton's luggage. "How much do you require?"

Voma inspected the coins. "What are these?"

"Interplanetary valuta," barked Fanton. "Have you never had off-world visitors?"

"I'm lucky to get some from off the canal and then they want me to write 'em a tab. But don't take me for a dolt, sir, because I'm inclined to outrages of the spirit, and I've been known to pull noses."

"Show us our rooms then. You will be paid, never fear."

The rooms were reasonably clean, but the food—boiled black tubers with a rancid odor—was beyond the noble-folks' eating. Ghyl asked, "These are 'reebers', no doubt?"

"Reebers they are and right. Tingled with pap and bug-spice. I can't touch them myself, or I pay for it."

"Bring us fresh fruit," suggested Fanton. "Or some plain broth."

"Sorry, sir. I can get you a pot of swabow wine, now."

"Very good, bring the wine, and perhaps a crust of bread."

So passed the day. During the course of the evening Ghyl, sitting in the pot-room, mentioned that they had walked down from the south, after leaving a wrecked air-boat. Conversation halted. "Down from the south? Across the Rakanga?"

"I guess that's what it's called. Something attacked us in the deserted village. Who or what would that be?"

"The Bouns, most likely. Some say they are men. It's why the village is deserted. Bouns got them all. Crafty cruel things."

The following day Ghyl came upon Shanne, strolling alone beside the canal. She made no protest to his joining her, and presently they sat on the bank, shaded from Capella by a tinkling silver and black disk-tree.

For a space they watched the canal boats ease past, powered by billowing square sails, in some cases by electric-field engines. Ghyl reached to put his arms around her, but she primly evaded him.

"Come now," said Ghyl. "When we sat by another river you were not so hoity-toity."

"That was the County Ball: a different case. And you were not then a vagabond and a pirate."

"I thought that the piracy had been put by the boards."

"No indeed. My father plans to denounce you the instant we reach Daillie."

Ghyl raised on his elbow. "But he promised, he gave me his word!"

Shanne looked at him in smiling surprise. "You can't believe that he would hold to an agreement with an underling? A contract is struck between equals. He always intended that you should be punished, and severely."

Ghyl nodded slowly. "I see…Why did you warn me?"

Shanne shrugged, pursed her lips. "I suppose I am perverse. Or coarse. Or bored. There is no one to talk with but you. And I know that you are not innately vicious, like the others."

"Thank you." Ghyl rose to his feet. "I believe I will be returning to the inn."

"I will come along too…In so much light and air I easily become nervous."

"You are a bizarre people."

"No. You are—unperceptive. You are not aware of texture and shadows."

Ghyl took her hands and for a moment they stood face to face on the riverbank. "Why not forget you are a lady and come with me? It would mean sharing the life of a vagabond; you would be giving up all that you are accustomed to—"

"No," said Shanne, with a cool smile for the opposite bank of the river. "You must not misunderstand me—as you most obviously do."

Ghyl bowed as formally as he knew how. "I am sorry if I have caused you embarrassment."

He walked back to the inn and sought out Voma. "I am departing. Here—" he gave her coins "—this should cover what I owe."

She gazed slack-mouthed down at the coins. "What of the others? That sour Lord Fanton, he told me that you would pay for all."

Ghyl laughed scornfully. "What kind of a fool do you take me for? See that he pays his score."

"Just as you say, sir." Voma dropped the coins into her pouch. Ghyl went to his room, took his parcel, ran down to the canal, arriving just in time to leap aboard a passing barge. It was piled high with hides and tubs of pickled reebers and reeked with an offensive odor; nevertheless it was transportation. Ghyl came to an arrangement with the boatman and took himself and his parcel to the windward section of the foredeck. He settled himself to watch the passing countryside and considered his circumstances. Travel, adventure, financial independence: this was the life he had yearned for, and this was the life he had achieved. All but the financial independence. He counted his money: two hundred and twelve interplanetary exchange units: the so-called valuta. Enough for three or four months living expenses, perhaps more if he were careful. Financial independence of a sort. Ghyl leaned back against a bale of hides and, looking up at the slowly passing tree-tops, mused of the past, the malodorous present, and wondered what the future would bring.

CHAPTER XVII

A week later the barge verged alongside a concrete dock on the outskirts of Daillie. Ghyl jumped ashore, half-expecting to be greeted by welfare agents, or whatever the nature of the local police. But the dock was vacant except for a pair of roustabouts handling lines for the barge and they paid him no heed.

Ghyl found his way to the street. To either side were warehouses and manufacturing plants built of white concrete, panels of blue-green ripple glass, soft convex roofs of white solidified foam: all glaring and flashing in the light of Capella. Ghyl set off to the northeast, toward the center of the city. A fresh wind blew briskly down the street, fluttering

Ghyl's ragged clothes and, he hoped, blowing away the reek of hides and reebers.

Today seemed to be a holiday: the streets were uncannily empty; the clean crisp structures were silent; there was no sound except for the rush of the wind.

For an hour Ghyl walked along the bright street, seeing not a single person. The street lifted over the brow of a low hill; beyond spread the immense city, dominated by a hundred glass prisms of various dimension, some as tall or taller than the skeletal structures of Vashmont Precinct, all glittering and winking in the blaze of Capella-light.

Ghyl set off down the sun-swept street, into a district of cubical white dwellings. Now there were people to be seen: brown-skinned folk of no great stature, with heavy features, black eyes, black hair, not a great deal different from the inhabitants of Attegase. They paused in their occupations to watch as Ghyl passed; he became ever more conscious of the reek of hides, his stained off-world garments, his growth of beard, his untidy hair. Down a side street he spied a market: an enormous nine-sided structure under nine translucent roof-panels, each a different color. An aged man, leaning on a cane, gave him counsel and directed him to a money-changer's booth. Ghyl gave over five of his coins and received a handful of metal wafers in return. He bought local garments and boots, went to a public rest-room, cleaned himself as well as possible, changed clothes. A barber shaved and trimmed him to the local mode; cleaner and less conspicuous. Ghyl continued toward the center of Daillie, riding most of the way on a public slideway.

He took a room at an inexpensive hostelry overlooking the river and immediately bathed in a tall octagonal room paneled with strips of aromatic wood. Three children, shaved bald and of indeterminate sex, attended him. They sprayed him with unctuous foam, beat him with whisks of soft feathers, turned gushes of effervescent water over him, the first warm, the second cold.

Much refreshed Ghyl resumed his new clothes and sauntered out into the late afternoon. He ate in a riverside restaurant with windows shaded by screens much like those carved at Ambroy. Ghyl's interest, momentarily aroused, waned when he saw the material to be a homogeneous synthetic substance. It occurred to him that he had seen little natural material in Daillie. There were vast masses of concrete foam, glass, synthetic stuff of one sort or another, but little wood or stone or fired clay, and the lack invested Daillie with a curious sterility, a clean sun- and wind-swept emptiness.

Capella sank behind the glass towers. Dusk fell over the city; the interior of the restaurant grew dim. To each table was brought a glass bulb containing a dozen luminous insects, glowing various pale colors. Ghyl leaned back in his seat and, sipping pungent tea, divided his attention between the luminous insects and the vivacious folk of Daillie at nearby tables. Rakanga Steppe, the Bouns of the deserted village, Attegase and Voma's Inn were remote. The events aboard the space-yacht were a half-forgotten nightmare. The woodworking shop on Undle Square? Ghyl's mouth moved in a wistful half-smile. He thought of Shanne. How pleasant it would be to have her across the table, chin on knuckles, eyes reflecting the insect lights. What sport they could have exploring the city together! Then traveling on to other strange planets!

Ghyl gave his head a wry shake. Impossible dream. He would be sufficiently fortunate if Lord Fanton, through impatience or press of circumstances, failed to lodge a complaint against him...Had he remained with the group, always within eye-range, a continual reminder of outrages and offenses, nothing could have deterred Lord Fanton from charging him with piracy. But out of sight, out of mind: Lord Fanton might well conceive it beneath his dignity to exert himself against an underling...Ghyl returned to the inn and went to sleep, certain that he had seen the last of Lord Fanton, Lady Radance and Shanne.

Daillie was a city vast in area and population, with a character peculiarly its own yet peculiarly fugitive and hard to put a name to. The components were readily identifiable: the great expanses of sun-dazzled streets constantly swept by wind; the clean buildings essentially homogeneous in architecture, cleverly built of synthetic substances: a population of mercurial folk who nevertheless gave the impression of self-restraint, conventionality, absorption in their own affairs. The spaceport was close to the center of the city; ships from across the human universe came to Daillie but seemed to arouse little interest. There were no enclaves of off-world folk, few restaurants devoted to off-world cuisines; the newspapers and journals concerned themselves largely with local affairs: sports, business events and transactions, the activities of the Fourteen Families and their connections. Crime either was non-existent or purposely ignored. Indeed, Ghyl saw no law enforcement apparatus: no police, militia, or uniformed functionaries.

On the third day of his stay, Ghyl moved to a less expensive hostelry near the space-port; on the fourth day he learned of the Civic Bureau of Information, to which he immediately took himself.

The clerk noted his requirements, worked a few moments at an encoding desk, then punched buttons on a sloping keyboard. Lights blinked and flashed, a strip of paper was ejected into a tray. "Not much here," the clerk reported. "Enverios, a pathologist of Gangalaya, died last century, according to the H.I....No? Here's an Emphyrio, early despot of Alme, wherever that is. H.I....Is that your man? There's also an Enfero, a Third Era musician."

"What of Emphyrio, despot of Alme? Is there further information?"

"Only what you have heard. And the H.I. reference, of course."

"What is 'H.I.'?"

"The Historical Institute of Earth, which provided the item."

"The Institute could provide more information?"

"So I would suppose. It has detailed records of every important event in human history."

"How can I get this information?"

"No problem whatever. We'll put through a research requisition. The charge is thirty-five bice. There is, of course, a wait of three months, the schedule of the Earth packet."

"That's a long time."

The clerk agreed. "But I can't suggest anything quicker—unless you go to Earth yourself."

Ghyl departed the Bureau of Information and rode by surface car to the space-port. The terminal was a gigantic half-bubble of glass surrounded by green lawn, white concrete runways, parking plats. Magnificent! thought Ghyl, recalling the dingy space-port at Ambroy. Nonetheless, he felt a lack. What could it be? Mystery? Romance? And he wondered if the lads of Daillie, visiting their space-port, could feel the awe and wonder that had been his when he had skulked the Ambroy space-port with Floriel...Perfidious Floriel. The train of thought thus stimulated set Ghyl to wondering about Lord Fanton. He had barely set foot into the terminal when his speculations were resolved. Hardly fifty feet away stood Shanne. She wore a fresh white gown, silver sandals; her hair was glossy and clean; nevertheless, she herself seemed haggard and worn, and her complexion showed an unhealthy pink flush.

Making himself inconspicuous behind a stanchion, Ghyl sought around the terminal. At a counter stood Lord Fanton and Lady Radance, both harsh and gaunt, as if even now the hardships they had undergone preyed on them. They completed their transaction; Shanne joined them; the three moved off across the terminal, conspicuous even here, where travelers from half a hundred worlds mingled, for their aloofness and withdrawal: for the Difference!

Ghyl now felt assured that Lord Fanton had not denounced him to the authorities: in fact, Fanton probably believed that Ghyl had departed the planet.

Keeping a wary lookout, Ghyl conducted his own business. He learned that any of five different shipping lines would convey him to Earth, in whatever degree of luxury and style he chose. Minimum fare was twelve hundred bice: far more than the sum in Ghyl's possession.

Ghyl departed the space-port and returned to the center of Daillie. If he wished to visit Earth he must earn a large sum of money, though by what means he had not the slightest idea. Perhaps he would simply request the Bureau of Information to secure the information he sought...Thus musing, Ghyl strolled along the Granvia, a street of luxury shops dealing in all variety of goods, and here he chanced upon an object which diverted him completely from his previous concerns.

The object, a carved screen of noble proportions, occupied a prominent position in the display window of Jodel Heurisx, Mercantile Factor. Ghyl stopped short, approached the window. The screen had been carved to represent a lattice festooned with vines. Hundreds of small faces looked earnestly forth. REMEMBER ME, read the plaque. Near the lower right-hand corner Ghyl found his own childhood face. Close at hand, the face of his father Amiante peered forth.

Ghyl's gaze seemed to blur; he looked away. When once more he could see, he returned to study the screen. The price was marked at four hundred and fifty bice. Ghyl converted the sum into valuta, then into welfare vouchers. He performed the calculation again. A mistake, surely: only four hundred and fifty bice? Amiante had been paid the equivalent of five hundred bice: little enough, certainly, considering the pride and love and dedication which Amiante gave his screens. Curious, thought Ghyl; curious indeed. In fact—astonishing.

He entered the shop; a clerk in a black and white robe of a mercantile functionary approached him. "Your will, sir?"

"The screen in the window—the price is four hundred and fifty bice?"

"Correct, sir. Somewhat costly, but an excellent piece of work."

Ghyl grimaced in puzzlement. Going to the cabinet, he inspected the screen carefully, to learn if it might have been damaged or misused. It seemed in perfect condition. Ghyl peered close, then all his blood turned cold and seemed to drain to his feet. He turned slowly to the clerk. "This screen is a reproduction."

"Of course, sir. What did you expect? The original is priceless. It hangs in the Museum of Glory."

Jodel Heurisx was an energetic, pleasant-faced man of early middle-age, stocky, strong and decisive in his manner. His office was a large room flooded with sunlight. There was little furniture: a cabinet, a table, a sideboard, two chairs and a stool. Heurisx half-leaned half-sat on the stool; Ghyl perched on the edge of a chair.

"Well then, young man, and who are you?" asked Heurisx.

Ghyl had difficulty framing a coherent statement. He blurted: "The screen in your window, it is a reproduction."

"Yes, a good reproduction: in pressed wood rather than plastic. Nothing as rich as the original, of course. What of it?"

"Do you know who carved the screen?"

Heurisx, watching Ghyl with a speculative frown, nodded. "The screen is signed 'Amiante'. He is a member of the Thurible Co-operative, no doubt a person of prestige and wealth. None of the Thurible goods come cheap, but they are all of superlative quality."

"May I ask from whom you obtained the screen?"

"You may ask, I will answer: from the Thurible Co-operative."

"It is a monopoly?"

"For such screens, yes."

Ghyl sat a half-minute, chin resting on his chest. Then: "Suppose that someone were able to break the monopoly?"

Heurisx laughed and shrugged. "It is not a question of breaking a monopoly, but destroying what appears to be a strong co-operative organism. Why, for instance, should Amiante care to deal with a newcomer when he already has a good thing going for himself?"

"'Amiante' was my father."

"Indeed? 'Was', did you say?"

"Yes. He is dead."

"My condolences." And Jodel Heurisx inspected Ghyl with cautious curiosity.

"For carving that screen," said Ghyl, "he received about five hundred bice."

Jodel Heurisx leaned back in shock. "What? Five hundred bice? No more?"

Ghyl gave a snort of sad disgust. "I have carved screens for which I earned seventy-five vouchers. About two hundred bice."

"Astounding," murmured Jodel Heurisx. "Where is your home?"

"The city Ambroy on Halma, far from here, beyond Mirabilis."

"Hmm." Heurisx plainly knew nothing of Halma nor perhaps of the great Mirabilis Cluster. "The craftsmen of Ambroy sell, then, to Thurible?"

"No. Boimarc is our trade organization. Boimarc must deal with Thurible."

"Perhaps they are one and the same," suggested Heurisx. "Perhaps you are being cheated by your own folk."

"Impossible," muttered Ghyl. "Boimarc sales are verified by the guild-masters, and the lords take their percentage from this sum. If there were peculation, the lords would be cheated no less than the underlings."

"Someone enjoys vast profits," mused Heurisx. "So much is clear. Someone at the top end of the monopoly."

"Suppose then as I asked before, that you were able to break the monopoly?"

Heurisx tapped his chin with his finger. "How would this be accomplished?"

"We would visit Ambroy in one of your ships and buy from Boimarc."

Heurisx held up his hands in protest. "Do you take me for a mogul? I am small beer compared with the Fourteen. I own no space-ships."

"Well then, can a space-ship be chartered?"

"At considerable expense. Of course the profit likewise would be large—if the Boimarc group would sell to us."

"Why should they not? If we offer double or triple the previous rate? Everyone gains: the craftsmen, the guilds, the welfare agents, the lords. No one loses but Thurible, who has enjoyed the monopoly long enough."

"It sounds reasonable." Heurisx leaned back against the table. "How do you envisage your own position? As of now you have nothing further to contribute to the enterprise."

Ghyl stared incredulously. "Nothing but my life. If I were caught I'd be rehabilitated."

"You are a criminal?"

"In a certain sense."

"You might do best to disengage yourself at this moment."

Ghyl could feel the warmth of anger on the skin of his face; but he carefully controlled his voice. "Naturally I would like financial independence. But no matter about that. My father was exploited; he was robbed of his life. I want to destroy Thurible. I would be happy to achieve no more than this."

Heurisx gave a short bark of a laugh. "Well, you can be assured I do not care to cheat you nor anyone else. Suppose, after due reflection, that I agree to provide the ship and assume all financial risks—then I believe that I should receive two-thirds of the net profit, and you one-third."

"That is more than fair."

"Come back tomorrow and I'll communicate my decision."

Four days later Jodel Heurisx and Ghyl met at a riverside café where the factors of Daillie consummated much of their business. With Heurisx was a young man, ten years or so older than Ghyl, who had little to say.

Heurisx said, "I have obtained the use of a ship: the *Grada*. It is larger than I had intended; on the other hand it costs no charter fee, and in fact belongs to my brother Bonar Heurisx." He indicated his companion. "We will participate jointly in the venture; he will convey a cargo of specialty instruments to Luschein, on Halma, where, according to Rolver's Directory, there is a ready market for such articles. There will be no great profit, but enough to defer costs. Then, you and he will take the *Grada* to Ambroy, to buy craft-goods in the manner you describe. The financial risk is reduced to a minimum."

"My personal risk unfortunately remains."

Heurisx tossed a strip of enamel upon the table. "This, when impressed with your photograph will identify you as Tal Gans, resident of Daillie. We will dye your skin, depilate your scalp, and fit you with fashionable clothing. No one will recognize you, unless it be an intimate friend, whom you will no doubt take pains to avoid."

"I have no intimate friends."

"I consign you then to the care of my brother. He is somewhat more wayward than myself, somewhat less cautious: in short, just the man for such a venture." Jodel Heurisx rose to his feet. "I will leave the two of you together, and I wish you both good luck."

CHAPTER XVIII

Strange to return to Ambroy! How familiar and dear, how remote and dim and hostile was the ramshackle half-ruined city!

They had found no difficulties at Luschein, though the instruments sold for considerably less than Bonar Heurisx had anticipated, causing him despondency. Then up and around the planet, over the Deep Ocean, north beside the Baro Peninsula and Salula, out over the Bight, with the low coast of Fortinone ahead. For the last time Ghyl rehearsed the various aspects of his new identity. Ambroy spread below. The *Grada* accepted a landing program from the control tower and descended upon the familiar space-port.

The landing formalities at Ambroy were notoriously tedious; two hours passed before Ghyl and Bonar Heurisx walked through the wan midmorning sunlight to the depot. Calling the Boimarc offices by Spay, Ghyl learned that, while Grand Lord Dugald was on the premises, he was extremely busy, and could not be seen without prior appointment.

"Explain to Lord Dugald," said Ghyl, "that we are here from the planet Maastricht to discuss the Thurible marketing organization; that it will be to his advantage to see us immediately."

There was a wait of three minutes, after which the clerk somewhat sourly announced that Lord Dugald would be able to give them a very few minutes if they would come immediately to the Boimarc offices.

"We will be there at once," said Ghyl.

By Overtrend they rode out to the far verge of East Town, a district of abandoned streets, flat areas strewn with rubble and broken glass, a few buildings yet occupied: a forlorn region not without a certain dismal beauty.

In a thirty-acre compound were two structures, the Boimarc administrative center and the Associated Guilds warehouse. Ghyl and Bonar

Heurisx, passing through a portal in the barbed fence, proceeded to the Boimarc offices.

From a cheerless foyer they were admitted to a large room where twenty clerks worked at desks, calculators, filing devices. Lord Dugald sat in an alcove with glass walls, slightly elevated from the main floor, and, like the other Boimarc functionaries, appeared to be extremely busy.

Ghyl and Bonar Heurisx were taken to a small open area directly before Lord Dugald's alcove, under his gaze to a somewhat uncomfortable degree. Here they waited, on cushioned benches. Lord Dugald, after a swift glance through the glass, paid them no heed. Ghyl examined him with vast curiosity. He was short and heavy and sat slumped in his chair like a half-filled sack. His black eyes were close together; tufts of dark gray hair rose above his ears; there was an unnatural purplish overtone to his complexion. He was, almost comically, the realization of a caricature Ghyl had somewhere seen...Of course! Lord Bodbozzle, of Holkerwoyd's Puppets! And Ghyl worked hard to restrain a grin.

Ghyl watched while Lord Dugald examined, one after another, yellow sheets of parchment, apparently invoices or requisitions, and stamped each with a handsome instrument topped with a great globe of polished red carnelian. The invoices, so Ghyl noted, were prepared by a clerk sitting before an illuminated inventory board, of a sort he had seen at Daillie; the stiff sheets so prepared were then presented to Lord Dugald for the validation of his personal stamp.

Lord Dugald approved the last of the requisitions and hung the stamp by its carnelian globe under his desk. Only then did he make a curt signal to indicate that Bonar Heurisx and Ghyl were to come forward.

The two stepped up into the glass-enclosed alcove; Lord Dugald signaled them to seats. "What is this of Thurible Co-operative? Who are you? Traders, you say?"

Bonar Heurisx spoke carefully. "Yes, this is correct. We have only just arrived from Daillie, on Maastricht, in the *Grada*."

"Yes, yes. Speak then."

"Our research," Bonar Heurisx went on more briskly, "leads us to believe that Thurible Co-operative is performing inefficiently. To be brief, we can do a better job with considerably greater return for Boimarc. Or if you prefer, we will buy directly from you, at a schedule also yielding greatly augmented profits."

Lord Dugald sat immobile except for his eyes, which flicked back and forth, from one to the other. Curtly he responded, "The suggestion is not feasible. We enjoy excellent relations with our various trading organizations. In any case, we are bound by long-term contracts."

"But the system is not to your best advantage!" Bonar protested. "I will offer new contracts at double payment."

Lord Dugald rose to his feet. "I am sorry. The subject is not open to discussion."

Bonar Heurisx and Ghyl looked at him crestfallen. "Why not give us a try, at least?" argued Ghyl.

"Absolutely not. Now, if you will please excuse me…"

Outside, walking west along Huss Boulevard, Bonar said despondently, "So much for that. Thurible holds a long-term contract." After a moment's reflection he grumbled, "Obvious, of course. We're beaten."

"No," said Ghyl. "Not yet. Boimarc has contracted with Thurible, but not the guilds. We shall go to the source of the merchandise, and bypass Boimarc."

Bonar Heurisx gave a skeptical snort. "To what avail? Lord Dugald spoke with clear authority."

"Yes, but he has no authority over the recipients. The guilds are not bound to sell to Boimarc, craftsmen need not produce for the guilds. Anyone can go noncup as he wishes, if he cares to lose his welfare benefits."

Bonar Heurisx shrugged. "I suppose that it does no harm to try."

"Exactly my feeling. Well then, first to the Scriveners' Guild, to inquire about hand-crafted books."

They walked south through the old Merchants' Quarter into Bard Square, upon which most of the guild-houses fronted. Bonar Heurisx, who had been glancing over his shoulder, presently muttered, "We're being followed. Those two men in black capes are watching our every move."

"Special Agents," said Ghyl with a glum smile. "Hardly a surprise… Well, we're doing nothing irregulationary, so far as I know. But I'd better not appear too well-acquainted with the city."

So saying he halted, looked around Bard Square with an expression of perplexity and asked directions of a passerby who pointed out the Scriveners' Hall, a tall structure of black and brown brick with four looming gables of ancient timber. Evincing uncertainty and hesitation for the benefit of the Special Agents, Ghyl and Bonar Heurisx considered the building, then chose one of the three portals and entered.

Ghyl had never before visited the Scriveners' Hall and was taken aback by the almost indecorous volume of chatter and badinage, deriving from apprentice classes in rooms to either side of the foyer. Climbing a staircase hung with samples of calligraphy, the two found their way to the Guild-master's office. In the ante-room sat a score of fidgeting, impatient scriveners, each clutching a case containing his work-in-progress.

In dismay Bonar Heurisx looked at the crowd. "Must we wait?"

"Perhaps not," said Ghyl. He crossed the room, knocked on a door which swung open to reveal an elderly woman's peevish countenance. "Why do you pound?"

Ghyl spoke in his best Daillie accent. "Please announce us to his excellency, the Guild-master. We are traders from a far world; we wish to arrange new business with the Scriveners of Ambroy."

The woman turned away, spoke over her shoulder, then looked back to Ghyl. "Enter, if you please."

The Scriveners' Guild-master, a waspish old man with a wild ruff of white hair, sat behind a vast table littered with books, posters, calligraphic manuals. Bonar Heurisx stated his proposal, to the Guild-master's startlement. "Sell you our manuscripts? What an idea! How could we be sure of our money?"

"Cash is cash," declared Bonar.

"But—how absurd! We use a long-established method; this is how we have derived our livelihood for time out of mind."

"All the more reason then to consider a change."

The Guild-master shook his head. "The current system works well; everyone is satisfied. Why should we change?"

Ghyl spoke. "We will pay double the Boimarc rate, or triple. Then everyone would be even more satisfied."

"Not so! How would we calculate the welfare deduction, the special assessments? These are handled now with no effort on our part!"

"With all charges met you would still receive twice your previous income."

"What then? The craftsmen would become avaricious. They would work two times less carefully and two times as fast, hoping for financial independence or some such nonsense. They know now that they must use scrupulous care to secure an Acme or a First. If they were teased by prosperity and set up a great clamor, what of our standards? What of our quality? What of our future markets? Should we throw away security for a few paltry vouchers?"

"Well then, sell us your 'Seconds'. We will take them across the galaxy and dispose of them there. The craftsmen will double their income and your present markets are safe."

"And thereafter produce only 'Seconds', since they sell as well as 'Firsts'? The same considerations apply! Our basic stock-in-trade is high quality; if we abandon this principle we debase our merchandise and become mere triflers."

In desperation Ghyl exclaimed, "Well then, let us be the agent for your sales. We will pay the going rate, we will pay twice this sum into a fund for the benefit of the city. We can clear ruined areas, finance institutes and entertainments."

The Guild-master glared in outrage. "Are you attempting to deceive me? How can you do so much on the output of the scriveners?"

"Not just the scriveners alone! On the output of all the guilds!"

"The proposal is far-fetched. The old way is tried and true. No one becomes financially independent, no one becomes pompous and self-willed; everyone works meticulously and there is no contention or complaint. Once we introduce innovation, we destroy equilibrium. Impossible!"

The Guild-master waved them away; the two left the Guild Hall in discouragement. The Special Agents standing nearby, discreet rather than surreptitious, watched with open curiosity.

"Now what?" asked Bonar Heurisx.

"We can try the other important guilds. If we fail at least we will have tried our hardest."

Bonar Heurisx agreed to this; they continued to the Jewellers' Syndicate, but when finally they gained the ear of the Guild-master and made their proposal, the response was as before.

The Glassblowers' Guild-master refused to speak to them; at the Lute-makers' they were referred to the Guild-masters' Conclave, eight months hence.

The Enamel, Faience and Porcelain-workers' Guild-master put his head into an anteroom long enough to hear their proposition, said "No" and backed out.

"The Wood-carvers' Guild remains," said Ghyl. "It is probably the most influential; if we receive a negative response here, we might as well return to Maastricht."

They crossed Bard Square to the long low building with the familiar façade. Ghyl decided that he dared not go in. The Guild-master, while no intimate acquaintance, was a man with a keen eye and a sharp memory. While Ghyl waited in the street Bonar went into the office alone. The Welfare Specials who had been following approached Ghyl. "May we ask why you are visiting the guild-masters? It seems a curious occupation for persons new to the planet."

"We are inquiring after trading possibilities," said Ghyl shortly. "The Boimarc Lord would not listen to us; we thought to try the guilds."

"Mmf. The Welfare Agency would disapprove such an arrangement in any case."

"It does no harm to try."

"No, of course not. Where is your native planet? Your speech is almost that of Ambroy."

"Maastricht."

"Maastricht, indeed."

The after-work movement to the Overtrend kiosk had begun; people were pushing past. A lank well-remembered female figure loped by, then stopped short, turned to stare. Ghyl looked away. The young woman craned her neck, peered into Ghyl's face. "Why, it's Ghyl Tarvoke!" cawed Gedée Anstrut. "What in the world are you doing in that outlandish costume?"

The Welfare Specials leaned forward. One cried: "Ghyl Tarvoke? Have I not heard that name?"

"You have made a mistake," Ghyl told Gedée.

Gedée drew back, her mouth open. "I forgot. Ghyl Tarvoke went off with Nion and Floriel...Oh my!" She put her hand to her mouth, backed away.

"Just a moment, please," said the Welfare Special. "Who is Ghyl Tarvoke? Is that your name, sir?"

"No, no, of course not."

"Yes it is too!" shrieked Gedée. "You're a filthy pirate, a murderer. You are the terrible Ghyl Tarvoke!"

At the Welfare Agency, Ghyl was thrust before the Social Problems Clinic. The members, sitting in a long box behind desks of iron, examined him with expressionless faces.

"You are Ghyl Tarvoke."

"You have seen my identification."

"You have been recognized by Gedée Anstrut, by welfare agent Schute Cobol and by others as well."

"As you like then. I am Ghyl Tarvoke."

The door opened; into the room came Lord Fanton the Spay. He approached, stared into Ghyl's face. "This is one of them."

"Do you admit to piracy and murder?" the chairman of the Social Clinic asked Ghyl.

"I admit to confiscating the ship of Lord Fanton."

"'Confiscate'? A pretentious word."

"My ambitions were not ignoble. I intended to learn the truth of the Emphyrio legend. Emphyrio is a great hero; the truth would inspire the people of Ambroy, who are sorely in need of truth."

"This is beside the point. You are accused of piracy and murder."

"I committed no murder. Ask Lord Fanton."

Lord Fanton spoke in a pitiless voice: "Four Garrion were killed, I know not by which of the pirates. Tarvoke stole my money. We made a terrible march during which the Lady Jacinth was devoured by a beast and Lord Ilseth was poisoned. Tarvoke cannot avoid responsibility for their deaths. Finally he left us stranded in a squalid village without a check. We were forced to make the most unpleasant compromises before we reached civilization."

"Is this true?" the chairman asked Ghyl.

"I saved the lords and ladies from slavery and from death, several times."

"But you originally put them into the predicament?"

"Yes."

"No more need be said. Rehabilitation is denied. You are sentenced to perpetual expulsion from Ambroy, via Bauredel. Expulsion will occur at once."

Ghyl was taken to a cell. An hour passed. The door opened; an agent motioned to him. "Come. The lords want to question you."

Two Garrion took Ghyl into custody. He was thrust into a sky-flitter, conveyed up through the sky toward Vashmont. Down to an eyrie the flitter descended, landing upon a blue-tiled terrace. Ghyl was taken within.

His clothes were removed; he was led stark naked into a high room at the top of a tower. Three lords came into the room: Fanton the Spay, Fray the Underline and Grand Lord Dugald the Boimarc.

"You have been a busy young man," said Dugald. "Exactly what did you have in mind?"

"Breaking the trade monopoly which strangles the folk of Ambroy."

"I see. What is this hysterical yammer in regard to 'Emphyrio'?"

"I am interested in the legend. It holds a special meaning for me."

"Come, come!" demanded Dugald with surprising sharpness. "This cannot be truth! We demand that you be frank!"

"How do I help myself telling other than the truth?" asked Ghyl. "Or anything but untruth, for that matter."

"You are quick as mercury!" stormed Dugald. "You shall not evade us, I warn you! Tell us all, or we will be forced to process you, so that you cannot help yourself."

"I have told the truth. Why do you not believe me?"

"You know why we do not believe you!" And Dugald motioned to the Garrion. They seized Ghyl, propelled him, sick and trembling through a narrow trapezoidal portal into a long narrow room. They seated him in a heavy chair, clamped him so that he could not move.

Dugald said, "Now we shall proceed."

The inquiry was over. Dugald sat spraddle-legged, looking at the floor. Fray and Fanton stood across the room studiously avoiding each other's eyes. Dugald suddenly turned to stare at them. "Whatever you heard, whatever you presumed, whatever you even conjectured must be forgotten. Emphyrio is a myth; this young would-be Emphyrio will shortly be less than a myth." He signaled the Garrion. "Return him to the Welfare Agency. Recommend that expulsion occur at once."

A black air-wagon waited at the rear of the Welfare Agency. Wearing only a white smock Ghyl was brought forth, thrust into the air-car. The port clanged shut; the air-car throbbed, lifted and swept off to the north. The time was late afternoon; the sun wallowed in a bank of yeast-colored clouds; a wan and weary light bathed the landscape.

The air-car bumped to a landing beside a concrete wall which marked the Bauredel frontier. A brick road between two subsidiary walls led up to an aperture in the boundary wall. A two-inch stripe of white paint marked the exact Fortinone-Bauredel boundary.

Immediately behind the stripe the aperture was stopped by a plug of concrete stained and spotted a horrid dull brown.

Ghyl was seized and turned out upon the brick road, between the walls which led to the frontier. A Welfare Special clapped on the traditional broad-brimmed black hat and in a portentous voice read the banishment decree: "Depart from our cherished land, oh evil man who have been proved guilty of great harm! Glorious Finuka has proscribed killing throughout the cosmic realm; thank Finuka then for the mercy to be bestowed upon you, more than you showed your own victim! You are then to be banished perpetually, and for all time, from the territory of Fortinone, and into the land of Bauredel. Do you care to leap a final rite?"

"No," said Ghyl in a husky voice.

"Go then as best you may, go with Finuka's aid into the land of Bauredel!"

A great concrete piston, entirely filling the alley, moved forward, thrusting Ghyl toward that single inch of Bauredel territory available for his occupancy.

Ghyl backed up against the piston, planted his feet against the crumbling brick. The piston thrust forward. Sixty feet to the border. A film of sunlight, pale as lymph, slanted into the avenue, outlining uneven edges of the brick, framing the concrete plug of the portal with a black shadow.

Ghyl stared at the bricks. He ran forward, tugged at a brick, then another, then another, until his fingernails broke and his fingertips were bloody. By the time he found a loose brick, the piston had denied him all but forty feet of avenue. But after the first brick came up, others pulled up without difficulty. He rushed to carry the bricks to the wall, stacked them into a pile, ran back for more.

Bricks, bricks, bricks: Ghyl's head pounded; he gasped and wheezed. Thirty feet of avenue, twenty feet, ten feet. Ghyl scrambled up the pile of bricks; they collapsed below him; frantically he stacked them again, with the piston looming over his shoulder. Up once more, and as the pile gave way he scrambled to the top of the wall. The piston thrust upon the bricks. A crunch, a crush: the bricks compressed into a friable red cake.

Ghyl lay flat on top of the wall, concealed by the walls of the avenue and by the piston, ready to drop over into Bauredel territory should the welfare agents see fit to investigate.

Ghyl lay flat as a limpet. The sun fell behind clouds; sunset was a somber display of dark yellow, watery browns. A cold breeze blew in across the waste.

Ghyl could hear no sound. The machinery of the piston was silent. The Welfare Specials had departed. Ghyl rose cautiously to his knees, peered in all directions. Bauredel to the north was dark: a waste swept by a sighing wind. To the south a few far lights glimmered.

Ghyl rose to his feet, stood swaying. The air-car had departed; the shack which housed the piston machinery was dark, but Ghyl was only half-convinced that he was alone. The area was pervaded with terror. The thin wailing of the wretches expelled in the past still seemed to hang in the air.

Ghyl looked south toward Ambroy, forty miles distant, where the *Grada* represented security.

Security? Ghyl gave a hoarse laugh. He wanted more than security. He wanted vengeance: retribution for years upon years of fraud, dreary malice, the sadness of wasted lives. He dropped to the ground and started south across the barrens, toward the lights of the village. His legs, at first limp, regained their strength.

He came to a fenced pasture, where biloa stalked sedately back and forth. In the dark, when aroused, biloa had been known to attack men. Ghyl veered around the pasture and presently came to an unpaved road, which he followed to the village.

He halted at the edge of town. The white smock rendered him conspicuous: if seen he would be recognized for what he was, and the local welfare agent would be summoned...Ghyl moved stealthily through the shadows, down a side lane and to the rear of the town's beer garden, where he conducted a careful reconnaissance. Dropping to his hands and knees he crawled around the periphery to where a portly gentleman had draped his beige and black cloak over the railing. While the gentleman engaged the bar-maid in conversation, Ghyl took possession of the cloak, and retreating under the trees threw it over his shoulders and drew the hood over his head, to hide his Daillie hair-cut. Across the square he noted an Overtrend station with a concrete rail receding to the south.

Hoping that the portly gentleman would not immediately notice the loss of his cloak, Ghyl walked briskly to the station.

Three minutes later a car arrived; with a last look over his shoulder toward the beer garden Ghyl stepped aboard and was whisked south.

Mile after mile after mile: into Walz and Batra, then Elsen and Godero. The car halted; Ghyl stepped out upon the slideway, was carried to the escalator, raised and discharged into the space terminal. He swung back the hood of the stolen cloak, advanced with a forthright tread to the north gate. The control officer stepped forward. "Identification, sir?"

"I have lost it," said Ghyl, striving for a Daillie accent. "I am from the *Grada*—that ship yonder." He leaned over the book. "Here is my signature: Tal Gans. This official here—" Ghyl indicated a clerk, who stood nearby "—passed me through the gates."

The guard turned to the clerk indicated. "Correct?"

"Correct."

"Please be more careful with your papers, sir. They might be misused by some unscrupulous person."

Ghyl gave a lofty nod, and strode out upon the field. Five minutes later he was aboard the *Grada*.

Bonar Heurisx regarded him with astonishment. "I have been intensely concerned! I thought never to see you again!"

"I have had a fearful day. Only by chance am I alive." He told Heurisx of his adventures; and Heurisx, looking at him, marveled at the changes done in a single day. Ghyl's cheeks were hollow, his eyes burned; he had put the trust and hope of his youth forever behind him.

"Well then," said Bonar Heurisx, "so much for our plans, which were chancy at best."

"Not so fast," said Ghyl. "We came here to trade; trade we will."

"Surely you're not serious?" demanded Heurisx.

"Something may still be possible," said Ghyl. He went to his locker, threw off the white smock, donned dark Daillie trousers, a tight dark shirt.

Bonar Heurisx watched in puzzlement. "We're not going forth again tonight?"

"I, not you. I hope to make some sort of arrangement."

"But why not wait till tomorrow?" complained Bonar Heurisx.

"Tomorrow will be too late," said Ghyl. "Tomorrow I'll be calm, I'll be reasonable, I won't be desperate with anger."

Bonar Heurisx made no response. Ghyl finished his preparations. Because of the officials at the control gate, he dared not carry the articles he might have wished, and so contented himself with a roll of adhesive tape, a dark beret over his shaved head. "I'll be gone possibly two hours. If I do not return by morning, you had best depart."

"All very well, but what do you plan?"

"Trade. Of one sort or another."

Ghyl departed the ship. He returned to the control gate, submitted to a lackadaisical search for contraband, and was issued a new landing permit. "Be more careful of this than the last, if you please. And mind the tavern girls. They'll importune, and you'll wake in the morning with a sour taste and never a coin in your pocket."

"I'll take care."

Ghyl once more rode Overtrend to East Town: by night the most forlorn and dismal of regions. Once again he approached the thirty-acre compound surrounding the Associated Guilds warehouse and the Boimarc offices. Furtive as an animal, he approached the fence. The warehouse was dark save for a light in the guards' office. The Boimarc offices showed a set of illuminated windows. A pair of floodlights, to either side, shone across the compound, where during the day lift-trucks worked loading and unloading air-vans and drays.

Standing in the shadow of a broken signal stanchion, Ghyl examined the entire vicinity. The night was dark and damp. To the east were gutted ruins of ancient row-houses. Far south the Vashmont eyries showed a few high yellow lights; much closer he saw the red and green glimmer of a local tavern. In the compound, mist blowing in from the ocean swirled around the floodlights.

Ghyl approached the gate which was closed and barred, and undoubtedly equipped with sensor alarms. It offered no hope of access. He started around the periphery of the compound and presently came to a spot where wet earth had collapsed into a ditch, leaving a narrow gap. Ghyl dropped to his knees, enlarged the gap and presently was able to roll under the fence.

Crouching, sliding through the dark, he approached the Boimarc offices from the north, peered through a window, into the empty rooms. There was ample illumination, but no sound, no sense of occupancy.

Ghyl looked right and left, backed away, circled the building, cautiously testing doors and windows, but as he expected all were locked. At the east end a small annex was under construction. Ghyl clambered up the new masonry to a setback in the main structure and thence to the roof. He listened. No sound.

Ghyl stole across the roof and presently found an insecure ventilator which he detached and so was able to drop down into an upper storage chamber.

Quietly he made his way to the ground floor, his senses sharp and questing, and at last peered into the main offices. Light exuded calmly, evenly from glow-panels. He heard the ticking of an automatic instrument. The room, as before, was empty.

Ghyl made a quick investigation, taking note of the various doors, should he need to make a hurried exit. Then more confidently he turned back toward Lord Dugald's alcove. He peered behind the desk; there in its socket, hung the stamp. On the desk were new requisitions, as yet unvalidated. Ghyl took three of these, and going to the inventory mechanism, set himself to puzzle out the form and coding and the method by which the requisitions were printed. Then he studied the read-outs on the automatic inventory calculator.

Time passed. Ghyl essayed a few sale requisitions; then referring constantly to the sample forms and the operator's schedule, he prepared a requisition. He checked it with care. So far as he could see—perfect.

He removed the evidences of his work and replaced the sample requisitions. Then, taking Lord Dugald's stamp from its socket, he validated the requisition.

And now: what to do with the requisition? Ghyl studied a notice taped to the console of the computer: a schedule of lead times and deadlines, and verified his supposition: the requisition must be conveyed to the despatcher in the warehouse.

Ghyl departed the offices the way he had come, not daring to use the doors for fear of exciting an alarm.

Standing in the shadows he looked across at the warehouse, which was dark except for lights in the watchman's cabin.

Ghyl approached the warehouse from the rear, climbed up a ramp to the loading dock, went in a stealthy half-run to a corner of the building. He peered around and saw nearby the booth in which sat two guards. One knit a garment, the other rocked back and forth with his feet on a shelf.

Ghyl backed away, walked along the dock, testing doors. All were securely locked. Ghyl heaved a sad sigh. He found a length of half-rotten wood, took up a position and waited. Fifteen minutes passed. The guard who knitted glanced at a timepiece, arose, flicked on a lantern, spoke a word to his comrade. Then he went forth to make his rounds. He came past Ghyl whistling tunelessly between his teeth. Ghyl shrank back in the shadows. The watchman stopped by a door, fumbled with his keys, inserted one in the lock.

Ghyl crept up behind, struck down with the length of wood. The guard dropped in his tracks. Ghyl took his weapon, his lantern, bound and gagged the man with adhesive tape.

With a final glance to right and left he eased open the door, entered the dark warehouse. He flashed the light here and there: up and down bales of merchandise, crates and boxes, in bays marked *Acme, First, Second.* The despatcher's office was immediately to the left. Ghyl entered, turned his light along the counters, the desks. Somewhere he should see a sheaf of stiff yellow sheets…There, in a cubicle to the side. Ghyl stepped forward, inspected the requisitions. The top sheet was the earliest, carrying the lowest number. Ghyl removed this sheet, wrote its number on his own requisition, added it to the pile.

He ran back to the door. The watchman lay groaning, still unconscious. Ghyl dragged him into the warehouse, near a pile of crates. He lifted two crates to the floor, beside the watchman's head, disarranged the remaining crates. He replaced the lantern, the weapon, the keys, on the watchman's person, removed the adhesive bonds, and departed hastily.

Three-quarters of an hour later Ghyl was back and aboard the *Grada*, to find Bonar Heurisx taut with anxiety. "You've been gone so long! What have you accomplished?"

"A great deal! Almost everything! Or so I hope. We'll know in the morning." In exultation Ghyl explained the circumstances. "—and all 'Acmes' and 'Acme Reserve'! I ordered out the choicest goods in the warehouse! The best of the best! Oh what a trick to play on Lord Dugald!"

Heurisx heard him aghast. "The risk! Suppose the substitution is detected?"

Ghyl gave a reckless fling of the arms. "Unthinkable! But still—we want to be ready to leave, and leave at once. I agree as to that."

"Never have I stolen a copper!" cried Bonar Heurisx in distress. "I will not steal now!"

"We do not steal! We take—and pay!"

"But when? And to whom?"

"In due course. To whomever will accept the money."

Bonar sunk into a chair, rubbed his forehead wearily. "Something will go wrong. You will see. Impossible to steal—"

"Excuse me: to 'trade'."

"—to steal, trade, swindle, whatever you care to call it, with such facility."

"We shall see! If all goes well, the drays will arrive soon after sunrise."

"And if all goes ill?"

"As I said before—be ready to leave!"

The night passed; dawn came at last. On tenterhooks Ghyl and Bonar Heurisx waited, either for loaded drays or the black five-wheeled cars of the Special Agents.

An hour after dawn a port official mounted the loading ladder. "Ahoy, aboard the *Grada*."

"Yes, yes?" called Bonar Heurisx. "What is it?"

"Are you expecting cargo?"

"Certainly."

"Well, then, open your hatches, prepare to stow. We like to do things efficiently here at Ambroy."

"Just as you say."

Ten minutes later the first of the drays pulled up beside the *Grada*. "You must rate highly," said the driver. "All 'Acmes' and 'Acme Reserves'."

Bonar Heurisx made only a non-committal sound.

Six drays in all rolled up to the *Grada*. The driver of the sixth dray said, "You're cleaning us out of Acmes. I've never seen such a cargo. Everyone at the warehouse is wondering about it."

"Just another cargo," said Ghyl. "We're full to our chocks; don't bring any more."

"Precious little more to bring," grumbled the driver. "Well then, sign the receipt."

Ghyl took the invoice and prompted by a sudden whimsey scrawled 'Emphyrio' across the paper.

Bonar Heurisx called to the crew: "Close the hatches, we're taking off!"

"Only just soon enough," said Ghyl. He pointed. "There come the Special Agents."

Up into the air lifted the *Grada*; on the field below a dozen Special Agents jumped from their black cars to stand looking after them.

Ambroy dwindled below; Halma became a sphere. Damar, lowering and purple-brown, fell back to the side. The propulsors whined more hoarsely, the *Grada* went into space-drive.

✦

Jodel Heurisx was stupefied by the quality and quantity of the cargo. "This is not merchandise; this is treasure!"

"It represents the hoard of centuries," said Ghyl. "All goods of 'Acme' grade. Notice this screen, the Winged Being—the last screen my father carved. I polished and waxed it after his death."

"Put it aside," said Jodel Heurisx. "Keep it for your own."

Ghyl shook his head glumly. "Sell it with the rest. It brings me melancholy thoughts."

But Jodel Heurisx would not allow Ghyl his sentimentality. "Some day you will have a son. Would not the screen be a fine present to make to him?"

"If such an unlikely event ever comes to pass."

"The screen then is yours, and it will be kept in my home until you need it."

"Oh, very well. Who knows what the future holds?"

"The rest of the cargo we will convey to Earth. Why trifle with provincial markets? On Earth are the great fortunes, the ancient palaces; we will attract the money of connoisseurs. A sum shall be reserved for the Ambroy guilds. We shall deduct the expenses of the voyage. The remainder will be divided into three parts. There will be wealth for all of us. You shall be financially independent, Ghyl Tarvoke!"

CHAPTER XIX

All his life Ghyl had heard speculation as to the provenance of man. Some declared Earth to be the source of the human migration; another group inclined toward Triptolemus; others pointed to Amenaro, the lone planet of Deneb Kaitos; a few argued spontaneous generation from a universal float of spores.

Jodel Heurisx resolved Ghyl's uncertainty. "You may be sure: Earth is the human source! All of us are Earthmen, no matter where we were born!"

In many ways the reality of Earth was at odds with Ghyl's preconceptions. He had thought to find a dismal world, the horizon spiked with rotting ruins, the sun a flaming red eye, the seas oily and stagnant from the seepage of ages.

But the sun was warm and yellow-white, much like the sun of
Maastricht; and the sea seemed considerably more fresh than Deep
Ocean to the west of Fortinone.

The people of Earth were another surprise. Ghyl had been ready for
weary cynicism, a jaded autumnal lassitude, inversions, eccentricities,
subtle sophistications; and in this expectation he was not completely
wide of the mark. Certain of the people he met displayed these qualities, but others were as easy and uncomplicated as children. Still others
perplexed Ghyl by their fervor, the intensity of their conduct, as if the
day were too short for the transaction of all their business. Sitting
with Jodel Heurisx at an outdoor café of old Cologne, Ghyl remarked
upon the variety of people who walked past their table.

"True enough," said Jodel Heurisx. "Other cities on other planets
are cosmopolitan enough, but Earth is a universe in itself."

"I expected the people to seem old—sedate—wise. Some do, of
course. But others—well, look at that man in the green suede. His eyes
glitter; he looks right and left as if he were seeing everything for the first
time. Of course, he might be an outworlder, like us."

"No, he's an Earthman," said Jodel Heurisx. "Don't ask me how
I know; I couldn't tell you. A matter of style: small signs that betray
a man's background. As for his air of restlessness, sociologists declare that material well-being and psychic stability vary in counter-
proportion. Barbarians have no time either for idealism or its obverse,
psychosis. The people of Earth, however, concern themselves with
'justification' and 'fulfillment' and a few, such as, perhaps, that man
in green, become over-intense. But there are enormous variations.
Some devote their energies to visionary schemes. Others turn inward
to become sybarites, voluptuaries, connoisseurs, collectors, aesthetes;
or they concentrate upon the study of some arcane specialty. To be
sure, there are numerous ordinary folk, but somehow they are
never noticed, and only serve to heighten the contrast. But then, if you
remain on Earth for a period, you will discover much of this for
yourself."

❋

The *Grada's* cargo was sold, and profitably. At Tripoli Ghyl took
leave of Jodel and Bonar Heurisx. He promised some day to return to
Daillie. Jodel Heurisx told him, "On that day my home will be your

home. And never forget that I hold for you your wonderful screen: the 'Winged Being'."

"I won't forget. For now—goodbye."

"Goodbye, Ghyl Tarvoke."

Feeling somewhat melancholy, Ghyl watched the *Grada* lift into the windy blue African sky. But when the ship at last dwindled and disappeared, his spirits rapidly rose: far worse fates than to be on Earth for the first time, with the equivalent of a million vouchers in his pouch! Ghyl thought of his childhood: a time unreal behind a golden haze. How often he and Floriel had lain in the yellow grass on Dunkum's Heights, talking of travel and financial independence! Both, in separate ways, had achieved their ambition. And Ghyl wondered what region of space Floriel now wandered; whether he were alive or dead…Poor Floriel! thought Ghyl, to be so lost.

For a month Ghyl roamed Earth, exploring the cloud-towers of America, the equally marvelous submarine cities of the Great Barrier Reef, the vast wilderness parks over which air-cars were not permitted to fly. He visited the restored dawn-cities of Athens, Babylon, Memphis, medieval Bruges, Venice, Regensburg. Everywhere, often light but sometimes so heavy as to be oppressive, lay the weight of history. Each trifling area of soil exhaled a plasm: the recollection of a million tragedies, a million triumphs; of births and deaths; kisses exchanged; blood spilled; the char of fire and energy; songs, glees, incantations, war-chants, frenzies. The soil reeked of events; history lay in strata, in crusts; in eras, continuities, discontinuities. At night ghosts were common, so Ghyl was told: in the precincts of old palaces, in the mountains of the Caucasus, on the heaths and moors of the north.

Ghyl began to believe that Earth-folk were preoccupied with the past, a theory reinforced by the numerous historical pageants, the survival of anachronistic traditions, the existence of the Historical Institute which recorded, digested, cross-filed and analyzed every shred of fact pertinent to human origin and development…The Historical Institute! Presently he would visit the Institute's headquarters in London, although—for some reason he did not care to analyze—he was in no great hurry to do so.

At St. Petersburg he met a slim blonde Norwegian girl named Flora Eilander who occasionally reminded him of Shanne. For a period they traveled together, and she pointed out aspects of Earth he had not before noticed. In particular she scoffed at his theory that Earth folk were preoccupied with the past. "No, no, no!" she told him with a delightful lilting emphasis. "You miss the whole point! We are concerned with the soul of events, the intrinsic essences!"

Ghyl could not be sure that he had comprehended her exposition, but this was no longer a novelty. He found the people of Earth bewildering. In every conversation he felt a thousand subtleties and indirections, a frame of mind which found as much meaning in the unstated as the stated. There were, he finally decided, niceties of communication which forever would be denied him: allusions through twitches of mannerism, distinctions of a hundredth of a second between a pair of contradictory significances, nameless moods which must instantly be countered or augmented in kind.

Ghyl became angry with himself and quarreled with Flora, who compounded the situation by condescension. "You must remember that we have known everything, tried every pang and exhilaration. Therefore it is only natural—"

Ghyl gave a harsh laugh. "Nonsense! Have you ever known grief or fear? Have you ever stolen a space-yacht and killed Garrion? Have you known a County Ball at Grigglesby Corners with the lords and ladies coming forth like magicians in their wonderful costumes? Or stumbled through a rite at Finuka's Temple? Or looked down dreaming from the Meagher Mounts across old Fortinone?"

"No, of course; I have done none of these." And Flora, giving him a long slow inspection, said no more.

For another month they wandered from place to place: Abyssinia where the sunlight evoked aloes, bitumen, old dust; Sardinia with its olive trees and asphodel; the haze and murk of the Gothic north.

One day in Dublin Ghyl came upon a placard which froze him in his tracks:

FRAMTREE'S ORIGINAL PERIPATEZIC ENTERCATIONERS

The Wonderful Trans-Galactic Extravaganza!

Hear the blood-curdling screams of the Maupte Bacchanids!
Goggle at the antics of Holkerwoyd's puppets!
Smell the authentic fetors of two dozen far planets!
Much more! Much more!

At Casteyn Park, Seven days only

Flora was uninterested but Ghyl insisted that they instantly take themselves to Casteyn Park, and for once Flora was the one to be perplexed. Ghyl told her nothing other than that he had known the show in his childhood; there was nothing more he could tell her.

Beside a stand of giant oaks Ghyl found the same gaudy panels, the same placards, the same sounds and outcries he had known as a child. He sought out Holkerwoyd's Puppet Show and sat through a mildly amusing revue. The puppets squeaked and capered, trilled topical songs, caricatured local personalities, then a group dressed as punchinellos performed a series of farces.

After the show, leaving the bored but indulgent Flora in her seat, Ghyl approached the curtain at the side of the stage: it might have been the identical curtain that once before he had pushed through, and he fought the impulse to look over his shoulder to where his father must surely be sitting. Slowly he pulled aside the curtain and there, as if he had not moved during all the years, sat Holkerwoyd, mending a bit of stage property.

Holkerwoyd had aged; his skin was waxen, his lips had drawn back; his teeth seemed yellow and prominent; but his eyes were as keen as ever. Seeing Ghyl he paused in his work, cocked his head. "Yes, sir?"

"We have met before."

"I know this." Holkerwoyd looked away, rubbed his nose with a gnarled knuckle. "So many folk I've seen; so many places I've been; a task to set all out in order…Let me see. We met long years ago, on a far planet, in the ditch at the edge of the universe. Halma. It hangs below the green moon Damar, where I buy my puppets."

"How could you remember? I was a small boy."

Holkerwoyd smiled, wagged his head. "You were a serious fellow, puzzled at the way the world went. You were with your father. What of him?"

"Dead."

Holkerwoyd nodded without surprise. "And how goes your life? You are far from Ambroy."

"My life goes well enough. But there is a question which troubles me to this day. You performed the legend of Emphyrio. And the puppet was executed."

Holkerwoyd shrugged and returned to his mending. "The puppets are not useful forever. They become aware of the world, they begin to feel real. Then they are spoiled and must be destroyed before they infect the troupe."

Ghyl grimaced. "Puppets presumably are cheap."

"Cheap enough. But just barely. The Damarans are sly dealers, cold as steel. How they love the chink of valuta! To good effect! They live in palaces while I sleep on a cot, starting up at odd noises." Holkerwoyd became agitated and waved his mending in the air. "Let them lower prices, and lavish less splendor on themselves! They are deaf to all my remonstrances. Would you like to see Emphyrio once more? I have a puppet who is becoming perverse. I have warned and scolded but I continually find him looking across the footlights at the audience."

"No," said Ghyl. He backed toward the curtain. "Well then, for the second time I bid you goodby."

Holkerwoyd gave a casual wave. "We may yet meet again, though I suspect not. The years come fast. Some morning they'll find me lying stark, with the puppets climbing over me, peering in my mouth, tweaking my ears…"

Back at the Black Swan Hotel, Ghyl and Flora sat in the saloon bar, with Ghyl staring glumly into a glass of wine. Flora made several attempts to speak but Ghyl's mind had wandered far away, beyond Mirabilis, and he gave back monosyllabic answers. Looking into the wine he saw the narrow-fronted house on Undle Square. He heard Amiante's quiet voice, the thin scrape of chisels on wood. He felt the wan Ambroy sunlight, the drifting across the mudflats at the mouth of the Insse; he recalled the smells of the docks of Nobile and Foelgher, the gaunt Vashmont towers, the moldering ruins below.

Ghyl was homesick, even though Ambroy could no longer be considered home. Meditating on Amiante's humiliation and futile death, Ghyl became so bitter that he turned the whole glass of wine down his throat. The decanter was empty. A waiter in a white apron, sensing Ghyl's mood, hastened to bring a new decanter.

Flora rose to her feet, looked down at Ghyl a second or two, then sauntered from the room.

Ghyl thought of his expulsion, of the looming piston, the crushed bricks, the hour he lay huddled on the wall while the sad twilight gathered around him. Perhaps he had deserved the punishment; undeniably he had stolen a space-yacht. Still, was not the crime justifiable? Did not the lords use Boimarc, or Thurible Co-operative, what-ever the case, to swindle and cheat and victimize the recipients? Ghyl brooded and sipped wine, wondering how best to disseminate his knowledge to the recipients. Useless to work either through the guilds or the Welfare Agency; both were conservative to the point of obsession.

The problem required reflection. Ghyl turned the last of the wine down his throat and went up to his suite. Flora was nowhere in evidence. Ghyl shrugged. He would never see her again: this he knew. Perhaps it was just as well.

On the following day he crossed the Irish Channel to ancient London. Now, at last, he would visit the Historical Institute.

But the Historical Institute was not to be approached so easily. Ghyl's questions to Telescreen Information met first bland evasiveness then a recommendation to a guided tour of Oxford and Cambridge Universities. When Ghyl persisted, he was referred to the Bureau of Weights and Measures, who passed him on to Dundee House. This proved to be the headquarters of some sort of intelligence agency, whose function Ghyl never fully understood. A clerk politely inquired the reason for his interest in the Historical Institute, whereupon Ghyl, controlling his impatience, mentioned the legend of Emphyrio.

The clerk, a golden-haired young man with crisp mustache, turned away and spoke a few quiet words, apparently to the empty air, then listened, apparently to the air itself. He turned back to Ghyl. "If you will remain at your hotel, an agent of the Institute will shortly make contact with you."

Half-amused, half-irritated, Ghyl set himself to wait. An hour later he was met by an ugly little man in a black suit and a gray cloak: Arwin Rolus, sub-director of Mythological Studies at the Institute. "I understand that you are interested in the legend of Emphyrio."

"Yes," said Ghyl. "But first: explain to me the reason for so much stealth and secrecy?"

Rolus chuckled, and Ghyl saw that he was not really ugly after all. "The situation may seem extravagant. But the Historical Institute, by the very nature of its being, accumulates a great deal of secret intelligence. This is not the Institute's function, you understand: we are scholars. Still, from time to time we are able to resolve difficulties for more active folk." He looked Ghyl up and down with an appraising eye. "When an outworlder comes inquiring about the Institute, the authorities ensure that he doesn't intend to bomb the place."

"No danger of that," said Ghyl. "I want information, no more."

"Precisely what information?"

Ghyl handed him the fragment from Amiante's portfolio. Without apparent difficulty Rolus read the crabbed old characters. "Well, well, indeed. Interesting. And now you want to find what happened? How the story ended, so to speak?"

"Yes."

"May I ask why?"

The Earthers were a suspicious lot! thought Ghyl. In a measured voice he stated: "I have known half the legend since my childhood. I promised myself that if I ever were able to learn the rest, I would do so."

"And this is the only reason?"

"Not altogether."

Rolus did not pursue the question. "Your home-planet is—" He raised his bushy gray eyebrows.

"Halma. It is a world back of the Mirabilis Cluster."

"Halma. A remote world...Well, perhaps I can gratify your curiosity." He turned to the wall-screen, tapped with his fingertips to project a coded signal. The screen responded with a run of references, one of which Rolus selected. "Here," he said, "is the entire chronicle, indited by an unknown writer of the world Aume, or, as some say, Home, about two thousand years ago."

The screen displayed a message, printed in Archaic. The first few paragraphs were those of Ghyl's fragment; then:

In the Catademnon sat those without ears to hear, who owned no souls and knew neither ease nor fellowship. Emphyrio brought forth his tablet and called for peace. They gave alarms and waved green pennants. Emphyrio urged fellowship; without ears to hear and eyes averted, none would understand, and they waved blue pennants. Emphyrio pled for the kindness which differentiated man from monster, or lacking that, mercy. They broke the tablet of truth underfoot and waved red pennants. Then they lifted Emphyrio in their hands aloft, they held him high to a wall, and through his skull they drove a great nail so that he hung on the wall of the Catademnon. When all had looked to see how fared the man who would have spoken truth, they took him down and under the beam where they nailed him, there in the crypt they immured him forever!

But what was their profit?

Who was the victim?

On the world Aume, or Home, the brutes of Sigil no longer wasted the land. They looked eye to eye and asked: "Is it true, as Emphyrio avers, that we are creatures for whom there is dawn and dusk, pain and pain's ease? Why then do we waste the land? Let us make our lives good; for we have none other." And they threw down their arms and retired to those places which were the most pleasant to them, and at once became the easiest of folk, so that all men wondered at their first ferocity.

Emphyrio died imploring the dark ones to the ways of man, and that they should curb their begotten monsters. They refuted him; they hung him to the wall on a nail. But the monsters, at first insensate, were now, through truth, of all folk the easiest. If there be here lesson or moral, it lies beyond the competence of him who inscribes this record.

CHAPTER XX

A sheet printed with the message issued from the wall; Rolus handed it to Ghyl, who read it a second time, then placed it with Amiante's fragment.

"The world Aume—is it Halma? Is Sigil the moon Damar?"

Rolus brought further information to the screen, in a script unfamiliar to Ghyl. "Aume is Halma," he said. "A world with a complicated history: do you know it?"

"I suspect not," said Ghyl. "We learn very little at Ambroy." He could not keep the bitterness from his voice. "Very little indeed."

Without comment Rolus read from the screen, occasionally expanding or interpolating. Two or three thousand years before Emphyrio, and long before men appeared, the Damarans had established colonies on Halma, using space-ships provided by a race of star-wanderers. But war came; the Damarans were expelled and forced back to Damar, where they contrived a means to destroy the star-wanderers. Through the facility of their procreative systems, the Damarans were able to duplicate whatever genetic material might be presented to their glands. They decided to produce an army of irresistible warriors, ruthless and ferocious, who would tear the star-wanderers into shreds. First they prepared a prototype, then built artificial glands to produce the creatures in quantity. When the army was assembled they sent it down from Sigil, or Damar, but isolated in their caves they had lapsed half a thousand years behind the times. The star-wanderers were gone, no one knows where, and men had arrived to take possession of the planet. The army from Damar seemed an act of wanton aggression. The Wirwan—to name the monsters—seemed like fiends from hell. In certain details they were similar to their progenitors. They lacked an accurate sense of hearing, and communicated by means of radio waves. Emphyrio apparently devised a mechanism which translated human words into Wirwan radiation. He was the first man to communicate with the invaders. They were singularly innocent, he discovered, having been trained to one purpose. He made them aware of themselves; he corrupted their innocence, so to speak. Almost magically they became hesitant and retiring, and retreated into the mountains. Encouraged by his success, Emphyrio traveled across the gap to Sigil, hoping to pacify those who had despatched the army.

"Emphyrio's ultimate fate is uncertain," said Rolus. "The account you just read states that the Damarans drove a nail through his head and killed him. Another source declares that Emphyrio negotiated a truce and returned to Aume, where he became the first lord. There are other reports to the effect that the folk of Sigil held Emphyrio a prisoner in perpetuity, preserving him in a state of suspended life. The facts are uncertain. All is changed now. The Damarans produce puppets and manikins in their artificial glands. The Wirwans, a forlorn race, survive on the slopes of Mount Meagher. The men are as you know."

Ghyl heaved a sigh. So then: the tale was told. Fortinone, scene of the early campaigns, was now placid. On Damar the puppet-makers catered to the tourists and bred puppets. And Emphyrio? His fate was uncertain. Ghyl recalled his childhood visit to the Meagher Mounts when he had traced imaginary campaigns upon the topography. He had been more accurate than he ever could have dreamed.

Arwin Rolus was preparing to take his departure. "Is there anything more you wish to know?"

"Does the Institute collect information from Halma now? From Fortinone?"

"Yes, of course."

"You have a correspondent at Ambroy?"

"Several."

"Their identity is secret?"

"Of course. If they were known, they might be compromised. We are required to stay aloof from events. Not all are able to do this. Your father, for instance."

Ghyl turned to stare at Rolus. "My father? Amiante Tarvoke? Was he a correspondent?"

"Yes. For many years."

Ghyl took himself to a cosmetic surgeon. His nose was narrowed, bridged and peaked; his eyebrows set in a new slant. The tattoo on his shoulder was expunged; the prints of his tongue, fingers, palms and soles were altered. His skin was toned dull olive-bronze, his hair was dyed black and finally only the contents of his brain remained to identify him as Ghyl Tarvoke.

At Ball and Sons, Haberdashers, Ghyl fitted himself out with Earth-style garments and was astounded by the hologram. Who would associate this debonair young gallant with poor harried Ghyl Tarvoke of old?

Fictitious identification papers were hard to come by. Finally Ghyl called Dundee House and presently was connected with Arwin Rolus.

Rolus recognized Ghyl at once which caused Ghyl exasperation and uneasiness. Ghyl stated his requirements but Rolus was reluctant to offer assistance. "Please understand the Institute's position. We profess didactic dispassion and nonpartisanship in all circumstances. We record, analyze, interpret—but we do not interfere or promulgate. If I, as an officer of the Historical Institute, were to assist your intrigue, I would be intruding the Institute upon a flow of history."

Ghyl thought that Rolus had unnecessarily emphasized one of his phrases. Ghyl said quickly, "I did not mean this to be an official call. I thought only to turn to you, as my single acquaintance on Earth, for some quiet advice."

"I see," said Rolus. "Well, in that case—" He thought a moment. "Of course I know nothing of these matters. But—" a slip of paper issued from the wall-slot in Ghyl's room "—if you call this code, some-one at least will listen to you without wincing."

"I also have a question for you in your official capacity."

"Well then. What is the question?"

"Where is the Catademnon, where on Damar?"

Rolus gave a brisk nod, as if Ghyl's question came as no surprise. "I will put the question into process; the information will reach you shortly and the service charge will be added to your hotel addition."

Ten minutes later a sheet of paper issued from the wall-slot. The message read:

> The Catademnon, hall of the war lords of ancient Sigil, now known as Damar, is a ruin in the mountains ten miles southwest of the present Old City.

During the evening Ghyl made contact with the man whose code Arwin Rolus had supplied. The next day he picked up his new documents, and assumed the identity of Sir Hartwig Thorn, Grandee. He immediately booked passage for Damar, and the same evening departed Earth.

CHAPTER XXI

Damar was an eery little world, half the diameter of Halma, but with one-sixth Halma's mass and two-thirds its surface gravity. There were great expanses of bog across the polar regions, mountains and crags of astonishing dimension in the middle latitudes, an arid zone where grew Damar's unique equatorial thicket: a tangle of barbs and tendrils ten miles wide and occasionally a half-mile high. What with bogs, crags, gorges and the thicket, there were few areas convenient for habitation. Garwan, the tourist center, and Damar Old City were at opposite ends of the Great Central Plain, this apparently a scar inflicted by the glancing blow of a meteor.

At Garwan were hotels, restaurants, baths, sporting areas; luxury in bizarre surroundings. Puppet theaters provided spectacle and diversion: farce, historical pageants, macabre drama, erotic display. The puppet performers were a special breed: handsome little creatures four or five feet tall, vastly different from the half-simian imps supplied to such as Holkerwoyd.

The Damarans themselves seldom ventured from their residences under the hills, upon which they spent prodigious fortunes. The typical residence was a complex system of chambers swathed in soft fabrics, illuminated with meticulous nicety. Silver light shone on gray and nacreous curtains; red, carmine and magenta were used against blues and pale pink. Globes giving off deep purple or plangent sea-green hung behind films and layers of gauze. The residences were never complete, always in the process of alteration and extension. On rare occasions a man whom the Damaran wished to please, or one who paid a sufficiently large fee, might be invited into a residence: a visit preceded by an extraordinary ritual. Twittering puppets bathed the visitor, sprayed him with mist, muffled him head to foot in a white robe, fitted him with sandals of white felt. Thus sanitized, deodorized and padded, he would be conducted along interminable vistas of hangings and draperies, into grottoes hung with waving webs and gauzes, through blue lights and gray-green lights, finally to emerge awed and bewildered, if by nothing else but the vast expenditures of wealth. The average excursionist, however, saw the Damarans only as silent shapes to the back of an office or shop.

Arriving at Garwan, Ghyl established himself at one of the 'Old Damar' hotels: a pyramidal heap of white domes and hemispheres, with a few small windows placed seemingly at random. Ghyl was lodged in two domed rooms on different levels, draped with panels of pale green, and floors cushioned by a heavy black carpet.

Leaving the hotel, Ghyl entered a tour and travel agency. On a shadowed balcony stood a Damaran, eye-bulbs each glinting with a luminous star: a creature smaller, softer, more flexible than a Garrion, but otherwise much the same. On the counter a screen responding to a radio-frequency projection showed luminous characters: "You wish?"

"I want to hire an air-car." The words became tremulous shapes on the screen, which the Damaran read at a glance.

The response came: "This is possible, though expensive. A tour by sight-seeing tube costs no more and is preferable, in safety and deluxe comfort."

"No doubt," said Ghyl. "But I am a scholar at a university of Earth. I wish to look for fossils. I want to visit the puppet factories and look through the old ruins."

"It is possible. There is a depletion fee upon the export of fossils. It is not advisable to visit the puppet factories, due to the delicacy of

procedures. A visitor would not be amused. There are no ruins of inter-
est. The sight-seeing tube will offer greater value, and will cost less."
"I prefer to hire an air-car."
"You must post a bond for the value of the car. When do you want it?"
"Early tomorrow morning."
"Your name?"
"Hartwig Thorn."
"Tomorrow morning the car will be at the back of the hotel. You
may now pay three thousand one hundred standard valuta units. Three
thousand is the deposit. It will be returned to you. The air-car charge is
one hundred units a day."

Ghyl walked about the city for an hour or two. With the coming of
evening, he seated himself in an open-air café, to drink ale imported
from Fortinone. Halma swam up into the sky, an enormous amber half-
disk, vaguely marked with familiar outlines.

A man walked into the café, followed by a woman; each in turn was
silhouetted against Halma. Ghyl altered the focus of his vision, watched
the couple settle themselves at a nearby table. The man was Schute Cobol;
the woman no doubt was his wife; they had come to Damar to spend their
hoarded vouchers like any other recipients. Schute Cobol glanced at Ghyl,
studied his Earth-style garments, muttered something to his wife, who
likewise inspected Ghyl. Then they gave their attention to the menu.
Ghyl, with a wry grin, looked up through the air toward Halma.

CHAPTER XXII

The days and nights of Damar were short. After dining and musing
long into the night over a map of Damar, Ghyl had hardly retired to his
suite before the sky began to lighten.

He arose with a sense of fatefulness. Long ago Holkerwoyd had pronounced him 'fey': laboring under a burden of doom. He dressed slowly,
aware of the weight. It seemed that his whole life had been directed
toward this day.

The air-car was waiting on a stage behind the hotel. Ghyl examined
the controls, decided that they were standard. He climbed in, latched
the dome, hitched the control wheel up to a convenient position and
locked it. He checked the energy level: the cells were charged; he touched
the ON button, pulled up on the wheel. The car lifted into the air.

Ghyl slid the wheel forward, tilted it back: the car slid up at a slant.

So far so good. Ghyl sent the car higher, up over the mountains. Far to the south was the equatorial thicket, a formless gray-brown smudge. Ghyl steered to the north.

The miles slipped past; the thin upper air hissed past the dome. Ahead glinted a single rime-crusted peak: a landmark. Ghyl steered to the north of the peak and saw ahead Damar Old City: an unlovely jumble of long sheds and warehouses. Instinctively preferring that his presence not be noted Ghyl dropped the air-car low, to within a hundred feet of the surface, and veered to the southeast of Old City.

He searched an hour before he found the ruins: a tumble of stone lost among the rocky debris of the mountainside.

He landed the air-car on a little flat of drifted gravel fifty yards from a low wall, and now Ghyl wondered how he had searched so long, for the structure was of monumental scope and walls were yet standing. He alighted and stood by the car, listening, to hear only the sigh of wind across the harsh surface of the scree. The Old City, ten miles distant, was a formless jumble of grey and white tablets. He could see no moving object, no sign of life.

He took his lamp and hand-gun, approached the broken wall, which was half-drifted over with soil. Beyond was a depression, then a heavier wall of lichen-stained concrete: cracked, sagging, but still upright. Ghyl moved closer, trying to control his awe. This was a hall of giants; Ghyl felt dwarfed and trivial. Still—Emphyrio had been a man like himself, with a man's courage and a man's fear. He had come to the Catademnon—and then?

Ghyl crossed the fosse between the two walks and came to a portal, choked with rubble. He scrambled up and peered within, but the sunlight, slanting across the sky, avoided the gap and he saw only black shadows.

Ghyl switched on his lamp, slid down over the debris, into a dank corridor cluttered with the drift of centuries. On the wall hung tatters of fabric spun, perhaps, from fibers of melted obsidian, stained with metal oxides. The patterns were crusted with grime, but nonetheless heroic. They reminded Ghyl of hangings he had seen elsewhere, in circumstances he could not recall…The corridor opened into an oval hall, the roof of which had collapsed. The floor was open to the sky.

Ghyl halted. He stood in the Catademnon. Here Emphyrio had confronted the tyrants of Sigil. There was no sound, not even the rasp of the wind, but the pressure of the past was almost tangible.

At the far end of the hall was a gap with tatters of ancient regalia to either side. Here might Emphyrio have been lifted and nailed to a beam—if this had indeed been his fate.

Ghyl crossed the floor. He halted, looked up at the stone beam over the gap. There was certainly a scar, an eroded hole, a socket. If Emphyrio had been suspended here, his feet would have dangled to the level of Ghyl's shoulders, his blood would have stained the stone by Ghyl's feet...The stone was crusted with a gray efflorescence.

Ghyl walked under the beam, turned his flash down into the opening. Dust, debris, bits of dry vegetation clogged the first part of a wide set of stairs. Ghyl clambered through, flashing the light to all sides. "Under the beam where they had nailed him, there in their crypt did they immure him forever." The steps gave upon an oval chamber, with three passages leading off into the darkness. The chamber was floored with a dull stone on which lay an undisturbed layer of dust. The crypt? Ghyl turned the light around the chamber, and walked in the direction where the crypt must lie. He looked into a long room, cold and still. On the floor, helter-skelter, were half a dozen cases molded of glass, coated heavily with dust. Each contained organic remains: chitinous plates; strips of withered black leather...In one of the cases was a human skeleton, the joints wasted apart, the bones collapsed. The vacant eyeholes looked up at Ghyl. In the center of the forehead was a round hole.

Ghyl took the air-car back to Garwan, set it down on the pad behind the hotel, collected his deposit. Then he went to his suite where he bathed and changed into fresh garments. He went to sit on the terrace overlooking the plaza. He felt flat, deflated. He had not expected to find what he had found. The skeleton had been anticlimactical.

He had hoped for more. What of the sense of portent with which he had started the day? His instinct had played him false. Everything had gone with footling ease, with such small difficulty and so little incident that the whole affair seemed shameful. Ghyl felt uneasy, dissatisfied. He had found the remains of Emphyrio: as to this there was no doubt. But drama? There was none. He knew no more than before. Emphyrio had died uselessly, his glorious life ending in failure and futility. But there was no surprise: so much had been set forth in the legend.

The sun fell behind the western hills. Garwan's shape—receding domes, superimposed one on the other, pile on pile—was black against the ash-brown sky. From an alley beside the hotel came a dark figure: a Damaran. It sidled along the jetta hedge that bordered the terrace, halted to look across the plaza. Then it turned to examine the terrace, as if calculating the worth of the night's business. Avaricious, hyper-luxurious beasts, thought Ghyl, with every sequin, every voucher, every bice poured into their already extravagant residences. He wondered if in the old heroic days, during the time of Emphyrio, the Damarans had been equally sybaritic...The Catademnon had suggested no great refinement. Perhaps in those days they had lacked the financial means to gratify their tastes...Sensing Ghyl's attention, the Damaran turned its queer tufted head, stared for several seconds, the yellow-green star in the dull eyes expanding and contracting. Ghyl stared back, exploring a sudden startling speculation.

The Damaran abruptly turned, disappeared behind the hedge. Ghyl leaned back in his seat. He sat for a long while in a half-mesmerized state of detachment, while excursionists came, dined, departed. And the twilight faded to a luminous umber and disappeared.

The situation had a queer ambivalence. Ghyl swung between nervous amusement for his own whimsies and a dreadful bleakness of spirit.

As an exercise in abstract logic the problem resolved into a starkly simple solution.

When the arguments were transposed into human terms, the force of the logic remained, but the solution implied such heart-breaking tragedy that it transcended belief.

Still: facts were facts. So many curious little trifles which he had observed with wonder now became firm segments of an intricate whole. Ghyl gave a giddy wild laugh which drew glances of censure from a nearby group of Ambroy excursionists. Ghyl choked back his mirth. They would consider him a maniac. If he went to their table, told them his thoughts, how he would shock them! Their trip, for which they had saved all their lives, would be ruined. Would they welcome such knowledge?

Here was a new predicament: What should he do, what steps should he take?

There was no one to give him counsel; he was alone.

What, given the circumstances, would have been Emphyrio's course of action?

Truth.

Very well, thought Ghyl: it shall be Truth, and let the consequences fall where they may.

Another incidental thought occurred to him, nearly occasioning another outburst of lunatic mirth. What of his premonitions of destiny now? They had been fulfilled, ten times over.

Ghyl signaled for a menu and ordered his dinner. In the morning he would depart for Ambroy.

CHAPTER XXIII

Ghyl arrived at the familiar old Godero space-port late in the afternoon, Ambroy time. He waited until the excursionists had pushed off the ship, then strolled down the ramp in a manner of languid condescension, hoping to camouflage his inner trepidation.

The control official was a man of bitter disposition. He scowled at Ghyl's Earth-style garments, studied his documents with discouraging skepticism. "Earth, is it? What do you do here in Ambroy?"

"I travel."

"Hmf. Sir Hartwig Thorn. A grandee. We have them here as well. It's all the same. The grandees do the traveling; the underlings work. Duration of stay?"

"Perhaps a week."

"There's nothing here to see. A day is sufficient."

Ghyl shrugged. "It well may be."

"Nothing but drabness and drudgery. You'll find no splendor here, save up on the eyries. Do you know they just raised our percentage? It's 1.46 percent now, when for so long it was 1.18. Do you charge a percentage on Earth?"

"A different system is in force."

"I take it that you are importing no duplicated, machine-manufactured or plagiarized articles for distribution either gratis or for profit?"

"None."

"Very well, Sir Hartwig. Pass on, if you will."

Ghyl walked out into the well-remembered hall. At a Spay booth he placed a call to Grand Lord Dugald the Boimarc, at his eyrie in Vashmont Precinct.

The screen displayed a white disk on a dark blue ground. A courteous voice spoke: "Grand Lord Dugald is away from his eyrie. He will be pleased for you to leave a memorandum of your business."

"I am a grandee of Earth, just now arrived. Where may I find Lord Dugald?"

"He attends a fête, at the eyrie of Lord Parnasse the Underline."

"I will call there."

A lordling, thin of face, with varnished black hair dressed in a fanciful sweep over his forehead, responded to the second call. He listened with exquisite hauteur, turned away without a word. A moment later Lord Parnasse appeared.

Ghyl put on a style of amused condescension. "I am Sir Hartwig Thorn, touring from Earth. I called to pay my respects to Grand Lord Dugald, and was referred to your eyrie."

Parnasse, thin and keen like the lordling, with a darkly florid complexion, examined Ghyl up and down. "I am honored to make your acquaintance. Lord Dugald is at my eyrie, enjoying an entertainment." He hesitated a barely perceptible instant. "I would be glad to welcome you to my eyrie, especially if your business with Lord Dugald is urgent."

Ghyl laughed. "It has waited many years, and could well wait a day or so longer; but I would be pleased to settle it as soon as possible."

"Very good, sir. You are where?"

"At the Godero space-port."

"If you will go to Bureau C and mention my name, a conveyance will be put at your disposal."

"I will arrive shortly."

It was the common assumption among ordinary recipients that the lords lived in splendor, surrounded by exquisite objects, breathing delightful odors, attended by beautiful youths and maidens. Their beds, by repute, were air-fluff and wildflower down; each meal was said to be a banquet of delicious confections and the choicest Gade wines. Even under the load of his preoccupations, Ghyl felt something of the old thrill and wonder as the air-car rose toward the eyrie. He was discharged upon a terrace enclosed by a white balustrade, with all the expanse of Ambroy below. Two wide steps led to an upper terrace, with the palace of Lord Parnasse beyond.

Ghyl instructed the air-car to wait. He mounted the steps, approached the portal, beside which stood a pair of Garrion in dull red livery. Through tall windows swagged with golden-satin drapes a splendid assembly of lords and ladies was visible.

Ghyl entered the palace without challenge from the Garrion and halted to watch the lords and ladies at their entertainment. There was little noise. All spoke in fluttering arch whispers, and laughed, when they did so, almost soundlessly, as if each were vying to produce the most animation, the most entrancing visual display with the least sound.

Ghyl looked around the room: elegance, certainly, and a subtle suffusion of light which disguised and dissembled rather than illuminated. The floor was a checker of moth-wing brown and mustard yellow. For furniture there were couches upholstered in bottle-green plush—to Ghyl's eyes of an eccentric and over-refined design, certainly not the work of the Ambroy furniture-makers. The walls were hung with tapestries, apparently imported from Damar. Splendor and luxury indeed, thought Ghyl, but there was also a curious intimation of shabbiness: the makeshift insubstantiality of a stage-set. The air, despite the soft lights and sumptuous drapes, lacked ease and richness; the activity lacked spontaneity. It was, thought Ghyl, like watching puppets play at festivity, rather than watching festivity itself. Small wonder, he thought, that lords and ladies attended such functions as the County Ball, where they could participate in the passions of the underlings...As he thought of the County Ball, he saw Shanne, wearing a wonderful gown of muted lemon yellow, with ribbons and flounces of ivory. Ghyl watched in fascination as she stood talking in hushed half-whispers to a gallant young lord. With what charming eagerness did she perform her wiles: smiles, pouts, roguish tilts of the head, pretty little outrages, sham startlements, mock provocations, grimaces of delight, dismay, bewilderment, consternation.

A tall thin lord approached: Lord Parnasse. He halted, bowed. "Sir Hartwig Thorn?"

Ghyl bowed in return. "I am he."

"I trust you find my eyrie to your liking?" Lord Parnasse's voice was light, dry, with the faintest possible overtone of condescension.

"It is delightful."

"If your business with Lord Dugald is urgent, I will take you to him. When you have finished, you may enjoy yourself without restraint."

"I would not wish to presume upon your hospitality," said Ghyl.

"As you see, I have ordered the air-car to wait. My business probably will require no great time."

"As you wish. Be good enough, then, to follow me."

Shanne had noticed Ghyl; she stared at him in fascination. Ghyl gave her a smile and a nod; it made no great difference if she recognized him. Puzzled and thoughtful, she turned to watch as Ghyl followed Lord Parnasse to a small side-room hung with blue satin. At a little marquetry table sat Grand Lord Dugald the Boimarc.

"Here is Sir Hartwig Thorn of Earth who has a matter to discuss with you," said Parnasse. He gave a stiff bow, departed.

Grand Lord Dugald, portly, middle-aged, with a plum-colored complexion, stared at Ghyl. "Do I know you? You have aspects I find familiar. What was your name once more?"

"My name is irrelevant," said Ghyl. "You may think of me as Prince Emphyrio of Ambroy."

Dugald stared at him coldly. "This seems an over-extravagant joke."

"Dugald, Grand Lord as you are called, your entire life is an extravagant joke."

"Eh? What's this?" Dugald heaved himself to his feet. "What is all this about? You are no man of Earth! You have the voice of an underman. What farce is this?" Dugald turned to summon the Garrion who stood at the end of the hall.

"Wait," said Ghyl. "Listen to me, then decide what to do. If you call the Garrion now, you lose all of your options."

Dugald stared, his face an apoplectic purple, his mouth opening and closing. "I know you, I have seen you. I remember your way of speaking...Can it be? You are Ghyl Tarvoke, who was expelled! Ghyl Tarvoke, the pirate! The great thief!"

"I am Ghyl Tarvoke."

"I should have known, when you said 'Emphyrio'. What an outrage to find you here! What do you want of me? Revenge? You deserved your punishment!" Lord Dugald looked at Ghyl in new wrath. "How did you escape? You were expelled!"

"True," said Ghyl. "Now I am back once more. You destroyed my father, you set about to destroy me. I feel no great pity for you."

Lord Dugald once more turned toward the Garrion; once again Ghyl held up his hand. "I carry a weapon; I can kill you and the Garrion as well. You would do best to hear me out; it will take no great time. Then you can decide upon your course of action."

"Speak then!" bugled Lord Dugald. "Say what you must and go!"

"I spoke the name Emphyrio. He lived two thousand years ago, and thwarted the puppet-masters of Damar. He awoke the Wirwans to their own sentience; he persuaded them to peace. Then he went to Damar, and spoke in the Catademnon. Do you know of the Catademnon?"

"No," said Lord Dugald contemptuously. "Speak on."

"The puppet-makers drove a spike through Emphyrio's head, then they contrived a new campaign. What they had not gained by violence, they hoped to take by craft. After the Empire Wars they repaired the city; they installed Overtrend and Underline, they established Boimarc. They also organized Thurible Co-operative and thereafter Boimarc sold to Thurible, and perhaps bought from Thurible as well. Puppet-makers indeed! What need had the Damarans of puppets? They used the folk of Fortinone for their puppets, and robbed us of our wealth."

Dugald rubbed his nose with his two forefingers. "How do you know all this?"

"How could it be otherwise? You called me a thief, a pirate. But you are the thief and pirate! More accurately, you are a puppet controlled by thieves."

Lord Dugald seemed to swell in his chair. "So now. So now you insult me as well?"

"No insult: the literal truth. You are a puppet of a type created long ago in the Damaran glands."

Lord Dugald stared hard at Ghyl. "You are certain of this?"

"Of course. Lords? Ladies?" Ghyl gave a harsh laugh. "What a joke! You are excellent replicas of man—but you are puppets."

"Who infected you with such fantastic views?" demanded Lord Dugald in a stifled voice.

"No one. At Garwan I watched a Damaran walk; it walked with soft feet, as if its feet hurt. On Maastricht I remembered the lords and ladies walking just so. I remembered how they dreaded the light, the open sky; how they wished to run to the mountains to hide: like Wirwans, like Damarans. I remembered the color of their skin: the tone of pink that sometimes tends toward Damaran purple. On Maastricht I wondered how human-seeming folk could act so strangely. How was I so innocent? And so many generations of men and women: how could they have been so stupid, so unperceptive? Simple enough. A fraud so large cannot be comprehended: the idea is rejected."

As Ghyl spoke Dugald's face began to quiver and work in a most peculiar fashion, his mouth pulling in and out, his eyes bulging, the side of his head quivering and pulsing, so that Ghyl wondered whether he might be undergoing a seizure. Finally Dugald blurted: "Foolishness…Trash…Wicked nonsense…"

Ghyl shook his head. "No. Once the idea takes hold, everything is clear. Look!" He pointed to the hangings. "You stifle yourself in cloth like the Damarans; you have no music; you cannot breed children with true men; you even have a strange odor."

Dugald sank slowly into his chair, and for a moment was silent. Then he glanced craftily sidewise at Ghyl. "How far have you communicated these wild suppositions?"

"Widely enough," said Ghyl. "I would not care to come here otherwise."

"Hah! Who have you informed?"

"First, I sent a memorandum to the Historical Institute."

Dugald gave a sick groan. Then, with a pitiful attempt at bravado, he declared: "They will never heed such a farrago! Who else?"

"It would avail you nothing to kill me," said Ghyl politely. "I realize that you would like to do so. I assure you it would be useless. Worse than useless. My friends would spread the news, not only throughout Fortinone, but across the human universe: how the lords are but puppets, how their pride is play-acting, how they have cheated the folk who trusted them."

Dugald hunched down into his chair. "The pride is not counterfeit: it is true pride. Shall I tell you something? Only I, Grand Lord Dugald the Boimarc, of all the lords, have no pride. I am humble, I am purple with care—because only I know the truth. All the others—they are blameless. They realize their difference; they assume this to be the measure of their superiority. Only I am not proud; only I know who I am." He gave a piteous groan. "Well, I must pay your demands. What do you want? Wealth? A space-yacht? A town-house? All these?"

"I want only truth. Truth must be known."

Dugald gave a croak of protest. "What can I do! Would you have me destroy my people? Honor is all we have: what else? I alone am without honor, and look at me! See how I fare! I am different from all the rest. I am a puppet!"

"You alone know?"

"I alone. Before I die I will instruct another and doom him as I long ago was doomed."

Into the alcove came Lord Parnasse. He looked with inquisitive eyes from Ghyl to Lord Dugald. "You are still at your business? We are almost ready to dine." He addressed Ghyl: "You will join us?"

Ghyl gave a strained laugh. Lord Parnasse lifted his eyebrows. "Certainly," said Ghyl. "I will be pleased to do so."

Lord Parnasse bowed curtly, departed the alcove.

Lord Dugald contrived a face of bluff bonhomie. "Well, then let us consider the matter. You are not a Chaoticist; I'm sure you do not wish to destroy a time-tested socialty; after all—"

Ghyl held up his hand. "Lord Dugald, whatever else, the deception must be ended, and restitution must be made to the people you have cheated. If you and your 'socialty' can survive these steps, well and good. I bear malice only toward you and Damarans, not the Lords of Ambroy."

"What you demand is impossible," declared Dugald. "You have come here swaggering and threatening, now my patience is exhausted! I warn you, with great fervor, to spread no falsehoods or incitements."

Ghyl turned toward the door. "The first folk to know shall be Lord Parnasse and his guests."

"No!" cried Dugald in anguish. "Would you destroy us all?"

"The deception must be ended; there must be restitution."

Dugald held out his arms in despair and pathos. "You are obdurate!"

"'Obdurate'? I am passionate. You killed my father. You have robbed and cheated for two thousand years. You expect me to be otherwise?"

"I will mend matters. The rate will return to 1.18 percent. The underlings will receive an appreciably higher return; I will so demand. You cannot imagine how insistent are the Damarans!"

"The truth must be known."

"But what of our honor?"

"Depart Halma. Take your folk to a far planet, where none know your secret."

Dugald gave a cry of wild anguish. "How would I explain so drastic an act?"

"By the truth."

Dugald stared Ghyl eye to eye, and Ghyl, for a strange brief instant, felt himself looking into unfathomable Damaran emptiness.

Dugald must also have found a quality to daunt him. He turned, strode from the alcove, out into the great hall, where he climbed up on a chair. His voice rasped through the murmur, the half-heard whispers. "Listen to me! Listen, everyone! The truth must be told."

The company swung around in polite surprise.

"The truth!" cried Dugald, "the truth must be told. Everyone must know at last."

There was silence in the hall. Dugald looked wildly right and left, struggling to bring forth words. "Two thousand years ago," he declared, "Emphyrio delivered Fortinone from those Damaran monsters known as Wirwan.

"Now another Emphyrio has come, to expel another race of Damaran monsters. He has insisted upon truth. Now you will hear truth.

"Almost two thousand years ago, with Ambroy in ruins, a new set of puppets were sent from Damar. We are those puppets. We have served our masters the Damarans, and have paid to them money wrung from the toil of the underfolk. This is the truth; now that it is known the Damarans no longer can coerce us.

"We are not lords; we are puppets.

"We have no souls, no minds, no identities. We are synthetics.

"We are not men, not even Damarans. Most of all, we are not lords. We are whimsies, fancies, contrivances. Honor? Our honor is as real as a wisp of smoke. Dignity? Pride? Ridiculous even to use the words."

Dugald pointed to Ghyl. "He came here tonight calling himself Emphyrio, impelling me to truth.

"You have heard the truth.

"When the truth is finally told, there is no more to say."

Dugald stepped down from his chair.

The room was silent.

A chime sounded. Lord Parnasse stirred, looked around at his guests. "The banquet awaits us."

Slowly the guests filed from the room. Ghyl stood aside. Shanne passed near him. She halted. "You are Ghyl. Ghyl Tarvoke."

"Yes."

"Once, long ago, you loved me."

"But you never loved me."

"Perhaps I did. Perhaps I loved you as much as I was able."

"It was long ago."

"Yes. Things are different now." Shanne smiled politely, and gathering her skirts went her way.

Ghyl spoke to Lord Dugald. "Tomorrow you must speak to the undermen. Tell them the truth, as you have told the truth to your own folk. Perhaps they will not tear down your towers. If they are enraged beyond control, you must be prepared to depart."

"Where? To the Meagher Mounts to join the Wirwans?"

Ghyl shrugged. Lord Dugald turned, Lord Parnasse waited. They passed into the banquet hall leaving Ghyl standing alone.

He turned and went out on the terrace, and stood for a moment looking over the ancient city which spread with faint lights glowing, to the Insse and beyond. Never had he seen so beautiful a sight.

He went to the air-car. "Take me to the Brown Star Inn."

CHAPTER XXIV

The folk of Ambroy, so careful, so diligent, so frugal, were dazed for several hours after the announcement came over the Spay public announcement system. Work halted, folk went out into the streets, to look blankly into the sky toward Damar, up to the eyries on the Vashmont towers, then across town toward the Welfare Agency.

People spoke little to each other. Occasionally someone would give a short bark of harsh laughter, then become silent once more. Folk began to drift toward the Welfare Agency and by mid-day a great crowd stood in the surrounding plaza, staring at the grim old building.

Within was gathered the Cobol clan, holding an emergency meeting.

The crowd began to move restlessly. There were mutters, which swelling, became a vast susurrus. Someone, perhaps a Chaoticist, threw a stone, which broke a window. A face appeared in the gap, and an arm made admonitory motions, which seemed to irritate the crowd. Before there had been hesitancy and doubt as to the role of the Agency. But the angry gestures from the window seemed to put the Agency in the camp of those who had victimized the recipients; and, after all, had not the welfare agents enforced the regulations which made the swindle possible?

The crowd stirred; the mutter became an ugly growling sound. More rocks were thrown, more windows broken.

A loudspeaker on the roof suddenly brayed: "Recipients! Return to your work! The Welfare Agency is studying the situation, and in due course will make the proper representations. Everyone! Disperse, depart at once: to your homes or places of work. This is an official instruction."

The crowd paid no heed; more rocks and bricks were thrown; and suddenly the Agency had become a place in a state of siege.

A group of young men surged up to the locked portal, tried to force it open. Gun-fire sounded; several were laid low. The crowd pushed forward, entered the Agency through the broken windows. There was more gun-fire, but the crowd was within the building and many horrible deeds occurred. The Cobols were torn to bits, the structure put to the torch.

Hysteria continued throughout the night. The eyries remained undamaged mainly because the mob had no feasible mode of attack. On the next day the Guild Council attempted to restore order, with some success, and the Mayor set to work organizing a militia.

Six weeks later a hundred space-craft of every description—passenger packets, cargo vessels, space-yachts—departed Ambroy and crossed to Damar. A few Damaran were killed, a few more captured. The rest took refuge in their residences.

A deputation of the captured Damaran was handed an ultimatum:

> For two thousand years you have plundered us without pity or regret. We demand total retribution. Bring forth all of your wealth: every thread of fabric, every precious artifact, all your treasure, in money, credits, foreign accounts and exchange, and all other property of value. These articles and this wealth will thereupon become ours. We will then destroy the residences with explosives. The Damarans must henceforth live on the surface in conditions as bleak as those you inflicted upon us. Thereafter you must pay to the State of Fortinone an indemnity of ten million vouchers each year, for two hundred Halma years.
>
> If you do not immediately agree to these terms you will be destroyed, and not one Damaran will remain alive.

Four hours later the first precious articles began to be conveyed from the residences.

In Undle Square a shrine was erected to shelter a crystal case containing the skeleton of Emphyrio. On the door of a nearby narrow-fronted house with amber glass windows hung a plaque of polished black obsidian. Silver characters read:

In this house lived and worked the son of Amiante Tarvoke, Ghyl, who, taking the name of Emphyrio for his own, did the name, his father and himself great credit.

THE LANGUAGES OF PAO

INTRODUCTION

by Ursula K. Le Guin (2007)

Jack Vance loved to invent elaborate, gorgeous pageantries of costumes and manners, castes and classes, and recount histories of
powerful men scheming and striving for more power, set in countries
with remarkable geographies and exotic names, on distant worlds, in a
far future. Returning to those Vancean worlds after many years, the first
thing I noticed, with surprise and affection, was how familiar they are.
Despite the science-fictional apparatus of spaceflight and super-high-
technology, they aren't alien worlds, or future worlds. They are our own
lost world. They are Earth before the airplane, Earth in all the centuries
when it was boundless, endlessly rich in mystery and strangeness—
when there were blanks on the map—when Samarkand or Timbuctu or
California were names of legend, when Marco Polo was a stranger in
Cathay, when Baghdad was where the Thief lived…

About the time we started to destroy that world, industriously
shrinking it to the size of a theme park or a shopping mall, we started
writing about worlds out in space and their alien beings and ways.
When the *National Geographic* ran short of exoticism, science fiction
took over. Jack Vance seems to have enjoyed that compensatory inven-
tion immensely for its own sake; and he did it with the true Thousand
and One Nights flair, the deadpan realism of the best traveler's tales.

The Languages of Pao was my favorite of the many Vance novels I bought in the sixties, because I liked its subject. Vance was always aware that language is an interesting and tricky business—unlike many science-fiction writers, who still routinely present a whole planet or even galaxy of people(s) all speaking the same tongue. It is easier to explain airily that everybody speaks Ing-Lish ever since Urth installed the Galactic Empire than it is to cope realistically with Babel. But the trouble with a monolinguistic universe is, it's shrunken, artificial—we're back in the theme park, the shopping mall. Vance didn't share the imperial, reductionist mindset, common to his generation of sf writers, that dismisses variety as unimportant. Rather, he revels in it; his various peoples speak variously, and their names reflect the different phonologies of their languages.

Vance's writing style is certainly that of one to whom words, both the meaning and the sound, are important. He has—and it was a rare thing in science fiction in 1958—a real and personal literary style. His dialogue is often dignified and formal to the point of being stilted; people say things like, "This credence which you deprecate may be no more than fact." [p. 327] This is a mannerism, but, if you accept it, a rather endearing one. The rhythm of his narrative is calm, sedate, musical; his descriptive passages are direct and exact. He gives you a sense of what the weather is, what the colors of things are, he places you in a setting:

> Above reared the rock slope, far up to the gray sky, where the wild little white sun swerved like a tin disc on the wind. Beran retraced his steps. [p. 241]

This little passage is typical, the first sentence for its vivid description, poetic, exact, restrained; the second for its slightly old-fashioned phrasing and its simplicity. Vance did not waste words. He is as far as possible from the grab-'em-by-the balls school of action writing, yet he was an action writer: his plots move forward, not rapidly but steadily, with an impetus that carries the reader right along. He was in full charge of his story. The characters, the plot, the scenes, descriptions, actions, all are under control. And control is, perhaps, one of his great subjects.

The Languages of Pao concerns a struggle for the control of a people: a political conflict, a moral debate. As in others of his books, it involves a vast population, but is acted out by a very few characters.

One is a boy, Beran, inheritor of a world empire but reduced to dependence on a man of enormous power, Palafox. The plot is in fact the classic duel of father and son, complicated wonderfully by the fact that the father has literally hundreds of other sons. Pitting the father's pitiless megalomania against the boy's struggling sense of justice, Vance sets up his conflict cannily. Palafox, for all his power, is utterly controlled by the perverse society that formed him, and even the language which gives him his power; while Beran, because he is not committed to any one alternative, has a hope of freedom.

The element of speculative science informing the plot is known as the Sapir-Whorf Hypothesis, which says (stated crudely) that our mental outlook is formed by our language: what one can think depends, to a large extent, on the words one has to think with. Because linguistics is a "soft" or social science, diehards of "hard sci-fi" must dismiss this book as fantasy; but such quibbles grow ever quainter. Meeting the reasonable requirement of using a durable, if much-questioned, scientific hypothesis as a major element of the plot, *Pao* is excellent, solid science fiction. Vance understands Sapir-Whorf and, while applying it with due caution, elaborates it convincingly and spins a lively yarn out of it.

I feel a certain old-fashioned quality to *Pao*. Perhaps it was always there, inherent in Vance's dignified language, his unhurried pacing, and his avoidance of ubiquitous, gratuitous violence. But it may also have something to do, now, with Vance's inescapable masculism—an almost universal failing of the genre at that time. Women are perceived, if at all, as contingent on men—appurtenances. A shadowy girl, Gitan, plays a brief, passive role. Some nameless victims of Palafox's lust are glimpsed. Beran has a father but no mother. He neither seeks nor finds a wife. Male interests are the only concern, men perform all actions except domestic service, men fill every leading position; even madness is gendered, for Palafox's psychotic plan to populate the world with his sons is merely a hideous exaggeration of the male sex-drive, the selfish gene embodied. What women want, feel, think, or are plays no part whatever in the book. This is of course true of many novels, even now, even those with nominally female characters. Vance's lack of interest in half the population of the world was, at least, undisguised by hypocritical pieties.

Respecting his writing as I do, I tried to see the story as a critique of male dominance, and it can be read so, but the reading is unconvincing in the complete absence of active women characters. So this fine novel may seem, to a modern eye, maimed. It is benign and thoughtful, yet its omission of half humankind from agency cripples an otherwise just, subtle, and generous moral stance.

Jack Vance made no pretense to literary greatness, I think, but he held himself to a far higher literary standard than most pulp-fiction and genre writers of his time, and he was true to his own vision. For that he deserves lasting honor. May a new generation of readers discover the joys of traveling far beyond the shopping mall and the theme park, to the eight continents of Pao, and the bleak heights of Breakness.

THE LANGUAGES OF PAO

CHAPTER I

In the heart of the Polymark Cluster, circling the yellow star Auriol, is the planet Pao, with the following characteristics:

Mass:	1.73 (in standard units)
Diameter:	1.39
Surface Gravity:	1.04

The plane of Pao's diurnal rotation is the same as its plane of orbit; hence there are no seasons and the climate is uniformly mild. Eight continents range the equator at approximately equal intervals: Aimand, Shraimand, Vidamand, Minamand, Nonamand, Dronamand, Hivand and Impland, after the eight digits of the Paonese numerative system. Aimand, largest of the continents, has four times the area of Nonamand, the least. Only Nonamand, in the high southern latitudes, suffers an unpleasant climate.

An accurate census of Pao has never been made. Eiljanre on Minamand is the largest city, with six million inhabitants. The twin cities Koroi and Sherifte on Impland share another six million between them. There are perhaps a hundred other cities of over half a million, but the great mass of the population—estimated at fifteen billion persons—lives in country villages.

The Paonese are a homogeneous people, of medium stature, fair-skinned with hair-color ranging from tawny-brown to brown-black, with no great variations of feature or physique. They are so similar the extra-planetary visitor, traveling from continent to continent, has the peculiar sense of meeting the same persons again and again.

Paonese history previous to the reign of Panarch Aiello Panasper is uneventful. The first settlers, finding the planet hospitable, multiplied to an unprecedented density of population. Their system of life minimized social friction; there were no large wars, no plagues, no disasters except recurrent famine, which was endured with fortitude. A simple uncomplicated people were the Paonese, without religion or cult. They demanded small material rewards from life, but gave a correspondingly large importance to shifts of caste and status. They knew no competitive sports, but enjoyed gathering in enormous clots of ten or twenty million persons to chant the ancient drones. The typical Paonese farmed a small acreage, augmenting his income with a home craft or special trade. He showed small interest in politics; his hereditary ruler, the Panarch, exercised an absolute personal rule which reached out, through a vast civil service, into the most remote village. The word 'career' in Paonese was synonymous to employment with the civil service.

In general, the government was sufficiently efficient, the Panarch not too flagrantly corrupt. In the event of unusual abuse the people countered with passive resistance, a vast surly inanition which neither threat, penalty nor blandishment could dissolve. It was a weapon used only seldom, but the fact of its existence held the normal human peccancy of the ruling caste within reasonable bounds.

The language of Pao was derived from Waydalic but molded into peculiar forms. The Paonese sentence did not so much describe an act as it presented a picture of a situation. The language might be said to consist of nouns, suffixed post-positions, and temporal indexes; there were no verbs, no adjectives; no formal word comparison such as 'good', 'better', 'best'. There were no words for 'prestige', 'integrity', 'individuality', 'honor', or 'justice'; for the typical Paonese saw himself as a cork on a sea of a million waves, lofted, lowered, thrust aside by incomprehensible forces—if he thought of himself as a discrete personality at all. He was one of a uniform mass, a crowd of men distinguished only by the color, cut and weave of their clothes—highly significant symbols on Pao.

He held his ruler in awe, but felt neither admiration, envy, loyalty nor reverence. He gave unquestioning obedience, and asked in return only dynastic continuity, for on Pao nothing must vary, nothing must change. The Panarch occupied a paradoxical position. He ruled, he made decisions, he loomed over the population like a mountain over the plain, and for this reason excited fearful respect. The average man faced only the most trivial choices: ritual and precedent shaped his every act. He prospered and suffered with the mass of his fellows, and could not help but feel that a person who lived unsupported, who dealt death and bestowed life, must be a man apart, with ice in his veins and a special fire burning inside his skull.

But the Panarch, absolute tyrant though he might be, was also forced to conform. Here lay the paradox: the single inner-directed individual of Pao was allowed vices unthinkable and abhorrent to the average man. But he might not appear gay or frivolous; he must hold himself aloof from friendship; he must show himself seldom in public places. Most important of all, he must never seem indecisive or uncertain. To do so would break the archetype.

CHAPTER II

Pergolai, an islet in the Jhelianse Sea between Minamand and Dronamand, had been pre-empted and converted into an Arcadian retreat by Panarch Aiello Panasper. Every trace of former habitancy had been removed; forests had been transplanted into the old paddies, wildflowers seeded, a stream diverted to form a chain of ponds. At the head of a meadow bordered by Paonese bamboo and tall myrrh trees stood Aiello's lodge, an airy structure of white glass, carved stone and polished wood. The plan was simple: a residential tower, a service wing, and an octagonal pavilion with a pink marble dome. Here in the pavilion, at a carved ivory table, sat Aiello to his midday repast, wearing the Utter Black of his position. He was a large man, small-boned, well-fleshed. His silver-gray hair shone fine as a baby's; he had a baby's clear skin and wide unwinking stare. His mouth drooped, his eyebrows arched high, conveying a perpetual sense of sardonic and skeptical inquiry.

To the right sat his brother Bustamonte, bearing the title Ayudor— a smaller man, with a shock of coarse dark hair, quick black eyes, knobs of muscles in his cheeks. Bustamonte was energetic beyond the usual Paonese norm. He had toured two or three nearby worlds, returning with a number of alien enthusiasms which had gained him the dislike and distrust of the Paonese population.

On Aiello's other side sat his son, Beran Panasper, the Medallion. He was a thin child, hesitant and diffident, with fragile features and long black hair, resembling Aiello only in his clear skin and wide eyes.

Across the table sat a score of other men: functionaries of the government, petitioners, three commercial representatives from Mercantil, and a hawk-faced man in brown and gray who spoke to no one. With greater or less appetite they devoted themselves to food served in mother-of-pearl tureens by small sober-faced girls. Aiello was attended by special maids wearing long gowns striped with black and gold. Each dish served him was first tasted by Bustamonte—a custom residual from times when assassination was the rule rather than the exception. Another manifestation of this ancient caution could be found in the three Mamarone standing vigilant behind Aiello. These were enormous creatures tattooed dead-black—neutraloids with reservoirs of synthetic hormones in place of their procreative glands. They wore magnificent turbans of cerise and green, tight pantaloons of the same colors, chest emblems of white silk and silver, and carried shields of refrax to be locked in front of the Panarch in the event of danger.

Aiello morosely nibbled his way through the prolonged meal and finally indicated that he was ready to conduct the business of the day.

Vilnis Therobon, wearing the ocher and purple of Public Welfare, arose and came to stand before the Panarch. He stated his problem: the cereal farmers of the South Impland savannahs were beset by drought; he, Therobon, wished to bring water from across the Central Impland watershed, but had been unable to work out a satisfactory arrangement with the Minister of Irrigation. Aiello listened, asked a question or two, then, in a brief sentence, authorized a water-purification plant at the Koroi-Sherifte Isthmus, with a ten-thousand mile pipe-line network to take the water where needed.

The Minister of Public Health spoke next. The population of Dronamand's central plain had expanded past available housing. To build new dwellings would encroach upon land assigned to food production, and would hasten the famine already threatening. Aiello, munching a crescent of pickled melon, advised transportation of a million persons weekly to Nonamand, the bleak southern continent. In addition, all infants arriving to parents with more than two children should be subaqueated. These were the classical methods of population control; they would be accepted without resentment.

Young Beran watched with fascination, awed by the vastness of his father's power. He was seldom allowed to witness state business, for Aiello disliked children and showed only small concern for the upbringing of his son. Recently the Ayudor Bustamonte had interested himself in Beran, talking for hours on end, until Beran's head grew heavy and his eyes drooped. They played odd games which bewildered Beran and left with him a peculiar uneasiness. And of late there had been blank spaces in his mind, lapses of memory.

As Beran sat now at the ivory table in the pavilion, he held a small unfamiliar object in his hand. He could not recall where he had found it, but it seemed as if there were something he must do. He looked at his father, and felt a sudden hot panic. He gasped, clamped his teeth on his lower lip. He whispered feverishly to himself, *Why should I do that, why do I feel this way?* He found no answer. There was a roiling inside his head, a series of strains which left him dizzy. Bustamonte was looking at him, frowning. Beran felt awkward and guilty. He made a great effort, pulled himself erect in his chair. He must watch and listen, as Bustamonte had instructed him. Furtively he inspected the object he held in his hand. It was at once familiar and strange. As if in recollection from a dream, he knew he had use for this object—and again came the wave of panic.

Beran tasted a bit of toasted fish-tail, but as usual lacked appetite. He felt the brush of eyes; someone was watching him. Turning his head, he met the gaze of the hawk-faced stranger in brown and gray. The man had an arresting face, long and thin with a high forehead, a wisp of mustache, a nose like the prow of a ship. His hair was glossy black, thick and short as fur. His eyes were set deep; his gaze, dark and magnetic, awoke all of Beran's uneasiness. The object in his hand felt heavy and hot. He wanted to fling it down, but could not. His fingers refused to relax their grip. He sat sweating and miserable.

The last man to be heard was Sigil Paniche, business representative from Mercantil, the planet of a nearby sun. Paniche was a thin man, quick and clever, with copper-colored skin and burnished hair, which he wore wound into knobs and fastened with turquoise clasps. He was a typical Mercantil, a salesman and trader, as essentially urban as the Paonese were people of soil and sea. His world sold to the entire cluster; Mercantil space-barges roved everywhere, delivering machinery, vehicles, air-craft, communication equipment, tools, weapons, power-generators, returning to Mercantil with food-stuffs, luxury hand-crafts and whatever raw material might be cheaper to import than to synthesize.

Bustamonte whispered to Aiello, who shook his head. Bustamonte whispered more urgently; Aiello turned him a slow caustic side-glance. Bustamonte sat back sullenly.

At a signal from Aiello, the captain of the Mamarone guard addressed the table in his soft scraped-steel voice. "By the Panarch's order, all those who have completed their business will depart." Chairs slid softly on the marble floor. The ministers arose, spread their arms in the Paonese gesture of respect, and departed.

Across the table, only Sigil Paniche, his two aides, and the stranger in brown and gray remained.

The Mercantil moved to a chair opposite Aiello; he bowed, seated himself, his aides coming to stand at his back.

Panarch Aiello spoke an off-hand greeting; the Mercantil responded in broken Paonese.

Aiello toyed with a bowl of brandied fruit, appraising the Mercantil. "Pao and Mercantil have traded for many centuries, Sigil Paniche."

The Mercantil bowed. "We fulfill the exact letter of our contracts—this is our creed."

Aiello laughed shortly. The Mercantil looked at him in surprise, but said nothing. "Trade with Pao has enriched you."

"We trade with twenty-eight worlds, Supremacy."

Aiello leaned back in his chair. "There are two matters I wish to discuss with you. You have just heard our need for water on Impland. We require an installation to demineralize an appropriate quantity of ocean-water. You may refer this matter to your engineers."

"I am at your orders, sir."[*]

Aiello spoke in a level emotionless voice, almost casual. "We have ordered from you, and you have delivered, large quantities of military equipment."

Sigil Paniche bowed agreement. With no outward sign or change he suddenly seemed uneasy. "We fulfilled the exact requirements of your order."

---

[*]The Paonese and Mercantil languages were as disparate as the two ways of living. The Panarch, making the statement, 'There are two matters I wish to discuss with you', used words which, accurately rendered, would read: *Statement-of-importance* (a single word in Paonese)—*in a state of readiness*—two; ear—of Mercantil—*in a state of readiness;* mouth—of this person here—*in a state of volition.* The italicized words represent suffixes of condition.

The necessary paraphrasing makes the way of speaking seem cumbersome. But the Paonese sentence, *'Rhomel-en-shrai bogal-Mercantil-nli-en mous-es-nli-ro.'* requires only three more phonemes than, "There are two matters I wish to discuss with you."

The Mercantil express themselves in neat quanta of precise information. 'I am at your orders, sir.' Literally translated this is: *I—Ambassador—here-now gladly-obey the just-spoken-orders of-you—Supreme Royalty—here-now heard and understood.*

"I cannot agree with you," Aiello responded.

Sigil Paniche became stiff; his words were even more formal than before. "I assure Your Supremacy that I personally checked delivery. The equipment was exactly as described in order and invoice."

Aiello went on in his coldest tones. "You delivered sixty-four[*] barrage monitors, 512 patrol flitters, a large number of multiple resonators, energetics, wasps and hand-weapons. These accord with the original order."

"Exactly, sir."

"However, you knew the purpose behind this order."

Sigil Paniche bowed his copper-bright head. "You refer to conditions on the planet Batmarsh."

"Just so. The Dolberg dynasty has been eliminated. A new dynasty, the Brumbos, have assumed power. New Batch rulers customarily undertake military ventures."

"Such is the tradition," agreed the Mercantil.

"You have supplied these adventurers with armament."

Sigil Paniche once again agreed. "We sell to any who will buy. We have done so for many years—you must not reproach us for this."

Aiello raised his eyebrows. "I do not do so. I reproach you for selling us standard models while offering the Brumbo Clan equipment against which you guarantee we will be powerless."

Sigil Paniche blinked. "What is the source of your information?"

"Must I divest myself of every secret?" inquired Aiello, curling his lip.

"No, no," exclaimed Paniche. "Your allegations, however, seem mistaken. Our policy is absolute neutrality."

"Unless you can profit by double-dealing."

Sigil Paniche drew himself erect. "Supremacy, I am official representative of Mercantil on Pao. Your statements to me, therefore, must be regarded as formal insults."

Aiello appeared to be faintly surprised. "Insult a Mercantil? Preposterous!"

Sigil Paniche's skin burnt vermilion.

Bustamonte whispered in Aiello's ear. Aiello shrugged, turned back to the Mercantil. His voice was cool, his words carefully measured. "For the reasons I have stated, I declare that the Mercantil contract has not

---

[*]The Paonese number system is based on the number 8. Hence, a Paonese 100 is 64, 1000 is 512, etc.

been fulfilled. The merchandise will not perform its function. We will not pay."

Sigil Paniche affirmed, "The delivered articles meet the contractual specifications!" By his lights nothing more need be said.

"But they are useless to our need, a fact known on Mercantil."

Sigil Paniche's eyes gleamed. "No doubt Your Supremacy has considered the long-range effects of such a decision."

Bustamonte could not restrain a retort. "Better had the Mercantil consider the long-range effect of double-dealing."

Aiello made a small gesture of annoyance, and Bustamonte sat back.

Sigil Paniche looked over his shoulder to his two subordinates; they exchanged emphatic whispers. Then Paniche asked, "May I inquire as to what 'long-range effects' the Ayudor alluded?"

Aiello nodded. "I direct your attention to the gentleman at your left hand."

All eyes swung to the stranger in brown and gray. "Who is this man?" Sigil Paniche asked sharply. "I do not recognize his clothes."

Aiello was served a bowl of green syrup by one of the black and gold-clad maidens. Bustamonte dutifully sampled a spoonful. Aiello drew the bowl close to him, sipped. "This is Lord Palafox. He is here to offer us advice." He sipped once more from the bowl, pushed it aside. The maiden quickly removed it.

Sigil Paniche surveyed the stranger with cold hostility. His aides muttered to each other. Bustamonte sat slumped into his seat, as if disassociating himself from whatever understanding existed between Aiello and the stranger.

"After all," said Aiello, "if we can not rely upon Mercantil for protection, we must seek elsewhere."

Sigil Paniche once more turned to whisper with his counselors. There was a hushed argument; Paniche snapped his fingers in emphasis, the counselors bowed and became silent. Paniche turned back to Aiello. "Your Supremacy naturally will act as he thinks best. I must point out that the products of Mercantil are surpassed nowhere."

Aiello glanced at the man in brown and gray. "I am not disposed to dispute this point. Lord Palafox might have something to say."

Palafox, however, shook his head.

Paniche motioned to one of his subordinates, who advanced reluctantly. "Allow me to display one of our new developments." The counselor handed him a case, from which Paniche withdrew a pair of small transparent hemispheres.

The neutraloid bodyguards, at the sight of the case, had leapt in front of Aiello with their refrax shields; Sigil Paniche grimaced painfully. "No need for alarm—there is no danger here."

He displayed the hemispheres to Aiello, then placed them over his eyes. "Our new optidynes! They function either as microscope or telescope! The enormous range of their power is controlled by the ocular muscles and the eyelids. Truly marvellous! For instance—" he turned, looked out the window of the pavilion "—I see quartz crystals in the stones of the sea-wall. A gray chit stands under that far funella bush." He turned his gaze to his sleeve. "I see the threads, the fibers of the threads, the laminae of the fibers."

He looked at Bustamonte. "I note the pores of the Ayudor's estimable nose. I observe several hairs in his nostril." He glanced at the Medallion, carefully avoiding the solecism of staring at Aiello. "The brave lad is excited. I count his pulse: one, two, three, four, five, six, seven, eight, eleven, twelve, thirteen…He holds a tiny object between his fingers, no larger than a pill." He turned, inspected the man in gray. "I see…" he stared; then with a sudden gesture, removed the optidynes from his eyes.

"What did you see?" Bustamonte inquired.

Sigil Paniche studied the tall man in perturbation and awe. "I saw his sign. The tattoo of a Breakness wizard!"

The words seemed to arouse Bustamonte. He glared in accusation at Aiello, gave Palafox a look of loathing, then glowered down at the carved ivory of the table.

"You are correct," said Aiello. "This is Lord Palafox, Dominie of Breakness Institute."

Sigil Paniche bowed his head frigidly. "Will your Supremacy allow me a question?"

"Ask what you will."

"What does Lord Palafox do here on Pao?"

Aiello said blandly, "He came at my behest. I need expert advice. Certain of my confidants—" he glanced rather contemptuously toward Bustamonte "—feel that we can buy Mercantil co-operation. He believes that for a price you will betray the Brumbos of Batmarsh in the same way you have already betrayed us."

Sigil Paniche said in a brittle voice, "We deal in all types of merchandise. We can be engaged for special research."

Aiello twisted his pink mouth into a sneer of repugnance. "I would rather deal with Lord Palafox."

Paniche could hardly contain his anger. "Why are you telling me this?"

"I would not have your syndics think that their treachery goes unnoticed."

Sigil Paniche made a great effort. "I urge you to reconsider. In no way have we cheated you. We delivered exactly what was ordered. Mercantil has served you well in the past—we hope to serve you in the future. If you deal with Breakness, think what the bargain entails!"

"I have made no bargains with Lord Palafox," said Aiello, with a swift glance toward the man in brown and gray.

"Ah, but you will—and, if I may speak openly..." He waited.

"Speak," said Aiello.

"...to your eventual dismay." He became emboldened. "Never forget, Supremacy, that they build no weapons on Breakness. They make no application of their science." He looked to Palafox. "Is this not true?"

"Not altogether," replied Palafox. "A Dominie of the Institute is never without his weapons."

"And Breakness manufactures weapons for export?" Paniche persisted.

"No," answered Palafox with a slight smile. "It is well-known that we manufacture only knowledge and men."

Sigil Paniche turned to Aiello. "Only weapons can guard you against the fury of the Brumbos. Why not examine, at least, some of our new products?"

"This can do no harm," Bustamonte urged. "And perhaps we will not require Palafox after all."

Aiello turned him a peevish glance, but Sigil Paniche already was displaying a globe-shaped projector with a hand grip. "This is one of our most ingenious developments."

The Medallion Beran, watching in absorption, felt a sudden quiver, a pang of indescribable alarm. Why? How? What? He half-raised in his seat, then, turning his head, met Bustamonte's eyes. They were bright with meaning. Beran's mind filled with dread. He must leave the pavilion, he must go! But he could not move from his seat. He bowed his head, waited.

Paniche was directing his tool toward the pink marble dome. "Observe, if you will." The top half of the room went black, as if concealed by a black shutter, as if snatched from existence. "The device seeks out, attracts and absorbs energy of the visual phase," explained the Mercantil. "It is invaluable for the confusion of an adversary."

Beran turned his head, looked helplessly toward Bustamonte.

"Now notice!" cried Sigil Paniche. "I turn this knob here…" He turned the knob; the room was blotted out entirely.

Bustamonte's cough was the only sound to be heard.

Then there was a hiss of surprise, a rustle of movement, a choking sound.

Light returned to the pavilion. A great horrified gasp sounded; all eyes went to the Panarch. He lay back into his pink silk divan. His leg jerked up, kicked, set dishes and flagons on the table rattling.

"Help, doctor!" cried Bustamonte. "To the Panarch!"

Aiello's fists beat a spasmodic tattoo on the tabletop; his eyes went dim, his head fell forward in the complete lassitude of death.

The doctors gingerly examined Aiello, a gross hulk with arms and legs sprawled in four directions. Beran, the new Panarch, Deified Breath of the Paonese, Tyrant-Absolute of Eight Continents, Ocean-Master, Suzerain of the System and Acknowledged Leader of the Universe (among his other honorary titles), sat fidgeting, evidencing neither comprehension nor grief. The Mercantil stood in a taut group, muttering to each other; Palafox, who had not moved from his seat at the table, watched with completely impassive features.

Bustamonte, now Ayudor-Senior, lost no time in asserting the authority which, as regent for the new Panarch, he might be expected to employ. He waved his hand; a squad of Mamarone leapt to stations surrounding the pavilion.

"None will leave," declared Bustamonte, "until these tragic circumstances are clarified." He turned to the doctors. "Have you determined the cause of death?"

The first of the three doctors bowed. "The Panarch succumbed to poison. It was administered by a sting-missile, thrust into the left side of his throat. The poison…" He consulted the dials, the shadow-graphs and color-wheels of an analyzer into which his colleagues had inserted samples of Aiello's body-fluids. "The poison appears to be a mepothanax derivative, extin most probably."

"In that case," spoke Bustamonte, and his gaze swung from the huddle of Mercantil traders to the grave Lord Palafox, "the crime was committed by someone in this room."

Sigil Paniche diffidently approached the corpse. "Allow me to examine this sting."

The chief doctor indicated a metal plate. Here rested the black sting with its small white bulb.

Sigil Paniche's face was strained. "This object is that which I glimpsed in the hand of the Medallion, no more than a few moments ago."

Bustamonte succumbed to rage. His jowls went pink, his eyes swam with fire. "This accusation from you—a Mercantil swindler!—is a horror of impertinence, an epic of cruelty! You accuse the lad of killing his father?"

Beran began to whimper; his head wobbled from side to side. "Quiet," hissed Bustamonte. "The nature of the deed is clear!"

"No, no," protested Sigil Paniche, and all the Mercantil stood blanched and helpless.

"There is no room for doubt," Bustamonte stated inexorably. "You came to Pergolai aware that your duplicity had been discovered. You were resolved to evade the penalties."

"This is nonsense!" cried the Mercantil. "How could we plan so idiotic an act?"

Bustamonte ignored the protest. In a voice of thunder he continued. "The Panarch would not be mollified. You hid yourself in darkness, you killed the great leader of the Paonese!"

"No, no!"

"But you will derive no benefit from the crime! I, Bustamonte, am even less placable than Aiello! As my first act I pronounce judgment upon you."

Bustamonte held up his arm, palm outward, fingers clenched over thumb—the traditional death-signal of the Paonese. He called to the commander of the Mamarone. "Subaqueate these creatures!" He glanced into the sky; the sun was low. "Make haste, before sundown!"

Hurriedly, for a Paonese superstition forbade killing during the hours of darkness, the Mamarone carried the traders to a cliff overlooking an arm of the sea. Their feet were thrust into ballasted tubes, they were flung out through the air. They struck the water, sank, and the surface was calm as before.

Twenty minutes later, by order of Bustamonte, the body of Aiello was brought forth. Without ceremony it was weighted and cast after the

Mercantil. Once again the sea showed a quick white blossom of foam; once again it rolled quiet and blue.

CHAPTER III

The sun hovered at the rim of the sea. Bustamonte, Ayudor-Senior of Pao, walked with nervously energetic steps along the terrace.

Lord Palafox sat nearby. At each end of the terrace stood a Mamarone, fire-sting aimed steadily at Palafox, to thwart any possible act of violence.

Bustamonte stopped short in front of Palafox. "My decision was wise—I have no doubt of it!"

"What decision is this?"

"In connection with the Mercantil."

Palafox considered. "You may now find trade relations difficult."

"Pah! What do they care for the lives of three men so long as there is profit to be obtained?"

"Very little, doubtless."

"These men were cheats and swindlers. They deserved no more than they received."

"In addition," Palafox pointed out, "the crime has been followed by an appropriate penalty, with no lack of equilibrium to disturb the public."

"Justice has been done," said Bustamonte stiffly.

Palafox nodded. "The function of justice, after all, is to dissuade any who might wish to perform a like misdeed. The execution constitutes such a dissuasion."

Bustamonte swung on his heel, paced up and down the terrace. "It is true that I acted partly from considerations of expediency."

Palafox said nothing.

"In all candor," said Bustamonte, "I admit that the evidence points to another hand in the affair, and the major element of the difficulty remains, like the bulk of an iceberg."

"What difficulty is this?"

"How shall I deal with young Beran?"

Palafox stroked his lean chin. "The question must be considered in its proper perspective."

"I fail to understand you."

"We must ask ourselves, did Beran actually kill the Panarch?"

Protruding his lips, bulging his eyes, Bustamonte contrived to become a grotesque hybrid of ape and frog. "Undoubtedly!"

"Why should he do so?"

Bustamonte shrugged. "Aiello had no love for Beran. It is doubtful if the child were actually fathered by Aiello."

"Indeed?" mused Lord Palafox. "And who might be the father?"

Bustamonte shrugged once more. "The Divine Petraia was not altogether fastidious in her indiscretions, but we will never know the truth, since a year ago Aiello ordained her subaqueation. Beran was grief-stricken, and here might be the source of the crime."

"Surely you do not take me for a fool?" Palafox asked, smiling a peculiar fixed smile.

Bustamonte looked at him in startlement. "Eh? What's this?"

"The execution of this deed was precise. The child appeared to be acting under hypnotic compulsion. His hand was guided by another brain."

"You feel so?" Bustamonte frowned. "Who might such 'another' be?"

"Why not the Ayudor-Senior?"

Bustamonte halted in his pacing, then laughed shortly. "This is fantasy indeed! What of yourself?"

"I gain nothing from Aiello's death," said Palafox. "He asked me here to a specific purpose. Now he is dead, and your own policy faces a different direction. There is no further need for me."

Bustamonte held up his hand. "Not so fast. Today is not yesterday. The Mercantil, as you suggest, may prove hard to deal with. Perhaps you will serve me as you might have served Aiello."

Palafox rose to his feet. The sun was settling past the far horizon into the sea; it swam orange and distorted in the thick air. A breeze tinkled among glass bells and drew sad flute-sounds from an aeolian harp; feathery cycads sighed and rustled.

The sun flattened, halved, quartered.

"Watch now!" said Palafox. "Watch for the green flash!"

The last fiery bar of red sank below the horizon; then came a flickering shaft of pure green, changing to blue, and the sunlight was gone.

The two men were silent, watching the afterglow. Bustamonte spoke in a heavy voice, "Beran must die. The fact of patricide is clear."

"You over-react to the situation," observed Palafox mildly. "Your remedies are worse than the ailment."

"I act as I think necessary," snapped Bustamonte.

"I will relieve you of the child," said Palafox. "He may return with me to Breakness."

Bustamonte inspected Palafox with simulated surprise. "What will you do with young Beran? The idea is ridiculous. I am prepared to offer you a draft of females to augment your prestige, or for whatever peculiar purpose you require these female herds."

"Our purposes are hardly peculiar."

"Well," Bustamonte shrugged, "we will discuss this later. But now I give orders in regard to Beran."

Palafox looked away into the dusk, smiling. "You fear that Beran will become a weapon against you. You want no possible challenge."

Bustamonte's round face twisted into a cunning leer. "It would be banal to deny it."

Palafox stared into the sky. "You need not fear him. He would remember nothing."

"What is your interest in this child?" demanded Bustamonte.

"Consider it a whim."

Bustamonte was curt. "I must disoblige you."

"I make a better friend than enemy," Palafox said softly.

Bustamonte stopped short in his tracks. He nodded, suddenly amiable. "Perhaps I will reconsider. After all, the child can hardly cause trouble…Come along, I will take you to Beran; we will observe his reaction to the idea."

Bustamonte marched off, rocking on his short legs. Smiling faintly, Palafox followed.

At the portal, Bustamonte muttered briefly to the captain of the Mamarone. Palafox, coming after, paused beside the tall black neutraloid, let Bustamonte proceed out of earshot. He spoke, tilting his head to look up into the harsh face.

"Suppose I were to make you a true man once more—how would you pay me?"

The eyes glowed, muscles rippled under the black skin. The neutraloid replied in the strange soft voice of its kind: "How would I pay you? By smashing you, by crushing your skull. I am more than a man, more than four men—why should I want the return of weakness?"

"Ah," marveled Palafox. "You are not prone to weakness?"

"Yes," sighed the neutraloid, "indeed I have a flaw." He showed his teeth in a ghastly grin. "I take an unnatural joy in killing; I prefer nothing to the strangling of small pale men."

Palafox turned away, entered the pavilion.

The door closed behind him. He looked over his shoulder. The captain stood glaring through the transparent panel. Palafox looked to the other entrances; Mamarone stood at vigilance everywhere.

Bustamonte sat in one of Aiello's black foam chairs. He had flung a black cloak over his shoulders, the Utter Black of a Panarch.

"I marvel at you men of Breakness," said Bustamonte. "Your daring is remarkable! So casually do you put yourselves into desperate danger!"

Palafox shook his head gravely. "We are not so rash as we seem. No dominie walks abroad without means to protect himself."

"Do you refer to your reputed wizardry?"

Palafox shook his head. "We are not magicians. But we have surprising weapons at our command."

Bustamonte surveyed the brown and gray costume which afforded no scope for concealment. "Whatever your weapons, they are not now in evidence."

"I hope not."

Bustamonte drew the black cloak over his knees. "Let us put ambiguity aside."

"Gladly."

"I control Pao. Therefore I call myself Panarch. What do you say to that?"

"I say that you have performed an exercise in practical logic. If you now bring Beran to me, the two of us will depart and leave you to the responsibilities of your office."

Bustamonte shook his head. "Impossible."

"Impossible? Not at all."

"Impossible for my purposes. Pao is ruled by continuity and tradition. Public emotion demands Beran's accession. He must die, before news of Aiello's death reaches the world."

Palafox thoughtfully fingered the black mark of his mustache. "In that case it is already too late."

Bustamonte froze. "What do you say?"

"Have you listened to the broadcast from Eiljanre? The announcer is speaking at this moment."

"How do you know?" demanded Bustamonte.

Palafox indicated the sound-control in the arm of Bustamonte's chair. "There is the means to prove me wrong."

Bustamonte thrust down the knob. A voice issued from the wall, thick with synthetic emotion. "Pao, grieve! All Pao, mourn! The great Aiello, our noble Panarch is gone! Dole, dole, dole! Bewildered we search the sad sky, and our hope, our only sustention in this tragic hour is Beran, the brave new Panarch! Only let his reign prove as static and glorious as that of great Aiello!"

Bustamonte swung upon Palafox like a small black bull. "How did the news get abroad?"

Palafox replied with easy carelessness. "I myself released it."

Bustamonte's eyes glittered. "When did you do this? You have been under constant surveillance."

"We Breakness dominie," said Palafox, "are not without subterfuge."

The voice from the wall droned on. "Acting under the orders of Panarch Beran, the Mamarone have efficiently subaqueated the responsible criminals. Ayudor Bustamonte is serving Beran with wholehearted loyalty, and will help maintain equilibrium."

Bustamonte's fury seethed to the surface. "Do you think you can thwart me by such a trick?" He signaled the Mamarone. "You wished to join Beran. So you shall—in life and, at tomorrow's first light, in death."

The guards were at Palafox's back. "Search this man!" cried Bustamonte. "Inspect him with care!"

The guards subjected Palafox to a most minute scrutiny. Every stitch of his clothes was examined; he was patted and prodded with complete lack of regard for dignity.

Nothing was discovered; no tool, weapon or instrument of any kind. Bustamonte watched the search in unashamed fascination, and seemed disappointed at the negative result.

"How is this?" he asked scornfully. "You, a Wizard of Breakness Institute! Where are the devices, the infallible implements, the mysterious energetics?"

Palafox, who had submitted to the search without emotion, replied in a pleasant voice, "Alas, Bustamonte, I am not at liberty to answer your questions."

Bustamonte laughed coarsely. He motioned to the guard. "Take him to confinement."

The neutraloids seized Palafox's arms.

"One final word," said Palafox, "for you will not see me again on Pao."

Bustamonte agreed. "Of this I am sure."

"I came at Aiello's wish to negotiate a contract."

"A dastardly mission!" Bustamonte exclaimed.

"Rather an exchange of surpluses to satisfy each of our needs," said Palafox. "My wisdom for your population. It is a sensible offer."

"I have no time for abstruseness." Bustamonte motioned to the guards. They urged Palafox toward the door.

"Allow me my say," spoke Palafox gently. The guards paid him no heed. Palafox made a small twitch; the neutraloids cried out and sprang away from him.

"What's this?" cried Bustamonte, jumping to his feet.

"He burns! He radiates fire!"

Palafox spoke in his quiet voice, "As I say, we will not meet again on Pao. But you will need me, and Aiello's bargain will seem very reasonable. And then you must come to Breakness." He bowed to Bustamonte, turned to the guards. "Come, now we will go."

CHAPTER IV

Beran sat with his chin on the window sill, looking out into the night. The surf phosphoresced on the beach, the stars hung in great frosty clots. Nothing else could be seen.

The room was high in the tower; it seemed very dreary and bleak. The walls were bare fiber; the window was heavy cleax; the door fitted into the aperture without a seam. Beran knew the room for what it was—a confinement chamber.

A faint sound came from below, the husky grunting of a neutraloid's laugh. Beran was sure that they were laughing at him, at the miserable finale to his existence. Tears rose to his eyes but in the fashion of Paonese children he made no other show of emotion.

There was a sound at the door. The lock whirred, the door slid back. In the opening stood two neutraloids and, between them, Lord Palafox.

Beran came hopefully forward—but the attitudes of the three halted him. The neutraloids shoved Palafox forward. The door whirred shut. Beran stood in the center of the room, crestfallen and dejected.

Palafox glanced around the room, seeming instantly to appraise every detail. He put his ear to the door, listened, then took three long elastic strides to the window. He looked out. Nothing to be seen, only stars and surf. He touched his tongue to a key area on the inside of his cheek; an infinitesimal voice, that of the Eiljanre announcer, spoke inside his inner ear. The voice was excited. "Word has reached us from Ayudor Bustamonte on Pergolai: serious events! In the treacherous attack upon Panarch Aiello, the Medallion was likewise injured, and his survival is not at all likely! The most expert doctors of Pao are in constant attendance. Ayudor Bustamonte asks that all join to project a wave of hope for the stricken Medallion!"

Palafox extinguished the sound with a second touch of his tongue; he turned to Beran, motioned. Beran came a step or two closer. Palafox bent to his ear, whispered, "We're in danger. Whatever we say is heard. Don't talk. Just watch me—and move quickly when I give the signal!"

Beran nodded. Palafox made a second inspection of the room, rather more slowly than before. As he went about his survey, a section of the door became transparent; an eye peered through.

In sudden annoyance Palafox raised his hand, then restrained himself. After a moment the eye disappeared, the wall became once more opaque.

Palafox sprang to the window; he pointed his forefinger. A needle of incandescence darted forth, cut a hissing slot through the cleax. The window fell loose, and before Palafox could catch it, disappeared into the darkness.

Palafox whispered, "Over here now! Quick!" Beran hesitated. "Quick!" whispered Palafox. "Do you want to live? Up on my back, quick!"

From below came the thud of feet, voices growing louder.

A moment later the door slid back; three Mamarone stood in the doorway. They stopped, stared all around, then ran to the open window.

The captain turned. "Below, to the grounds! It's deep water for all if they have escaped!"

When they searched the gardens they found no trace of Palafox or Beran. Standing in the starlight, darker than the darkness, they argued in their soft voices, and presently reached a decision. Their voices ceased; they themselves slid away through the night.

CHAPTER V

Any collocation of persons, no matter how numerous, how scant, how even their homogeneity, how firmly they profess common doctrine, will presently reveal themselves to consist of smaller groups espousing variant versions of the common creed; and these sub-groups will manifest sub-sub-groups, and so to the final limit of the single individual, and even in this single person conflicting tendencies will express themselves.

—Adam Ostwald: *Human Society.*

The Paonese, in spite of their fifteen billion, comprised as undifferentiated a group as could be found in the human universe. Nevertheless, to the Paonese the traits in common were taken for granted and only the distinctions, minuscule though they were, attracted attention.

In this fashion the people of Minamand—and especially those in the capital city of Eiljanre—were held to be urbane and frivolous. Hivand, flattest and most featureless of the continents, exemplified bucolic naïveté. The people of Nonamand, the bleak continent to the south, bore the reputation of dour thrift and fortitude; while the inhabitants of Vidamand, who grew grapes and fruits, and bottled almost all the wine of Pao, were considered large-hearted and expansive.

For many years, Bustamonte had maintained a staff of secret informants, stationed through the eight continents. Early in the morning, walking the airy gallery of the Pergolai lodge, he was beset by worry. Events were not proceeding at their optimum. Only three of the eight continents seemed to be accepting him as de facto Panarch. These were Vidamand, Minamand and Dronamand. From Aimand, Shraimand, Nonamand, Hivand and Impland, his agents reported a growing tide of recalcitrance.

There was no suggestion of active rebellion, no parades or public meetings. Paonese dissatisfaction expressed itself in surliness, a work-slowdown throughout the public services, dwindling cooperation with the civil service. It was a situation which in the past had led to a breakdown of the economy and a change of dynasty.

Bustamonte cracked his knuckles nervously as he considered his position. At the moment he was committed to a course of action. The Medallion must die, and likewise the Breakness Wizard.

Daylight had come; now they could properly be executed.

He descended to the main floor, signaled to one of the Mamarone. "Summon Captain Mornune."

Several minutes passed. The neutraloid returned.

"Where is Mornune?" demanded Bustamonte.

"Captain Mornune and two of the platoon have departed Pergolai."

Bustamonte wheeled around, dumbfounded. "Departed Pergolai?"

"This is my information."

Bustamonte glared at the guard, then looked toward the tower. "Come along!" He charged for the lift; the two were whisked high. Bustamonte marched down the corridor, to the confinement chamber. He peered through the spy-hole, looked all around the room. Then he furiously slid aside the door, crossed to the open window.

"It is all clear now," he ranted. "Beran is gone. The dominie is gone. Both are fled to Eiljanre. There will be trouble."

He went to the window, stood looking out into the distance. Finally he turned. "Your name is Andrade?"

"Hessenden Andrade."

"You are now Captain Andrade, in the place of Mornune."

"Very well."

"We return to Eiljanre. Make the necessary arrangements."

Bustamonte descended to the terrace, seated himself with a glass of brandy. Palafox clearly intended Beran to become Panarch. The Paonese loved a young Panarch and demanded the smooth progression of the dynasty; anything else disturbed their need for timeless continuity. Beran need only appear at Eiljanre, to be led triumphantly to the Great Palace, and arrayed in Utter Black.

Bustamonte took a great gulp of brandy. Well then, he had failed. Aiello was dead. Bustamonte could never demonstrate that Beran's hand had placed the fatal sting. Indeed, had not three Mercantil traders been executed for the very crime?

What to do? Actually, he had no choice. He could only proceed to Eiljanre and hope to establish himself as Ayudor-Senior, regent for Beran. Unless guided too firmly by Palafox, Beran would probably overlook his imprisonment; and if Palafox were intransigent, there were ways of dealing with him.

Bustamonte rose to his feet. Back to Eiljanre, there to eat humble-pie; he had spent many years playing sycophant to Aiello, and the experience would stand him in good stead.

In the hours and days that followed, Bustamonte encountered three surprises of increasing magnitude.

The first was the discovery that neither Palafox nor Beran had arrived at Eiljanre, nor did they appear elsewhere on Pao. Bustamonte, at first cautious and tentative, began to breathe easier. Had the pair met with some unforeseen disaster? Had Palafox kidnapped the Medallion for reasons of his own?

The doubt was unsettling. Until he was assured of Beran's death he could not properly enjoy the perquisites of the Panarch's office. Likewise, the doubt had infected the vast Paonese masses. Daily their recalcitrance increased; Bustamonte's informers reported that everywhere he was known as Bustamonte Bereglo. 'Bereglo' was a word typically Paonese, applied to an unskillful slaughter-house worker, or a creature which worries and gnaws its victim.

Bustamonte seethed inwardly, but comforted himself with outward rectitude, hoping either that the population would accept him as Panarch or that Beran would appear to give the lie to rumors, and submit to a more definite assassination.

Then came the second unsettling shock.

The Mercantil Ambassador delivered Bustamonte a statement which first excoriated the Paonese government for the summary execution of the three trade attachés, broke off all trade relations until indemnification was paid, and set forth the required indemnification—a sum which seemed ridiculously large to a Paonese ruler, who every day in the course of his duties might ordain death for a hundred thousand persons.

Bustamonte had been hoping to negotiate a new armament contract. As he had advised Aiello, he offered a premium for sole rights to the most advanced weapons. The note from the Mercantil Ambassador destroyed all hope of a new agreement.

The third shock was the most devastating of all, and indeed reduced the first two to the proportion of incidents.

The Brumbo Clan of Batmarsh, elevated to primacy over a score of restless competitors, needed a glory-earning coup to cement its position. Eban Buzbek, Hetman of the Brumbos, therefore gathered a hundred ships, loaded them with warriors and set forth against the great world of Pao.

Perhaps he had only intended a foray: a landing, a vast orgiastic assault, a quick garnering of booty, and departure—but passing the outer ring of monitors he met only token resistance, and landing on Vidamand, the most disaffected continent, none at all. This was success of the wildest description!

Eban Buzbek took his ten thousand men to Donaspara, first city of Shraimand; and there was no one to dispute him. Six days after he landed on Pao he entered Eiljanre. The populace watched him and his glory-flushed army with sullen eyes; none made any resistance, even when their property was taken and their women violated. Warfare—

even hit-and-run guerilla tactics—was not in the Paonese character. They had relied on the Mamarone for protection, but Bustamonte had prudently departed the capital; there had been confusion and disorganization, and the Mamarone, although completely fearless, lacked initiative and were never called into action.

In any event only a small percentage of the population was touched by the Batch conquest; the others thought their deep slow thoughts and the rhythm of Paonese life proceeded much as before.

CHAPTER VI

Beran, Medallion and son of Panarch Aiello, had lived his life under the most uneventful circumstances. With his diet carefully prescribed and scheduled, he never had known hunger and so had never enjoyed food. His play was supervised by a corps of trained gymnasts and was considered 'exercise'; consequently he had no inclination for games. His person was tended and groomed, every obstacle and danger was whisked from his path; he had never faced a challenge, and had never known triumph.

Sitting on Palafox's shoulders, stepping out through the window into the night, Beran felt as if he were living a nightmare. A sudden weightlessness—they were falling! His stomach contracted, the breath rose in his throat. He squirmed and cried out in fear. Falling, falling, falling; when would they strike?

"Quiet," said Palafox shortly.

Beran's eyes focused. He blinked. A lighted window moved past his vision. It passed below; they were not falling; they were rising! They were above the tower, above the pavilion! Up into the night they drifted, light as bubbles, up above the tower, up into the star-bright sky. Presently, Beran convinced himself that he was not dreaming; it was therefore through the magic of the Breakness wizard that they wafted through the middle-air, light as thistle-down. As his wonder grew, his fear lessened, and he peered into Palafox's face. "Where are we going?"

"Up to where I anchored my ship."

Beran looked wistfully down to the pavilion. It glowed in many colors, like a sea-anemone. He had no wish to return; there was only a vague regret. Up into the sky they floated, for fifteen quiet minutes, and the pavilion became a colored blot far below. His eyes flooded with tears; he lapsed into a state of apathy, hardly caring what happened to him.

Palafox held out his left hand; impulses from the radar-mesh in his palm were reflected back from the ground, converted into stimulus. High enough. Palafox touched his tongue to one of the plates in the tissue of his cheek, spoke a sharp syllable.

Moments passed; Palafox and Beran floated like wraiths. Then a long shape came to blot out the sky. Palafox reached, caught a hand-rail, swung himself and Beran along a hull to an entrance hatch. He pushed Beran into a staging chamber, followed and closed the hatch.

Interior lights glowed.

Beran, too dazed to take an interest in events, sagged upon a bench. He watched Palafox mount to a raised deck, flick at a pair of keys. The sky went dull, and Beran was caught in the pulse of sub-space motion.

Palafox came down from the platform, inspected Beran with dispassionate appraisal. Beran could not meet his gaze.

"Where are we going?" asked Beran, not because he cared, but because he could think of nothing better to say.

"To Breakness."

Beran's heart took a queer jump. "Why must I go?"

"Because now you are Panarch. If you remained on Pao, Bustamonte would kill you."

Beran recognized the truth of the statement. He felt bleak, lost, forlorn. He knew nothing of Breakness, except what had been conveyed by the attitudes and voice-tones of others. The image so formed in his mind was not reassuring.

He stole a look at Palafox—a man far different from the quiet stranger at Aiello's table. This Palafox was tall as a fire-demon, magnificent with pent energy. A wizard, a Breakness wizard!

Palafox glanced down at Beran. "How old are you, boy?"

"Nine years old."

Palafox rubbed his long chin. "It is best that you learn what is to be expected of you. In essence, the program is uncomplicated. You will live on Breakness, you shall attend the Institute, you shall be my ward, and the time will come when you serve me as one of my own sons."

"Are your sons my age?" Beran asked hopefully.

"I have many sons!" said Palafox with grim pride. "I count them by the hundreds!" Becoming aware of Beran's bemused attention, he laughed humorlessly. "There is much here that you do not understand...Why do you stare?"

Beran said apologetically, "If you have so many children you must be old, much older than you look."

Palafox's face underwent a peculiar change. The cheeks suffused with red, the eyes glittered like bits of glass. His voice was slow, icy cold. "I am not old. Never make such a remark again. It is an ill thing to say to a Breakness dominie!"

"I'm sorry!" quavered Beran. "I thought…"

"No matter. Come, you are tired, you shall sleep."

Beran listlessly rose to his feet.

Palafox, displaying neither kindliness nor severity, lifted him into a bunk. Heat rays warmed Beran's skin; turning his face to the dark-blue bulkhead, he fell asleep.

Beran awoke in puzzlement to find himself not in his pink and black bed. After contemplating his position, he felt relatively cheerful. The future promised to be interesting, and when he returned to Pao he would be equipped with all the secret lore of Breakness.

He rose from the bunk, shared breakfast with Palafox, who seemed to be in high spirits. Beran took sufficient courage to put to him a few further inquiries. "Are you actually a wizard?"

"I can perform no miracles," said Palafox, "except perhaps those of the mind."

"But you walk on air! You shoot fire from your finger!"

"As does any other Breakness dominie."

Beran looked wonderingly at the long keen visage. "Then you are all wizards?"

"Bah!" exclaimed Palafox. "These powers are the result of bodily modification. I am highly modified."

Beran's awe became tinged with doubt. "The Mamarone are modified, but…"

Palafox grinned down at Beran like a wolf. "This is the least apt comparison. Can neutraloids walk on air?"

"No."

"We are not neutraloids," said Palafox decisively. "Our modifications enhance rather than eliminate our powers. Anti-gravity web is meshed into the skin of my feet. Radar in my left hand, at the back of my neck, in my forehead provides me with a sixth sense. I can see three colors below the red and four over the violet. I can hear radio waves. I can walk under water, I can float in space. Instead of bone in my forefinger, I carry a projection tube. I have a number of other powers, all drawing energy from a pack fitted into my chest."

Beran was silent for a moment. Then he asked diffidently, "When I come to Breakness, will I be modified too?"

Palafox considered Beran as if in the light of a new idea. "If you do exactly as I say you must do."

Beran turned his head. "What must I do?" he asked in a restrained voice.

"For the present, you need not concern yourself."

Beran went to the port and looked out, but nothing could be seen but speed-striations of gray and black. "How long before we reach Breakness?" he asked.

"Not so very long…Come away from the port. Looking into sub-space can harm a susceptible brain."

Indicators on the control panel vibrated and fluttered; the space-boat gave a quick lurch.

Palafox stepped up to look from the observation dome. "Here is Breakness!"

Beran, standing on his tiptoes, saw a gray world, and behind, a small white sun. The space-boat whistled down into the atmosphere, and the world grew large.

Beran glimpsed mountains enormous beyond imagination: claws of rock forty miles high trailing plumes of vapor, rimed by ice and snow. The boat slipped across a gray-green ocean, mottled by clumps of float-ing weed, then once more rode over the crags.

The boat, now moving slowly, dipped into a vast valley with rock-slab walls and a bottom hidden by haze and murk. Ahead a rocky slope, wide as a prairie, showed a trifle of gray-white crust. The boat approached, and the crust became a small city clinging to the shoulder of the mountain-side. The buildings were low, constructed of rock-melt with roofs of russet brown; some of them joined and hung down the crag like a chain. The effect was bleak and not at all imposing.

"Is that Breakness?" asked Beran.

"That is Breakness Institute," said Palafox.

Beran was vaguely disappointed. "I had expected something different."

"We make no pretensions," Palafox remarked. "There are, after all, a very few dominie. And we see very little of each other."

Beran started to speak, then hesitated, sensing that he was touching upon a sensitive subject. In a cautious voice he asked, "Do your sons all live with you?"

"No," said Palafox shortly. "They attend the Institute, naturally."

The boat sank slowly; the indicators on the control board fluttered and jumped as if alive.

Beran, looking across the chasm, remembered the verdant landscape and blue seas of his homeland with a pang. "When will I go back to Pao?" he asked in sudden anxiety.

Palafox, his mind on other matters, answered offhandedly. "As soon as conditions warrant."

"But when will that be?"

Palafox looked swiftly down at him. "Do you want to be Panarch of Pao?"

"Yes," said Beran decidedly. "If I could be modified."

"Perhaps you may be granted these wishes. But you must never forget that he who gets must give."

"What must I give?"

"We will discuss this matter later."

"Bustamonte will not welcome me," said Beran gloomily. "I think he wants to be Panarch too."

Palafox laughed. "Bustamonte is having his troubles. Rejoice that Bustamonte must cope with them and not you."

CHAPTER VII

Bustamonte's troubles were large. His dreams of grandeur were exploded. Instead of ruling the eight continents of Pao and holding court at Eiljanre, his retinue consisted of a dozen Mamarone, three of his least desirable concubines, and a dozen disgruntled officials of magisterial rank. His realm was a remote village on the rain-swept moors of Nonamand; his palace a tavern. He enjoyed these prerogatives only on the sufferance of the Brumbos who, enjoying the fruits of their conquest, felt no great urge to seek out and destroy Bustamonte.

A month passed. Bustamonte's temper grew short. He beat the concubines, berated his followers. The shepherds of the region took to avoiding the village; the innkeeper and the villagers every day became more taciturn, until one morning Bustamonte awoke to find the village deserted, the moors desolate of flocks.

Bustamonte despatched half the neutraloids to forage for food, but they never returned. The ministers openly made plans to return to a more hospitable environment. Bustamonte argued and promised, but the Paonese mind was not easily amenable to any sort of persuasion.

Early one dreary morning the remaining neutraloids decamped. The concubines refused to bestir themselves, but sat huddled together, sniffling with head colds. All forenoon a miserable rain fell; the tavern became dank. Bustamonte ordered Est Coelho, Minister of Inter-Continental Transport, to arrange a blaze in the fireplace, but Coelho was in no mood to truckle to Bustamonte. Tempers seethed, boiled over; as a result the entire group of ministers marched forth into the rain and set out for the coastal port of Spyrianthe.

The three women stirred, looked after the ministers, then like a single creature, turned to look slyly toward Bustamonte. He was alert. At the expression on his face, they sighed and groaned.

Cursing and panting Bustamonte broke up the tavern furniture and built a roaring blaze in the fireplace.

There was a sound from outside, a faint chorus of yells, a wild *Rip-rip-rip!*

Bustamonte's heart sank, his jaw sagged. This was the hunting chivvy of the Brumbos, the clan call.

The yelling and *rip-rip-rip!* grew keener, and finally came down the single street of the village.

Bustamonte wrapped a cloak about his stocky frame, went to the door, flung it open, stepped out upon the cobbles.

Down the road from the moors came his ministers at a staggering lope. Above, a dozen warriors of the Brumbo Clan rode air-horses, cavorting, whooping and shouting, herding the ministers like sheep. At the sight of Bustamonte they screamed in triumph, swung down, grounded their air-horses, sprang forward, each anxious to be first to lay hands on the nape of Bustamonte's neck.

Bustamonte retreated into the doorway, resolved to die with dignity intact. He brought out his wasp, and blood would have flowed had not the Batch warriors stood back.

Down flew Eban Buzbek himself, a wiry jug-eared little man, his yellow hair plaited into a foot-long queue. The keel of his air-horse clattered along the cobbles; the tubes sighed and sputtered.

Eban Buzbek marched forward, pushed through the sobbing huddle of ministers, reached to seize Bustamonte by the nape and force him to his knees. Bustamonte backed further into the doorway, pointed his wasp. But the Brumbo warriors were quick; their shock-pistols bellowed;

Bustamonte was buffeted against the wall. Eban Buzbek seized him by the neck and hurled him into the mud of the street.

Bustamonte slowly picked himself up to stand shaking in rage.

Eban Buzbek waved his hand. Bustamonte was seized, trussed with belts, rolled into a net. Without further ado, the Brumbos climbed into the saddles and rode through the sky, with Bustamonte hanging below like a pig for the market.

At Spyrianthe the group transferred into a domed air-ship. Bustamonte, dazed from the buffeting wind, half-dead of chill, slipped to the deck, and knew nothing of the trip back to Eiljanre.

The air-ship landed in the court of the Grand Palace; Bustamonte was hustled through the ravaged halls and locked in a sleeping-chamber.

Early the next day two women servants roused him. They cleaned him of mud and grime, dressed him in clean clothes, brought him food and drink.

An hour later the door opened; a clansman signaled. Bustamonte came forth, pallid, nervous but still uncowed.

He was taken to a morning room overlooking the famous palace florarium. Here Eban Buzbek waited with a group of his clansmen and a Mercantil interpreter. He seemed in the best of spirits, and nodded jovially when Bustamonte appeared. He spoke a few words in the staccato language of Batmarsh; the Mercantil translated.

"Eban Buzbek hopes you have passed a restful night."

"What does he want of me?" growled Bustamonte.

The message was translated. Eban Buzbek replied at considerable length. The Mercantil listened attentively, then turned to Bustamonte.

"Eban Buzbek returns to Batmarsh. He says the Paonese are sullen and stubborn. They refuse to cooperate as a defeated people should."

The news came as no surprise to Bustamonte.

"Eban Buzbek is disappointed in Pao. He says the people are turtles, in that they will neither fight nor obey. He takes no satisfaction in his conquest."

Bustamonte glowered at the pig-tailed clansman slouching in the Black Chair.

"Eban Buzbek departs and leaves you as Panarch of Pao. For this favor you must pay one million marks each Paonese month for the duration of your reign. Do you agree to the arrangement?"

Bustamonte looked from face to face. No one looked at him directly; the expressions were empty. But each warrior seemed peculiarly taut, like runners crouched at the start of a race.

"Do you agree to the arrangement?" the Mercantil repeated.

"Yes," muttered Bustamonte. There was an imperceptible rustle of motion around the room; a regretful relaxation.

The Mercantil translated. Eban Buzbek made a sign of assent, rose to his feet. A piper bent to his *diplonet*, blew a brisk march. Eban Buzbek and his warriors departed the hall without so much as a glance for Bustamonte.

An hour later, Buzbek's red and black corvette knifed up and away; before the day's end no single clansman remained on Pao.

With a tremendous effort Bustamonte asserted his dignity, and assumed the title and authority of Panarch. His fifteen billion subjects, diverted by the Batch invasion, showed no further recalcitrance; and in this respect Bustamonte profited from the incursion.

CHAPTER VIII

Beran's first weeks on Breakness were dismal and unhappy. There was no variety, inside or out; all was rock-color, in varying tones and intensities, and the look of distance. The wind roared incessantly, but air was thin, and the effort of breathing left an acrid burn in Beran's throat. Like a small pale house-sprite, he wandered the chilly corridors of Palafox's mansion, hoping for diversion, finding little.

The typical residence of a Breakness dominie, Palafox's house hung down the slope on the spine of an escalator. At the top were workrooms not permitted to Beran, but where he glimpsed marvellously intricate mechanisms. Below were rooms of general function panelled in dark board, with floors of russet rock-melt, generally unoccupied except for Beran. At the bottom, separated from the main chain of rooms was a large circular structure, which Beran eventually discovered to be Palafox's private dormitory.

The house was austere and chilly, without devices of amusement or ornament. No one heeded Beran; it was as if his very existence were forgotten. He ate from a buffet in the central hall, he slept where and when it suited him. He learned to recognize half a dozen men who seemed to make Palafox's house their headquarters. Once or twice in the lower part of the house he glimpsed a woman. No one spoke to him except Palafox, but Beran saw him only rarely.

On Pao there was small distinction between the sexes; both wore similar garments and enjoyed identical privileges. Here the differences were emphasized. Men wore dark suits of close-fitting fabric and black skull-caps with pointed bills. Those women whom Beran had glimpsed wore flouncing skirts of gay colors—the only color to be seen on Breakness—tight vests which left the midriff uncovered, slippers tinkling with bells. Their heads were uncovered, their hair was artfully dressed; all were young and handsome.

When he could tolerate the house no longer, Beran bundled himself into warm garments and ventured out on the mountainside. He bent his head into the wind and pushed to the east until he reached the verge of the settlement, where the Wind River dwindled in mighty perspective. A mile below were a half dozen large structures: automatic fabrication plants. Above reared the rock slope, far up to the gray sky, where the wild little white sun swerved like a tin disc on the wind. Beran retraced his steps.

A week later he ventured forth again, and this time turned west with the wind at his back. A lane melted from the rock wound and twisted among dozens of long houses like that of Palafox, and other lanes veered off at angles, until Beran became concerned lest he lose his way.

He halted within sight of Breakness Institute, a group of bleak buildings stepped down the slope. They were several stories high, taller than other buildings of the settlement, and received the full force of the wind. Streaks of sooty gray and black-green ran across the gray rock-melt, where years of driven rime and sleet had left their marks.

As he stood, a group of boys several years older than himself came up the road from the Institute; they swerved up the hill, marching in a solemn line, apparently bound for the space-port.

Curious! thought Beran. How unsmiling and silent they seemed. Paonese lads would have been skipping and skylarking.

He found his way back to Palafox's manse, puzzling over the lack of social intercourse on Breakness.

❂

The novelty of life on the new planet had worn smooth; the pangs of homesickness stabbed Beran hard. He sat on the settee in the hall tying aimless knots in a bit of string. There was the sound of footsteps; Beran looked up. Palafox entered the hall, began to pass through, then noticed Beran and came to a halt. "Well, the young Panarch of Pao—why do you sit so quietly?"

"I have nothing to do."

Palafox nodded. The Paonese were not ones to undertake gratuitously any arduous intellectual program; and Palafox had intended that Beran should become utterly bored, to provide incentive for the task.

"Nothing to do?" inquired Palafox, as if surprised. "Well, we must remedy that." He appeared to cogitate. "If you are to attend the Institute, you must learn the language of Breakness."

Beran was suddenly aggrieved. "When do I go back to Pao?" he asked querulously.

Palafox shook his head solemnly. "I doubt if you'd wish to return at this moment."

"But I do!"

Palafox seated himself beside Beran. "Have you heard of the Brumbos of Batmarsh?"

"Batmarsh is a small planet three stars from Pao inhabited by quarrelsome people."

"Correct. The Batch are divided into twenty-three clans, which continually compete in valor. The Brumbos, who are one of these clans, have invaded Pao."

Beran heard the news without total comprehension. "Do you mean…"

"Pao is now the personal province of Eban Buzbek, Hetman of the Brumbos. Ten thousand clansmen in a few painted war-ships took all Pao, and your uncle Bustamonte lives in forlorn circumstances."

"What will happen now?"

Palafox laughed shortly. "Who knows? But it is best that you remain on Breakness. Your life would be worth nothing on Pao."

"I don't want to stay here. I don't like Breakness."

"No?" Palafox pretended surprise. "Why is that?"

"Everything is different from Pao. There isn't any sea, no trees, no…"

"Naturally!" exclaimed Palafox. "We have no trees, but we have Breakness Institute. Now you will start learning, and then you'll find Breakness more interesting. First, the language of Breakness! We start at once. Come!" He rose to his feet. Beran's interest in the Breakness language was minuscule, but activity of any kind would be welcome—as Palafox had foreseen.

Palafox stalked to the escalator, with Beran behind; they rode to the top of the house—rooms heretofore barred to Beran—and entered a wide workshop exposed to the gray-white sky through a ceiling of glass. A young man in a skin-tight suit of dark brown, one of Palafox's many sons, looked up from his work. He was thin and taut, his features hard and bold. He resembled Palafox to a marked degree, even to tricks of gesture and poise of head. Palafox could take pride in such evidence of genetic vigor, which tended to shape all of his sons into near-simulacra of himself. On Breakness, status was based on a quality best described as 'creative and procreative efficacy', the forcible imprinting of self upon the future. For this reason there existed between high-status dominie and their sons a paradoxical discord of empathy, which tended to draw them close—and antagonism, which thrust them apart.

Between Palafox and Fanchiel, the young man in the dark brown suit, neither empathy nor hostility evinced itself openly: indeed the emotion was so all-pervasive throughout the houses, dormitories, and halls of the Institute as to be taken for granted.

Fanchiel had been tinkering with a minute fragment of mechanism clamped in a vise. He watched a magnified three-dimensional image of the device on a stage at eye-level; he wore gauntlets controlling micro-tools, and easily manipulated components invisible to the naked eye. At the sight of Palafox, he rose from his work, subordinating himself to the more intense ego of his progenitor.

The two men spoke in the language of Breakness for several minutes. Beran began to hope that he had been forgotten—then Palafox snapped his fingers. "This is Fanchiel, thirty-third of my sons. He will teach you much that is useful. I urge you to industry, enthusiasm and application—not after the Paonese fashion, but like the student at Breakness Institute, which we hope you shall become." He departed without further words.

Fanchiel unenthusiastically put aside his work. "Come," he said in Paonese, and led the way into an adjoining room.

"First—a preliminary discussion." He pointed to a desk of gray metal with a black rubber top. "Sit there, if you please."

Beran obeyed. Fanchiel appraised him carefully, without regard for Beran's sensibilities. Then, with the faintest of shrugs, he dropped his own taut-muscled body into a chair.

"Our first concern," he said, "will be the language of Breakness."

Accumulated resentments suddenly merged inside Beran: the neglect, the boredom, the homesickness, and now this last cavalier disregard for his personal individuality. All contributed to a spasm of sullen Paonese obstinacy. He lowered his head, tightened his mouth.

"I don't care to learn Breakness. I want to return to Pao."

Fanchiel seemed vaguely amused. "In time you certainly will return to Pao—perhaps as Panarch. If you returned at this moment you would be killed."

Beran's eyes stung with loneliness and misery. "When can I go back?"

"I don't know," said Fanchiel. "Lord Palafox is undertaking some great plan in connection with Pao—you will undoubtedly return when he thinks best. In the meanwhile, you would do well to accept such advantages as are offered you."

Beran's reason and native willingness to oblige struggled with the obstinacy of his race. "Why must I go to the Institute?"

Fanchiel replied with ingenuous candor. "Lord Palafox apparently intends that you should identify with Breakness and so feel sympathetic to his goals."

Beran could not grasp this; however, he was impressed by Fanchiel's manner. "What will I learn at the Institute?"

"A thousand things—more than I can describe to you. In the College of Comparative Culture—where Lord Palafox is Dominie—you will study the races of the universe, their similarities and differences, their languages and basic urges, the specific symbols by which you can influence them.

"In the College of Mathematics you learn the manipulation of abstract ideas, various systems of rationality—likewise you are trained to make quick mental calculations.

"In the College of Human Anatomy you learn geriatry and death prevention, pharmacology, the technique of human modification and augmentation—and possibly you will be allowed one or two modifications."

Beran's imagination was stimulated. "Could I be modified like Palafox?"

"Ha hah!" exclaimed Fanchiel. "This is an amusing idea. Are you aware that Lord Palafox is one of the most powerfully modified men of Breakness? He controls nine sensitivities, four energies, three projections, two nullifications, three lethal emanations, in addition to miscellaneous powers such as the mental slide-rule, the ability to survive in a de-oxygenated atmosphere, anti-fatigue glands, a sub-clavicle blood chamber which automatically counteracts any poison he may have ingested. No, my ambitious young friend!" For an instant the jutting features became soft with amusement. "But if ever you rule

Pao, you will control a world full of fecund girls, and thus you may command every modification known to the surgeons and anatomists of Breakness Institute."

Beran looked blankly at Fanchiel, quite at a loss. Modification, even under these incomprehensible but questionable terms, seemed a long way in the future.

Fanchiel paused an instant, then said briskly, "And now, to our first concern, the language of Breakness."

With the prospect of modification removed to the far future, Beran's obstinacy returned. "Why can't we speak Paonese?"

Fanchiel explained patiently. "You will be required to learn a great deal that you could not understand if I taught in Paonese."

"I understand you now," muttered Beran.

"Because we are discussing the most general ideas. Each language is a special tool, with a particular capability. It is more than a means of communication, it is a system of thought. Do you understand what I mean?"

Fanchiel found his answer in Beran's expression.

"Think of a language as the contour of a watershed, stopping flow in certain directions, channeling it into others. Language controls the mechanism of your mind. When people speak different languages, their minds work differently and they act differently. For instance: you know of the planet Vale?"

"Yes. The world where all the people are insane."

"Better to say, their actions give the impression of insanity. Actually they are complete anarchists. Now if we examine the speech of Vale we find, if not a reason for the behavior, at least a parallelism. Language on Vale is personal improvisation, with the fewest possible conventions. Each individual selects a speech as you or I might choose the color of our garments."

Beran frowned. "We Paonese are not careless in such matters. Our dress is established, and no one would wear a costume unfamiliar to him, or one which might cause misunderstanding."

A smile broke the austere cast of Fanchiel's face. "True, true; I forgot. The Paonese make no virtue of conspicuous dress. And—possibly as a corollary—mental abnormality is rare. The Paonese, fifteen billion of them, are pleasantly sane. Not so the people of Vale. They live to complete spontaneity—in clothes, in conduct, in language. The question arises: does the language provoke or merely reflect the eccentricity? Which came first: the language or the conduct?"

Beran admitted himself at a loss.

"In any event," said Fanchiel, "now that you have been shown the connection between language and conduct, you will be anxious to learn the language of Breakness."

Beran was unflatteringly dubious. "Would I then become like you?"

Fanchiel asked sardonically, "A fate to be avoided at all costs? I can relieve your anxiety. All of us change as we learn, but you can never become a true man of Breakness. Long ago you were shaped into the Paonese style. But speaking our language, you will understand us—and if you can think as another man thinks, you cannot dislike him. Now, if you are ready, we commence."

CHAPTER IX

On Pao there was peace and the easy flow of life. The population tilled their farms, fished the oceans, and in certain districts sieved great wads of pollen from the air, to make a pleasant honey-tasting cake. Every eighth day was market day; on the eight-times-eighth day, the people gathered for the drones; on the eight-times-eight-times-eighth day, occurred the continental fairs.

The people had abandoned all opposition to Bustamonte. Defeat at the hands of the Brumbos was forgotten; Bustamonte's taxes were easier than those of Aiello, and he ruled with a lack of ostentation befitting his ambiguous accession to the Black.

But Bustamonte's satisfaction at the attainment of his ambition was not complete. A dozen aspects of his new life exasperated him; fears he had never suspected affected him with an intense disquiet. An impulsive man, his reaction to these unpleasant stimuli was often more violent than the occasion demanded. He was by no means a coward, but personal safety became an obsession; a dozen casual visitors who chanced to make abrupt motions were exploded by Mamarone hammer-guns. Bustamonte likewise imagined himself the subject of contemptuous jest, and other dozens lost their lives for displaying a merry expression when Bustamonte's eye happened to fall upon them. The bitterest circumstance of all was the tribute to Eban Buzbek, Hetman of the Brumbos.

Each month Bustamonte framed a stinging defiance to send Eban Buzbek in lieu of the million marks, but each month caution prevailed; Bustamonte, in helpless rage, despatched the tribute.

Four years passed; then one morning a red, black and yellow courier ship arrived at the Eiljanre spaceport, to discharge Cormoran Benbarth, scion of a junior branch of the Buzbeks. He presented himself at the Grand Palace as an absentee landlord might visit an outlying farm and greeted Bustamonte with casual amiability.

Bustamonte, wearing the Utter Black, maintained an expressionless face with great effort. He made the ceremonial inquiry: "What fortunate wind casts you upon our shores?"

Cormoran Benbarth, a tall young bravo with braided blond hair and magnificent blond mustaches, studied Bustamonte through eyes blue as cornflowers, wide and innocent as the Paonese sky.

"My mission is simple," he said. "I have come into possession of the North Faden Barony, which as you may or may not know is hard against the south countries of the Griffin Clan. I require funds for fortification and recruitment of followers."

"Ah," said Bustamonte. Cormoran Benbarth tugged at the drooping blond mustache.

"Eban Buzbek suggested that you might spare a million marks from your plenty, in order to incur my gratitude."

Bustamonte sat like an image of stone. His eyes held the innocent blue gaze for thirty seconds while his mind raced furiously. Submission to the extortion might entice an endless series of needy clansmen to the palace. The idea was intolerable. But could he deny this young brigand without fear of retaliation?

To Bustamonte's devious Paonese mind, it was inconceivable that the request could be anything other than a demand backed by an implicit threat of violence, to which he could offer no resistance. He threw up his arms in frustration, ordered forth the required sum and received Cormoran Benbarth's thanks in baleful silence.

Benbarth returned to Batmarsh in a mood of mild gratitude; Bustamonte's fury induced an abdominal acerbation, and his resolve to defy the Brumbos became the guiding force of his life.

* * *

Bustamonte spent moody weeks in reflection. It presently became clear that he must swallow his pride and petition those whose offices he had once rejected: the dominies of Breakness Institute.

Assuming the identity of an itinerant engineer, Bustamonte took passage to the depot planet Journal and there boarded a packet for the voyage through the outer Marklaides.

Presently he arrived at Breakness. A lighter came up to meet the packet. Bustamonte gratefully departed the cramped hull, and was conveyed down through gigantic crags to the Institute.

At the terminus he encountered none of the formalities which gave occupation to a numerous branch of the Paonese civil service; in fact he was given no notice whatever.

Bustamonte became vexed. He went to the portal, looked down across the city. To the left were factories and workshops, to the right the austere mass of the Institute, in between the various houses, manors and lodges, each with its appended dormitory.

A stern-faced young man—hardly more than a lad—tapped him on the arm, motioned him to the side. Bustamonte stepped back as a draft of twenty young women with hair pale as cream moved past him. They entered a scarab-shaped car, which slid away down-slope.

No other vehicle could be seen, and the terminal was now almost empty. Bustamonte, white with anger, the knobs of muscles twitching in his cheeks, at last admitted that either he was not expected, or that no one had thought to meet him. It was intolerable! He would command attention; it was his due!

He strode to the center of the terminus, and made imperious motions. One or two persons paused curiously, but when he commanded them in Paonese to fetch a responsible authority, they looked at him blankly and continued on their way.

Bustamonte ceased his efforts; the terminus was vacant except for himself. He recited one of the rolling Paonese curses, and went once more to the portal.

The settlement was naturally unfamiliar; the nearest house was a half-mile distant. Bustamonte glanced in alarm toward the sky. The little white sun had fallen behind the crag; a murky fog was flowing down Wind River; light was failing over the settlement.

Bustamonte heaved a deep breath. There was no help for it; the Panarch of Pao must tramp his way to shelter like a vagabond. Grimly he pushed open the door, and stepped forth.

The wind caught him, wheeled him down the lane; the cold ate through his thin Paonese garments. He turned, ran on his short thick legs down the lane.

Chilled to the bone, his lungs aching, he arrived at the first house. The rock-melt walls rose above him, bare of opening. He trudged along the face of the building, but could find no entrance; and so crying out in anguish and rage, he continued down the road.

The sky was dark; small pellets of sleet began to sting the back of his neck. He ran to another house, and this time found a door, but no one responded to his pounding. He turned away, shivering and shaking, feet numb, fingers aching. The gloom was now so thick he could barely distinguish the way.

Lights shone from windows of the third house; again no one responded to his pounding at the door. In fury Bustamonte seized a rock, threw it at the nearest window. The glass clanged: a satisfying noise. Bustamonte threw another rock, and at last attracted attention. The door opened; Bustamonte fell inside stiff as a toppling tree.

The young man caught him, dragged him to a seat. Bustamonte sat rigid, feet sprawled, eyes bulging, breath coming in sobs.

The man spoke; Bustamonte could not understand. "I am Bustamonte, Panarch of Pao," he said, the words coming blurred and fuzzy through his stiff lips. "This is an ill reception—someone shall pay dearly."

The young man, a son of the resident Dominie, had no acquaintance with Paonese. He shook his head, and seemed rather bored. He looked toward the door and back to Bustamonte, as if preparing to eject the unintelligible intruder.

"I am Panarch of Pao!" screamed Bustamonte. "Take me to Palafox, Lord Palafox, do you hear? Palafox!"

The name evoked a response. The man signaled Bustamonte to remain in his seat and disappeared into another room.

Ten minutes passed. The door opened, Palafox appeared. He bowed with bland punctilio. "Ayudor Bustamonte, it is a pleasure to see you. I was unable to meet you at the terminal, but I see that you have managed very well. My house is close at hand, and I would be pleased to offer you hospitality. Are you ready?"

The next morning Bustamonte took a tight check-rein on himself. Indignation could accomplish nothing, and might place him at embarrassing odds with his host, although—he looked contemptuously around the room—the hospitality was poor quality indeed. Why would men so knowledgeable build with such austerity? In point of fact, why would they inhabit so harsh a planet?

Palafox presented himself, and the two sat down to a table with a carafe of peppery tea between them. Palafox confined himself to bland platitudes. He ignored the unpleasantness of their last meeting on Pao, and showed no interest in the reason for Bustamonte's presence.

At last Bustamonte hitched himself forward and spoke to the point. "The late Panarch Aiello at one time sought your aid. He acted, as I see now, with foresight and wisdom. Therefore I have come in secrecy to Breakness to arrange a new contract between us."

Palafox nodded, sipping his tea without comment.

"The situation is this," said Bustamonte. "The accursed Brumbos exact a monthly tribute from me. I pay without pleasure—nevertheless I make no great complaint, for it comes cheaper than maintaining arms against them."

"The worst loser appears to be Mercantil," observed Palafox.

"Exactly!" said Bustamonte. "Recently, however, an additional extortion occurred. I fear it to be the forerunner of many more similar." Bustamonte described the visit of Cormoran Benbarth. "My treasury will be open to endless forays—I will become no more than a paymaster for all the bravos of Batmarsh. I refuse to submit to this ignoble subservience! I will free Pao: this is my mission! For this reason I come for counsel and strategic advice."

Palafox arranged his goblet of tea with a delicacy conveying an entire paragraph of meaning. "Advice is our only export. It is yours—at a price."

Bustamonte frowned. "And this price?" he asked, though he well knew.

Palafox settled himself more comfortably in his chair. "As you know this is a world of men, and so has been since the founding of the Institute. But necessarily we persist, we sire offspring, we rear our sons—those whom we deem worthy of us. It is the lucky child who wins admission to Breakness Institute. For each of these, twenty depart the planet with their mothers, when the indenture expires."

"In short," said Bustamonte crisply, "you want women."

Palafox nodded. "We want women—healthy young women of intelligence and beauty. This is the only commodity which we wizards of Breakness cannot fabricate—nor would we care to."

"What of your own daughters?" Bustamonte asked curiously. "Can you not breed daughters as easily as sons?"

The words made no impression upon Palafox; it was almost as if he had not heard them. "Breakness is a world of men," he said. "We are Wizards of the Institute."

Bustamonte sat in pensive consideration, unaware that to a man of Breakness, a daughter was scarcely more desirable than a two-headed Mongoloid. The Breakness dominie, like the classical ascetics, lived in the present, certain only of his own ego; the past was a record, the future an amorphous blot waiting for shape. He might lay plans for a hundred years ahead; for while the Breakness wizard paid lip-service to the inevitability of death, emotionally he rejected it, convinced that in the proliferation of sons he merged himself with the future.

Bustamonte, ignorant of Breakness psychology, was only reinforced in the conviction that Palafox was slightly mad. Reluctantly he said, "We can arrive at a satisfactory contract. For your part, you must join us in crushing the Batch, and ensuring that never again…"

Palafox, smiling, shook his head. "We are not warriors. We sell the workings of our minds, no more. How can we dare otherwise? Breakness is vulnerable. A single missile could destroy the Institute. You will contract with me alone. If Eban Buzbek arrived here tomorrow he could buy counsel from another wizard, and the two of us would pit our skills."

"Hmmph," growled Bustamonte. "What guarantee have I that he will not do so?"

"None whatever. The policy of the Institute is passionless neutrality—the individual wizards, however, may work where they desire, the better to augment their dormitories."

Bustamonte fretfully drummed his fingers. "What can you do for me, if you cannot protect me from the Brumbos?"

Palafox meditated, eyelids half-closed, then said, "There are a number of methods to achieve the goal you desire. I can arrange the hire of mercenaries from Hallowmede, or Polensis, or Earth. Possibly I could stimulate a coalition of Batch clans against the Brumbos. We could so debase Paonese currency that the tribute became valueless."

Bustamonte frowned. "I prefer methods more forthright. I want you to supply us tools of war. Then we may defend ourselves, and so need be at no one's mercy."

Palafox raised his crooked black eyebrows. "Strange to hear such dynamic proposals from a Paonese."

"Why not?" demanded Bustamonte. "We are not cowards."

A hint of impatience entered Palafox's voice. "Ten thousand Brumbos overcome fifteen billion Paonese. Your people had weapons. But no one considered resistance. They acquiesced like grass-birds."

Bustamonte shook his head doggedly. "We are men like other men. All we need is training."

"Training will never supply the desire to fight."

Bustamonte scowled. "Then this desire must be supplied!"

Palafox showed his teeth in a peculiar grin. He pulled himself erect in his chair. "At last we have touched the core of the matter."

Bustamonte glanced at him, puzzled by his sudden intensity.

Palafox continued. "We must persuade the amenable Paonese to become fighters. How can we do this? Evidently they must change their basic nature. They must discard passivity and easy adjustment to hardship. They must learn truculence and pride and competitiveness. Do you agree?"

Bustamonte hesitated. Palafox had outdistanced him, and seemed bent on a course other than he had envisioned. "You may be right."

"This is no overnight process, you understand. A change of basic psychology is a formidable process."

Bustamonte was touched by suspicion. There was strain in Palafox's manner, an effort at casualness.

"If you wish an effective fighting force," said Palafox, "here is the only means to that end. There is no short-cut."

Bustamonte looked away, out over the Wind River. "You believe that this fighting force can be created?"

"Certainly."

"And how much time might be required?"

"Twenty years, more or less."

"Twenty years!"

"We must begin with children, with babies."

Bustamonte was silent several minutes. "I must think this over." He jumped to his feet, strode back and forth shaking his hands as if they were wet.

Palafox said with a trace of asperity: "How can it be otherwise? If you want a fighting force you must first create fighting spirit. This is a cultural trait and cannot be inculcated overnight."

"Yes, yes," muttered Bustamonte. "I see that you are right, but I must think."

"Think also on a second matter," Palafox suggested. "Pao is vast and populous. There is scope not merely for an effective army, but also a vast industrial complex might be established. Why buy goods from Mercantil when you can produce them yourself?"

"How can all this be done?"

Palafox laughed. "That is where you must employ my special knowledge. I am Dominie of Comparative Culture at Breakness Institute."

"Nevertheless," said Bustamonte obstinately, "I still must know how you propose to bring about these changes—never forgetting that Paonese resist change more adamantly than the advent of death."

"Exactly," replied Palafox. "We must alter the mental framework of the Paonese people—a certain proportion of them, at least—which is most easily achieved by altering the language."

Bustamonte shook his head. "This process sounds indirect and precarious. I had hoped..."

Palafox interrupted incisively. "Words are tools. Language is a pattern, and defines the way the word-tools are used."

Bustamonte was eyeing Palafox sidelong, his expression suggesting that he considered the dominie no more than an impractical academician. "How can this theory be applied practically? Do you have a definite detailed plan?"

Palafox inspected Bustamonte with scornful amusement. "For an affair of such magnitude? You expect miracles even a Breakness Wizard cannot perform. Perhaps you had best continue with the tribute to Eban Buzbek of Batmarsh."

Bustamonte was silent.

"I command basic principles," said Palafox presently. "I apply these abstractions to practical situations. This is the skeleton of the operation, which finally is fleshed over with detail."

Bustamonte still remained silent.

"One point I will make," said Palafox, "that such an operation can only be effectuated by a ruler of great power, one who will not be swayed by maudlin sentiment."

"I have that power," said Bustamonte. "I am as ruthless as circumstances require."

"This is what must be done. One of the Paonese continents—or any appropriate area—will be designated. The people of this area will be persuaded to the use of a new language. That is the extent of the effort. Presently they will produce warriors in profusion."

Bustamonte frowned skeptically. "Why not undertake a program of education and training in arms? To change the language is going far afield."

"You have not grasped the essential point," said Palafox. "Paonese is a passive, dispassionate language. It presents the world in two dimensions, without tension or contrast. A people speaking Paonese, theoretically, ought to be docile, passive, without strong personality development—in fact, exactly as the Paonese people are. The new language will be based on the contrast and comparison of strength, with a grammar simple and direct. To illustrate, consider the sentence, 'The farmer chops down a tree.'* In the new language the sentence becomes: 'The farmer overcomes the inertia of the axe; the axe breaks asunder the resistance of the tree.' Or perhaps: 'The farmer vanquishes the tree, using the weapon-instrument of the axe.'"

"Ah," said Bustamonte appreciatively.

"The syllabary will be rich in effort-producing gutturals and hard vowels. A number of key ideas will be synonymous; such as 'pleasure' and 'overcoming a resistance'—'relaxation' and 'shame'—'out-worlder' and 'rival'. Even the clans of Batmarsh will seem mild compared to the future Paonese military."

"Yes, yes," breathed Bustamonte. "I begin to understand."

"Another area might be set aside for the inculcation of another language," said Palafox off-handedly. "In this instance, the grammar will be extravagantly complicated but altogether consistent and logical. The vocables would be discrete but joined and fitted by elaborate rules of accordance. What is the result? When a group of people, impregnated with these stimuli, are presented with supplies and facilities, industrial development is inevitable.

"And should you plan to seek ex-planetary markets, a corps of salesmen and traders might be advisable. Theirs would be a symmetrical language with emphatic number-parsing, elaborate honorifics to teach hypocrisy, a vocabulary rich in homophones to facilitate ambiguity, a syntax of reflection, reinforcement and alternation to emphasize the analogous interchange of human affairs.

"All these languages will make use of semantic assistance. To the military segment, a 'successful man' will be synonymous with 'winner of a

---

*Literally rendered from the Paonese in which the two men spoke, the sentence was: 'Farmer in state of exertion; axe agency; tree in state of subjection to attack.' the italicized words denoting suffixes of condition.

fierce contest'. To the industrialists, it will mean 'efficient fabricator'. To the traders, it equates with 'a person irresistibly persuasive'. Such influences will pervade each of the languages. Naturally they will not act with equal force upon each individual, but the mass action must be decisive."

"Marvellous!" cried Bustamonte, completely won over. "This is human engineering indeed!"

Palafox went to the window and looked across Wind River. He was faintly smiling and his black eyes, usually so black and hard, were softly unfocused. For a moment his real age—twice Bustamonte's and more—was apparent; but only for a moment, and when he swung about, his face was as emotionless as ever.

"You understand that I merely talk at random—I formulate ideas, so to speak. Truly massive planning must be accomplished: the various languages must be synthesized, their vocabularies formulated. Instructors to teach the languages must be recruited. I can rely on my own sons. Another group must be organized, or perhaps derived from the first group: an elite corps of coordinators trained to fluency in each of the languages. This corps will ultimately become a managerial corporation, to assist your present civil service."

Bustamonte raised his eyebrows, blew out his cheeks. "Well…possibly. So far-reaching a function for this group seems unnecessary. Enough that we create a military force to smite Eban Buzbek and his bandits!"

Bustamonte jumped to his feet, marched back and forth in excitement. He stopped short, looked slyly toward Palafox. "One further point we must discuss: what will be the fee for your services?"

"Four brood of women a month," said Palafox calmly, "of optimum intelligence and physique, between the ages of fourteen and twenty-four years, their time of indenture not to exceed fifteen years, their transportation back to Pao guaranteed, together with all substandard and female off-spring."

Bustamonte, with a knowing smile, shook his head. "Four brood—is this not excessive? Surely you cannot successfully breed sixty-four women a month?"

Palafox darted him a burning glance. To question the genetic strength of a Breakness dominie was a prime solecism. Bustamonte, aware of his mistake, added hastily, "However, I will agree to this figure. In return you must return me my beloved nephew, Beran, so that he may make preparation for a useful career."

"As a visitor to the floor of the sea?"

"We must take account of realities," murmured Bustamonte.

"I agree," said Palafox in a flat voice. "They dictate that Beran Panasper, Panarch of Pao, complete his education on Breakness."

Bustamonte broke out into furious protest; Palafox responded tartly; there was contention, with Bustamonte erupting into rage. Palafox remained contemptuously calm, and Bustamonte at last acceded to his terms.

The bargain was recorded upon film and the two parted, if not amicably, at least in common accord.

CHAPTER X

Winter on Breakness was a time of chill, of thin clouds flying down Wind River, of hail fine as sand hissing along the rock. The sun careened only briefly above the vast rock slab to the south, and for most of the day Breakness Institute was shrouded in murk.

Five times the dismal season came and passed, and Beran Panasper acquired a basic Breakness education.

The first two years Beran lived in the house of Palafox, and much of his energy was given to learning the language. His natural preconceptions regarding the function of speech were useless, for the language of Breakness was different from Paonese in many significant respects. Paonese was of that type known as 'polysynthetic', with root words taking on prefixes, affixes and post-positions to extend their meaning. The language of Breakness was basically 'isolative', but unique in that it derived entirely from the speaker: that is to say, the speaker was the frame of reference upon which the syntax depended, a system which made for both logical elegance and simplicity. Since Self was the implicit basis of expression, the pronoun 'I' was unnecessary. Other personal pronouns were likewise non-existent, except for third person constructions—although these actually were contractions of noun phrases.

The language included no negativity; instead there were numerous polarities such as 'go' and 'stay'. There was no passive voice—every verbal idea was self-contained: 'to strike', 'to receive impact'. The language was rich in words for intellectual manipulation, but almost totally deficient in descriptives of various emotional states. Even if a Breakness dominie chose to break his solipsistic shell and reveal his mood, he would be forced to the use of clumsy circumlocution.

Such common Paonese concepts as 'anger', 'joy', 'love', 'hate', 'grief', were absent from the Breakness vocabulary. On the other hand, there were words to define a hundred different types of ratiocination, subtleties unknown to the Paonese—distinctions which baffled Beran so completely that at times his entire stasis, the solidity of his ego, seemed threatened. Week after week Fanchiel explained, illustrated, paraphrased; little by little Beran assimilated the unfamiliar mode of thought, and, simultaneously, the Breakness approach to existence.

Then...one day Palafox summoned him and remarked that Beran's knowledge of the language was adequate for study at the Institute; that he would immediately be enrolled for the basic regimen.

Beran felt hollow and forlorn. The house of Palafox had provided a certain melancholy security; what would he find at the Institute?

Palafox dismissed him, and half an hour later Fanchiel escorted him to the great rock-melt quadrangle, saw him enrolled and installed in a cubicle at the student dormitory. He then departed, and Beran henceforth saw nothing either of Fanchiel or of Palafox.

So began a new phase of Beran's existence on Breakness. All his previous education had been conducted by tutors; he had participated in none of the vast Paonese recitatives, wherein thousands of children chanted in unison all their learning—the youngest piping the numbers "Ai! Shrai! Vida! Mina! Nona! Drona! Hivan! Imple!"; the oldest the epic drones with which Paonese erudition concerned itself. For this reason Beran was not as puzzled by the customs of the Institute as he might have been.

Each youth was recognized as an individual, as singular and remote as a star in space. He lived by himself, shared no officially recognized phase of his existence with any other student. When spontaneous conversations occurred, the object was to bring an original viewpoint, or novel sidelight, to the discussion at hand. The more unorthodox the idea, the more certain that it would at once be attacked. He who presented it must then defend his idea to the limits of logic, but not beyond. If successful he gained prestige; if routed, he was accordingly diminished.

Another subject enjoyed a furtive currency among the students: the subject of age and death. The topic was more or less taboo—especially in the presence of a dominie—for no one died of disease or corporeal degeneration on Breakness. The dominies ranged the universe; a certain number met violent ends in spite of their built-in weapons and defenses. The greater number, however, passed their years on Breakness, unchanging except for perhaps a slight gauntness and angularity of the bone structure. And then, inexorably the dominie would approach his Emeritus status: he would become less precise, more emotional; egocentricity would begin to triumph over the essential social accommodations; there would be outbursts of petulance, wrath, and a final megalomania—and then the Emeritus would disappear.

Beran, shy and lacking fluency, at first held aloof from the discussions. As he acquired facility with the language, he began to join the discussions, and after a period of polemic trouncings, found himself capable of fair success. These experiences provided him the first glow of pleasure he had known on Breakness.

Interrelationships between the students were formal, neither amiable nor contentious. Of intense interest to the youth of Breakness was the subject of procreation in every possible ramification. Beran, conditioned to Paonese standards of modesty, was at first distressed, but familiarity robbed the topic of its sting. He found that prestige on Breakness was a function not only of intellectual achievement but also of the number of females in one's dormitory, the number of sons which passed the acceptance tests, the degree of resemblance in physique and mind with the sire, and the sons' own achievements. Certain of the dominies were highly respected in these regards, and ever more regularly was the name of Lord Palafox heard.

When Beran entered his fifteenth year, Palafox's repute rivalled that of Lord Karollen Vampellte, High Dominie of the Institute. Beran was unable to restrain a sense of identification and so pride.

A year or two after puberty, a youth of the Institute might expect to be presented with a girl by his sire. In expectation of this occasion, the pubescent youths spent considerable time at the space terminal where they might inspect the broods of incoming women.

In solemn groups they stood to the side, making grave appraisals, speculating on the planet of origin of some particular individual, calling to mind the sexual customs of the particular planet, and occasionally, if language permitted, verifying their speculations by putting a series of searching questions.

Beran, attaining this particular stage in his development, was a youth of pleasant appearance, rather slender, almost frail. His hair was a dark brown, his eyes gray and wide, his expression pensive. Due to his exotic origin and a certain native diffidence, he was seldom party to what small group activity existed. When he finally felt the pre-adult stirrings in his blood and began to think of the girl whom he might expect to receive from Palafox, he went alone to the space terminal.

He chose a day on which the transport from Journal was due, and arriving just as the lighter dropped down from the orbiting ship, found the terminal in apparent confusion. To one side, in quiet, almost stolid ranks, stood women at the end of their indentures, together with their girl children and those boys who had failed the Breakness tests. Their ages ranged from twenty-five to thirty-five; they would now return to their home-worlds as wealthy women, with most of their lives before them.

The lighter slid its nose under the shelter, the doors opened; young women trooped forth, looking curiously to right and left, swaying and dancing to the blast of the wind. Unlike the women at the ends of their indentures, these were volatile and nervous, parading their defiance, concealing their apprehension. Their eyes roved everywhere, curious to find what sort of man would claim them.

Beran looked on in fascination. The women in their early maturity he disregarded, but the girls seemed easy and graceful, visions of erotic delight. Almost all were older than himself; but a few were barely past the age of puberty.

The newcomers noticed the other women, those waiting to depart; the two groups examined each other in covert fascination.

A squad-leader gave a terse order; the incoming broods filed across the terminal to be registered and receipted; Beran strolled closer, sidling toward one of the younger girls. She turned wide sea-green eyes on him, then swung suddenly away. Beran moved forward—then stopped short. These women puzzled him. There was a sense of familiarity to them, the redolence of a pleasant past. He listened as they spoke among themselves. Their language was one he knew well.

He stood beside the girl. She observed him without friendliness.

"You are Paonese," Beran exclaimed in wonder. "What do Paonese women do on Breakness?"

"The same as any other."

"But this has never been the case!"

"You know very little of Pao," she said bitterly.

"No no," said Beran, anxious for the girl's approval. "I am Paonese!"

"Then you must know what occurs on Pao."

Beran shook his head. "I have been here since the death of Panarch Aiello."

She spoke in a low voice, looking off across the terminal. "You chose well, for things go poorly. Bustamonte is a madman."

"He sends women to Breakness?" Beran asked in a hushed husky voice.

"A hundred* a month—we who have been dispossessed or made orphans by the turmoil."

Beran's voice failed. He tried to speak; while he was stammering a question, she began to move away. "Wait!" croaked Beran, running along beside. "What turmoil is this?"

"I cannot wait," the girl said bitterly. "I am indentured, I must do as I am bid."

"Where do you go? To the dormitory of what lord?"

"I am in the service of Lord Palafox."

Beran stopped short. He stared after the retreating figure. A vehicle waited at the door. Beran ran forward, to the side of the girl who ignored him.

"What is your name?" Beran demanded. "Tell me your name!"

Embarrassed and uncertain, she said nothing. Two paces more and she would be gone, lost in the anonymity of the dormitory. "Tell me your name! I shall claim you as my bride. Lord Palafox, whom I know well, who is all powerful here, will not refuse me."

She spoke swiftly over her shoulder: "Gitan Netsko—" then passed through the door and out of his sight. The vehicle moved off the ramp, swayed in the wind, drifted down slope and was gone.

Beran walked slowly down from the terminal, a small figure on the mountainside, leaning and stumbling against the wind. He passed among the houses, and arrived at the house of Palafox.

Outside the door he hesitated, picturing the tall figure within. He summoned the whole of his resources, tapped the escutcheon plate. The door opened; he entered.

At this hour Palafox might well be in his lower study. Down the familiar steps Beran walked, past the remembered rooms of stone and valuable Breakness hardwood. At one time he had considered the house

*(In Paonese, 64.)

harsh and bleak; now he could see it to be subtly beautiful, perfectly suited to the environment.

As he had expected, Palafox sat in his study; and, warned by a stimulus from one of his modifications, was expecting him.

Beran came slowly forward, staring into the inquiring but unsympathetic face, and plunged immediately into the heart of his subject. It was useless to attempt deviousness with Palafox. "I was at the terminal today. I saw Paonese women, who came here unwillingly. They speak of turmoil and hardship. What is happening on Pao?"

Palafox considered Beran a moment, then nodded with faint amusement. "I see. You are old enough now to frequent the terminal. Do you find any women suitable for your personal use?"

Beran bit his lips. "I am concerned by what must be happening on Pao. Never before have our people been so degraded!"

Palafox pretended shock. "But serving a Breakness dominie is by no means degradation!"

Beran, feeling that he had scored a point on his redoubtable opponent, took heart. "Still you have not answered my question."

"That is true," said Palafox. He motioned to a chair. "Sit down—I will describe to you exactly what is taking place." Beran gingerly seated himself. Palafox surveyed him through half-closed eyes. "Your information as to turmoil and hardship on Pao is half-true. Something of this nature exists, regrettably but unavoidably."

Beran was puzzled. "There are droughts? Plagues? Famines?"

"No," said Palafox. "None of these. There is only social change. Bustamonte is embarked on a novel but courageous venture. You remember the invasion from Batmarsh?"

"Yes, but where…"

"Bustamonte wants to prevent any recurrence of this shameful event. He is developing a corps of warriors for the defense of Pao. For their use he has appointed the Hylanth Littoral of the continent Shraimand. The old population has been removed. A new group, trained to military ideals and speaking a new language, has taken their place. On Vidamand, Bustamonte is using similar means to create an industrial complex, in order to make Pao independent of Mercantil."

Beran fell silent, impressed by the scope of these tremendous schemes, but there were still doubts in his mind. Palafox waited patiently. Beran frowned uncertainly, bit at his knuckle, and finally blurted out: "But the Paonese have never been warriors or mechanics—

they know nothing of these things! How can Bustamonte succeed with this plan?"

"You must remember," said Palafox drily, "that I advise Bustamonte."

There was an unsettling corollary to Palafox's statement—the bargain which evidently existed between himself and Bustamonte. Beran suppressed the thought of it, put it to the back of his mind. He asked in a subdued voice, "Was it necessary to drive the inhabitants from their homes?"

"Yes. There could be no tincture of the old language or the old ways."

Beran, a native Paonese, aware that mass tragedy was a commonplace of Paonese history, was able to accept the force of Palafox's explanation. "These new people—will they be true Paonese?"

Palafox seemed surprised. "Why should they not? They'll be of Paonese blood, born and bred on Pao, loyal to no other source."

Beran opened his mouth to speak, closed it again dubiously.

Palafox waited, but Beran, while patently not happy, could find no logical voice to give his emotions.

"Now tell me," said Palafox, in a different tone of voice, "how goes it at the Institute?"

"Very well. I have completed the fourth of my theses—the provost found matter to interest him in my last independent essay."

"And what was the subject?"

"An expansion upon the Paonese vitality-word *praesens*, with an effort at transposition into Breakness attitudes."

Palafox's voice took on something of an edge. "And how do you so easily analyze the mind of Breakness?"

Beran, surprised at the implied disapproval, nevertheless answered without diffidence. "Surely it is a person such as I, neither of Pao nor of Breakness, but part of both, who can best make comparisons."

"Better, in this case, than one such as I?"

Beran considered carefully. "I have no basis for comparison."

Palafox stared hard at him, then laughed. "I must call for your essay and study it. Are you determined yet upon the basic direction of your studies?"

Beran shook his head. "There are a dozen possibilities. At the moment I find myself absorbed by human history, by the possibility of pattern and its peculiar absence. But I have much to learn, many authorities to consult, and perhaps this form will eventually make itself known to me."

"It seems that you follow the inspiration of Dominie Arbursson, the Teleologist."

"I have studied his ideas," said Beran.

"Ah, and they do not interest you?"

Beran made another careful reply. "Lord Arbursson is a Breakness dominie. I am Paonese."

Palafox laughed shortly. "The form of your statement implies an equivalence between the two conditions of being."

Beran, wondering at Palafox's testiness, made no comment.

"Well then," said Palafox, a trifle heavily, "it seems as if you are going your way and making progress." He eyed Beran up and down. "And you have been frequenting the terminal."

Beran, influenced by Paonese attitudes, blushed. "Yes."

"Then it becomes time that you began practicing procreation. No doubt you are well-versed in the necessary theory?"

"The students of my age talk of little else," said Beran. "If it please you, Lord Palafox, today at the terminal..."

"So now we learn the source of your trouble, eh? Well then, what is her name?"

"Gitan Netsko," Beran said huskily.

"Await me here." Palafox strode from the room.

Twenty minutes later he appeared in the doorway, signaled to Beran. "Come."

A domed air-car waited outside the house. Within, a small forlorn figure sat huddled. Palafox fixed Beran with a stern gaze.

"It is customary that sire provide son with education, his first female, and a modicum of dispassionate counsel. You already are profiting by the education—in the car is the one of your choice, and you may also retain the car. Here is the counsel, and mark it well, for never will you receive more valuable! Monitor your thoughts for traces of Paonese mysticism and sentimentality. Isolate these impulses—make yourself aware of them, but do not necessarily try to expunge them, because then their influence subverts to a deeper, more basic, level." Palafox held up his hand in one of the striking Breakness gestures. "I have now acquitted myself of my responsibilities. I wish you a successful career, a hundred sons of great achievement, and the respectful envy of your peers." Palafox bowed his head formally.

"Thank you," said Beran with equal formality. He turned and walked through the howl of the wind to the car.

The girl, Gitan Netsko, looked up as he entered, then turned her eyes away and stared out across great Wind River.

Beran sat quiet, his heart too full for words. At last he reached out, took her hand. It was limp and cool; her face was quiet.

Beran tried to convey what was in his mind. "You are now in my care...I am Paonese..."

"Lord Palafox has assigned me to serve you," she said in a measured passionless voice.

Beran sighed. He felt miserable and full of qualms: the Paonese mysticism and sentimentality Palafox had expressly counseled him to suppress. He raised the car into the wind; then slid downhill to the dormitory. He conducted her to his room with conflicting emotions.

They stood in the austere little room, surveying each other uneasily. "Tomorrow," said Beran, "I will arrange for better quarters. It is too late today."

The girl's eyes had been growing fuller and fuller; now she sank upon the couch, and suddenly began to weep—slow tears of loneliness, humiliation, grief.

Beran, feeling full of guilt, went to sit beside her. He took her hand, stroked it, muttered consoling words, which she clearly never heard. It was his first intimate contact with grief; it disturbed him tremendously.

The girl was speaking in a low monotone. "My father was a kind man—never did he harm a living creature. Our home was almost a thousand years old. Its timber was black with age and all the stone grew moss. We lived beside Mervan Pond, with our yarrow field behind, and our plum orchard up the slope of Blue Mountain. When the agents came and ordered us to leave, my father was astonished. Leave our old home? A joke! Never! They spoke only three words and my father was angry and pale and silent. Still we did not move. And the next time they came..." the sad voice dwindled away; tears made soft marks on Beran's arm.

"It will be mended!" said Beran, his abstract humanitarianism forgot, his mind fired with fury.

She shook her head. "Impossible...And I would as soon be dead too."

"No, never say that!" Beran sought to comfort her. He stroked her hair, kissed her cheek. He could not help himself—the contact aroused him, his caresses became more intimate. She made no resistance. Indeed she seemed to welcome the love-making as a distraction from her grief. Presently, in their various ways exhausted, they fell asleep.

＊

They awoke early in the morning dimness, while the sky was still the color of cast iron, the slope black and featureless as tar, Wind River a roaring darkness.

After a while Beran said, "You know so very little about me—are you not curious?"

Gitan Netsko made a noncommittal sound, and Beran felt a trifle nettled.

"I am Paonese," he said earnestly. "I was born in Eiljanre fifteen years ago. Temporarily I live on Breakness."

He paused, expecting her to inquire the reason for his exile, but she turned her head, looking up through the high narrow window into the sky.

"Meanwhile I study at the Institute," said Beran. "Until last night I was uncertain—I knew not where I would specialize. Now I know! I will become a Dominie of Linguistics!"

Gitan Netsko turned her head, looked at him. Beran was unable to read the emotion in her eyes. They were wide eyes, sea-green, striking in her pale face. He knew her to be younger than himself by a year, but meeting her gaze, he felt unsure, ineffectual, absurd.

"What are you thinking?" he asked plaintively.

She shrugged. "Very little…"

"Oh, come!" He bent over her, kissed her forehead, her cheek, her mouth. She made neither resistance nor response. Beran began to worry. "Do you dislike me? Have I annoyed you?"

"No," she said in a soft voice. "How could you? So long as I am under indenture to a man of Breakness, my feelings mean nothing."

Beran jerked upright. "But I am no man of Breakness! It is as I told you! I am Paonese!"

Gitan Netsko made no response and seemed to lapse into a private world.

"Someday I will return to Pao. Perhaps soon, who knows? You will come back with me."

She made no comment. Beran was exasperated. "Don't you believe me?"

In a muffled voice she said, "If you were truly Paonese, you would know what I believe."

Beran fell silent. At last he said, "Regardless of what I may be, I see you do not believe me to be Paonese!"

She burst out furiously, "What difference does it make? Why should you take pride in such a claim? The Paonese are spineless mud-worms—they allow the tyrant Bustamonte to molest them, despoil them, kill them, and never do they raise a hand in protest! They take refuge like sheep in a wind, rumps to the threat. Some flee to a new continent, others..." she darted him a cool glance "...take refuge on a distant planet. I am not proud to be Paonese!"

Beran somberly rose to his feet looking blindly away from the girl. Seeing himself in his mind's-eye he grimaced: what a paltry figure he cut! There was nothing to say in his own defense; to plead ignorance and helplessness would be an ignoble bleating. Beran heaved a deep sigh, began to dress himself.

He felt a touch on his arm. Gitan Netsko, kneeling on the bed, smiled uncertainly at him. "Forgive me—I know you meant no harm."

Beran shook his head, feeling a thousand years old. "I meant no harm, that is true...But so is everything else you said...There are so many truths—how can anyone make up his mind?"

"I know nothing of these many truths," said the girl. "I know only how I feel, and I know that if I were able I would kill Bustamonte the Tyrant!"

As early as Breakness custom allowed, Beran presented himself at the house of Palafox. One of the sons-in-residence admitted him, inquired his business, which question Beran evaded. There was a delay of several minutes, while Beran waited nervously in a bleak little ante-room near the top of the house.

Beran's instinct warned him to circumspection, to a preliminary testing of the ground—but he knew, with a sinking feeling at the pit of his stomach, that he lacked the necessary finesse.

At last he was summoned and conducted far down the escalator, into a wood-paneled morning room, where Palafox, in a somber blue robe, sat eating bits of hot pickled fruit. He regarded Beran without change of expression, nodded almost imperceptibly. Beran made the customary gesture of respect and spoke in the most serious voice he could muster: "Lord Palafox, I have come to an important decision."

Palafox looked at him blankly. "Why should you not? You have reached the age of responsibility, and none of your decisions should be frivolous."

Beran said doggedly, "I want to return to Pao."

Palafox made no immediate response, but it was clear that Beran's request struck no sympathetic fire. Then he said in his driest voice, "I am astonished at your lack of wisdom."

Again the subtle diversion, the channeling of opposing energy into complicated paths. But the device was wasted on Beran. He plowed ahead. "I have been thinking about Bustamonte's program, and I am worried. It may bring benefits—but I feel there is something abnormal and unnatural at work."

Palafox's mouth compressed. "Assuming the correctness of your sensations—what could you do to counter this tendency?"

Beran spoke eagerly, "I am the true Panarch, am I not? Is not Bustamonte merely Ayudor-Senior? If I appear before him, he must obey me."

"In theory. How will you assert your identity? Suppose he claims you to be a madman, an impostor?"

Beran stood silently; it was a point which he had not considered.

Palafox continued relentlessly. "You would be subaqueated, your life would be quenched. What would you have achieved?"

Beran tightened his lips. "Perhaps I would not announce myself to Bustamonte. If I came down on one of the islands—Ferai or Viamne..."

"Very well. Suppose you convinced a certain number of persons of your identity, Bustamonte would still resist. You might precipitate disturbances—even civil war. If you consider Bustamonte's actions ruthless, consider your own intentions in this light."

Beran smiled, at last sure of his ground. "You do not understand the Paonese. There would be no war. Bustamonte would merely find himself without authority."

Palafox did not relish the correction of Beran's views. "And if Bustamonte learns of your coming, and meets the ship with a squad of neutraloids, what then?"

"How would he know?"

Palafox ate a bit of spiced apple. He spoke deliberately. "I would tell him."

Beran was astounded—but perhaps only at the top of his mind. "Then you oppose me?"

Palafox smiled his faint smile. "Not unless you act against my interests—which at this time coincide with those of Bustamonte."

"What are your interests, then?" cried Beran. "What do you hope to achieve?"

"On Breakness," said Palafox softly, "those are questions which one never asks."

Beran was silent a moment. Then he turned away, exclaiming bitterly, "Why did you bring me here? Why did you sponsor me at the Institute?"

Palafox, the basic conflict now defined, relaxed and sat at his ease. "Where is the mystery? The able strategist provides himself as many tools and procedures as possible. Your function was to serve as a lever against Bustamonte, if the need should arise."

"And now I am of no further use to you?"

Palafox shrugged. "I am no seer—I cannot read the future. But my plans for Pao…"

"Your plans for Pao!" Beran interjected.

"…develop smoothly. My best estimate is that you are no longer an asset, for now you threaten to impede the smooth flow of events. It is best, therefore, that our basic relationship is clear. I am by no means your enemy, but neither do our interests coincide. You have no cause for complaint. Without my help you would be dead. I have provided you sustenance, shelter, an unexcelled education. I will continue to sponsor your career unless you take action against me. There is no more to say."

Beran rose to his feet, bowed in formal respect. He turned to depart, hesitated, looked back. Meeting the black eyes, wide and burning, he felt shock. This was not the notably rational Dominie Palafox, intelligent, highly-modified, second in prestige only to Lord Dominie Vampellte; this man was strange and wild, and radiated a mental force over and beyond the logic of normality.

Beran returned to his cubicle, where he found Gitan Netsko sitting on the stone window-ledge, chin on knees, arms clasped around her ankles.

She looked up as he came in, and in spite of his depression, Beran felt a pleasurable, if wistful, thrill of ownership. She was charming, he thought: a typical Paonese of the Vinelands, slender and clear-skinned with fine bones and precisely-modeled features. Her expression was unreadable; he had no hint as to how she regarded him, but this was how it went on Pao, where the intimate relationships of youth were traditionally shrouded in indirection and ambiguity. A lift of an eyebrow could indicate raging passion; a hesitancy, a lowered pitch of the voice absolute aversion…Abruptly Beran said, "Palafox will not permit my return to Pao."

"No? And so then?"

He walked to the window, looked somberly across the mist-streaming chasm. "So then—I will depart without his permission…As soon as opportunity offers."

She surveyed him skeptically. "And if you return—what is the use of that?"

Beran shook his head dubiously. "I don't know exactly. I would hope to restore order, bring about a return to the old ways."

She laughed sadly, without scorn. "It is a fine ambition. I hope I shall see it."

"I hope you shall, too."

"But I am puzzled. How will you effect all this?"

"I don't know. In the simplest case I will merely issue the orders." Observing her expression, Beran exclaimed, "You must understand, I am the true Panarch. My uncle Bustamonte is an assassin—he killed my father, Aiello."

Her eyes widened and she leapt to her feet and stared at him for an instant in stunned disbelief. Then—and the gesture seemed as natural to her as breathing—she sank to her knees, placing both of her hands, palms upward, upon his sandaled feet, whispering words of almost worshipful import.

Slowly he bent, and raised her up, shaking his head over and over, "No, no, no." Then: "You mustn't. I am only a man—like other men. A man in love."

CHAPTER XI

Beran's resolve to return to Pao was difficult to implement. He had neither funds to buy, nor authority to commandeer, transportation. He tried to beg passage for himself and the girl; he was rebuffed and ridiculed. At last frustrated, he sulked in his rooms, ignoring his studies, exchanging hardly a word with Gitan Netsko, who spent most of her time staring blankly along the windy chasm. Beran one time inquired what she found of interest in barren stone and windy haze, to which she replied that she saw none of it, nothing except the thoughts which passed before her eyes.

Three months passed. And one morning Gitan Netsko remarked that she thought herself pregnant.

Beran stared at her incredulously. Barely adolescent himself, he had never envisioned fathering a child. He took Gitan Netsko to the clinic, registered her for the pre-natal regimen. His appearance aroused surprise and amusement among the staff of the clinic.

"You bred the child without assistance? Come now, tell us: who is the actual father?"

"She is indentured to me," Beran stated, indignant and angry. "I am the father!"

"Forgive our skepticism, but you appear hardly the age of virility."

"The facts seem to contradict you," Beran retorted.

"We shall see, we shall see." They motioned to Gitan Netsko. "Into the laboratory with you."

At the last moment the girl became afraid. "Please, I'd rather not."

"It's all part of our usual routine," the reception clerk assured her. "Come, this way, if you please."

"No, no," she muttered, and shrank back. "I don't want to go!"

Beran was puzzled. He turned to the reception clerk. "Is it necessary that she go now?"

"Certainly!" said the clerk in exasperation. "We make standard tests against possible genetic discord or abnormality. These factors, if discovered now, prevent difficulty later."

"Can't you wait until she is more composed?"

"We'll give her a sedative." They laid hands on the girl's shoulder. As they took her away, she turned an anguished glance back to Beran that told him many things that she had never spoken.

Beran waited—an hour, two hours. He went to the door, knocked. A young medic came forth and Beran thought to detect discomfort in his expression.

"Why the delay? Surely by now..."

The medic held up his hand. "I fear that there have been complications. It appears that you have not sired after all."

A chill began to spread through Beran's viscera. "What sort of complications?"

The medic moved away, back through the door. "You had best return to your dormitory. There is no need to wait longer."

Tears swelling at his eyes, Beran ran forward, groping to hold back the door. "Tell me, tell me!"

But the door closed in his face, and there was no further response to his signals...

Gitan Netsko was taken to the laboratory, where she submitted to a number of routine tests. Presently she was laid, back down, on a pallet and rolled underneath a heavy machine. An electric field damped her cephalic currents, anaesthetized her while the machine dipped an infinitesimally thin needle into her abdomen, searched into the embryo and withdrew a half-dozen cells.

The field died; Gitan Netsko returned to consciousness. She was now conveyed to a waiting room, while the genetic structure of the embryonic cells was evaluated, categorized and classified by a calculator.

The signal returned: "A male child, normal in every phase. Class AA expectancy." The index to her own genetic type was shown, and, likewise, that of the father.

The operator observed the paternal index without particular interest, then looked again. He called an associate, they chuckled, and one of them spoke into a communicator.

The voice of Lord Palafox returned. "A Paonese girl? Show me her face...I remember—I bred her before I turned her over to my ward. It is definitely my child?"

"Indeed, Lord Palafox. There are few indices we are more familiar with."

"Very well—I will convey her to my dormitory."

Palafox appeared ten minutes later. He bowed with formal respect to Gitan Netsko, who surveyed him with fear. She had experienced nothing but pain at his hands; none of her imaginings had prepared her for the callousness of his breeding.

Palafox spoke politely. "It appears that you are carrying my child, of Class AA expectancy, which is excellent. I will take you to my personal lying-in ward, where you will get the best of care."

She looked at him blankly. "It is your child that I carry?"

"So the analyzers show. If you bear well, you will earn a bonus. I assure you, you will never find me niggardly."

She jumped to her feet, eyes blazing. "This is horror—I won't bear such a monster!"

She ran wildly down the room, out the door, with the medic and Palafox coming behind.

She sped past the door which led to the room where Beran waited, but saw only the great spine of the escalator which communicated with levels above and below.

At the landing she paused, looked behind with a wild grimace. The spare shape of Palafox was only a few yards behind. "Halt!" he cried in passion. "You carry my child!"

She made no answer, but turning, looked down the staircase. She closed her eyes, sighed, let herself fall forward. Down and down she rolled, bumping and thudding, while Palafox stared after her in amazement. At last she came to rest, far below, a limp huddle, oozing blood.

The medics took her up on a litter, but the child was gone and Palafox departed in disgust.

There were other injuries, and since Gitan Netsko had decided on death, the Breakness medicine could not force life upon her...and she died an hour or two after her fall.

✹

When Beran returned the next day he was told that the child had been that of Lord Palafox; that, upon learning of this fact, the girl had returned to the dormitory of Palafox in order to collect the birth-bonus. The actual circumstances were rigidly suppressed; in the society of Breakness Institute, nothing could so reduce a man's prestige, or make him more ridiculous in the eyes of his peers, than an episode of this sort: that a woman had killed herself rather than bear his child.

For a week Beran sat in his cubicle, or wandered the windy streets as long as his flesh could withstand the chill. And indeed it was by no conscious will that his feet took him trudging back to the dormitory.

Why had she gone to Palafox? Had she been promised swifter return to Pao?...Pao! Waves of homesickness swept over Beran. Pao, blue with water, green with leaves, warm from the sunlight! Pao! His only escape from misery was to return to Pao! Never had life seemed so dismal a panorama.

He reacted from his stupor and dullness with an almost vicious emotion. He flung himself into his work at the Institute, wadding knowledge into his mind to serve as poultice against his grief.

Two years passed. Beran grew taller; the bones of his face showed hard through his skin. Gitan Netsko receded in his memory, to become a bittersweet dream.

One or two odd things occurred during these years—affairs for which he could find no explanation. Once he met Palafox in a corridor of the Institute; Palafox turned him a glance so chill that Beran stared in wonder. It was himself who bore the grievance, not Palafox. Why then Palafox's animosity?

On another occasion he looked up from a desk in the library to find a group of high-placed dominies standing at the side, looking at him. They were amused and intent, as if they shared a private joke. Indeed this was the case—and poor Gitan Netsko had provided its gist. The facts of her passing had been too good to keep, and now Beran was pointed out among the knowledgeable as the stripling who had, to paraphrase, 'out-bred' Lord Palafox to such an extent that a girl had killed herself rather than return to Palafox.

The joke at last became stale and half-forgotten; only emotional scar-tissue remained.

After the passing of Gitan Netsko, Beran once more began to frequent the space-port—as much in hopes of garnering news of Pao as watching the incoming women. On his fourth visit he was startled to see debarking from the lighter a large group of young men—forty or fifty—almost certainly Paonese. When he drew close enough to hear their speech, his assumption was verified; they were Paonese indeed!

He approached one of the group as they stood waiting for registration, a tall sober-faced youth no older than himself. He forced himself to speak casually. "How goes it on Pao?"

The newcomer appraised him carefully, as if calculating how much veracity he could risk. In the end he made a non-committal reply. "As well as might be, times and conditions as they are."

Beran had expected little more. "What do you do here on Breakness, so many of you in a group?"

"We are apprentice linguists, here for advanced study."

"'Linguists'? On Pao? What innovation is this?"

The newcomer studied Beran. "You speak Paonese with a native accent. Strange you know so little of current affairs."

"I have lived on Breakness for eight years. You are the second Paonese I have seen in this time."

"I see…Well, there have been changes. Today on Pao one must know five languages merely to ask for a glass of wine."

The line advanced toward the desk. Beran kept pace, as one time before he had kept pace with Gitan Netsko. As he watched the names being noted into a register, into his mind came a notion which excited him to such an extent that he could hardly speak…"How long will you study on Breakness?" he asked huskily.

"A year."

Beran stepped back, made a careful estimate of the situation. The plan seemed feasible; in any case, what could he lose? He glanced down at his clothes: typical Breakness wear. Retiring to a corner, he pulled off his blouse and singlet; by reversing their order, and allowing them to hang loose outside his trousers, he achieved an effect approximately Paonese.

He fell in at the end of the line. The youth ahead of him looked back curiously, but made no comment. Presently he came to the registration desk. The clerk was a young Institute don four or five years older than himself. He seemed bored with his task and barely glanced up when Beran came to the desk.

"Name?" asked the clerk in heavy Paonese.

"Ercole Paraio."

The clerk broodingly scanned the list. "What are the symbols?"

Beran spelled forth the fictitious name.

"Strange," muttered the clerk. "It's not on the roster…Some inefficient fool…" His voice dwindled; he twitched the sheet. "The symbols again?"

Beran spelled the name, and the clerk added it to the registration manifest. "Very well—here is your pass-book. Carry it at all times on Breakness. You will surrender it when you return to Pao."

Beran followed the others to a waiting vehicle, and in the new identity of Ercole Paraio, rode down the slope to a new dormitory. It seemed a fantastic hope…And yet—why not? The apprentice linguists had no reason to accuse him; their minds were occupied by the novelty of Breakness. Who would investigate Beran, the neglected ward of Palafox? No one. Each student of the Institute was responsible only to himself. As Ercole Paraio, he could find enough freedom to maintain the identity of Beran Panasper, until such time as Beran should disappear…and if his ploy were discovered, what then? What harm could come?

Beran, with the other apprentice linguists from Pao, was assigned a sleeping cubicle and a place at the refectory table. In the morning the lessons would begin.

※

The class was convocated the next morning in a bare stone hall roofed with clear glass. The wan sunlight slanted in, cut the wall with a division between light and shade.

A young Institute don named Finisterle, one of Palafox's many sons, appeared to address the group. Beran had noticed *him* many times—in the corridors of the Institute, tall, even more gaunt than the Breakness norm, with Palafox's prow-like nose and commanding forehead, but with brooding brown eyes and a dark-oak skin inherited from his nameless mother. He spoke in a quiet, almost gentle voice, looking from face to face, and Beran wondered whether Finisterle would recognize him, and if he did, what his reaction might be.

"In a sense, you are an experimental group," said Finisterle. "It is necessary that many Paonese learn many languages swiftly. Training here on Breakness may be a means to this end.

"Perhaps in some of your minds is confusion. Why, you ask, must we learn three new languages?

"In your case, the answer is simple: you will be an elite managerial corps—you will coordinate, you will expedite, you will instruct.

"But this does not completely answer your question. Why, you ask, must anyone learn a new language? The response to this question is found in the science of dynamic linguistics. Here are the basic precepts, which I will enunciate without proof or argument, and which, for the time being at least, you must accept arbitrarily.

"Language determines the pattern of thought, the sequence in which various types of reactions follow acts.

"No language is neutral. All languages contribute impulse to the mass mind, some more vigorously than others. I repeat, we know of no 'neutral' language—and there is no 'best' or 'optimum' language, although Language A may be more suitable for Context X than Language B.

"In an even wider frame of reference, we note that every language imposes a certain world-view upon the mass mind. What is the 'true' world-picture? Is there a language to express this 'true' world-picture? First, there is no reason to believe that a 'true' world-picture, if it existed, would be a valuable or advantageous tool. Second, there is no standard to define the 'true' world-picture. 'Truth' is contained in the preconceptions of him who seeks to define it. Any organization of ideas whatever presupposes a judgment on the world."

Beran sat listening in vague wonder. Finisterle spoke in Paonese, with very little of the staccato Breakness accent. His ideas were considerably more moderate and equivocal than any others that Beran had heard expressed around the Institute.

Finisterle spoke further, describing the routine of study, and as he spoke it seemed that his eyes rested ever more frequently and frowningly upon Beran. Beran's heart began to sink.

But when Finisterle had finished his speech, he made no move to accost Beran, and seemed, rather, to ignore him. Beran thought perhaps he had gone unrecognized after all.

Beran tried to maintain at least the semblance of his former life at the Institute, and made himself conspicuous about the various studios, research libraries and classrooms, so that there should be no apparent diminution in his activity.

On the third day, entering a depiction booth at the library, he almost bumped into Finisterle emerging. The two looked eye to eye. Then Finisterle stepped aside with a polite excuse, and went his way. Beran, his face hot as fire, entered the booth, but was too upset to code for the film he had come to study.

Then the next morning, as luck would have it, he was assigned to a recitation class conducted by Finisterle, and found himself seated across a dark teak table from this ubiquitous son of Palafox.

Finisterle's expression did not change; he was grave and polite when he spoke to Beran—but Beran thought he saw a sardonic spark in the other man's eyes. Finisterle seemed too grave, too solicitous, too courteous.

Beran's nerves could stand no further suspense. After the class he waited in his seat while the others departed.

Finisterle, likewise, had risen to leave. He lifted his eyebrows in polite surprise when Beran spoke to him. "You have a question, Student Paraio?"

"I want to know what you plan toward me. Why don't you report me to Palafox?"

Finisterle made no pretense of incomprehension. "The fact that as Beran Panasper you attend the Institute, and as Ercole Paraio you study languages with the Paonese? What should I plan, why should I report you?"

"I don't know. I wonder if you will."

"I cannot understand how your conduct affects me."

"You must know I am here as ward of Lord Palafox."

"Oh indeed. But I have no mandate to guard his interests. Even," he added delicately, "if I desired to do so."

Beran looked his surprise. Finisterle went on in a soft voice. "You are Paonese; you do not understand us of Breakness. We are total individuals—each has his private goal. The Paonese word 'co-operation' has no counterpart on Breakness. How would I advance myself by monitoring your case to Sire Palafox? Such an act is irreversible. I commit myself without perceptible advantage. If I say nothing, I have alternate channels always open."

Beran stammered, "Do I understand then, that you do not intend to report me?"

Finisterle nodded. "Not unless it reacts to my advantage. And this I can not envision at the moment."

CHAPTER XII

A year passed—a year of anxiety, inward triumph, carefully stifled hope; a year of artifice, of intense study in which the necessity to learn seemed to kindle the powers of learning; a year during which Beran Panasper, the Paonese exile, was an attentive if irregular student at the Institute and Ercole Paraio, the Paonese apprentice linguist, made swift progress in three new languages: Valiant, Technicant and Cogitant.

To Beran's surprise and to his great advantage, Cogitant proved to be the language of Breakness, modified considerably against the solipsism latent in the original tongue.

Beran thought it best not to display ignorance of current conditions on Pao, and restrained his questions. Nevertheless, by circuitous methods, he learned much of what was transpiring on Pao.

On sections of two continents, the Hylanth Littoral of Shraimand, and along the shores of Zelambre Bay on the north coast of Vidamand, dispossession, violence and the misery of refugee camps still continued. No one knew definitely the scope of Bustamonte's plans—no doubt as Bustamonte intended. In both areas, the original population had been and were being disestablished, while the enclave of new speech expanded, a tide pressing against the retreating shores of the old Paonese customs. The areas affected were still comparatively small, and the new populations very young: children in the first and second octads of life, guided by a sparse cadre of linguists who under pain of death spoke only the new language.

In subdued voices the apprentices recalled scenes of anguish: the absolute passive obduracy of the population, even in the face of starvation; the reprisals, effected with true Paonese disregard for the individual life.

In other respects Bustamonte had proved himself a capable ruler. Prices were stable, the civil service was reasonably efficient. His personal scale of living was splendid enough to gratify the Paonese love of pomp, but not so extravagantly magnificent as to bankrupt the treasury. Only on Shraimand and Vidamand was there real dissatisfaction—and here of course dissatisfaction was a mild word for the sullen rancor, the pain and grief.

Of the infant societies which in due course would expand across the vacated lands, little was known and Beran found it hard to distinguish between speculation and fact.

A person born to the Paonese tradition inherited insensitivity toward human suffering—not so much callousness as an intuition of fate. Pao was a world of vast numbers and cataclysm automatically affected great masses of people. A Paonese hence might be touched by the plight of a bird with a broken wing, even as he ignored news of ten thousand drowning in a tidal wave.

Beran's Paonese endowment had been modified by his education; for no one could regard the population of Breakness as anything other than a set of discrete units. Perhaps for this reason he was moved by the woe of Shraimand and Vidamand. Hate, an element hitherto foreign to his nature, began to find a place in his mind. Bustamonte, Palafox—these men had vast horrors to answer for!

The year moved to its completion. Beran, through a combination of natural intelligence, zeal and his prior knowledge of the Breakness language, achieved a creditable record as apprentice linguist, and likewise sustained something of his previous program. In effect Beran lived two distinct existences, each insulated from the other. His old life, as student at Breakness Institute, offered no problem, since no one spent an iota of attention on any but his own problems.

As an apprentice linguist, the situation was more difficult. His fellow students were Paonese, gregarious and inquisitive, and Beran won a reputation for eccentricity, for he had neither time nor inclination to join the spare time recreations.

In a jocular moment the students contrived a bastard mish-mash of a language, assembled from scraps of Paonese, Cogitant, Valiant, Technicant, Mercantil and Batch, with a syncretic syntax and heterogeneous vocabulary. This patchwork tongue was known as Pastiche.

The students vied in fluency and used it to the disapproval of the instructors, who felt that the effort might better be spent in their studies. The students, referring to the Valiants, the Technicants and the Cogitants, argued that in all logic and consistency the Interpreters should likewise speak a characteristic tongue—so why not Pastiche?

The instructors agreed in principle, but objected to Pastiche as a formless mélange, a hodge-podge without style or dignity. The students were unconcerned, but nevertheless made amused attempts to contrive style and dignity for their creation.

Beran mastered Pastiche with the others, but took no part in its formulation. With other demands on his attention, he had small energy for linguistic recreations. And ever as the time of return to Pao drew near, Beran's nerves tautened, and his fear of apprehension increased. A year of hope blasted; how could he bear it?

One month remained, then a week, and the linguists spoke of nothing but Pao. Beran remained apart from the others, pale and anxious, gnawing his lips.

He met Finisterle in one of the dark corridors, and stopped short. Would Finisterle, now reminded, report him; would Finisterle set at nought his work of an entire year? But Finisterle walked past, gaze fixed on some inner image.

Four days, three days, two days—and then during the final recitations the instructor exploded a bombshell. The shock came with such sudden devastation that Beran was frozen in his seat and a pink fog blurred his vision.

"...you will now hear the eminent Dominie who initiated the program. He will explain the scope of your work, the responsibilities that are yours. Here is Lord Palafox."

Palafox strode into the room, looking neither right nor left. Beran crouched helplessly in his seat, a rabbit hoping to evade the notice of an eagle.

Palafox bowed formally to the class, making a casual survey of faces. Beran sat with head ducked behind the youth ahead; Palafox's eyes did not linger in his direction.

"I have followed your progress," said Palafox. "You have done creditably. Your presence here on Breakness was frankly an experiment, and your achievements have been compared to the work of similar groups studying on Pao. Apparently the Breakness atmosphere is a stimulus—your work has been appreciably superior. I understand that you have even evolved a characteristic language of your own—Pastiche." He smiled indulgently. "It is an ingenious idea, and though the tongue lacks elegance, a real achievement.

"I assume that you understand the magnitude of your responsibilities. You comprise nothing less than the bearings on which the machinery of Pao will run. Without your services, the new social mechanisms of Pao could not mesh, could not function."

He paused, surveyed his audience; again Beran ducked his head.

Palafox continued in a slightly different tone of voice. "I have heard many theories to explain Panarch Bustamonte's innovations, and they have been for the most part fallacious. The actuality is basically simple, yet grand in scope. In the past, Paonese society was a uniform organism with weaknesses that inevitably attracted predators. The new diversity creates strength in every direction, protects the areas of former weakness. Such is our design—but how well we succeed only the future can tell. You linguists will contribute greatly to any eventual success. You must school yourselves to flexibility. You must understand the peculiarities of each of the new Paonese societies, for your main task will be to reconcile conflicting interpretations of the same phenomena. In a large measure your efforts will determine the future of Pao."

He bowed once more and marched for the door. Beran watched him approach with thumping heart. He passed an arm's length away; Beran could feel the air of his passage. With the utmost difficulty, he prevented himself from hiding his face in his hands. Palafox's head did not turn; he left the room without slackening his stride. Beran sagged sprawled out, his arms and legs limp. Palafox was not infallible—Palafox had not seen him.

On the day following, the class with great jubilation departed the dormitory and rode the air-bus to the terminal. Among them, concealed by his identity with the others, was Beran.

The class entered the terminal, filed toward the check-off desk. The line moved forward; his mates spoke their names, turned in their passbooks, received passage vouchers, departed through the gate into the waiting lighter. Beran came to the desk. "Ercole Paraio," he said huskily, putting his passbook down.

"Ercole Paraio." The clerk checked off the name, pushed across a voucher.

Beran took the voucher with trembling fingers, moved forward, walked as fast as he dared to the gate. He looked neither right nor left, afraid to meet the sardonic gaze of Lord Palafox.

He passed through the gate, into the lighter. Presently the port closed, the lighter rose from the rock-melt flat, swung to the blast of the wind. Up and away from Breakness, up to the orbiting ship. And finally Beran dared hope that his plan of a year's duration, his scheme to escape Breakness, might succeed.

The linguists transferred into the ship, the lighter fell away. A pulse, a thud—the voyage had begun.

Breakness astern, Pao ahead. Beran's escape was reality. He had eluded the vigilance of the Institute, the outwardly insurmountable forces arrayed against him, the merest accident, a blind fluke...the simple wonder of it! But—Beran speculated—was that so incredible, really? Did not many of the great turning points in the history of civilizations, the great changes that shook established customs to their foundations, have their origin in some trivial incident—a shrewd man's accidental, momentary carelessness, a breakdown or lapse of authority at some vital point? No, it was not too incredible. Many times before, a prisoner, with the lightning at his fingertips, had simply walked out, unobserved and unchallenged. It was one of the recurrent ironies of life.

CHAPTER XIII

The small white sun dwindled, became a single glitter in the myriad; the ship floated in black space, imperceptibly shifting through the stars of the cluster.

At last yellow Auriol grew bright, tended by blue-green Pao. Beran could not leave the bulls-eye. He watched the world expand, lurch from a disk to a sphere. He traced the configuration of the eight continents, put names to a hundred islands, located the great cities. Nine years had passed—almost half of his life; he could not hope to find Pao the world of his recollections. His perspectives had changed, and Pao had by no means enjoyed nine years of tranquillity. Still, the blue oceans, the verdant islands would be the same; the innumerable villages with whitewashed walls and brown tile roofs, the masses of people—to alter all these would require a greater power than Bustamonte's.

What if his absence from Breakness Institute had been detected, what if Palafox had communicated with Bustamonte? It was an apprehension that Beran had toyed with all during the voyage. If it were accurate, then awaiting the ship would be a squad of Mamarone, and Beran's homecoming would be a glimpse or two of the countryside, a lift, a thrust, the rushing air with cloud and sky whirling above, the wet impact, the deepening blue of ocean water as he sank to his death.

The idea seemed not only logical but likely. The lighter drew alongside; Beran went aboard. The other linguists broke into an old Paonese chant, waggishly rendered into Pastiche.

The lighter eased down upon the field; the exit ports opened. The others tumbled happily forth; Beran pulled himself to his feet, warily followed. There was no one at hand but the usual attendants. He drew a great breath, looked all around the field. The time was early afternoon; fleecy clouds floated in a sky which was the very essence of blue. The sun fell warm on his face. Beran felt an almost religious happiness. He would never leave Pao again, in life or in death; if subaqueation awaited him, he preferred it to life on Breakness.

The linguists marched off the field, into the shabby old terminal. There was no one to meet them, a fact which only Beran, accustomed to the automatic efficiency of Breakness, found extraordinary. Looking around the faces of his fellows, he thought, I am changed. Palafox did his worst upon me. I love Pao, but I am no longer Paonese. I am tainted with the flavor of Breakness; I can never be truly and wholly a part of this world again—or of any other world. I am dispossessed, eclectic; I am Pastiche.

Beran separated himself from the others, went to the portal, looked down the tree-shaded boulevard toward Eiljanre. He could step forth, lose himself in a moment.

But where would he go? If he appeared at the palace, he would receive the shortest of shrift. Beran had no wish to farm, to fish, to carry loads. Thoughtfully he turned back, rejoined the linguists. It was always possible that his imposture might be discovered, but Paonese records were hardly precise enough to make this event likely.

The official welcoming committee arrived; one of the dignitaries performed a congratulatory declamation, the linguists made formal appreciation. They were then ushered aboard a bus and taken to one of the rambling Eiljanre inns.

Beran, scanning the streets, was puzzled. His imagination had depicted repression and terror; he saw only the usual Paonese ease. Naturally, this was Eiljanre, not the resettled areas of Shraimand and Vidamand—but surely the sheer reflection of Bustamonte's tyranny must leave a mark! Yet...the faces along the avenue were placid.

The bus entered the Cantatrino, a great park with three artificial mountains and a lake, the memorial of an ancient Panarch for his dead daughter, the fabulous Can. The bus passed a moss-draped arch, where the park authority had arranged a floral portrait of Panarch Bustamonte. Someone had expressed his feelings with a handful of black slime. A small sign—but it revealed much, for the Paonese seldom made political judgments.

Ercole Paraio was assigned to the Progress School at Cloeopter, on the shores of Zelambre Bay, at the north of Vidamand. This was the area designated by Bustamonte to be the manufacturing and industrial center for all Pao. The school was located in an ancient stone monastery, built by the first settlers to a purpose long forgotten.

In the great cool halls, full of green leaf-filtered sunlight, children of all ages lived to the sound of the Technicant language, and were instructed according to a special doctrine of causality in the use of power machinery, mathematics, elementary science, engineering and manufacturing processes. The classes were conducted in well-equipped rooms and work-shops; although the students were quartered in hastily erected dormitories of poles and canvas to either side of the monastery. Girls and boys alike wore maroon coveralls and cloth caps, studied and worked with adult intensity. After hours there were no restraints upon their activities so long as they remained on school grounds.

The students were fed, clothed, housed and furnished only with the essentials. If they desired luxuries, play equipment, special tools, private rooms, these could be earned by producing articles for use elsewhere in Pao, and almost all of the students' spare time was devoted to small industrial ventures. They produced toys, pottery, simple electrical devices, aluminum ingots reduced from nearby ore, and even periodicals printed in Technicant. A group of eight-year students had joined in a more elaborate project: a plant to extract minerals from the ocean, and to this end spent all their funds for the necessary equipment.

The instructors were for the most part young Breakness dons. From the first, Beran was perplexed by a quality he was unable to locate, let alone identify; only after he had lived at Cloeopter two months did the source of the oddness come to him. It lay in the similarity which linked these Breakness dons. Once Beran had come this far, total enlightenment followed. These youths were all sons of Palafox. The name was never spoken in Beran's hearing, and probably—so Beran conjectured—never out of it.

Surely they were aware of their common parentage. The situation was strange, provocative to the imagination. What could they gain on this alien planet? By all tradition they should be engrossed in their most intensive studies at the Institute, preparing themselves for the Authority, earning modifications. But no, here they worked at an occupation they must regard as menial. Beran found the entire situation mysterious.

His own duties were simple enough, and in terms of Paonese culture, highly rewarding. The director of the school, an appointee of Bustamonte's, in theory, controlled the scope and policy of the school, but his responsibility was only nominal. Beran served as his interpreter, translating into Technicant such remarks that the director saw fit to make. For this service he was housed in a handsome cottage of cobbles and hand-hewn timber, a former farmhouse, paid a good salary and allowed a special uniform of gray-green with black and white trim.

A year passed. Beran took a melancholy interest in his work, and even found himself participating in the ambitions and plans of the students. He tried to compensate by describing with cautious enthusiasm the ideals of old Pao, but met blank unconcern. More interesting were the technical miracles they believed he must have witnessed in the Breakness laboratories.

During one of his holidays Beran made a dolorous pilgrimage to the old home of Gitan Netsko, a few miles inland. With some difficulty he found the old farm beside Mervan Pond. It was now deserted; the green glass windows were dusty and cracked, the timber dry, the fields of yarrow overgrown with thief-grass. He seated himself on a rotting bench under a low tree, and to his mind came sad images...

He climbed the slope of Blue Mountain, looked back over the valley. The solitude astonished him. Across all the horizon, over a fertile land once thronged with population, there was now no movement other than the flight of birds. Millions of human beings had been removed, most to other continents, but others had preferred to lie with their ancestral earth over them. And the flower of the land—the most beautiful and intelligent of the girls—had been transported to Breakness, to pay the debts of Bustamonte.

Beran despondently returned to Zelambre Bay. Theoretically it lay within his power to rectify the injustice—if he could find some means to regain his rightful authority. The difficulties seemed insuperable. He felt inept, incapable...

Driven by his dissatisfaction, he deliberately put himself in the way of danger, and journeyed north to Eiljanre. He took a room in the old Moravi Inn, on the Tidal Canal, directly opposite the walls of the Grand Palace. His hand hesitated over the register; he restrained the reckless impulse to scrawl *Beran Panasper,* and finally noted himself as Ercole Paraio.

The capital city seemed gay enough. Was it his imagination that detected an underlying echo of anger, uncertainty, hysteria? Perhaps not: the Paonese lived in the present, as the syntax of their language and the changeless rhythm of the Paonese day impelled them.

In a mood of cynical curiosity, he checked through the archives of the Muniment Library. Nine years back, he found the last mention of his name: "During the night the alien assassins poisoned the beloved young Medallion. Thus, tragically, the direct succession of the Panaspers ends, and the collateral line stemming from Panarch Bustamonte begins, with all auspices indicating tenure of extreme duration."

Irresolute, unconvinced, without power to enforce any resolution or conviction he might have settled upon, Beran returned to the school on Zelambre Bay.

Another year passed by. The Technicants grew older, more numerous, and greatly more expert. Four small fabrication systems were established, producing tools, plastic sheet, industrial chemicals, meters and gauges; a dozen others were in prospect, and it seemed as if this particular phase of Bustamonte's dream, at least, were to prove successful.

At the end of two years Beran was transferred to Pon, on Nonamand, the bleak island continent in the southern hemisphere. The transfer came as an unpleasant surprise, for Beran had established an easy routine at Zelambre Bay. Even more unsettling was the discovery that routine had become preferable to change. At the age of twenty-one, was he already enervated? Where were his hopes, his resolutions; had he so easily discarded them? Angry at himself, furious at Bustamonte, he rode the transport southeast across the rolling farmlands of South Vidamand, over the Plarth, across the orchards and vines of Minamand's Qurai Peninsula, across that long peculiar bight known as The Serpent, over the green island Fraevarth with its innumerable white villages, and across the Great Sea of the South. The Cliffs of Nonamand rose ahead, passed below, fell behind; they flew into the barren heart of the continent. Never before had Beran visited Nonamand, and the wind-whipped moors covered with thunder-stones, black gorse, contorted cypress seemed completely un-Paonese.

Ahead loomed the Sgolaph Mountains, the highest of all Pao. And suddenly they were over ice-crusted crags of basalt, in a land of glaciers, barren valleys, rushing white rivers. The transport circled the shattered cusp of Mount Droghead, swung quickly down upon a bare plateau, and Beran had arrived at Pon.

The settlement was reminiscent in spirit, if not in appearance, of Breakness Institute. A number of dwellings spread haphazardly to the contour of the terrain, surrounding a central clot of more massive buildings. These, so Beran learned, comprised laboratories, classrooms, a library, dormitories, refectories and an administration building.

Almost immediately Beran conceived a vast dislike for the settlement. Cogitant, the language spoken by the Paonese indoctrinees, was a simplified Breakness, shorn of several quasi-conditional word-orders, and with considerably looser use of pronouns. Nonetheless the atmosphere of the settlement was pure Breakness, even to the costumes affected by the 'dominies'—actually high-ranking dons. The countryside, while by no means as fierce as that of Breakness, was nevertheless forbidding. A dozen times Beran contemplated requesting a transfer, but each time restrained himself. He had no wish to call attention to himself, with the possibility of exposing his true identity.

The teaching staff, like that of the Zelambre schools, consisted primarily of young Breakness dons, and, again, they were all sons of Palafox. In residence were a dozen Paonese sub-ministers, representatives of Bustamonte, and Beran's function was to maintain coordination between the two groups.

A situation which aroused considerable uneasiness in Beran was the fact that Finisterle, the Breakness don who knew Beran's true identity, also worked at Pon. Three times Beran, with pounding heart, managed to slip aside before Finisterle could notice him, but on the fourth occasion the meeting could not be avoided. Finisterle made only the most casual of acknowledgements and passed on, leaving Beran staring after him.

In the next few weeks Beran saw Finisterle a number of times, and at last entered into guarded conversation. Finisterle's comments were the very definition of indirection.

Beran divined that Finisterle was anxious to continue his studies at the Institute, but remained at Pon for three reasons: first, it was the wish of his sire, Lord Palafox. Second, Finisterle felt that opportunity to breed sons of his own was easier on Pao than on Breakness. With so much, he was comparatively candid; the third reason was told more by his silences than his words. He seemed to regard Pao as a world in flux, a place of vast potentialities, where great power and prestige might be had by a person sufficiently deft and decisive.

What of Palafox? Beran wondered.

What of Palafox indeed, Finisterle seemed to say, and looking off across the plateau, apparently changed the subject. "Strange to think that even these crags, the Sgolaph, will some day be eroded to pene-plain. And on the other hand, the most innocent hillock may erupt into a volcano."

These concepts were beyond dispute, said Beran.

Finisterle propounded another apparently paradoxical law of nature: "The more forceful and capacious the brain of a dominie, the more wild and violent its impulses when it succumbs to sclerosis and its owner becomes an Emeritus."

But it was not Finisterle who gave Beran the greatest jolt. Several months later, Beran, leaving the administration headquarters, came face to face with Palafox.

Beran froze in his tracks; Palafox stared down from his greater height.

Summoning his composure, Beran performed the Paonese gesture of greeting. Palafox returned a sardonic acknowledgement. "I am surprised to see you here," said Palafox. "I had assumed that you were diligently pursuing your education on Breakness."

"I learned a great deal," said Beran. "And then I lost all heart for further learning."

Palafox's eyes glinted. "Education is not achieved through the heart—it is a systematization of the mental processes."

"But I am something other than a mental process," said Beran. "I am a man. I must reckon with the whole of myself."

Palafox was thinking, his eyes first contemplating Beran, then sliding along the line of the Sgolaph crags. When he spoke his voice was amiable, although the sense of his words was obscure. "There are no absolute certainties in this universe. A man must try to whip order into a yelping pack of probabilities, and uniform success is impossible."

Beran understood the meaning latent in Palafox's rather general remarks. "Since you had assured me that you took no further interest in my future, it was necessary that I act for myself. I did so, and returned to Pao."

Palafox nodded. "Beyond question, events took place outside the radius of my control. Still these rogue circumstances are often as advantageous as the most carefully nurtured plans."

"Please continue to neglect me in your calculations," said Beran in a carefully passionless voice. "I have learned to enjoy the sense of free action."

Palafox laughed with an untypical geniality. "Well said! And what do you think of new Pao?"

"I am puzzled. I have formed no single conviction."

"Understandable. There are a million facts at a thousand different levels to be assessed and reconciled. Confusion is inevitable unless you are driven by a basic ambition, as I am and as is Panarch Bustamonte. For us, these facts can be separated into categories: favorable and unfavorable."

He stepped back a pace, inspected Beran from head to foot. "Evidently you occupy yourself as a linguist."

Beran made a rather reluctant admission that this was so.

"If for no other reason," said Palafox, "you should feel gratitude to me and Breakness Institute."

"Gratitude would be a misleading oversimplification."

"Possibly so," agreed Palafox. "And now, if you will excuse me, I must hurry to my appointment with the Director."

"One moment," said Beran. "I am perplexed. You seem not at all disturbed by my presence on Pao. Do you plan to inform Bustamonte?"

Palafox showed restiveness at the direct question; it was one which a Breakness dominie would never have deigned to make. "I plan no interference in your affairs." He hesitated a moment, then spoke in a new and confidential manner. "If you must know, circumstances have altered. Panarch Bustamonte becomes more headstrong as the years go by, and your presence may serve a useful purpose."

Beran angrily started to speak, but observing Palafox's faintly amused expression held his tongue. After all, Palafox need speak but a single sentence to bring about his death.

"I must be on to my business," said Palafox. "Events proceed at an ever accelerating tempo. The next year or two will resolve a number of uncertainties."

Three weeks after his encounter with Palafox, Beran was transferred to Deirombona on Shraimand, where a multitude of infants, heirs to five thousand years of Paonese placidity, had been immersed in a plasm of competitiveness. Many of these were now only a few years short of manhood.

Deirombona was the oldest inhabited site on Pao, a sprawling low city of coral block in a forest of phaltorhyncus. For some reason not readily apparent, the city had been evacuated of its two million inhabitants. Deirombona Harbor remained in use; a few administrative offices had been given over to Valiant affairs; otherwise the old buildings lay stark as skeletons, bleaching under the tall trees. In the Colonial Sector, a few furtive vagrants lurked among the apartment blocks, venturing forth at night to scavenge and loot. They risked subaqueation, but since the authorities would hardly comb the maze of streets, alleys, cellars, houses, stores, warehouses, apartments and public buildings, the vagrants considered themselves secure.

Ten Valiant cantonments had been established at intervals up the coast, each headquarters to a legion of Myrmidons, as the Valiant warriors called themselves.

Beran had been assigned to the Deirombona Legion, and had at his disposal all the abandoned city in which to find living quarters. He selected an airy cottage on the old Lido, and was able to make himself extremely comfortable.

In many ways the Valiants were the most interesting of all the new Paonese societies. They were easily the most dramatic. Like the

Technicants of Zelambre Bay and the Cogitants of Pon, the Valiants were a race of youths, the oldest not yet Beran's age. They made a strange glittering spectacle as they strode through the Paonese sunlight, arms swinging, eyes fixed straight ahead in mystical exaltation. Their garments were intricate and of many colors, but each wore a personal device on his chest, legion insignia on his back.

During the day the young men and women trained separately, mastering their new weapons and mechanisms, but at night they ate and slept together indiscriminately, distinction being only one of rank. Sexual contacts were common, casual, barren of any sublimation or fervor. Emotional import was given only to organizational relationships, to competition for rank and honor.

On the evening of Beran's arrival at Deirombona, a ceremonial convocation took place at the cantonment. At the center of the parade ground a great fire burnt on a platform. Behind rose the Deirombona stele, a prism of black metal emblazoned with emblems. To either side stood ranks of young Myrmidons, and tonight all wore common garb: a plain dark gray leotard. Each carried a ceremonial lance, with a pale flickering flame in the place of a blade.

A fanfare rang out. A girl in white came forward, carrying an insignia of copper, silver and brass. While the Myrmidons knelt and bowed their heads, the girl carried the insignia three times around the fire and fixed it upon the stele.

The fire roared high. The Myrmidons rose to their feet, thrust their lances into the air. They formed into ranks and marched from the square.

The next day Beran received an explanation from his immediate superior, Sub-Strategist Gian Firanu, a soldier-of-fortune from one of the far worlds. "You witnessed a funeral—a hero's funeral. Last week Deirombona held war-games with Tarai, the next camp up the coast. A Tarai submarine had penetrated our net and was scoring against our base. All the Deirombona warriors were eager, but Lemauden was first. He dove five hundred feet with a torch and cut away the ballast. The submarine rose and was captured. But Lemauden drowned—possibly by accident."

"'Possibly by accident'? How else? Surely the Tarai…"

"No, not the Tarai. But it might have been a deliberate act. These lads are wild to place their emblems on the stele—they'll do anything to create a legend."

Beran went to the window. Along the Deirombona esplanade swaggered groups of young bravos. Was this Pao? Or some fantastic world a hundred light-years distant?

Gian Firanu was speaking; his words at first did not penetrate Beran's consciousness. "There's a new rumor going around—perhaps you've already heard it—to the effect that Bustamonte is not the true Panarch, merely Ayudor-Senior. It's said that somewhere Beran Panasper is alive and grows to manhood, gaining strength like a mythical hero. And when the hour strikes—so the supposition goes—he will come forth to fling Bustamonte into the sea."

Beran stared suspiciously, then laughed. "I had not heard this rumor. But it may well be fact, who knows?"

"Bustamonte will not enjoy the story!"

Beran laughed again, this time with genuine humor. "Better than anyone else, he'll know what truth there is in the rumor. I wonder who started this rumor."

Firanu shrugged. "Who starts any rumor? No one. They come of idle talk and misunderstanding."

"In most cases—but not all," said Beran. "Suppose this were the truth?"

"Then there is trouble ahead. And I return to Earth."

Beran heard the rumor later in the day with embellishments. The supposedly assassinated Medallion inhabited a remote island; he trained a corps of metal-clad warriors impervious to fire, steel or power; the mission of his life was to avenge his father's death—and Bustamonte walked in fear.

The talk died away, then three months later flared up again. This time the rumor told of Bustamonte's secret police combing the planet, of thousands of young men conveyed to Eiljanre for examination, and thereafter executed, so that Bustamonte's uneasiness should not become known.

Beran had long been secure in the identity of Ercole Paraio; but now all complacency left him. He became distrait and faltered in his work. His associates observed him curiously and at last Gian Firanu inquired as to the nature of his preoccupation.

Beran muttered something about a woman in Eiljanre who was bearing his child. Firanu tartly suggested that Beran either expel so trivial a concern from his attention or take leave of absence until he felt free to concentrate on his work. Beran hastily accepted the leave of absence.

He returned to his cottage and sat several hours on the sun-flooded verandah, hoping to strike upon some sensible plan of action. The linguists might not be the first objects of suspicion, but neither would they be the last.

He could immerse himself in his role, make the identity of Ercole Paraio a trustworthy disguise. He could conceive no means to this end, and the secret police were a good deal more sophisticated than himself.

He could seek help from Palafox. He toyed with the idea only an instant before discarding it with a twinge of self-disgust. He considered leaving the planet, but where would he go—assuming that he were able to book passage?

He felt restless. There was urgency in the air, a sense of pressure. He rose to his feet, looked all around him: up the deserted streets, out across the sea. He jumped down to the beach, walked along the shore to the single inn still functioning in Deirombona. In the public tavern he ordered chilled wine, and taking it out on the rattan-shaded terrace, drank rather more deeply and hastily than was his custom.

The air was heavy, the horizons close. From up the street, near the building where he worked, he saw movement, color: several men in purple and brown.

Beran half-rose from his seat, staring. He sank slowly back, sat limp. Thoughtfully he sipped his wine. A dark shadow crossed his vision. He looked up; a tall figure stood in front of him: Palafox.

Palafox nodded a casual greeting and seated himself. "It appears," said Palafox, "that the history of contemporary Pao has not yet completely unfolded."

Beran said something indistinguishable. Palafox nodded his head gravely, as if Beran had put forward a profound wisdom. He indicated the three men in brown and purple who had entered the inn and were now conferring with the major-domo.

"A useful aspect of Paonese culture is the style of dress. One may determine a person's profession at a glance. Are not brown and purple the colors of the internal police?"

"Yes, that is true," said Beran. Suddenly his anxiety was gone. The worst had occurred, the tension was broken: impossible to dread what had already happened. He said in a reflective voice, "I suppose they come seeking me."

"In that case," said Palafox, "it would be wise if you departed."

"Departed? Where?"

"Where I will take you."

"No," said Beran. "I will be your tool no more."

Palafox raised his eyebrows. "What do you lose? I am offering to save your life."

"Not through concern for my welfare."

"Of course not." Palafox grinned, showing his teeth in a momentary flash. "Who but a simpleton is so guided? I serve you in order to serve myself. With this understanding I suggest we now depart the inn. I do not care to appear overtly in this affair."

"No."

Palafox was roused to anger. "What do you want?"

"I want to become Panarch."

"Yes, of course," exclaimed Palafox. "Why else do you suppose I am here? Come, let us be off, or you will be no more than carrion."

Beran rose to his feet; they departed the inn.

CHAPTER XIV

The two men flew south, across the Paonese countryside, rich with ancient habitancy; then over the seas, flecked with the sails of fishing craft. League after league they flew, and neither man spoke, each contained in his own thoughts.

Beran finally broke the silence. "What is the process by which I become Panarch?"

Palafox said shortly, "The process began a month ago."

"The rumors?"

Palafox was perhaps irritated by the implied deprecation. He answered in a metallic voice, "It is necessary that the people of Pao realize that you exist."

"And why am I preferable to Bustamonte?"

Palafox laughed crisply. "In general outline, my interests would not be served by certain of Bustamonte's plans."

"And you hope that I will be more sympathetic to you?"

"You could not be more obstinate than Bustamonte."

"In what regard was Bustamonte obstinate?" Beran persisted. "He refused to concede to all your desires?"

Palafox chuckled hollowly. "Ah, you young rascal! I believe you would deprive me of all my prerogatives."

Beran was silent, reflecting that if he ever became Panarch, this indeed would be one of his primary concerns.

Palafox spoke on in a more conciliatory tone. "These affairs are for the future, and need not concern us now. At the present we are allies. To signalize this fact, I have arranged that a modification be made upon your body, as soon as we arrive at Pon."

Beran was taken by surprise. "A modification?" He considered a moment, feeling a qualm of uneasiness. "Of what nature?"

"What modification would you prefer?" Palafox asked mildly.

Beran darted a glance at the hard profile. Palafox seemed completely serious. "The total use of my brain."

"Ah," said Palafox. "That is the most delicate and precise of all, and would require a year of toil on Breakness itself. At Pon it is impossible. Choose again."

"Evidently my life is to be one of many emergencies," said Beran. "The power of projecting energy from my hand might prove valuable."

"True," reflected Palafox. "And yet, on the other hand, what could more completely confuse your enemies than to see you rise into the air and float away? And since, with a novice, the easy projection of destruction endangers friends as well as enemies, we had better decide upon levitation as your first modification."

The surf-beaten cliffs of Nonamand rose from the ocean; they passed above a grimy fishing village, rode over the first ramparts of the Sgolaphs, flew low over the moors toward the central spine of the continent. Mount Droghead raised its cataclysmic crags; they swept close around the icy flanks, swerved down to the plateau of Pon. The car settled beside a long low building with rock-melt walls and a glass roof. Doors opened; Palafox floated the car within. They grounded on a floor of white tile; Palafox opened the port and motioned Beran out.

Beran hesitated, dubiously inspecting the four men who came forward. Each differed from the others in height, weight, skin and hair-color, but each was like the others.

"My sons," said Palafox. "Everywhere on Pao you will find my sons...But time is valuable, and we must set about your modification."

Beran alighted from the car; the sons of Palafox led him away.

They laid the anaesthetized body on a pallet, injected and impregnated the tissues with various toners and conditioners. Then standing far back, they flung a switch. There was a shrill whine, a flutter of violet light, a distortion of the space as if the scene were observed through moving panels of poor glass.

The whine died; the figures stepped forward around the body now stiff, dead, rigid. The flesh was hard, but elastic; the fluids were congealed; the joints firm.

The men worked swiftly, with exceeding deftness. They used knives with entering edges only six molecules thick. The knives cut without pressure, splitting the tissues into glass-smooth laminae. The body was laid open halfway up the back, slit down either side through the buttocks, thighs, calves. With single strokes of another type of knife, curiously singing, the soles of the feet were removed. The flesh was rigid, like rubber; there was no trace of blood or body fluid, no quiver of muscular motion.

A section of lung was cut out, an ovoid energy-bank introduced. Conductors were laid into the flesh, connecting to flexible transformers in the buttocks, to processors in the calves. The antigravity mesh was laid into the bottom of the feet and connected to the processors in the calves by means of flexible tubes thrust up through the feet.

The circuit was complete. It was tested and checked; a switch was installed under the skin of the left thigh. And now began the tedious job of restoring the body.

The soles were dipped in special stimulating fluid, returned precisely into place, with accuracy sufficient to bring cell wall opposite cell wall, severed artery tight to severed artery, nerve fibril against nerve fibril. The slits along the body were pressed tightly together, the flesh drawn back into place over the energy bank.

Eighteen hours had passed. The four men now departed for rest, and the dead body lay alone in the darkness.

Next day the four men returned. The great machine whined again, and the violet light flickered around the room. The field which had gripped the atoms of Beran's body, in theory reducing his temperature to absolute zero, relaxed, and the molecules resumed their motion.

The body once more lived.

A week passed, while Beran, still comatose, healed. He returned to consciousness to find Palafox standing before the pallet.

"Rise," said Palafox. "Stand on your feet."

Beran lay quiet for a moment, aware by some inner mechanism that considerable time had passed.

Palafox seemed impatient and driven by haste. His eyes glittered; he made an urgent gesture with his thin strong hand. "Rise! Stand!"

Beran slowly raised himself to his feet.

"Walk!"

Beran walked across the room. There was a tautness down his legs, and the energy-bulb weighed on the muscles of his diaphragm and rib-sheathing.

Palafox was keenly watching the motion of his feet. "Good," he exclaimed. "I see no halting or discoordination. Come with me."

He took Beran into a high room, hitched a harness over his shoulders, snapped a cord into a ring at his back.

"Feel here." He directed Beran's left hand to a spot on his thigh. "Tap."

Beran felt a vague solidity under his skin. He tapped. The floor ceased to press at his feet; his stomach jerked; his head felt like a balloon.

"This is charge one," said Palafox. "A repulsion of slightly less than one gravity, adjusted to cancel the centrifugal effect of planetary rotation."

He made the other end of the cord fast on a cleat. "Tap again."

Beran touched the plate, and instantly it seemed as if the entire environment had turned end for end, as if Palafox stood above him, glued to the ceiling, as if he were falling head-first at a floor thirty feet below him. He gasped, flailed out his arms; the cord caught him, held him from falling. He turned a desperate glance toward Palafox, who stood faintly smiling.

"To increase the field, press the bottom of the plate," called Palafox. "To decrease, press the top. If you tap twice, the field goes dead."

Beran managed to return to the floor. The room righted, but swung and bobbed with nauseating effect.

"It will be days before you accustom yourself to the levitation mesh," said Palafox briskly. "Since time is short, I suggest that you practice the art diligently." He turned toward the door.

Beran started to reply, but Palafox silenced him with a gesture.

Beran watched him walk away, frowning in puzzlement. "Just why is time short, then?" he called to the spare retreating back.

Palafox swung around. "The date," he said, "is the fourth day of the third week of the eighth month. On Kanetsides Day I plan that you shall be Panarch of Pao."

"Why?" asked Beran.

"Why do you continually require that I expose myself to you?"

"I ask from both curiosity and in order to plan my own conduct. You intend that I be Panarch. You wish to work with me." The gleam in Palafox's eyes brightened. "Perhaps I should say, you hope to work through me, in order to serve your ends. Therefore, I ask myself what these ends are."

Palafox considered him a moment, then replied in a cool even voice. "Your thoughts move with the deft precision of worm-tracks in the mud. Naturally I plan that you shall serve my ends. You plan, or, at any rate, you hope, that I shall serve yours. So far as you are concerned, this process is well toward fruition. I am working diligently to secure your birthright, and if I succeed, you shall be Panarch of Pao. When you demand the nature of my motives, you reveal the style of your thinking to be callow, captious, superficial, craven, uncertain and impudent."

Beran began to sputter a furious refutal, but Palafox cut him off with a gesture. "Naturally you accept my help—why should you not? It is only right to strive for your goals. But, after accepting my help, you must choose one of two courses: serve me or fight me. Forward my aims or attempt to deny me. These are positive courses. But to expect me to continue serving you from a policy of abnegation is negative and absurd."

"I cannot consider mass misery absurd," snapped Beran. "My aims are…"

Palafox held up his hand. "There is nothing more to say. The scope of my plans you must deduce for yourself. Submit or oppose, whichever you wish. I am unconcerned, since you are powerless to deflect me."

Day after day Beran practiced the use of his modification, and gradually became adjusted to the sensation of falling head-first away from the ground.

He learned how to move through the air, by leaning in the direction he wished to travel; he learned how to descend, falling so fast the air sang past his ears, then braking with deft timing to land without a jar.

On the eleventh day, a boy in a smart gray cape, no more than eight years old, with the typical Palafox cast to his features, invited Beran to Palafox's apartments.

Crossing the concrete quadrangle, Beran armed his mind and arranged his emotions for the interview. He marched through the portal stiff with resolution.

Palafox was sitting at his desk, idly arranging polished trapezoids of rock crystal. His manner was almost affable as he directed Beran to a chair.

Beran warily seated himself.

"Tomorrow," said Palafox, "we enter the second phase of the program. The emotional environment is suitably sensitive: there is a general sense of expectation. Tomorrow, the quick stroke, the accomplishment! In a suitable manner we affirm the existence of the traditional Panarch. And then—" Palafox rose to his feet "—and then, who knows? Bustamonte may resign himself to the situation, or he may resist. We will be prepared for either contingency."

Beran was not thawed by unexpected cordiality. "I would understand better had we discussed these plans over a period of time."

Palafox chuckled genially. "Impossible, estimable Panarch. You must accept the fact that we here at Pon function as a General Staff. We have prepared dozens of programs of greater or less complexity, suitable for various situations. This is the first pattern of events to mesh with one of the plans."

"What, then, is the pattern of events?"

"Tomorrow three million persons attend the Pamalisthen Drones. You will appear, make yourself known. Television will convey your face and your words elsewhere on Pao."

"Tomorrow?"

"Tomorrow."

Beran chewed his lips, angry both at his own uneasiness and at Palafox's indomitable affability. "What exactly is the program?"

"It is of the utmost simplicity. The Drones commence at an hour after dawn and continue until noon. At this time is the pause. There will be a rumor-passing, and you will be expected. You will appear wearing Black. You will speak." Palafox handed Beran a sheet of paper. "These few sentences should be sufficient."

Beran dubiously glanced down the lines of script. "I hope events work out as you plan. I want no bloodshed, no violence."

Palafox shrugged. "It is impossible to foretell the future. If things go well, no one will suffer except Bustamonte."

"And if things go poorly?"

Palafox laughed. "The ocean bottom is the rendezvous for those who plan poorly."

CHAPTER XV

Across the Hyaline Gulf from Eiljanre was Mathiole, a region of special and peculiar glamour. There were romantic dells and waterfalls, mountains which swept across the sky with dashing and delicate outlines. The trees of the land grew with a distinctive flair, the flowers glowed with prismatic light, the waters seemed derived from dew. In the folktales of early Pao, when episodes of fantasy and romance occurred, Mathiole was inevitably the locale.

To the south of Mathiole was the Pamalisthen, a verdant plain of farms and orchards arranged like pleasure-glades. Here were seven cities, forming the apices of a great heptagon; and at the very center was Festival Field, where drones took place. Among all the numerous gatherings, convocations and Grand Massings of Pao, the Pamalisthen Drones were accorded the highest prestige.

Long before dawn, on the Eighth Day of the Eighth Week of the Eighth Month, Festival Field began to fill. Small fires flickered by the thousands; a susurration rose from the plain.

With dawn came throngs more: families gravely gay, in the Paonese fashion. The small children wore clean white smocks, the adolescents school uniforms with various blazons on their shoulders, the adults in the styles and colors befitting their place in society.

The sun rose, generating the blue, white and yellow of a Paonese day. The crowds pressed into the field: millions of individuals standing shoulder to shoulder, speaking only in hushed whispers, but for the most part silent, each person testing his identification with the crowd, adding his soul to the amalgam, withdrawing a sense of rapturous strength.

The first whispers of the drone began: long sighs of sound, intervals of silence between. The sighs grew louder and the silences shorter, and presently the drones were in full pitch—a not-quite-inchoate progression, without melody or tonality: a harmony of three million parts, shifting and fluctuating, but always of definite emotional texture.

The moods shifted in a spontaneous but ordained sequence, moods stately and abstract, in the same relationship to jubilation or woe that a valley full of mist bears to a fountain of diamonds.

Hours passed, the drones grew higher in pitch, rather more insistent and urgent. When the sun was two-thirds up the sky, a long black saloon-flyer appeared from the direction of Eiljanre. It sank quietly to a low eminence at the far end of the field. Those who had taken places here were thrust down into the plain, barely escaping the descending hull. A few curious loitered, peering in through the glistening ports. A squad of neutraloids in magenta and blue debarked and drove them off with silent efficiency.

Four servants brought forth first a black and brown carpet, then a polished black wooden chair with black cushioning.

Across the plain, the drones took on a subtly different character, perceptible only to a Paonese ear.

Bustamonte, emerging from the black saloon, was Paonese. He perceived and understood. His round white face compacted into a frown, he glanced from right to left across the multitude as if seeking one to fix guilt upon.

The drones continued. The mode changed once more as if Bustamonte's arrival were no more than a transient trifle—a slight more pungent, even, than the original chord of dislike and mockery.

Down the ordained progression of changes went the drones. Shortly before noon the sound ceased. The crowd quivered and moved; a sigh of satisfied achievement rose and died. The crowd changed color and texture, as all who could do so squatted to the ground.

Bustamonte grasped the arms of his chair to rise. The crowd was in its most receptive state, sensitized and aware. He clicked on his shoulder microphone, stepped forward to speak.

A great gasp came from the plain, a sound of vast astonishment and delight.

All eyes were fixed on the sky over Bustamonte's head, where a great rectangle of rippling black velvet had appeared, bearing the blazon of the Panasper Dynasty. Below, in mid-air, stood a solitary figure. He wore short black trousers, black boots, and a rakish black cape clipped over one shoulder. He spoke; the sound echoed over all Festival Field.

"Paonese: I am your Panarch. I am Beran, son to Aiello, scion of the ancient Panasper Dynasty. Many years I have lived in exile, growing to my maturity. Bustamonte has served as Ayudor. He has made mistakes—now I have come to supersede him. I hereby call on Bustamonte to acknowledge me, to make an orderly transfer of authority. Bustamonte, speak!"

Bustamonte had already spoken. A dozen neutraloids ran forward with rifles, knelt, aimed. Lances of white fire raced up to converge on the figure in black. The figure seemed to shatter, to explode; the crowd gasped in shock.

The fire-lances turned against the black rectangle, but this appeared impervious to the energy. Bustamonte swaggered truculently forward. "This is the fate meted to idiots, charlatans and all those who would violate the justice of the government. The impostor, as you have seen..."

Beran's voice came down from the sky. "You shattered only my image, Bustamonte. You must acknowledge me: I am Beran, Panarch of Pao."

"Beran does not exist!" roared Bustamonte. "Beran died with Aiello!"

"I am Beran. I am alive. Here and now you and I will take truth-drug, and any who wishes may question us and bring forth the truth. Do you agree?"

Bustamonte hesitated. The crowd roared. Bustamonte turned, spoke terse orders to one of his ministers. He had neglected to turn off his microphone; the words were heard by three million people. "Call for police-craft. Seal this area. He must be killed."

The crowd-noise rose and fell, and rose again, at the implicit acknowledgement. Bustamonte tore off the microphone, barked further orders. The minister hesitated, seemed to demur. Bustamonte turned, marched to the black saloon. Behind came his retinue, crowding into the craft.

The crowd murmured, and then as if by a single thought, decided to leave Festival Field. In the center, at the most concentrated node, the sense of constriction was strongest. Faces twisted and turned; from a distance the effect was rapid pale twinkling.

A milling motion began. Families were wedged apart, pushed away from each other. Then shouts and calls were the components of a growing hoarse sound. The fear became palpable; the pleasant field grew acrid with the scent.

Overhead the black rectangle disappeared, the sky was clear. The crowd felt exposed; the shoving became trampling; the trampling became panic. Screaming began to sound; the noise bred hysteria; Paonese men and women climbed over each other, walking on squirming flesh.

Overhead appeared the police craft. They cruised back and forth like sharks; the panic became madness; screams became a continuous shrieking. But the crowd at the periphery was fleeing, swarming along the various roads and lanes, dispersing across the fields. The police craft swept back and forth indecisively; then turned and departed the scene. For moments the panic persisted; then the crowd came to its senses. The screams became moans, and the fear became grief...

✸

Beran seemed to have shrunk, collapsed in on himself. He was pallid, bright-eyed with horror. "Why could we not have foreseen such an event? We are as guilty as Bustamonte!"

"It serves no purpose to become infected with emotion," said Palafox.

Beran made no response. He sat crouched, staring into space.

The countryside of South Minamand fell astern. They crossed the long narrow Serpent and the island Fraevarth with its bone-white villages, and swept out over the Great Sea of the South. There was a period when nothing could be seen but rolling gray water; then the ramparts of Nonamand rose into view, with the eternal white surf crashing at the base. Then on to the moors and the Sgolaph crags, then around Mount Droghead to settle on the desolate plateau.

In Palafox's rooms they drank spiced tea, Palafox sitting in a tall-backed chair before a desk, Beran standing glumly by a window.

"You must steel yourself to unpleasant deeds," said Palafox. "There will be many more before the issues are resolved."

"What advantage to resolve issues, if half the people of Pao are dead?" asked Beran bitterly.

"All persons die. A thousand deaths represent, qualitatively, no more than one. Emotion increases merely in one dimension, that of intensity, but not of multiplicity. We must fix our minds on the final..." Palafox stopped short, tilted his head, listened to the speaker concealed inside his aural passages. He spoke in a tongue unknown to Beran; there was the inner reply, to which Palafox responded curtly. Then he sat back, regarding Beran with a kind of contemptuous amusement. "Bustamonte is settling your qualms for you. He has thrown a blockade around Pon. Mamarone are advancing across the plateau."

Beran asked in puzzlement, "How does he know that I am here?"

Palafox shrugged. "Bustamonte's spy service is efficient enough, but he vitiates it by his arrogant stupidity. His tactics are inexcusable. He attacks when clearly his best policy is compromise."

"Compromise? On what basis?"

"He might undertake a new contract with me, in return for the delivery of your person to the Grand Palace. He could thereby prolong his reign."

Beran was astounded. "And you would accede to this bargain?"

Palafox displayed wonder of his own. "Certainly. How could you think otherwise?"

"But your commitment to me—that means nothing?"

"A commitment is good only so long as it is advantageous."

"This is not always true," said Beran in a stronger voice than he had heretofore employed. "A person who fails one commitment is not often entrusted with a second."

"'Trust'? What is that? The interdependence of the hive; a mutual parasitism of the weak and incomplete."

"It is likewise a weakness," retorted Beran in fury, "to take advantage of trust in another—to accept loyalty, then fail to return it."

Palafox laughed in real amusement. "Be that as it may, the Paonese concepts of 'trust', 'loyalty', 'good faith' are not a part of my mental equipment. We dominie of Breakness Institute are individuals, each his own personal citadel. We expect no sentimental services derived from clan loyalty or group dependence; nor do we render any. You would do well to remember this."

Beran made no reply. Palafox looked at him curiously. Beran had stiffened, seemed lost in thought. In fact, a curious event had occurred inside his mind; there had been a sudden instant of dizziness, a whirl and a jerk which seemed to bypass an entire era of time, and he was a new Beran, like a snake sloughed of an old skin.

The new Beran turned slowly, inspected Palafox with dispassionate appraisal. Behind the semblance of agelessness, he saw a man of great age, with both the strengths and weaknesses of age.

"Very well," said Beran. "I necessarily must deal with you on this same basis."

"Naturally," said Palafox, but nonetheless with a trace of irritation. Then once more his eyes went vague; he tilted his head, listening to the inaudible message.

He rose to his feet, beckoned. "Come. Bustamonte attacks us."

They went out on a roof-top, under a transparent dome.

"There..." Palafox pointed to the sky "...Bustamonte's miserable gesture of ill-will."

A dozen of the Mamarone sky-sleds showed as black rectangles on the streaked gray sky. Two miles away a transport had settled and was exuding a magenta clot of neutraloid troops.

"It is well that this episode occurred," said Palafox. "It may dissuade Bustamonte from another like impertinence." He tilted his head, listening to the inner sound. "Now—observe our deterrent against molestation!"

Beran felt, or perhaps heard, a pulsating whine, so shrill as to be only partially in perception.

The sky-sleds began to act peculiarly, sinking, rising, jostling. They turned and fled precipitously. At the same time, there was excitement among the troops. They were in disarray, flourishing their arms, bobbing and hopping. The pulsating whine died; the Mamarone collapsed on the ground.

Palafox smiled faintly. "They are unlikely to annoy us further."

"Bustamonte might try to bomb us."

"If he is wise," said Palafox negligently, "he will attempt nothing so drastic. And he is wise at least to that extent."

"Then what will he do!"

"Oh—the usual futilities of a ruler who sees his regnum dwindling…"

Bustamonte's measures in truth were stupid and harsh. The news of Beran's appearance flew around the eight continents, in spite of Bustamonte's efforts to discredit the occurrence. The Paonese, on the one hand drawn by their yearning for the traditional, on the other repelled by Bustamonte's sociological novelties, reacted in the customary style. Work slowed, halted. Cooperation with civil authority ceased.

Bustamonte attempted persuasion, grandiose promises and amnesties. The disinterest of the population was more insulting than a series of angry demonstrations. Transportation came to a standstill, power and communications died, Bustamonte's personal servants failed to report for work.

A Mamarone, impressed into domestic service, scalded Bustamonte's arms with a hot towel: this was the trigger which exploded Bustamonte's suppressed fury. "I have sung to them! They shall now sing in their turn!"

At random he picked half a hundred villages. Mamarone descended upon these communities and were allowed complete license. Sadism was a prominent facet of the neutraloid nature, a substitute for creativity. They were sufficiently ingenious, and they hated natural men and women. The combination produced the most hideous events yet known on Pao.

Atrocity failed to move the population—already an established principle of Paonese history. Beran, learning of the events, felt all the anguish of the victims. He turned on Palafox, reviled him.

Palafox, unmoved, commented that all men die, that pain is transitory and in any event the result of faulty mental discipline. To demonstrate, he held his hand in a flame; the flesh burnt and crackled; Palafox watched without concern.

"These people lack this discipline—they feel pain!" cried Beran.

"It is indeed unfortunate," said Palafox. "I wish pain to no man, but until Bustamonte is deposed—or until he is dead—these episodes will continue. There is no way we can prevent them."

"Why do you not restrain these monsters?" raged Beran. "You have the means. You are as guilty as he is!"

"The word 'guilt' implies uncertainty," said Palafox. "I cannot profess to omniscience; but I can plan as well as I can, and regard these plans as definite. I am not uncertain; I am not guilty. And in any event you can restrain Bustamonte as readily as I."

Beran replied with fury and scorn. "I understand you now. You want me to kill him. Perhaps you have planned this entire series of events. I will kill him gladly! Arm me, tell me his whereabouts—if I die, at least there shall be an end to all."

"Come," said Palafox, "you receive your second modification."

Bustamonte was shrunken and haggard. He paced the black carpet of the foyer, holding his arms stiff, fluttering his fingers as if to shake off bits of grit.

The glass door was closed, locked, sealed. Outside stood four black Mamarone.

Bustamonte shivered. Where would it end? He went to the window, looked out into the night. Eiljanre spread ghostly white to all sides. Three points on the horizon glowed angry maroon where three villages and those who had dwelt there felt the weight of his vengeance.

Bustamonte groaned, chewed his lip, fluttered his fingers spasmodically. He turned away from the window, resumed his pacing. At the window there was a faint hiss which Bustamonte failed to notice.

There was a thud, a draft of air.

Bustamonte turned, froze in his tracks. In the window stood a glaring-eyed young man, wearing black.

"Beran," croaked Bustamonte. "Beran!"

Beran jumped down to the black carpet, came quietly forward.

Bustamonte tried to turn, tried to scuttle and dodge. But his time had come; he knew it, he could not move. His knees went limp, his bowels churned, relaxed.

Beran raised his hand. From his finger darted blue energy.

The affair was accomplished. Beran stepped over the corpse, unsealed the glass doors, flung them aside.

The Mamarone looked around, sprang back, squinted in wonder.

"I am Beran Panasper, Panarch of Pao."

CHAPTER XVI

Pao celebrated the accession of Beran in a frenzy of joy. Everywhere, except in the Valiant camps, along the shore of Zelambre Bay, at Pon, there was rejoicing of so orgiastic a nature as to seem non-Paonese. In spite of a vast disinclination, Beran took up residence in the Grand Palace and submitted to a certain degree of the pomp and ritual expected of him.

His first impulse was to undo all Bustamonte's acts, to banish the entire ministry to Vredeltope, the penal isle in the far north. Palafox, however, counseled restraint. "You act emotionally—there is no point in discarding the good with the bad."

"Show me something good," responded Beran. "I might then be less determined."

Palafox thought a moment, seemed to be on the point of speaking, hesitated, then said, "For instance: the Ministers of Government."

"All cronies of Bustamonte's. All nefarious, all corrupt."

Palafox nodded. "This may be true. But how do they comport themselves now?"

"Ha!" Beran laughed. "They work night and day, like wasps in autumn, convincing me of their probity."

"And so they perform efficiently. You would only work confusion in de-robing the lot. I advise you to move slowly—discharge the obvious sycophants and time-servers, bring new men into the ministry only whenever opportunity presents itself."

Beran was forced to admit the justice of Palafox's remarks. But now he sat back in his chair—the two were taking a lunch of figs and new wine on the palace roof garden—and seemed to brace himself. "These are only the incidental alterations I wish to make. My main work, my dedication, is to restore Pao to its former condition. I plan to disperse the Valiant camps to various parts of Pao, and do something similar with the Technicant installations. These persons must learn Paonese, they must take their places in our society."

"And the Cogitants?"

Beran rapped his knuckles on the table. "I want no second Breakness on Pao. There is scope for a thousand institutes of learning—but they must be established among the Paonese people. They must teach Paonese topics in the Paonese language."

"Ah yes," sighed Palafox. "Well, I expected nothing better. Presently I will return to Breakness, and you may restore Nonamand to the shepherds and furze-cutters."

Beran concealed his surprise at Palafox's docility. "Evidently," he said at last, "you plan something quite different. You assisted me to the Black Throne only because Bustamonte would not cooperate with you."

Palafox smiled to himself as he peeled a fig. "I plan nothing. I merely observe and, if requested to do so, advise. Whatever is to occur stems from plans long ago formulated and given momentum."

"It may become necessary to frustrate these plans," said Beran.

Palafox ate his fig without concern. "You are naturally at liberty to make such attempts."

During the next few days Beran pondered at great length. Palafox seemed to regard him as a predictable quantity, one which would automatically react in a direction favorable to Palafox. This consideration moved him to caution and he delayed immediate action against the three non-Paonese enclaves.

Bustamonte's splendid harem he sent packing, and began the formation of his own. It was expected of him; a Panarch without suitable concubines would be regarded with suspicion, and his masculinity called to question.

Beran felt no disinclination on this score; and since he was young, well-favored, and a popular hero, his problem was not so much one of seeking as of selection.

However, the affairs of state left him little time for personal indulgence. Bustamonte had overcrowded the penal colony on Vredeltope, with criminals and with political offenders mingled indiscriminately.

Beran ordered an amnesty for all except confirmed felons. In the latter part of his reign, Bustamonte likewise had raised taxes until they approached those of Aiello's reign, with peculant officials absorbing the increment. Beran dealt decisively with these, setting the peculators to unpleasant types of menial labor, with earnings applied to their debts.

One day, without warning, a red, blue and brown corvette dropped down from space. The sector monitor issued the customary challenge; the corvette, disdaining response other than to break out a long serpent-tongue banderole, landed with insolent carelessness on the roof of the Grand Palace.

Eban Buzbek, Hetman of the Batmarsh Brumbos, and a retinue of warriors debarked. Ignoring the palace preceptors, they marched to the great throne-room, called loudly for Bustamonte.

Beran, arrayed in formal black, entered the hall.

By this time Eban Buzbek had heard a report of Bustamonte's death. He gave Beran a hard quizzical stare, then called to an interpreter. "Inquire if the new Panarch acknowledges me his overlord."

To the interpreter's timid question, Beran made no immediate reply. Conflict was the least of his desires; yet tribute was a humiliation he did not wish to prolong.

Eban Buzbek barked out, "What is the new Panarch's reply?"

The interpreter translated. "In truth," said Beran, "I have no reply ready. I wish to reign in peace, still I feel that the tribute to Batmarsh has been paid long enough."

Eban Buzbek roared a quick gust of laughter when he heard the interpreter's translation. "This is not the manner in which realities arrange themselves. Life is a pyramid—only one may stand at the top. In this case it is I. Immediately below are others of the Brumbo Clan. In the remaining levels I have no interest. You must win the stage to which your prowess entitles you. My mission here is to demand more money from Pao. My expenses are increasing—therefore, the tribute must increase. If you agree, we part in amity. If not, my restive clansmen will visit Pao and you will regret your obstinacy."

Beran said, "I have no alternative. Under protest I pay you your tribute. I will say also that you would profit more as a friend to us than as an overlord."

In the Batch tongue the word 'friend' could only be interpreted as 'companion-in-arms'. Upon receiving Beran's reply, Eban Buzbek laughed. "Paonese as companions-at-arms? They who turn up their rumps for a kicking when so ordered? Better warriors are the Dinghals of Fire Planet, who march behind a shield of their grandmothers. No—we Brumbos have no need of such an alliance."

Retranslated into Paonese, the words became what seemed a series of gratuitous insults. Beran swallowed his wrath. "Your money shall be transmitted to you." He bowed stiffly, turned, strode from the room. One of the warriors, deeming his conduct disrespectful, leapt forward to intercept him. Beran's hand came up, his finger pointed—but again he restrained himself. The warrior somehow sensed that his doom had been close at hand, and stood back.

Beran left the hall unmolested. Eban Buzbek ordered a banquet set before him and demanded women. These were supplied from the harlots' guild-house, and the Batch clansmen passed a merry evening.

Beran, trembling with anger, went to the quarters of Palafox, who displayed no great interest at the news. "You acted correctly," he said. "It is hopeless quixotry to defy such experienced warriors."

Beran assented gloomily. "No question but what Pao needs protection against brigands...Still, we are well able to afford the tribute, and it is cheaper than maintaining a large military establishment."

Palafox agreed. "The tribute is a decided economy."

Beran searched the long lean face for the irony he suspected, but finding none, took his leave.

The next day, after the Brumbos had departed, he called for a map of Shraimand, and studied the disposition of the Valiant camps. They occupied a strip along the coast ten miles wide by a hundred long, although the hinterland area had been depopulated another ten miles in anticipation of their increase.

Recalling his term of duty at Deirombona, Beran remembered the ardent young men and women, the tense faces, the steady undeviating expressions, the dedication to glory...He sighed. Such traits had their uses. These were men and women of Paonese blood! If only they spoke the true language, shared the ancient traditions! In this case, he reflected sadly, they would no longer be warriors...

But such enclaves were intolerable. Tribute or no tribute, the Valiant camps must be abandoned, the Myrmidons re-educated and merged with the rest of the population. Yet, after preparing the decree which would activate this principle, he hesitated, and finally put it aside.

He called Palafox to him, and began arguing heatedly, although Palafox had said nothing. "Theoretically, I agree to the need for an army, and also an efficient industrial establishment. But Bustamonte's procedure is cruel, artificial, disruptive!"

Palafox spoke gravely. "Suppose that by some miracle you were able to recruit, train and indoctrinate a Paonese army—then what? Whence will come their weapons? Who will supply warships? Who will build instruments and communications equipment?"

"Mercantil is the present source of our needs," Beran said slowly. "Perhaps one of the out-cluster worlds might supply us."

"The Mercantil will never conspire against the Brumbos," said Palafox. "And to procure merchandise from an out-cluster world, you must pay in suitable exchange. To acquire this foreign exchange, you must engage in trading."

Beran gazed bleakly from the window. "When we have no cargo ships, we can not trade."

"Precisely true," said Palafox, in high good humor. "Come, I would show you something of which you are perhaps not aware."

❂

In a swift black torpedo, Palafox and Beran flew to Zelambre Bay. In spite of Beran's questions, Palafox said nothing. He took Beran to the eastern shore, to an isolated area at the root of Maesthgelai Peninsula. Here was a group of new buildings, stark and ugly. Palafox landed the boat, took Beran inside the largest. They stood before a long cylinder.

Palafox said, "This is the secret project of a group of advanced students. As you have deduced, it is a small space-ship. The first, so I believe, ever built on Pao."

Beran surveyed the vessel without comment. Clearly Palafox was playing him as a fisherman plays a fish. It was impossible not to feel resentment.

He went closer to the ship. The finish was rough, the detailing crude; the general impression however was one of rugged serviceability. "Will it fly?" he asked Palafox.

"Not now. But undoubtedly it shall—in another four or five months. Certain delicate components are on order from Breakness.

Aside from these, it is a true Paonese production. With such a fleet of ships you may make Pao independent of Mercantil. I do not doubt that you will find sufficient trade, since the Mercantil screw the maximum advantage from any transaction."

"Naturally, I am—gratified," said Beran reluctantly. "But why was this work held secret from me?"

Palafox held up his hand and spoke in a soothing voice. "There was no attempt to keep you from knowledge. This is one project of many. These young men and women attack the problems and lacks of Pao with tremendous energy. Every day they undertake something new."

Beran grunted skeptically. "As soon as possible, these isolated groups shall be returned into the main current of Paonese life."

Palafox demurred. "In my opinion, the time is hardly ripe for any dilution of Technicant enthusiasm. Admittedly there was inconvenience to the displaced population, but the results seem to vindicate the conception."

Beran made no reply. Palafox signaled to the quietly observing group of Technicants. They came forward, were introduced, showed mild surprise when Beran spoke to them in their own language, and presently conducted him through the ship. The interior reinforced Beran's original conception of rough but sturdy serviceability. And when he returned to the Grand Palace it was with an entirely new set of doubts and speculations in his mind. Could it be possible that Bustamonte had been right, and he, Beran, wrong? The miseries inflicted upon the displaced Paonese, on the indentured girls, on the children abstracted from the rich old culture of Pao and trained in raw new ways—were they after all justifiable means to a necessary end? The question was one which Beran could not answer. But when he once again considered the decree which merged the neo-lingual enclaves with the rest of Pao, again he set it aside.

CHAPTER XVII

A year went by. The prototype space-ship of the Technicants was completed, tested and put into service as a training ship. On plea of the Technicant Coordinating Council, public funds were diverted to a large-scale ship-building program.

Valiant activity proceeded as before. A dozen times Beran decided to curtail the scope of the camps, but on each occasion the face of Eban Buzbek appeared to his mind's-eye and his resolve diminished.

The year saw great prosperity for Pao. Never had the people fared so well. The civil service was uncharacteristically self-effacing and honest; the taxes were light; there was none of the fear and suspicion prevalent during Bustamonte's reign. In consequence the population lived with almost non-Paonese gusto. The neo-lingual enclaves, like tumors, neither benign nor malignant, were not forgotten, but tolerated. Beran paid no visit to the Cogitant Institute at Pon; he knew however that it had expanded greatly: that new buildings were rising, new halls, dormitories, workshops, laboratories—that the enrollment increased daily, derived from youths arriving from Breakness, all bearing an unmistakable resemblance to Lord Palafox, and from other youths, rather younger, graduating from the Institute crèches—children of Palafox and children of his children.

Another year passed, and down from space came the gay-colored corvette of Eban Buzbek. As before, it ignored the challenge of the monitor, and landed on the roof-deck of the Grand Palace. As before, Eban Buzbek and a swaggering retinue marched to the great hall, where they demanded the presence of Beran. There was a delay of ten minutes, during which the warriors stamped and jingled impatiently.

Beran entered the room, and halted, surveying the clansmen, who turned cold-eyed faces toward him.

Beran came forward. He made no pretense of cordiality. "Why do you come to Pao this time?"

As before, an interpreter transferred the words into Batch.

Eban Buzbek sat back into a chair, motioned Beran to another nearby. Beran took the seat without comment.

"We have heard unpleasant reports," said Eban Buzbek, stretching forth his legs. "Our allies and suppliers, the artifactors of Mercantil, tell us that you have lately sent into space a fleet of cargo-vessels—that you bargain and barter, and eventually bring back to Pao great quantities of technical equipment." The Batch warriors moved behind Beran; they towered over his seat.

He glanced over his shoulder, turned back to Eban Buzbek. "I cannot understand your concern. Why should we not trade where we will?"

"Sufficient should be the fact that it is contrary to the wish of Eban Buzbek, your liege-lord."

Beran spoke in a conciliatory voice. "But you must remember that we are a populous world. We have natural aspirations..."

Eban Buzbek leaned forward; his hand rang on Beran's cheek. Beran fell back into the chair, stunned by surprise, face white but for the red welt. It was the first blow he ever had received, his first contact with violence. The effect was peculiar—it was a shock, a stimulus, not altogether unpleasant, the sudden opening of a forgotten room. Eban Buzbek's voice sounded almost unheard: "...your aspirations must at all times be referred to Clan Brumbo for judgment."

One of the warriors of the retinue spoke. "Only small persuasion is needed to convince the *ocholos*."

Beran's eyes once more focussed on the broad red face of Eban Buzbek. He raised himself in his seat. "I am happy you are here, Eban Buzbek. It is better that we talk face to face. The time has come when Pao pays no further tribute to you."

Eban Buzbek's mouth opened, curved into a comical grimace of surprise.

"Furthermore, we shall continue to send our ships across the universe. I hope you will accept these facts in good spirit and return to your world with peace in your heart."

Eban Buzbek sprang to his feet. "I will return with your ears to hang in our Hall of Arms."

Beran rose, backed away from the warriors. They advanced with grinning deliberation. Eban Buzbek pulled a blade from his belt. "Bring the rascal here." Beran raised his hand in a signal. Doors slid back on three sides; three squads of Mamarone came forward, eyes like slits. They carried halberds with cusped blades a yard long, mounted with flame sickles.

"What is your will with these jackals?" the sergeant rasped.

Beran said, "Subaqueation. Take them to the ocean."

Eban Buzbek demanded the sense of the comments from the interpreter. On hearing it, he sputtered, "This is a reckless act. Pao shall be devastated! My kinsmen will leave no living soul in Eiljanre. We shall sow your fields with fire and bone!"

"Will you then go home in peace and bother us no more?" Beran demanded. "Come, the choice is yours. Death—or peace."

Eban Buzbek looked from right to left; his warriors pressed close together, eyeing their black adversaries.

Eban Buzbek sheathed his blade with a decisive snap. He muttered aside to his men. "We go," he said to Beran.

"Then you choose peace?"

Eban Buzbek's mustaches quivered in fury. "I choose—peace."

"Then throw down your weapons, leave Pao and never return."

Eban Buzbek, wooden-faced, divested himself of his arms. His warriors followed suit. The group departed, herded by the neutraloids. Presently the corvette rose from the palace, darted up and away.

Minutes passed; then Beran was called to the telescreen. Eban Buzbek's face glowed, glistening with hate. "I left in peace, young Panarch, and you shall have peace—only so long as it takes to bring the clansmen back to Pao. Not only your ears but your head will be mounted among our trophies."

Beran said, "Come at your own risk." He motioned; the screen went blank; he left the room and retired to his chambers...

❂

Three months later the Batch clansmen attacked Pao. A fleet of twenty-eight warships, including six round-bellied transports, appeared in the sky. The monitors made no attempt either to challenge or defend, and the Batch warships slid contemptuously down into the atmosphere.

Here they were attacked by rocket-missiles, but counter-missiles harmlessly exploded the barrage.

In tight formation, they settled toward north Minamand and landed a score of miles north of Eiljanre. The transports debarked a multitude of clansmen mounted on air-horses. They darted high into the air, dashing, cavorting, swerving in a fine display of braggadocio.

A school of anti-personnel missiles came streaking for them, but the defenses of the ships below were alert, and anti-missiles destroyed the salvo. However, the threat was sufficient to hold the riders close to the flotilla.

Evening came and night. The riders wrote vainglorious slogans in the sky with golden gas, then retired to their ships, and there was no further activity.

❂

Another set of events had already occurred on Batmarsh. No sooner had the twenty-eight ship flotilla set forth for Pao, when another ship, cylindrical and sturdy, evidently converted from a cargo-carrier, dropped down into the dank forested hills at the south end of the Brumbo domain. A hundred young men disembarked. They wore ingenious segmented suits of transpar, which became streamlined shells when the wearer's arms hung by his sides. Anti-gravity mesh made them weightless, electric jets propelled them with great speed.

They flew low over the black trees, along the bottom of the wild valleys. Lake Chagaz glimmered ahead, reflecting the glowing constellations of the cluster. Across the lake was the stone and timber city Slagoe, with the Hall of Honors looming tall over the lesser buildings.

The flyers swooped like hawks to the ground. Four ran to the sacred fire, beat down the aged fire-tenders, quenched the blaze except for a single coal which they packed in a metal pouch. The remainder had continued past up the ten stone steps. They stunned the guardian vestals, charged into the tall smoky-beamed hall.

Down from the wall came the tapestry of the clan, woven with hair from the head of every Brumbo born to the clan. Helter-skelter into bags and gravity boxes went the trophies, the sacred fetishes: old armor, a hundred tattered banners, scrolls and declamations, fragments of rock, bone, steel and charcoal, vials of dried black blood commemorating battles and Brumbo valor.

When Slagoe at last awoke to what was taking place, the warriors were in space, bound for Pao. Women, youths, old men, ran to the sacred park, crying and shouting.

But the raiders had departed, taking with them the soul of the clan, all the most precious treasure.

On dawn of the second day the raiders brought forth crates and assembled eight battle-platforms, mounting generators, anti-missile defenses, dynamic stings, pyreumators and sonic ear-blasters.

Other Brumbo bravos came forth on air-horses, but now they rode in strict formation. The battle platforms raised from the ground and exploded. Mechanical moles, tunneling through the soil, had planted mines to the bottom of each raft.

The air-cavalry milled in consternation. Without protection they were easy targets for missiles—cowardly weapons by the standards of Batmarsh.

The Valiant Myrmidons likewise disliked missiles. Beran had insisted on every possible means to minimize bloodshed, but when the battle-rafts were destroyed, he found it impossible to restrain the Myrmidons. In their transpar shells they darted into the sky and plunged down at the Brumbo cavalry. A furious battle swirled and screamed over the pleasant countryside.

There was no decision to the battle. Myrmidons and Brumbo air-horsemen fell in equal numbers, but after twenty minutes, the air-horsemen suddenly disengaged and plunged to the ground, leaving the Myrmidons exposed to a barrage of missiles. The Myrmidons were not taken entirely unawares, and dove headfirst for the ground. Only a few laggards—perhaps twenty—were caught and exploded.

The horsemen retreated under the shadow of their ships; the Myrmidons withdrew. They had been fewer than the Brumbos; never-theless, the clansmen had given way, puzzled and awed by the ferocity of the resistance.

The remainder of the day was quiet, likewise the next day, while the Brumbos sounded and probed under the hulls of their ships to disen-gage any mines which might have been planted.

This accomplished, the fleet rose into the air, lumbered out over the Hylanthus Sea, crossed the isthmus just south of Eiljanre, settled on the beach within sight of the Grand Palace.

The next morning the Brumbos came forth on foot, six thousand men guarded by anti-missile defenders and four projectors. They moved cautiously forward, directly for the Grand Palace.

There was no show of resistance, no sign of the Myrmidons. The marble walls of the Grand Palace rose over them. There was motion on top; down rolled a rectangle of black, brown and tawny cloth. The Brumbos halted, staring.

An amplified voice came from the palace. "Eban Buzbek—come forth. Come inspect the loot we have taken from your Hall of Honors. Come forth, Eban Buzbek. No harm shall come to you."

Eban Buzbek came forth, called back through an amplifier. "What is this fakery, what cowardly Paonese trick have you contrived? Speak quickly; I will not listen long!"

"We possess all your clan treasures, Eban Buzbek: that tapestry, the last coal of your Eternal Fire, all your heraldry and relics. Do you wish to redeem them?"

Eban Buzbek stood swaying as if he would faint. He turned and walked unsteadily back to his ship.

An hour passed. Eban Buzbek and a group of noblemen came forth. "We request a truce, in order that we may inspect these articles you claim to have in your possession."

"Come forward, Eban Buzbek. Inspect to your heart's content."

Eban Buzbek and his retinue inspected the articles. They spoke no word—the Paonese who conducted them made no comment.

The Brumbos silently returned to their ships.

A nunciator called, "The time is at hand! Coward Paonese—prepare for death!"

The clansmen charged, driven by the most violent emotion. Halfway across the beach they were met by the Myrmidons, and engaged in hand to hand combat, with swords, pistols and bare hands.

The Brumbos were halted; for the first time their battle-lust met another more intense. They knew fear, they fell back, they retreated.

The voice from the Grand Palace called out, "You cannot win, Eban Buzbek, you cannot escape. We hold your lives, we hold your sacred treasures. Surrender now or we destroy both."

Eban Buzbek surrendered. He bent his head to the ground before Beran and the Myrmidon captain, he renounced all claim to Paonese overlordship, and kneeling before the sacred tapestry swore never more to molest or plan harm against Pao. He was then permitted the treasures of his clan, which the sullen clansmen carried aboard the flotilla. Eban Buzbek turned abruptly to Beran. "You have defeated us in craft as well as valor. It is a small heart therefore which would hold hate against you. I leave Pao feeling only woe that we have met a band of warriors more skillful and more gallant than we. From what far planet did you recruit them, that we may give them all possible avoidance?"

Beran smiled with mingled pride and misgiving. "They are from no far planet; they are Paonese."

Eban Buzbek was shocked. He gave Beran a hard stare. "Paonese? Surely not, for I have heard them speak, and the language is not Paonese."

"Nevertheless, Paonese is their blood. If you doubt, I can direct you to their camp, or you may question them yourself through an interpreter."

Beran signaled to one of the Interpreter Corps, who was never far distant during these times. But Eban Buzbek declined the opportunity. He boarded the flagship of his flotilla, and so departed Pao.

CHAPTER XVIII

Time after time Pao traced its orbit around Auriol, marking off five complex and dramatic years. For Pao at large they were good years. Never had living been so easy, hunger so rare. To the normal goods produced by the planet was added a vast variety of imports from far-off worlds. To every corner of the cluster the Technicant ships plied, and many a commercial battle was waged between Mercantili and Technicants. As a result, both enterprises expanded their services, and sought farther afield for trade.

The Valiants likewise became more numerous, but on a restricted basis. There was no further recruiting from the population at large, and only a child of Valiant father and mother could be received into the caste.

At Pon, the Cogitants increased in numbers, but even more slowly than the Valiants. Three new Institutes were established in the misty hills, and high upon the most remote crag of all Pao, Palafox built a somber castle.

The Interpreter Corps was now largely derived from the Cogitants; in fact, the Interpreters might be said to be the operative function of the Cogitants. Like the other groups, the Interpreters had expanded both in numbers and importance. In spite of the separation of the three neo-linguistic groups, from each other and from the Paonese population, there was a great deal of interchange. When an Interpreter was not at hand, the business might be transacted in Pastiche—which by virtue of its relative universality, was understood by a large number of persons. But when communication of any precision was necessary, an Interpreter was called for.

So the years passed, fulfilling all the changes conceived by Palafox, initiated by Bustamonte, and reluctantly supported by Beran. The fourteenth year of Beran's reign saw the high-tide of prosperity and well-being.

Beran had long disapproved of the Breakness concubinage system, which had taken unobtrusive but firm root at the various Cogitant Institutes.

Originally there had been no lack of girls to indenture themselves for eventual financial advantage, and all the sons and grandsons of Palafox—not to speak of Palafox himself—maintained large dormitories in the neighborhood of Pon. But when prosperity came to Pao, the number of young women available for indenture declined, and presently peculiar rumors began to circulate. There was talk of drugs, hypnotism, black magic.

Beran ordered an investigation of the methods by which the Cogitants secured women for indenture. He realized he would be treading on sensitive toes—but he did not suspect the response would be so instant and so direct. Lord Palafox himself came to Eiljanre.

He appeared one morning on an upper terrace of the palace where Beran sat contemplating the sea. At the sight of the tall spare frame, the angular features, Beran reflected how little this Palafox differed, even to the cloak of heavy brown cloth, the gray trousers, the peaked cap with a sharp bill, from the Palafox he had first seen so many years before. How old was Palafox?

Palafox wasted no time in preliminary small-talk. "Panarch Beran, an unpleasant situation has arisen, concerning which you will wish to take steps."

Beran nodded slowly. "What is this 'unpleasant situation'?"

"My privacy has been invaded. A clumsy gang of spies dogs my footsteps, annoys the women in my dormitory with impertinent surveillance. I beg that you discover who has ordered this persecution and punish the guilty party."

Beran rose to his feet. "Lord Palafox, as you must know, I personally ordered the investigation."

"Indeed? You astonish me, Panarch Beran! What could you hope to learn?"

"I expected to learn nothing. I hoped you would interpret the act as a warning, and make such changes in your conduct as the fact of the investigation would suggest. Instead you have chosen to contend the issue, which may make for difficulty."

"I am a Breakness dominie. I act directly, not through devious hints." Palafox's voice was like iron, but the statement had not advanced his attack.

Beran, a student of polemics, sought to maintain his advantage. "You have been a valuable ally, Lord Palafox. In recompense, you have received what amounts to control over the continent of Nonamand. But this control is conditional upon the legality of your acts. The indenture of willing females, while socially offensive, is not a crime. However, when these females are unwilling..."

"What basis do you have for these remarks?"

"Popular rumor."

Palafox smiled thinly. "And if by chance you could verify these rumors, what then?"

Beran forced himself to stare into the obsidian gaze. "Your question has no application. It refers to a situation already of the past."

"Your meaning is obscure."

"The way to counter these rumors," said Beran, "is to bring the situation into the open. Henceforth, women willing to indenture themselves will appear at a public depot here in Eiljanre. All contracts will be negotiated at this depot, and any other traffic is declared a crime equivalent to kidnapping."

Palafox was silent several seconds. Then he asked softly, "How do you propose to enforce this decision?"

"'Enforce'?" asked Beran in surprise. "On Pao it is not necessary to enforce the orders of the government."

Palafox curtly inclined his head. "The situation, as you say, is clarified. I trust neither of us will have cause for complaint." He took his departure.

Beran drew a deep breath, leaned back in his chair, closed his eyes. He had won a victory—to a certain degree. He had asserted the authority of the state and had wrung tacit acknowledgement of this authority from Palafox.

Beran was clever enough not to gloat. He knew that Palafox, utterly secure in his solipsism, probably felt nothing of the emotional umbra surrounding the occurrence, considered the defeat no more than a momentary irritation. Indeed, there were two highly significant points to consider: first, something in Palafox's manner which suggested that, in spite of his anger, he had been prepared to accept at least temporary compromise. 'Temporary' was the key word. Palafox was a man biding his time.

Second, there was the phrasing of Palafox's last sentence: "I trust that neither of us shall have cause for complaint." Implicit was an assumption of equal status, equal authority, equal weight, indicating the presence of a disturbing ambition.

To the best of Beran's recollection Palafox had never so spoken before. Religiously he had maintained the pose of a Breakness dominie, temporarily on Pao as an advisor. Now it seemed as if he regarded himself a permanent inhabitant, with a proprietary attitude to boot.

Beran contemplated the events leading to the present tangle. For five thousand years Pao had been homogeneous, a planet directed by tradition, somnolent in an ageless tranquillity. Panarchs succeeded each other, dynasties came and went, but the blue oceans and green fields were eternal. The Pao of these times had been easy prey for corsairs and raiders, and there had been much poverty.

The ideas of Lord Palafox, the ruthless dynamism of Bustamonte, in a single generation had changed all. Now Pao was prosperous and sent its merchant fleet cruising throughout the star-system. Paonese traders out-bargained the Mercantil, Paonese warriors out-fought the clansmen of Batmarsh, Paonese intellectuals compared favorably with the so-called wizards of Breakness.

But—these men who excelled, who out-traded, out-fought, out-produced, out-thought their planetary neighbors—were they Paonese? The Cogitants now numbered close to ten thousand and all had Palafox either for sire or grandsire. Palafoxians: a better name for these people!

The Valiants and the Technicants, what of them? Their blood was pure Paonese, but they lived as far from the stream of Paonese tradition as the Brumbos of Batmarsh or the Mercantil.

Beran jumped to his feet. How could he have been so blind, so negligent? These men were not Paonese, no matter how well they served Pao: they were aliens, and it was questionable where their ultimate loyalties lay.

The divergence between Valiant, Technicant and basic Paonese had gone too far. The trend must be reversed, the new groups assimilated.

Now that he had defined his ends, it was necessary to formulate the means. The problem was complex; he must move cautiously. First of all—to establish the agency where women could present themselves for indenture. He would give Palafox no 'cause for complaint'.

CHAPTER XIX

At the eastern outskirts of Eiljanre, across the old Rovenone Canal, lay a wide commons, used principally for the flying of kites and festival mass-dancing. Here Beran ordered the erection of a large tent-pavilion, where women wishing to hire themselves to the Cogitants might exhibit themselves. Wide publicity had been given the new agency, and also to the edict that all private contracts between women and Cogitant would henceforth be illegal and felonious.

The opening day arrived. At noon Beran went to inspect the pavilion. Construction was in the best tradition of Paonese craftsmanship.

Pillars plaited of glass ropes supported a red velvet parasol, the floor was clean shell crushed into a matrix of blue gel. Around the wall were benches and booths of blackwood, comprising accommodation for four hundred applicants and sixty Cogitants.

On the benches sat a scattered handful of women, a miserable group by any standards, unlovely, harassed, peaked—perhaps thirty in all.

Beran stared in surprise. "Is this the lot of them?"

"That is all, Panarch!"

Beran rubbed his chin ruefully. He looked around to see the man he wished least to see: Palafox.

Beran spoke first, with some effort. "Choose, Lord Palafox. Thirty of Pao's most charming women await your whim."

Palafox replied in a light voice. "Slaughtered and buried, they might make acceptable fertilizer. Other than that, I see no possible use for them." He peered to left and right. "Where are the hundreds of prime maidens you promised to display? I see only these charwomen and empty benches."

Implicit in the remark was a challenge: failure to recognize and answer it was to abandon the initiative. "It appears, Lord Palafox," said Beran, "that indenture to the Cogitants is as objectionable to the women of Pao as I had supposed. The very dearth of persons vindicates my decision." And Beran contemplated the lonely pavilion.

There was no sound from Palafox, but some intuition flashed a warning to Beran's mind. He turned his head, and his startled eyes saw Palafox, face like a death-mask, raising his hand. The forefinger pointed; Beran flung himself flat. A blue streak sizzled overhead. He pointed his hand; his own finger-fire spat forward, ran up Palafox's arm, through the elbow, the humerus and out the shoulder.

Palafox jerked his head up, mouth clenched, eyes rolled back like a maddened horse. Blood sizzled and steamed where the mangled circuits in his arm had heated, fused and broken.

Beran pointed his finger once more; it was urgent and advisable to kill Palafox; more than this, it was his duty. Palafox stood watching, the look in his eyes no longer that of a human being; he stood waiting for death.

Beran hesitated, and in this instant, Palafox once more became a man. He flung up his left hand; now Beran acted and again the blue fire-pencil leapt forth; but it impinged on an essence which the left hand of Palafox had flung forth, and dissolved.

Beran drew back. The thirty women had flung themselves quaking and whimpering to the floor; Beran's attendants stood lax and limp. There was no word spoken. Palafox backed away, out the door of the pavilion; he turned and was gone.

Beran could find no energy to pursue. He returned to the palace, closed himself in his private rooms. Morning became the gold Paonese afternoon, day faded into evening.

Beran roused himself. He went to his wardrobe, dressed in a suit of skin-tight black. He armed himself with knife, hammer-beam, mind-blinder, swallowed a pellet of nerve-tonic, then unobtrusively made his way to the roof-deck.

He slipped into an air car, wafted high into the night and flew south.

The dreary cliffs of Nonamand rose from the sea with phosphorescent surf at the base and a few wan lights flickering along the top. Beran adjusted his course over the dark upland moors toward Pon. Grim and tense he sat, riding with the conviction that doom lay before him. Far from making him uneasy, the prospect filled him with a ghastly exhilaration. Flying over the bleak moors, he felt like a man already dead, a ghost, a fleeting wraith.

There: Mount Droghead, and beyond, the Institute! Every building, every terrace, walk, out-building and dormitory, was familiar to Beran: the years he had served here as Interpreter would now stand him in good stead.

He landed the car out on the moor, away from the field, then activating the anti-gravity mesh in his feet, he floated into the air and leaning forward, drifted over the Institute.

He hovered high in the chill night wind, surveying the buildings below. There—Palafox's dormitory, and there, through the triangular translux panels, a glow of light.

Beran alighted on the pale rock-melt of the dormitory roof. The wind swept past, droning and whistling; there was no other sound.

Beran ran for the roof door. He burnt out the seal with a flicker of finger-fire, slid the door back, entered the hall.

The dormitory was silent; he could hear neither voice nor movement. He set out down the corridor with long swift steps.

The top floor was given over to the day rooms, and was deserted. He descended a ramp, turned to the right, toward the source of the light he had seen from above. He stopped outside a door, listened. No voices—but a faint sense of motion within: a stir, a shuffle.

He touched the latch. The door was sealed.

Beran readied himself. All must go swiftly. Now! Flick of fire, door free, door aside—stride forward! And there in the chair beside the table, a man.

The man looked up, Beran stopped short. It was not Palafox; it was Finisterle.

Finisterle looked at the pointed finger, then up to Beran's face. "What do you do here?" His exclamation was in Pastiche, and in this tongue Beran replied.

"Where is Palafox?"

Finisterle laughed weakly, let himself sink back into the chair. "It seems as if I nearly met the fate of my sire."

Beran came a step closer. "Where is Palafox?"

"You are too late. Palafox is gone to Breakness."

"Breakness!" Beran felt limp and tired.

"He is broken, his arm is a shred. No one here can repair him." Finisterle appraised Beran with cautious interest. "And this the unobtrusive Beran—a demon in black!"

Beran clenched his fists, beat them together. "Who could do it but I?" He glanced suddenly at Finisterle. "You are not deceiving me?"

Finisterle shook his head. "Why should I deceive you?"

"He is your sire!"

Finisterle shrugged. "This means nothing, either to sire or to son."

Beran slowly seated himself in a nearby chair, watching Finisterle all the while. "The death of Palafox is hardly to your advantage."

Finisterle made a non-committal gesture. "A man no matter how remarkable, has only a finite capability. It is no longer a secret that Lord Palafox has come to the margin, and indeed has passed beyond. He has succumbed to the final sickness, he is an Emeritus. The world and his brain are no longer separate—to Palafox they are one and the same."

Beran rubbed his chin, frowned. Finisterle leaned forward. "Do you know his ambition, do you understand his presence on Pao?"

"I guess, but I do not know."

"Some weeks ago he gathered together his sons. He spoke to us, explained his ambition. He claims Pao as a world of his own. Through his sons, his grandsons, and his own capabilities, he will outbreed the

Paonese, until eventually there will be only Palafox and the seed of Palafox on Pao."

Beran heaved a deep sigh. "How long will he stay on Breakness?"

"Who knows? His arm is mangled; there is much repair to be done."

Beran rose heavily to his feet.

"What will you do now?" asked Finisterle.

"I am Paonese," said Beran. "I have been passive in the Paonese fashion. But I have also studied at Breakness Institute, and now I shall act. And if I destroy what Palafox has worked so long to build—perhaps he will not return." He looked around the room. "I will start here, at Pon. You all may go where you will—but go you must. Tomorrow the Institute will be destroyed."

Finisterle leapt to his feet, restraint forgotten. "Tomorrow? That is fantastic! We can not leave our research, our library, our precious possessions!"

Beran went to the doorway. "There will be no more delay. You certainly have the right to remove your personal property. But the entity known as the Cogitant Institute will vanish tomorrow."

Esteban Carbone, Chief Marshal of the Valiants, a muscular young man with an open pleasant face, was accustomed to rise at dawn for a plunge into the surf.

On this morning he returned naked, wet and breathless from the beach, to find a silent man in black awaiting him.

Esteban Carbone halted in confusion. "Panarch, as you see, I am surprised. Pray excuse me while I clothe myself."

He ran into his quarters, and presently reappeared in a striking black and yellow uniform. "Now, Supremacy, I am ready to hear your commands."

"They are brief," said Beran. "Take a warship to Pon, and at twelve noon, destroy Cogitant Institute."

Esteban Carbone's amazement reached new heights. "Do I understand you correctly, Supremacy?"

"I will repeat: take a warship to Pon, destroy Cogitant Institute. Explode it to splinters. The Cogitants have received notice—they are now evacuating."

Esteban Carbone hesitated a perceptible instant before replying. "It is not my place to question matters of policy, but is this not a very drastic act? I feel impelled to counsel careful second thought."

Beran took no offense. "I appreciate your concern. This order however is the result of many more thoughts than two. Be so good as to obey without further delay."

Esteban Carbone touched his hand to his forehead, bowed low. "Nothing more need be said, Panarch Beran." He walked into his quarters, spoke into a communicator.

Beran watched the warship, a barrel-shaped black hulk, wallow up into the sky and head south. Then he went slowly to his air-car and returned to Eiljanre.

At noon precisely the warship hurled an explosive missile at the target, a small cluster of white buildings on the plateau behind Mount Droghead. There was a dazzle of blue and white, and Cogitant Institute was gone.

When Palafox heard the news, his face suffused with dark blood; he swayed back and forth. "So does he destroy himself," he groaned between his teeth. "So should I be satisfied—but how bitter the insolence of this young coxcomb!"

The Cogitants came to Eiljanre, settling in the old Beauclare Quarter, south of the Rovenone. As the months passed they underwent a change, almost, it seemed, with an air of joyous relief. They relaxed the doctrinaire intensity which had distinguished them at the Institute, and fell into the ways of a bohemian intelligentsia. Through some obscure compulsion, they spoke little or no Cogitant, and likewise, disdaining Paonese, conducted all their affairs in Pastiche.

CHAPTER XX

Beran Panasper, Panarch of Pao, sat in the rotunda of the pink-colonnaded lodge on Pergolai, in the same black chair where his father Aiello had died.

The other places around the carved ivory table were vacant; no one was present but a pair of black-dyed neutraloids, looming outside the door.

Presently there was motion at the door, the Mamarone's challenge in voices like ripping cloth. Beran identified the visitor, signaled the Mamarone to open.

Finisterle entered the room, gravely deigning no notice of the hulking black shapes. He stopped in the center of the room, inspected Beran from head to foot. He spoke in Pastiche, his words wry and pungent as the language itself. "You carry yourself like the last man in the universe."

Beran smiled wanly. "When today is over, for better or worse, I will sleep well."

"I envy no one!" mused Finisterle. "Least of all, you."

"And I, on the other hand, envy all but myself," replied Beran morosely. "I am truly the popular concept of a Panarch—the overman who carries power as a curse, delivers decisions as other men hurl iron javelins…And yet I would not change—for I am sufficiently dominated by Breakness Institute to believe that no one but myself is capable of disinterested justice."

"This credence which you deprecate may be no more than fact."

A chime sounded in the distance, then another and another.

"Now approaches the issue," said Beran. "In the next hour Pao is ruined or Pao is saved." He went to the great black chair, seated himself. Finisterle silently chose a seat down near the end of the table.

The Mamarone flung back the fretwork door; into the room came a slow file—a group of ministers, secretaries, miscellaneous functionaries: two dozen in all. They inclined their heads in respect, and soberly took their places around the table.

Serving maidens entered, poured chilled sparkling wine.

The chimes sounded. Once more the Mamarone opened the door. Marching smartly into the room came Esteban Carbone, Grand Marshal of the Valiants, with four subalterns. They wore their most splendid uniforms and helms of white metal which they doffed as they entered. They halted in a line before Beran, bowed, stood impassively.

Beran had long realized this moment must come.

He rose to his feet, returned a ceremonious greeting. The Valiants seated themselves with rehearsed precision.

"Time advances, conditions change," said Beran in an even voice, speaking in Valiant. "Dynamic programs once valuable become harmful exaggerations when the need has passed. Such is the present situation on Pao. We are in danger of losing our unity.

"I refer in part to the Valiant camp. It was created to counter a specific threat. The threat has been rebuffed; we are at peace. The Valiants, while retaining their identity, must now be reintegrated into the general population.

"To this end cantonments will be established among all the eight continents and the larger isles. To these cantonments the Valiants shall disperse, in units of fifty men and women. They shall use the cantonment as an organizational area and shall take up residence in the countryside, recruiting locally as becomes necessary. The areas now occupied by the Valiants will be restored to their previous use." He paused, stared from eye to eye.

Finisterle, observing, marvelled that the man he had known as a moody hesitant youth should show such a strong face of decision.

"Are there any questions or comments?" asked Beran.

The Grand Marshal sat like a man of stone. At last he inclined his head. "Panarch, I hear your orders but I find them incomprehensible. It is a basic fact that Pao requires a strong arm of offense and defense. We Valiants are that arm. We are indispensable. Your order will destroy us. We will be diluted and dispersed. We will lose our esprit, our unity, our competivity."

"I realize all this," said Beran. "I regret it. But it is the lesser of the evils. The Valiants henceforth must serve as a cadre, and our military arm will once again be truly Paonese."

"Ah, Panarch," spoke the Grand Marshal abruptly, "this is the crux of the difficulty! You Paonese have no military interest, you..."

Beran held up his hand. "We Paonese," he said in a harsh voice. "All of us are Paonese."

The Grand Marshal bowed. "I spoke in haste. But, Panarch, surely it is clear that dispersion will lessen our efficiency! We must drill together, engage in exercises, ceremonies, competitions..."

Beran had anticipated the protest. "The problems you mention are real, but merely pose logistical and organizational challenges. I have no wish to diminish either the efficiency or the prestige of the Valiants. But the integrity of the state is at stake, and these tumor-like enclaves, benign though they be, must be removed."

Esteban Carbone stared glumly at the ground a moment, then glanced left and right at his aides for support. Their faces were bleak and dispirited.

"A factor you ignore, Panarch, is that of morale," Carbone said heavily. "Our effectiveness..."

Beran interrupted briskly. "These are problems which you, as Grand Marshal, must solve. If you are incapable, I will appoint someone else. There will be no more discussion—the basic principle as I have outlined it must be accepted. You will confer with the Minister of Lands over details."

He rose to his feet, bowed in formal dismissal. The Valiants bowed, marched from the room.

As they left a second group entered, wearing the simple gray and white of the Technicants. They received, in general, the same orders as the Valiants, and put forward the same protests. "Why need the units be small? Surely there is scope on Pao for a number of industrial complexes. Remember that our efficiency depends on a concentration of skill. We cannot function in such small units!"

"Your responsibility is more than the production of goods. You must educate and train your fellow Paonese. There will undoubtedly be a period of confusion, but eventually the new policy will work to our common benefit."

The Technicants departed as bitterly dissatisfied as the Valiants.

Later in the day Beran walked along the beach with Finisterle, who could be trusted to speak without calculation as to what Beran might prefer to hear. The quiet surf rolled up the sand, retreated into the sea among glistening bits of shell, fragments of bright blue coral, strands of purple kelp.

Beran felt limp and drained after the emotional demands which had been made upon him. Finisterle walked with an air of detachment, and said nothing until Beran asked directly for his opinions.

' Finisterle was dispassionately blunt. "I think that you made a mistake in issuing your orders here on Pergolai. The Valiants and Technicants will return to familiar environments. The effect will be that of returning to reality, and in retrospect the instructions will seem fantastic. At Deirombona and at Cloeopter, the orders would have had more direct reference to their subject."

"You think I will be disobeyed?"

"The possibility appears strong."

Beran sighed. "I fear so myself. Disobedience may not be permitted. Now we must pay the price for Bustamonte's folly."

"And my sire, Lord Palafox's ambition," remarked Finisterle.

Beran said no more. They returned to the pavilion and Beran immediately summoned his Minister of Civil Order.

"Mobilize the Mamarone, the entire corps."

The Minister stood stupidly. "Mobilize the Mamarone? Where?"

"At Eiljanre. Immediately."

Beran, Finisterle and a small retinue flew down out of the cloudless Paonese sky to Deirombona. Behind them, still beyond the horizon, came six sky-barges, bearing the entire Mamarone corps, growling and mumbling to each other.

The air-car grounded. Beran and his party alighted, crossed the vacant plaza, passed under the Stele of Heroes, and entered the long low structure which Esteban Carbone used for his headquarters, as familiar to Beran as the Grand Palace at Eiljanre. Ignoring startled expressions and staccato questions, he walked to the staff room, slid back the door.

The Grand Marshal and four other officers looked up in an irritation which changed to guilty surprise.

Beran strode forward, impelled by an anger which over-rode his natural diffidence. On the table lay a schedule entitled: 'Field Exercises 262: Maneuver of Type C Warships and Auxiliary Torpedo-Units'.

Beran fixed Esteban Carbone with a lambent glare. "Is this the manner in which you carry out my orders?"

Carbone, after his initial surprise, was not to be intimidated.

"I plead guilty, Panarch, to delay. I was certain that after consideration you would understand the mistake of your first command…"

"It is no mistake. Now—at this very moment—I order you: implement the instructions I gave you yesterday!"

The men stared eye to eye, each determined to pursue the course he deemed vital, neither intending to yield.

"You press us hard," said the Marshal in a glacial voice. "Many here at Deirombona feel that we who wield the power should enjoy the fruits of power—so unless you wish to risk…"

"Act!" cried Beran. He raised his hand. "Or I kill you now!"

Behind him there was sudden movement, a spatter of blue light, a hoarse cry, a clatter of metal. Wheeling, Beran saw Finisterle standing over the body of a Valiant officer. A hammer-gun lay on the floor; Finisterle held a smoking energy-needle.

Carbone struck out with his fist, hit Beran hard on the jaw. Beran toppled back upon the desk. Finisterle turned to shoot, but was forced to hold his fire for the confusion.

A voice cried, "To Eiljanre! Death to the Paonese tyrants!"

Beran rose to his feet, but the Marshal had departed. Nursing his sore jaw, he spoke into a shoulder microphone; the six sky-barges, now above Deirombona, swooped down to the square; the monstrous black Mamarone poured forth.

"Surround the corps headquarters," came Beran's orders. "Allow neither entrance nor exit."

Carbone had broadcast orders of his own; from nearby barracks came hasty sounds, and into the plaza poured groups of Valiant warriors. At sight of the neutraloids they stopped short. Mamarone in magenta and green stared at the young Valiants, and the air seemed to harden with hate along the line of sight.

Squad leaders sprang forward; the Valiants became a disciplined force instead of a mob. For a space there was silence, while Mamarone and Myrmidon weighed each other.

At the necks of the squad leaders vibrators pulsed. The voice of Grand Marshal Esteban Carbone issued from a filament. "Attack and destroy. Spare no one, kill all."

* * *

The battle was the most ferocious in the history of Pao. It was fought without words, without quarter. The Myrmidons outnumbered the Mamarone, but each neutraloid possessed three times the strength of an ordinary man.

At a signal the Myrmidons came running forward, weaving and dodging. The neutraloids opened fire with shatter-beams and killed several dozen Myrmidons. The Myrmidons, lying prone, returned the fire; the neutraloids, secure behind absorption shields, waited.

The Myrmidons advanced in enveloping waves, one segment forcing the neutraloids to shelter behind their shields, while the other advanced, and so they leapfrogged across the plaza, fifty feet at a time.

Within the headquarters Beran called into his microphone.

"Marshal, I beseech you, prevent this spilling of blood. It is unnecessary, and good Paonese will die!"

There was no response. In the plaza only a hundred feet separated

Mamarone from Myrmidon; they stood almost eye to eye, the neutral-oids grinning in humorless rancor, contemptuous of life, unconscious of fear; the Myrmidons seething with impatience and verve, anxious for glory. The neutraloids, behind their screens and with backs against the wall of the corps headquarters, were secure from small weapons; however once they should move away from the wall, their backs would be vulnerable.

Suddenly they dropped the screens; their weapons poured death into the nearby ranks: a hundred men fell in an instant. The screens returned into place and they took the retaliating fire without casualty.

The gaps in the front line were filled instantly. Horns blew a brilliant fanfare; the Myrmidons drew scimitars and charged against the black giants.

The neutraloids dropped the screens, the weapons poured out death, a hundred, two hundred warriors were killed. But twenty or thirty sprang across the final few yards. The neutraloids drew their own great blades, hacked, hewed; there was the flash of steel, hisses, hoarse calls, and again the Mamarone stood free. But while the shields had been down, lances of fire from the rear ranks of the Myrmidons found targets, and a dozen neutraloids were fallen.

Stolidly the black ranks closed. Again the Myrmidon horns sounded, again the charge, and again the hack and splinter of steel. It was late afternoon; ragged clouds low in the west veiled the sun, but an occasional beam of orange light played across the battle, glowing on the splendid fabrics, reflecting from glistening black bodies, shining dark on spilled blood.

Within the staff headquarters Beran stood in bitter frustration. The stupidity, the arrogance of these men! They were destroying the Pao he had hoped to build—and he, lord of fifteen billion, could find insufficient strength to subdue a few thousand rebels.

In the plaza the Myrmidons at last split the neutraloid line into two, battered back the ends, bunched the giant warriors into two clots.

The neutraloids knew their time had come, and all their terrible detestation for life, for men, for the universe boiled up and condensed in a clot of pure fury. Swinging their great swords with one hand, grasping necks and heads with the other, they waded back and forth across the plaza, and the ground was littered with corpses and parts of corpses. One by one they succumbed, to a thousand hacks and cuts. Their number dwindled—to fifty, to thirty, to twenty, to ten, to five.

These last few looked at each other, and laughed, inhuman hoarse bellows, and presently they too died, and the plaza was quiet except for subdued sobbing. Then behind, by the Stele, the Valiant women set up a chant of victory, forlorn but exulting, and the survivors of the battle, gasping and sick, joined the paean.

Beran and his small company had already departed, flying back to Eiljanre in the air-boat. Beran sat steeped in misery. His body shook, his eyes burnt in their sockets, his stomach felt as if it were caked with lye. Failure, the breaking of his dreams, the beginning of chaos! All to the score of Palafox!

He thought of the tall spare form, the lean face with the wedge-shaped nose and opaque black eyes. The image carried such intensity of emotion as to become almost dear to him, something to be cherished from all harm, except that destruction which he himself would deal—in the event, of course, that he himself should survive. Because now hostility had erupted into bloodshed, and it was inconceivable that the Myrmidons should not go on the offensive. With what weapons could he subdue them? He had no army, no air-force, no space-navy, not even the Mamarone. He had his own two hands, no more.

Beran laughed aloud. Could he enlist the aid of Palafox?

With the last rays of sunset flickering over the roofs of Eiljanre, he arrived at the Palace.

In the great hall sat Palafox, in his usual gray and brown, a wry sad smile on his mouth, a peculiar shine to his eyes.

Elsewhere in the hall sat Cogitants, Palafox's sons for the most part. They were subdued, grave, respectful. As Beran came into the room, the Cogitants averted their eyes.

Beran ignored them. Slowly he approached Palafox, until they stood only ten feet apart.

Palafox's expression changed no whit; the sad smile trembled on his mouth; the dangerous shine glittered in his eyes.

It was clear to Beran that Palafox had completely succumbed to the Breakness syndrome. Palafox was an Emeritus.

CHAPTER XXI

Palafox saluted Beran with a gesture of apparent affability; but there was no corresponding change in his expression. "My wayward young disciple! I understand that you have undergone serious reverses."

Beran came forward another step or two. He need only raise his hand, point, expunge this crafty megalomaniac. As he marshaled himself to act, Palafox uttered a soft word, and Beran found himself seized by four men strange to him, wearing garments of Breakness. While the Cogitants looked on soberly these men flung Beran flat on his face, opened his clothes, touched metal to his skin. There was an instant of piercing pain, then numbness along his back. He heard the click of tools, felt the quiver of manipulation, a wrench or two, and then they were done with him.

Pale, shaken, humiliated, he regained his feet, rearranged his garments.

Palafox said easily, "You are careless with the weapon provided you. Now it is removed and we can talk with greater relaxation."

Beran could find no answer. Growling deep in his throat, he marched forward, stood before Palafox. He opened his mouth to speak, but the only words which came to mind were such paltry vehicles for his hate that he stood in silence.

Palafox smiled slightly. "Once again, Pao is in trouble. Once again, it is Lord Palafox of Breakness to whom appeals are made."

"I made no appeals," said Beran in a husky voice.

Palafox ignored him. "Ayudor Bustamonte once needed me. I aided him, and Pao became a world of power and triumph. But he who profited—Panarch Beran Panasper—broke the contract. Now, again the Paonese government faces destruction. And only Palafox can save you."

Realizing that exhibitions of rage merely amused Palafox, Beran forced himself to speak in a voice of moderation. "Your price, I assume, is as before? Unlimited scope for your satyriasis?"

Palafox grinned openly. "You express it crudely but adequately. I prefer the word 'fecundity'. But such is my price."

A Cogitant came into the room, approached Palafox, spoke a word or two in Breakness. Palafox looked to Beran. "The Myrmidons are coming. They boast that they will burn Eiljanre, destroy Beran and set forth to conquer the universe. This, they claim, is their destiny."

"How will you deal with the Myrmidons?" asked Beran tartly.

"Easily," said Palafox. "I control them because they fear me. I am the most highly modified man on Breakness, the most powerful man ever to exist. If Esteban Carbone fails to obey me, I will kill him. To their plans for conquest I am indifferent. Let them destroy this city, let them destroy all the cities, as many as they will." His voice was rising— he was becoming excited. "So much the easier for me, for my seed! This is my world, this is where I shall live magnified by a million, a billion sons. I shall fructify a world; there never shall have been so vast a siring! In fifty years the planet will know no name other than Palafox, you shall see my face on every face. The world will be I, I will be the world!"

The black eyes glowed like opals, pulsing with fire. Beran became infected with the madness; the room was unreal, hot gases swirled through his mind. Palafox, losing the appearance of a man, took on various semblances in rapid succession: a tall eel, a phallus, a charred post with knotholes for eyes, a black nothingness.

"A demon!" gasped Beran. "The Evil Demon!" He lunged forward, caught Palafox's arm, hurled Palafox stumbling to the floor.

Palafox struck with a thud, a cry of pain. He sprang to his feet holding his arm—the same arm that Beran had wounded before—and he looked an Evil Demon indeed.

"Now is your end, gad-fly!" He raised his hand, pointed his finger. From the Cogitants came a mutter.

The finger remained pointed. No fire leapt forth. Palafox's face twisted in passion. He felt his arm, inspected his finger. He looked up, calm once more, signaled to his sons. "Kill this man, here and now. No longer shall he breathe the air of my planet."

There was dead silence. No one moved. Palafox stared incredulously; Beran looked numbly about him. Everywhere in the room faces turned away, looking neither toward Beran nor Palafox.

Beran suddenly found his voice. He cried out hoarsely, "You talk madness!" He turned to the Cogitants. Palafox had spoken in Breakness, Beran spoke in Pastiche.

"You Cogitants! Choose the world you would live in! Shall it be the Pao you know now, or the world this Emeritus proposes?"

The epithet stung Palafox; he jerked in anger, and in Breakness, the language of insulated intelligence, he barked, "Kill this man!"

In Pastiche, language of the Interpreters, a tongue used by men dedicated to human service, Beran called, "No! Kill this senile megalomaniac instead!"

Palafox motioned furiously to the four men of Breakness—those who had de-energized Beran's circuits. His voice was deep and resonant. "I, Palafox, the Great Sire, order you, kill this man!"

The four came forward.

The Cogitants stood like statues. Then they moved as if at a single decision. From twenty parts of the room streaks of flame leapt forth.

Transfixed from twenty directions, eyes bulging, hair fluffing into a nimbus from the sudden charge, Lord Palafox of Breakness died.

Beran fell into a chair, unable to stand. Presently he took a deep breath, staggered to his feet. "I can say nothing to you now—only that I shall try to build the sort of world that Cogitants as well as Paonese can live in with satisfaction."

Finisterle, standing somberly to the side, said, "I fear that this option, admirable as it is, lies not entirely in your hands."

Beran followed his gaze, through the tall windows. High up in the sky appeared bursts of colored fire, spreading and sparkling, as if in celebration for some glory.

"The Myrmidons," said Finisterle. "They come for vengeance."

The sky was filled with explosions of colored sparks in flower-like garlands, three-dimensional snowflakes, heraldic medallions. A dozen great black warships cruised over Eiljanre, circled over the palace, in tighter and tighter circles, funnelling down toward the landing deck.

Finisterle touched Beran's arm. "Best had you flee while there is yet time. They will show you no mercy."

Beran made no answer. Finisterle took his arm. "You accomplish nothing here but your own death. There is no guard to protect you— we are all at their mercy."

Beran gently disengaged himself. "I shall remain here; I shall not flee."

"They will kill you!"

Beran gave the peculiar Paonese shrug. "All men die."

"But you have much to do, and you can do nothing dead! Leave the city, and presently the Myrmidons will tire of the novelty and return to their games."

"No," said Beran. "Bustamonte fled. The Brumbos pursued him, ran him to the ground. I will no longer flee anyone. I will wait here with my dignity, and if they kill me, so shall it be."

An hour passed, the minutes ticking off slowly, one by one. The warships dropped low, hovered only yards from the ground. The flag-ship settled gingerly upon the palace deck.

Within the great hall Beran sat quietly on the dynastic Black Chair, his face drawn with fatigue, his eyes wide and dark. The Cogitants stood in muttering groups, watching Beran from the corners of their eyes.

From far off came a whisper of sound, a deep chant, growing louder, a chant of dedication, of victory, sung to the organic rhythm of pumping heart, of marching feet.

Louder and louder—the sound of a hundred voices, and now the tread of heavy steps could likewise be heard.

The chant swelled, the door burst open: into the great hall marched Esteban Carbone, the Grand Marshal. Behind him came a dozen young Field Marshals, and behind these, ranks of staff officers.

Esteban Carbone strode up to the Black Chair and faced Beran.

"Beran," spoke Esteban Carbone, "you have done us unforgivable injury. You have proved a false Panarch, unfit to govern the planet Pao. Therefore we have come in force to pull you down from the Black Chair and to take you away to your death."

Beran nodded thoughtfully, as if Esteban Carbone had come urging a petition.

"To those who wield the power shall go the direction of the state: this is the basic axiom of history. You are powerless, only we Myrmidons are strong. Hence we shall rule, and I now declare that the Grand Marshal of the Myrmidons shall now and forever function as Panarch of Pao."

Beran said no word; indeed, there was no word to be said.

"Therefore, Beran, arise in what little dignity you retain, leave the Black Chair and walk forth to your death."

From the Cogitants came an interruption. Finisterle spoke out angrily. "One moment; you go too far and too fast."

Esteban Carbone swung about. "What is this you say?"

"Your thesis is correct: that he who wields power shall rule—but I challenge that you wield power on Pao."

Esteban Carbone laughed. "Is there anyone who can deter us in any course we care to pursue?"

"That is not altogether the point. No man can rule Pao without consent of the Paonese. You do not have that consent."

"No matter. We shall not interfere with the Paonese. They can govern themselves—so long as they supply us our needs."

"And you believe that the Technicants will continue to supply you with tools and weapons?"

"Why should they not? They care little who buys their goods."

"And who shall make your needs known to them? Who will give orders to the Paonese?"

"We shall, naturally."

"But how will they understand you? You speak neither Technicant nor Paonese, they speak no Valiant. We Cogitants refuse to serve you."

Esteban Carbone laughed. "This is an interesting proposition. Are you suggesting that Cogitants, by reason of their linguistic knack, should therefore rule the Valiants?"

"No. I point out that you are unable to rule the planet Pao, that you cannot communicate with those you claim to be your subjects."

Esteban Carbone shrugged. "This is no great matter. We speak a few words of Pastiche, enough to make ourselves understood. Soon we will speak better, and so shall we train our children."

Beran spoke for the first time. "I offer a suggestion which perhaps will satisfy the ambitions of everyone. Let us agree that the Valiants are able to kill as many Paonese as they desire, all those who actively oppose them, and so may be said to exercise authority. However, they will find themselves embarrassed: first, by the traditional resistance of the Paonese to coercion, and secondly, by inability to communicate either with the Paonese or the Technicants."

Carbone listened with a grim face. "Time will cure these embarrassments. We are the conquerors, remember."

"Agreed," said Beran in a tired voice. "You are the conquerors. But you will rule best by disturbing the least. And until all Pao shares a single language, such as Pastiche, you cannot rule without great disturbance."

"Then all Pao must speak one language!" cried Carbone. "That is a simple enough remedy! What is language but a set of words? This is my first command: every man, woman and child on the planet must learn Pastiche."

"And in the meantime?" inquired Finisterle.

Esteban Carbone chewed his lip. "Things must proceed more or less as usual." He eyed Beran. "Do you, then, acknowledge my power?"

Beran laughed. "Freely. In accordance with your wish, I hereby order that every child of Pao: Valiant, Technicant, Cogitant and Paonese, must learn Pastiche, even in precedence to the language of his father."

Esteban Carbone stared at him searchingly, and said at last, "You have come off better than you deserve, Beran. It is true that we Valiants do not care to trouble with the details of governing, and this is your one bargaining point, your single usefulness. So long as you are obedient and useful, so long may you sit in the Black Chair and call yourself Panarch." He bowed, turned on his heel, marched from the hall.

The Field Marshals swung smartly after him, and next the officers. The chant began, the rhythm pounding to the beat of steps on marble: it dwindled in volume and presently was heard no more. Shortly the black warships lifted from Eiljanre, climbed into the sky amid triumphant showers of colored fire, and sailed southwest to Deirombona.

Beran sat slumped in the Black Chair. His face was white and haggard, but his expression was calm.

"I have compromised, I have been humiliated," he said to Finisterle, "but in one day I have achieved the totality of my ambitions. Palafox is dead, and we are embarked on the great task of my life—the unifying of Pao."

Finisterle handed Beran a cup of mulled wine, drank deep from a cup of his own. "Those strutting cockerels! At this moment they parade around their stele, beating their chests, and at any instant…" He pointed his finger at a bowl of fruit. Blue flame lanced forth, the bowl shattered.

"It is better that we allowed them their triumph," said Beran. "Basically, they are decent people, if naïve, and they will cooperate much more readily as masters than as subjects. And in twenty years…"

He rose to his feet; he and Finisterle walked across the hall, looked out over the roofs of Eiljanre. "Pastiche—composite of Breakness, Technicant, Valiant, Paonese. Pastiche—the language of service. In twenty years, everyone will speak Pastiche. It will fertilize the old minds, shape the new minds. What kind of world will Pao be then?"

They looked out into the night, across the lights of Eiljanre, and wondered.

THE DOMAINS OF KORYPHON

INTRODUCTION

by Mike Resnick

I have a confession to make. Few things in science fiction annoy me more than having to learn a few dozen new words and as many not-quite-human names simply to be able to work my way through a single book. And one of the things that does annoy me more is a novel with forty or fifty footnotes (or feetnote, as the late James Blish dubbed them.)

I have another confession to make: I find that I don't mind new names, new words, or footnotes at all when a master like Jack Vance incorporates them into one of his books, such as, for example, *The Domains of Koryphon*, originally published as *The Grey Prince,* and appearing here under the author's preferred title.

I first read this novel more than thirty years ago. I wasn't aware of all the controversy it was engendering; I read it simply because I made it my business to read all of Jack's books as they came out. I thought it was pretty typical, which is to say, a fast-paced novel with interesting characters and beautiful word-pictures, crafted by one of our master stylists.

So you can imagine my surprise when I started reading reviews and reader comments to the effect that it was racist, or a right-wing polemic, or both.

(A few years later I would be accused, by an equally small handful of critics, of writing racist and sexist tracts in my "Kirinyaga" stories, which are about the Kikuyu people of East Africa trying to form a Utopian colony on a terraformed planetoid. Oddly enough, at the same time those stories came out, I wrote a science fictional allegory of Kenya's history titled *Paradise*, but although my Kikuyu analogs shared every trait and belief with the Kikuyu of "Kirinyaga," they were alien in shape and had alien names—and not a single one of those critics thought *Paradise* was racist or sexist, which I think says a little more about the critics than about the author or the literature. Jack clearly made his aliens a little *too* human.)

This is a very tricky book, *The Domains of Koryphon*. Not only did it fool some of the knee-jerk critics, but it approaches everything in a very indirect manner. (Well, why *shouldn't* a wordsmith of prodigious talent be subtle?)

For example, the viewpoint character is clearly Schaine Madduc, but she is missing from large parts of the narrative, and a strong case can be made that she is too naïve for her own good.

For example, Jorjol is the Grey Prince, but he is *not* the viewpoint character, nor in the end is he an especially nice person, though he is surely a motivated one. There are times when you think he's a bit of an ass who just happens to be on the side of Right and Justice, and there are times when you think he is a reasonably decent character who just happens to be dead wrong. There are as many opinions about him as there are characters in the story who know him, which is precisely as it should be (and so rarely is in a work of fiction.)

As for the true subject of the book, it's as difficult to define in a single sentence or paragraph as the Grey Prince himself, though possibly not to the critics who claim this is a right-wing diatribe. They would tell you, when speaking of the Land-barons, that it is evil and immoral to take land from an indigenous people—and they would be right as far as that argument goes. But what Vance points out is that the "indigenous people" weren't born there, any more than the Apaches or Commanches or Maasai or Kikuyu were born on *their* "ancestral land," that they simply took it from someone else just as surely as various people took it from them.

Not so simple when viewed that way (which is to say, Jack Vance's way), is it?

Then there's the charge of racism.

I suppose you could make a case (or at least *I* could) that the book's Nomads are Amerind analogs, that the Erjin slaves are analogs of the

Negro race of perhaps two centuries ago, and so on. But again, nothing in *The Domains of Koryphon* is ever quite as simple and clear-cut as it seems. You have a slaveholding culture secure in its moral superiority to the Land-baron culture that "steals" the Nomad's land…while the Land-barons know *they* are the superior culture because they do not keep slaves. If you are a Nomad or an Erjin, you don't think too highly of *either* of them.

And finally there are the Morphotes, the true indigenous race, who have a bone to pick with just about everybody.

I have a feeling that the critics who screamed "right-wing tract" and "racist trash" the loudest not only completely misunderstood the book, but also ignored or never understood the fact that guilt is not eternal, that after a certain number of generations have passed most people no longer feel responsible or guilty for the actions of their distant progenitors, but learn to live with the conditions as they now exist. (Actually, most people don't feel guilty ten minutes later or they wouldn't have done whatever it is that inspires guilt, but that has nothing to do with the point I'm making.)

I think I know which side Jack Vance is on, but he makes sure every side is represented by the arguments a believer would make. There comes a point in Patrick McGoohan's still-popular television series of four decades back, *The Prisoner,* when McGoohan runs for office of the mysterious Village, promising to find out "who are the warders and who are the prisoners." You might make a case that, below the surface sheen of exotic other-world adventure, Vance is concerned here with who are truly the oppressed and who are truly the oppressors. I think it was his temerity in even asking the question that upset that small handful of critics I mentioned earlier. After all, this is supposed to be mindless escapist fiction, or if not mindless, at least it should direct the mind to problems of science.

To which I reply: welcome to the works and worlds of Jack Vance.

THE DOMAINS OF KORYPHON

PROLOGUE

The space age is thirty thousand years old. Men have moved from star to star in search of wealth and glory; the Gaean Reach encompasses a perceptible fraction of the galaxy. Trade routes thread space like capillaries in living tissue; thousands of worlds have been colonized, each different from every other, each working its specific change upon those men who live there. Never has the human race been less homogenous.

The outward surge has been anything but regular or even. Men have come and gone in waves and fluctuations, responding to wars, to religious impetus, to compulsions totally mysterious.

The world Koryphon is typical only in the diversity of its inhabitants. On the continent Uaia, the Uldras inhabit that wide band along the southern littoral known as the Alouan, while to the north the Wind-runners sail their two- and three-masted wagons across the Palga plateau. Both are restless nomadic peoples; in almost every other respect they differ. South across the Persimmon Sea the equatorial continent Szintarre is inhabited by a cosmopolitan population of Outkers*, distinguished from both Uldras and Wind-runners by several orders of sociological magnitude.

---

*Outker: The general term for tourists, visitors, recent immigrants: essentially all persons other than Uldra or Wind-runner.

Considered indigenous to Koryphon are a pair of quasi-intelligent races: the erjins and the morphotes. The Wind-runners domesticate and offer for sale erjins of a particularly massive and docile variety, or perhaps they breed and train ordinary erjins to such characteristics. The Wind-runners are secretive in this regard, inasmuch as the trade provides them wheels, bearings and rigging for their wind-wagons. Certain Uldras of the Alouan capture, mount and ride wild erjins, controlling their ferocity with electric curbs. Both domesticated and wild erjins have telepathic capacity by which they communicate with each other and with a few Wind-runner adepts. Unrelated to the erjins are the morphotes, a malicious, perverse and unpredictable race, esteemed only for their weird beauty. At Olanje on Szintarre the Outkers have gone so far as to form morphote-viewing clubs, a recreation all the more titillating for the macabre habits of the morphotes.

Two hundred years ago a group of off-planet freebooters dropped down upon Uaia, surprised and captured a conclave of Uldra chieftains and compelled cession of title to certain tribal lands: the notorious Submission Treaties. In such a fashion each member of the company acquired a vast tract ranging from twenty thousand to sixty thousand square miles. In due course these tracts became the great 'domains' of the Alouan, upon which the 'land-barons' and their descendants lived large and expansive lives in mansions built on a scale to match the holdings.

The tribes signatory to the Submission Treaties found their lives affected to no great extent: if anything, improved. The new dams, ponds and canals provided dependable sources of water; intertribal warfare was proscribed and the domain clinics provided at least a modicum of medical care. A few Uldras attended domain schools and trained to become clerks, storekeepers and domestic servants; others took jobs as ranch-hands.

In spite of such improvement, many Uldras resented the simple fact of inferior status. On a subconscious and unacknowledged level but perhaps a source of equal exacerbation was the land-barons' disinclination for the Uldra females. A certain amount of rape or seduction, while resented, might have been accepted as a sordid but inevitable adjunct to the conquest. In point of fact, while the Uldra men, with their tall nervous physiques, gray skins dyed ultramarine blue and aquiline features, were in general personable, the same could not be said for the women. The girls, squat and fat, with their scalps shaved bald against the onslaught of vermin, lacked charm. As they matured, they retained their heavy hips and short legs, but elongated their torsos, arms and faces. The typically long Uldra nose became a drooping icicle; the gray skins became muddy; the hair, verminous or not, was allowed to grow into a heavy orange nimbus. Toward these Uldra girls and women the Outker land-barons* maintained a scrupulously correct indifference, which eventually, by a paradoxical reverse effect, came to be regarded by the Uldras as a humiliation and an insult.

South across the Persimmon Sea lay the long narrow island Szintarre and its pleasant capital Olanje, a fashionable resort for out-worlders. These folk, sophisticated, urbane, articulate, had little in common with the land-barons whom they regarded as pompous martinets, without style, grace or humor.

At Olanje in an eccentric old edifice known as Holrude House sat Koryphon's single organ of government: the Mull, a council of thirteen notables. The Mull's charter asserted control across Szintarre and Uaia alike, but in practice it avoided any interest in Uaian affairs. The land-barons considered the Mull an organ for the production of inconsequential sophistry; the Treaty Uldras were apathetic; the Retent Uldras rejected even the theory of centralized authority; the Wind-runners were ignorant of the Mull's very existence.

The cosmopolitan population of Olanje generated for itself an almost hyperactive intellectualism. Social activity was incessant; committees and societies existed to accommodate almost any special interest: a yacht club; several artists' associations; the Morphote-Watchers; the Szintarre Hussade Association; the Library of Gaean Musical Archives; an association to sponsor the annual fête: Parilia; a college of the dramatic arts; Dionys: that organization dedicated to hyperaesthesia. Other groups were philanthropic or altruistic, such as the Ecological Foundation, which enjoined the importation of alien flora and fauna, no matter how economically useful or aesthetically gratifying. The Redemptionist Alliance crusaded against the Submission Treaties; they advocated dissolution of the Uaian domains and return of the lands to the Treaty tribes. The Society for the

---

*No satisfactory equivalent for the word *eng'sharatz* (literally: the revered master of a large domain) exists. 'Baron' or 'lord' implies a formal aristocracy; a 'squire' is master of a small property; 'rancher' implies emphasis upon agricultural activity. 'Land-baron' is awkward and somewhat labored but is perhaps closer to the sense of *eng'sharatz* than any other term.

Emancipation of the Erjin, or SEE, asserted that erjins were intelligent beings and might not legally be enslaved. The SEE was possibly the most controversial organization of Olanje, inasmuch as an increasing number of erjins were being imported from the Palga for domestic service, farm labor, garbage pick-up and the like. Other less disputatious groups sponsored education and employment for Uldras immigrant to Szintarre from Uaia. These Uldras, derived in about equal proportion from Retent and Treaty tribes, tended to excoriate the land-barons. Often their grievances were real; often they complained from sheer petulance. The Redemptionists sometimes brought Uldra immigrants before the Mull, the better to prod that often discursive, airy, didactic and capricious group into action. With practiced skill the Mull fended off such importunities or appointed a study commission, which invariably reported the Treaty lands to be havens of peace compared to the Retent, where the independent tribes conducted feuds, raids, assassinations, retaliations, outrages, massacres, atrocities and ambushes. The Redemptionists declared such considerations to be irrelevant. The Treaty tribes, so they pointed out, had been deprived of their ancestral lands through violence and deceit. The perpetuation of such a condition was intolerable, nor could the passage of two hundred years legitimize an originally wrongful situation. Most residents of Szintarre tended generally to endorse the Redemptionist doctrine.

CHAPTER 1

In the foyer at the Olanje space port Schaine Madduc and her brother Kelse examined each other with affectionate curiosity. Schaine had expected changes in Kelse; changes there were indeed—five years' worth and more. She had left him a bedridden cripple, pallid and desperate; he now seemed strong and well, if a trifle gaunt. His artificial leg carried him with only the suggestion of a limp; he worked his left arm as capably as he did his right, although he disdained simulated flesh and kept the metal hand encased in a black glove. He had grown taller: this she had expected, but not the change in his face which had lengthened and hardened and taken on an acerb refinement. His cheekbones had become prominent; his jaw was a jut; his eyes were narrow, and he had acquired a habit of glancing sidewise in a wary or suspicious or challenging squint: a signal, thought Schaine, of the true changes in Kelse: the alteration from a trusting generous boy to this austere man who looked ten years older than his age.

Kelse had been reflecting along similar lines. "You're different," he said. "Somehow I was expecting the merry, frivolous, silly old Schaine."

"Both of us are different."

Kelse glanced contemptuously down at his arm and leg. "Quite a bit different. You never saw these before."

"Are they easy to use?"

Kelse shrugged. "The left hand is stronger than the right. I can crack nuts in my fingers and do all sorts of interesting jobs. Otherwise I'm much the same."

Schaine could not restrain the question: "Have I changed so very much?"

Kelse looked at her dubiously. "Well, you're five years older. You're not quite so skinny. Your clothes are very nice; you look quite smart. You always were pretty, even as a ragtag tomboy."

"'Ragtag tomboy' indeed!" Schaine's voice was soft with melancholy. As they walked across the depot memories and images flooded her mind. The girl they spoke about was distant by not five but by five hundred years; she had inhabited a different world, where evil and woe were unknown. The verities were simple and obvious to all. Morningswake Manor was no more and no less than the center of the universe; each of those who lived there had a predestined role to fulfill. Uther Madduc was the font of authority. His decisions, sometimes benign, sometimes mysterious, sometimes awful, were as definite as the motion of the sun. Concentric to Uther Madduc had been herself and Kelse; in an orbit less stable, sometimes near, sometimes far, was Muffin. In general the roles were uncomplicated, except again in the case of Muffin whose status was often ambiguous. Schaine had been the 'ragtag tomboy', nonetheless charming and pretty—so much went without saying—just as Kelse had always been proud and handsome and Muffin always dashing and brave and gay. Such attributes were implicit in the very fabric of existence, just as the sun Methuen was unalterably pink and the sky immutably ultramarine. Looking back across the years she saw herself against a backdrop of Morningswake: a girl of medium height, neither tall nor short, engagingly lanky but durable, as if she were good at swimming and running and climbing, which of course she had been and still was. Her skin shone tawny-gold from the sunlight; her dark hair was a loose curly tangle. She was the girl with the sweet wide mouth and the alert marveling expression, as if each successive instant brought some new wonder. She had loved with innocence and hated without calculation; she had been mercurial, gentle with small creatures, quick with gleeful gibes...Now she was five years older and five years wiser, or so she hoped.

Kelse and Schaine walked out into the soft Szintarre morning. The air smelled as Schaine remembered: fragrant with the essence of leaves and flowers. Down from the dark green juba trees hung strands of scarlet blossoms; sunlight seeped through the foliage to spatter patterns of pink and black on Kharanotis Avenue.

"We're staying at the Seascape," Kelse told her. "There's a party at Aunt Val's this afternoon, ostensibly to welcome you home. We could have stayed at Mirasol, of course, but..." His voice trailed off. Schaine recalled that Kelse had never been overfond of their Aunt Val. He asked: "Shall I call a cab?"

"Let's walk. Everything looks so beautiful. I've been cooped up aboard the *Niamatic* for a week." She drew a deep breath. "It's wonderful to be back. I feel like I'm home already."

Kelse gave a sour grunt. "Why did you wait so long?"

"Oh—various reasons." Schaine made a flippant gesture. "Obstinacy. Willfulness. Father."

"You're still obstinate and willful—so I presume. Father is still Father. If you think he's changed, you're in for a shock."

"I'm under no illusions. Someone has to give in, and I can do it as easily as anyone. Tell me about Father. What has he been doing?"

Kelse considered before answering: a trait Schaine could not recall from five years ago. Kelse's youth had passed all too swiftly, she thought. "Father is by and large the same. Since you've been gone there's been a lot of new pressure, and—well, you've heard of the Redemptionist Alliance."

"I suppose so. I don't remember much about it."

"It's a society based here in Olanje. They want us to tear up the Submission Treaties and leave Uaia. Nothing new, of course; but now it's a fashionable cause, and in the 'Gray Prince', as he calls himself, they have a fashionable figurehead."

"'Gray Prince'? Who is he?"

Kelse's mouth twitched in a crooked grin. "Well—he's a young Uldra, a Garganche, with some education; he's voluble, quaint and vivacious—in fact, he's the darling of all Olanje. No doubt he'll be at Aunt Val's party this evening."

They passed an expanse of blue-green sward, extending from the avenue up the slope to a tall mansion with five gables, towers to right and left, a façade of mustard-yellow tiles relieved by slabs of glossy black skeel: a structure conceived in eclectic caprice, yet impressive by virtue of sheer size and a certain careless magnificence. This was Holrude House, seat of the Mull. Kelse gave his head a gloomy shake. "The Redemptionists are up there now, trying to indoctrinate the Mull...I speak figuratively of course. I don't know that they're in Holrude at this specific instant. Father is pessimistic; he thinks the Mull will eventually issue an edict against us. I got a letter from him this morning." He reached into his pocket. "No, I left it at the hotel. He's planning to meet us at Galigong."

Schaine asked in perplexity: "Why Galigong? He could as easily meet us here."

"He won't come to Olanje. I don't think he wants to see Aunt Valtrina; she might make him come to a party. That's what she did last year."

"It wouldn't hurt him. Aunt Val's parties were always fun. At least I liked them."

"Gerd Jemasze is coming with us; in fact we flew here in his Apex, and he'll take us across to Galigong."

Schaine made a sour face; she had never liked Gerd Jemasze, whom she considered surly.

A pair of columns marked the entrance to the Seascape. Schaine and Kelse rode a slideway down the vestibule. Kelse arranged for the transfer of Schaine's luggage from the space port, then they sauntered out upon the terrace close beside the Persimmon Sea and refreshed themselves with goblets of pale green cloudberry juice, glinting with ice crystals. Schaine said: "Tell me what's been happening at Morningswake."

"Ordinary routine for the most part. We stocked Fairy Lake with a new mix of fish. I went prospecting south of the Burrens and found an ancient kachemba*."

"Did you go in?"

Kelse shook his head. "Those places give me cold chills. I told Kurgech about it; he said it was probably Jirwantian."

---

*Kachemba: a secret Uldra cult-place, dedicated to divination and sorcery, usually located in a cave.

"Jirwantian?"

"They occupied South Morningswake for five hundred years, before the Hunge annihilated them. Then the Aos drove out the Hunge."

"How are all the Aos? Is Zamina still matriarch?"

"Yes, she's still alive. Last week they shifted camp into Dead Rat Gulch. Kurgech dropped by the manor and I told him you were coming home. He said you'd get in less trouble on Tanquil."

"Wretched old creature! What did he mean by that?"

"I don't believe he meant anything. He was merely 'tasting the future'."

Schaine sipped the fruit juice and looked out over the sea. "Kurgech is a mountebank. He can't foresee or draw fates or cold-eye or transmit thoughts any better than I can."

"Not true. Kurgech has some amazing skills...Ao or not, he's Father's closest friend."

Schaine snorted. "Father is too much of a tyrant to be good friends with anyone—most especially an Ao."

Kelse gave his head a sad shake. "You just don't understand him. You never have."

"I understand him as well as you do."

"That may well be true. He's a hard man to know. Kurgech provides him exactly the right kind of companionship."

Schaine snorted again. "He's undemanding, loyal and knows his place—like a dog."

"Absolutely wrong. Kurgech is an Uldra, Father is an Outker. Neither wants it any different."

With an extravagant flourish Schaine drained the goblet. "I certainly don't intend to debate anything whatever with either you or Father." She rose to her feet. "Let's walk over to the river. Is the morphote fence still up?"

"So far as I know. I haven't been here since you left for Tanquil."

"A melancholy occasion which I'd just as soon forget. Let's go find a twelve-spine devil-chaser with triple fans and a purple lattice."*

A hundred yards along the beach a path led inland to the swamp at the mouth of the Viridian River and ended beside a tall fence of steel mesh. A sign read:

---

*Morphote viewing is a sport on many levels. The morphotes stimulate upon themselves all manner of growths: spines, webs, wens, fans, prongs, to make themselves objects of fantastic splendor. Morphote viewers have contrived an elaborate nomenclature to define the elements of their sport.

CAUTION!
Morphotes are dangerous and cunning! Consider none of
their proffers; accept none of their gifts! Morphotes come to
this fence with a single purpose in mind: to mutilate, insult,
or frighten those Gaeans who come to view them.
TAKE WARNING!
Morphotes have injured many persons;
they may kill YOU.
NEVERTHELESS, WANTON MOLESTATION OF
THE MORPHOTES IS
ABSOLUTELY FORBIDDEN.

Kelse said, "A month ago some tourists from Alcide came to view
morphotes. While the mother and father joked with a beautiful red-
ringed bottle-face at the fence, another tied a butterfly on a string and
lured away the three-year-old child. When Mama and Daddy looked
around, Baby was gone."

"Disgusting beasts. There should be controls on morphote viewing."

"I think the Mull is considering along those lines."

Ten minutes passed and no morphotes came up from the swamp to
make horrifying proposals. Schaine and Kelse returned to the hotel,
descended to the submarine restaurant and lunched on a ragout of cray-
fish, pepper-pods and wild onion, a salad of chilled cress and flat-bread
baked from the flour of wild brown ferris. Luminous blue-green space
surrounded them; at their very elbows swam, grew or drifted the flora
and fauna of the Persimmon Sea: white eels and electric blue scissor-
fish darting through the thickets of water-weed; schools of blood-red
spark-fish, green serpents, yellow twitters, twinkling and darting, the
myriads occasionally sifting through each other in a pointillistic confusion, finally to emerge as before. On three occasions purple and silver
spangs, ten feet of prongs, barbs, hooks and fangs, came to grind
against the crystal in an attempt to seize one of the folk who lunched
in the half-light; once the dire bulk of a black matador slid past; once
off in the distance appeared the jerking form of a swimming morphote.

A man two or three years older than Kelse approached the table.
"Hello, Schaine."

"Hello, Gerd." Schaine's greeting was cool; all her life she had disliked
Gerd Jemasze, for reasons she could never quite define to herself. His
conduct was reserved, his manner polite, his features undistinguished:

blunt at the cheekbones, flat in the cheeks, with short thick black hair above a low broad forehead. His clothes—a dark gray blouse and blue trousers—seemed, in the context of Olanje where everyone wore gay colors and exaggerated fashions, almost ostentatiously severe. Schaine suddenly understood why he repelled her: he totally lacked the idiosyncrasies and easy little vices which endowed all her other acquaintances with charm. Gerd Jemasze's physique was not noticeably large or heavy, but when he moved, the clothes tightened to the twist of his muscles; in just such a fashion, thought Schaine, did his quiet appearance mask an innate arrogance. She knew why her father and Kelse liked Gerd Jemasze; he outdid them both in rigidity and resistance to change; his opinions, once formed, became impervious as stone.

Gerd Jemasze took a seat at their table. Schaine asked politely, "And how goes life at Suaniset?"

"Very quietly."

"Nothing ever happens out in the domains," said Kelse.

Schaine looked from one to the other. "You two are teasing me."

Gerd Jemasze displayed a twitch of a smile. "Not altogether. Whatever happens usually goes on out of sight."

"What's happening out of sight, then?"

"Well—wittols* out of the Retent have been skulking through the domains talking coalition of all Uldras under the Gray Prince, presumably to chase us into the sea. There's been a lot of sky-shark** attacks on air traffic—just last week Ariel Farlock of Carmione was shot down."

"For a fact there's a strange mood over Uaia," said Kelse somberly. "Everybody feels it."

"Even Father," said Schaine, "rejoicing over his wonderful joke. Have you any idea what he finds so funny?"

---

*Wittols: One of every thousand Uldras is born albino, eunuchoid, short of stature and round-headed. These are the wittols, treated with a mixture of repugnance, contempt and superstitious awe. They are credited with competence at small magic and witchcraft; occasionally they deal in spells, curses and potions. Major magic remains the prerogative of the tribal warlocks. The wittols bury dead, torture captives and serve as emissaries between tribes. They move with safety across the Alouan, since no Uldra warrior would either deign or dare to kill a wittol.

**Sky-shark: A crude one-man aircraft, little more than a flying plank fitted with a gun or some other weapon, used by Uldra nobles for attacks upon enemy tribes or duels among themselves.

"I don't even know what you're talking about," said Gerd Jemasze.

"I had a letter from Father," Kelse explained. "I told you that he'd gone up on the Palga. Well, the trip seems to have exceeded his expectations." Kelse brought forth the letter and read: "'I've had some remarkable adventures and I have a wonderful story to tell you, a most wonderful joke, a most prodigious and extraordinary joke, which has put ten years on my life.'" Kelse skipped down across a line or two. "Then he says: 'I'll meet you at Galigong. I don't dare come to Olanje, which would mean suffering through one of Valtrina's awful parties, complete with all the pussy-footers, logic-choppers, aesthetes, four-flushers, sybarites and sycophants in Szintarre. Make sure Gerd comes back to Morningswake with us; he, no less than you, will appreciate this situation, and express to Schaine my great pleasure at having her home once again...'

There's more along this line but that's the gist of it."

"Very mysterious," said Gerd Jemasze.

"Yes, that's how I feel. What is there up on the Palga to cause Father such merriment? He's not famous for his humor."

"Well—tomorrow we'll know." Gerd rose to his feet. "If you'll excuse me, I have a few errands to do." He bowed with rather cursory politeness to Schaine.

Kelse asked: "You're coming to the party at Aunt Valtrina's?"

Gerd Jemasze shook his head. "It's not really my kind of affair."

"Oh come along," said Kelse. "You might have a chance to meet the Gray Prince—among other local notables."

Gerd Jemasze reflected a moment or two as if Kelse had scored a point in a profound and complicated argument. "Very well. I'll come. What time and where?"

"Four o'clock at Villa Mirasol."

CHAPTER 2

The road to Villa Mirasol, departing Kharanotis Avenue, wound back and forth up the side of Panorama Mountain under stands of gonaive, native teak, langtang and mace. Passing under an arch, the road circled a wide lawn and ended at the villa: an elegant construction of glass, fluted posts, white walls, a roof of many angles and levels, designed in a light and easy spirit of rococo decadence.

Valtrina Darabesq, maternal great-aunt to Schaine and Kelse, welcomed both with an enthusiasm none the less real for its impersonal facility. Schaine had always marveled at her energy and her remarkable gregariousness; Kelse considered her a bit over-stylish, though he could not help but approve her expansive generosity. Both were prepared for her insistence that they transfer from the Seascape to Villa Mirasol and stay a week, two weeks, a month. "I've seen neither of you for so long. Schaine, it's been at least—how many years?"

"Five."

"So long? How time goes! I never really understood why you went flouncing off to Tanquil. Your father is a dinosaur, of course, but he's a dear for all that, even if he refuses to come across to Olanje. What can he find to amuse him in Uaia? A wilderness, a dreadful emptiness!"

"Come now, Aunt Val, it's not that bad! In fact Uaia is full of magnificent scenery."

"Perhaps so, but why Uther and the others insist on living out where they're not wanted, I'll never understand. Morningswake is like a border fortress."

"Someday you should come pay us a visit," said Kelse.

Valtrina gave her head a decisive shake. "I haven't been to Morningswake since I was a girl. Your grandfather Norius was a gentleman of style for all of being a land-baron. He hosted several parties—rather stuffy occasions, to be absolutely candid, and took us for a picnic to an enormous pillar of red rock; what's it called?"

"The Skaw."

"The Skaw, of course. And when the tribesmen came past and looked at us, the aliens who had taken their land, I felt frightened and oppressed, for all the space. It was as if we were besieged!"

"Our Aos have never given us trouble," said Kelse patiently. "We help them and they help us. Neither resents the other."

Valtrina gave her head a smiling shake. "My dear boy, you can't possibly divine what goes on in an Uldra mind. Of course they resent your presence, even though they show you blank faces. I know, because I have Uldra friends! But I shouldn't remonstrate with you; you're just a boy. Come along then, I'll introduce you to my friends. Or perhaps you'd prefer just to wander about?"

"We'd rather just wander," said Kelse.

"Just as you like. Have Alger fix you drinks. Kelse, please don't draw a gun and shoot my erjins; their names are Sim and Slim and they're extremely expensive. We'll have a good chat later on this evening." Valtrina moved off to welcome a new group of guests; Kelse took Schaine's arm and led her to the buffet where Alger the steward dispensed refreshment, using formulas older than memory. Kelse and Schaine accepted goblets of punch, and paused to take their bearings. Schaine saw no one she knew among the guests. Half a dozen Uldras were present: tall, thin, long-nosed bravos, their slate-gray skin dyed ultramarine, their wads of pale russet hair confined within the tall spikes of a fillet.

Kelse muttered to Schaine: "Trust Aunt Val to be fashionable; in Olanje no party is complete without an Uldra or two."

Schaine retorted: "Why shouldn't Uldras be invited to parties? They're human."

"Approximately human. Their weldewiste* is alien to ours. They've drifted quite a distance on the evolutionary floe."

Schaine sighed and turned to inspect the Uldras. "Is one of them the Gray Prince?"

"No."

Valtrina approached with a handsome man in his middle maturity: a person of obvious distinction, wearing a dark gray suit embroidered with pale gray arabesques. She brought her companion to a halt. "Erris, my niece and nephew Schaine and Kelse Madduc. Schaine is just home from Tanquil, where she's been at school. Schaine, Kelse, this is Erris Sammatzen, who sits on the Mull: a man of great importance." She added with perhaps a hint of malice: "Schaine and Kelse live on Morningswake Domain in the Alouan, which they claim to be the single habitable area of Koryphon."

"Perhaps they know more than we do."

Schaine asked, "Are you native to Olanje, Dm.** Sammatzen?"

"No, I'm an Outker like almost everyone else. I came here twelve years ago to rest, but who can rest when Valtrina and a dozen like her

---

*Weldewiste: a word from the lexicon of social anthropology, to sum up a complicated idea comprising the attitude with which an individual confronts his environment; his interpretation of the events of his life; his cosmic consciousness; his perception of self vis-à-vis the universe; his character and personality from the purview of comparative culture.

**The two most common appellatives of the Gaean Reach are Dm., for Domine, which may properly be applied to all persons of distinguished or exalted station, and Vv., a contraction of Visfer (originally Viasvar, an Ordinary of the ancient Legion of Truth, then a landed gentleman, finally the common polite appellative).

insist on keeping me alert? This is the most intellectually alive community I've ever known. Really, it's most exhausting."

Valtrina beckoned to a tall woman with long blonde ringlets. Her overlarge features were exaggerated by cosmetics into a clown's mask; Schaine wondered if she mocked the world or herself. Valtrina spoke in her hoarsest contralto: "This is Glinth Isbane, one of our celebrities: she taught three morphotes to play desisto and won all kinds of strange booty. She's secretary of SFS and far more profound than she likes to appear."

"What's SFS?" asked Schaine. "Excuse me, I'm just back on Koryphon."

"SFS means 'Society for a Free Szintarre'."

Schaine laughed incredulously. "Isn't Szintarre free now?"

"Not altogether," said Glinth Isbane in a cool voice. "No one wants—I should say, no one admits that he wants—to exploit toil or discomfort for gain, but everyone knows that this is often the case. Workers therefore have banded into guilds to protect themselves. And now, who wields more raw power than the Director of the Associated Guilds? I need not remind you of the abuses from this direction. The SFS has therefore organized a force which we hope will exactly counter-balance the excesses of the guilds."

Another person had joined the group: a tall young man with guileless gray eyes, soft blond hair, pleasant half-humorous features which instantly appealed to Schaine. He remarked: "Both groups—the SFS and the Associated Guilds—support my particular organization. Hence, both must be sound, and your conflicts are pettifoggery."

Glinth Isbane laughed. "Both groups endorse SEE, but for quite different reasons. Our reasons are the decent ones."

Schaine said to Valtrina, "I'm confused by all these organizations. What is SEE?"

Valtrina, rather than explaining, brought forward the blond young man. "Elvo, meet my charming niece, just arrived from Tanquil."

"With great pleasure."

"Schaine Madduc; Elvo Glissam. Now Elvo, explain the meaning of SEE, but don't mention me or my expensive footmen or I'll have them fling you out into the street."

"SEE is Society for Emancipation of the Erjins," said Elvo Glissam. "Please don't think us maudlin; we're truly attacking a serious injustice: the enslavement of intelligent beings. Valtrina, with her erjin servants, is one of our prime targets, and we'll have her behind bars yet. Unless she displays remorse and frees her slaves."

"Ha! First demonstrate two things—no, three. Prove to me that Sim and Slim are intelligent beings rather than domestic animals. Then prove that they would prefer to be emancipated. Then find me two other domestics with as much docility, style and dependability as my black-and-mustard beauties. In fact, I intend to buy three or four more and train them as gardeners."

One of the erjin footmen had just entered the chamber, rolling a service wagon. Looking over her shoulder Schaine cringed away. "Don't they frighten you? The buck that chewed up Kelse wasn't much bigger, if at all."

"If I were running things," said Kelse, "I'd shoot them all."

Glinth Isbane's voice took on an edge. "If they're intelligent, it's murder. If they're not, it's brutality."

Kelse shrugged and turned aside. A few minutes previously Gerd Jemasze had appeared on the scene; now he said: "We fear our erjins; you don't. Incidentally, I don't notice any societies which advocate taking erjin mounts away from the Uldras."

"Why don't you form one?" snapped Glinth Isbane.

Erris Sammatzen chuckled. "As for the erjins and Vv. Glissam's SEE, the labor guilds are understandably anxious: the erjins represent cheap labor. Vv. Glissam is presumably motivated by other concerns."

"Naturally. The Gaean Charter prohibits slavery, and the erjins are enslaved: benignly here at Olanje, not so benignly in Uaia. And the Wind-runners, whose role everyone ignores, are slavers, pure and simple."

"Or domesticators—if they conceive the erjins to be no more than clever beasts."

Schaine said: "I can't understand how erjins can be tamed; in fact, I can't believe it! An erjin is ferocious; it hates men!"

"Sim and Slim are quite docile," said Valtrina. "As to how and why: I can't even guess."

Sim the erjin footman once again passed by, splendid in its livery. Meeting the opaque orange gaze from among the black optical tufts, Schaine received the uncomfortable impression that it understood all which transpired. "Perhaps it would prefer not being gelded or altered or brainwashed—whatever the Wind-runners do to it."

"Ask it," Valtrina suggested agreeably.

"I don't know how."

Valtrina's contralto voice became lofty and careless. "So why worry? They're free to leave whenever they like. I don't keep them in chains.

Do you know why they work here? Because they prefer Villa Mirasol to the deserts of Uaia. No one complains except the Association of Labor Guilds which feels a threat to its absurdly high wage structure." Valtrina gave her head a lordly jerk and stalked across the room to where a pair of Uldras formed the nucleus of another group.

Gerd Jemasze spoke to no one in particular: "I won't say that all this talk is a waste of time, because people seem to enjoy it."

In a frigid voice Glinth Isbane said: "Words are the vehicle of ideas. Ideas are the components of intellectualization, which distinguished men from animals. If you object to the exchange of ideas, then—in essence—you reject civilization."

Jemasze grinned. "Not such a bad idea as you might think."

Glinth Isbane turned away and went off to join Valtrina. Jemasze and Kelse sauntered to the buffet where Alger supplied them refreshment. Schaine went to inspect a pair of Uldra lamps, carved from blocks of red chert in the distinctive Uldra style of reckless asymmetry. Elvo Glissam came to join her. "Do you like these lamps?"

"They're interesting to look at," said Schaine. "Personally, I wouldn't care to own them."

"Oh? They seem very dashing and adventurous."

Schaine gave a grudging nod. "I suppose it's a prejudice left over from my childhood, when everything Uldra was supposed to be erratic and uneven and wild. I realize now that the Uldras consider uniformity a kind of slavishness; they express their individualism in irregularity."

"Perhaps they try to suggest regularity by presenting something else: a very sophisticated technique."

Schaine pursed her lips. "I doubt if the Uldras would reason so methodically. They're extremely proud and truculent, especially the Retent Uldras, and I suspect that their art-work reflects as much. It's just as if the lamp-maker were saying: 'This is how I choose to make this lamp; this is my caprice; if you don't like it, seek elsewhere for light.'"

"That's the effect produced, certainly. At best: magnificence. At worst: a kind of strident peevishness."

"Which, in fact, expresses the Uldra temperament."

Elvo Glissam looked across the room toward the two Uldras. Schaine studied him from the corner of her eye. She liked him, so she decided; he seemed gentle and humorous and subtle in his perceptions. Additionally, he was nice to look at, with his soft blond hair and pleasantly regular features. He stood perhaps an inch taller than the average;

he appeared athletic, in an easy loose-limbed fashion... He turned to find her eyes on him and responded with a self-conscious smile. Schaine said rather hurriedly: "You're not a native to Szintarre?"

"I'm from Jennet on Diamantha. A dreary city on an unexciting world. My father publishes a pharmaceutical journal; right now I'd probably be writing an article on the latest foot powders if my grandfather hadn't given me a lottery ticket for my birthday."

"The ticket paid off?"

"A hundred thousand SLU*."

"What did you do with it?"

Elvo Glissam made a casual, or perhaps modest, gesture. "Nothing remarkable. I paid off the family debts, bought my sister a Cloud-hopper and put the rest out at interest. So here I am, living on a modest but adequate income."

"And what do you do besides just live?"

"Well, I've got two or three things going on. I work for SEE, as you know, and I'm putting together a collection of Uldra war songs. They're natural musicians and produce the most wonderful songs which don't get half the attention they deserve."

"I grew up with those songs," said Schaine. "In fact, I could sing a few blood-curdlers right now, if I were in the right mood."

"Some other time."

Schaine laughed. "I'm seldom anxious to burn my enemies, one by one, 'with six thousand fires and six thousand pangs'."

"The Gray Prince, incidentally, is supposed to be here tonight."

"The Gray Prince—isn't he the Uldra messiah, or rabble-rouser, or some such special agent?"

"So I'm told. He advocates what he calls 'Pan-Uldra'—an association of the Retent tribes, which then will absorb the Treaty tribes and ultimately eject the land-barons from Uaia. Over here he's sponsored by the Redemptionists, which means almost everyone in Szintarre."

"Including yourself?"

"Well—I don't like to admit it to the daughter of a land-baron."

Schaine sighed. "I don't really mind. I'm going back to live at Morningswake, and I've determined not to quarrel with my father."

---

*SLU: Standard Labor-value Unit; the monetary unit of the Gaean Reach, defined as the value of an hour of unskilled labor under standard conditions. The unit supersedes all other monetary bases, in that it derives from the single invariable commodity of the human universe: toil.

"Aren't you putting yourself in a very awkward position? I feel in you a certain awareness of justice and fair play—"

"In other words, am I a Redemptionist? I hardly know what to say. Morningswake is my home, so I've been brought up to believe. But what if I really didn't have any right to be there, would I still want to keep it? To be candid, I'm glad that my opinion carries absolutely no weight, so that I can enjoy going home without suffering pangs of conscience."

Elvo Glissam laughed. "At least you're honest. If I were you I might feel the same way. Kelse is your brother? Who is the grim dark-haired fellow with the stomach-ache?"

"That's Gerd Jemasze of Suaniset, the domain next east to ours. He's always been lofty and saturnine, ever since I can remember."

"I think someone said—probably Valtrina—that an erjin attacked Kelse."

"Yes, it was absolutely horrible, and erjins terrify me to this day. I can't believe those great beasts are tame."

"There are many different kinds of human beings; maybe there are different kinds of erjins."

"Perhaps…When I see those great maws and awful arms, I think of poor little Kelse, all chewed and ripped."

"It's a miracle he's alive."

"He'd be dead except for an Uldra boy we called Muffin, who came with a gun and blew the erjin's head off. Poor Kelse. Poor Muffin, for that matter."

"What happened to Muffin?"

"It's a long sordid story. I don't want to talk about it."

For a moment the two stood in silence. Elvo Glissam said: "Let's go out on the terrace and look over the sea—where you'll be flying tomorrow."

Schaine thought this was a pleasant idea, and they walked out into the warm night. Through the campander fronds the lights of Olanje were scattered in a long irregular crescent; overhead hung the stars of the Gaean Reach, many seeming to shimmer with an extra significance for the populated worlds surrounding.*

---

*On the worlds of the Gaean Reach and Alastor Cluster, especially those with rural populations, a new profession has come into existence: the man skilled in star-naming and star-lore. For a fee he enlivens nocturnal gatherings with his tales, marvels and descriptions of the worlds surrounding stars within the vision of those present.

Elvo Glissam said: "An hour ago you were not even a name, and now Schaine Madduc is you, and I'll be sorry to see you leave. Are you sure you prefer Uaia to Olanje?"

"I can hardly wait to get home."

"Isn't it bleak and drab and depressing?"

"Of course not! Where have you heard such nonsense? Uaia is magnificent! The sky is so wide, the horizons are so far, that mountains, valleys, forests and lakes are lost in the landscape. Everything swims in light and air; I can't describe the effect except to say that Uaia does something to your soul. I've missed Morningswake terribly these last five years."

"You make Uaia sound interesting."

"Oh, it's interesting, but it's not a soft place. Uaia is often cruel—more often than not. If you saw the wild erjins destroying our cattle, you might not be so pro-erjin."

"See? You completely misunderstand me! I'm not pro-erjin! I'm anti-slavery, and erjins are slaves."

"Not the wild erjins! Better if they were."

Elvo Glissam gave an indifferent shrug. "I've never seen a wild erjin, and I'm not likely to have the opportunity. They're quite extinct in Szintarre."

"Come out to Morningswake; you'll see wild erjins, as many as you like."

Elvo Glissam said rather wistfully: "I'd accept the invitation if I thought you were serious."

Schaine hesitated barely an instant, although her invitation had been intended in general rather than specific terms. "Yes, I'm serious."

"What of Kelse? What of your father?"

"Why should they mind? Guests are always welcome at Morningswake."

Elvo Glissam reflected a moment. "When do you leave?"

"First thing in the morning. We fly with Gerd Jemasze to Galigong, at the edge of the Retent; there my father meets us. Tomorrow at sunset we'll be at Morningswake."

"Your brother might consider me forward."

"Of course not! Why should he?"

"Very well then. I'll be more than happy to accept. In fact I'm tremendously excited." Elvo Glissam straightened up from the balustrade. "In which case I'll now have to leave this party, to pack some clothes and change some arrangements. And I'll meet you at your hotel early tomorrow morning."

Schaine held out her hand. "Goodby till then."

Elvo Glissam bent his head and kissed her fingers. "Good night." He turned and walked away. Schaine watched him go with a half-smile on her face and a soft warm pressure in her throat.

She followed Elvo inside and wandered from room to room until, in that chamber which Valtrina called the kachemba, after the sacred places of the Uldras, she found Kelse and Gerd Jemasze debating the authenticity of Valtrina's antique fetishes.

Kelse picked up a blasphemy mask* and raised it to his face. "I can smell gabbhout smoke, and there's a smear of what looks like dilf by the nostril holes."

Schaine chuckled. "I wonder how many masks in how many kachembas look like you two."

"No doubt several of both," said Gerd. "Our Faz aren't as docile as your Aos. Last year on the Kaneel Broads I looked into a kachemba. Sure enough, they built it to represent Suaniset."

"What about masks?"

"Just two: me and my father. My father's mask wore a red cap. Mission accomplished."

Two years before a letter from Kelse had apprised Schaine of the murder of Palo Jemasze, Gerd's father, through the instrumentality of an Uldra sky-shark.

"The tutelar in this case flying a sky-shark," Kelse observed.

Jemasze gave a curt nod. "Once or twice a week I take up my Dacy and go hunting. No luck, so far."

Schaine decided to change the subject. "Kelse, I've invited Elvo Glissam to Morningswake."

"Elvo Glissam? The SEE advocate?"

"Yes. He's never seen a wild erjin. I told him we'd find one for him. Do you mind?"

"Why should I mind? He seems decent enough."

---

*Blasphemy mask: the Uldra warlocks array themselves in a burnt-clay mask in the likeness of their enemy, with whatever of his accoutrements they are able to possess, together with his caste tassels; then they visit the kachemba, or secret fane, pertaining to the tribe of the enemy, and there blaspheme the tutelars of this tribe, in the expectation that the tutelars will revenge themselves upon the person represented.

The three returned to the main salon. Glancing across the room Schaine noticed a tall young Uldra in the robes of an Alouan chieftain, though the robes, rather than red or rose or pink, were unrelieved gray. He was a man remarkably handsome, with a skin blue as the sea and hair bleached glistening white. Schaine stared in shock and wonder, then turned wide-eyed to Kelse. "What is he doing here?"

"That's the Gray Prince," said Kelse. "He's seen everywhere around Olanje."

"But how—why—"

"In some fashion," said Kelse, "he was encouraged to become the savior of his race."

Gerd Jemasze gave a snort of sardonic amusement, and Schaine became furiously angry with both. Gerd was innately a boor; Kelse had become as crabbed and obstinate as her father...She took command of herself. Kelse, after all, had suffered the loss of a leg and an arm. Her own loss—if 'loss' were the appropriate word—was trivial in comparison...The Gray Prince, swinging his gaze around the room, saw Schaine. He tilted his head forward, then jerked it back in a motion of glad surprise. He strode across the room to stand in front of Schaine.

Kelse said in a bored voice, "Hello, Muffin. What brings you here?"

The Gray Prince, throwing up his head, laughed. "'Muffin' no more! I must reckon with my public image." A trace of Uldra accent gave his voice a gay and urgent quality. "To the friends of my childhood I am 'Jorjol', or if you insist upon formality: 'Prince Jorjol'."

"I hardly think we'll insist upon formality," said Kelse. "You probably remember Gerd Jemasze from Suaniset."

"I remember him most distinctly." Jorjol took Schaine's hand, bent his head and kissed it. "You can still call me 'Muffin' if you like but—" he looked around the room; his gaze, slipping past Kelse and Gerd, relegated them to the background "—I'd prefer not here. Where have you been? Has it been five years?"

"Quite five years."

"It seems forever. So much has changed."

"You seem to have done very well for yourself. You're the talk of Olanje, so I understand—although I wasn't aware that the Gray Prince was Muffin."

"Yes, Muffin has come a vast distance, and I intend to go as far again—even at the risk of inconveniencing my old friends." His glance now included Kelse and Gerd; then he turned back to Schaine. "And what will you do now?"

"I'm returning to Morningswake tomorrow. We meet Father in Galigong and fly home from there."

"As an 'intransigent'?"

"What's an 'intransigent'?"

Kelse said in a bored voice: "The opposite of 'Redemptionist', or so I suppose."

Schaine said: "I'm going as myself, nothing more, and I intend to quarrel with no one."

"You might find it more difficult than you think."

Schaine smilingly shook her head. "Father and I can accommodate to each other. He's neither cruel nor unreasonable, as you well know."

"He's a force of nature! Storms, lightning, torrents—they're not cruel or unreasonable either, but they cannot be defeated by kindness and rationality."

Schaine laughed sadly. "And you intend to defeat my poor father?"

"I must. I am a Redemptionist. I intend to win back for my people the lands they lost to the violence of your people."

Gerd looked up toward the ceiling and turned half away. Kelse said: "Speaking of my father, I had a letter from him today: a most curious letter. He mentions you as well. Listen. 'You might be seeing that scamp Jorjol. If so, try to bring him to his senses, for his own sake. Perhaps the prospect of a career at Morningswake no longer appeals to him; tell him nevertheless that when his bubble breaks he is always welcome here, for reasons of which we are all aware.

"'I have just returned from the Volwodes and I can't wait to see you. I've had some remarkable adventures and I have a wonderful story to tell you, a most wonderful joke, a most prodigious and extraordinary joke which has put ten years on my life, and which might well amuse and edify Jorjol...' That's about all here to interest you."

Jorjol raised his bleached white eyebrows. "What kind of joke? I am not interested in jokes."

"I don't know what his joke might be; I'm anxious to find out."

Jorjol pulled at his long nose, which apparently had been surgically cropped of its drooping Uldra tip. "Uther Madduc was never a great humorist, to my recollection."

"True," said Kelse. "Still, he's a more complex person than you might think."

Jorjol reflected a minute. "I remember your father principally as a man dominated by the strictures of etiquette. Who knows what sort of person he really is?"

"External events have shaped us all," said Kelse.

Jorjol grinned, showing teeth whiter than his hair, in gleaming contrast to his blue skin. "Never! I am I, because I have willed myself thus!"

Schaine could not restrain a nervous laugh. "Heavens, Muffin—Jorjol—Gray Prince—whatever your name is—your intensity startles us all!"

Jorjol's grin diminished somewhat. "You know me for an intense person." From across the room Valtrina called him; he bowed, and with a final quick glance at Schaine took his leave.

Schaine heaved a sigh. "Quite true; he's always been intense."

Erris Sammatzen came to join them. "You seem to know the Gray Prince intimately."

"Yes, that's Muffin," said Kelse. "Father found him out at the edge of the Retent when he was little: he'd been abandoned. Father brought him home and put him into the care of an Ao bailiff, and we all grew up together."

"Father always had a soft spot for Muffin," mused Schaine. "When we were caught in some really flagrant mischief, Kelse and I would get a whack or two, but Muffin always got off with a lecture."

"Actually," said Kelse, "that's not so much forbearance as the etiquette we just heard about. One never strikes a Blue."

Sammatzen glanced across the room to the group of Uldras. "They look pretty formidable. I don't think I'd want to strike one."

"He'd kill you with a knife, but he wouldn't strike back. Among the Uldras only women fight barehanded; woman-fights are a popular spectacle."

Sammatzen looked curiously at Kelse. "You don't like the Uldras very much."

"I like some of them. Our Aos are well-behaved. Kurgech the shaman is one of Father's cronies. We've put a stop to the woman-fights and a few other unpleasant customs. They still work sorcery which we can't stop."

"It would seem that Jorjol wasn't brought up as an Uldra."

"He wasn't brought up as anything. He lived with the Ao bailiff, but he took lessons with us and played with us and wore Gaean clothes. We really never thought of him as a Blue."

"I used to adore him," said Schaine, "especially after he saved Kelse from the erjin."

"Indeed! This was the erjin that took your arm and leg?"

Kelse gave a curt nod and would have changed the subject but Schaine said: "It happened only two miles south of the house. An erjin came around the Skaw and proceeded to tear Kelse to bits. Jorjol ran up to the beast and blew its head off with a gun, and just in time or Kelse wouldn't be here now. Father wanted to do something wonderful for Jorjol..." Schaine paused, thinking back across scenes five years old. "But there were emotional problems. Jorjol went *aurau**. He ran away and we never saw him again, although we learned from Kurgech that he'd crossed into the Retent and joined the Garganche. He was originally Garganche—we knew that from his birth tattoo—so there was no question about their 'land-scouring' him."

"'Land-scouring' is what the Blues do to enemy tribesmen," remarked Kelse. "One of the things, I should say."

Schaine glanced across the room toward Jorjol. "And tonight we find him here at Villa Mirasol. We expected him to make a career for himself, but nothing like this."

Kelse said dryly, "Father had in mind head stockman, or bailiff."

"You'll have to agree," Sammatzen observed, "that for an ambitious Uldra very little opportunity exists to better himself."

Gerd Jemasze snorted in sour amusement. "The ambitious Blue wants to raid or ransom or steal enough money to buy a sky-shark. He doesn't want to be a teacher or an engineer—any more than you want to ride an erjin."

"That's a yearning I'm able to control."

"Reflect a moment," Kelse told him. "The Blues can come to Szintarre whenever they want; they can attend school at Olanje and learn a profession. How many do so? Few, if any. All the Blues in Olanje are agitators and Redemptionist house pets; they exist only to get the land-barons out of the Treaty Lands."

"They seem to feel that the land is theirs," remarked Sammatzen.

"It's theirs if they can force us off it," said Kelse. "If they can't, it's ours."

Sammatzen shrugged and turned away. Kelse said to Schaine, "We'd better be leaving; we've got a long day tomorrow."

---

*Aurau: untranslatable; said of a tribesman afflicted with revulsion against civilized restrictions, and sometimes of a caged animal yearning for freedom.

Schaine made no protest. With Gerd Jemasze they bade farewell to Valtrina and departed Villa Mirasol.

The hour was late. Schaine was restless. She stepped out on her balcony and stood under the stars. The sea was quiet; the town had gone to sleep; a few lights twinkled up and down the shore and through the foliage of the hillside. No sound could be heard but the sigh of the surf...An eventful day. Kelse, Gerd Jemasze, Aunt Val, Muffin (the Gray Prince!)—all components of her childhood, all now with their elemental natures refined and intensified. The tranquility she had come home to find seemed forever lost and gone. She brought faces into her mind. Kelse: more terse and cynical than she could have expected. Kelse had aged very quickly; all his boyish grace had departed...Gerd Jemasze: a hard harsh man with a soul of stone...Muffin, or Jorjol as now he must be called: as gallant and clever as ever. How fateful that the agency which had given him sustenance, education, even life itself—namely Morningswake—should now be the target of Redemptionist attack!... Elvo Glissam! Schaine felt a warm flush, a pulse of eagerness. She hoped that he would stay weeks, months, at Morningswake. She would take him up to the Opal Pits, to the Lake of the Veils, to Sanhredin Glade, to the Magic Forest and the lodge on Mount May; she would ask Kurgech to organize a Grand Karoo*. Elvo Glissam would bring fun to Morningswake where none had existed for five years: five bitter wasted years.

CHAPTER 3

Across the Persimmon Sea flew the Suaniset utility vehicle, an ungainly Apex A-15, lacking all style or flair and Schaine suspected that Gerd Jemasze intended nothing less than a demonstration of contempt for the fads of Olanje. She remarked: "All this is very luxurious, but where's the Hybro Saloon?"

---

*Karoo: Uldra festivities, including feasting, music, dancing, declaiming, athletic contests. An ordinary karoo occupies a night and a day; a Grand Karoo continues three days and nights, or longer. The karoos of the Retent tribes are wild and often macabre.

Gerd Jemasze fixed the auto-pilot upon Galigong and swung around in his seat. "The Hybro is in the shop. I'm waiting for new dexodes."

Schaine remembered the Suaniset Hybro from her childhood. She asked Kelse: "I suppose Father is still flying our dilapidated Sturdevant with the broken window?"

"Yes, it's ageless. I fixed the window last year."

Schaine informed Elvo Glissam: "Out on the domains life flows at a serene pace. Our ancestors were wise and industrious; what's good enough for them is good enough for us."

"We're not altogether torpid," said Kelse. "Twelve years ago we planted two hundred acres to vines and next year we'll start producing wine."

"That sounds interesting," said Schaine. "We should be able to undersell the imports; we might end up as tycoons of the wine trade."

Elvo Glissam said: "I thought you were all rich, with so much land and mountains and streams and minerals."

Kelse gave a wry chuckle. "We're subsistence farmers. We don't see much cash."

"Perhaps you can advise us on the lottery," suggested Schaine.

"Gladly," said Elvo Glissam. "Invest your money elsewhere. For instance, a resort marina on one of those beautiful islands down there, for the convenience of yachtsmen."

"Cruising the Persimmon Sea is a chancy business," said Kelse. "Sometimes morphotes climb aboard and kill everybody and sail the yacht away."

"That must be quite a sight," said Gerd Jemasze.

Elvo Glissam grimaced. "Koryphon is a cruel world."

"Suaniset is peaceful enough," said Gerd Jemasze.

"So is Morningswake," said Kelse. "Jorjol tries to tell our Aos how bad things are and they don't know what he's talking about. So now Jorjol does his talking in Olanje."

"Jorjol hardly seems a classical reformer," said Elvo Glissam. "He's really a most perplexing individual. What could be his motives? After all, your father was his benefactor."

Schaine sat silent. Gerd Jemasze scowled down at the Mermione Islands. Kelse said: "There's really no great mystery. Father has a most rigid set of values. It might seem that Jorjol and Schaine and I grew up as playmates and equals, but there was never any attempt to gloss over the real situation. We were Outkers; Jorjol was a Blue. He never took a meal in the Great Hall; instead he ate in the kitchen, which I suppose rankled much more than he cared to admit. Then summers, when we visited Aunt Val in Olanje, Jorjol was sent out to learn ranch business, because Father intended Jorjol to become head stockman."

Elvo Glissam nodded soberly and asked no more questions.

The pink sun floated up the sky; the Apex broke through a shoal of cumulus to discover the loom of Uaia across the northern horizon. Details appeared through the haze: bluffs, beaches, promontories; colors gradually clarified to pale dun, ocher, black, white-buff and brown. The shore approached; a peninsula detached itself from the hulk of the continent to enclose a long narrow bight. At the tip clustered a half-dozen warehouses, a few rows of huts and cabins, a rickety hotel of white-painted timber built half over the water on a pier of a hundred crooked stilts. "Galigong," said Kelse. "The chief seaport of the Retent."

"And how far to Morningswake?"

"About eight hundred miles." Kelse studied the landscape through binoculars. "I don't see the Sturdevant, but we're a bit early. The Hilgads are having a karoo at their shore camp. I think there's a woman-fight in progress." He offered the binoculars to Elvo Glissam, who was just as pleased to see only a confused surge of tall blue-faced forms in white, pink and buff robes.

The sky-car landed; the four stepped out upon the chalky soil of Uaia and hurried across the crackling pink glare to the shelter of the hotel. They entered a dim tavern, illuminated only by a row of green glass bull's-eyes. The inn-keeper came forward: a short fat Outker with a few whorls of brown hair, a splayed nubbin of a nose, melancholy brown eyes drooping at the outer corners.

Kelse asked: "Are there messages from Morningswake?"

"No sir, not a word."

Kelse looked down at his watch. "I suppose we're still a bit early." He went to the door, looked around the sky and returned. "We'll take lunch. What can you provide us?"

The inn-keeper dolefully shook his head. "Very little, I fear. I might fry up a bit of spernum. There's a jar or two of preserved polyps, and I can send the boy out for a salad of rockwort. You can have that sugar tart yonder in the case, although I can't overly vouch for it."

"Well, do the best you can. Meanwhile bring us jars of cold ale."

"As cold as may be, sir."

The lunch appeared: a meal somewhat less makeshift than the landlord's diffidence had suggested. The four sat out on the pier in the shade of the hotel, facing north across the water to the Hilgad camp. The landlord confirmed that a karoo was in progress. "But don't be tempted by curiosity; they're drunk on raki; they'd treat you very unfairly if you ventured near. Already this morning there's been three woman-fights and eight rascolades, and tonight they'll throw from the wheel." He made a sign of caution and returned into the hotel.

"These terms are all mysterious," said Elvo Glissam. "None sound appealing."

"Your instincts are accurate," said Kelse. He pointed to the sunburnt hillside. "Can you make out those little cages and hutches? That's where captives wait for ransom. After a year or two, if ransom isn't paid, the captive is brought out to run down a course. After him come warriors on erjins, armed with lances. If he reaches the other end of the course he's set free. That's rascolade. The wheel—see that tall structure with the counterweight? The counterweight is hoisted; the captive is tied to the wheel. The counterweight is cut loose; the wheel spins. At a certain point the captive is cut loose and thrown toward that jut of rock you see offshore. Sometimes he lands in the water and the morphotes get him. The fun goes on until they run out of captives. Meanwhile they're all eating barbecued morphote and drinking skull-buster and plotting where to get more captives."

Schaine was displeased by the flavor of the conversation; she did not want Kelse and Gerd Jemasze impinging their prejudices upon Elvo Glissam's still open mind. She said: "The Hilgad aren't representative Uldras; in fact they're pariahs."

Gerd Jemasze said: "They're pariahs because they lack traditional lands and kachembas, not because their customs are unusual."

Schaine started to point out that the remark applied only to the Retent tribes, that Treaty Uldras, such as the Morningswake Aos, were considerably less savage and ruthless; then noticing the sardonic gleam in Gerd Jemasze's eyes, she held her tongue.

The hours passed. At mid-afternoon Kelse telephoned Morningswake; on the dusty insect-spotted screen in the corner of the tavern appeared the image of Reyona Werlas-Madduc, housekeeper at Morningswake and third cousin to Schaine and Kelse. Her image flared and wavered; her voice vibrated through the antique filaments. "He's not yet at Galigong? Stars, he should be there by now; he left this morning."

"Well, he's not here. Did he mention another destination, or an errand somewhere along the way?"

"He said nothing to me. Is Schaine there? Let me say a word to dear little Schaine."

Schaine came forward and exchanged greetings with Reyona; then Kelse returned to the telephone. "If Father calls, explain that we're waiting at Galigong Hotel."

"He should be there any minute…Might he have stopped off at Trillium to take a glass or two with Dm. Hugo?"

"Hardly likely," said Kelse. "We'll just have to wait until he arrives."

The afternoon passed; the sun sank into the Persimmon Sea among flaring clouds and darting rays. Schaine, Kelse, Elvo Glissam and Gerd Jemasze sat out on the dock, facing westward over the placid water. Worry now hung in the air.

"He wouldn't be this late unless he ran into trouble," Kelse declared. "It's almost certain that he's been forced down along the way. And two-thirds of the route is over Retent land: Garganche and Hunge and Kyan."

"Why wouldn't he radio for help?" Schaine asked.

"A dozen things might have happened," said Gerd Jemasze. "We'll surely find him somewhere along the route between here and Morningswake."

Kelse cursed under his breath. "We can't find him in the dark; we'll have to wait for morning." He went off to arrange for accommodations and returned more disconsolate than ever. "The landlord has two rooms with beds, and he'll hang up a pair of hammocks. But he doesn't know whether he'll be able to feed us supper."

Supper nonetheless consisted of an adequate platter of sand-creepers poached in sea-water, with a garnish of soursops and fried kale. After the meal the four went once more to sit out on the pier. In a spasm of zeal the inn-keeper threw a cloth over his bait table and served a dessert of biscuits and dried fruit, with a pot of verbena tea.

Conversation among the four dwindled. For a period the Hilgad fires burned high, then subsided to quivering red sparks. Languid swells surging under the pier made soft sad sounds; in the sky constellations began to appear: the magnificent Griffeides, Orpheus with his lute of eight blue stars, Miraldra the Enchantress with blazing Fenim for her diadem, and low in the southeast the star-veils of Alastor Cluster. How pleasant this evening might have been, thought Schaine, had circumstances been different! She felt depressed, a mood distinct from her worry in regard to Uther Madduc. Lovely old Morningswake had become a vortex of ugly emotions, and she was uncertain as to her ultimate sympathies. Not, she suspected, with her father, although it made no difference; she loved him anyway. Why then, she wondered, did she detest Gerd Jemasze so intensely? His opinions were identical to those of her father; he was no less resourceful and self-sufficient. She looked toward the rail where Elvo Glissam and Gerd Jemasze spoke together. Both were about the same age; both were physically personable; both were individuals with pride in their own identities. Elvo was warmhearted, impulsive and happy; he was sympathetic and idealistic; he concerned himself with moral ultimates. In contrast Gerd Jemasze guarded his feelings behind a cool mask; his humor was sardonic; his code of ethics—if such it could be called—was based upon a self-serving pragmatism…Their conversation drifted across the night; they spoke of morphotes and erjins. Schaine listened.

"—somewhat peculiar," Gerd was saying. "The palaeontologists find a fossil record of morphote evolution, all the way up from a creature similar to the creeper we ate for supper. The erjins have left no fossils. Their skeletal substance disintegrates over just a few years so that the evolutionary sequence isn't at all clear; no one even knows how they breed."

"Except the Wind-runners," said Kelse.

"How do the Wind-runners domesticate erjins? Do they capture cubs? Or work with adults?"

"Uther Madduc can tell you more than I can; he's just come down from the Palga."

"Maybe that's his 'wonderful joke'," suggested Kelse.

Gerd Jemasze shrugged. "So far as I know, the Wind-runners hatch out erjin eggs and train the cubs. Wild erjins are telepathic; maybe the Wind-runners block off the faculty. How? I've no more idea than you."

❋

374

Kelse and Gerd Jemasze elected to sleep on the ample settees of the Apex and presently took themselves off to bed. Elvo and Schaine walked out to the end of the pier, where they sat on an overturned skiff. Stars reflected along the dark water. The Hilgad fires had guttered low; from somewhere along the shore came music: quavering wails accented by plangent bass outcries. Elvo Glissam listened. "What dire sounds!"

"Blue music is never cheerful," said Schaine. "The Blues, on the other hand, consider all our music insipid tinkling."

The Hilgad music dwindled off into silence. The two sat listening to the wash of the waves through the piers. Schaine said: "For you this can't be a very exciting occasion. Naturally we didn't plan so much inconvenience."

"Don't speak of it! I only hope it's just inconvenience."

"I hope so too. As Gerd says, Father carries weapons, and even if his car has gone down we'll find him tomorrow."

"Not that I'm pessimistic," said Elvo, "but how can you be so sure? It's a long way to Morningswake. There's a great deal of territory he might have flown over."

"We always fly by auto-pilot, from destination to destination, just in case our air-cars do come down. It's an elementary safety precaution. Tomorrow we'll fly back along the flight line, and unless Father deviated from course we're certain to find him." She rose to her feet. "I think I'll go to bed."

Elvo stood up and kissed her forehead. "Sleep well and don't worry—about anything."

CHAPTER 4

Under the gray and rose-pink sky of dawn, the sea lay motionless. From the Hilgad camp smoke drifted across the inlet, carrying a pleasant spicy reek.

Within the tavern the landlord, grumbling and yawning, set forth a breakfast of boiled clams, porridge and tea over which the four wasted little time. Kelse paid the score; a few minutes later the Apex rose into the sky. Jemasze set the auto-pilot to the referents of Morningswake; the Apex slid off to the northwest: across the inlet, over the Hilgad camp. Warriors ran forth, leapt on their erjin mounts, stung them into action with electric prods. Hopping, bounding, running on hind legs, massive heads thrust forward, the erjins followed below, the warriors screaming insane imprecations.

The Hilgad were left behind. The sky-car rose to clear the stony coastal slopes, then flew to an altitude of fifteen hundred feet, to allow maximum visibility right and left across that band of territory over which Uther Madduc would have passed. The Alouan spread away past the range of vision: a rolling plain splotched with clumps of gray thorn, bottle-bush, an occasional thick-trunked hag-tree with branches that seemed to claw at the air. The Apex flew slowly, the four within scanning every square foot of ground.

Miles went past, and hours; the plain sagged and became a basin swimming with heat haze and pocked with salt sinks. Ahead rose the white cliffs of the Lucimer Mountains. "Not very inviting territory," Elvo Glissam remarked, "which probably explains why it's still Retent."

Kelse grinned. "It suits the Kyan well enough. So everybody's satisfied."

"They must have simple tastes," said Elvo Glissam. "I don't see how a lizard could survive down there."

"This is dry season. The Kyan are off in those mountains there to the west. During the rains they'll migrate down into the limestone hills yonder, where they maintain their kachembas."

"Have you ever explored a kachemba?"

Kelse shook his head. "Never. They'd kill me."

"How would they know?"

"They'd know."

Schaine said: "Since we don't invite them into our drawing rooms, they don't ask us into their kachembas."

"Tit for tat, so to speak."

"And again," said Kelse, "everyone is well pleased."

"Except Jorjol," said Schaine.

Flying over the Lucimer Range Jemasze reduced speed, the better to examine slopes and gullies. Nowhere could be found a trace of Uther Madduc's Sturdevant air-car.

Beyond the Lucimers lay a rolling savanna watered by a dozen streams which merged to become the Lela River. A swampy thicket grew alongside the river; Jemasze slowed the Apex until it barely moved, but the Sturdevant had not come down in the swamp.

Elvo Glissam asked: "This land is still Retent?"

"Still Retent: Hunge territory. A hundred miles east is Trillium. Morningswake is still four hundred miles north."

The landscape slid below; the savanna became a dry plain covered with smokeweed. Along the horizon hulked a dozen buttes like a group of monstrous gray animals. Jemasze took the Apex higher to gain a wider vantage, but to no immediate avail.

Below passed the buttes; the countryside became a broken waste-land of dry water-courses and rocky knolls, given contrast and color by clumps of tangle-tree and jossamer and isolated ibix trees with black trunks and flapping mustard-colored foliage: a tract of land known as the Dramalfo.

Two hours after noon, close upon the edge of the Retent with Morningswake Manor still a hundred miles north, they discovered the Sturdevant. It appeared to be wrecked, as if it had fallen from a height. No sign of life was evident. Jemasze hovered over the broken black car and scanned the ground through binoculars. "There's something strange about all this." Looking westward he halted the sweep of the binoculars. "Blues—about thirty. They're riding this way."

He lowered the Apex to the wreck while Kelse studied the riders. "They're coming fast, as if they know what they'll find."

"Loot."

"Which means they know the wreck is here."

"And that means—" Jemasze looked around the sky. He jerked at the controls. "Sky-shark!"

Not fast enough. An explosion: metal cracked and groaned; the Apex shuddered and sagged by the stern. Down to the side swooped the sky-shark—a narrow platform with a curved windshield and a long concave bow-cone, which functioned both as gun and lance on those occasions when the pilot might wish to dart low and spit an enemy.

The sky-shark swerved, rolled and went streaking high. The Apex hung dangerously down by the stern. Jemasze manipulated the controls and managed to control the rate of descent. Down swung the sky-shark; the Apex shuddered to another impact. Jemasze cursed under his breath. The ground came up to meet them; Jemasze used every ounce of thrust remaining to break the fall, almost toppling the Apex over on its back.

The Apex settled upon the flinty soil. Jemasze seized a gun from a locker and jumped to the ground but the sky-shark, fleeting into the west, had disappeared.

Kelse staggered to the radio and attempted a call. "Nothing. No power."

Jemasze said, "He shot away our rear pods—to bring us down, not to kill us."

"Rather sinister," said Kelse. "We might learn more about rascolade than we want to know."

"Get the guns from the locker," said Jemasze. "There should be a grenade tube there as well."

Schaine, Elvo and Kelse joined Jemasze on the ground. Kelse went over to the wrecked Sturdevant and peered within. He returned with a grim face. "He's there. Dead."

Elvo Glissam looked in bewilderment from wrecked Sturdevant to wrecked Apex to Kelse. He started to speak, then held his tongue. Schaine blinked back tears. Five years wasted on Tanquil; five years gone because of arrogance and pride and reckless emotions—and now she'd never see her father again.

Gerd Jemasze asked Kelse: "Did you identify the Blues?"

"Most likely Hunge. They're certainly not Ao. The erjins show a white ruff, so they're not Garganche."

"You three take shelter behind the Apex," said Jemasze. "If they come around from the north, open fire. I'm going out yonder to intercept them, and maybe reduce the odds a bit."

Kelse went behind the Apex; Schaine followed and Elvo more slowly, looking doubtfully after Jemasze who was trotting off in a half-crouch toward a knoll of compacted sand a quarter-mile west. "Why is he going out there?"

"To kill some Blues," said Kelse. "Do you know how to use this gun?"

"I'm afraid not."

"It's quite simple. Fix that yellow dot on your target and touch this button. Trajectory is automatically computed. You're shooting OB-16 explosive pellets which should take out a Blue and an erjin together."

Elvo Glissam scowled down at the gun. "Are you sure they're hostile?"

"If they're Hunge, they're hostile. They've got no business here on the Dramalfo; this is Garganche territory. Even if they're Garganche they're hostile, unless they keep clear of us. They know the rules."

"If there are thirty of them, I wouldn't think we have much chance. Shouldn't we try to parley with them?"

"Pointless. As for the odds, Gerd went out to even things up a bit."

Reaching the knoll, Jemasze scrambled up to a clump of dwarf ibix on the crest. The Uldras, still a mile distant, came bounding forward at full speed, flourishing their ancient Two Star thio-manuals. Jemasze scanned the sky. No sign of the sky-shark; perhaps it hung somewhere up against the sun, unseen in the pink dazzle.

The Uldras approached and Jemasze saw that they were Hunge indeed. They came directly toward him, apparently ignoring the possibility of ambush, which suited Jemasze very well. He settled himself comfortably, arranged the grenade tube to the side, and thrust his gun forward. The Hunge bounded close; he could hear the panting cries of the erjins. Jemasze selected the leader: a tall man in flapping gray and yellow robes, with a headdress fashioned from a human skull. He touched the trigger button, then immediately aimed and fired again, and again and again. At the explosions, the erjins squealed in outrage and halted, digging talons into the soil. Jemasze discharged the grenade launcher at the knot of riders: a shattering blast and the survivors wheeled their mounts to the side. Jemasze rose to his feet and fired after the scattering Uldras…On the ground erjins lay kicking and roaring. A wounded Uldra groped for his gun and fired at Jemasze; the pellet whistled close past Jemasze's head. He lobbed across a second grenade and all motion ceased.

From above came the shock of a concussion; Jemasze knew what had occurred before he turned to look. The sky-shark had swung down from out of the sun; anticipating such a move, Kelse had fired on the sky-shark. Jemasze looked up, and as he had expected, the sky-shark was swerving and jerking, apparently out of control. Jemasze aimed and fired, without effect; the pilot applied thrust and sent the sky-shark limping into the west.

Jemasze approached the dead bodies. He counted fourteen Blue corpses; about as many had escaped. He gathered the guns, stacked them in a pile and destroyed them with a grenade, then returned to his knoll. Two miles away the surviving Hunge had halted to take counsel. The range was extreme, but Jemasze aimed his gun, and allowing a trifle for the breeze, fired, but the pellet fell short.

Jemasze returned to the wrecked air-car. Kelse, Schaine and Elvo Glissam already were digging a grave in the sandy soil, using sticks to loosen the dirt. Kelse and Jemasze dragged the body of Uther Madduc forth and lowered it into the grave. Schaine looked off into the sky, while Elvo Glissam stood uncertainly to the side. Kelse and Gerd Jemasze filled the grave and covered it with stones. Whatever the wonderful joke, they would never hear it now from Uther Madduc.

Gerd Jemasze and Kelse sought through both the Sturdevant and the Apex, bringing forth Uther Madduc's weapons and the contents of the water tank: about three gallons. The Apex yielded a map, a compass,

binoculars, several packets of emergency rations and another four gallons of water. "We've got about a hundred miles to go; four or five days
cross-country," said Jemasze. "We're not in bad shape—if the Blues don't
come back. I fear they will. Keep your eyes open for dust or movement
along the skyline."

Elvo Glissam asked: "We can't call for help by radio?"

"No chance whatever," said Jemasze. "Our power-banks are gone.
The attacker apparently wanted to take us alive."

Kelse shouldered his pack. "The sooner we start, the sooner we
arrive."

Schaine looked him over dubiously. "Will your leg hold up?"

"I hope so."

The four set off to the north and had proceeded only a mile when
the Hunge reappeared on the skyline. They ranged themselves into a
line: sixteen silhouettes on restive erjins, arms groping forward, great
bearded heads outthrust, and above, straddling sling-saddles, the
Hunge warriors. They looked across the plain without display or gesture in a silence more sinister than cries and whoops. Elvo Glissam
asked uncertainly: "If they attack—what are we supposed to do?"

"They won't attack," said Kelse shortly. "Not here; their old Two
Stars don't have the range. They'll wait for an ambush, or they might try
to take us by night."

Jemasze pointed ahead to a set of grotesque sandstone pinnacles
carved by the wind. "And there's good ambush country."

"I make it about ten miles," said Kelse. "Say three hours, or an hour
before sunset."

The four trudged onward across the waste. The Uldras watched for
two minutes, then swung their mounts about and riding northward disappeared behind the skyline.

Schaine spoke to Elvo Glissam: "You'll long remember your visit to
Uaia."

"If I live to think about it."

"Oh, you'll live. Gerd Jemasze will see to that. His self-esteem
would suffer if anything happened to us."

Elvo Glissam glanced at her sidewise but made no comment.

As they walked Kelse and Gerd Jemasze exchanged muttered comments and occasionally indicated one or another aspect of the landscape. In the shade of a sprawling hag-tree they halted to rest. Kelse
said to Elvo Glissam and Schaine: "We've got to keep clear of those

buttes ahead, because the Blues could get up within range of us. The butte on the far right is somewhat safer, with open ground to the side. We'll pass around it to the east."

The four trudged onward through the hot afternoon. Schaine noticed that Kelse's limp was becoming more pronounced…They came to a dry watercourse a hundred yards across, with a sandy bed and banks supporting a growth of poison cassander and junkberry bushes. Jemasze signaled a halt and drew the group into the shade of the purple cassander foliage. "They might have ridden ahead of us and crossed the gully. If so they're waiting behind the far bank, to get us as we cross…We'd better continue along this side for a mile or two."

"Then what?" demanded Elvo Glissam.

"Then we'll see how the land lies."

They continued, wary and uneasy. A half-mile along, Jemasze pointed to tracks on the sand of the riverbed. "There's where they crossed. They're over there now, waiting for us." He reflected a moment. "You three continue along the bank, as far as that big jossamer tree."

The three set off. Jemasze crouched low and slid away to where he could not be seen from the opposite bank, then loped back the way they had come. He went three hundred yards, then cautiously returned to the top of the bank. He looked behind him, then scanned the opposite bank. He saw no movement; he felt no tension of danger. He waited another minute, then slid down into the watercourse and ran crouching across the pink sand and quartz pebbles toward the opposite side, every instant expecting the impact of a bullet, although both his reason and his instinct assured him that the Hunge had left no one to guard this area of the watercourse. Without molestation he made it to the far bank and gratefully climbed into the cover of the junkberry bushes. Gaining the top of the bank he looked north and, as he expected, discovered the party of Hunge approximately opposite the big jossamer tree where Kelse, Schaine and Elvo Glissam waited. Jemasze returned to the riverbed and keeping close under the shrubbery, ran north a hundred yards, then made another reconnaissance. Still too far. He returned to the riverbed and ran crouching another hundred yards. Now when he clambered up through the vegetation the Hunge were barely a hundred yards distant.

He watched a moment, selecting the rider who now seemed to be the leader. He aimed his gun and without further ado opened fire. Three Blues fell sprawling to the soil; erjins screamed in fury and shock. The survivors jerked instantly into flight. They crashed down through the shrubbery into the riverbed and charged at a zig-zag toward the jossamer tree, shooting as they rode.

Kelse instantly opened fire. He looked toward Elvo Glissam who lay looking in numb fascination toward the charging Hunge.

"Shoot, man, shoot!"

Elvo Glissam shook his head in distress, then gritting his teeth fired the gun.

Pellets sang over their heads; the riverbed seemed littered with flapping erjins and dying Blues. Five still survived and clambered up through the shrubbery. Schaine and Kelse fired at point-blank range; three neared the top of the bank. Elvo Glissam, motivated by a complex mixture of outrage, humiliation, fear and fury, gave an inarticulate yell of passion and hurled himself upon the back of one of the Blues and tore him down from his mount. The two thrashed among the junkberries; the erjin, roaring and hissing, stamped upon them both, then bounded down into the watercourse and away on enormous exultant strides. The Blue drew his dagger and slashed at Elvo's arm which encircled his neck. Jemasze, arriving on the scene, clubbed the Blue with the butt of his gun, and the Blue sprawled back into the bushes.

Silence, except for panting and the sounds of riderless erjins trying to dislodge their fang-guards and electric gyves against the rocks. Elvo Glissam sat staring at the blood flowing from his forearm. Schaine uttered an exclamation and went to help him. Kelse produced a flask of all-purpose medicament and sprayed the wounds, which almost instantly stopped bleeding. When the protective membrane had formed, Schaine poured water over Elvo's arms and washed away the blood. In a shaky voice he said: "Sorry to be so bemused; I'm afraid I've led a sheltered life."

"Shock has nothing to do with a sheltered life," said Schaine. "It can happen to anyone. You're very brave."

Jemasze went back for his pack; the party once more set out toward the north, leaving behind the dry watercourse and the Blue corpses.

Methuen sank behind the far Lucimers; the four made camp on the slope of a butte. To avoid attracting the attention of such Uldras as might still be near, they built no fire, and supped on emergency rations and water. The sky faded through phases of vermilion, scarlet, ruby and purple; dusk fell across the landscape. Schaine went to sit by Elvo Glissam. "How is your arm?"

Elvo looked down at the gash. "It aches a bit, but it could be far worse. I also resent that erjin kicking me in the ribs."

Schaine said gloomily: "I wonder if you'll ever forgive me for inviting you to Morningswake."

Elvo Glissam replied and in so doing initiated a conversation which, when later he consulted his recollections, seemed more unreal and incongruous than any other aspect of the adventure.

"I forgive you right now," said Elvo Glissam. "If nothing else, the trip is an education. I see myself from a new perspective."

Schaine objected vigorously. "Not at all. The surroundings have changed. You're the same!"

"It amounts to the same thing. Delicate sensibilities are of small assistance when a person is fighting for his life."

Schaine glanced from Kelse, propped against a tree trunk with what she suspected to be a half-smile on his face, to Gerd Jemasze who sat on a flat rock, arms around knees brooding across the twilight; and she felt impelled to put Elvo Glissam's self-deprecation into proper perspective. "In civilized surroundings it's not necessary to fight for your life."

Kelse chuckled mirthlessly. Schaine looked at him coldly. "Did I say something foolish?"

"A fire department isn't necessary except when there's a fire."

"Civilization is a very normal ordinary condition," said Schaine. "Civilized people don't need to fight for their lives."

"Not often," said Kelse laconically. "But you can't kill a Blue by invoking an abstraction."

"Did I suggest as much?"

"In a manner of speaking."

"I agree that I must be confused, since I have no such recollection."

Kelse shrugged and raised his eyes to the sky, as if to indicate that he did not care to pursue the topic any further. But he said, "You used the word 'civilization', which means a set of abstractions, symbols, conventions. Experience tends to be vicarious; emotions are predigested and electrical; ideas become more real than things."

Schaine was taken somewhat aback. She said: "That's rather all-inclusive."

"I don't think so," said Kelse mildly.

Elvo Glissam said, "I can't understand your objection to ideas."

"I can't either," said Schaine. "I think Kelse is indulging in whimsey."

"Not altogether," said Kelse. "Urban folk, dealing as they do in ideas and abstractions, become conditioned to unreality. Then, wherever the fabric of civilization breaks, these people are as helpless as fish out of water."

Elvo Glissam heaved a sigh. "What could be more unreal than sitting out here in the wilderness discussing civilization? I can't believe it. In passing, I might point out that Kelse's remarks indicate considerable skill in urbane and civilized abstraction."

Kelse laughed. "Also in passing, I might mention that urbane folk make up the membership of the Redemptionist Alliance, the Vitatis Cult, the Cosmic Peace Movement, Panortheism, a dozen more: all motivated by abstractions four or five or six times removed from reality."

"Reality, so-called, is itself an abstraction," Elvo Glissam remarked.

"It's an abstraction with a difference, because it can hurt, as when your sky-car comes down in the wilderness with a hundred miles to walk. That's real. Aunt Val's chamber of winds at Villa Mirasol isn't real."

Schaine said: "You're simply beating a horse to death. Because a person can deal with ideas doesn't signify that, ergo, he's helpless."

"In an urban environment he's quite safe; in fact, he prospers. But such environments are fragile as cobwebs, and when they break— chaos!"

Gerd Jemasze joined the conversation. "Reflect on human history."

"I've done so," said Kelse. "History describes the destruction of a long series of urban civilizations because the citizens preferred intellectualism and abstraction to competence in basic skills, such as self-defense. Or attack, for that matter."

Schaine said in disgust: "You've become awfully crabbed and illiberal, Kelse. Father certainly stamped his opinions upon you."

"Your theory has its obverse," said Elvo Glissam. "From this viewpoint, history becomes a succession of cases in which barbarians, renouncing crassness, develop a brilliant civilization."

"Usually destroying older civilizations in the process," remarked Kelse.

"Or exploiting other less capable barbarians. Uaia is a case in point. Here a group of civilized men attacked and plundered the barbarians. The barbarians were helpless in the face of energy weapons and sky-cars—all contrived through the use of abstractions, and, incidentally, built by urbanites."

Gerd Jemasze chuckled, a sound which annoyed Schaine. She said: "These are merely facts."

"But not all the facts. The barbarians weren't plundered; they use their lands as freely as before. I must concede that torture and slavery have been discouraged."

"Very well then," said Elvo Glissam. "Imagine yourself an Uldra: disenfranchised and subject to alien law. What would you do?"

Gerd Jemasze pondered a moment or two. "I suppose it would depend on what I wanted. What I wanted I'd try to get."

❋

Before dawn the party was astir and away. A great reef of clouds obscured the east and the party walked in maroon gloom. At noon lightning began to strike down at the buttes, now lonely shapes in the southern distance, and draughts of dank air blew north across the plain. Halfway into the afternoon a rain squall raced past, drenching the group to the skin and laying the dust; shortly after, the sun found gaps in the clouds and sent remarkable pink rays slanting down at the ground. Jemasze led the way, accommodating his pace to that of Kelse, whose limp had become somewhat more noticeable. Schaine and Elvo Glissam sauntered along to the rear. Had the circumstances been different, had her father been alive and Kelse not so obviously contriving each separate step by an effort of will, she might almost have enjoyed the adventure.

The land sloped down into a sink paved with pale hardpan. At the far verge stood a cluster of sandstone pinnacles and beyond, an irregular scarp of pink, mauve and russet sandstone. Schaine called ahead to Kelse: "There's Bottom Edge!"

"Almost like home," said Kelse.

Schaine excitedly told Elvo Glissam: "Morningswake starts at the brink of the cliff. Beyond is our land—all the way north to the Volwodes."

Elvo Glissam shook his head in sad disapproval, and Schaine looked at him wonderingly. She thought a moment, reflecting upon what she had said, then laughed but made no comment. Clearly she was not a Redemptionist by instinct, or by innate conviction...How to reconcile her love for Morningswake with the guilty suspicion that she had no right to the property? Kelse and Gerd Jemasze had no such qualms. On an impulse she asked Elvo Glissam: "Suppose you owned Morningswake: what would you do?"

Elvo Glissam smiled and shook his head. "It's always easier to relinquish somebody else's property...I'd like to believe that my principles would dominate my avarice."

"So you'd give up Morningswake?"

"I honestly don't know. I hope that's what I'd do."

Schaine pointed toward a cluster of tung-beetle mounds about a hundred yards west. "Look: in the shadow to the right! You wanted to see a wild erjin—there it is!"

The erjin stood seven feet tall, with massive arms banded with stripes of black and yellow fur. Tufts of stiff golden fiber stood above the head; folds of gunmetal cartilage almost concealed the four small eyes in the neck under the jutting frontal bone. The creature stood negligently, showing neither fear nor hostility. Gerd Jemasze and Kelse became aware of the beast. Kelse stared in fascination, and slowly brought forth his gun.

Elvo asked in dismay: "Is he going to shoot it? It's such a magnificent creature!"

"He's always hated erjins—worse since he lost his arm and leg."

"But this one isn't threatening us. It's almost murder."

Gerd Jemasze suddenly turned and fired to the east at a pair of erjins lunging forward from a thicket of greasebush. One sprawled forward and fell only four feet from Schaine and Elvo Glissam, to lie with great six-fingered hands twitching; the other jerked up into a grotesque backward somersault and fell with a thump. The first erjin, who had acted as a decoy, slipped behind the tung mounds before Kelse could aim his gun. Jemasze ran off to the side to get another shooting angle, but the creature had disappeared.

Elvo Glissam stood looking down at the quivering hulk of the near erjin. He noticed the hand-palps, as sensitive as human fingers, and the talons which extended themselves when the erjin made a fist. He examined the tuft of bronze bristles on the scalp, which some authorities declared to be telepathy receptors. Another bound and the creature would have been at his throat. In a subdued voice he said to Gerd Jemasze, "That was a close call...Do the erjins often use tricks like that?"

Jemasze nodded curtly. "They're intelligent brutes, and unforgiving. How they can be domesticated is a mystery to me."

"Maybe the secret was Uther Madduc's 'wonderful joke'."

"I don't know. I plan to find out."

Kelse asked: "How do you propose to do that?"

"As soon as we get to Morningswake we'll fly back to the Sturdevant and rescue the log," said Gerd Jemasze. "Then we'll have an idea where he went."

The afternoon waned. At sunset the party camped among the sandstone pinnacles, with the southern edge of Morningswake Domain still three miles to the north. Jemasze stalked, killed and cleaned a ten-pound bustard, the wild descendant of fowl imported from beyond the stars. Schaine and Elvo Glissam gathered fuel and built a fire, and the four toasted chunks of the bird on twigs.

"Tomorrow we'll find water," said Gerd. "Three or four streams cross South Morningswake, so I recall."

"It's about ten miles to South Station," said Kelse. "There's a windmill and maybe a few stores there. But no radio, worse luck."

"Where are the Aos?"

"They might be anywhere, but I suspect they're moving north. No help for it; we've still got sixty miles to go."

"How's your leg holding up?"

"Not too good. But I'll get there."

Elvo Glissam leaned back and lay staring up at the stars. His own life, he thought, seemed relatively simple compared to that of a land-baron…Schaine! What went on in her mind? One moment she seemed intensely subtle and sympathetic, then naïve, then caught up in some emotion beyond his knowing. Beyond question she was brave and kind and cheerful. He could well imagine passing the rest of his life in her company…At Morningswake? He was not so sure. Would she agree to live elsewhere? He was not sure of this either…Three days more of this arduous marching. He wished he could in some manner help Kelse. Perhaps in the morning he'd inconspicuously take part of Kelse's backpack and hang it on his own.

In the morning Elvo Glissam put his plan into effect. Kelse noticed and protested, but Elvo Glissam said: "This is just simple common sense. You're already working twice as hard as I am, and it's in everybody's interest that you stay healthy."

Gerd Jemasze said, "Glissam's right, Kelse. I'd rather carry your pack than carry you."

Kelse said no more; the group set forth and an hour later reached the base of the South Rim. By a dry gulch they ascended five hundred feet, then toiled another hundred feet up a face of rotting conglomerate and finally stood at the lip. Behind spread the Retent, melting into the southern haze; ahead the ground fell away to a pleasant valley grown with green-gum, dragon-eye, slender black-green gadroon, and copses of orange vandalia. A mile to the north the sunlight glinted on a shallow pond. "Morningswake!" cried Schaine huskily. "We're home."

"With about sixty miles to go," said Kelse.

Jemasze looked back over the Retent. "We're past the worst of it. The going should be easier."

There was a day of silent trudging across the south prairie; another day was spent toiling up and down the Tourmaline Hills. Kelse now moved in awkward hops and lurches. There was a long sweaty morning in the marsh north of Skyflower Lake. At noon the party struggled through a thicket of coarse vines to reach solid terrain. They halted to rest. Kelse looked ahead. "Fourteen more miles…We'll never make it tonight. Perhaps you'd better go on to the house and send a wagon back for me."

"I'll wait here with you," said Schaine. "It's a good idea."

Gerd Jemasze said: "It would be a good idea—except that we're being kept under observation." He pointed toward the sky. "Three times in the last two days I've seen a sky-shark hanging in the clouds."

All stared toward the sky. "I don't see anything," said Schaine.

"Right now he's in the fold of that cumulus cloud."

"But what could he want? If he's hostile, why doesn't he try to shoot us?"

"I would guess that he wants to take us alive. Or some of us alive. If we separated, the chances would be much improved. There might even be another party of Hunge on the way to intercept us before we reach Morningswake."

Schaine said in a hushed voice: "Would they dare come in so far from the Retent? Our Aos would kill them."

"The sky-shark would observe the Aos and provide warning."

Elvo Glissam licked his lips. "I wouldn't care to be captured now. Or even killed."

Kelse struggled to his feet. "Let's get started."

Twenty minutes later Gerd Jemasze once more searched the landscape. Looking to the northwest he became still. He lowered the binoculars and pointed. "Uldras. About twenty."

Schaine peered wearily through the pink dust-haze. More fighting, more killing; and in this region of thickets and clumps of vandalia there was small hope—in fact, no hope—of beating off an attack. Fourteen miles to Morningswake. So near and so far.

Elvo Glissam had arrived at the same conclusion. His face became pinched and gray; a husky sound forced its way up his throat.

Gerd Jemasze looked through the binoculars again. "They're riding criptids."

Schaine released her pent breath. "They're Aos!"

Gerd Jemasze nodded. "I can make out their headdress. White plumes. They're Ao."

Schaine's breath came in a rasping guttural sob. Elvo Glissam asked in a soft strained voice: "Are they hostile?"

"No," said Kelse shortly.

The riders approached, raising a trail of dust behind them. Gerd Jemasze studied the sky through his binoculars. "There he goes!" He pointed to a minute mark among the clouds, which drifted slowly west, then picked up speed and presently disappeared.

The Aos rode in a ritual circle around the group, the soft-footed criptids* running easily and low to the ground. They halted; an old man, somewhat shorter and more sturdy than the ordinary Uldra, dismounted and came forward. Schaine took his hand. "Kurgech! I've come home to Morningswake."

Kurgech touched the top of her head, a gesture half caress, half formal salute. "It gives us pleasure to see you home, Mistress."

Kelse said: "Uther Madduc is dead. He was shot down over the Dramalfo by a sky-shark."

Kurgech's gray face—he wore no azure oil—showed no twitch of emotion, and Schaine surmised that the information had already reached his mind. She asked: "Do you know who killed my father?"

"The knowledge has not come to me."

Kelse, hobbling forward, said hoarsely: "Search for the knowledge, Kurgech. When it comes—tell me."

---

*Criptid: a long low pad-footed variant of the terrestrial horse. The Uldras of the Retent disdain criptids as mounts fit only for wittols, sexual deviates and women.

Kurgech gave a curt nod which might have meant anything, then turned and signaled to four of the tribesmen, who dismounted and brought their mounts forward. Gerd Jemasze half-lifted Kelse into the saddle. Schaine told Elvo Glissam: "Just sit quietly and hang on; it doesn't need guidance."

She herself mounted, as did Gerd Jemasze, and the four Aos mounted double. The party rode north toward Morningswake.

Two hours later, past the Skaw and across the South Savanna, Schaine saw her home. She blinked back tears, unable to restrain her pent-up emotion any longer. She looked at Kelse, who rode beside her. His face was strained with pain and as gray as Kurgech's; his eyes also glinted with tears. Gerd Jemasze's dark face was unreadable; who could fathom this man? Elvo Glissam, far too polite to betray any excess of relief, rode in grave silence. Schaine watched him covertly. For all his lack of wilderness craft, he had by no means disgraced himself. Kelse clearly liked him and even Gerd Jemasze treated him with civility. When he left Uaia and returned to Olanje, he would have memories to last him a lifetime.

And there ahead: Morningswake, serene among tall frail green-gums and lordly transtellar oaks, with the brimming Chip-chap flowing to the side: the landscape of a dear reverie; a place forever precious; and tears once more flooded Schaine's eyes.

CHAPTER 5

Across two hundred years Morningswake had been built and rebuilt, extended, remodeled, subjected to a dozen modifications and improvements as each land-baron in turn attempted to impinge some trace of his identity upon the hereditary manse. Morningswake therefore lacked a definable style and showed a different aspect from each perspective. The roof of the central structure stood tall and steep, with a dozen high-pitched dormers, a curious little observation deck overlooking Wild Crake Pond, and along the high central ridge a line of black iron ghost-chasers in the shape of trefoils. From either flank extended a rambling two-story wing with verandahs at each level; the double colonnades were overgrown with arabella vine. The framing timbers were gadroon from Fairy Forest; the exterior clapboards were green-gum, equally durable; the interior stairs, balusters, floors, moldings and wainscotings were ironwood, pearl sachuli, verbane, Szintarre teak. The chandeliers, furniture and rugs had been imported, not from Olanje (the products of which were considered cheap and unsubstantial), but from one of the far Old Worlds.

The central structure enclosed the Great Hall which was the heart of Morningswake, where the family celebrated important occasions, entertained guests and took its evening meal in an atmosphere which Schaine remembered as portentously formal. Everyone dressed for dinner; the table was laid with fine porcelain, silver and crystal; the conversation was confined to dignified subjects and lapses of decorum were not tolerated. As a child Schaine had found these dinners tedious and she could never understand why Muffin was not allowed to dine in the Great Hall where his fancies and drolleries would certainly have enlivened matters. But Muffin was excluded; he dined alone in the kitchen.

When Schaine was eleven her mother drowned in a boating accident on Shadow Lake. Dinners in the Great Hall became subdued rather than merely decorous, and Uther Madduc inexplicably—to Schaine— turned gruff and unreasonable; frequently she had been aroused to anger and even rebellion. Not that she did not love her father; Schaine was too warm not to love everything connected with her life; still Schaine had decided that her father must be taught a lesson on how to get along with people and how not to be so arrogant with the Uldras, specifically poor Muffin.

Uther Madduc at this time had been a man of remarkable appearance, straight and tall, with thick gray hair worn in a style of elegant simplicity, clear gray eyes, features of classical regularity. He had been neither easy nor gregarious. Schaine remembered him as a man of brooding imagination and sudden impulses, simultaneously calm and restless, lacking all talent or taste for frivolity. His rare angers were cold and controlled, and diminished without perceptible aftermath; neither Schaine nor Kelse had ever incurred punishment at his hands except possibly on that last climactic night—if being sent to an expensive boarding school on Tanquil could be reckoned as punishment. Really, thought Schaine, I was an arrogant feckless self-important little wretch...And yet, and yet...

Kelse and Gerd Jemasze had flown south in the Morningswake cargo carrier to salvage the Apex and the Sturdevant. With them flew two of Gerd Jemasze's cousins and a pair of Ao ranch-hands. An automatic cannon had been mounted on the cargo deck, to fend off sky-shark attacks.

Elvo Glissam had not been invited to join the party, and he had not volunteered his services; instead he and Schaine enjoyed a leisurely breakfast under the green-gums. Elvo Glissam told Schaine: "By no means feel that you must entertain me; I know you have a hundred things on your mind."

Schaine grinned. "I'm not worried about entertaining you. I've already shown you a wild erjin, as I said I'd do—and whatever the hundred affairs on my mind, I don't intend to consider them for several days, if ever. In fact, I may very well decide to do nothing at all for the next month or two."

"When I think back now," said Elvo Glissam, "I can't believe it all happened. And yet it did."

"It's certainly one way of getting acquainted," said Schaine. "On a five-day march, a certain intimacy is almost unavoidable."

"Yes. At least with you, and with Kelse. Gerd Jemasze—I don't know. He puzzles me."

"Me no less, and I've known him all my life."

"I'd swear that he enjoys killing Uldras," said Elvo Glissam. "It seems churlish to cavil at his motives. He brought us home alive—as you predicted."

"He's not bloodthirsty," said Schaine. "He just doesn't consider the Hunge human beings, especially when they're attacking us."

"He amazes me," said Elvo Glissam thoughtfully. "Killing just isn't one of my skills."

"You did yourself credit," said Schaine. "Kelse and Gerd both respect you, and I do too, so don't go agonizing over imaginary deficiencies."

"Oh, I'm not agonizing. Still, I can't believe I did anything noteworthy."

"You made no complaints. You did your share and usually more of whatever work was needful; you were always cheerful. I think that's all very commendable."

Elvo Glissam made a careless gesture. "Inconsequentialities. I'm back in an environment I prefer, and whatever good qualities I possess will go back into hiding."

Schaine looked off across the South Savanna. "Do you really like it here at Morningswake?"

"Yes, of course."

"And you're not bored?"

"Not with you here." Elvo Glissam's glance was unmistakably ardent.

Schaine smiled absently off across the distance. "It's been very quiet at Morningswake since my mother died. Before, there were parties every week. We always had guests, from other domains, from Olanje, or even off-planet. Several times a year the Aos would organize a karoo. Often we'd go up to Twin Lake Lodge, or Snowflower Lodge in the Suaniset Crags. There was always excitement and fun—before my mother died. You mustn't think we live like hermits."

"And then?"

"Father became—well, 'recluse' is too strong a word. Then I went off to Tanquil, and for the last five years Morningswake has been very quiet. Kelse says Father's closest friend has been Kurgech!"

"And now?"

"I'd like Morningswake to be a happy place again."

"Yes. That would be pleasant. Except…" Elvo Glissam paused.

"Except what?"

"I suspect that the days of the great domains are numbered."

Schaine grimaced. "What a dismal thought."

Kelse and Gerd Jemasze returned to Morningswake towing the hulks of the Apex and the Sturdevant on float pods. A coffin of white glass contained the body of Uther Madduc, and Kelse carried a notebook which he had found in a locker.

Two days later a funeral took place, and Uther Madduc was buried in the family graveyard, across the Chip-chap River in the park beside the Fairy Forest. Two hundred family friends, relatives and folk from neighboring domains came to pay their last respects to Uther Madduc.

Elvo Glissam watched in fascination, marveling at the conduct of these folk so different from himself. The men, he thought, were a matter-of-fact lot, while the women lacked a certain quality he could not quite define. Frivolity? Mischief? Artfulness? Even Schaine seemed rather more direct than he might have preferred, leaving small scope for teasing or flirtation or any of the subtle games which made urban society so amusing. Worse? Better? Adaptation to the environment? Elvo Glissam only knew for certain that he found Schaine as beautiful as some magnificent natural process, like a sunrise, or a surge of breaking surf, or stars in the midnight sky.

He met dozens of folk: cousins, aunts, uncles, with their sons and daughters, and fathers and mothers, and cousins, aunts and uncles, none of whom he remembered. He saw no evidence of grief, nor even fury against the assassin; the prevailing mood seemed, rather, a grim smoulder which in Elvo Glissam's opinion boded ill for any accommodation with the Redemptionists.

He listened to a conversation between Kelse Madduc and Lilo Stenbaren of Doradus Domain. Kelse was speaking: "—not a random act. There was planning involved, and precise calculation. First Uther Madduc and then ourselves."

"What of the 'wonderful joke' of the letter? Is there some connection?"

"Impossible to say. We've taken the auto-pilot from the Sturdevant and we'll trace my father's route, and perhaps join him in his 'wonderful joke' yet."

Kelse brought Elvo Glissam forward and performed an introduction. "I'm sorry to say that Elvo Glissam, without shame, admits himself a Redemptionist."

Dm. Stenbaren laughed. "Forty years ago I remember a 'Society for Uaian Justice', ten years later a 'League Against the Land-looters', and sometime afterward a group which simply called itself 'Apotheosis'. And now of course the Redemptionists."

"All of which reflect a deep and lasting concern," remarked Elvo Glissam. "'Decency', 'security against pillage', 'justice', 'restoration of sequestered property' are timeless concepts."

"Concepts don't bother us," said Dm. Stenbaren. "So far as I am concerned, you may continue to harbor them."

On the morning after the funeral a sparkling blue Hermes sky-boat, with silver flare-bars and a jaunty four-foot probe, swooped out of the sky and, ignoring the landing area to the side, came down on the promenade directly before Morningswake Manor.

Schaine, looking forth from the library, noticed the sky-boat on the neatly dressed gravel and reflected that Kelse would be irritated, especially since the occupant was Jorjol, who should have known better.

Jorjol jumped to the ground and stood a moment surveying Morningswake with the air of a person contemplating purchase. He wore a pale leather split-skirt, hide sandals, a rock-crystal sphere on his right big toe, the 'revelry-bonnet' of a Garganche bravo: an intricate contrivance of silver rods on which Jorjol's white-bleached hair was tied and twined and tasseled. Fresh azure oil had been applied to his face; his skin shone as blue as the enamel of his Hermes.

Schaine shook her head in amused vexation for Jorjol's bravado. She went out on the front piazza to meet him. He came forward, took her hands, bent forward and kissed her forehead. "I learned of your father's death, and felt that I must come to express my sentiments."

"Thank you, Jorjol. But yesterday was the funeral."

"Pshaw. I would have found you occupied with dozens of the dullest people imaginable. I wished to express myself to you."

Schaine laughed tolerantly. "Very well, express yourself."

Jorjol cocked his head and inspected Schaine sharply. "In reference to your father, condolence is of course in order. He was a strong man, and a man to be respected—even though, as you know, I stand opposite to his views."

Schaine nodded. "Do you know, he died before I had a chance to speak to him. I came home hoping to find him a softer easier man."

"Softer? Easier? More reasonable? More just? Hah!" Jorjol threw his fine head back as if in defiance. "I think not. I doubt if Kelse intends to alter by so much as a whit. Where is Kelse?"

"He's in the office, going over accounts."

Jorjol looked up and down the quaint old façade of Morningswake. "The house is as pleasant and inviting as ever. I wonder if you know how lucky you are."

"Oh yes indeed."

"And I am committed to bringing this era to an end."

"Come now, Jorjol, you can't deceive me. You're just Muffin in fancy clothes."

Jorjol chuckled. "I must admit that I came half to express sympathy and half—rather more than half—to see you. To touch you." He took a step forward. Schaine retreated.

"You mustn't be impulsive, Jorjol."

"Aha! but I'm not impulsive! I'm determined and wise, and you know how I feel about you."

"I know how you *felt* about me," said Schaine, "but that was five years ago. Let me go tell Kelse you're here. He'll want to see you."

Jorjol reached out, took her hand. "No. Let Kelse drudge among the accounts. I came to see you. Let's walk by the river where we can be alone."

Schaine glanced down at the long blue hand, with the long fingers and black fingernails. "It's almost lunch-time, Jorjol. Perhaps after lunch. You'll stay, won't you?"

"I will be happy to lunch with you."

"I'll go find Kelse. And here's Elvo Glissam, whom you met at Aunt Val's. I'll be back in a few minutes."

Schaine went to the office. Kelse looked up from the calculator. "Jorjol is here."

Kelse nodded shortly. "What does he want?"

"He made a nice speech in regard to Father. I've invited him to lunch."

Into their field of vision came Jorjol and Elvo Glissam on the lawn under the clump of parasol trees. Kelse grunted, rose to his feet.

"I'll come out and talk to him. We'll take lunch on the east terrace."

"Wait, Kelse. Let's be nice to Jorjol. He deserves to be treated like any other guest. It's a warm day and the Hall would be perfectly suitable."

Kelse said patiently: "In two hundred years no Uldra has entered our Great Hall. I don't care to break this tradition. Not even for Jorjol."

"But it's a cruel tradition and not worth keeping. We're not bigots, you and I—even if Father was. Let's live our lives more reasonably."

"I am not a bigot; I am very reasonable indeed. In fact, I realize that Jorjol cunningly chose this time—today—to try to force a submission upon us. He won't succeed."

"I can't understand you!" cried Schaine in a passion. "We've known Jorjol since we were little. He saved your life at risk of his own and it's absolutely absurd that he can't have lunch with us as any ordinary person might."

With raised eyebrows Kelse looked Schaine up and down. "I'm surprised that you don't understand the significance of all this. We hold Morningswake not through the forbearance of others, but because we are strong enough to protect what is ours."

Schaine said in disgust: "You've been talking to Gerd Jemasze. He's worse even than Father."

"Schaine, my naïve little sister, you simply don't understand what's going on."

Schaine controlled her exasperation. "I know this: Jorjol the Gray Prince is welcome anywhere in Olanje; it seems strange that he can't be treated equally well here, where he grew up."

"Circumstances are different," said Kelse patiently. "In Olanje there's nothing to lose; the folk can afford the luxury of abstract principles. We're Outkers in the middle of the Alouan; if we falter, we're done."

"What's that got to do with treating Jorjol in a civilized manner?"

"Because he's not here in a civilized manner! He's here as a Blue of the Retent. If he came here in Outker clothes, using Outker manners and not reeking of azure oil—in other words, if he came here as an Outker, then I would treat him as an Outker. But he doesn't do this. He comes flaunting his Uldra clothes, his blue skin, his Redemptionist bias—in short, he challenges me. I react. If he wants to enjoy Outker privileges, such as dining in our Great Hall, then he must make himself respectable by my standards. It's as simple as that."

Schaine could think of nothing to say. She turned away. Kelse said to her back: "Go talk to Kurgech; ask his opinion. In fact, we'll ask Kurgech to join us for lunch."

"Now you're really trying to offend Jorjol."

Kelse uttered a wild bitter laugh. "You want it both ways! We mustn't invite one Uldra because that would offend another."

"You don't reckon with Jorjol's opinion of himself—his self-image."

"And he intends to make me accept this self-image. I won't do it. I didn't invite him here; since he comes of his own volition, then he must adapt himself to us, not we to him."

Schaine stalked from the room and returned to the front piazza. "Kelse is up to his ears in the accounts," she told Jorjol. "He sends his apologies and he looks forward to seeing you at lunch...Let's all walk out to the river."

Jorjol's face twitched. "Certainly; just as you like. In fact, I'll enjoy revisiting the scenes of my most happy childhood."

The three wandered up the river to Shadow Lake where Uther Madduc had built a boathouse to house three skimmer sailboats. Elvo Glissam was his usual self; Jorjol's mood altered each minute. At times he prattled nonsense, as light-hearted and charming as Elvo Glissam, then he would sigh and become melancholy over some reminiscence of his childhood, only to turn on Elvo Glissam to argue some minor point with fierce intensity. Schaine watched him in fascination, wondering at the emotions which surged through the proud narrow skull. She would not have wished to walk out alone with Jorjol; he would certainly have become ardent.

Jorjol resented Elvo Glissam's presence and disguised the fact with obvious effort. Once or twice Schaine thought he was on the verge of asking Elvo Glissam to leave, at which times she quickly intervened.

Jorjol at last resigned himself to the circumstance and began to exhibit a new set of moods: mocking, self-pitying, sentimental, as surroundings called to mind this or that incident of his childhood. Schaine began to feel a nervous embarrassment; Jorjol was so clearly striking poses. She wanted to tease him and perhaps deflate him a bit, but in doing so she might wound him and perhaps provoke a new and more passionate drama. So she held her tongue. Elvo Glissam, wearing a bland expression, kept the conversation almost foolishly impersonal and elicited glares of contempt from Jorjol.

Meanwhile Schaine had been wondering how to announce that lunch was not to be served in the Great Hall. The problem solved itself; as they returned around the house, the buffet table on the eastern lawn was plain to see, and Kelse stood nearby, in conversation not only with Kurgech but with Julio Tanch the head stockman. Both Julio and Kurgech wore Outker garments: twill trousers, boots and a loose white shirt; neither had oiled his skin.

Jorjol stopped short, staring at the three men. Slowly he moved forward. Kelse raised his hand in a polite salute. "Jorjol, you'll remember Kurgech and Julio."

Jorjol gave a curt nod of recognition. "I remember both well. Much water has flowed down Chip-chap River since last we met." He drew himself to his full height. "Changes have occurred. There are more to come."

Kelse's eyes glittered. "We're going to stop assassinations from the Retent. That's one change. You might find the Retent gone and Treaty Lands all along the Alouan. That's another."

Schaine cried out, "Please, let's all eat our lunch."

Jorjol stood rigid. "I do not care to eat out in the open like a servant. I prefer to take my meal in the Great Hall."

"I'm afraid that this is impossible," said Kelse politely. "None of us are dressed for the occasion."

Schaine laid her hand on Jorjol's arm. "Muffin, please don't be difficult. None of us are servants; we're eating outside by preference."

"This is not the point! I am a man of character and reputation; I am as good as any Outker, and I wish to be treated with dignity!"

Kelse replied in a neutral voice: "When you come here in Outker costume, when you show respect for our institutions and our sensibilities, the situation might change."

"Aha, well then—what of Kurgech and Julio? They meet these standards; take them into the Great Hall and feed them and I will eat alone out here."

"At an appropriate occasion, this might occur, but not today."

"In that case," said Jorjol, "I find that I cannot take lunch with you, and I will now be away and about my business."

"As you wish."

Schaine walked with Jorjol to the Hermes. She spoke in a subdued voice: "I'm sorry things turned out so badly. But really, Jorjol, you need not have been so irascible."

"Bah! Kelse is an ingrate and a fool. Does he think his great army can frighten me? He will learn one day how things go!" He seized her shoulders. "You are my sweet Schaine. Come with me now! Jump into the sky-boat and we'll leave them all behind."

"Muffin, don't be silly. I wouldn't dream of such a thing."

"One time you did!"

"Long long ago." She drew back as Jorjol attempted to kiss her. "Muffin, please stop."

Jorjol stood stiff with emotion, gripping her shoulders so tightly that she cringed in pain. A sound: Jorjol looked wildly toward the house, to see Kurgech sauntering forward, apparently lost in thought. Schaine jerked herself free.

Jorjol jumped into the Hermes like a man bereft and shot off into the sky. Schaine and Kurgech watched the aircraft disappear into the west. Schaine turned and looked up into the seamed gray face. "What has come over Jorjol? He's become so wild, so outrageous!" Even as she spoke she recollected that Jorjol had always been wild and outrageous.

Kurgech said: "He smells of doom; he carries disaster on his back as an animal carries its cub."

"Changes are in the air," said Schaine. "I feel them; they press on us all. Tell me: what do the Aos feel? Do they want us to leave Morningswake?"

Kurgech looked south, across the landscape which for thousands of years had been Ao land. "Certain young men have listened to the wittols; they model themselves upon the Gray Prince and call themselves the Vanguard of the Uldra Nation. Others feel that the Alouan is too large to be affected by words. If the Outkers claim the land: well and good; let them do so. The accommodation costs us little and we gain advantages. Then the Vanguard cries out: 'What of the future, when hundreds of new manses are built, and we are forced out into the desert? This is our land of which we were plundered and we must regain control now!' And the other group says: 'These hundreds of new manses are not in evidence; is there not enough trouble in the world without anticipating more?' And so the argument goes."

"And what of today, when Jorjol wanted to take his lunch in the Great Hall?"

"Jorjol attempted too much."

"What of yourself? Do you want to sit in the Great Hall?"

"If I were invited I would feel honored to accept. The Great Hall is a sanctuary which no one should violate. Uther Madduc knew the location of our kachembas; many times he could have violated them, but never did so. Had he undergone certain rites, and worn ceremonial clothing, and come in the proper frame of mind, he could have visited any of our sacred places, except those concerned with himself, and then only for his own safety. Certainly he would have lent me Outker garments and taken me into his Great Hall had I asked him to do so."

Schaine pursed her lips dubiously. "Father was a strict man."

"Someday perhaps you will learn the truth."

Schaine was startled. "The truth about what?"

"In due course you will know."

Lunch was served by Wonalduna and Saravan, two of the constantly shifting succession of Ao girls who chose to work a year or two at the great house. The cook at Morningswake was Hermina Lingolet, a second cousin to Kelse and Schaine, who, like Reyona Werlas-Madduc the housekeeper, considered herself a member of the family rather than a servant. For lunch she had prepared a peppery *halash*, or stew in the Ao style, with a garnish of wild parsley, a platter of steamed barley, a salad of fresh herbs from the kitchen garden. Jorjol's going had left a constraint on the company. Only when Elvo Glissam mentioned erjins and their intelligence did the conversation move. Kurgech had anecdotes to tell: of four erjins, communicating telepathically, attempting to trick a party of Somajji outriders into an ambush; of battle between erjins and morphotes; of meeting an erjin face to face on a mountain trail.

So went the lunch. Without perceptible signal Julio and Kurgech simultaneously rose to their feet, expressed polite gratitude and took their leave. Kelse, Elvo Glissam and Schaine remained in the pleasant coolness under the green-gums. Schaine said: "Well, lunch is over and once again Muffin has been barred from the Great Hall. I wonder what's going on in his mind."

"Devil take Muffin—Jorjol—Gray Prince, whatever he calls himself," declared Kelse irritably. "I wish he'd go back to Olanje and take up residence. He can go to as many Outker parties as he likes."

Elvo Glissam said cautiously: "He's a spirited fellow, to say the least."

"He's insane," growled Kelse. "Megalomania, delusion, hysteria—he's afflicted with everything."

Schaine looked off over the savanna. "What could he mean 'the great army' that you are raising?"

Kelse grinned sourly. "His spies tell him more than we know ourselves. The 'great army' is nothing more than a few marks on a paper. Gerd and I have been working on a scheme we'd hoped to keep quiet for at least a few weeks longer."

"I'm not really interested in your secrets."

"It's not really a secret; in fact it's an obvious step we should have taken years ago: political organization. Gerd and I have worked out a tentative charter of federation."

"This is quite an undertaking," said Elvo Glissam. "You two have been busy."

"Someone had to get in motion. We've telephoned all the domains; without exception every one favors political unity. Jorjol naturally has heard the news and assumes that we're organizing for military purposes."

"No doubt true," said Schaine.

Kelse nodded. "We plan to protect ourselves."

Elvo asked tentatively: "What of the Mull? Doesn't it control the Treaty Lands?"

"In theory, yes. In actuality, no. If the Mull minds its own business, we'll mind ours."

Elvo Glissam sat silent. Schaine heaved a mournful sigh. "Everything seems so fragile and uncertain. If only we could feel that Morningswake was truly ours."

"It's ours until we let someone take it away from us. And that's not going to happen."

CHAPTER 6

Schaine and Elvo went out riding on a pair of criptids. Kelse insisted that they carry guns and that two of the ranch-hands accompany them, to Schaine's annoyance. But as they rode south toward the Skaws she conceded that the precaution was probably well taken. She told Elvo Glissam: "We're not all that far from the Retent and, as you know, wicked things can happen."

"I'm not complaining."

They halted in the shadow of the Great Skaw: a spire of sandstone two hundred feet tall, stratified beige, buff, pink and gray. Mornings-wake Manor could hardly be seen under the pale green-gums and the darker transtellar oaks. Beyond, the yet darker line of Fairy Forest lay along the horizon. To the west the Chip-chap wandered back and forth and disappeared into the southwest, eventually to flow into Massacre Lake. "When we were little," said Schaine, "we often came out here on picnics and to look for tourmalines; there's a pegmatite dike over yonder...This is where the erjin attacked Kelse, incidentally."

Elvo appraised the surroundings. "Right here?"

"I was over on the pegmatite; Kelse and Muffin were climbing the pinnacle. The erjin came out of that cleft and scrambled up after the boys. It caught Kelse and pulled him down; I heard the noise and ran around to help, but Muffin had shot the erjin, and it was flailing around right where you're standing. Kurgech arrived and tied up Kelse's arm and leg and carried him home, and Muffin became the big hero. For about a week."

"Then what happened?"

"Oh—there was a big quarrel. I flounced off to Tanquil. Then Muffin took himself off to the Retent and now he's the Gray Prince." Schaine looked around the area. "I guess I don't really like it here after all...Poor Kelse."

Elvo looked uneasily over his shoulder. "Do erjins come here often?"

"Once in a while they'll come to look over the cattle, but our Aos are marvellous trackers; they'll follow a trail which you can't even see. The erjins have learned this and generally they keep to the far wilderness."

Returning to Morningswake Manor, they found Gerd Jemasze's battered old Dacy sky-boat on the landing area. Kelse and Gerd were busy in the library and failed to appear until dinner was served in the Great Hall. In accordance with Morningswake custom all had dressed in formal evening wear—Gerd Jemasze and Elvo Glissam in costumes maintained for the use of casual guests. No question, thought Schaine, but what the ritual enhanced the occasion; casual clothes and casual manners would have gone incongruously with the high-backed chairs, the enormous old umberwood table, the chandelier imported from the Zitz Glass Works at Gilhaux on Darybant, and the heirloom dinnerware. Tonight Schaine had taken unusual pains with her appearance. She wore a simple dark green gown and had piled her hair on top of her head after the fashion of Pharistane water nymphs, with an emerald starburst at her forehead.

Reyona Werlas-Madduc had already taken her meal with Hermina Lingolet; four persons only sat at the umberwood table in the Great Hall: those four who had shared the march across a hundred miles of wasteland. As they sipped wine, Schaine leaned back and looked at the men through half-closed eyelids, pretending they were strangers so that she might appraise them objectively. Kelse, she thought, looked older than his relatively few years. He could never be a man as imposing as his father. His face was thin and keen; ridges of assertion clamped his mouth. In contrast Elvo Glissam looked easy and light-hearted, without a care in the world. Gerd Jemasze, to Schaine's detached view, looked surprisingly elegant. He turned his head and their glances met. Schaine, as usual, felt a small pulse of antagonism or challenge or some other such emotion. Gerd Jemasze dropped his gaze to the goblet of wine; Schaine was both amused and amazed to discover that he had become aware of her presence; through all the years of her life he had ignored her.

"The charter is now circulating around the domains," said Kelse. "If we get general approval, and I believe we shall, then, ipso facto, we become a political unit."

"What if you don't get general approval?" Schaine asked.

"Unlikely. We've taken up the matter with everyone."

"What if they don't like the structure of your charter and insist on changes?"

"The charter has no structure. It's merely a statement of common cause, an agreement to agree, a pledge to abide by the will of the majority.

This is the basic first step which must be taken; then we'll approve a more detailed document."

"So now you must wait. How long?"

"A week or two. Perhaps three."

"Long enough," said Gerd Jemasze, "to discover the humor in Uther Madduc's 'wonderful joke'."

Elvo Glissam was immediately interested. "And how do you do this?"

"Follow his route. Somewhere along the way I'll discover what he considered so funny."

"And what was his route?" asked Schaine.

"From Morningswake he flew three hundred and twelve miles north, seventeen miles northeast—in other words, to the No. 2 Palga Depot. There he landed." Gerd Jemasze brought out Uther Madduc's notebook. "Listen to this: 'No man dares fly the skies above the Palga. Astonishing paradox! The Wind-runners, so meek, so vague, become demons of ferocity at the sight of an aircraft. Out come the ancient light-cannons; the aircraft is exploded into shreds and shards. I put the question to Filisent: "Why do you shoot sky-craft?"

"""Because," said he, "they are likely to be Blue raiders." "Oh?" said I. "When have the Uldra raided last?" "Not in my memory, nor in my father's memory," said he. "Nevertheless that is how things must be; we will have no flyers in our air." He gave me leave to examine his cannon: a marvellous implement, and I wondered who had crafted so fine a weapon. Filisent could tell me little. The weapon, with its intricate scrolling and amazing engravements, was an heirloom, reached down father to son over years beyond memory; it might well have arrived with that long forgotten first exploration of Koryphon; who knows?'"

Gerd Jemasze looked up. "He wrote this, so it appears, a few days after landing at No. 2 Depot. Unfortunately there's not much more. He says: 'The Palga is a most remarkable land and Filisent is a most remarkable fellow. Like all Wind-runners he is a deft and enthusiastic thief unless dissuaded by fiap or vigilance. Otherwise he is quite a good chap. He owns a barkentine and thirty-seven separate plots of ground which he cultivates along the passage. How closely these people are meshed with wind and sun, cloud and weather! To see them at the steering rod, with the sails billowing above them and great wheels trundling, is to see men rapt in a religious rite. And yet, ask them does three twos equal six and they respond with a blank stare. Ask them of erjins, who trains them and how? and the stare becomes a look of bewilderment. Ask them how they pay for their fine wheels and sailcloth and metal fittings and they gape as if they suspect you to be lacking in reason.'"

Gerd Jemasze turned a page. "Here's a section which he calls 'Notes for a treatise':

"'Srenki: that amazing and awesome caste, or is it a cult? The knowledge comes to the child through recurrent dreams. He becomes pale and thin and troubled, and eventually wanders away from his wagon. Presently he performs his first wanton deed; and thereafter, in this strange placid land, he concentrates within himself and dissipates the elemental turpitude of all the others, who respond to this now-creature of horror with pity and forbearance. The Srenki are few; in all the Palga they number perhaps only twenty; it can be well understood how ghastly and deep within them runs the cloacal seep.'"

Silence; no one spoke.

Gerd Jemasze turned the page. "Here's about the last of it. He says: 'The man's name is Poliamides. I have swindled him with Kurgech's trick, and he admits he has seen the erjin training center. "Then take me there!" He demurs. I twirl the prism and my voice comes to him from the sky within his brain. "Take me there!"—the voice of a sun-eyed god! Poliamides accepts the inevitable though he knows he is churning a million destinies into a kind of chaotic soup. "Where and how far?" I ask. "Yonder and at some good distance," is his reply; and so we will see.'" Gerd Jemasze turned a page. "Next a list of numbers I can't interpret, and that's about all. Except for this last page. First two words: 'Splendor! Marvel!' and then: 'Of bittersweet ironies this is the prime. How slow tolls the chime of the centuries! How plangent and sweet is the justice of the tones!' And then a final paragraph: 'The situation is so clear that a demonstration is hardly necessary; still this wonderful demonstration now exists, and if any dare to question our right and our justice, I can and I will pin him to the wall of his own doctrinaire absurdity.'"

Gerd Jemasze closed the notebook and tossed it on the table. "That's all of it. He returned to the Sturdevant. The auto-pilot shows that he flew directly back to Morningswake. Two days later he was dead over the Dramalfo."

Elvo Glissam said: "I'm puzzled why he went up to the Palga in the first place. To trade?"

"Oddly enough," said Kelse, "on a mission dear to your heart. Last spring he visited Olanje and took note of Aunt Val's erjins. No one seemed to know how the erjins were trained so Father went up on the Palga to find out."

"And did he find out? Is this his 'wonderful joke'?"

Kelse shrugged. "We don't know."

"The Palga must be a remarkable place."

Schaine said: "I remember all kinds of strange tales—half of them false, no doubt. Babies are traded between wagons, on the theory that a child raised by its own parents becomes overindulged."

Kelse said, "Remember our old nurse Jamia? She'd scare us silly with bedtime stories about the Srenki."

"I remember Jamia very well," said Schaine. "Once she told us how the Wind-runners hang up their corpses in trees, to keep them safe from the wild dogs, so that when you'd walk through a forest, every tree had a skeleton grinning down at you."

"And not just corpses do they hang up in the trees," said Jemasze. "The ailing old grandparents, it's up the tree with them, to save the trouble of returning to the grove later."

"Charming people," said Elvo Glissam. "So what do you plan to do?"

"I'll fly up to No. 2 Depot and pick up Uther Madduc's trail, by one means or another."

Kelse shook his head. "The trail's too old; you'll never find it."

"I won't, but Kurgech will."

"Kurgech?"

"He wants to come along. He's never been up on the Palga and he wants to see the wind-wagons."

Elvo Glissam said expansively: "I'd like to go along myself, if I could be at all useful."

Schaine clamped her mouth shut; impossible to protest or mention hardship and danger without embarrassing Elvo, nor could she gracefully point out that Elvo had consumed several goblets of heady amber wine.

Gerd Jemasze's face twitched so slightly that perhaps only Schaine noticed, and her always smouldering dislike of Jemasze flared; again she restrained herself from speaking. Jemasze said politely: "Your company of course is welcome—still we'll be gone for a week or more, perhaps under rough conditions."

Elvo Glissam laughed. "It couldn't be any worse than the trip up from the Dramalfo."

"I hope not."

"Well, I'm not exactly frail, and I have a particular interest in the matter."

Kelse spoke in the most sober of voices, further infuriating Schaine: "Elvo wants to look into the enslavement of erjins at first hand."

Elvo grinned, showing no embarrassment. "Quite true."

Without enthusiasm Gerd Jemasze said: "I imagine Kelse can fit you out with boots and a few oddments of gear."

"No trouble as to that," said Kelse.

"Very well then; we'll leave tomorrow morning, if I can find Kurgech."

"He'll be up at the old Apple Orchard with his tribe."

For a reckless instant Schaine thought herself to join the venture, then reluctantly put the idea by. It wouldn't be fair to Kelse to fly off to the Palga and leave him alone.

CHAPTER 7

The sky-car flew north across a land of low hills, wide valleys, winding streams, forests of gadroon, flame-tree, mangoneel, an occasional giant Uaian jinko. Elvo Glissam rode with a feeling of unreality, already dubious in regard to his bravado of the night before. He glanced back the way they had come...By no means, he told himself firmly; he had joined himself to the expedition for good and sufficient reasons: to examine the basic facts of erjin enslavement, a course of action to which he was impelled by moral commitment. And another more visceral reason. What Gerd Jemasze could do, he could do.

Elvo Glissam looked across the car. He was perhaps an inch taller than Gerd Jemasze. Gerd was broader in the shoulders, heavier in the chest, decisive, definite and efficient in his movements; he used no unnecessary flourishes nor any of those idiosyncratic gestures which gave flavor to a personality. In fact, at first impression, and perhaps second and third, Gerd Jemasze's personality was spare, drab, grim and colorless; he evinced neither dash nor flair nor pungency. Elvo Glissam's own attitude toward the world was optimistic, positive, constructive: Koryphon, indeed the whole of the Gaean Reach, needed improvement and only through the efforts of well-meaning folk could these changes be effected.

Gerd Jemasze, while sufficiently courteous and considerate, could never be called a sympathetic individual and he certainly viewed the cosmos through a lens of egocentricity. By this same token, Gerd

Jemasze was superbly self-assured; the possibility of failure in any undertaking whatever obviously had never crossed his mind, and Elvo felt a twinge of envy or irritation, or even a faint sense of dislike—which he instantly realized to be petty and unworthy. If only Gerd were less arrogant in his unconscious assumptions, less innocent—for Gerd Jemasze's impervious self-confidence after all could be nothing less than naïveté. In hundreds of capabilities he would show to poor advantage indeed. He knew next to nothing of human achievement in the realms of music, mathematics, literature, optics, philosophy. By any ordinary consideration, Gerd Jemasze should feel uneasy and resentful in regard to Elvo Glissam, not the reverse. Elvo Glissam managed a sour chuckle. The situation was as it was, for better or worse.

Once again he looked down at the terrain passing below. They would still take him back, if he so requested, perhaps pleading illness. Gerd Jemasze's reaction would be only mild puzzlement; he wouldn't care enough one way or the other to feel disgust…Elvo scowled. Enough of all this self-pity and hand-wringing. He'd do his best to be a competent companion; if he failed, he failed, and that was that; he refused to think any more about it.

Gerd Jemasze pointed down to where three enormous gray beasts wallowed in a mudhole. One stood erect and shambled ashore, to stare vacuously up at the sky-car.

"Armored sloths," said Gerd Jemasze. "Close cousins to the morphotes. Evolution left them far behind."

"But no relation to the erjins."

"None whatever. Some people say the erjins developed from the mountain gergoid: half-rat half-scorpion; other people say no. Erjins don't leave fossils."

The sky-car slid north. Ahead loomed the Palga, with the Volwodes stabbing the sky to the west. Gerd Jemasze took the sky-car higher, to fly just below the vast cumulus pillars which basked in the sunlight. The ground below heaved and rolled as if under pressure, then suddenly thrust up three thousand feet, the face of the scarp eroded into thousands of spurs and ravines. Beyond, far off and away across sunny distances, extended the Palga.

Close by the brink of the escarpment clustered a dozen whitewashed buildings with black-brown roofs. "No. 2 Depot," said Gerd Jemasze succinctly. "You'll probably see some export erjins…It won't help to express your outrage."

Elvo managed a good-natured laugh. "I'm here as an observer only." He now reflected that he had never heard Gerd Jemasze voice an opinion one way or another on the matter of erjin enslavement. "What of yourself? What do you feel about the business?"

Gerd Jemasze considered a moment or two. "Personally, I wouldn't care to be a slave." He stopped talking and after a moment Elvo saw that he intended to express no further opinion—perhaps because he had formed none. Then, frowning at his own insensitivity, Elvo corrected this thinking. Gerd Jemasze had a subtle way of implying his point of view, and it would appear that he had expressed something like: "Offhand, the situation seems dirty and disreputable, but since we know so little about the total picture, I am reserving final judgment. As for the anguish of the Olanje Labor Guilds and the hurt feelings of the Society for the Emancipation of the Erjins, I can hardly take them seriously." Elvo grinned. Such, translated into the language of Villa Mirasol, were Gerd Jemasze's opinions.

The sky-car settled into the central compound at No. 2 Depot. To the left rambled a long low irregular structure of cemented soil, whitewashed, with a roof of haphazard angles and slopes supported by heavy poles: evidently an inn. Ahead, along the western edge of the compound, stood three barn-like structures with tall doors open at front and rear to reveal a number of vehicles in the process of construction. A rack supported a dozen large light pneumatic wheels, as high as a man or higher; beyond and through the construction sheds could be glimpsed other vehicles incongruously equipped with masts, yards, booms, sprits and rigging. To the right, along the northern edge of the compound, was ranged another complex of open sheds; some containing empty cages, others fitted with screened enclosures from which a dozen erjins looked stolidly forth.

In the construction shops the workmen had halted their activity. A half-dozen came out into the compound and approached the sky-car: sturdy brown men of no great stature. Several wore what Elvo considered absolutely preposterous headgear: horizontal disks of wood four feet in diameter and an inch thick secured to an iron casque strapped under the chin and around the nape of the neck. How could anyone work in such ungainly contraptions?

Gerd Jemasze now performed a most curious act. As the workmen came closer, he picked up a small stick and scratched a circle in the dirt of the compound to enclose the sky-car. The workmen halted, then came forward more slowly, to stop at the circumference of the circle. They were the first Wind-runners Elvo had seen: representatives of a race totally different from the Uldras. Their pale brown skin seemed colored by an innate pigment, rather than by exposure to the sun, and evinced the peculiar property of showing neither shadows nor highlights. Some wore cloth caps, others disks of wood and iron casques; where hair could be seen, it showed as a tousle of pale brown curls and was worn without evident attention to style. Their features were small and blunt except for rather heavy jaws; their eyes showed a haunting pale buff color. Certain of the men wore small mustaches; several had plucked away their eyebrows to give themselves a bland and quizzical expression. All wore short trousers of pale blue, gray or pale green, with loose shirts of similar material; all wore in their hair or on their caps what appeared to be ornaments of glass blown into intricate shapes and tied with colored ribbons.

Gerd Jemasze spoke: "Good luck; fair wind to all."

The workers mumbled a responsive benediction. One asked: "Do you trade or do you buy?"

"My business has not yet been made clear to me. It will come in a dream."

The workmen nodded in comprehension and muttered to each other. Elvo gaped in surprise; he had expected no such flights of fancy from the matter-of-fact Jemasze, who now indicated the circle. "Observe this fiap. It is enforced not by Ahariszeio, but by ourselves, our fists and the sting of our guns. Is this clearly understood?"

The workmen shrugged, shuffled their feet and craned their necks to examine the sky-car and its contents.

Jemasze asked: "Where is the priest?"

"Yonder, in his compartments, beyond the inn."

Jemasze looked around at Kurgech, who leaned against the sky-car, a handgun significantly displayed. Jemasze turned back to the Wind-runners. "You can depart without regret; our property is neither loose nor free, but carefully guarded."

The workers made polite signs and returned to the sheds. Elvo asked in bewilderment: "What is the meaning of all that?"

"The Wind-runners steal anything they can lay their hands on," said Gerd Jemasze. "The protective signs, or talismans, are called fiaps; you'll see them everywhere. The Wind-runners wear them in their hair."

"Why do they wear those wooden disks?"

"They've violated some sort of religious ordinance. There's no authority up here but the priesthood."

Elvo grunted. "It gives me a headache just to think about it."

"Sometimes the disks are four inches thick, or even six inches. The culprit in such a case usually dies in a week or two, unless someone takes care of him."

"What does he do to earn a disk?"

Gerd Jemasze shrugged. "Spitting against the wind. Talking in his sleep. I'm not all that familiar with Wind-runner law. Come along; we'll go find the priest and get ourselves some fiaps."

The priest wore a white gown; his hair, dyed stark black, hung to his shoulders and terminated in small onyx balls. His round face was bare of hair and he had painted black circles around his eyes, giving himself an expression of owlish intensity. He showed no surprise at the sight of Gerd Jemasze and Elvo Glissam, though he had been asleep on his couch when they entered the compartment.

Gerd Jemasze now began a conversation which once again left Elvo Glissam wilted with astonishment: "Good winds to you, priest. We require a set of fiaps, covering all phases of life."

"Indeed, indeed," said the priest. "You intend to trade? You will not need so many fiaps."

"We are not traders; we come to the Palga for pleasure and novelty."

"Hi-ho! You must be easy men to please then. We offer neither carnivals nor melodious girls nor banquets of fat flesh. For a fact, we see very few if any of your ilk."

"My friend Uther Madduc passed this way recently," said Gerd Jemasze. "He tells me that you provided him fiaps and gave him counsel."

"Not I, not I. Poliamides then held tenure. I am Moffamides."

"In that case we will pay our respects to Poliamides."

Moffamides' eyes became round and brilliant; he pursed his mouth and gave his head a shake of disapprobation. "Poliamides has proved inconstant; he has abandoned the priesthood and gone out across the sarai*. Perhaps he was unduly responsive to your friend Uther Madduc."

"In the name of Ahariszeio then, provide us fiaps; and make them strong."

The priest went to look into a black leather case lined with pink felt, where rested a dozen rock-crystal spheres. He touched them,

---

*Sarai: Untranslatable: a limitless expanse, horizon to horizon, of land or water, lacking all impediment or obstacle to travel and projecting an irresistible urgency to be on the way, to travel toward a known or unknown destination.

rearranged them, and jerked back with a small exclamation of surprise. "The portents are unfavorable! You must return to the Alouan."

Gerd Jemasze said brusquely: "You have misused the spheres; the portents are favorable."

Moffamides turned him a sharp sidelong look, the agate beads in his black hair clicking and softly clattering. "How can you say so? Are you priests?"

Jemasze gave his head a curt shake. "Uther Madduc is dead, as you know."

Moffamides' eyes bulged in apparently genuine surprise. "How should I know?"

"Through telepathy, which is one of your priestly skills, so I am told."

"In certain circumstances only, and never as to events on the Alouan, where I know no more than you of the Palga."

"Uther Madduc's ghost has laid a charge on us. He and Poliamides became companions and each for assurance allowed the other a taste of his soul."

Elvo Glissam listened in awe. And he had considered Gerd Jemasze dull and stolid!

Moffamides sat with owl eyes now half-closed and thoughtful. "I have heard nothing of this."

"You have so been told, and if we must return to the Alouan without Uther Madduc's soul, I will ask you to return with us and console his ghost."

"Utterly impossible," declared the priest. "I dare not leave the Palga."

"In that case we must have a few words with Poliamides."

Moffamides nodded slowly, thoughtfully, his eyes unfocused.

"First," said Gerd Jemasze, "you must provide us fiaps."

Moffamides once more became alert. "Fiaps of what nature?"

"Contrive us a fiap so that we may fly our sky-car across the Palga."

Moffamides drew down the corners of his mouth and held up his forefinger. "Belches of gas and whines of energy on the excellent winds of Ahariszeio? Unthinkable! Nor will I work you a fiap of fair venture because I am aware of bodes and umbras, and all may not go well. At best I can contrive a general talisman commending you to the mercy of Ahariszeio."

"Very good; we will accept this fiap with gratitude. Additionally, the sky-car must be protected against every manner of damage, nuisance and misfortune, including pilferage, destruction, curiosity, tampering, vandalism, defilement, removal or concealment. I want fiaps for myself and my companions, guarding us against molestation, harm, magic, beguilement, exploitation, capture or immobility, and the various stages and conditions of death. We will also need a suitable set of fiaps for our vehicle, assuring us of good winds, smooth turf, stability and fair destiny."

"You require a great deal."

"For a priest as close to Ahariszeio as yourself, our requirements are small. We could ask more."

"It is quite enough. You must pay a fee."

"We will discuss the fee on our return, after the fiaps have been proved."

Moffamides opened his mouth to speak, then closed it again. "How far do you fare?"

"As far as necessary. Where is Poliamides?"

"Not close at hand."

"You must then direct us to him."

Moffamides nodded thoughtfully. "Yes. I will give you direction and I will provide fiaps. They must be strong; and their power must not fade. Tomorrow they will be charged with force."

Gerd Jemasze gave a curt nod. "Give us now a temporary fiap to secure the sky-car, and others to guard ourselves and our belongings overnight."

"Take your sky-car behind the wagon shops. I will bring the fiaps."

Gerd Jemasze returned to the sky-car, floated it over the wagon shops to the indicated area: a storage lot for dozens of vehicles, of various styles and sizes, old and new, from a three-masted cargo schooner on eight ten-foot wheels, to a three-wheeled skimmer with a single unstayed mast. Attached to each was a confection of twisted glass bulbs and rods of various colors from which depended ribbons long enough to drop past the side of the wagon.

Moffamides awaited them with a basket. "These are fiaps of general potency." He brought the objects forth. "This red and green fiap is standard and will guard your sky-car indefinitely. These blue and whites will secure your belongings so long as you remain at the inn. The black, green and white fiap will guard this Uldra against vengeance, malice and ghost-clutch. The two black, blue and yellow fiaps will suffice for you Outkers."

Jemasze attached the red and green fiap to the sky-car, distributed the others among Elvo, Kurgech and himself. "Quite correct," said Moffamides, and without further ceremony departed the yard.

Jemasze regarded the fiaps dubiously. "Hopefully they're operative and not just junk."

"They are good fiaps," said Kurgech. "They carry magic."

"I don't notice anything," said Elvo in a subdued voice. "I suppose my sensibilities are atrophied."

Jemasze went to inspect a tall-masted sloop on four six-foot wheels with a wicker deck and a small cabin. "All my life I've wanted to sail one of these wagons…This is probably too light and too small. That ketch yonder would be more suitable."

The three repaired to the inn and entered a foyer, separated by a chest-high bar of scrubbed pale wood from the kitchen, where a stocky brown man, naked to the waist and glistening with sweat, tended a row of iron pots which bubbled and seethed on a great iron range. The three waited; the cook darted them a severe glance and seizing a cutlass began to dice a parsnip.

Into the chamber came a young woman, tall and slender, with a face impassive as that of a somnambulist. Elvo, always on the alert for odd human variants, was instantly fascinated. With any degree of animation this young woman might have manifested a most unusual beauty, comprising the languor of a nenuphar and the elegance of some swift white winter beast. But her face was still and the beauty was absent. Or almost absent, thought Elvo; perhaps it was there, stranger than ever, by implication. Her ivory skin was paler than that of the ordinary Wind-runner and showed a most subtle luster or bloom of an indefinable color: blue? blue-green? green-violet? Her hair, dark brown, hung to her shoulders and was contained at the forehead by a black fillet with a purple, black and scarlet fiap at the back.

In a soft voice the woman asked their needs and Gerd Jemasze rather brusquely spoke for three beds, supper and breakfast, and Elvo wondered at his indelicacy. The woman stepped back, as graceful and easy as a retreating wave and signaled to them; the three men followed her into a cavernous common room, dim and moving with mysterious shadows. Slabs of dark gray stone paved the floor; posts of smoke-stained timber supported the ceiling rafters, from which depended hundreds of barely visible fiaps. A long clerestory of a hundred purple and brown panes admitted a warm umbrous light which enhanced the quality of posts, beams and panels, enriched the dark red cloth which covered the tables, and as if by purposeful chiaroscuro dramatized the features of the other persons in the room. These were five men who sat gambling at a table, pounding with heavy fists and cursing for emphasis, while a pot-boy in a white apron served mugs of beer.

The young woman led the way across the common room, through a short passage and out upon a balcony which seemed to overlook nothing but sky. Elvo looked over the rail. The inn had been built on the very brink of the escarpment; the balcony hung out over emptiness. Between wall and posts were strung a number of hammocks, any of which, so the woman indicated, were at the disposal of the travelers. A walkway supported by long spider-leg stilts extended over the chasm; at the far end was the privy, consisting of a bar hanging over the windy emptiness and a pipe trickling cold water. Far below could be seen the twinkle of running water, which Elvo hoped was not the source of the Chip-chap.

The three men brought mugs of beer out upon the balcony: a soft pale brew fragrant of Palga sunshine and wortleberries. They sat drinking while Methuen the sun went down in a cataclysm of scarlet, rose, pink and red, like a king advancing to his doom.

Silence on the balcony. The tall woman came forth with new mugs of beer, then stood a moment staring at the sunset as if never in her life had she witnessed a sight so remarkable; after a moment she stirred and returned into the common room.

Elvo Glissam, half-intoxicated from the beer and the sunset, lost his misgivings; here, beyond question, was the richest moment of his life— and yet in such bizarre surroundings, with such inexplicable companions! Questions thronged his mind. He spoke to Kurgech: "The fiaps: do they actually control the Wind-runners?"

"They know no other control."

"What would happen if a person disobeyed a fiap?"

Kurgech made a small motion, implying that the question hardly need be asked. "The offenders suffer, and often die."

"How did you know that the priest's fiaps held magic?"

Kurgech merely shrugged.

Jemasze said, "If you live where magic is unknown, you'll never recognize it."

Elvo looked out over the sky. "I've had no experience with magic... until now."

Dusk began to blur the panorama; the woman made a stately appearance to announce that supper had been laid out. The three men followed her into the common room and dined on saltbread, broad beans and sausage, a pickle of unknown ingredients, a salad of sweet grasses. The gamblers ignored all but their game, which was played with four-inch rods of polished wood, tipped at each end with daubs of bright color, usually, but not always, different end from end. Each player in turn took a rod from a receptacle, concealing the tips from the sight of the opposing players until, usually after deliberation, he displayed one or the other end in his rack. After each draw a discard might or might not be made into the center of the table, usually with a curse or an exclamation. The game occasioned considerable tension, with glances of surprise and frowns of calculation being exchanged among the players.

Jemasze and Kurgech presently went out to their hammocks. Elvo sat watching the game, which he found to be more complicated than first appearances suggested. The hundred and five rods were divided into twenty-one sorts, ringing the combinations of red, black, orange, white, blue, green. To start a game the rods were placed in the receptacle, which was then agitated until a rod fell horizontally down a slot which concealed both ends. The player took the rod, examined it surreptitiously then thrust one end up through a hole in the rack on the table before him. Each player drew in turn, holding or discarding until each player had five rods protruding from his rack, these displaying a variation of colors, with another variation of colors concealed and known only to the player holding the rack. The players bet after each round of draws, meeting or raising the bets or dropping from the game as they deemed their chances warranted. Each player then drew another rod and either discarded it or thrust it up into his rack, usually discarding one of the rods he previously held; and so on until all the rods had been drawn, selected or discarded. The players now considered the discards, the colors displayed above the boxes, and with this information each attempted to calculate the colors hidden by the racks of his opponents: all of which served as a basis for a final round of bets. The players then displayed the concealed ends of their rods. The high-ranking set of rods took the accumulation of bets. Elvo, somewhat intimidated by the visceral grunts of emotion, let diffidence be the better part of curiosity and kept a respectful distance from the game; he was therefore unable to learn the hierarchy of combinations.

The young woman came forward once again to serve a mug of unrequested beer, which Elvo was pleased to accept. He tried to catch the woman's eye so that he might have a friendly word with her when into the room came a man of most extraordinary appearance and mien. His face exhibited a range of mismatched over-large features: an odd wide jaw, sunken cheeks, heavy cheekbones, a splayed nose, a tall round forehead, a wide flexible slit of a mouth twisted in a mindless grin. His eyes, round and pale buff, blinked and winced as if the light were uncomfortable. Long heavy arms dangled from burly shoulders; his torso was knotted and knobbed with bone and muscle; his long legs terminated in massive feet. He looked, thought Elvo, both imbecilic and cunning; simple yet rich in fancy.

The gamblers saw him with little side-flicks of vision but paid him no heed; the pot-boy ignored him as if he had not existed. He approached the woman and spoke to her; then, with a soft sad grin on his face, struck her an open-handed blow on the side of the head, creating a sound which caused Elvo's stomach to churn. The woman fell to the floor; the man kicked her in the neck.

An instantaneous image struck into Elvo's mind which never would leave him: the pale young woman on the floor, blood oozing from her mouth, face placid, eyes staring; the man looking down in proud delight, heavy foot raised to kick again, like a man performing a grotesque jig; the players at the table showing glittering side-glances but indifferent and remote; himself, Elvo Glissam of Olanje, sitting astounded and horrified. To his amazement he saw himself reach out, catch the foot and pull, so that the man fell sprawling, only to leap up with incredible lightness, and still smiling his soft sad smile, aim a kick for Elvo's head. Never in his life had Elvo fought with his hands; he hardly knew what to do except jerk back, so that the force of the kick thrust air against his face. In desperation he seized the foot and ran forward. The man, face suddenly contorted in dismay, hopped back with lurching foolish hops, out the door, out across the balcony, over the rail, out into the void.

With nothing better to do, Elvo tottered back to his seat. He sat panting and presently he drank from the mug of beer. The players occupied themselves with their game. The woman hobbled away. The room was quiet except for the sounds at the gaming table. Elvo rubbed his forehead and stared down into the beer. The episode evidently had been a hallucination...For several minutes Elvo sat immobile. An odd

417

thought occurred to him: the man had worn no fiaps, no talismans of protection. Elvo thoughtfully finished the mug of beer, then rose to his feet and went out to his hammock.

CHAPTER 8

In the morning no reference was made to the episode. The innkeeper served a breakfast of bread, tea and cold meat, and took coins from Gerd Jemasze in settlement of the account. The three departed Sailmaker's Inn, crossed the compound to the area behind the workshops. The sky-car rested as they had left it. Jemasze turned his attention to the sail-wagons. At a big eight-wheeled beer-cart, with three masts, a multiplicity of yards, shrouds, sprits and halyards, he merely glanced; the six-wheeled and four-wheeled house-wagons he gave more consideration. Their pneumatic wheels stood eight feet tall; the house hung on spring suspensions with less than two feet of ground clearance; most were rigged as schooners or two-masted brigantines; like the cargo-wagons, they seemed more adapted to passages down the monsoon winds than to speed or maneuverability.

Jemasze turned his attention to a land-yawl about thirty feet long, with four independently sprung wheels, a flat bed with a pair of cuddies fore and aft. The shop foreman had been unobtrusively watching; now he came forward to ascertain Jemasze's requirements, and the two engaged in negotiations which occupied the better part of an hour. Jemasze finally obtained a rental rate for the land-yawl at a figure he considered tolerable, and the shop foreman went off to find sails for the craft. Jemasze and Kurgech returned to the inn to buy provisions, while Elvo transferred luggage and personal belongings from the sky-car to the land-yawl.

Moffamides the priest sauntered across the yard. "You have selected a good wagon for your journey," he told Elvo. "Sound and stiff, fast and easy."

Elvo Glissam politely acquiesced in the priest's judgment. "What kind of sail-wagon did Uther Madduc use?"

Moffamides' eyes went blank. "A wagon somewhat similar, so I would suppose."

Several men came forth from the shop with sails which they proceeded to bind to the masts. Moffamides watched with an air of benign approval. Elvo wondered whether he should refer to the events of the night before, which now seemed totally unreal. Some kind of conversation seemed in order. He çounterfeited a tone of ease and lightness. "My home is in Szintarre; at Olanje, actually. I've become interested in the erjins. How in the world do you tame such creatures?"

Moffamides slowly turned his head and inspected Elvo through heavy-lidded eyes. "The process is complicated... We start with erjin cubs and train them to our commands."

"I assumed as much, but how can a ferocious beast become a semi-intelligent domestic servant?"

"Ha ha! The ferocious beasts are semi-intelligent at the start! We convince them that they live better as Uldra mounts than as starvelings running naked across the desert, and better still as Outker house servants."

"Then you communicate with them?"

Moffamides raised his eyes to the sky. "To some extent."

"Telepathically?"

Moffamides frowned. "We are not truly adept."

"Hmm. In Olanje an important society intends to stop the enslavement of erjins. What do you think of this?"

"Foolishness. The erjins are otherwise wasted and we are supplied good wheels and bearings and metal parts for our sail-wagons. The commerce is profitable."

"Don't you consider the commerce immoral?"

Moffamides looked at Elvo in what seemed mild perplexity. "It is work approved by Ahariszeio."

"I would like to visit the laboratories, or camps, whatever they are called. Could such a visit be arranged?"

Moffamides gave a curt laugh. "Impossible. Here are your friends."

Jemasze and Kurgech returned to the land-yawl. Moffamides gave them a sedate greeting. "Your craft is eager and yearns for the sarai. A fair wind offers; it is time you were away."

"All very well," said Jemasze, "but how do we find Poliamides?"

"You would do best to forget Poliamides. He is far away. Like all Outkers you brood too much upon the evanescent."

"I concede the fault; where is Poliamides?"

Moffamides made an easy gesture. "I cannot say; I do not know."

Kurgech leaned forward to stare into the priest's pale buff eyes. Moffamides' face went lax. Kurgech said softly: "You are lying."

Moffamides became angry. "Practice none of your Blue magic here on the Palga! We are not without defenses!" He recovered his poise almost instantly. "I only try to protect you. The omens are bad. Uther Madduc came to grief, and now you go forth to repeat his mistake. Is it any wonder that I perceive false winds?"

"Uther Madduc was killed by a Blue," said Gerd Jemasze. "So far as I know, there was no connection between his death and his trip across the Palga."

Moffamides smiled. "Perhaps you are wrong."

"Perhaps. Do you intend to help us or hinder us?"

"I help you best by urging your return to the Alouan."

"What danger would we encounter? The Palga is famous for its tranquility."

"Never thwart the Srenki," said Moffamides. "They work their tragic deeds and so protect us all."

Enlightenment came to Elvo; the terrible man of the night before had been one of them. Was Moffamides now conveying an oblique warning or reproach?

"They bear their unhappy lot with pain," intoned Moffamides. "If one is mishandled, the others exact an exaggerated retribution."

"This is nothing to us," said Jemasze. "Inform us as to Poliamides and we will be on our way."

Elvo Glissam frowned off into the sky. Moffamides said: "Fare northeast on a broad reach. Turn into the third track which you will discover on the third day. Follow the track four days to the Aluban, which is a great forest, and at the white pillar ask for Poliamides."

"Very good. You have prepared our fiaps?"

Moffamides stood silent a moment; then he turned and walked away. Five minutes later he returned with a wicker box. "Here are potent fiaps. The green-yellow guards your land-yawl. The orange-black-whites provide for your personal protection. I wish you the joy of whatever fair winds Ahariszeio sees fit to send you."

Moffamides stalked from the yard.

Elvo, Kurgech and Gerd Jemasze climbed aboard the land-yawl; Jemasze activated the auxiliary motor and the yawl rolled out upon the sarai. From the south blew the monsoon breeze. Elvo took the wheel while Kurgech and Jemasze hoisted jib, mainsail and mizzen; off across the resilient soum*

---

*Soum: the thick tough dun lichen which carpets most of the Palga.

rolled the land-yawl. Elvo leaned back in the seat, looked up at the sky, surveyed the landscape, where the only contrast came from moving cloud-shadows, and glanced astern at the diminishing No. 2 Depot. Freedom! Out upon the windy sarai with only space around him! Oh for the life of a Wind-runner!

Jemasze trimmed the sails; the land-yawl jerked forward and gained a speed which Elvo estimated to be quite thirty miles an hour.

The yawl needed little attention at the helm; Elvo used a claw-shaped device to engage the wheel and rose to his feet to revel in the motion. Kurgech and Gerd Jemasze were similarly affected. Kurgech stood by the mainmast, the wind ruffling his sparse amber curls; Jemasze stretched out in the cockpit and broached one of the casks of beer with which he had provisioned the yawl. "No question but what there are worse ways to live," he said.

Methuen rose up the sky. No. 2 Depot had disappeared astern. The sarai looked as before: a dun flatland, relieved here and there by wisps of crisp yellow straw and an occasional low flat flower. Cloud shadows coursed across the soum; the air was fresh, neither cool nor warm, and smelled faintly of straw and a more subtle fragrance from the lichen. There was nothing to be seen, yet Elvo found the landscape anything but monotonous; it changed constantly in a manner he could not easily define: perhaps through clouds and shadows. The wheels, whispering with speed, left a dark track across the soum; occasionally other traces indicated that at some time in the past other sail-wagons had come this way.

Elvo noticed Kurgech and Jemasze talking together and staring astern. Elvo rose to his feet and scanned the southern horizon. He saw nothing and resumed his seat. Since neither Kurgech nor Jemasze saw fit to enlighten him, he asked no questions.

Halfway through the afternoon a group of small humps marked the horizon, which as they approached proved to be sizable hillocks flanked by fields of growing stuff: grain, melons, fruit trees, bread-and-butter plant, pepper plants, elixir vines. The plots were each about an acre in extent; each was watered by a system of tubes radiating from a pond, and each was guarded by a conspicuous fiap.

The time was now late afternoon, and with the pond affording a pleasant place to bathe, Jemasze elected to camp. Elvo looked at the fruit trees, but Jemasze indicated the fiaps. "Beware!"

"The fruit is ripe! In fact some is rotting, going to waste!"

"I advise you to leave it alone."

"Hmmf. What would happen if I ate, say, one of those tangerines?"

"I only know that your madness or death would inconvenience us all, so please control your appetite."

"Certainly," said Elvo stiffly. "By all means."

The three lowered sails, blocked the wheels, bathed in the pond, prepared a meal over a small campfire, then sat back over cups of tea and watched another magnificent sunset.

Twilight became night; the sky shone with stars beyond number. The constellation Gyrgus looped across the zenith; to the southwest shone the Pentadex; in the east rose the blazing miracle which was Alastor Cluster. The men put down pads loose-packed with aerospore on the deck of the yawl and lay down to sleep.

At midnight Elvo half-awoke and lay drowsily musing over the episode of the night before. Reality? Hallucination?...Out on the Palga sounded a soft eery whistle, followed a few minutes later by another such whistle from a different direction. Elvo quietly rose to his feet and went to stand by the mast. A man loomed above him in the starlight. Elvo's heart jumped up in his throat; he gave a croak of dismay. The man turned and made a gesture of annoyance; Elvo recognized Kurgech. He whispered: "Did you hear the whistles?"

"Insects."

"Then why are you standing here?"

"The insects whistle when they are disturbed—perhaps by a night-hawk or a walkinger."

From a distance of no more than ten yards sounded a clear fluting warble. "Gerd Jemasze is down there," muttered Kurgech. "He watches against the skyline."

"For what?"

"For whatever has been following us."

The two stood quiet in the starlight. Half an hour passed. The yawl quivered; Gerd Jemasze spoke in a soft voice. "Nothing."

"I felt nothing," said Kurgech.

"I should have brought a set of sensors," grumbled Jemasze. "Then we could sleep in peace."

"The bugle-bugs serve us as well."

Elvo said: "I thought the Wind-runners molested no one."

"The Srenki molest as they see fit."

Jemasze and Kurgech returned to their pads; Elvo Glissam presently followed.

Dawn flooded the east with pink-crimson light. Clouds burned red, and the sun appeared. No breath of air fluttered the silk whisks on the yawl's shrouds, and the three made no haste over breakfast.

With the wagon becalmed Elvo climbed to the summit of a nearby hill and descended the opposite side, where he discovered a copse of wild pawpaws, apparently unguarded by fiap. The fruit appeared ripe and succulent: round red globes with orange stars at the ends, surrounded by black voluted foliage. Elvo nonetheless eyed the fruit askance and passed it by.

Returning around the base of the hill he met Kurgech with a sack of crayfish he had taken from an irrigation ditch. Elvo mentioned the pawpaws and Kurgech agreed that a good lunch could be made of boiled crayfish and fruit; the two returned to the copse. Kurgech searched for fiaps and found none; the two men picked as much fruit as they could carry and returned around the hill.

Arriving at the land-yawl, they found it looted of all portable gear, equipment and provisions. Gerd Jemasze, coming from a morning plunge in the pond, joined them a moment after they discovered the loss.

Kurgech uttered a set of sibilant Uldra curses directed at Moffamides. "His fiaps were as weak as water; he sent us forth naked."

Gerd Jemasze gave his characteristic curt nod. "Nothing unexpected, of course. What do you see for tracks?"

Kurgech examined the soum. His nose twitched; he leaned closer to the ground and sighted along the surface. "A single man came and went." He moved off twenty yards. "Here he climbed on his vehicle and departed yonder." Kurgech pointed west, around the base of the hills.

Jemasze considered. "There's still only a trace of wind. He can't move at any speed—if he's in a sail-wagon." He squinted along the trail of the vehicle, a pair of dark marks on the soum. "The trail curves; he's sailing around the hill. You follow the track; I'll cut across the hill; we'll catch him on the other side. Elvo, you stay and guard the yawl before someone steals the whole affair."

The two men set off, Kurgech trotting after the tracks; Jemasze scrambling up the hillside.

Kurgech came in sight of the thief-wagon first: a small tall-masted skimmer with three spindly wheels and slatting sails, moving no faster than a walk. At the sight of Kurgech the occupant trimmed his sail, scanned the sky and looked around the circle of the horizon, but saw nothing except Gerd Jemasze approaching from the direction in which he was headed.

Jemasze reached the craft first and held up his hand. "Stop."

The occupant, a middle-aged man of no great stature, turned pale buff eyes up and down Jemasze's frame, luffed his sail and applied the brake. "Why do you hinder my passage?"

"Because you have stolen our belongings. Turn around."

The Wind-runner's face became mulish. "I took only what was available."

"Did you not see our fiaps?"

"The fiap is dead; it spent its magic last year. You have no right to transfer fiaps; such an act is the paltry play of children."

"Last year's fiaps, eh?" mused Jemasze. "How do you know?"

"Isn't it evident? Do you not see the pink strand on the orange? Stand aside; I am not a man for idle conversation."

"Nor are we," said Jemasze. "Turn your craft and sail back to our yawl."

"By no means. I do as I please and you cannot protest; my fiap is fresh and strong."

Jemasze approached the hull of the skimmer. He pointed to the hillside. "See those stones yonder? What if we pile them in front of you and astern? Will your fiap carry you over two piles of rocks?"

"I will sail on before you pile the rocks."

"Then you will sail over my body."

"What of that? Your personal fiap is a joke. Who do you think to befuddle? The fiap was hung on a beer vat to guard the malt from going sour."

Jemasze laughed and pulling the fiap from his head threw it to the ground. "Kurgech, bring stones. We'll wall in this thief so that he'll never depart."

The Wind-runner gave a passionate cry of outrage. "You are morphotes in disguise! Must I always lose my gains to plunderers? Is justice gone from the Palga?"

"We will talk philosophy after we regain our belongings."

Cursing and muttering, the Wind-runner came about and sailed back the way he had come, with Kurgech and Jemasze walking behind.

Halting beside the land-yawl the Wind-runner ill-naturedly passed across the goods he had taken.

Jemasze asked: "Where are you bound?"

"To the depot; where else?"

"Seek out Moffamides the priest; tell him you have met us; tell him what occurred, and tell him that if the fiaps guarding the sky-car are as false as those he gave us, we'll take him down to the Alouan and lock him in a cage forever. He'll never escape us; we'll follow his track wherever he goes. Take him that message, and be certain that he hears you out!"

The Wind-runner, clench-mouthed with rage, tacked off into the south on a freshening breeze.

Elvo and Jemasze loaded the yawl while Kurgech boiled the cray-fish for lunch to be consumed on the way. The sails were hoisted; the yawl rolled briskly into the northeast.

At noon Kurgech pointed across the bow to the sails of three lofty brigantines bellying in the wind. "The first of the tracks."

"If Moffamides gave us proper directions."

"He gave us proper directions; I read at least this much truth in his mind. I read mischief as well, and this has been demonstrated."

"I understand now why Outkers seldom visit the Palga," said Elvo glumly.

"They are not welcomed; this is true."

The brigantines passed in front of the yawl: three beer-wagons, each loaded with three enormous hogsheads. The crews watched the yawl incuriously and ignored Elvo Glissam's wave.

The yawl crossed the track—an avenue of compressed soum—and pointed once more across the open sarai.

An hour later they sailed past another set of irrigated tracts. Wind-runner families worked at the plots: tilling, pulling weeds, harvesting legumes, plucking fruit; their sail-wagons standing nearby. At mid-afternoon the yawl overtook just such a wagon: a six-wheeled schooner with a pair of high masts, three jibs and topsails. Two men leaned on the after rail; children played on the deck; a woman peered through the casements of the aft cabin as the yawl approached. Elvo steered to pass downwind, which he deemed to be the courteous tactic. The Wind-runners however failed to recognize the nicety and gave no acknowledgment to Elvo's cheerful wave. Peculiar people, thought Elvo glumly. Shortly after, the schooner changed course and trundled off to the north, to become a far white spot, then disappear.

The wind had become gusty; to the south a scurf of black clouds rose up into the sky. Jemasze and Kurgech reefed the mainsail, lowered the mizzen and took in the jib; still the yawl bowled across the soum on hissing wheels.

The clouds raced overhead; rain began to fall. The three men hauled down all sails, braked and blocked the wheels, tossed to the ground a heavy metal chain connected through the shrouds to the lightning rod, then took refuge in the aft cuddy. For two hours lightning clawed at the sarai, generating an almost continuous reverberation of thunder; then the storm drifted north; the rain stopped; the wind died, leaving behind an uncanny silence.

The three men crawled forth from the cuddy to find the sun setting through a confused storm-wrack and the sky an inverted carpet of flaring purple-red. While Gerd Jemasze and Elvo put the yawl to rights, Kurgech boiled up a soup in the forward cuddy, and the three men took a supper of pawpaws, soup and hard-bread.

A slow and easy breeze came to blow the remaining storm clouds north; the sky was clear and effulgent with stars. The sarai seemed utterly vacant and lonely, and Elvo was surprised to find Kurgech in a state of obvious uneasiness. After a few minutes Elvo became infected with nervousness and asked: "What's the trouble?"

"Something is drawing upon us."

Jemasze raised his hand to feel the wind. "Shall we sail for an hour or two? There's nothing we can run into."

Kurgech readily agreed. "I will be happy to move."

The sails were hoisted; the yawl swerved around and bore off on a quartering reach into the northeast at an easy ten miles an hour. Kurgech steered by Koryphon's North Star Tethanor, the Toe of the Basilisk.

Four hours they sailed, until midnight, when Kurgech declared: "The imminence is gone. I no longer feel pressure."

"In that case, it is time to stop," said Jemasze. The sails were dropped; the brakes were set; the three laid out their beds and slept.

At dawn they hoisted sail in preparation for the morning wind, which once more came tardily, and the three men sat silently waiting. At last the monsoon arrived and the yawl slid off into the northeast.

After an hour of sailing they crossed the second track, though no sails were visible save a tall narrow triangle far astern.

The sarai began to rise and fall, at first almost imperceptibly, then in long wide hills and dales. Ledges of black trap slanted up from the soum, and for the first time navigation demanded a degree of foresight and strategy. The easiest route most usually lay along the ridges, where the wind blew most freshly and where the ground lay generally flat. Often these ridges ran in inconvenient directions; then the helmsman must direct the craft down one slope and up the one opposite, and often the auxiliary motor was needed to propel the yawl the last fifty or hundred feet to the ridge.

A river meandered across the countryside, at the bottom of a steep-sided terraced valley where the land-yawl could not go, and for several miles they sailed along the brink of the valley, until the river once more swung north.

The tall-sailed wagon they had noticed previously had gained appreciably upon them. Jemasze took binoculars and inspected the craft, then handed the glasses to Kurgech who looked and uttered a soft Uldra curse.

Taking the binoculars, Elvo saw a long black articulated wagon of three segments, each with a notably tall mast and narrow sail: a vehicle intended for high speed and high capability into the wind. Five men rode the deck, hanging to the shrouds or crouched in the cockpit. They wore loose black pantaloons; their torsos were naked and showed the typical cream-brown Wind-runner color. Several wore red scarves to bind their hair. As they moved about the deck they displayed a peculiar jerking agility, which by some trick of association recalled to Elvo the fearsome man who had entered the inn three nights previously. So then: these were Srenki, men whose virtue was the excess of vice, who with leaden zest performed quintessential evil and so redeemed their fellows from turpitude. Elvo's stomach felt cold and heavy. He looked toward Gerd Jemasze, who seemed interested only in the terrain ahead. Kurgech stood by the mast, looking vaguely off into the sky. Elvo began to feel a sweaty desperation; he had come on this trip for complicated reasons, but certainly not in search of death. With loose knees he crossed the cockpit to where Gerd Jemasze stood by the wheel. "Those are Srenki."

"I supposed as much."

"What are you going to do?"

Jemasze glanced over his shoulder at the racing black schooner. "Nothing, unless they molest us."

"Isn't that what they plan?" cried Elvo, his voice rather more shrill than he had intended.

"It looks that way." Jemasze looked up at the sail. "We could probably outrun them straight downwind; their sails tend to blanket each other."

"Then why don't we sail downwind?"

"Because the river valley lies yonder."

Through the binoculars Elvo inspected the black wagon. "They're carrying guns—long rifles."

"Hence I don't shoot at them. They'd shoot back. Apparently they want to take us alive."

Again Elvo studied the onrushing black schooner, until the gestures and grimaces of the Srenki affected him with nausea. In a stifled voice he asked: "What will they do with us?"

Jemasze shrugged. "They're wearing red, which means they've taken vows of revenge. Somehow we've offended them, though I can't imagine how or where or when."

Elvo Glissam scanned the downwind terrain through the binoculars. He called out to Jemasze: "There's a hill ahead! It's too steep to cross and it slopes down into the river valley; we'll have to come about!"

Jemasze demurred. "They'd have us in twenty seconds."

"But—what can we do?"

"Sail. You stand by the reef-roller and make ready to shorten sail when I give you the signal."

Elvo stared numbly at Jemasze. "Shorten sail?"

"Not until I give you the signal."

Elvo hunched to the mast and stood by the reefing gear. The Srenki had narrowed the gap to a hundred yards; the three tall sails seemed to overhang the yawl. To Elvo's amazement Jemasze slackened the sheets to slow the yawl and to allow the schooner to gain even more swiftly. The Srenki could now be perceived in detail. Three stood on the foredeck straining forward, their gaunt faces shadowed under the vertical pink sunlight... To Elvo's consternation, Jemasze once again eased the sheets, allowing the Srenki to gain at an even faster rate. Elvo opened his mouth to scream a protest, then in blind desperation clamped his teeth together and turned away.

Ahead the ground began to slope down toward the river gorge on one hand, up to a round-topped bluff on the other; the yawl heeled and skidded. Behind, the black schooner came rushing, so close that Elvo could hear the hoarse calls of the crew. The slope steepened; the yawl tilted precariously; Elvo, peering over the gunwale, looked a sickening distance down, down, down into the river gorge; he squeezed shut his eyes and clung to the mast. The wind swept down the hillside; the yawl bounced crab-wise down-slope.

"Reef!" called Jemasze. Elvo cast a wild glance astern. The schooner, careening along the slope, was closing in fast; a Srenki on the foredeck hefted a grapnel, preparing to throw it into the cockpit of the yawl. "Reef!" Jemasze called in a voice of brass.

With numb fingers Elvo turned the handle and the mainsail rolled down the mast. A gust hit the yawl; the weather wheels lifted. Elvo's stomach lifted with vertigo; he scrambled for the high side of the deck. The same gust struck the tall sails of the schooner and applied an inexorable leverage. As the weather wheels left the ground, the helmsman put down the helm to prevent a capsize; the schooner trundled wildly down-slope, out of control. The wheels bounded off rocks and bumps; the tall masts jerked and shivered; the sails bulged and flapped. On one of the wilder lurches the mizzen jibed, the helmsman spun the wheel; the schooner bounced off a boulder, flew off a ledge and toppled upside down into the river.

"Reef down!" bawled Jemasze. Elvo cranked the sail almost to invisibility. Jemasze cut on the auxiliary motor. At a careful pace the yawl negotiated the slope of the hill and reached the flatland beyond. Jemasze set the course into the northeast as before.

The yawl sailed across the deserted sarai, through an afternoon so peaceful that Elvo began to doubt the accuracy of his recollection; had the Srenki existed? Surreptitiously he studied Kurgech and Gerd Jemasze, one hardly more cryptic than the other.

The sun sank in a clear sky. The sails were lowered, the wheels locked, and camp made for the night out in the middle of the trackless sarai.

After a supper of potted meat, biscuit and Depot beer, the three men sat on the foredeck, leaning against the cuddy. Elvo could not restrain a question to Gerd Jemasze: "Did you plan that the Srenki schooner should be wrecked?"

Jemasze nodded. "I claim no great wisdom. With their narrow beam and three tall masts they obviously couldn't reach along much of a slope. So I thought to tease them until they sailed themselves down to the river."

Elvo gave a shaky chuckle. "Suppose they didn't go over?"

"We'd have set them back some other way," said Jemasze indifferently.

Elvo fell silent, reflecting that Jemasze's confidence, while reassuring, perfectly typified that quality which Elvo found so exasperating...

Elvo managed a sad chuckle. Jemasze felt competent to meet any challenge. He, Elvo, did not, and in consequence felt resentful: there was the truth of the matter. Elvo assuaged his abraded self-esteem with the reflection that here, at least, was a faculty in which he excelled Gerd Jemasze: he was capable of self-analysis. Gerd Jemasze had obviously never troubled to ponder his own psyche.

He turned to Kurgech and asked a question he never could have asked two weeks previously: "Is anyone on our trail now?"

Kurgech stared off across the twilight. "I feel no near threat. A dark mist hangs around the horizon, far away. Tonight we are safe."

CHAPTER 9

Morning brought a brisk cool breeze and with all sail set, the yawl bowled across the gently heaving sarai: a landscape, thought Elvo, fresh and sweet as springtime. Bustards flew up from under the singing wheels; patches of pink and black periwinkles splotched the otherwise dun soum.

Halfway through the morning they sighted a fleet of brigantines sailing northward, sails straining to the wind: a signal that they had arrived at the third trail, as stipulated by Moffamides. A few minutes later they reached the trail itself, which to Elvo's puzzlement led not north but definitely into the northwest. "We've come a hundred miles or more out of the way," he complained to Jemasze. "If we had sailed north out from the Depot instead of northeast we might have saved ourselves a day's sail."

Jemasze gave somber agreement. "Moffamides evidently preferred that we come this route."

The yawl overtook the house-wagons. Tousle-headed children hung on the rail and pointed; men stood up from the cockpit to stare; women came forth from the cabins, their expressions neither affable nor hostile. As usual Elvo essayed a friendly salute, which the Windrunners ignored.

The trail descended from a region of great heaves and swales upon a flat plain reaching north beyond the horizon. At intervals sink-holes brimming with clear water irrigated fields and plots where grew melons, pulses, sweet vetch and cereals, each area guarded by its fiap.

Northwest across the plain sailed the yawl, sometimes in company with Wind-runner brigantines, more often alone. Long sunny days alternated with nights glittering with stars. Elvo often reflected that here was a life to be envied, a life without circumscription and no routine other than that imposed by the winds and the seasons. Perhaps the Wind-runners were the most sensible folk of all Koryphon, scudding as they did across the open places, with great clouds towering above and glorious sunsets to mark the end of each day.

On the fourth afternoon along the northwest trail, a dark smudge appeared on the horizon, which the binoculars revealed to be a forest of massive dark trees of a species Elvo had never seen before. "This must be Aluban forest," said Jemasze. "We now proceed to a white pillar."

Presently the pillar appeared—an object thirty feet high, constructed of a white lumpy stucco-like substance. At the base of the pillar an old man in a white cassock worked a pestle in a large iron mortar. The yawl coasted to a halt beside the pillar; the old man rose to his feet and, showing the clench-faced glare of a zealot, backed protectively against the white pillar. "Take care with your vehicle; this is the Great Bone; steer aside."

Jemasze performed a courteous gesture to which the old man made no response. "We seek a certain Poliamides," said Jemasze. "Can you direct us?"

Before the old man deigned to answer he dipped a brush in the mortar and applied a white wash to the pillar. Then he pointed the brush toward the forest and spoke in a harsh croaking voice: "Follow the trail; inquire at the hexagon."

Jemasze released the brake; the yawl sailed past the Great Bone toward the Aluban.

At the forest's edge Jemasze halted the wagon; the three men descended warily to the ground. The trees were the most ponderous growths Elvo had yet observed on Uaia: great twisted baulks the color and apparent density of black iron, with sprawling heavy branches and masses of pale gray and gray-green foliage. For several silent moments the three men stood peering into the forest, where the trail wound away among slanting sun-rays and black shadows. Listening, they heard only a dank stillness.

Kurgech said in a heavy voice: "We are expected."

Elvo suddenly became aware that by some tacit understanding leadership of the group had transferred to Kurgech, who now muttered to

Jemasze: "Let Elvo stay with the wagon; you and I will go forward."

Elvo attempted an uneasy protest, but the words stuck in his throat. In an awkward attempt at facetiousness he said: "If you run into trouble, call out for help."

Kurgech said: "There will be no trouble. No hot blood spills in this sacred forest."

Jemasze said softly: "I fear Moffamides has played us a sour joke."

"So much was clear from the first," said Kurgech. "Still, it is better to play the game out, and to act in certitude."

The two set off into the forest and immediately foliage closed out the sky; the trail became narrow and wound back and forth, past banks of moss and clusters of pale star-flowers; in and out of small glades, along dim aisles with pink rays slanting across the vistas. Kurgech moved with a peculiar delicacy, striding on the balls of his feet, turning his head first one way, then the other. Jemasze felt only stillness and peace; he apprehended no danger, nor did Kurgech's attitude suggest more than wariness in the proximity of the unknown.

A glade carpeted with purple sedum opened before them; here stood a hexagonal structure of white stone, twice as tall as a man, open on all sides to the slow airs of the forest. In front of the structure a priest in a white cassock awaited them: a man frail and cold-faced. "Outkers," said the priest, "you have come far, and you are welcome to share the peace of our forest Aluban."

"We have come far indeed," said Jemasze. "As you know we have come in search of Poliamides. Will you take us to him?"

"Certainly, if this is your wish. Come then." The priest set off through the forest; Jemasze and Kurgech followed. The sun was low; the forest had become dim and dark. Looking up, Jemasze stopped short at the sight of a white object: a skeleton in the crotch of the tree. The priest said: "There sits Windmaster Boras Mael, who suspires his soul through the leaves, and who has given his right toe to the Great Bone." He signaled them forward.

Jemasze looking aloft saw skeletons in many of the trees.

The priest, halting once more, spoke in a plangent voice: "Here all weary or troubled souls make their peace with Ahariszeio. Their transitory flesh is buried; their bones embrace the tree; the soul is absorbed and purified and suspired into the holy air of the Palga, to ride the blissful clouds."

"And Poliamides?"

The priest pointed aloft. "There sits Poliamides."

Jemasze and Kurgech studied the skeleton for a moment. Jemasze asked: "How did he die?"

"He went into an introspection so earnest that he neglected to eat or drink, and presently his condition became indistinguishable from death. The errors of his gross vitality are now forgotten and his soul breathes out from the leaves."

With an edge in his voice, Jemasze asked: "Moffamides told you of our coming?"

Kurgech spoke in a low profound voice: "Speak truth!"

The priest replied: "Moffamides explained your presence, as was his duty."

"Moffamides has used us poorly," said Jemasze. "He has wantonly dealt us deceit. We have quite a score to settle with him."

"Patience, my friends, patience and forbearance! Go back now to your Outker lands in humility rather than anger."

"First we will deal with Moffamides."

"Surely you have no grievance with Moffamides," declared the priest. "You required the presence of Poliamides and behold! you have been vouchsafed your desire."

"So we are sent forth on a week's journey with useless fiaps to look at a set of bones? Moffamides will not long enjoy his triumph."

The priest spoke gravely: "It might be wise to moderate your anger. Moffamides truly did you a beneficial service. If you take his intimations to heart, you will apprehend the sorry consequences of ignoble curiosity. Such knowledge is beyond value. Poliamides, for instance, so far overlooked propriety as to accept an Outker's bribe. When he recognized his fault, he suffered a pang of guilt and became moribund."

"I feel that you exaggerate the benign effects of Moffamides' treachery," said Jemasze. "He will not soon again deceive trusting strangers, I assure you of this."

"The Palga is vast," murmured the priest.

"The spot on which Moffamides stands is small," said Jemasze. "We can discover this spot through Blue magic. As for now, we have seen sufficient of Poliamides."

The priest turned wordlessly and led the way back through the forest to the hexagon. Mounting the white stone porch, he stood smiling impassively. Kurgech stared up at him. Slowly Kurgech raised his right hand. The priest's eyes followed the movement. Kurgech raised his left hand, and the priest smiling a now strained smile seemed to watch both hands separately, an eye for each. From Kurgech's left palm came a sudden shattering blast of white light. Kurgech called out in a deep calm voice: "Speak what is in your mind!"

Thrusting through the priest's lips, as if of their own volition, came words: "You will never live to see Outker land, poor fools!"

"Who will kill us?"

The priest had recovered his poise. "You have seen Poliamides," he said shortly. "Now go your way."

Jemasze and Kurgech returned by the now nearly invisible track to the edge of Aluban the sacred forest.

Elvo, standing against the stern of the yawl, was a forlorn and worried figure; at the sight of Gerd Jemasze and Kurgech, he came forward in obvious relief. "You've been gone so long; I began to wonder what had happened to you."

"We found Poliamides," said Jemasze. "His right toe is part of the Great Bone. In short—he is a dead skeleton."

Elvo stared toward the forest indignantly. "Why did Moffamides send us here?"

"This is as good a place as any to hang up our bones."

Elvo stared at Jemasze as if doubting his seriousness, then turned and looked dubiously into the Aluban. "What does he gain?"

"I guess they don't want Outkers investigating the erjin trade—especially members of the SEE."

Elvo grinned wanly at the pleasantry. Jemasze held up his hand to a faint cool breeze seeping down from the north. "Hardly enough to move us."

"This is not a good place," said Kurgech. "We should depart."

Jemasze and Elvo Glissam hoisted the sails. The yawl responded sluggishly and rolled south along the edge of the forest.

The breeze died; with limp sails the yawl coasted to a stop, only fifty feet distant from the loom of the trees. "It appears that we camp here," said Jemasze.

Kurgech looked toward the forest but said nothing.

Jemasze lowered the sails and blocked the wheels; Kurgech rummaged among the stores in the forward cuddy; Elvo gingerly approached the edge of the forest and returned with an armful of fuel. Jemasze grunted with something like disapproval but made no protest as Elvo kindled a fire beside the yawl.

For supper they ate bread and dry meat, a few morsels of dried fruit and drank the last of the Depot beer. Elvo discovered himself to be neither hungry nor thirsty; he felt rather a strong lassitude and could think only of stretching himself out beside the fire and drowsing away…What a curious fire, thought Elvo. The flames seemed to be made not of hot leaping gases, but syrup or jelly; they moved sluggishly, like the petals of a monstrous red flower blowing in a warm wind. Elvo looked languidly toward Gerd Jemasze to see whether or not he had noted this odd phenomenon…Jemasze conversed with Kurgech; Elvo heard what they were saying:

"—strong and near."

"Can you break it?"

"Yes. Bring wood from the forest—and six long poles."

Jemasze spoke to Elvo. "Wake up. You're being hypnotized. Help me bring wood."

Numbly Elvo lurched to his feet and followed Jemasze to the forest. He now felt alert and awake, and burning with rage. Jemasze's arrogance for a fact knew no bounds; an outrage the way he presumed to give orders! Well then, what of this heavy gnarled branch? An excellent club.

"Elvo!" rasped Jemasze. "Wake up!"

"I am awake," muttered Elvo.

"Well then, carry wood to the fire."

Elvo blinked, yawned, rubbed his eyes. He had been asleep. Sleepwalking, thinking terrible thoughts. He dragged dead branches to the fire. Kurgech cut six crooked poles and planted them into the ground to form a hexagon twelve feet in diameter, and connected the top ends with lengths of cord. Between the poles he built six small fires and on the cords he hung small trifles of equipment: clothes, binoculars, handguns: all articles imported to the Palga.

"Stay inside the ring of fires," said Kurgech. "We have made this alien land; they must now put forth great force to reach us."

Elvo said plaintively: "I don't understand anything of what's happening."

"The priests are using mind-magic against us," said Kurgech. "They use their holy objects and ancient instruments, and they can exert great power."

"Don't allow yourself to daydream or go drowsy," Jemasze told him. "Keep the fires alight."

Elvo said shortly, "I'll do my best."

Minutes passed: ten, fifteen, twenty.Peculiar, thought Elvo, how the fires tended to smoulder rather than burn. The flames guttered and recoiled in smoky red wallows of flame. Out in the darkness he sensed squat shapes watching him with eyes like puddles of ink.

Jemasze said: "Don't panic; just ignore them."

Elvo laughed hoarsely. "I'm sweating; I'm panting; my teeth are chattering. I'm not about to panic, but the fires are going out."

"I guess it's time I used some Outker magic," said Jemasze. He spoke to Kurgech: "Ask how they'd like a forest fire."

A queer stillness gripped the air. Jemasze picked up a flaming brand from the central fire and took a step toward the Aluban.

Tension broke like a snapping twig. The fires blazed normally; Elvo saw no more crouching shapes: only the starlit landscape. Gerd Jemasze dropped the brand back in the fire and stood watching the forest in that pose of negligent disdain which Elvo had so often found irritating. He felt for breeze; the night was dead calm; they lacked the option to move away, out upon the wholesome sarai.

Kurgech remarked: "Rage and fear hang in the air. They may attempt more ordinary work."

Suddenly in a mood of urgency, Jemasze said: "To the forest then, where at least we are safe from ambush."

The three men climbed into trees and became invisible in the deep gloom under the foliage. Twenty yards away, out on the sarai, the land-yawl stood alone in the firelight. For the hundredth time, Elvo reflected that if by some lucky chance he eventually were restored to the security of Olanje, he would have memories to color the remainder of his life-time. He doubted if ever again he would undertake a journey across the Palga...He strained his ears. Silence. He could see neither Kurgech nor Jemasze who had ensconced themselves somewhere off to his left. Elvo gave a sad humorless chuckle. The whole affair seemed absurd and melodramatic—until he remembered how the landscape surrounding the yawl had constricted and pressed in upon him.

Time passed. Elvo began to feel uncomfortable. The time must be midnight. He wondered how long Jemasze proposed to stay in the tree. Surely not till dawn! In another five or ten minutes either Jemasze or Kurgech must certainly decide that the threat had diminished, that it was time to get some rest.

Ten minutes went by, and fifteen, then half an hour. Elvo took a breath in preparation for calling cautiously across the dark to find how much longer they meant to perch in the trees. He opened his mouth, then closed it again. Jemasze might disapprove of such a call. He had not expressly commanded silence, but Elvo could see that silence might be considered an integral adjunct to the circumstances. He decided to hold his tongue. Kurgech and Jemasze no doubt were also uncomfortable; if they could endure the inconvenience, he could do so as well. To ease his cramped legs Elvo cautiously rose to a standing position. His head bumped on a branch which swung away and scraped his cheek. Elvo leaned back to see silhouetted against the sky, not a branch, but a skeleton, the bones wired together. Beside his face dangled the right foot. Heart pumping, Elvo quickly returned to his former position.

A sound, a thud, muffled noises, a thrashing among the dry leaves. Elvo jumped to the ground, to find Jemasze and Kurgech looking down at the hulk of a man prone on the ground. Elvo started to speak: Jemasze signaled him to silence…No sound. A minute passed. The man at their feet began to stir. Jemasze and Kurgech dragged him toward the yawl. Elvo picked up a long metal object and followed; he discovered the object to be a Wind-runner rifle. Jemasze and Kurgech dropped the man into the glow of the firelight. Elvo uttered an ejaculation of surprise. "Moffamides!"

Moffamides stared into the fire with eyes like cusps of polished flint. He made no move when Kurgech bound his ankles and wrists, then with Jemasze's help tossed him up onto the deck of the yawl like a sack of beans.

Jemasze hoisted the sail, which bellied to a cold night breeze Elvo had not even noticed. The yawl rolled away to the southeast, leaving the sacred forest Aluban astern.

CHAPTER 10

Dawn flooded the sarai with wan pink illumination. Clouds to south and west glowed crimson and rose; Methuen climbed into the sky.

At an oasis surrounded by feathery Uaian acacia the yawl made a breakfast halt. Moffamides had not yet spoken a word.

Beside the pond were neglected plots where fruit and berries grew wild. The fiaps were weathered and inoperative, and Elvo went off with a bucket to harvest whatever he found ripe.

When he returned he found Kurgech busy at the construction of a most peculiar device. From acacia withes he built a cubical frame two feet on the side, lashing the corners with twine. He cut up an old blanket and attached it to the frame to make a rude box. Across one side of the box he attached a board through which he bored a hole half an inch in diameter.

The work was being accomplished out of Moffamides' range of vision. Elvo could no longer contain his curiosity; he asked Jemasze: "What is Kurgech making?"

"The Uldras call it a 'crazy-box'."

Jemasze spoke so shortly that Elvo, sensitive to real or imagined slights, forbore to ask any further questions. He watched in fascination as Kurgech cut a circle of fiberboard about six inches in diameter and painted it with a pair of black and white spirals. Elvo marveled to watch the deftness of his touch. Suddenly he saw Kurgech in a new light: not the semi-barbarian with peculiar customs and odd garments, but a proud man of many talents. With embarrassment Elvo recalled his previously half-condescending attitude toward Kurgech—and this in spite of the fact that he was a member of the Redemptionist League!

Kurgech's work was now more intricate, and an hour passed before he was satisfied with his contraption. The disk now turned on the inside of the box and was connected by a shaft to a small wind-powered propeller.

Elvo decided that he did not entirely approve of the device and what he divined to be its purpose; he watched in a mixture of repugnance and fascination as Kurgech, intent and earnest, completed his 'crazy-box'. In a somewhat sardonic voice Elvo asked: "Will it work?"

Kurgech turned him a cool clear glance and asked softly: "Would you care to test it?"

"No."

Meanwhile Moffamides had sat propped on the deck of the yawl, in the full glare of Methuen, with neither food nor drink. Kurgech went to the forward cuddy and from his case of effects brought forth a vial of dark liquid. He poured water into a mug, mixed in a small quantity of the liquid and brought it to Moffamides.

"Drink."

Without words Moffamides drank. Kurgech applied a blindfold to the priest's eyes, then went to sit on the foredeck. Jemasze meanwhile bathed in the pond.

Half an hour passed. Kurgech rose to his feet. He cut a pair of slits at right angles to each other in the cloth covering the bottom of the box, and a circular hole at the top. He now took up the box and placed it over Moffamides' head and arranged a pair of sticks across the priest's shoulders to support the device. After assuring himself that the propeller turned freely in the wind, Kurgech reached inside the box and removed the blindfold.

Elvo started to speak; Gerd Jemasze, returning from his bath, sternly signaled him to silence.

Ten minutes passed. Kurgech went to crouch beside Moffamides. He began to chant in a soft voice: "Peace; you rest at ease; sleep is sweet, when troubles dissolve and fear is gone. Sleep is sweet; tranquility is near. It is good to ease yourself; to rest and forget."

The propeller slowed as the wind eased; Kurgech flicked it with his finger to keep it turning and inside the box the spiral-painted disk turned in front of Moffamides' eyes.

"The spiral turns," crooned Kurgech. "It brings out to in. It also brings you yourself from out to in, and you rest at ease. From out to in, from out to in, and I say to you: how pleasant to relax where nothing can hurt you. Can anyone or anything hurt you?"

From within the box came Moffamides' voice: "Nothing."

"Nothing can hurt you unless I command, and now there is nothing but peace and rest and the ease of helping your friends. Whom do you wish to help?"

"My friends."

"Your friends are here. The people here are your friends, and only these people here. Notice, they cut your bonds and make you comfortable." Kurgech released the cords binding Moffamides' arms and legs. "How pleasant to be happy and comfortable with your friends. Are you happy?"

"Yes, I am happy."

"The spiral has wound your attention into your brain and the only outside channel is my voice. You must now be deaf to other thoughts and the complaints of others. Only your friends, who give you peace and ease deserve your loyalty. Whom do you trust, whom do you wish to help?"

"My friends."

"And where are they?"

"They are here."

"Yes, of course. I will now take the box from your head and you will see your friends. Once, long ago, there were some trivial differences, but no one cares anymore about these matters. Your friends are here; nothing else is important."

Kurgech lifted the box from Moffamides' head. "Breathe the fresh air and look at your friends."

Moffamides drew a deep breath and looked from face to face. His eyes were glazed; the pupils had constricted, perhaps under the influence of Kurgech's drug.

Kurgech asked: "Do you see your friends?"

"Yes, they are here."

"Of course! You are now one with your friends, and you want to help them in everything they do. The old ways were bad; your friends want to learn about the old ways so that you can rest at ease. There are no secrets among friends. What is your cult name?"

"Inver Elgol."

"And your private name, known only to yourself, which knowledge you now want to provide your friends?"

"Totulis Amedio Falle."

"How pleasant to share secrets with friends. It eases the soul. Where did Poliamides take the Outker?"

"To the Place of Rose-and-Gold."

"Ah, indeed! And what is this 'Place of Rose-and-Gold'?"

"It is where the erjins are trained."

"It must be an interesting place to visit. Where is it?"

"At Al Fador in the mountains west of Depot No. 2."

"And this is where Poliamides took the Outker Uther Madduc?"

"Yes."

"Is there danger there?"

"Yes, much danger."

"How could we go and be safe?"

"We could not go safely to Al Fador."

"Uther Madduc and Poliamides went to Al Fador and returned safely. Could we not do the same?"

"They saw Al Fador but made no close approach."

"We will do the same, if it is still safe to do so. How shall we steer?"

"Southwest, hard on the wind."

The land-yawl careened across the sarai. Moffamides sat hunched in a corner of the cockpit, apathetic, morose, silent. Elvo watched him in fascination. What went on in the priest's mind? Elvo attempted conversation to no avail; Moffamides merely stared at him.

Five days the yawl sailed, from dawn until dark, and later yet when the sarai lay flat and the stars provided guidance for the helmsman. The two trails were crossed; the yawl sailed a region to the north of the hill where they had made their first camp, then entered a hot and dreary tract where dust lay on the soum and lifted under the wheels as they passed. The Volwodes came into view: a far shadow across the south which became a cluster of steel-gray crags high against the sky.

Elvo was now as apathetic as Moffamides. He had lost all interest in the enslavement of the erjins, which at any rate could most expeditiously be attacked from the forums of Olanje. Only a day's run to the south lay No. 2 Depot but he dared not suggest any truncation of the journey. As always, he found Gerd Jemasze's moods impenetrable. As for Kurgech, Elvo had reverted to his earlier opinions. The man was cunning and wise, competent in his own milieu, which was not necessarily the environment where Elvo himself cared to excel. All things considered, he would be pleased to return to Olanje. Schaine Madduc? A girl delicious to look at, with a head full of charming notions: by now she also must be bored with Uaia and might well choose to accompany him back to Szintarre.

If he survived the visit to Al Fador…Elvo examined Moffamides, wondering as to his mental condition. Hypnotic suggestion, so he had been given to understand, could not be relied upon to persist. A clever ill-intentioned man like Moffamides might feign subservience, the more effectively to work an act of treachery. He voiced none of his suspicions to Jemasze or Kurgech who presumably knew as much about the matter as he did.

The Volwodes reached high into the pink-blue sky: barren crags marked with black thorn-bush and a few stunted sere-trees. When the yawl halted for the night, an erjin came to watch from a distance of about fifty yards. It slowly raised its massive arms and extended its talons to attack position; the ruff at its neck began to bristle. Jemasze brought forth his gun, but the erjin suddenly abandoned its aggressive posture. Its ruff subsided and after watching another minute it trotted off to the west.

"Curious conduct," mused Jemasze. Through his binoculars he watched the creature lope away. Elvo turned to find Moffamides staring after the erjin, and his posture was not that of a man dazed and subservient.

A few minutes later Elvo voiced his apprehensions to Gerd Jemasze.

"So far he's still under control," said Jemasze. "Kurgech has tested him. What may happen I don't know. If he wants to live he won't betray us."

"What of erjins? Won't they attack us tonight?"

"Erjins don't see well in the dark. They're not likely to attack by night."

Elvo nevertheless went to his bed in a state of uneasiness. Far into the night he lay awake listening to the sounds of the sarai: a low moaning from the direction of the foothills which presently faded into silence; a chittering close at hand; an angry whirring at various pitches; from far away a throbbing gong-like sound so exquisite that something strange rose up within Elvo's mind to terrify him. Kurgech had tied a steel cord from Moffamides' ankle to his own, then had rubbed it with a dry rag until it squeaked and set Elvo's nerves on edge; whether for this reason or from the effect of the crazy-box, Moffamides lay inert the whole of the night.

Elvo awoke to find dawn-light burning the upper crags of the Volwodes.

Breakfast was brief and meager. Moffamides seemed more glum than ever and sat to the edge of the deck staring north, away from the mountains.

Jemasze went to squat beside him. "How far now to the training area?"

Moffamides looked up with a start, and the expressions of his face underwent a set of quicksilver changes: from abstraction to surly contempt, to affability and candor, to something swift and wild, like desperation. Elvo, watching, suspected that Kurgech's suggestions had ceased to exert an absolute influence over Moffamides.

Jemasze patiently repeated his question. Moffamides rose to his feet and pointed. "It lies somewhere beyond that ridge, toward the grim Volwodes. I have never been there. I can guide you no further."

Kurgech spoke in a mild voice: "I notice tracks yonder: perhaps they were laid by Uther Madduc."

Jemasze asked Moffamides, "Is this the case?"

"I suppose it is possible."

Hard on a breeze from the west, the yawl followed the tracks presumably laid by Uther Madduc's skimmer. A second set of tracks joined those which guided them, to Elvo's mystification. "It looks as if Uther Madduc had been followed!"

"More probably they are the tracks of Uther Madduc coming and Uther Madduc going," said Jemasze.

"I suppose you're right."

Below a bluff of red and gray sandstone Uther Madduc's trail came to an end. Jemasze dropped the sails and secured the brakes. Moffamides climbed laboriously to the ground and stood with shoulders hunched. "You need me no more," said Moffamides. "I have done my best for you; I will now take my leave."

"Here?" asked Jemasze. "In the wilderness? How will you survive?"

"I can reach the Depot in three or four days. There is food and water to be had along the way."

"What of the erjins? They infest the region."

"I fear no erjins; I am a priest of Ahariszeio."

Kurgech came forward and touched Moffamides on the shoulder; Moffamides leaned away quivering but seemed unable to detach himself. Kurgech said: "Totulis Amedio Falle, you may now forget your worries; you are with your friends whom you wish to help and protect."

The priest's head jerked back; his eyes took on a flinty glaze. "You are my friends," he declared without conviction. "This I know; hence, by corollary, I would grieve to see your corpses. So I must state that even now an erjin prince watches you. He has been talking to my mind; he wonders if he should attack."

"Tell him no," said Kurgech. "Explain that we are your friends."

"Yes, I have already done so, although my thoughts are somewhat confused."

Jemasze asked, "Where is the erjin?"

"He stands among the rocks."

"Invite him to come forth," said Jemasze. "I prefer erjins in full view to those skulking among the rocks."

"He is fearful of your guns."

"We will do him no harm if he restrains his own hostility."

Moffamides looked toward the rocks, and the erjin came forward: a magnificent creature as large as any Jemasze had ever seen; mustard-yellow on chest and belly, brown-black on back and legs. A russet ruff, starting between the ridges of cartilage shielding the optical processes, hung down across the bone-plated shoulders. It approached without haste, apparently neither fearful nor hostile, and halted at a distance of fifty feet.

Moffamides spoke to Jemasze: "It wants to know why we are here, instead of elsewhere."

"Explain that we are travelers from the Alouan, interested in the scenery."

Facing the erjin, Moffamides flourished his arms and uttered a set of hissing vocables. The erjin stood immobile except for a jerking of its ruff.

Kurgech instructed the priest: "Inquire the easiest route to the training station."

Moffamides performed new flourishes and uttered another set of sounds. The erjin responded as a man might, by turning and raising one of its massive arms, to indicate the southwest.

"Ask how far," said Jemasze.

Moffamides put the question; the erjin responded with a set of soft sibilants. "No great distance," said Moffamides. "Two hours more or less."

Jemasze looked skeptically sidewise at the erjin. "Why is it here to meet us?"

Kurgech interposed a gentle remark: "Perhaps our friend Moffamides sent a mind-message ahead."

Moffamides said weakly: "Sheer chance, undoubtedly."

"Does it plan to attack us?"

"I can declare nothing with assurance."

Jemasze grunted. "I have never before seen a wild erjin so mild."

"The Volwode erjin is different from the wild erjin of the Alouan," said Moffamides. "It is a different race, so to speak."

Kurgech walked off in the direction the erjin had indicated and scrutinized the ground. He called back to Jemasze: "The trail is here."

Jemasze looked at the yawl, then glanced at Elvo, who divined that Jemasze was about to require that he remain to guard the vehicle. Jemasze however turned to Moffamides. "We need a fiap to guard the wagon: of better quality than you provided before."

"The vehicle is safe," said Moffamides bluffly, "unless a band of Srenki pass by, which is hardly likely."

"Nevertheless, I would prefer to hang a strong fiap on the yawl."

With poor grace Moffamides took bangles and ribbons from the previous fiaps and contrived a new device. "It lacks magic; it is only an admonitory fiap but it will serve adequately."

The four men set forth up a barren gully, with Kurgech leading the way. Moffamides walked second, then Elvo, and Gerd Jemasze brought up the rear. The erjin followed at a discreet distance.

The way became steep; the gully caught and reflected the sun's pink heat; when the group reached the ridge they stood panting and sweating. The erjin came up to join them, standing so close to Elvo that his skin prickled. From the corner of his eye he glanced along the creature's arm, with its curious black talons and the finger-like palps sprouting from the base of the talons. With a single quick motion, thought Elvo, the erjin could rip him to ribbons. Elvo gingerly sidled two or three steps away. He asked Moffamides: "Why is this creature so different from the Alouan erjins?"

Moffamides showed no interest in the subject. "There is no great difference."

"I notice considerable difference," said Elvo. "This creature is docile. Has it been tamed or trained?"

Moffamides put a question to the erjin, then replied to Elvo: "Kurgech is what it calls the 'ancient enemy' who displays a 'green soul' and hence the erjin's kill-fury* is not aroused. You and Gerd Jemasze are Outkers, and inconsequential."

Jemasze asked: "So why does it follow us?"

Moffamides replied in a dispirited voice: "It has nothing better to do; perhaps it intends to be of help."

Jemasze gave a snort of skepticism and studied the landscape through binoculars, while Kurgech cast about the wind-scoured barrens for the trail of Uther Madduc, without immediate success.

The erjin moved forward past Elvo to attract the attention of Moffamides; a half-telepathic colloquy ensued. Moffamides called to Jemasze: "It says Uther Madduc crossed the plateau and traversed that middle ridge."

The erjin loped across the flat and stood waiting; when the men failed to respond briskly, it made urgent signals.

Kurgech went to investigate; the others followed more slowly. Kurgech scanned the seared rubble and somewhere saw signs to reassure him. "This is the trail."

The erjin led the way up a tumble of granite boulders, jumping from surface to surface without effort. At the ridge it paused and seemed almost to strike a conscious pose.

The men reached the ridge and again halted to rest. Beyond, a slope supporting a sparse growth of brown scutch and wire-weed descended to the lip of a great gorge. The erjin started off again, on a long slant-wise course, across a field of loose pebbles.

---

*Kill-fury: a weak rendering of a word signifying the explosive release of a vast pent quantity of emotion, like the breaking of a dam or throwing wide a gate.

Elvo marveled at the trust Jemasze and Kurgech allowed the creature, which must by any sane reckoning be considered baleful. He put a tentative question to Jemasze: "Where do you think it's taking us?"

"Along Uther Madduc's trail."

"Aren't you suspicious of its good intentions? Suppose it's taking us on a wild goose chase?"

"Kurgech isn't worried. He's the tracker."

Elvo went to walk beside Kurgech. "Is this the way Uther Madduc came?"

Kurgech signified assent.

"How can you be sure? These rocks don't take tracks."

"The trail is evident. Notice: there a pebble has been disturbed. It shows a side which is not sunburned. See there: the web of dust has been broken. The erjin leads us accurately."

For a period the course led down-slope; then, where a gully seemed to afford a route to the bottom of the gorge, the erjin veered away. Kurgech stopped short. Jemasze asked: "What's the trouble?"

"Madduc and Poliamides went down that gully. The trail does not go where he wants to lead us."

They looked after the erjin, who had paused to make urgent signals. Moffamides said uneasily: "It takes you the way your friends came."

"Their trail leads down into the gorge."

"The erjin gives me information. The way is difficult here, but easier ahead."

Jemasze stood looking first one way, then the other. Elvo thought that he had never before seen Jemasze indecisive. Finally, without enthusiasm, Jemasze said: "Very well, we'll see where he takes us."

The erjin took them along a laborious route indeed: up a steep bank of crumbling conglomerate, across a tumble of boulders where small blue lizards basked and glided, up to a ridge and down the slope opposite. The erjin ran at an easy lope; the men strained and panted to maintain the pace. Sunlight glared from the rocks and shimmered in the air across the gorge; the erjin danced ahead like a fire demon.

The erjin halted as if in sudden doubt as to its destination; Jemasze spoke tersely over his shoulder to Moffamides: "Find out where it's taking us."

"Where the other Outker went," said Moffamides hurriedly. "This way is easier than clambering down a cliff. You can see for yourself!" He indicated the terrain ahead, where the walls of the gorge relaxed and fell back.

The erjin once more loped ahead, and led the way down to the floor of the valley, a place in dramatic contrast to the stark upper slopes. The air was cool and shadowed; a slow full stream welled quietly from pool to pool under copses of pink and purple fern-trees and dark Uaian cypress.

Kurgech studied the pale sand beside the stream and gave a grunt of grudging surprise: "The creature has not misled us. There are tracks; for a fact, Uther Madduc and Poliamides came this way."

The erjin moved off down the valley and signaled again, as urgent and impatient as before. The men followed more deliberately than it thought appropriate; it ran ahead, halted to look back, signaled and ran forward again. Kurgech, however, stopped short and bent his head over the tracks. "There is something peculiar here."

Jemasze bent over the tracks; Elvo looked from the side, while Moffamides stood fretting and nervous. Kurgech pointed down at the sand. "This is the track left by Poliamides. He wears the flat-toed Windrunner sandal. This, with the hard heel-mark, is the track of Uther Madduc. Before Poliamides walked first; he led the way with a nervous step, as might be expected. Here Uther Madduc walks first; he strides in excitement and haste. Poliamides comes behind, and notice where he pauses to look behind him. They are not approaching their goal; they are leaving, in stealth and haste."

All turned to look back up the valley, except Moffamides who watched the other three men and made small nervous gestures. The erjin whistled and fluted. Moffamides said fretfully: "Let us not delay; the erjin is becoming captious and may refuse to assist us."

"We need no more assistance," said Jemasze. "We're going back up the valley."

"Why go to the trouble?" cried Moffamides. "The tracks lead downstream!"

"Nevertheless, this is where we wish to go. Inform the erjin that we no longer need its help."

Moffamides transmitted the message; the erjin gave a rumble of displeasure. Moffamides turned once more to Jemasze: "There is no need to go into the canyon!" But Jemasze had already started along Uther Madduc's trail. The erjin approached on long silky strides, then uttered an appalling scream and bounded forward with arms extended and talons spread. Elvo stood paralyzed; Moffamides cowered; Kurgech jerked aside; Jemasze aimed his hand-gun and destroyed the creature as it sprang through the air.

The four men stood motionless, staring at the corpse. Moffamides began to moan softly under his breath.

"Quiet!" growled Kurgech. Jemasze thrust the gun back into his waistband, then turned and continued up the canyon, the others following. Moffamides came at the rear, walking lethargically. He began to lag behind; Kurgech fixed him with a glare, and Moffamides obediently hurried his steps.

The valley walls, gradually steepening, became sheer precipices, reaching from the valley floor to the brink. In the soil grew copses of trees: jinkos, banglefruit, Uaian willow, blue-baise. Presently patches of cultivation became evident: yams, pulse, yellow-pod, tall white stalks of cereal molk, red pongee bushes burdened with purple-black berries. Here was a secret Arcadia, thought Elvo, still and quiet and solemn. He found himself walking with soft steps and holding his breath to listen. The trail became a narrow road; apparently they were close upon habitation.

The four men went forward even more warily, using the trees for cover, keeping to the shadow of the steep south walls. Underfoot the ground suddenly became a pavement of pink marble, cracked and discolored. A great grotto opened into the side of the cliff, sheltering what appeared to be a temple of most intricate construction fabricated from rose quartz and gold.

Entranced, the four men approached the shrine, if such it were, and saw, to their stupefaction, that the entire edifice had been carved from a single mass of pink quartz, heavily shot with gold. The front façade, forty feet high, was disposed into seven tiers, each showing eleven niches. The quartz everywhere glowed with sheets and filaments of gold; with consummate craft the artisans had worked their scenes to the shape of the natural metal, and the carving of each niche seemed immanent to the rock itself, as if it had always existed, as if the scenes and subjects of the carvings were possessed of natural truth.

The subject matter of the carvings was battle, between stylized erjins and morphotes, both caparisoned in a strange and particular kind of armor or battle dress, using what appeared to be energy weapons of sophisticated design.

Elvo, in a rapturous daze, touched a carving, and where his fingertips removed a film of dust the rose quartz glowed with a light so vital that it seemed to pulse like blood.

In the bottom tier, or gallery, six openings penetrated the shrine. Elvo entered the aperture farthest left and found himself in a tall narrow hall curving so as to emerge at the aperture farthest right. The light in the passage, filtered through several panes and screens of rose quartz, seemed almost palpably dark rose-red, heavy as old wine. Every square inch had been carved with microscopic precision; gold shone bright, and every detail was evident. In awe Elvo walked the length of the hall. Emerging, he re-entered the shrine, using the next aperture toward the center; here the light was livelier and rose-coral, like the flesh of a canchineel plum. This passage was two-thirds the length of the first. Upon his exit he turned into the central passage, where the light glowed ardent pink, and the gold plaques and filaments glistened against the outside light.

Returning to the front he stood contemplating the seven-tiered façade. A treasure, he thought, to amaze the world, and worlds beyond, and the entire Gaean Reach! He approached and studied the detail. The stylistic conventions were almost incomprehensible; the organization of the various segments could not at once be grasped. It seemed that erjins battled morphotes, each group almost unrecognizable for its grotesque accoutrements; erjins flew through the air in vehicles like none seen across the Gaean Reach; erjins stood triumphant above corpses of what seemed to be men. An insight came to Elvo; he turned in excitement to Gerd Jemasze: "This must be a memorial, or an historical record! In the passages are detail; the exterior niches are like a table of contents."

"As good a guess as any."

Kurgech had gone off to cast for tracks; he now returned and indicated a ravine choked with blue jinkos, with a dozen pink parasol trees tilting crazily above. "Up on the brink we discovered Uther Madduc's tracks. They led down yonder gulch. Poliamides brought him here, then took him up the valley."

Elvo pondered the seven-tiered shrine of rose quartz and gold. He asked: "Is this Uther Madduc's wonderful joke? Why should he laugh at this?"

"There is more to see," said Jemasze. "Let's go on up the valley."

"Caution," said Kurgech. "Uther Madduc returned much faster than he went."

For a quarter-mile the track led beside the river, then into a copse of solemn black-gums which choked the valley floor.

Kurgech led the way, step by silent step. Methuen hung directly above; pink glimmer from ahead seeped through the forest, where the shadows were velvety black.

The path left the forest. Standing in concealment, the four men looked out at the compound from which erjins were sent forth to servitude.

Elvo's first emotion was deflation. Had he come so far, endured so much only to look at a few nondescript stone buildings around a dusty compound? He could sense that neither Jemasze nor Kurgech intended to make any closer investigation, and Moffamides displayed anxiety tantamount to sheer funk.

Moffamides tugged at Jemasze's arm. "Let us go at once. We stand here in peril of our lives!"

"Strange! You gave us no such previous warning."

"Why should I?" Moffamides spoke in spiteful desperation. "The erjin intended to take you to Tanglin Falls. By now you would be far away and gone."

"There's little to see," said Jemasze. "Where is the danger?"

"It is not for you to ask."

"Then we will wait and see for ourselves."

Into the compound came a dozen erjins, to stand in a desultory group. Four men in priestly white gowns emerged from one of the stone buildings; from another came two more erjins and another man, also dressed as a priest. Without warning, Moffamides lunged forward from the forest and ran yelling toward the compound. Jemasze cursed under his breath and snatched out his gun; he aimed, then made an exasperated sound and held his fire. Elvo, watching in horror, felt a surge of gratitude toward Jemasze: unjust to kill the miserable Moffamides, who owed them no loyalty.

"We'd better leave," said Jemasze, "and quick. We'll go up the gulch where Madduc came down; that should be the shortest route back to the wagon."

They ran through the forest, along the trail beside the cultivation. They forded the river and made for the wooded ravine opposite the shrine.

From the forest burst a group of erjins. They saw the three men and veered in pursuit. Jemasze fired his handgun; one of the erjins, pierced by a needle of dexax, collapsed in a broken heap; the others fell flat and brought forth long Wind-runner guns. Jemasze, Kurgech and Elvo scrambled for the shelter of the trees at the mouth of the gully, and the pellets passed harmlessly by.

Jemasze aimed the gun carefully and killed another erjin, but behind came a dozen more, and Elvo cried out in frustration: "Run! It's our only chance! Run!"

Jemasze and Kurgech ignored him. Elvo looked frantically around the landscape, hoping for some miraculous succor. The sun had passed to the side; pink light suffused the gorge, and the seven-tiered shrine gave back an eery beauty. Even in his terror Elvo wondered who had built it. Erjins, undoubtedly. How long ago? Under what circumstances?

Jemasze and Kurgech fired again and again at the erjins, who retreated into the forest. "They'll be climbing up from the valley and shooting down on us," said Jemasze. "We've got to reach the top first!"

Up the gully they climbed, hearts pounding in their chests, lungs aching for air. The sky began to open out; the rim of the tableland hung close above. From below came desultory shots, striking and exploding much too close for comfort; glancing back, Elvo saw erjins running easily after them up the trail.

They gained the rim of the tableland to stand sobbing for breath. Elvo dropped to his hands and knees, breath rasping in his throat, only to hear Jemasze's remark: "There they come. Let's get going!"

Elvo staggered to his feet and saw a dozen erjins at the edge of the plateau a quarter-mile to the north. Jemasze took a moment to scan the landscape. Due east, beyond a succession of descending ridges, slopes and gullies, the land-yawl awaited them. If they attempted to flee in this direction they would present targets to the long rifles of the erjins and soon be killed. A hundred yards south rose a broken pyramid of rotten gneiss: a natural redoubt which offered at least temporary protection. The three men scrambled up the loose scree to the top, finding an almost flat area fifty feet in diameter. Jemasze and Kurgech immediately threw themselves flat and crawling to the edge began to shoot at the erjins on the plateau below. Elvo crouched low and, bringing forth his own weapon, aimed it but could not bring himself to fire. Who was right and who was wrong? The men had come as interlopers; did they have the right to punish those whose rights they had invaded?

Jemasze noted Elvo's indecision. "What's wrong with your gun?"

"Nothing. Just futility. That's all that's wrong. We're trapped up here; we can't escape. What's one dead erjin more or less?"

"If thirty erjins attack and we kill thirty, then we go free," explained Jemasze. "If we only kill twenty-five, then we are, as you point out, trapped."

"We can't hope to kill all thirty," Elvo muttered.

"I hope to do so."

"Suppose there are more than thirty?"

"I'm not interested in hypotheses," said Jemasze. "I merely want to survive." Meanwhile he aimed and fired his gun to such good effect that the erjins retreated.

Kurgech made a survey to the south. "We're surrounded."

Elvo went to sit on a ledge of rock. The sun, halfway down the western sky, threw his shadow across the barren surface. No water, thought Elvo. In three or four days they would be dead. He sat torpid, elbows on knees, head hanging low. Jemasze and Kurgech muttered together for a period, then Kurgech went off to sit where he could overlook the eastern horizon. Elvo looked at him in wonder: the eastern side of the crag was the least vulnerable to assault...He took a deep breath and tried to pull himself together. He was about to die but he'd face the unpleasant process as gracefully as possible. He rose to his feet and walked across the flat. At the sound of his footsteps, Jemasze turned his head. His face became instantly harsh. "Get down, you fool!"

A pellet sang through the air. Elvo jerked to a cruel enormous blow. He fell to the ground and lay staring up at the sky.

CHAPTER 11

At Morningswake the days passed, one much like the next. Schaine and Kelse examined the casual and often enigmatic records left by Uther Madduc and instituted a new system to facilitate management of the domain.

Each morning the two conferred over breakfast, sometimes harmoniously, sometimes in a state of contention. Schaine was forced to admit that, despite her natural affection for Kelse, she often did not like him very much. Kelse had become crabbed, rigid and humorless, for reasons beyond her understanding. Certainly Kelse had suffered greatly; still his loss of arm and leg inconvenienced him little. In his place, she would never allow herself to brood! Another thought occurred to her. Perhaps Kelse loved someone who had rejected him because of his handicap.

The idea fascinated her. Who could it be?

Social life back and forth across the domains was gay; there were house parties, balls, fiestas, 'karoos': these latter pale imitations of the Uldra carnivals of lust, gluttony and psychological catharsis. Kelse agreed that he seldom attended such functions, so when from Ellora Domain arrived an invitation to an all-day picnic in the wonderful Ellora Garden, Schaine accepted for both herself and Kelse.

The picnic was a most delightful affair. Two hundred guests roamed the fifty-acre park which the Lilliet family had now maintained for two hundred years, each generation augmenting and improving the work of those before. Schaine enjoyed herself immensely and meanwhile kept an interested eye upon Kelse. As she had expected he made no attempt to mingle with younger folk—after all, he was only two years her senior—but kept to the company of those land-barons present.

Schaine renewed many old acquaintances and learned that, as she suspected, Kelse was considered shy and abrupt by the girls.

Schaine sought Kelse out and said, "You've just had some dazzling compliments. I probably shouldn't explain, because you might become vain."

"Small chance of that," grumbled Kelse, which Schaine took as an invitation to proceed.

"I've been talking to Zia Forres; she considers you most attractive, but she's afraid to talk to you for fear you might destroy her."

"I'm not all that irascible; and certainly not vain. Zia Forres can talk to me anytime she likes."

"You don't seem elevated by the compliment."

Kelse gave her a sickly grin. "It startles me."

"Well then—look pleasantly startled at least, not as if someone had dropped a rock on your foot."

"Which foot?"

"On your head then."

"To be quite honest my mind is on other things. There's been news from Olanje. The Redemptionists have finally persuaded the Mull to issue a definitive mandate—directed against us, naturally."

Schaine began to feel despondent. If only these discouraging problems would go away, or at least be forgotten, just for today! In a resigned voice she asked: "What kind of mandate?"

"The land-barons are ordered to meet with a council of tribal hetmen. We must abandon all pretense to legal title; said title must be affirmed to reside with the tribes traditionally resident on the domains. We retain the manors and ten acres surrounding, and at the pleasure and discretion of the tribal councils, may apply for leaseholds not to exceed terms of ten years on other lands, and not to exceed one thousand acres per domain."

Schaine said flippantly, "It could be worse. They could sequester title to the houses as well."

"They've sequestered nothing as yet. A manifesto is words. We hold the land and we'll continue to hold it."

"That's not realistic, Kelse."

"It seems realistic to me. We've declared ourselves a political entity independent of the Mull; they no longer exert authority over us—if ever they did."

"Realism is this: Szintarre has a population of millions. The political entity you speak of has a population of a few thousand. The Mull exerts much more power. We've got to obey."

"Don't equate power with population," said Kelse. "Especially urban population. But there's no immediate worry—not from our side at least. We won't kill any Redemptionists unless they come here to kill us. I hope they think better of it."

Schaine turned away, furiously angry with Kelse and in the mood to do something wild and outrageous. She restrained herself and went to visit with her old friends, but the day had lost its zest.

Returning to Morningswake, Kelse and Schaine were surprised to find six Ao elders encamped on the lawn in front of the house, in a manner which Schaine thought portentous and somber . Kelse muttered, "Now what's the emergency?"

Schaine said: "They've also had the news from Olanje. They're here to get your signature on the lease."

"Not likely." Kelse nonetheless hesitated before he went to investigate. "You'd better wait in the house—just in case." And so Schaine, standing in the grand front parlor, watched through the window as Kelse crossed the lawn to where the Aos waited.

Kelse returned to the house faster than he had departed. Schaine ran out into the hall to meet him. "What's wrong?"

"I've got to take the Standard north. Zagwitz has had a message from Kurgech. A mind-message, needless to say, the substance of which is trouble."

Schaine's heart went up in her throat. "Do they know how, or why, or where?"

"I'm not sure what they know. They want me to take them up into the Volwodes."

"What about Gerd and Elvo?"

"They've nothing to say."

"I'll come with you."

"No. There's danger. I'll keep in touch with you by radio."

*

At midnight the sky-car returned, with Kurgech, Gerd Jemasze, and Elvo Glissam barely conscious on an improvised stretcher. Kelse had already administered an all-purpose disinfectant and pain-suppressant from the sky-car's emergency kit. Gerd and Kurgech carried the stretcher into the sick-bay where Cosmo Brasbane the domain medic removed Elvo's clothes and gave him further medical attention.

Kurgech started to leave the house; Gerd called him back. "Where are you going?"

Kurgech said soberly: "This is Morningswake Manor and the traditions of your people are strong."

Gerd said, "You and I have been through too much together; if it weren't for you we'd all be dead. What's good enough for me is good enough for you."

Schaine, looking at Gerd Jemasze, felt an almost overwhelming suffusion of warmth; she wanted to laugh and she wanted to cry. Of course, of course! She loved Gerd Jemasze! Through prejudice and incomprehension she had not allowed herself to recognize the fact. Gerd Jemasze was a man of the Alouan; she was Schaine Madduc of Morningswake. Elvo Glissam? No.

Kelse said gruffly, and perhaps only Schaine apprehended the nearly imperceptible reluctance: "Gerd is quite right; formality can't apply to situations like this."

Kurgech shook his head and half-smiling, took a step backward. "The expedition is over; conditions are once more as before. Our lives go differently, and this is as it should be."

Schaine ran forward. "Kurgech, don't be so solemn and fateful; I want you to stay with us. I'm sure you're hungry and I'm having a meal laid out."

Kurgech went to the door. "Thank you, Lady Schaine, but you are Outker, I am Uldra. Tonight I will be more comfortable with my own people." He departed.

*

In the morning Elvo Glissam, his shoulder bandaged and his left arm in a sling, limped down to the breakfast table to find the others there before him, and all talking. Everyone felt at the same time emotionally flat but superficially stimulated and almost euphoric, so that all kinds of remarks and opinions came forth that might not have been broached under different circumstances.

The talk went quickly and lightly, glancing on many subjects. In a weak but marveling voice, like a man describing a nightmare, Elvo Glissam recounted his version of the events of the past two weeks which provided Schaine and Kelse a more particularized and personal account than that which they had gleaned from Gerd Jemasze.

Schaine asked in bewilderment: "But where is the 'wonderful joke'? I haven't heard anything even remotely funny."

"Father had an odd sense of humor," said Kelse, "if any."

"He must have had a sense of humor," declared Elvo. "From all I've heard of him he was a remarkable man."

"Well then," Schaine challenged him, "where is the great joke?"

"It's too subtle for me."

Glancing sidewise at Gerd Jemasze, Schaine thought to detect a half-smile. "Gerd! You know!"

"Only a guess."

"Tell me! Please!"

"Let me think about it; I don't know whether it's a joke or a tragedy."

"Tell us! Let us all judge!"

Gerd Jemasze started to speak but hesitated too long, and Elvo, almost intoxicated from relief of tension, spoke first. "Joke or no joke, the shrine is a remarkable discovery. Morningswake will soon be a name as familiar as Gomaz and Sadhara! There'll be guided tours flying out from Olanje!"

"We could put up a hotel and make a fortune," Schaine suggested.

"What would we do with a fortune?" growled Kelse. "We have all the money we need."

"If we're allowed to keep Morningswake."

"Bah. Who's to stop us? Don't say the Mull."

"The Mull."

"Once again—bah."

"I'll take the fortune. We need another big saloon," said Schaine. "Remember, the Sturdevant is wrecked. I say, let's buy another Sturdevant."

Kelse threw up his hands. "How will we pay for it? Do you know how much a sound saloon car costs?"

"What's money? We'll run our own guided tours out to this wonderful exhibit. And don't forget: the hotel!"

Elvo asked: "Is that valley the Palga or the Retent or what?"

"I've been thinking about that," said Gerd Jemasze. "The gorge runs west and south out of the Volwodes. That's Ao country and Mornings-wake domain."

"No problem then," declared Elvo. "You own a magnificent histor-ical monument, and you have every right to build a hotel!"

"Not so fast," said Kelse. "The Mull and the Redemptionists say we own no more than the clothes on our back; who is right?"

"I agree the matter must be adjudicated," said Elvo. "Still, Redemp-tionist though I am, I wish the best for my friends here at Morningswake."

"Strange that the Aos know nothing about the shrine," said Gerd Jemasze. "I've checked the map; it's on Ao tribal land."

"It's also next to the Retent," said Kelse. "The Garganche might know about it."

"Aha!" cried Schaine. "All is clear. Jorjol has learned of the shrine; he wants to build a hotel; and that's why he wants to kick us out of Morningswake!"

"I wouldn't put anything past Jorjol," said Kelse.

"You wrong poor Muffin," said Schaine. "He's really very simple, very straightforward, very open. I understand him completely."

"Then you're the only one," said Kelse.

"I also disagree," said Elvo. "Jorjol is a very complex person. He has no choice. Let's view him from the standpoint of the psychologist. He's an Outker and an Uldra at the same time: two sets of ideas work in his one brain. He can't have a thought without finding an instant contra-diction. It's a wonder he's as effective as he is!"

"No puzzle there," said Kelse. "Outker or Uldra, first and last, back-ward and forward, Jorjol is an egotist. He switches back and forth between roles as it suits him. At this moment he's a Garganche bucko: the swashbuckling Gray Prince. Do you know, it's quite likely that he drove the sky-shark that shot down Father, and the Apex as well!"

Schaine produced an indignant refutal. "What utter nonsense! You know Jorjol better than that! He's proud and gallant! A ruthless assas-sin? Never!"

Kelse was not convinced. "By Garganche theories, ruthless assassi-nation is equivalent to pride and gallantry."

"You're not at all fair to Jorjol," said Schaine. "His 'pride and gal-lantry', or however you want to put it, saved your life. He deserves at least credit for bravery."

"I'll concede him that," said Kelse. "Still, I don't think much of his loyalty."

Schaine laughed. "Loyalty to whom? To what? I never had reason to complain."

"Naturally not; you were in love with him."

Schaine heaved a patient sigh. "I'd prefer to call it infatuation."

"Father, it would seem, is now vindicated."

With an effort Schaine decided not to quarrel with Kelse. She responded quietly and, she hoped, rationally. "Father meant well. He gave Muffin a great deal, up to a carefully defined limit. Muffin naturally resented the limit more than he appreciated the generosity. And why not? Put yourself in his place: half part of the family, half a Blue ragamuffin who ate his meals in the kitchen. He was allowed to look at the cake and even taste it, but never eat any of it."

Elvo Glissam ventured a facetious quip: "And you were the cake?— I hope not!"

Schaine raised her eyebrows and looked away with pointed coolness. The remark seemed in poor taste—especially in view of the fact that immediately following Jorjol's rescue of Kelse, she had allowed Jorjol considerably more than a taste. The discovery of the affair had provoked a wrathful explosion in Uther Madduc, which had sent Jorjol flying in one direction and Schaine thirty-two light years in another.

Schaine said evenly: "Those times are quite remote." She rose to her feet. "The conversation is becoming dull."

CHAPTER 12

Gerd Jemasze, with his younger brother Adare, two cousins and a nephew, flew the Standard utility up to the Palga across to where the sarai broke against the Volwode foothills. They found the land-yawl undisturbed. Gerd and Adare Jemasze and the nephew sailed the yawl east, while the cousins flew overhead in the sky-car.

A day's brisk sail brought them to No. 2 Depot. Jemasze paid rent for the use of the land-yawl and examined the Dacy sky-boat, which Moffamides' fiaps had kept inviolate. A new priest was on hand, a thin young man with burning eyes and a thin quivering mouth, who watched intently but spoke not a word. Jemasze wondered if Moffamides had gone to sit high in the Aluban, but forbore to question the young priest, who stood glowering at them from across the compound.

No sooner had Gerd Jemasze returned to Suaniset than news arrived from Morningswake of an extraordinary incursion from the Retent. The raiders numbered over four hundred elite warriors, mixed Hunge, Garganche, Aulk and Zeffir: an amazing circumstance in itself to discover traditional enemies acting in concert. A few Ao scouts skirmished with the outriders, then fell back before the main force, which proceeded to Lake Dor where three Ao kachembas were discovered and defiled.

Kelse immediately broadcast a call for assistance, and the Order of Uaia found itself required to fight before it had fully defined itself as an entity. A heterogeneous and rather casual assortment of utility flyers, passenger saloons, sky-cars, runabouts and inspection drifters, to the number of sixty, each with a complement of from two to eight armed men, assembled at Morningswake, then flew down to Lake Dor, to discover that the Uldra raiders were already retreating across the rocky barrens west of the lake. The aircraft from the domains attacked with guns and energy-projectors; the Uldras dispersed in all directions. On their lunging mounts they made the poorest of targets and the punitive fleet inflicted minimal damage...A score of sky-sharks dropped from the upper atmosphere and in the twinkling of an eye a dozen aircraft were disabled and sent plunging to the ground. Then, before adequate retaliation could be effected, the sky-sharks dashed away to the west.

In a dour mood the land-barons rescued those who had been shot down and returned to their domains. The foray had been ineffectual; they had been defeated by tactics more clever than their own.

A number of land-barons gathered at Morningswake to discuss the cheerless events of the day. They had ventured forth overconfidently; they had been tricked; they had paid the price of vanity.

Dm. Ervan Collode, a portly and rather bombastic man whom Schaine had always disliked, was one of those who had been shot down by the sky-sharks. He had escaped with a severe jolting and various bruises, but the experience had stimulated him to a vindictive rage. "We'll never have peace until we absolutely break the Retent tribes. We must put them in such fear that they'll never again attack us!"

Dm. Joris made a wry observation: "I fear that we lack capacity to cow them. For thousands of years they've been cutting up each other, and it only whets their appetite for more."

"They don't go far enough," declared Dm. Collode. "They never press to a decision! If we destroy their herds, poison their water, we'll force their submission."

Dm. Joris demurred. "I don't believe such tactics would work; they live too easily off the land, and we'd simply have our trouble for nothing."

"There is an important first step we should undertake," said Jemasze. "The Retent tribes are theoretically wards of the Mull, and we should demand that the Mull assert control."

Dm. Collode blew through his teeth. "What good will that do? The Mull is dominated by Redemptionists! Have you forgotten their manifesto?"

Kelse likewise took exception to the proposal. "We can't declare ourselves independent, then in the next breath appeal for help."

"I suggest no appeal, but a formal notice, from one sovereign entity to another," said Jemasze. "I would notify them that the Retent Uldras are molesting not only us but the tribes under our protection; that we plan decisive action which might include seizure and permanent control of the Retent, unless they take steps to restrain their wards. Then, if the Mull doesn't act, and we do, they can't say that they haven't been warned. If finally we're forced to subdue the Garganche, we at least have a basis of legality."

"What good is legality to the Garganche?" grumbled Dm. Collode. "To an Uldra, might is right."

Schaine could not restrain a sardonic chuckle. "To avoid making fools of yourselves, I suggest that you forgo hypocrisy. For two hundred years the land-barons have asserted the right of might, so now, when the shoe is on the other foot, don't look askance at the maxim."

"Hypocrisy isn't an issue," Jemasze responded. "Whenever there's conflict the weaker side loses; and all else being equal, it's better to win than to lose."

"It depends on the company you keep," said Schaine, darting a glance toward Dm. Collode.

Dm. Joris said: "Undoubtedly Gerd Jemasze is right. To prepare a position, we first must notify the Mull."

Dm. Thanet of Balabar said, "Let us do so at this very moment. We are not precisely an official body, but surely we can function as an instrument to this particular end."

The group moved into the study. Kelse telephoned Holrude House in Olanje. The face of a secretary appeared on the screen. Kelse identified himself. "I am Dm. Kelse Madduc, and I represent the provisional executive committee of the Uaian Order. I have an important message to transmit to the Chairman of the Mull."

"The Chairman, Dm. Madduc, is currently Dm. Erris Sammatzen, and it so happens that he is at hand."

Erris Sammatzen's face appeared on the screen. "Kelse Madduc? We have met, at Villa Mirasol."

"Quite true. My purpose in calling you, however, is not social, but official. I speak for the provisional executive committee of the Uaian Order, and I inform you that a large group of Uldras from the Retent, nominally wards of the Mull, yesterday invaded our lands, specifically Morningswake Domain, and there committed acts of murder and vandalism. We have driven them back into the Retent and we now look to you to prevent any further incursions."

Erris Sammatzen reflected a moment. "Such raids, if they have in fact occurred, are a serious matter, and certainly cannot be condoned."

"'If' they have occurred?" cried Kelse angrily. "Of course they have occurred! I just now told you about them!"

Erris Sammatzen said, "Please, Dm. Madduc, don't take offense. As a private individual, of course I believe you. As Chairman of the Mull, I must take a more measured approach."

"I don't follow your distinctions," said Kelse. "The Order of Uaia notifies you, through me, that these raids have occurred, and requires that you ensure their permanent cessation; otherwise we must protect ourselves."

Erris Sammatzen spoke in a ponderous voice: "I must put certain matters into perspective. I remind you that the Mull is the organ of all the folk of Koryphon and must act in the best interests of all the folk. The land-barons of the Alouan are a minority even upon the so-called 'domains'; they therefore can claim neither autonomy nor any wide representative function. I also remind you of the recent ordinance proclaimed by the Mull which reconstructs the so-called Domains of Koryphon, regarding which we have received no acknowledgment."

Dm. Joris, perceiving that Kelse was about to make an immoderate reply, stepped forward. "The points you raise are at issue. We hope they may be resolved in a reasonable manner. Your remarks, however, are not responsive to the notification just made to you by Dm. Kelse Madduc."

"They are not responsive," said Erris Sammatzen, "because the Mull does not recognize the premises upon which they are based. Further, we have received information which contradicts your assertions. I therefore order you to desist from any further acts hostile to tribes of the Retent."

Kelse made a strangled sound of astonishment and displeasure. "Do you suggest that I have made a false report to you?"

"I state only that contradictory information has been put before the Mull."

Dm. Joris once more interposed himself. "In that case, we suggest that you come here to Morningswake and make your own investigations. Then, should you discover, as you surely will, that we have reported the facts accurately, you can make appropriate representation to the Retent tribes."

Erris Sammatzen reflected thirty seconds. Then he said: "I will do as you suggest, in company with other members of the Mull. In the meantime I ask that you refrain from any further attacks or reprisals, and I will transmit similar instructions to the other parties at contention."

Dm. Joris smiled a cool thin smile. "We will be most happy to meet with the Mull and work out a mutual accommodation: from our point of view the sooner the better. In the meantime, while we do not concede your authority either to instruct or to advise us, we intend to refrain from attacking the tribes of the Retent, except in defense of our sovereign territory."

Kelse asked: "When may we expect you at Morningswake?"

"The day after tomorrow will be convenient."

CHAPTER 13

The land-barons, all except Gerd Jemasze, had returned to their respective domains, and night had fallen over the Alouan. Schaine went to sit on the front lawn overlooking the starlit landscape. The knots in her mind began to unravel, and her conflicts resolved themselves in the simplest possible manner.

She loved Morningswake: this was the elemental fact; nothing was more real. Morningswake, with its history and traditions, breathed a life of its own; Morningswake was an entity yearning for survival. If she intended to live at Morningswake, then she must protect it. If she felt that she must advance a hostile cause, then she must leave and go elsewhere, which of course was unthinkable.

She thought of Elvo Glissam and smiled. Today, after the land-barons had gone off to punish the Uldras, Elvo had urged that he and she return to Olanje and there espouse each other, to which suggestion Schaine had given an offhand, almost absentminded, refusal. Elvo had accepted her decision without surprise and had voiced his intention of returning to Olanje as soon as possible. Ah well, thought Schaine, life went on.

She went back into the house. In the study lights still glowed; Gerd Jemasze and Kelse conferred late. Schaine went upstairs to her bedroom on the west verandah.

Schaine awoke. The night was dark, and all was quiet. Yet something had aroused her.

A soft *tap tap* at the door.

Schaine climbed drowsily from bed, stumbled to the door and slid it ajar. On the verandah a tall shape darker than the shadows awaited her. Recognition came instantly, and she was no longer half-asleep. She turned on the lights in her room. "Jorjol! What in the world are you doing here?"

"I came to see you."

Schaine peered in bewilderment up the dark verandah. "Who let you in?"

"No one." Jorjol gave a soft chuckle. "I arrived by the old route—up the corner column."

"Sheer insanity, Jorjol! What could you have in mind?"

"Need you ask that?" Jorjol leaned forward as if to enter the room but Schaine slipped past and stepped out upon the verandah.

The night was absolutely still. The arabella vine climbing the columns to the roof hung in festoons, and the white blossoms gave off a sweet perfume.

Jorjol stepped a trifle closer; Schaine went to the balustrade and looked out over the landscape, which was dark except for a few glints of starlight reflected from Wild Crake Pond. Jorjol put his arm around her waist and lowered his head to kiss her. Schaine turned away. "Stop it, Jorjol, I'm not at all interested. I haven't the faintest notion why you're here, and, really, you'd better go."

"Come now, don't be prim," whispered Jorjol. "You love me and I love you; it's been that way all our lives, and now more than ever!"

"No, Jorjol, not at all. I'm not the person I was five years ago, and you're not either."

"Quite true! I'm a man, a person of consequence! For five years I've burned for you, and longed for you, and since I saw you at Olanje I've thought of nothing else."

Schaine laughed uneasily. "Please be sensible, Jorjol! Go away and call tomorrow morning."

"Hah! I don't dare! I'm now the enemy; have you forgotten?"

"Well then, you'd better mend your ways and behave yourself. Now good night! I'm going back to bed."

"No!" Jorjol spoke with great earnestness. "Listen, Schaine! Come away with me! My dear girl Schaine! You're not one of these pompous tyrants who calls himself a land-baron! You're a free soul, so come with me now and be free! We will live as happy as birds, with the best of everything the world affords! You don't belong here; you know that as well as I do!"

"You're totally and absolutely wrong, Jorjol! This is my home and I love it dearly!"

"But you love me more! Tell me so, my dearest Schaine!"

"I don't love you, not in the slightest. In fact, I love someone else."

"Who? Elvo Glissam?"

"Of course not!"

"Then it must be Gerd Jemasze! Tell me! Is it he?"

"Isn't this a personal matter, Muffin?"

"Don't call me Muffin!" Jorjol's voice rose in pitch and intensity. "And it's not private because I want you for myself. You haven't denied it! So your new lover is Gerd Jemasze!"

"He's not my lover, Jorjol, new or old. And please take your hands off of me." For Jorjol, in his excitement, had clenched his fingers upon her two arms.

He whispered huskily: "Please, darling Schaine, tell me it isn't true; that you love me!"

"I'm sorry, Jorjol, it is true, and I don't love you. And now, good night. I'm going back to bed."

Jorjol gave a small ugly laugh. "Do you think I so easily accept defeat? You know me better! I came to get you and you're coming away with me. Very soon you'll learn to love me. I warn you, don't try to fight me!"

Schaine shrank back appalled, as Jorjol's fingers gripped her arms like steel tongs. She drew in her breath to scream; with one long-fingered hand, Jorjol seized her throat; with his other fist he struck her in the side at the bottom of the rib-cage in a clever way to cause an agony of pain, and Schaine's knees sagged…The porch lights went on; she felt a confused scuffle, saw a blur of movement, heard a grunt of shock and dismay.

Schaine staggered to the wall. Jorjol lay crumpled, half against the balustrade. A knife hung in a scabbard against his leg; in his sash gleamed the ivory handle of a pistol. His hands twitched, then jerked for the pistol. Gerd Jemasze stepped forward, struck down at Jorjol's arm, and the pistol went clattering across the floor. Schaine swiftly stooped and picked it up, even while she tingled with embarrassment. How much had Gerd Jemasze heard?"

The three stood motionless: Jorjol pale, blasted by emotion; Jemasze somber and brooding; Schaine tense with a not unpleasant excitement. Jorjol turned to Schaine and in the wild staring face she thought once more to see the face of Muffin the boy.

"Schaine, dear Schaine—will you come with me?"

"No, Jorjol, of course not! It's really absurd to think I might. I'm not an Uldra; I'd be miserable out there on the Retent."

Jorjol gave a poignant throbbing call, a cry from the heart. "You're like all the other Outkers."

"I hope not. I'm really just myself."

Jorjol drew himself stiffly erect. "I implore you, by your brother's life which I gave to him! This is a blood debt and cannot be denied!"

Gerd Jemasze made an odd sound: a choking gasping stammer as words rose too thickly in his throat to be enunciated. He finally spoke. "Shall I tell the truth?"

Jorjol blinked and cocked his head sidewise. "What truth?"

"You'd best apologize to Lady Schaine and assure her that no obligation exists and then go your way."

Jorjol spoke in a stony voice: "The debt exists, and I demand that she give me my due."

"The debt does not exist and never existed. When the erjin attacked Kelse, you climbed a rock and watched while the creature tore Kelse to pieces. When you saw Schaine come running, you carefully shot the beast from the top of the rock, then jumped down and pretended to be in the middle of the fight, and you even rubbed Kelse's blood on yourself. You did not try to save Kelse. You allowed him to be mutilated!"

Jorjol whispered: "You lie! You were not there."

Jemasze's voice was cold as fate. "Kurgech was there. He saw the whole thing."

Jorjol gave a sudden cry of despair: an oddly sweet contralto sound. He ran to the corner of the verandah, swung over the balustrade and was gone.

Schaine turned to Gerd Jemasze and spoke in a voice of horror. "Is this true?"

"It's true."

"It can't be true," muttered Schaine, looking back down the years. "It's too awful to be true." It seemed as natural as the wind and the movement of the stars across the sky to find herself sobbing against Gerd Jemasze's chest, his arms around her.

"It's true," said Kelse. He came slowly out on the verandah. "I heard what you told him. I've suspected it for five years. All his life he's hated us. Someday I'll kill him."

CHAPTER 14

To Morningswake in a black-and-silver Ellux saloon came a delegation from the Mull: Erris Sammatzen and six others. On hand to greet them was the Directive Committee of the Uaian Order: nine land-barons selected and given legitimacy by a hasty telephonic referendum across the Treaty Lands.

Dm. Joris made a rather dry and formal welcoming statement, his purpose being to establish at the outset an official tone to the meeting. In keeping with this concern, the land-barons wore formal dress and each wore his heraldic cap. In contrast, the members of the Mull were almost ostentatiously casual. "The Order of Uaia welcomes you to Morningswake," said Dm. Joris. "We earnestly desire that this conference will reduce the misunderstandings which trouble our two polities. We hope that you will approach the discussions constructively and realistically, and for our part we intend that our relations with Szintarre shall continue to be friendly and intimate."

Sammatzen laughed. "Dm. Joris, thank you for your welcome. As you're well aware, I can't accept, or even take seriously, your other remarks. We have come here to acquaint ourselves with local conditions, so that we can administrate the area in the best interests of the majority of its inhabitants; and hopefully to the ultimate satisfaction, or at least acceptance, of everyone."

"Our differences may or may not be irreconcilable," said Dm. Joris without emotion. "If you please, Dm. Madduc has provided refreshment for us; and then, when you are of a mind, we can resume our discussions in the Great Hall."

For half an hour the groups engaged in cautious pleasantries on the west lawn, then repaired to the Great Hall. The formal attire of the Directive Committee accorded with the nobility of the room, the grandeur of its proportions, the richness of the old wood. Kelse seated the Mull on one side of the table, the Directive Committee on the other.

Erris Sammatzen briskly assumed control of the meeting. "I won't pretend that our purpose here is anything other than what it is. The Mull is the single administrative body of Koryphon. We directly represent the population of Szintarre; we provide a forum for the inhabitants of Uaia. Over the Uldra we exercise a benevolent protectorate. The domains of the land-barons are included under our control, by protocols both formal and informal; they also have rights of petition and protest.

"As you know we have felt obliged to issue an edict, the articles of which are now familiar to you." Erris Sammatzen spoke now in a slow and meaningful voice. "We cannot and will not tolerate the recalcitrance of a few hundred stubborn men and women who wish to retain aristocratic perquisites to which they are not entitled. A more natural and equitable system is long overdue, and I remind you that the absolute authority of the land-barons across vast domains, achieved through violence and compulsion, is now terminated. Title is reinvested in those tribes which have traditional and legitimate ownership of the land. We intend to inflict hardship on no one, and will assist in the orderly transfer of authority."

Dm. Joris replied, again without heat: "We reject your edict. It obviously derives from altruism and in this sense does you credit, but it makes a number of doctrinaire assumptions. I point out that the option of self-determination is the inherent right of any community, no matter how small, provided that it conforms to the basic charter of the Gaean Reach. We adhere to these principles, and we claim this right. I now wish to anticipate your claim that the rights of the domain tribes are curtailed. To the contrary. The factors which contribute to what they consider an optimum life have never been more favorable. Our dams and flood-control projects guarantee them year-round water for themselves and their herds. When they need money to buy imported articles, they are able to take temporary or permanent employment, as they wish. Their freedom of movement is absolute, except upon the few acres immediately contiguous to the domain halls, so that in effect, there is dual occupancy of the land, to our mutual satisfaction and benefit. We exploit no one; we exert authority only in a protective sense. We provide medical assistance; we occasionally exert police powers, though not often, inasmuch as the tribes usually administer their own justice. We feel that you of the Mull have been stampeded into reckless decisions by the zealous and articulate group known as the Redemptionists, who deal in abstractions and not in facts.

"I ask: what is accomplished by your edict? Nothing. What would the Uldras have which they do not have now? Nothing. They would lose, and we would lose. Your edicts only bring mischief to all of us— assuming that we agreed to them, which we do not."

Dm. Joris was answered by Adelys Lam, a thin nervous woman with a bony face and restless eyes. She spoke in an urgent voice and punctuated her words with jabbing motions of her forefinger.

"I intend to speak of law and its innate nature. Dm. Joris, you have used the words 'doctrinaire' and 'abstraction' in a pejorative sense, and I must point out that all law, all ethical systems, all morality, are based upon doctrines and abstract principles by which we test specific cases. If we adopt a pragmatic attitude, we are lost and civilization is lost; morality becomes a matter of expedience or brute force. The edicts of the Mull therefore rest not so much upon exigencies of the moment as upon fundamental theorems. One of these is that title to pre-empted, stolen or sequestered property never becomes valid, whether the lapse of time be two minutes or two hundred years. The flaw in title remains, and reparation, no matter how dilatory, must be made. Again, you scorn the Redemptionists; as for me, I rejoice that the Redemptionists are sufficiently idealistic and sufficiently motivated that they have urged this sometimes sluggish Mull to decisive action."

Gerd Jemasze responded in a cold voice. "Your ideas might carry more weight were you not hypocrites and persons with an infinite capacity for—"

"'Hypocrites'?" flared Adelys Lam. "Dm. Jemasze, I am astounded by your use of the word!"

Erris Sammatzen said reproachfully: "I had hoped our discussions might proceed without fulmination, threats or invective. I am sorry to see that Dm. Jemasze has become intemperate."

"Let him call us names," Adelys Lam cried angrily. "Our consciences are clear, which is more than he can say for his own."

Jemasze listened imperturbably. "My remarks were not invective," he said. "I refer to demonstrable fact. You legislate against our imaginary crimes, and meanwhile you tolerate in Szintarre and across the Retent an offense proscribed everywhere in the Gaean Reach: slavery. In fact, I suspect that at least several of you are slave-keepers."

Sammatzen pursed his lips. "You refer to the erjins, no doubt. The facts of the matter are unclear."

Adelys Lam declared: "The erjins are not intelligent beings, by the legal definition of the term or by any other. They are clever animals, no more."

"We can demonstrate the opposite, beyond any argument," said Gerd Jemasze. "Before you reproach us for abstract transgressions, you should abate your own very real offenses."

Erris Sammatzen said uncomfortably: "You make a cogent point; I can't argue with you. However, I doubt that you can make so positive a demonstration."

Adelys Lam protested. "Surely we are being diverted from our principal task?"

"Our schedule is flexible," said Sammatzen. "I'm willing to clarify this other matter."

Another Mull member, the crusty Thaddios Tarr, said: "We can't avoid doing so and retain our credibility as an impartial administrative body."

Gerd Jemasze rose to his feet. "I think we'll be able to surprise you."

Erris Sammatzen cautiously asked: "How?"

"Uther Madduc called it his 'wonderful joke'. But I doubt if you'll laugh."

Schaine, listening from the side of the Great Hall, said to Elvo Glissam: "I don't understand why anyone should laugh. Do you understand this 'wonderful joke'?"

Elvo shook his head. "It escapes me completely."

The members of the Mull boarded the black-and-silver Ellux saloon. Gerd Jemasze went to the controls and took the craft aloft. Behind came a convoy of ten well-armed sky-cars. Gerd Jemasze set a course to the northwest, across the most beautiful region of Morningswake: a land of magnificent vistas and far perspectives.

The scarp which delineated the Palga loomed in the distance; the Volwodes rose into the sky; the land became bleak and broken. At the bottom of a wide valley flowed a glistening river: the Mellorus. Jemasze altered course and descended into the valley, to fly only a hundred yards above the river.

The valley walls grew steep and high and obscured part of the sky; a few moments later they passed over cultivated plots and irrigated orchards which Jemasze recognized. He slowed the Ellux until it barely drifted up the gorge, then turned to the members of the Mull. "What I'm about to show you has been seen by very few men indeed. Most of these have been Wind-runners—because we're close on the station where erjins are bred, trained and marshalled for export. There is definitely an element of danger in this demonstration, but when I am done you will agree that I am justified in bringing you here. In any case our assembled firepower provides protection, and the hull of this Ellux should be tough enough to turn back bullets from the Palga long-rifles."

"I hope," said Julias Metheyr, "that you intend to show us something more than erjins marching in formation or learning to put on their trousers."

Adelys Lam said crossly: "I personally don't care to be killed or even wounded for your personal gratification."

Gerd Jemasze made no response. He set the Ellux saloon down in front of the rose-quartz and gold shrine. He activated doors and descensor; the Mull trooped out upon the pink marble floor.

"What is it?" asked Julias Metheyr in awe.

"It appears to be a temple or historical monument constructed long before the first men arrived on Koryphon. The detail chronicles an erjin civilization."

"'Civilization'?" asked Adelys Lam.

"You can decide for yourself. Erjins are depicted riding in what appear to be spaceships. You'll see them fighting morphotes, who also use weapons and other adjuncts of a technical society; so the morphotes also have contrived a civilization in their time. Finally, the erjins record a war with men."

Erris Sammatzen strode forward to examine the seven-tiered fane; the others followed, muttering in amazement as they studied the intricate carving. One by one the escort sky-craft dropped down into the gorge and landed, and the occupants came forth to marvel at the shrine in company with the others.

Erris Sammatzen approached Jemasze. "And this is Uther Madduc's 'wonderful joke'?"

"So I believe."

"But what's funny?"

"The magnificent ability of the human race to delude itself."

"That's bathos, not humor," said Sammatzen shortly. "The joke, at least, is a hoax."

"No, I don't think so," said Jemasze.

Sammatzen ignored him. "The Wind-runner training station is nearby?"

"About half a mile up the gorge."

"Is there any reason why we should not go there now, and put a stop to the traffic?"

Jemasze shrugged. "I couldn't guarantee your safety. But I believe that we mount enough firepower to protect ourselves if the need arose."

"What do you know concerning this operation?"

"No more than you. I saw it for the first time a week or so ago."

Sammatzen rubbed his chin. "It occurs to me that the tribes of the Retent will resent the loss of their mounts. What is your opinion on this?"

Jemasze grinned. "They can buy criptids from the domains."

Erris Sammatzen went to confer with the other members of the Mull; they argued ten minutes, then Sammatzen approached Jemasze. "We want to examine the training station if it can be accomplished safely."

"We'll do our best."

The compound and the long buildings were as Jemasze remembered them, and even more somnolent than before. A pair of Wind-runners squatted beside one of the walls. At the sight of the descending sky-craft, they slowly rose to their feet and stood in postures of uncertainty, debating whether or not to take to their heels.

Jemasze dropped the Ellux to the ground directly before the largest of the stone structures. He opened the door, extended the descensor and alighted, followed by Sammatzen and more cautiously by the other members of the Mull.

Jemasze signaled to the Wind-runners; they approached without enthusiasm. Jemasze asked: "Where is the director of the agency?"

The Wind-runners looked bewildered. "Director?"

"The individual in authority."

The Wind-runners muttered together, then one asked: "Might you be referring to the Old Erjin? If so, there he stands."

Out of the interior of the stone building, like a fish rising from dark water, came an exceedingly large erjin; a creature bald, with neither ruff nor facial tufts, its skin a curious snake-belly white. Never had Gerd Jemasze seen an erjin of such proportions or such presence. It glanced aside; one of the Wind-runners stiffened as if by electric shock, then moved forward to stand beside the erjin, where he served as translator, converting telepathic messages into words. The erjin asked: "What do you want here?"

Sammatzen said: "We are the Mull, the primary administrative organ of Koryphon."

"Of Szintarre," said Jemasze.

Sammatzen continued. "The enslavement of intelligent beings is an illegal act, on Szintarre and throughout the Gaean Reach. We find that erjins are being enslaved as mounts for the Uldra tribes and as servants and workers on Szintarre."

"They are not slaves," the Old Erjin stated, through the agency of the Wind-runner.

"They are slaves by our definition, and we are here to stop the practice. No more erjins may be sold either to Uldras or to the Gaeans of Szintarre, and those already enslaved will be freed."

"They are not slaves," stated the Old Erjin.

"If they are not slaves—what are they?"

The Old Erjin transmitted his message. "I knew you were coming. You and your fleet of sky-ships were watched as you entered the valley of the monument; you have been expected."

Sammatzen said dryly: "For a fact there seems little activity around here."

"The activity is elsewhere. We sold no slaves; we sent forth warriors. The signal has been broadcast. This world is ours and we are now resuming control."

The men listened gape-mouthed.

The Old Erjin controlled the voice of the Wind-runner: "The signal has gone forth. At this instant, erjins destroy the Uldras who thought to master them. Those erjins whom you considered servants now domi-nate the city Olanje and all Szintarre."

Sammatzen stared toward Joris and Jemasze, his face contorted in disbelief and anguish. "Is the creature telling the truth?"

"I don't know," said Jemasze. "Call Olanje by radio and find out."

Sammatzen ran heavy-footed to the saloon. Jemasze watched the Old Erjin reflectively a moment or two, then asked: "Are you planning violence upon us, here and now?"

"Not unless you initiate such violence, inasmuch as you have a clear preponderance of force. So leave here as you came."

Jemasze and Joris retreated to the Ellux saloon, to find Sammatzen turning away from the radio. His face was pale; sweat beaded his fore-head. "Erjins are running rampant in Olanje; the city is a madhouse!"

Jemasze went to the controls. "We're leaving, and fast, before the Old Erjin changes its mind."

"Can't we persuade it to call off its warriors?" cried Adelys Lam. "They're killing, destroying, burning! Nothing but bloodshed! Let me out! I will entreat the Old Erjin to peace!"

Jemasze thrust her back. "We can't entreat it to anything. If it were rational it wouldn't have launched the attack to begin with. Let's leave here before the rest of us are dead."

CHAPTER 15

The erjin uprising achieved its most striking successes in Olanje, where fewer than a thousand erjins cowed and dominated the entire city. The residents hysterically submitted to slaughter, or fled pell-mell. Some hid in the jungles; some retreated to their villas in the Carnelian Mountains; a few boarded their yachts or the yachts of their friends; oth-ers flew aircraft to the Persimmon Islands or Uaia. Only the most negli-gible resistance was offered, and later, when historians and sociologists studied the episode, and the question was put: "Why did you not fight in defense of your homes?" the responses were generally similar: "We were not organized; we had no leadership; we did not know what to do." "I am not accustomed to the use of weapons; I have always been a peaceful per-son and I never thought that I might be required to defend myself."

The land-barons of the Uaian domains assembled an expeditionary force of three thousand men, including contingents from the Uldra tribes of the Treaty Lands. In two weeks of cautious probing, fusillades from the air and assaults in improvised armored cars, the erjins were blasted out of the once beautiful city and sent fleeing in bedraggled bands across the countryside. For another two weeks sky-ships and mobile patrols pursued and destroyed the fugitives*; then without formality the expeditionary force returned to Uaia, and the folk of Szintarre ruefully addressed themselves to the task of reconstruction.

The Uldras of the Retent, no less than the Outkers of Szintarre, suffered from the insurrection. Immediately upon receipt of the telepathic notice, the erstwhile mounts, ignoring pinch-snaffles and electric curbs, reared over backwards to throw their riders, then proceeded to rend them into fragments. Those in pens broke or climbed fences, disconnected electric circuitry and attacked members of the tribe. After recovering from the initial shock the Uldras fought back with a vindictiveness equal to that of the erjins and successfully defended themselves. Primitive and remote tribes such as Cuttacks and the Nose-talkers suffered the most severely, while the Garganche, the Blue Knights, the Hunge and the Noal took relatively few casualties.

Two weeks later the Gray Prince called a grand karoo of the Garganche, Hunge, the Long-lips, and several other tribes; in passionate terms he labeled the erjin insurrection a plot of the Treaty Land Outkers, and he performed the chilling howl of hate by which an Uldra warrior swore vengeance upon his enemies. Intoxicated with rage and xheng**, the tribesmen echoed his howl, and on the following day an Uldra horde marched off to the east, intending to purge the Alouan of Outkers.

Kurgech brought news of the imminent invasion to Kelse, who at once notified the Uaian Order War Council. For a second time the sky-army was mobilized and dispatched to the Manganese Cliffs, a great

---

*During the latter stages of this period the Board of Directors of the SEE (Society for the Emancipation of the Erjins), returning to Olanje from their places of refuge, decried 'this orgy of unnecessary and meaningless slaughter'. They recommended that, when feasible, the erjins be captured rather than killed, in order that the captives might be educated, rehabilitated and encouraged to create a new peaceful society, in some unspecified area of Uaia. In the emotional climate of the mop-up, the SEE doctrine received small implementation.

**Xheng: untranslatable; a dark and peculiar emotion which might most succinctly be translated *horror-lust*: a generalized desire to inflict torments and agonies, a fervent dedication to the achievement of sadistic excesses.

scarp of glossy black schist overlooking the Plain of Walking Bones, where a party of a hundred Aos mounted on criptids were conducting a cautious holding operation against the xheng-crazed warriors of the Retent. As the flotilla approached, sky-sharks plunged out of the clouds; but today they were anticipated and demolished by radar-aimed guns. The Retent Uldras, despite their fanaticism, scattered and retreated across the Plain of Walking Bones, and ultimately took cover in a forest of black jinkos on the slopes of the Gildred Mountains.

Kelse was on hand in the Morningswake utility vehicle which had been converted into a gunship, with a crew of twelve—seven of his cousins and four Ao ranch-hands. During the first few minutes of the encounter a Garganche pellet exploded against an interior bulkhead, breaking and lacerating the shoulder of Ernshalt Madduc. There was no longer any semblance of a battle; Kelse communicated with the flotilla commander and received permission to return to Morningswake with the wounded man.

As Kelse flew north, his attention was attracted by a plume of smoke on the horizon which aroused him to instant alarm. He radioed Morningswake Manor but made no contact, and his foreboding was intensified. He strained the sky-car to its utmost speed, and presently Morningswake appeared ahead.

Smoke arose from a field of dry grain across Wild Crake Pond; also ablaze was the little clapboard schoolhouse where those Ao children who so desired were educated. Morningswake Manor appeared undamaged; but looking through binoculars Kelse saw a sky-blue Hermes Cloudswift on the lawn before the house.

Kelse dropped the sky-car to the lawn. Eleven men jumped to the ground and with weapons ready ran to the house. In the Great Hall they found five Uldra nobles drinking the finest wines Morningswake cellars afforded. Jorjol sat in the place of the land-baron, his feet on the table. The appearance of Kelse took him by surprise; he gasped in wonder. Kelse loped across the room and struck him sprawling to the floor. The four other Uldras vented oaths and jumped to their feet to stand petrified at the sight of the drawn weapons.

"Where is Schaine?" demanded Kelse.

Jorjol picked himself up from the floor and mustered what dignity he was able. He jerked his thumb toward the study. His voice was blurred by wine. "She chose to lock herself away. She would have come forth when we fired the manor." He lurched a step closer to

Kelse and stood looking down his long drooping nose. "How I hate you," he said softly. "If hate were stone I could build a tower into the clouds. I have always hated you. The joy I felt when the erjin tore you apart was like rain on the hot desert and caused me as much pleasure as the attention I gave your sister. My life has not been good, except for those two moments and now I will add a third, for I mean to kill you. If I do nothing else, I will take the life from your wicked Outker body."

A long blade appeared in his hand, thrust forward from his sleeve by a spring. He lunged; Kelse jerked away from the stroke and caught Jorjol's wrist with his right hand; with his steel left hand he caught Jorjol's throat; with his steel arm he lifted him into the air and staggering to the door threw him out into the yard. He moved forward, and as Jorjol rose to his feet, seized him again and shook him like a rag. Jorjol's eyes bulged; his tongue lolled from his mouth. In Kelse's ears came a screaming: the voice of Schaine. "Kelse, Kelse, please don't! Don't, Kelse! We are land-barons; he is an Uldra!"

Kelse relaxed his grip; Jorjol sagged gasping to the ground.

Jorjol and his henchmen were locked in a cattle-shed and a pair of guards placed over them. During the night they dug under the back wall, garrotted the guards and escaped.

CHAPTER 16

The world Koryphon was at peace: a surly, roiling peace of unresolved hatreds and unpleasant insights. In Olanje the physical damage done by the erjins had been repaired; the city seemed as gay and insouciant as ever. Valtrina Darabesq opened Villa Mirasol to three parties in rapid succession to demonstrate that the erjin uprising had left her undaunted. Across the Persimmon Sea the tribes of the Retent sullenly sat in their camps nursing grievances and planning murders, raids and tortures for the future, though without any great zest. On the Palga the Wind-runners eyed the empty slave pens and wondered how they would buy wheels, bearings and hardware for their sail-wagons. Meanwhile, under the Volwode peaks in the gorge of the river Mellorus, groups of marveling scholars had already begun to examine the rose-quartz and gold fane. The Old Erjin and his associates had departed into regions even more remote than the

Volwodes. Jorjol the Gray Prince, however, had not been rendered apathetic by his reverses. The fervor of his emotions had no upper limit; rather than waning with time they had condensed and thickened and become more pungent.

About a month after the expulsion of the erjins from Olanje the Mull sat in formal session at Holrude House. Tuning in the broadcast of the proceedings, Kelse Madduc heard a familiar voice and saw the splendid figure of Jorjol the Gray Prince standing at that rostrum provided for petitioners, claimants and witnesses. Kelse summoned Schaine and Gerd Jemasze: "Listen to this."

"—this opinion I hold to be defeatist, vague and unprincipled," Jorjol was saying. "Certain conditions have changed, as agreed—but not those conditions under discussion, by no whit! Do ethical principles fluctuate overnight? Does good become bad? Does a wise decision become a trifle merely because a set of unrelated events have occurred? Certainly not!

"In its wisdom the Mull issued a manifesto terminating the control of the land-barons over domains illegally seized and maintained. The land-barons have defied the lawful commands of the Mull. I speak with the voice of public opinion when I call for enforcement of the Mull's edict. What then is your response?"

Erris Sammatzen, the current chairman, said: "Your remarks, on their face, are reasonable. The Mull indeed issued an edict which the land-barons have ignored, and intervening circumstances are not germane to the affair."

"In that case," stated Jorjol, "the Mull must compel obedience!"

"There," said Sammatzen, "is the difficulty, and it illustrates the fallacy of issuing large commands which we can't enforce."

"Let us examine the matter as reasonable men," said Jorjol. "The edict is just; we are agreed as to this. Very well! If you cannot enforce this edict, then obviously an organ of enforcement is needed; otherwise, your role in the world becomes no more than advisory."

Sammatzen gave a dubious shrug. "What you say may be true; still, I don't feel that we are ready to make such large readjustments."

"The process is not all that difficult," said Jorjol. "In fact I will now volunteer to organize this compulsive force! I will work diligently to strengthen the Mull! Give me authority; give me funds. I will recruit able men; I will procure powerful weapons; I will ensure that the law of the Mull is no longer ignored."

Sammatzen frowned and leaned back in his chair. "This is obviously a very large decision, and at first glance it seems over-responsive."

"Perhaps because you are reconciled to a Mull weak and toothless."

"No, not necessarily. But—" Sammatzen hesitated.

"Do you or do you not intend to enforce your edicts upon all the folk of Koryphon, high and low, without fear or favoritism?" asked Jorjol.

Sammatzen spoke in an easy voice: "We certainly intend justice and equity. Before we decide how to achieve these fugitive ideals, we must decide what kind of an agency we are, how powerful a mandate our people have given us, and whether we really want to expand our responsibilities."

"Agreed in all respects!" Jorjol declared. "The Mull must come to grips with reality and establish once and for all the nature of its role."

"We'll hardly achieve this task tonight," said Sammatzen dryly, "and in fact it's time to adjourn until tomorrow."

Kelse, Schaine and Gerd Jemasze watched while the members of the Mull slowly made their way to the retiring chambers. Schaine said in a voice half-amused, half-horrified: "In addition to his other talents, Muffin turns out to be a demagogue."

"Muffin is a dangerous man," said Kelse somberly.

"I think," said Gerd Jemasze, "that I would like to be on hand for tomorrow's session of the Mull."

"I want to be there too," said Kelse. "I think it's time to amuse the Mull with Father's wonderful joke."

"I'll come too," said Schaine. "Why should I miss the fun?"

The Mull convened at its appointed time in a chamber crowded to capacity by folk who scented momentous, or at least stimulating, events. Erris Sammatzen performed the usual convocation ceremonies and indicated that the business of the day might proceed.

Jorjol the Gray Prince immediately stepped forward. He bowed to the Mull: "Honorable persons! To reintroduce my proposals of yesterday, I call the attention of the Mull to the fact that, in defiance of the Mull's edict, the land-barons of Uaia retain control over lands seized by violence from my people. I request that the Mull implement their edict—by coercion, if necessary."

"The edict has indeed been issued," said Erris Sammatzen, "and to this date has met no compliance, and in fact—" He stopped short as he noticed Gerd Jemasze and Kelse Madduc who had come to stand before the railing which separated the Mull from the audience. "I see before me two land-barons of Uaia," said Sammatzen. "Perhaps they bring us notice in regard to the edict."

"We do indeed," said Gerd Jemasze. "Your edict is absurd, and you had best retract it."

Sammatzen raised his eyebrows, and the other members of the Mull stared down in displeasure. Jorjol stood stiff and alert, his head thrust forward.

Sammatzen spoke politely: "We are a sober honest group; we try our best but we are not infallible and sometimes make mistakes. But 'absurd'? I think you have selected an unsuitable adjective."

Gerd Jemasze responded no less equably. "In the light of recent events, the word does not appear too strong."

Sammatzen's voice became heavy. "Do you refer to the erjin insurrection? Ah, but we have learned a lesson indeed, and the Gray Prince, whom you see before you, has suggested a method to repair our weakness."

"You intend to recruit a mercenary army of barbarians? Is that your intent? Do you recall a hundred thousand historical parallels?"

Sammatzen started to speak, then checked himself. "The matter has by no means been decided," he said at last. "We have, however, issued a judgment that the land-barons must cease to assert title to the Treaty lands; and arguments to the effect that time lapse has sanctified title will not be considered."

Jemasze grinned at the Mull. "This then is your considered opinion?"

"It is indeed."

"Then, by precisely the same reasoning, Uldra tribes of the Retent must yield the territories they now control to the tribes from whom they seized them. These tribes in turn must yield to the tribes which claimed the land before themselves. Ultimately—and here is the idea which Uther Madduc found so amusing—all must yield to the prior habitancy of the erjins, from whom men originally seized the land. Indeed we have only just crushed their very reasonable and quite legitimate effort to regain these lost territories."

The Mull stared at Jemasze in bemusement. Sammatzen said in a tentative voice: "This is a facet of the case we had not considered. I agree that it is most challenging."

Jorjol strode forward. "Very well, do as he suggests! The Uldras support the concept! Give all Uaia back to the erjins; let them take ownership! We will roam the wild lands as before; only destroy the grotesque halls of the Outker land-barons! Break their fences and dams and canals! Expunge every suppurating vestige of the Outker presence! By all means deed the land to the erjins!"

"Not so fast," said Kelse. "There is more to come: the second part of my father's joke." He spoke to Sammatzen. "Do you recall the erjin shrine, or monument—whatever may be its function?"

"Naturally."

"This was the 'recent event' to which Dm. Jemasze referred a few moments ago—not to the erjin insurrection as you supposed. Perhaps you noticed that the erjins are depicted riding in what apparently are spaceships? You know that fossil traces of proto-erjins have never been found on Koryphon? The conclusion is clear. The erjins are invaders. They arrived from space; they conquered the morphote civilization. The morphotes are true indigenes; the fossil record is clear on this point. So the chain of conquest has yet another link. The erjins have no better title than the Uldras."

"Yes," admitted Erris Sammatzen, "this is very likely true."

Jorjol emitted a wild yell of laughter. "Now you award Uaia to the morphotes! Then be sure to give them Szintarre as well, and the villas of Olanje, and the luxurious hotels and all the property you believe yourselves to own!"

Kelse gave a sardonic nod. "This is the third part of my father's joke. You of the Mull, and all the Redemptionists, found it easy enough to give our land away, by reason of your ethical doctrine; now demonstrate your integrity and give away your own property."

Sammatzen showed him a sad twisted smile. "Today? At this instant?"

"Anytime you like, or not at all, so long as you rescind your edict in regard to us."

Voices called out from every corner in the chamber: protesting, jeering, applauding. Sammatzen at last restored order. For a period the Mull conferred in soft mutters but obviously came to no concerted opinion. Sammatzen turned back to Gerd Jemasze and Kelse. "I feel that somehow you are using casuistry to confuse us but for the life of me I can't define it."

Adelys Lam cried out bitterly: "It is clear to me that the land-barons not only profess a creed of violence, but that they also warp their creed into a travesty of an ethical system."

"Not at all," said Gerd Jemasze. "The travesty exists only because reliance upon abstraction has made reality incomprehensible to you. These issues aren't merely local; they extend across the Gaean Reach. Except for a few special cases title to every parcel of real property derives from an act of violence, more or less remote, and ownership is only as valid as the strength and will required to maintain it. This is the lesson of history, whether you like it or not."

"The mourning of defeated peoples, while pathetic and tragic, is usually futile," said Kelse.

Sammatzen shook his head in dismay. "I find such a doctrine repellent. The enjoyment of human rights should rest upon a base more noble than brute force."

Jorjol gave another caw of laughter. "You and your sheep-brained Mull: why don't you pass an edict to this effect?"

Kelse said: "When the galaxy is ruled by a single law, these ideals may have substance. Until then, that which a man, a tribe, a nation or a world, or the entire Gaean Reach possesses, it must be prepared to defend."

Sammatzen threw up his hands. "I move to rescind the edict dissolving the domains of Uaia. Who dissents?"

"I do," declared Adelys Lam. "I am yet a Redemptionist; I will never be anything else."

"Who assents?...I count eleven votes, including my own. The edict is canceled; and we now adjourn for the day."

Jorjol strode from the chamber, robes flapping about his long legs. Kelse, Gerd Jemasze and Schaine followed. Out upon the avenue Jorjol halted to look first one way then the other. To his left the way led across the Persimmon Sea, to Uaia and the lands of the Retent; to his right, only a hundred yards along Kharanotis Avenue, the space depot offered transit to other worlds.

"How he hates us!" mused Schaine. "And think! We nurtured this hate by our own deeds. We were so vain and proud that we refused to admit an Uldra waif into our Great Hall; think of the tragedy it brought to all of us! I wonder: have we learned our lesson?"

Kelse was silent for a moment. Then he said: "This is the language of Olanje and not the reality of Uaia. It contains bright glimmers of truth but not all the truth."

Jemasze said: "There are as many realities as there are people. At Suaniset any gentleman may dine at our table, no matter what clothes he wears."

Kelse gave a sour chuckle. "And at Morningswake as well. Uther Madduc fostered his private reality perhaps too rigidly."

"There goes Jorjol!" said Gerd Jemasze, "off to inflict himself upon another world." For Jorjol had chosen to turn right, toward the spaceport.

The three strolled along Kharanotis Avenue toward the Seascape Hotel. A tall mesh fence separated the road from the swamp, and a gap in the foliage afforded a view across the swamp, down to the slow water of the Viridian River. A morphote, resting on a log, made an incomprehensible gesture and slipped off into the undergrowth.

EDITOR BIOS

TERRY DOWLING

Terry Dowling (www.terrydowling.com) is one of Australia's most acclaimed and best-known writers of science fiction, fantasy and horror, the award-winning author of *Rynosseros, Blue Tyson, Twilight Beach, Rynemonn* (the Tom Rynosseros saga), *Wormwood, The Man Who Lost Red, An Intimate Knowledge of the Night, Blackwater Days, Basic Black: Tales of Appropriate Fear* and editor of *Mortal Fire: Best Australian SF, The Essential Ellison* and *The Jack Vance Treasury*. He has also written a number of articles on Jack's writing, among them "Kirth Gersen: The Other Demon Prince" (which won him the 1983 William Atheling Award for Criticism) and his 28,000 word "The Art of Xenography: Jack Vance's 'General Culture' Novels" (*Science Fiction # 3*, December 1978). Terry is a close friend of the Vances and a frequent visitor to their home in the Oakland hills. Jack wrote an Introduction to *Blue Tyson*, Terry's 1992 collection of Tom Rynosseros stories, and refers to a "Terence Dowling's World" in *Throy*. In *Ports of Call*, he mentions a drink called a "Wild Dingo Howler, which was invented by a reckless smuggler named Terence Dowling." Terry counts these things among his most treasured possessions.

JONATHAN STRAHAN

Jonathan Strahan (www.jonathanstrahan.com) is an editor, anthologist and reviewer from Perth, Western Australia. He established *Eidolon*, one of Australia's leading semiprozines, before moving on to work for *Locus* as an editor and book reviewer. He has been Reviews Editor for *Locus* since 2002, and has had reviews published in *Locus*, *Eidolon*, *Ticonderoga* and *Foundation*. Jonathan has won the William Atheling Jr. Award for Criticism and Review, the Ditmar Award a number of times, and is a recipient of the Peter McNamara Achievement Award. As a freelance editor, he has edited or co-edited 11 anthologies, with five more in the pipeline. Titles include *The Locus Awards*, *The Year's Best Australian Science Fiction and Fantasy*, *Science Fiction: Best of*, *Fantasy: Best of*, and the *Best Short Novels* anthology series, as well as *Eclipse One: New Fantasy and Science Fiction*. He recently completed *Science Fiction: The Very Best of 2005* and *Fantasy: The Very Best of 2005* and *Best Short Novels: 2006*, and is working on a YA SF anthology for Viking Penguin and an anthology of new space opera stories to be co-edited with Gardner Dozois for HarperCollins.